FROM
THE
FOREST

L. E. MODESITT, JR.

FROM
THE
FOREST

TOR

Tor Publishing Group

NEW YORK

This is a work of fiction. All of the characters, organizations, and events portrayed in this novel are either products of the author's imagination or are used fictitiously.

FROM THE FOREST

Some of the material in the first seven chapters appeared in the story "The Forest Girl" from *Recluce Tales* (Tor Books, 2017).

A Tor Book
Published by Tom Doherty Associates / Tor Publishing Group
120 Broadway
New York, NY 10271

www.torpublishinggroup.com

Tor® is a registered trademark of Macmillan Publishing Group, LLC.

The Library of Congress Cataloging-in-Publication Data is available upon request.

ISBN 978-1-250-32333-0 (trade paperback)
ISBN 978-1-250-88683-5 (ebook)

Our books may be purchased in bulk for promotional, educational, or business use. Please contact your local bookseller or the Macmillan Corporate and Premium Sales Department at 1-800-221-7945, extension 5442, or by email at MacmillanSpecialMarkets@macmillan.com.

First Tor Paperback Edition: 2024

Printed in the United States of America

0 9 8 7 6 5 4 3 2 1

For Carol Ann

ALYIAKAL

Northpoint, Jakaafra

I

A youth sits in a chair behind a writing desk in the corner of the study. He looks to the vacant white-oak desk, polished and without papers or any objects upon it, then toward the open door to the hallway before returning his attention to the small book he holds, the cover of which is white leather.

Sometime later, he hears steps approaching the study door, but he keeps his eyes on the angular letters on the page he has stopped reading.

"Alyiakal . . . have you finished your studies?" asks the wiry figure wearing the green-trimmed white uniform of a Mirror Lancer majer.

"Yes, ser." The youth immediately looks up, his eyes seeming to meet those of his father.

"What have you learned?"

"That chaos must be directed by the least amount of order possible. The greater the order, the more likely it is to weaken the force of chaos."

"What does that mean?"

"Mean, ser?"

"If you're going to aspire to the Magi'i, boy, you can't just parrot the words." The slightest hint of impatience colors the majer's words.

"So what do the words mean, ser?" Alyiakal is careful to keep his tone polite. He doesn't want another beating.

"You tell me." The majer's voice is hard. "Magus Triamon says that you can sense order and chaos, if barely. Your mother would have been disappointed by such sophistry."

Alyiakal holds the wince within himself at the reference to his mother. "Chaos has no order. It will go where it will. Order is necessary to direct chaos, but order reduces chaos. The skill is to direct chaos without reducing the power of that chaos."

"Alyiakal . . . you understand. From now on, every stupid question will merit a blow with a switch or lash."

"Yes, ser."

"Your supper should have settled. It's time for your blade exercises and lessons."

"Yes, ser."

The majer turns, heading for the rear terrace.

Alyiakal closes the white-leather book, sets it on the writing desk, and stands. While he is now nearly as tall as his father, he is only sixteen, and slender, so far lacking the physical strength of his father. Until the last season, he had dreaded the blade lessons. Although they practiced with wooden wands, he had always ended up with painful bruises. Now, as he walks to the rear terrace of the quarters, he is merely resigned to what may be. He understands all too well that if he fails to satisfy the Magi'i he will follow his father into the Mirror Lancers.

The practice wands—wooden replicas of Mirror Lancer sabres—hang on the rack by the door. As Alyiakal eases his wand from the rack, he considers his lesson. Order must direct chaos, but it also must direct a blade, for an undirected blade cannot be effective. Can he use his slight skills at sensing order to determine where his father's blade must go? He takes a deep breath. It is worth the effort. He cannot be more badly bruised than he has been in the past. He makes his way to the terrace and waits in the warm air of late Spring.

He does not wait long, for the majer appears in moments, his own wand in hand. "Ready?"

"Yes, ser." Instead of concentrating on his father's eyes, Alyiakal tries to sense where his father's wand will go before it does. For the first few moments, he is scrambling, dancing back, allowing touches—but not hard strikes. Then . . . slowly, he begins to feel the patterns and to anticipate them.

He slides his father's wand, and then comes over the top to pin it down, but he cannot hold the wand against Kyal's greater strength, and he has to jump back.

"Good technique . . . but you have to finish!" The majer is breathing hard. "Keep at it!"

By the end of half a glass, Alyiakal can slip, parry, or avoid almost every attack his father brings to bear, but he is sweating heavily enough that he can't see clearly when Kyal abruptly says, "That's enough for this evening."

Alyiakal lowers the wand.

"You worked hard, and your defense is much better. Just apply yourself that hard to your studies, and you shouldn't have that much trouble."

"I'm still bruised in places, ser."

"At your age, that's to be expected." His father nods. "You're free to do what you will until dark. Don't go too far. If you're going to walk the wall road, don't forget your sabre."

"Yes, ser. I won't." Alyiakal is sore enough that he isn't certain he wants to go anywhere. At the same time, being free for a glass or so is a privilege not to be wasted. Still . . .

After several moments, he decides to at least take a walk, if only to show that he appreciates and will use the privilege. He follows his father inside and carefully racks the wand, then goes to wash up and cool down.

Less than a quarter glass later, he walks out the front door and around the small and narrow privacy screen wall, the ancient Mirror Lancer cupridium blade in the scabbard at his waist. He does not breathe easily until the officers' quarters at Jakaafra are more than a hundred yards behind him, as is the tall building that holds the northernmost of the chaos towers. Before long he walks southeast along the white sunstone road paralleling the whitestone wall that, along with the wards powered by the chaos towers, confines the Accursed Forest.

Alyiakal glances to his right. Between the wall and road, there is neither vegetation nor grass, only bare salted ground. To the left are fields and orchards, and a few cots and barns, fewer with each kay from Jakaafra . . . until the next town, kays away.

He keeps walking along the road flanking the white wall, glancing back, but he sees no one, and no lancer patrols, not that he expects any. While his eyes remain alert for any movement, especially near the wall, his thoughts consider what had happened during his blade practice . . . and how he had not previously thought of using order to help in using a sabre.

How else might I use order? He doesn't have an answer to that question, but he does not have time to pursue it because, some fifty yards ahead, at the base of the whitestone wall is a black beast, a chaos panther, lowering itself, as if to spring and charge him. He draws the antique lancer sabre, knowing that its usefulness against such a massive beast is limited at best.

Then . . . the black predator is gone, and a girl—a young woman, he realizes—stands beside the wall. He starts to walk toward her . . . and as suddenly as she was there, she also has vanished. He looks around, bewildered, but the salted ground between the patrol road and the wall remains empty—for as far as he can see.

Carefully, if unwisely, he knows, he moves toward where both the black cat-like creature and the young woman had been.

Once there, he studies the ground. There are bootprints, but no pawprints, leading to the wall, not away from it, as if someone had walked from the road to the wall. He can find no bootprints leading away.

A concealing illusion? It had to be, but he can sense neither the heavy blackness of order nor the whitish red of chaos. *And from a woman, when there are no women Magi'i?*

Finally, after waiting and watching for perhaps a fifth of a glass, he turns and begins to walk back home, thinking.

II

On fourday morning, as on most mornings, except sevenday and eightday, Alyiakal sets out early on the three-kay walk to the house of Magus Triamon, carrying only the white leather-bound book, and not wearing the old Mirror Lancer sabre, since his father has made it more than clear that he may not wear it into the town. He makes his way east to the narrow stone road that runs northwest of the lancer compound, taking a last look at the whitestone wall that girdles the Accursed Forest, then turning toward Jakaafra. While he walks swiftly, nearly a glass passes before he steps onto the porch. He knocks three times, then once, before stepping back and waiting, standing between the privacy screen and the door. He is about to sit down on the wooden bench beside the door when it opens, and the gray-haired magus stands there, his angular countenance younger than his hair would indicate.

Triamon says nothing, just steps back and motions for the youth to enter, closing the heavy door behind them.

Alyiakal follows him to the study, which contains a tall and narrow bookcase, a desk and two chairs, an ancient white-oak cabinet that has aged to a golden shade, and a table slightly over waist-high topped with dark gray soapstone, on which rests a single candle in an unornamented bronze holder.

"Today, you're going to learn a bit more about the dangers of chaos, Alyiakal." Triamon gestures to the oak cabinet that is beside the stone-topped table. "How old would you say that cabinet is?"

"The wood is aged. It looks to be at least fifty years old."

"It does look that old. It's not. It's but ten years old. That's what too much chaos too close can do."

"You said that you always keep chaos under control, ser."

"I'm careful, but I've taught a few other would-be Magi'i besides you."

"They did that?"

"So will you, after a time, if you're not careful," Triamon says, eyes on his student.

For a moment, Alyiakal says nothing, then realizes that the magus expects a response, and blurts, "After a time? Is that because I can't muster enough chaos to affect the chest until I'm stronger?"

"That's one reason, but there's another."

"Because young mages use more chaos than they should?"

Triamon smiles momentarily, then says, "They often do, but that wouldn't matter, except for the reason I'm seeking."

Alyiakal tries to conceal the puzzlement he feels.

"For the present, I'll not tell you, and we'll see if you can come up with the answer over the next few eightdays. I will give you a hint. You won't find it in your text."

If it's not in Basics of Magery, *where am I supposed to find it?* Alyiakal is aware enough not to ask the question.

After a slight pause, Triamon says, "In the meantime, you must sharpen your awareness of order and chaos. Watch the candle, with your senses, not your eyes."

Alyiakal concentrates on the candle as a point of chaos touches the already blackened wick and as the heat of that chaos creates the usual flame of a lighted candle.

"Is there more chaos in the flame or in the candle?" asks Triamon.

"The flame," declares Alyiakal.

The magus shakes his head. "What does the book say about forms of chaos?"

"There are two basic forms of chaos, free chaos and order-bound chaos."

"And what is a candle composed of?"

"Order-bound chaos," replies Alyiakal, "but I can't use it or sense it. So it seems to me—"

"The failure is in your senses. What does the book say about the relative power of order-bound chaos and free chaos?"

"Free chaos is the more powerful."

"That's not quite what it states, Alyiakal. You need to read more carefully. I'll expect a better answer tomorrow."

"Yes, ser."

"Now, I'm going to gather points of free chaos. You compare the point I've gathered to the amount of free chaos in the candle flame, and tell me which contains more free chaos."

A larger point of chaos appears beside the candle flame.

"Your point contains more chaos."

Triamon reduces the amount of gathered chaos. "Now which one?"

"Yours."

Triamon moves the chaos point farther from the flame. "Now which?"

"Yours."

The magus moves the chaos point to the far side of the study. "And now?"

"They seem about the same."

"What they *seem* could kill you if it's not correct. Which has more?"

"The candle."

Triamon shakes his head. "I contracted the chaos so that it was more tightly packed, but it held more chaos. You went by the size you sensed, not the amount of chaos."

By the end of the glass that is the length of his lesson, Alyiakal has a headache, but he has improved greatly in his ability to sense the relative strength of the chaos point compared to the candle.

"You're getting much better ability. In the days ahead, I'll have you work on judging strengths of dissimilar or mixed forces."

"Mixed forces?"

"How else can a magus create and throw a chaos bolt? Some chaos bolts are deadlier than others. As a magus you need to sense immediately what you need to use and what you need in defending yourself." Triamon pauses. "Now . . . I'm going to give you an exercise you can do at home . . ."

Despite his headache, Alyiakal concentrates on Triamon's instructions.

When Alyiakal leaves the dwelling of the magus his steps are slow for several reasons. Even though it isn't even midday yet, the early Summer sun feels as hot as mid-Summer. Also, there is no real reason to hurry, since his father won't be home until late afternoon, if then, and Areya will not arrive until early afternoon to clean and then prepare dinner. His steps remain slow as he thinks over his lesson, trying to puzzle out why stronger mage students created more uncontrolled free chaos later in their studies, rather than earlier, especially since Magus Triamon had agreed with his suggestions, but had said there was another reason. He also frets over the fact that he had not read the text carefully enough, particularly if the magus reports that to his father. Carelessness or sloppiness—or stupidity—always results in punishment.

But you get privileges if you do well.

Except that it often seems he doesn't meet his father's standards.

Alyiakal smiles ruefully, recalling his father's words, words he has heard in one form or another more than once, usually when he thinks about complaining, not that he's actually said a word of complaint in years.

"That's life. Mistakes can cost everything. Rewards are few, and those rewards are to be cherished."

Despite his measured pace, Alyiakal has to blot the dampness from his forehead as he steps into the coolness of the quarters. The day is even warmer than he expected, and Summer swelters around the Accursed Forest on the best of days. After standing for a moment in the small entry, he walks into the kitchen, but finds little to eat except bread and cheese in the coolbox. Since bread and cheese is better than nothing, he eats what has been left for him, along with some water.

After eating, he takes the copy of *Basics of Magery* to the shaded corner of the rear terrace, sits on the bench, and begins to read, forcing himself to concentrate on the words and their meaning. After half a glass he has still not found the words or phrases that he must have misread . . . or that Magus Triamon may have remembered from another text. Another quarter glass passes before he finds what he seeks.

> . . . order and chaos comprise all objects, from the smallest grain of sand to the massive sunstone blocks that provide the foundation of the Palace of Light. The chaos in a mere pebble is scores upon scores more powerful than the firebolts of the greatest of the Magi'i, yet bound as it is to order, that power held within the pebble cannot be gathered by a magus unaided, and is as nothing, so that a magus must gather free chaos from where he can . . .

Alyiakal rereads the paragraph once more. *How did you miss that?*

He takes a deep breath and continues reading, forcing himself to read all the words, even the boring ones and those too often repeating the obligations laid upon any who would be Magi'i.

When he finishes rereading what he had obviously not read closely enough, as well as the next section of the text, equally closely, it is well past midafternoon.

Since Areya has finished her cleaning and is in the kitchen preparing the evening meal, Alyiakal will not disturb her if he goes into the study, which he does. There, he takes down two night candles in their holders and sets them side by side on the writing desk. Then he uses a striker to light one, an effort that takes more than a few attempts.

Following Triamon's instructions, he concentrates on the lit candle, as much with his senses and thoughts as with his eyes. In time, he begins to sense what is almost an image of golden reddish white around the tip of the candle wick . . . as well as a faint blackish mist above the point of the flame. Yet he sees neither the white nor the black with his eyes. Of that, he is certain . . . but they are there.

Next, he concentrates on replicating the pattern of golden whiteness around the tip of the wick of the unlit candle. Sweat beads on his forehead. Nothing happens.

"You must not be doing it right," he murmurs to himself.

He shakes his head, then closes his eyes, and takes a deep breath. Finally, he concentrates once more. The wick of the unlit candle remains dark.

Do you need to look at the candle?

He looks steadily at the candle, concentrating, but the blackened wick remains as it was. Next, he closes his eyes and tries to visualize the dark wick, and a pattern of golden whiteness around it. He opens his eyes quickly, only to see a tiny point of redness, visible to his eyes, wink out.

"You can do it," he says quietly, redoubling his efforts.

Sweat is running into his eyes a quarter glass later when the candle flickers alight . . . and stays lit. Alyiakal allows himself only a brief smile and a moment of rest before he blows out the candle and repeats the effort. After a deep breath, he once more blows out the candle . . . and relights it—just by focusing order on chaos.

He has repeated the process once more when he hears the door open, and the heavy footsteps of his father, steps seemingly far too ponderous for a man as small as the majer.

"What are you doing with the candles?" asks Kyal, not quite brusquely, as he steps into the study.

"Practicing an exercise that Magus Triamon gave me. He told me to work on it until I could do it instantly."

"Lighting a candle?"

"Lighting it without a striker, ser. That requires gathering chaos. He says it's the first step in mastering chaos."

Slowly, Kyal nods, as if he is not certain about the matter.

At that moment, there is a series of knocks on the front door, followed by a loud voice. "Majer! Ser!"

The majer turns and walks swiftly from the study to the front door, which he opens.

Alyiakal does not follow, but strains to listen intently.

"Majer Kyal . . . ser . . . it's happened again."

"What?" snaps the majer, whose voice is far larger than his stature.

"Another dispatch rider is gone. The incoming patrol found his mount and the dispatches. There's no sign of him. The men claim they saw a black chaos cat, one of the big ones. It was prowling outside the wall, just to the southwest of the northern point."

"Send a squad with fully charged firelances. I'd like a report of what they find. Or what they don't."

"Yes, ser."

Kyal closes the door and walks back to the archway into the small library. "We'd best eat early. There's no telling when we'll get another chance." He pauses. "Are you finished with the exercises?"

Alyiakal nods. "I did what the magus wanted."

"You can tell me about it at supper. We need to wash up. I'll tell Areya to get the plates ready."

When the two are finally seated at the table, Areya sets a platter of mutton slices covered with cheese and a yellow-green glaze of ground rosemary. One smaller platter holds lace potatoes, and another thinly sliced pearapples. The pitcher holds a decent, but not outstanding, red wine.

Kyal serves himself, then passes each platter to Alyiakal. "What about the exercises?"

"Every flame holds both chaos and order, but there's almost no order and much more chaos. Magus Triamon taught me how to sense both order and chaos in the flame. He says that's the easiest way to sense them at first. Once I could sense them, and he made sure of that by swirling the patterns, he made me try to move the chaos myself. Then he sent me home with the exercise. That was to light a candle, and then learn to light another one by duplicating the pattern of chaos around the wick. It took a while, but I did it three times in a row. Next, I have to light a candle without using another candle as a pattern."

"Do you think you'll ever be able to match a full magus?" asks the majer, not quite diffidently.

"Magus Triamon thinks I can . . . if I keep working."

Kyal nods slowly. "I'd advise you to work very hard, son."

"I will, ser." After a silence, Alyiakal looks at his father. "Is that because I will not match you in might?"

Kyal laughs. "Oh . . . you'll be able to do that in another year or so. You're still growing, and it looks like you'll be taller and broader than me. Your technique is far better than mine was at your age. No . . . it's because too many Mirror Lancers are being killed fighting the barbarians who swarm across the Grass Hills, especially to the north. We need better weapons. Perhaps you'll be able to become a great enough magus to create them. Even if you don't, the Magi'i are the only ones who can use the Mirror Towers to keep our firelances charged."

"You don't want me to be a Mirror Lancer officer like you?"

"I'd like it very much. But the son of a lancer majer from Jakaafra is likely to do no better than his sire, if his talents are limited to the blade and skill at arms alone. Why do you think I insist on your reading about tactics and logistics?"

"But . . . Magus Triamon . . ."

"You may become a great magus. You may not, but a lancer has three weapons— his sabre, his firelance, and his mind. Firelances are powered by chaos. If you do follow in my steps, the more you know and the more you can do with chaos, the better you will be with your weapons. The more you study with the magus, the more you will know what I cannot teach you, and that will sharpen your mind even more." Kyal clears his throat. "There is one more thing. All the senior Mirror Lancer officers come from the great families of Cyad. If you wish to rise further than I have, you must become more capable than all of them. You must be so clearly so superior that none can contest you." Kyal smiles wryly. "That, you will find, is true in all areas where a man must make his way." His words turn sardonic. "At times, even that is not sufficient."

Alyiakal sits, silent. Never has his father talked so bluntly.

"It's time you began to learn more of how the world works . . . really works. Now . . . eat your supper. I'll have to leave soon to see what that squad has found. You can walk a bit tonight, but go the southeast way. And be careful."

"Yes, ser."

Once they finish eating and after the majer leaves the quarters, Alyiakal fastens on the old sword belt and scabbard, checks the sabre, and then slips out into the early-evening air, still steaming, but not quite so unbearable as it was several glasses earlier. Once he is away from the quarters buildings of the Mirror Lancer outpost, he studies the wall even more closely, but he sees no sign of anyone or anything on the road or near it.

Then, after he has walked close to half a kay, in the early twilight, when his eyes move from the fields of a small stead on his left, whose house is out of sight, and likely as far from the wall as possible, to the cleared and salted strip of land on his right, he sees a large black panther-cat crouched at the base of the sunstone wall, where he had seen nothing at all a moment before.

Where did that come from? He stops and studies the beast. While his hand rests on the top of the hilt of his sabre, he does not attempt to draw the weapon. The black panther-cat's eyes remain fixed on him. There is something . . . something he cannot fathom . . . yet he has no doubt that his sabre will likely not suffice against such a creature. *What will?*

Fire! All wild animals fear—or are wary of—flame. *Can you create a flame large enough to startle it?* He smiles nervously. It cannot hurt to try.

He looks directly at the panther-cat, then concentrates on replicating the flame pattern of a candle—a very large candle.

A flare of light flashes up in front of the creature . . . then vanishes.

Alyiakal feels as though his head has been cleft in two. His eyes burn, and for several moments he cannot move.

Abruptly . . . the giant cat vanishes. A black-haired young woman, scarcely more than a girl, stands there, the same one as he saw before, he thinks.

She laughs. "Fair enough!"

"Who are you?" he asks, moving forward, if slowly.

"Someone of the Forest and the town," she replies, taking several steps toward him. "Nothing more."

He laughs softly. "Nothing more? When you can take on the semblance of a giant black panther and then vanish?"

She frowns.

Now that he is closer, he sees that her eyes are as black as her hair, for all that her skin is a lightly tanned creamy color. "I saw you do that eightdays ago. You didn't really vanish, did you? You only made it seem so."

She stops and asks, "Why do you say that?"

"Because I followed your bootprints, and you climbed over the whitestone wall into the Accursed Forest."

"It's not cursed. It's different."

"You've actually been in the . . . Forest . . . and you're alive?"

"You sound so surprised. Why?"

Despite her question, Alyiakal feels that she is somehow amused. "Lancers die every season from attacks by the black cats or the stun lizards."

"That's because they consider the cats and lizards enemies, and the cats and lizards can feel that."

"I think it's more than that," says Alyiakal, looking directly at her. Up close it is clear she must be at least several years older than he is; it is also obvious that she is striking. Not pretty, but something beyond. What that might be, he is far from certain.

"Why do you think that?" she asks.

"Because they have attacked those who have not attacked them."

"How is a stun lizard to determine which man is foe and which is not?" She lifts her eyebrows in quizzical amusement.

"You said they could tell the difference."

"Can you use that blade?" she asks, turning and walking parallel to the wall.

"Yes." He takes several quick steps to catch up to her.

"Then you must be Alyiakal."

"Why do you think that?"

"Magus Triamon said it was a pity you were already so proficient with such a weapon. No one else near Jakaafra uses a blade and can also sense both black and white."

"You're obviously far better at that than am I."

"I'm older."

"Not that much," he protests.

"You're young, and you're kind. Trust me. I am older."

"What do you do in the Forest?"

"You don't have to do anything in the Forest."

"You didn't answer my question."

She smiles. "No, I didn't."

"Then show me."

"I can't do that."

"Why not?"

"If anything happened to you, your father would seek those responsible. Magus Triamon would have to flee or die, and I could never see my father again—if he survived your father's wrath."

Alyiakal thinks, then says, "Could you show me some of the Forest from the wall?"

A smile that becomes a wide grin crosses her lips. "You'd do that after all the lancers your father has lost?"

"How do you . . . how much do you know about me . . . and my father?"

"He's in charge of the Mirror Lancers here in Jakaafra, and you live with him in the quarters, and you study with Master Triamon." She shrugs. "Other than that . . . very little, except that you have courage and are willing to look beyond walls."

"Will you show me?" he asks again.

"Since you're asking. But you must promise not to enter the Forest."

"You said it wasn't dangerous." He offers an impish grin.

"It isn't . . . if you know what you're doing. You don't."

Alyiakal can accept that. "I won't." *Not until I do know, at least.*

"Then climb up." She turns and scrambles up the whitestone so quickly that she is looking down at him before he even begins.

He discovers that the stone is smoother than it looks. He almost loses his grip twice, but soon he perches on the flat surface of the wall beside her, looking into the part of the Accursed Forest that cannot be seen from the wall road.

Less than thirty yards from the base of the wall beneath Alyiakal is the rounded end of a pool, whose still waters look to be a clear deep green in the gloom created by both the beginning of twilight and the high canopy of the taller trees and the lower canopy formed by the undergrowth, if it can be called that, for those trees are far taller than any Alyiakal has seen anywhere outside the Accursed Forest, not that he recalls much of anyplace that has not been near the Forest. A long greenish log lies half in, half out of the water, except that when the log moves, Alyiakal realizes that it is a stun lizard, not that he has ever seen one, but only drawings of the beasts.

"The stun lizard . . . are they all so big?"

"That's a small one. Some of them are more than ten yards from snout to tail, and they can stun an entire squad of lancers."

"How do you know that?"

"Shhhh . . . watch."

An enormous black panther-cat pads along the side of the pond opposite the stun lizard, which freezes back into resembling a log. A cream-colored crane, with silver-green wings, alights at the far end of the pond, standing motionless for the longest time. Then, suddenly, the long beak stabs into the water and comes up with a squirming flash of silver impaled on the beak almost as sharp as a cupridium blade.

"Try to see the order and the chaos in each of them," she suggests.

Alyiakal had not thought of that, and even as he wonders why he should, he attempts what she has suggested. At first, he can sense only swirling flows of order and chaos . . . but as he keeps watching, he can soon discern that the order and chaos within each of the Forest creatures is locked in a tight pattern, and that while the patterns are different, they share a similarity he cannot describe.

"You need to go," the woman who looks like a girl says quietly.

He glances to the west. While he cannot see the sun, the angles of the shadows tell him that it is far later than he realized. Has that much time passed? He looks to her. "Thank you."

After he drops to the salted ground beneath the wall, he looks back up. She remains there, looking at him.

"You didn't tell me your name," he says.

"No, I didn't."

"Why not?"

"It's better that way."

"Why don't you want me to know your name?"

"I'd be happy to have you learn my name . . . as long as you don't discover it from me." Then she smiles . . . and vanishes.

For several moments, Alyiakal can faintly sense a web of darkness on the wall, but he sees nothing. Then the darkness drops away, leaving the top of the wall empty of order . . . and her. The only sounds are those from the Accursed Forest, and they are muted.

He turns and begins the walk back toward the quarters, walking quickly and hoping he will not be so late that Areya will tell his father.

III

Now that the memorial for His Mightiness Kiedral'elth'alt'mer, Second Emperor of Light, is a year behind us, almost no one remembers Kiedral Daloren, Vice Marshal of the Anglorian Unity, yet they were one and the same.

Before him, there was chaos. Not the chaos confined within the Towers of Light, nor the chaos of the great and possibly accursed forest, but the chaos of power not understood and too often misused conflicting with ambitions formed in a past now unreachable by either machines or magery. He saw that chaos and the need for it to be channeled into productive use, and persuaded, sometimes violently, those of all manner of power and passions into the social-power triad all in Cyad and its lands call the Magi'i, the Mirror Lancers, and the Merchanters.

That accomplishment was far more difficult than the construction of the City of Light, and far, far more arduous than his taming of the great forest, or his cold-blooded dealing with the theft of a chaos tower in the brief schism of southeastern dissidents, or his insistence on the building of the first sunstone highways and the great canal, yet few today, even before his death, would consider the success of that social triad as an accomplishment. They regard it as something that merely happened, ignoring the schism as a symptom of what could have destroyed a united Cyador, and now believe that the triad was something absolutely inevitable, and that unthinking acceptance in itself marks the significance of that achievement.

The Second Emperor of Light was a greater magus than any of the First Magi'i who served him and Cyador, but he went out of his way to avoid showing that power. He was a greater strategist and tactician than any of the Majer-Commanders who have led the Mirror Lancers, but he let them take his "suggestions" as their own and then praised them for their leadership and acumen.

If the Emperors of Light who come after him try to follow his specific acts or deeds, or even principles, they will fail, for Kiedral'elth'alt'mer understood, as few do, that those who lead must do so from the true core of who they have been and who they are at each moment in time, and they must understand what they must become as they change the world in which they live . . .

Fragment, Mirror Lancer Archives
Zaenth'alt, Captain-Commander
Cyad, 45 A.F.

IV

The next morning, when Alyiakal arrives at the small square dwelling under the canopy of the overarching oak trees, as often occurs, he has to wait for Magus Triamon to open the door and admit him. Rather than sit on the bench on the porch, he finds himself pacing back and forth, debating how much he should say, until Triamon opens the door and motions for him to enter.

Alyiakal hurries inside and to the study.

"You seem eager this morning," says the gray-haired magus as he closes the study door.

"I came across another student of yours, Master Triamon."

"Oh? Which one?"

"The black-haired young woman."

Triamon nods and smiles. "She's not exactly a student of mine. And how did you meet her?"

"She gave the image of herself as a great black panther-cat. Except I just saw the Forest cat. So I created an image of a large flame because cats don't like fire. I don't know how good an image it was, but she dropped the image of the panther-cat and laughed."

Triamon frowns. "How did you manage that? We haven't gotten to illusions yet."

"Ser . . . you had me studying the sense and image of candle flames. I made it bigger. It probably didn't look real, but I thought it might scare off the panther-cat. Except it wasn't a panther-cat."

"You must have amused her. Otherwise, you never would have seen her." Triamon pauses. "A real panther-cat would have still sensed you. It might have attacked you, but the flame image wasn't a bad idea."

"I know it might not have worked, but I only had my sabre, and that wouldn't have been enough. That was the best I could do."

"I said it wasn't a bad thought, Alyiakal. If you have to do something like that again, try to put a few tiny points of chaos along the edges of your thought-image. That will help."

"Thank you, ser." After an instant, Alyiakal asks, "Who is she?"

"That, my young pupil, you will have to discover for yourself."

"She said the same thing. Are you both so frightened of my father?"

The magus shakes his head. "Your father is but an officer, a strong and honest one. But he is a Mirror Lancer, and one does not anger the Mirror Lancers."

"Why would telling me her name upset anyone?"

"She has the gift of the Magi'i, without any training. She cannot be a magus, and she refused to be just a healer. I understand some of the poorest folk seek her out for healing. For those reasons, and others, the powers of the altage and those of the Magi'i would be less than pleased if I facilitated any acquaintance between the two of you."

"But I've already met—" Alyiakal breaks off the remainder of what he had been about to say as the import of what Triamon said sinks in. Then he asks, "Because you are of the Magi'i?"

"Exactly. There are . . . agreements . . ."

"That's absurd. I don't intend to consort her."

"Consorting is not precisely the problem."

"Then why are you teaching me? I'm not from an elthage family."

"To determine if you can become a magus. Not all of the Magi'i come from elthage families, and not all elthage offspring can become Magi'i, as not all sons of Mirror Lancer officers continue in the lancers. If the Magi'i accept you, then the Mirror Lancers will not want you. If your talent is only of order and not excessive, then you might be acceptable to the Mirror Engineers. If your talent is broader but also not excessive, such as lighting candles and healing, then you will never become a magus, and you are acceptable to the Mirror Lancers."

"Just acceptable?"

"They prefer lancers who have no talent with order or chaos, but limited ability, especially healing, is acceptable in junior officers."

"Then why should I study with you?"

"Why indeed?" Triamon smiles.

"Another answer I must find for myself?"

"In the end, we all must find our own answers." Triamon's smile vanishes. "Do you wish to proceed with your lessons?"

"Why would I not?"

"Good. Have you considered the comparative power of the candle and the chaos of the flame?"

"I did. I misread that section of the text. I was thinking about the power of the chaos a magus could gather, not the amount of chaos locked within a candle or anything else." After a slight hesitation, Alyiakal asks, "Has any magus ever tried to unlock the chaos within objects?"

"It is said that the founders of Cyad who created the Mirror Towers built them so that they are powered in a way similar to that. That may be so. It may not. What is so is that no magus since then has been able to create a chaos tower or anything like it. It is also true that all Magi'i are strongly discouraged from attempting anything like that."

"But if they could—"

"If they were successful, the power released would likely shred their shields and destroy them and anything nearby." Triamon clears his throat. "Now . . . today, you will begin work on the importance of focus . . ."

After his glass of instruction and practice with Triamon, Alyiakal makes his way to the market square, rather than return immediately to quarters. He stands at the edge of the square, pondering where to start.

At last, he begins his inquiries with a young woman not that much older than he is who stands at a stall selling a range of plain bowls of various sizes.

She glances at him speculatively for a moment, then says, "You're not interested in bowls, and you're wasting your time."

"You're right about the bowls," Alyiakal admits. "I wondered if you knew anything about a black-haired, black-eyed woman who frequents the Accursed Forest."

"Never heard of such, and you'd be a fool to get close to anything like that."

"Thank you," replies Alyiakal politely as he moves to the next stall, one where a white-haired woman sells scarves of wool and cotton, but none of shimmersilk, not that he expected any, for the only shimmersilk scarf he ever saw was the blue one his mother had. For all its worth, it had burned with her. At the time, Alyiakal hadn't understood, because he'd wanted the scarf so much to remind him of her. Eight years later, his father still would have no blue cloth in their quarters.

"I've heard tales," the weaver says, "little else."

The grower woman with carrots and quilla for sale knows nothing, and neither does the apprentice coppersmith hawking some of his master's wares.

After asking a half score others, Alyiakal comes to a worn woman who sells grass and reed baskets.

"Good woman . . . would you know the black-eyed young woman with black hair who often goes to the Accursed Forest?"

"The child of forest and night?"

"Yes . . . I believe so."

"No . . . I have seen her. I do not know her."

"Do you know her name?"

"No. It would not be wise to ask."

Alyiakal refrains from asking why and merely says, "Thank you." Then he moves to the next stall, that of a spicemonger, who is haggling over the price of pepper so vociferously that Alyiakal moves to the cart beyond, which displays open kegs of salted fish, where he asks the same question.

"I know few here," replies the fishmonger. "Never saw one like her, though."

Next, he tries the woman selling pastries and meat pies.

"The spawn of the Accursed Forest? Best you stay away from her, young fellow."

"Do you know her name?"

"Why would I?" sneers the woman. "No good would come from that."

Alyiakal moves on, and over the next glass, he visits more than a score of carts and stalls before he comes to the one-eyed beggar propped against the wall. He has always avoided the beggar before, but ashamed of himself for his lack of compassion in the past, he places a copper in the near-empty bowl.

"Heard your question of the cheese-seller, boy. They all fear her, you know?"

"You don't, I think," replies Alyiakal with a half smile.

"What's to fear? Her name is Adayal, and her father is a carpenter. Her mother . . . who knows?"

"Thank you." Alyiakal puts another copper in the bowl.

"Be careful in what you'll be wanting, young fellow. Great wants call to great danger." With that, the old beggar closes his one good eye.

Great wants call to great danger? How could wanting to know Adayal's name be a great want?

With a puzzled smile, he turns and heads back toward the quarters, hoping to arrive before Areya so that he need not explain his absence, although it is unlikely she will ask. And, of course, he has much to read, and another exercise from Magus Triamon.

V

For Alyiakal, the Summer days pass slowly, although instruction from Magus Triamon widens, so that he can call up more than a limited concealment, momentary shields, and more illusions than merely flames. Even so, despite all his walks along the wall, and his forays into the town, Alyiakal does not see Adayal, or any large panther-cats, either.

Often he climbs the wall of the Accursed Forest and perches or sits there, watching what goes on beyond, trying to hold a concealment as he does, but when he does, he finds he cannot see, and can only sense through his use of order. But for all his efforts, he does not encounter the Forest girl. He thinks of her as such, even though it is more than clear that she is truly a woman . . . and definitely even more, but what more Alyiakal can only imagine.

At breakfast on threeday of the seventh eightday of Summer, the majer clears his throat. "I received a dispatch late last evening. You were not around."

"You said I could walk so long as I was careful. I've been careful." *If not exactly in ways you would approve.*

Kyal continues without addressing Alyiakal's observation. "I'm going to have to leave this morning and accompany Third Company to Geliendra. Commander Waasol wants to see all the majers posted to duty near the Accursed Forest to discuss possible changes in the standing orders." The majer adds, sardonically, "When senior officers say that they want to discuss something, that usually means they're making a change that will either cost lives or take more time to accomplish, if not both. That's true among the Magi'i as well."

"I'll remember that," replies Alyiakal.

"I'll likely be gone an eightday. Areya will come in daily to clean and prepare your dinner. You're to get your own breakfasts and clean up dinner. You're also to keep up with your lessons. I've sent word to Magus Triamon. You're to see him both morning and afternoon. I've instructed him to keep you challenged and busy. You're to do exactly what he tells you."

"Yes, ser." Alyiakal does not point out that he has never not followed the instructions of the magus. He also does not mention the times when he has done things that would have been forbidden, had he asked, such as his covert observations of the Accursed Forest from the top of the wall.

After the usual breakfast of porridge, bread, and fruit, the fruit being pear-apples for the present, Alyiakal cleans up the kitchen, then walks to the door

with his father, not quite knowing what to say. He finally manages, "Ser . . .
please take care."

Kyal smiles. "You're the one who needs to take care. I look forward to seeing
your progress in mastering order and chaos when I return."

"Yes, ser."

Alyiakal watches as his father carries a small duffel toward the Mirror
Lancer stables, then finally closes the door. The knowledge that he is free of
daily scrutiny is not particularly liberating, not when he knows that, when his
father returns, he will be judged on the state of the quarters, his courtesy to
Areya, his progress in magery, and whatever Magus Triamon may report.

He takes a deep breath, then walks to the rear terrace, where he seats himself
on the bench and quietly waits. After a time, a bird with yellow-banded black
wings alights on the wall behind the terrace, cocking its head and emitting an
irritatingly cheerful *twirrpp.*

Alyiakal concentrates on perceiving the patterns of chaos and order that flow
within the traitor bird. As he does, the bird emits another *twirrpp,* a sound so
irritating that Alyiakal wants to shoo it away, but he knows that its call is designed to bring hidden prey to the attention of mountain and forest cats, either
revealing the prey or causing the prey to move and become more vulnerable, so
that, in time, the traitor bird can scavenge the kill.

Not moving, Alyiakal continues to study the bird, until he can fix in his
mind the patterns he senses. Only then does he stand, and only then does the
traitor bird fly from the wall to the green apple tree farther from the terrace.

Alyiakal returns to the study, where he carefully takes a cupridium-tipped
pen and draws an outline of the bird, then painstakingly illustrates the concentrations of chaos with small dots, and those of order with thin dashes. Because
the only ink he has is black, he writes beneath the sketch of the bird that the
patch of chaos near the base of the left wing is white and reddish-orange. Then
he wipes the nib of the pen clean with a small rag and lets his rough sketch dry
before adding it to the one of the rat and the cat that he had done the afternoon
before. He has also studied an ant and a leafhopper, but they were too small for
him to sketch accurately; so he had written notes about them below the other
images.

Half a glass later, he gathers the papers and the copy of *Basics of Magery,*
then sets out on the long walk to Jakaafra and the house of Magus Triamon. He
still uses both his eyes and his developing order/chaos senses, always hoping to
see or discern Adayal in some fashion, but as it has been for the eightdays and
eightdays since he last met with her, his efforts are fruitless.

When he reaches Triamon's dwelling, the magus opens the door even before
Alyiakal can reach out to knock. The two walk to the study, where Alyiakal

hands the sketches and notes to Triamon, hoping that his tutor will not be too harsh.

In turn, the magus studies each of the sheets before speaking. Then he nods. "These are adequate. Perhaps slightly more than adequate. The detailing of the order flows . . . many Magi'i could not do that."

"They couldn't?" blurts Alyiakal.

"A significant number of Magi'i are so attuned to chaos that they have difficulty discerning order flows, particularly small order flows. The term you may hear, but should not use, is 'order-blind.' The use of those words offends many higher-level mages."

Alyiakal understands all too well that those with power do not like references to their faults or weaknesses.

"While you are not a student magus," Triamon goes on, "you are now close in ability to many of them, and your discernment of patterns of both order and chaos is far more than adequate." Triamon pauses, then asks, "What do you recall about the chaos pattern near the base of the wing of the traitor bird?"

"There was a small central point of whitish red—I know that doesn't make sense, but that was how it felt—and then outside that was a bit of orangish red, and outside of that was faint dull red, and the edge of the dull red . . . well, it faded into gray with tiny bits of dull red."

"Excellent!" declares Triamon.

So seldom has Alyiakal heard that word that he doesn't know what to say. Finally, he manages, "I should have written it all down."

"Most midlevel healers couldn't have done any better, and they have more experience with wounds and injuries. There are many shades to chaos, more than the shades of order. That is why even the lowest of healers need to know the shades and what each signifies, as you will need to know, one way or the other."

"Why do I need to know about healing? Are not the most valuable talents of a magus those that can be used to store and channel chaos?"

"They are . . . but even the most powerful of the Magi'i in handling chaos need to know how chaos damages the body. Also, you are more grounded in order, and order suits healing. If the Magi'i accept you for training, the more you know the better, and because many Magi'i deal more with chaos than is healthy, you should know your limits. Without understanding healing, you will not. If you do not become a magus, then you will be either a Mirror Engineer or a Mirror Lancer. Mirror Engineers deal with order flows to recharge firelances and other devices. If you are a lancer, it will help if you can aid healing of your men. That will keep you from losing too many rankers and give them cause to support you when you need it."

Alyiakal frowns.

"Mirror Lancer officers will always need the support of their men at least once, if not more often. The ones who don't get it generally die before they make major." Triamon's words are delivered in a dry, sardonic tone that emphasizes their verity.

Alyiakal starts to protest, then closes his mouth. His father does know field healing, even if he does not have the skill of even a beginning healer magus.

"The lowest and least focused chaos is a dull red, infused with gray, or gray with the slightest tinge of dull red, as you described with the traitor bird. It was likely stung by a fruit wasp."

Alyiakal winces. He has been stung only once, and he still remembers how it hurt for almost an eightday.

"Sometimes, even a bad bruise will show the dull red. If there is more than a point of intense whitish-red chaos, the wound is serious, and if that whiteness cannot be turned to the dull red with the careful infusion of free order, it is likely it will spread, and the injury will turn fatal . . ."

Alyiakal forces himself to concentrate, although it doesn't take that much effort, not when he recalls the sting of the fruit wasp.

VI

Even with two lessons a day for close to two eightdays, Alyiakal has more than enough time to continue his walks along the wall, but he sees neither Adayal nor any large panther-cats, either. He still studies the creatures of the Accursed Forest from the wall, and he can now distinguish most of them by their patterns of order and chaos, or rather chaos held in patterns by order. But Summer gives way to Harvest, and Alyiakal has yet to see Adayal, even though he now knows she must dwell there, at least part of the time.

He has realized in hindsight that inquiring about her at the market square was not the wisest of decisions, but as the eightdays have passed, he can hope that those he asked will forget, and since he and his father have never gone there together, it is likely few will even know who he is or link him to Kyal'alt, Mirror Lancer Majer.

But a young man asking about a young woman, even one touched by the Accursed Forest, isn't the greatest of indiscretions. *At least, you hope so.*

Still, he continues to observe the Forest and look for boot tracks, but he never sees or senses her. Then perhaps she is not there or has created a concealment so perfect that his order senses cannot penetrate it. How is he to know which it might be, or both . . . or neither?

He also tries a bit of limited healing, by adding a touch of order to wound chaos on one of the not-quite-stray dogs around the post and on one of the feral cats. Both seem to improve. At least, the wound chaos fades to dull red.

On the second threeday of Harvest, an eightday after his birthday, early on another evening when his father is away on patrol, for even majers must occasionally patrol, Alyiakal has removed himself from the quarters to a place on the wall from which he can watch one end of the pool some thirty yards away, the same pool that Adayal had shown him the first time he had looked into the Accursed Forest.

His awareness has expanded, and he can now sense the wards mounted on the outer side of the wall, and the intertwined pulsations of order and chaos that both link the wards and create the barrier that largely keeps the Forest from exceeding its boundaries. Even so, he can barely make out the stun lizard half-concealed by a fallen log, although it is small, from what he has seen over the past season, only two and a half yards from nose to tail. That is more than large enough to stun a man and a large horse.

He hears a rustling and the faintest of scrapings on the stone . . . and Adayal sits on the wall beside him. Yet he has sensed nothing.

"Why can't I even sense you?" he asks, trying not to sound annoyed.

"You will before long," she says. "You have grown. There is an order about you."

"Magus Triamon has been teaching me how to use order to manipulate chaos so that the chaos does not break down the order of my body."

"You've learned well. There is only a touch of the whiteness about you. If you keep working at that, and your shields, only the greatest magus would be able to tell that you are also a magus."

Alyiakal frowns for a moment. "You don't think the Magi'i will accept me?"

"You're inclined to order. Even I can sense that. Do you really want to be dominated by chaos?" She smiles gently, but ironically, then says, "I'm glad you're here."

"I've been looking for you all Summer and since."

"I know, but you needed to grow. Would you like to walk through a little part of the Great Forest with me?"

"Have I learned enough to be safe?"

"Even more than that."

"I would like that."

"Then let us go . . ." She slips down from the wall into the Forest and onto the mossy ground beside the sunstone.

Alyiakal follows, and when he stands beside her, she reaches out and takes his hand. "This way."

"Should I hold a concealment?"

"There is no need of that." Her voice is throaty yet warm.

She leads him down a path. "Look carefully, beyond that fallen trunk . . ."

He studies where she has pointed, then sees a tortoise, or perhaps it is a turtle, whose shell stretches two full yards and displays a pattern of light and dark green diamonds that hold the faintest light of their own. Farther on, he sees two gold-and-black birds perched on a limb, the like of which he has never seen.

Adayal stretches a hand out. "Wait."

Alyiakal waits. His mouth opens as a giant serpent slithers across the path some fifteen yards ahead of them, its scales a mixture of greens and browns that blend so well into the Forest that he can only make out the part of its body crossing the darker path.

In time, after she has shown him more creatures than he ever would have believed existed in such a small part of the Forest, they come to a tree whose trunk contains a small door. Adayal opens the door and gestures for him to enter.

He senses nothing within and follows her gesture. Once inside, after she closes the door, he can still see, because of a faint greenish illumination that somehow surrounds them.

"There is something else you need to learn, Alyiakal," she says gently, turning to him. "I would not have you too innocent or too unlearned about women . . . or learning from rough lancers, or women of pleasure who seek only coin." She reaches out and draws his head to her, and her lips are warm upon his.

"Slowly . . ." she murmurs, drawing him down onto the soft pallet he had not noticed. "Slowly . . . let me show you."

Alyiakal, surprised beyond belief, does . . . so afraid that the moments that follow will end, but they do not, not for glasses.

Finally, she draws her garments back on and around her. "I shouldn't keep you any longer. Try to keep some of that sweetness. The woman who best suits you will appreciate it more than you will ever know."

The woman who best suits me? Are you not that woman? How could you not be? But he does not dare to voice that question.

"It's time for you to go," she says gently.

He dresses slowly, not wanting the night to end.

Then they retrace their steps through the darkness that he scarcely notices back to the wall. After a time, they both stand at the base of the wall, outside the Forest. Alyiakal looks through the darkness, sensing Adayal as much as seeing her. He remains stunned by both the warmth and the fire Adayal had shown, and touched by the gentleness behind both.

"That is how it should be between a man and a woman," she says softly. "Never forget."

"How could I?" Abruptly, he adds, "You're not leaving Jakaafra and the Forest, are you?"

"No. I am part of the Forest, and it is part of me. I will always be here."

For all of her words, he can sense a sadness and a regret.

"You must go," she says. "It is late."

Too late, he thinks as they separate and leave the wall in different directions.

It is well past midnight when Alyiakal slips back into the quarters, only to find too many lamps lit. He sighs, if silently, and makes his way into the study.

"Where have you been?" asks the majer.

Alyiakal inclines his head politely, hoping his father will answer the question himself, as he sometimes does.

"Out walking the wall road, no doubt, and peering into the Forest." The majer shakes his head. "No matter."

Alyiakal tries not to stiffen at the resigned tone of voice.

"I've been talking to Master Triamon. He says that you have talent, but you are too rooted in order to be a magus. You also have too much ability with chaos for the Mirror Engineers, and your interests lie elsewhere. He feels that you'd never be more than the lowest of the Magi'i, if that."

Alyiakal does not sigh in relief, although relief is indeed what he feels, and he is surprised by that relief, even after what Adayal has said. *How did she know?* Except, in her own way, Adayal is as much a magus as Triamon. "Yes, ser."

"That being so . . . young man, next oneday you're leaving for Kynstaar."

"Kynstaar, ser?"

"That's where they take the sons of lancer officers and see if they can train them to be officers. Some of what they teach, you already know. Much you don't. It's time to see what you can be. There's nothing more you can learn here. You'll likely know more than some of the others and less than those from the high altage families."

"On oneday? So soon?"

"There's no point in putting it off. You'll spend two years at the lancer officer candidate school, then a year in officer training. You'll have to ride with the patrols to Geliendra, and then you'll take a firewagon from there to Kynstaar. You'll actually arrive there two eightdays late, maybe longer, but the school's used to that, because some candidates have to travel from places like Biehl or Summerdock or Syadtar, and you only get space available in the rear section of the firewagons." Kyal pauses. "There's a downside to this."

"Ser?"

"If you can't make it through the school, you'll spend at least four years as a lancer ranker."

Alyiakal manages not to swallow.

"You have the skills and the ability, son. If you fail, it will be only for lack of will."

"Yes, ser," replies Alyiakal, although he had no idea that the cost of failure would be that drastic, but there is little point in protesting. Already, he knows to pick his battles. That much he has learned from his father, from Magus Triamon, from watching the Accursed Forest . . . and from Adayal.

He does know that he cannot afford to fail, whatever it takes.

VII

On fourday, Alyiakal searches Jakaafra for Adayal, but can find no trace of her. Nor can he do so on fiveday, or sixday. On sevenday, he leaves the quarters right after dawn, determined to find her. Since he has walked all the streets of Jakaafra on the previous days, in vain, he hurries to where she had found him on threeday. She is not there. He looks to the wall, then nods. He quickly climbs the wall and stops on the top. Does he dare to enter the Forest without her protection?

Do you dare not to?

He takes some time to create both a shield and a concealment around himself, not one like he has raised before, but one more like the interlocked patterns of the great Accursed Forest creatures. Hoping that the concealment and shield will suffice, he eases himself down into the Forest and onto the shorter path, the one Adayal had led him back to the wall along at the end of their evening. He cannot see, not with his eyes, but relies on his senses. He walks as quietly as he can, not wishing to alarm any creature needlessly, but he must see Adayal one more time before he leaves for Kynstaar.

He slips around the last curve in the path before her tree bower . . . and senses that she stands by the door, as if she has expected him.

He hurries to her, dropping the concealment, then stops as he sees the sad smile. "Adayal . . . I have to leave."

"I know. I knew it would happen before long." She smiles warmly. "You can walk the Forest now, whenever you wish."

Now that I'm leaving. He pushes aside the bitterness, for it will do no good. "I learned it from you." Quickly, he adds, "I have to go to be trained as a Mirror Lancer officer . . . if I can be."

"You will be, if that is what you want."

"You and Magus Triamon both think that's what I should do."

She shakes her head. "Trying to be what we are not will destroy us. That is true for me, and it is true for you. Do you want to be a magus?" Her eyes meet his.

After a moment, he says, "No, but my choices are limited." *My realistic choices, anyway.* When she does not speak, he asks, "Will you be here when I finish training? I want you to be with me."

"Alyiakal, you have seen me. I cannot be far from the Forest, and you are meant for one kind of greatness. I cannot share that greatness. Nor would you be happy if I were by your side, because I would be but half there. We have different paths."

He finds he can say nothing.

"I will walk back to the wall with you," she says gently. "I cannot tell you how it moved me that you would enter the Forest for me."

Alyiakal's eyes burn, but he nods. He does not trust himself to speak.

She takes his hand in hers, and they begin to walk.

Two large tawny cougars, perhaps half the size of the great black panther-cats, appear and walk before them.

"They . . . they do your bidding."

"No . . . they are here to honor you. For your courage and your understanding of the Forest."

Alyiakal has his doubts, but he does not voice them.

When they reach the wall, there is a flicker, and Adayal appears as the great black panther-cat and springs to the top of the wall. Alyiakal studies her with his senses, but he can only sense what he sees. He climbs to the top of the wall, where Adayal has returned to being the black-haired, black-eyed striking woman who has loved him.

In her own fashion.

"Do you see now?" she asks softly.

He nods.

"Do great deeds, honest deeds, and do them with all your heart. You can, but they will not come soon . . . or easily. You know that. Do not forget it."

After a long moment, he slips down the wall and then steps back to look at her once more.

The two tawny cougars have joined her on the top of the whitestone wall, flanking her. She looks down at him, then speaks softly, as if to a beloved, yet her words are clear in his ears and thoughts. "You are a part of the Forest, and part of it will always be with you."

"Because of you."

"And you," she replies.

She stands there for a moment, then reappears as the great panther, framed by the two smaller tawny cougars. An instant later, the top of the wall is vacant.

Alyiakal just stares for long moments that seem to last forever, her words reverberating in his thoughts. *We have different paths.* Finally, he takes a deep breath.

After a last look at the empty wall, Alyiakal turns and begins the walk back to quarters.

VIII

Early on oneday morning, Alyiakal and his father walk through the misty air that often surrounds the Accursed Forest early in the day toward the lancer barracks—and the stables. Alyiakal carries a small duffel.

"You'll be riding with Captain Karoun and Seventh Company as far as East-end," says the majer in a matter-of-fact tone, "and then with either Captain Waelkyn or Captain Taazl to Geliendra . . ."

While Alyiakal has occasionally ridden, usually older and calmer mounts, he has never spent a day in the saddle, or even more than two glasses, but he has no doubts that his father has arranged matters so that he will be riding with Karoun, an older captain, and one of the few who has worked his way up through the ranks.

". . . If the patrols encounter Forest cats or stun lizards, stay out of the way . . ."

Since you won't let me take a sabre, what else could I do?

". . . but don't let the lancers leave you behind."

When they reach the stables, lancers are beginning to lead their mounts out, but have not begun to form up. Kyal walks toward an officer who is talking to a squad leader, then stops a good five yards away from the two . . . and two mounts tied to a short railing. The majer says nothing but does not approach the officer until the squad leader turns away.

"Good morning, Majer." Captain Karoun has a lined and weathered face and looks older than the majer to whom he reports, but his thick hair is jet black without a trace of white.

"Good morning, Captain. You've seen Alyiakal a few times before. I appreciate your escorting him to Eastend."

"My pleasure, Majer."

From what Alyiakal can sense of the captain's order/chaos flows, Karoun is neither disturbed nor pleased as he says, "You'll be riding the bay, here. She's solid and doesn't spook easily. Fasten your gear behind the saddle and the bed-roll there."

"Yes, ser." Alyiakal moves up to the mare's shoulder, and lets her register his presence before he slowly extends a hand for her to smell. After she has satisfied herself, he pats her shoulder, firmly but not hard . . . and extends a trace of what he can only think of as warm order. Only then does he step back and fasten the small duffel in place.

"Time to mount up," says the captain.

Alyiakal turns to his father. "Take care, ser."

"The same to you, son. Let me know how you're doing when you have time."

"I will." Alyiakal unties the mare, takes the reins in hand, and mounts, carefully, but not awkwardly, noting, once he is in the saddle, that there is also a water bottle in a holder.

The majer steps to the side, but Alyiakal can feel his father's eyes on his back as he rides beside the captain toward the front of the column.

"You're headed to Kynstaar, I hear," says Karoun, clearly to make conversation, since he has to know Alyiakal's destination.

"Yes, ser. The officer candidate school." Alyiakal would like to know what the captain thinks but decides not to ask immediately. There will likely be time over the next several days.

"Do you know why the majer wanted you to ride with companies patrolling the northeast and southeast walls, rather than the west walls?"

"He never said, ser, but I've heard that there are more incidents with growths and Forest creatures along the northwest wall."

"That's true, but we could still encounter stun lizards or the black Forest panthers, and I'll need to keep watch for those. You'll be riding with Lancer Raenyld, in the rank behind me. If we do encounter anything, you're to follow his orders. Do you understand?"

"Yes, ser." Alyiakal has no doubt that Raenyld has orders to keep him clear of any action, and given that he has no weapons, that makes sense, even as he wonders if he could use what he learned from Adayal to keep a Forest creature from attacking him.

Raenyld turns out to be one of the younger rankers, and doesn't look to be more than five years older than Alyiakal, if that.

Once the company is formed up and moving onto the whitestone road bordering the Forest wall, Raenyld asks, "Have you ever seen one of the giant black Forest cats?"

"Only from a distance," replies Alyiakal, which is true enough, given that he hasn't specified the distance.

"That's the best place to see them."

"Have you had to use your firelance against one?"

"Not yet, but I saw first squad take one down. It took the lances of three troopers, and it was a small one. That was when we were patrolling the northwest wall."

"Keep the talk down." That order doesn't come from the captain, but from the senior squad leader riding beside him.

Since there is to be no idle talk, or not much of it, while on patrol, Alyiakal decides to see what he can sense beyond the wall, possibly even to sense Adayal, unlikely as it may be, only to discover he can sense little. For a moment, he wonders why, because he's been able to sense the Accursed Forest before. Then he realizes that he has done so when he was on the top of the wall—*inside the wards.*

For a time, he tries to probe beyond the wards, since he feels that there must be a way, but he can find none, or perhaps his senses simply are not strong enough. Instead, he studies the lancers and their mounts, trying to discover if any show the kind of white free chaos that swirls around Magus Triamon, or the darkness of order.

Within a glass, he has studied all the lancers close enough for him to sense clearly. While a few show tiny bits of dull red in gray, he decides those instances are so small that they must be small cuts or bruises. He also can sense that the total amount of order and chaos varies slightly from individual to individual, but not by that much, and that most of it is bound in some fashion into their bodies, unlike Magus Triamon, who is surrounded with additional free order and chaos, but mostly chaos.

Almost two glasses pass without any sign of Forest creatures, trees fallen across the wall, or Forest sprouts. Then the captain says something to the senior squad leader, who in turn orders, "Company! Halt!"

Alyiakal is more than glad to dismount when that order comes and less enthused after the break when the command comes to mount once more and to form up. Over the next glass, Alyiakal concentrates on studying the mounts. The one thing he does discover is that the mare he rides seems to have slightly less order and chaos than most of the other horses, but she does not seem ill.

Because she's older and not up to supporting a lancer in fighting Forest creatures?

That is a guess on his part, but from what his father and Magus Triamon have said about how lancers are wary of those who have any order/chaos abilities, he's not about to ask, because he doesn't want to reveal his small skills and a question about the mare's age and ability to support a fighting lancer will mark him as trying to impress or complaining about the mount he has been given.

Riding for two glasses, resting and watering the horses, and then doing it all again is the pattern for the entire day, and it is close to twilight when Seventh Company reaches the lancer way station, located a third of the way to Eastend. By then, most of his muscles are sore, and his legs are unsteady for several moments when he dismounts.

Twoday and threeday are no different, except that on threeday evening he eats with the officers at Eastend and is introduced to Captain Taazl, and Third Company, which he will accompany the remainder of the way to Geliendra. Taazl is polite and formal, but, Alyiakal senses, not all that pleased to be escorting him to Geliendra.

On sixday evening, when Third Company rides into the Mirror Lancer post at Geliendra, Alyiakal studies the immaculate whitestone gateposts on the north side of the compound. Not only are they at least ten cubits tall, but they're set far enough apart that they can accommodate two carriages abreast and support polished white-oak gates that he suspects have seldom been closed. The compound walls run at least a kay on a side.

Seeing those walls so close to the Forest wall jolts Alyiakal. For a moment, he wonders why, before realizing that their positioning, comparatively close as they are, shows so clearly the separation between the Great Forest and the life and duty of a Mirror Lancer and what lies before him.

Thinking again of Adayal, he feels his eyes burn, and he swallows.

As the column rides through the gates, the lancer beside Alyiakal says quietly, "These are the patrol gates. The impressive gates are the ones on the south side. They face the town."

To Alyiakal, the north gates are impressive in themselves, and he nods, taking in all the white stonework as he rides to the patrol stable with the rest of the company. There he dismounts and unsaddles the mare. He is still working on grooming her, if with helpful hints from one of the rankers, when a junior squad leader wearing an immaculate green-trimmed cream-white uniform appears.

"Are you Alyiakal, the son of Majer Kyal, the officer in charge of Northpoint Post?"

"Yes, ser."

"Just 'Squad Leader.' The 'ser's only go to officers. You're to come with me to be signed in with the other candidate."

Alyiakal feels stupid. He *knows* that. "Yes, Squad Leader."

"This way, and bring whatever gear you have."

Alyiakal looks at the grooming brush in his hand.

"I'll take that," says the ranker. "Best of fortune."

"Thank you." Alyiakal hands over the brush, then picks up his duffel and follows the squad leader from the stable and along one of the sunstone walks past two low buildings and into a third, then down a hallway and into a small waiting room where another young man stands. Like Alyiakal, he is black-haired, but is several digits taller, and burlier. Alyiakal has the feeling that he is also older. At least, he looks older.

Before Alyiakal can even introduce himself, a Mirror Lancer captain appears. From the officer's apparent age, Alyiakal has no doubts that the captain is a former senior squad leader who won his rank through ability and survivability.

The captain surveys both young men, focusing more intently on Alyiakal, then asks, "You're Majer Kyal's son?"

"Yes, ser."

"Good. Baertal, this is Alyiakal. Alyiakal, this is Baertal." The captain nods to the taller youth, then goes on, "From this moment on, you're both Mirror Lancers, either as an officer candidate, or, if you're not suited for that, as a ranker-in-training. When you get to Kynstaar, you'll be issued your uniforms and gear. The first eightdays there will be similar to basic ranker training, except harder because you'll also have to keep up with your studies. You'll need to work hard because many of those at the candidate school have had the benefit of excellent instruction and arms training."

The captain looks to Alyiakal. "How much training in bladework have you had?"

"I can keep from getting badly bruised when sparring. I don't know how that compares to anything."

"That will be helpful."

Alyiakal notes that the captain does not ask the same question of Baertal.

"There's space for you two on the firewagon that leaves Geliendra eightday morning. You're to remain on the post until then. Failure to do so will be considered desertion, with the appropriate consequences. Tonight and tomorrow night, you two will share a room in the officers' quarters. You'll also eat in the officers' mess. Appreciate it while you can." The captain gestures to the squad leader. "Asquall will show you around briefly. Eat immediately when the mess opens on eightday morning and have your gear with you. A squad leader will meet you there with your orders." The captain pauses, then asks, "Any questions?"

"No, ser," replies Baertal.

"Thank you, ser," says Alyiakal. "I don't know enough to ask questions."

"Then it might be best not to say so," replies the captain, his tone politely pleasant, but not hard.

"Yes, ser."

"This way, Candidates," says Asquall.

Alyiakal picks up his duffel, letting Baertal be the first to follow the squad leader from the room.

After taking Alyiakal and Baertal to their quarters to leave their gear and then providing a hurried tour of the post, Squad Leader Asquall shows them to the mess, where several undercaptains stand near one wall and talk.

The squad leader points to the end of a table. "That's the junior officers' table. You two sit there. But you don't sit down until everyone else does. Stand when the officers do, and sit when they do. You'll be served last. Don't eat until the senior officer does, and stop eating, if you haven't finished, when he stands and leaves." After a pause, he adds, "At breakfast, you serve yourself, but defer to any officers." Then he turns and leaves.

Baertal eases away from the table and toward the wall.

Alyiakal follows his example.

After a short time, Baertal looks at Alyiakal. "You haven't said much. I don't even know where you're from."

"Jakaafra. What about you?"

"I'm from here, Geliendra."

While Alyiakal had noted that the captain seemed to know or know about Baertal, he is pleased to have his suspicion confirmed. "Have you lived here long?"

"For the past four years. Before that, my mother and I stayed with her parents in Fyrad. We couldn't go to Inividra or Assyadt. What about you?"

"The same sort of thing, except it was the last three years." Alyiakal isn't about to mention the time he'd spent with his great-aunt in Pyraan, little more than a hamlet north of Westend, after his mother's death when his father had commanded the Mirror Lancer post at Isahl.

"Your grandfather a lancer as well?" asks Baertal.

"He was. I never knew him." That was because he'd been killed by the barbarians of Cerlyn when Alyiakal's father hadn't been that much older than Alyiakal now happens to be.

"Barbarians or the Accursed Forest?" Baertal's tone is matter-of-fact, as if those two were the only causes of death for a lancer.

"Barbarians," returns Alyiakal. "What about your grandfather?"

"My father's the first Mirror Lancer in the family. My uncle was the second."

"Your father must be very good, then."

"He was. He's stipended now. Do you have any brothers?"

"No," replies Alyiakal. "No sisters, either. You?"

"One brother. He's a lot older. He's a Mirror Engineer in Fyrad."

"Could he have been a magus?"

"He likes order and devices too much." Baertal's words are both amused and wistful.

"While you have different interests?"

"Good horses and pretty girls," replies Baertal offhandedly.

"I haven't ridden that much. Well . . . except in the last eightday. I rode with the patrols from Jakaafra to Geliendra."

Baertal frowns momentarily, then asks, "Did you see any Forest creatures?"

"Not on the ride here."

"Then you've seen them before? Are they more common in the north part of the Accursed Forest?"

"Only once or twice. A great black panther and a small stun lizard. They were both close to the wall."

"And you're still here?"

"They seemed like other animals. I didn't bother them, and they didn't bother me. Besides, what else could I do?" Alyiakal sees more officers entering the mess, most of whom appear to be undercaptains and captains.

"You walked that close to the wall? That doesn't seem very smart."

"I was careful."

Baertal shakes his head. "Careful isn't enough, not around the Accursed Forest."

"Then I guess I was fortunate."

"You can't count on fortune, not as a Mirror Lancer," declares Baertal firmly. "Lancers have to create their own fortune."

"You think that lancers from altage families in Cyad don't have advantages?" asks Alyiakal.

"At first, but that doesn't last. Barbarians and stun lizards don't care about family or who you know."

Alyiakal nods, adding, "That's certainly true." *But position and wealth can purchase skilled instruction.* Just as his father has passed on what skills he can and paid a magus to expand Alyiakal's own talents.

"You'll see," replies Baertal, as if he senses doubt behind Alyiakal's words. "If you make it through training and survive your first duty post."

That goes for you as well. But all Alyiakal says is, "I'm sure I will."

Abruptly, the officers in the mess move to stand at places at the long junior officers' table and a much shorter table, where a majer and three overcaptains stand.

"As you were," orders the majer.

Alyiakal follows their example, taking his place across the table from Baertal.

IX

When Baertal says he wants to walk around the post after dinner to stretch his legs, he has more than that in mind, but Alyiakal merely nods and says, "Have a good walk. I could use the sleep."

That is true, since Alyiakal is indeed tired. He sleeps soundly, although he wakes briefly when Baertal enters the room they share well after midnight.

When Alyiakal rises for breakfast, Baertal is sound asleep, and Alyiakal does not wake him, but goes to the mess and eats a decent breakfast. Then he sets out to explore the post, discovering in the process that there is a section that holds modest family housing for consorted officers.

That suggests where Baertal may have been, but since the quarters are not for stipended officers, as Alyiakal already knew, it raises other questions. For the present, Alyiakal decides not to raise those questions, although the first chance he has is when he sees Baertal at the officers' mess on sevenday evening.

"Did you have a good day?" he asks Baertal as the two seat themselves.

"Very good. What about you?"

"I explored the post. It's rather large, and there's a lot to see. What about your day?"

"I spent some of it with friends. I didn't want to pass up the chance, since it will be some time before I'll see them again."

Once more, from the shades of chaos around the other, Alyiakal can tell that his words are less than the entire truth. "You're fortunate to have that opportunity. Everywhere I've been, there's been almost no one close to my age. I imagine there were at least a few for you when you lived in Fyrad."

"A few. Not many."

"Are any of them here now?"

Baertal shakes his head, then takes a small swallow of the ale in his mug.

"What do you know about the officer training in Kynstaar?" asks Alyiakal.

"It's hard. Less than a third of those who enter leave as undercaptains."

"What's the most difficult part?"

Baertal shrugs. "It's all hard. My brother says that whatever you're the weakest at is the hardest." He turns his attention to the emburhka dished out by the server—a fresh-faced ranker who looks no older than Alyiakal.

After the ranker serves Alyiakal, he says quietly, "Thank you."

Baertal frowns momentarily, but says nothing.

Tired of trying to draw out Baertal, Alyiakal concentrates on eating the emburhka, which is merely spiced to be hot, without subtlety, but more than acceptable, and the small loaf of warm bread, which is actually quite good. The wine is about the same as what he has had at home. He's glad he doesn't have to drink the ale served to rankers, although it's said to be decent, because he's never much cared for lager or ale.

As on sixday evening, Baertal takes his leave after dinner and does not return to the small shared room until late.

Both wake early, but because Baertal does not speak as they wash up, dress, and head for the mess, carrying their gear, neither does Alyiakal, especially since the shades of chaos around Baertal suggest that he is somewhat agitated, although his expression is merely stolid. At the mess, the two eat quickly.

Not totally surprising, the one who escorts them from the mess to the front gates is again Asquall.

"The firewagon should be here in less than a quint," Asquall announces. "You two will sit in the rear section."

Moments later, two captains appear, each with a single duffel. They stand well away from the squad leader and the two candidates.

Perhaps half a quint later, Alyiakal catches sight of the arriving firewagon, the early-morning sunlight reflected off the glass wind and rain screen of the driver's compartment as the firewagon nears the post gates. After the firewagon comes to a stop, the driver does not leave his position in the glass-fronted forward compartment, but the lancer ranker seated beside him opens the narrow side door and steps out. He opens the door to the forward passenger compartment, right behind the front wheels, and a Mirror Lancer subcommander and a majer step out.

Then the lancer announces, "Officers first."

The two captains step forward and enter the forward passenger compartment, designed to convey four passengers comfortably.

Only then does the lancer ranker turn to Asquall and his charges. "Just two from here?"

"That's all," replies Asquall.

"Be more comfortable, then. Leastwise, till you get to Chulbyn." The lancer leads Baertal and Alyiakal past the cargo compartment and the power section, with two wheels on each side, to the rear passenger compartment, where he opens the rear door. "Gear under the seat."

Four other young men sit in the rear section, two each on the two bench seats, each of which can hold five passengers, tightly. Baertal enters first and takes the middle front-facing seat, quickly sliding his duffel underneath the thinly padded bench. In turn, Alyiakal takes the middle rear-facing seat.

Unlike the forward passenger compartment, which has large windows, the two windows in the rear, one on each side, are small. As he slides his gear under the seat, Alyiakal notices that both windows have been lowered halfway. He suspects that is all the farther down they will go. He has barely seated himself before the driver's assistant closes the door.

As the firewagon begins to move, Alyiakal hears a faint whining, and the slight rumbling of the wheels on the sunstone of the avenue that will lead to the highway flanking the Great Canal. He can also sense what feels like a continual swirl of confined chaos from behind him.

The power compartment.

"What's your name?" asks the flame-haired youth to Alyiakal's left. "I'm Hyrsaal. That's Khaarl on your other side. We're both from Fyrad."

"Alyiakal. From Jakaafra."

"If you three wouldn't mind," says Baertal crossly, "some of us would like a chance to sleep. You might try it, too, while you can."

Alyiakal looks to Hyrsaal, who shrugs, as if it's of no import to him, then abruptly grins with an infectious warmth and mouths, "Once he's asleep . . ."

If he ever sleeps.

Except that Alyiakal knows that Baertal will sleep, sooner or later, because

they will not reach Chulbyn until dawn on oneday, and the trip from there to
Kynstaar will take almost as long, not counting the time they may have to wait
at Chulbyn.

He offers Hyrsaal an amused smile in return.

X

For the next three days, Alyiakal and the other candidates receive indifferent
food and sleep fitfully as they can seated on the hard benches of the firewagon
or on pallet beds at Chulbyn. Nine officer candidates finally emerge from the
firewagon at Kynstaar in midmorning on threeday, each carrying a bag, satchel,
or duffel of some sort.

Alyiakal is groggy and looks around the bare sunstone platform, taking in
the stone walls and the low buildings to the north of the highway. To the south
is a plain largely filled with golden-tan grass that is perhaps waist-high with
only scattered clumps of trees. In moments, his groggy stupor lifts as the cool
Autumn wind flows past him and he realizes how much cooler Kynstaar is than
either Jakaafra or Geliendra. He sees that Hyrsaal appears to be shivering, possibly because the redheaded candidate wears only a light hemp shirt without an
undertunic, although Alyiakal doesn't find the wind that cold.

Or is he worried about what comes next?

Alyiakal scarcely has a moment for that speculation, because a graying captain and a squad leader appear.

"Officer candidates," declares the captain, "I presume?"

"Yes, ser," responds Alyiakal before Hyrsaal and Baertal do.

"Three of you can get out the proper response when you're disoriented and
tired," the captain continues. "That should improve. The squad leader will get
you signed in, assigned bunks and uniforms. Then you'll get a basic orientation,
which will last until the evening mess. Get a good night's sleep. You'll need it."
After a pause, he goes on, "I'll leave you with one point. Right now, you are not
officer candidates. You are candidates to become officer candidates." The captain
turns. "They're all yours, Squad Leader."

Alyiakal can't say he's surprised as he follows the unnamed squad leader to a
stone building where a rank clerk takes names, checks them against a list, and
provides each candidate with a card listing his barracks and bed number.

From there, the nine go to the supply building, where they're given three
sets of uniforms, underclothes, socks, and boots. The uniforms are not the crisp

cream-whites of Mirror Lancers, but pale khaki brown without insignia. The boots Alyiakal is issued are dull brown, as is the belt he receives.

Next comes a visit to a lancer barber, followed by cold showers, donning uniforms, and turning over all personal gear for storage, after which the squad leader marches them to their quarters. The quarters consist of a long room in a one-story building that holds raised pallet beds, each one with a doorless chest holding open shelves and a space for boots below. The windows are unglazed, but have heavy shutters.

The squad leader demonstrates how the uniforms are to be folded and stored, then orders them to duplicate the process, following up with a polite but condescending critique of each candidate's failures, and a reminder that bunks and chests will be inspected regularly.

Following that exercise, the nine are marched to another stone building where Alyiakal is surprised to find small desks with chairs, beside which the nine stand, as ordered by the squad leader. That surprise is succeeded by another—the appearance of a Mirror Lancer subcommander.

"As you were," orders the subcommander, also gesturing for them to sit down and waiting for the nine to settle themselves before continuing. "You were told that you are only candidates to become officer candidates. That is true. There are two ways to become a Mirror Lancer officer, and both end here in Kynstaar. No new Mirror Lancer officer is commissioned except through a minimum of a year's training here. Candidates who have advanced education from other sources and who are found to have the potential to become officers still must finish that education and training here, and they will join those of you who succeed in your education and training over the next two years for the final year. How you perform over the next two years will determine whether you qualify for that final year. Most of you who succeed finishing the first two years will likely succeed in the third. That has not been the case with those who will join you in that third year . . ."

From what Alyiakal can sense, the subcommander is being completely truthful, since Alyiakal has observed that lying usually creates an increased flurry of personal chaos.

". . . some of you will silently question why we even allow the other avenue of training, when so many fail, but just as the Magi'i allow those with ability but not born into elthage families to become a magus, so must the Mirror Lancers offer an opportunity to others not born into altage families the chance to become a Mirror Lancer officer.

"Being either a Mirror Lancer officer or a magus requires discipline, dedication, and skill because each can control and wield great power. The next years will determine which of you will develop, master, and control those skills." The subcommander offers a cold smile, then adds, "Those of you who dismiss what I have said will likely fail. Some will be injured. A few may die. That is part of the price of being a Mirror Lancer officer." He pauses again. "Captain Traukyl will now provide the rest of your basic orientation."

"Attention!" snaps the squad leader.

Alyiakal knows enough to remain standing while the subcommander departs and the captain enters the instruction room.

"As you were," declares the captain, waiting for everyone to be seated before continuing. "Your time at Kynstaar will require the mastery of all manner of physical skills, not just skills in weapons and riding. It will require education not only in military matters and history, but also about the cultures and military tactics of the barbarians who live beyond the borders of Cyador. You will have to learn the basics of how magery operates and what its strengths and limits are. And those are but the beginning . . ."

Alyiakal listens carefully as the captain outlines what awaits him and what will be required of him. At the same time, he wonders how what he has learned of magery can be useful, besides in bladework.

ALYIAKAL'ALT

Kynstaar & Pemedra

XI

The early-fall sun warms the midmorning air of Kynstaar as Alyiakal dons for the first time the green-trimmed formal whites of a Mirror Lancer officer, if without the silver bars that will soon confirm his father's prediction. His eyes do not take in his image in the mirror, but are focused on certain pieces of the seemingly endless eightdays of the past three years . . .

* * *

The hard-faced squad leader extends a wooden wand with the grip of a lancer sabre to Alyiakal. "Take it."

Alyiakal takes the wand, and the squad leader steps back.

"Undercaptain Faaryn says you're pretty good with these, Candidate. That so?"

Alyiakal knows there is no good answer that is accurate and no accurate answer that will be acceptable. "I've had some training, Squad Leader, but I haven't sparred with enough people to know if I even compare to an experienced lancer."

The squad leader raises his sabre wand. "You're about to find out, Candidate."

Alyiakal raises his wand, but not too high, having seen earlier how the squad leader feints high and attacks low, except the instructor continues beyond the feint and Alyiakal barely slides the instructor's wand away from his own body. Still he recovers, ignoring the apparent opening that has to be a trap, and angles his wand toward the squad leader's knee, then shifts his attack as he senses the other's intent, sidestepping, and deciding not to strike the other's wrist, instead just deflecting another attack, before beating down the instructor's wand and circling.

"Defense means nothing against a barbarian with a heavy blade," declares the instructor, again attacking. "You have to strike quickly and move on to the next one."

Alyiakal senses his chance, and makes two quick moves, disarming the squad leader, and then tapping him on the shoulder before stepping back.

The squad leader frowns, and his eyes narrow.

Alyiakal picks up the dropped wand and tenders it to the other, alert and ready to move if the instructor tries a surprise attack.

"Where did you learn that?"

"From a Mirror Lancer majer, Squad Leader."

"How long did you work with him?"

"About three years."

"You'll spar with Squad Leader Ghaud or Captain Zuhland. If they're not here, you'll spend sparring time working with weights. Your technique's good, but one of those burly barbarians could force your sabre from your hand . . . or lift you from the saddle with the impact on your blade. Start on the weights now."

"Yes, Squad Leader," replies Alyiakal. He has seen Captain Zuhland use a blade, and Zuhland is better than Alyiakal's father. Much better . . . and that will lead to more bruises.

* * *

"Why do we use cupridium blades, Candidate Alyiakal?" asks the captain as he stands beside the classroom lectern.

Alyiakal can sense that the question is a trap. He knows that the Mirror Lancers have always used cupridium blades, and he knows their advantages, but not why they were first used. Or why they continue to be used. "Because they're stronger and hold an edge longer than iron blades, ser?"

"That's partly true enough, but only partly. Candidate Whasyl?"

"Because they're the best blades in the world, ser?"

The captain shakes his head. "They're not the best blades in the world. Does anyone know what the best blade in the world might be?"

Abruptly, Hyrsaal says, "The twin sabres of the second Emperor of Light, ser?"

"That's right, Candidate. Can any of you now answer the original question?"

"Is it that cupridium blades are the best we can make without spending an inordinate amount of time, order, and chaos?" asks Alyiakal.

"That's also true but not complete. Think about the processes."

Alyiakal does so, and then wants to shake his head.

"Candidate Alyiakal, are you in pain or do you have a thought?"

"Cupridium blades are cast, and order and chaos are imbued in the process. An iron blade with equal strength has to be forge-welded with the aid of a magus—"

"Precisely. A cast cupridium blade is superior to all but the finest of mage-forged iron blades, and it takes a tiny fraction of the time and effort. Scores of cupridium blades can be created by an engineer smith and a journeyman magus with far less cost and effort than embodied in just one blade that would be superior to a cupridium blade. The same process is used with firelances. In fact, spent firelances can be used as regular lances effectively. But only as a last resort. Why is that, Candidate Ghelmyn?"

"Because you'd waste chaos, ser?"

"You weren't listening. Candidate Whasyl?"

"Because you might damage the aiming or chaos mechanisms, ser?"

"Exactly, and that requires extensive engineering repairs." The captain turns. "Candidate Baertal, why don't we use firewagons to supply border outposts?"

Alyiakal remains intent on the captain, who can instantly discern who is tired or not paying attention . . .

*   *   *

The cold rain of early Winter pelts down on the roof as Alyiakal leaves the candidates' mess. Although he has yet to receive a letter, he checks his postbox before he heads back to the barracks and is surprised to see that it contains a letter. Puzzled, he extracts the missive and breaks the seal. He immediately recognizes the handwriting.

> Alyiakal—
>
>   I am certain that you have wondered why I have not written before this. It is not a lack of care or affection, but a result of the year I spent as an instructor at Kynstaar. Few candidates initially deluged by letters from family and others were successful. I would not do that to you. More than anything, I wish you success and fulfillment in what you set out to achieve.
>
>   As you have seen, the Rational Stars are far from rational in their impact on our lives. Happiness and love can be snatched away in an instant . . .

Alyiakal swallows at those words, words he had never heard from his father, then continues reading.

> . . . so can position and golds or silvers. Rivalry and pettiness exist even within the Mirror Lancers, and they can be as deadly as a barbarian's massive blade, both to the recipient of that pettiness and, in time, to the ones who foment evil out of their petty spirits. All we have, all you will ever have for certain, are the self-discipline you develop, the skills and knowledge you master, the affection you offer without conditions, and the respect others give you freely. Everything else can be taken in an instant. While this is more apparent to Mirror Lancers, and especially to officers, it is true for everyone in Cyador, from the lowest ranker to the Emperor of Light himself.
>
>   You have more raw ability than I ever had, and that is why I have always insisted on your doing the best you can do. All too often, those with great

natural abilities fail because they do not understand that any ability, by itself, without the hard work to perfect it, is a fatal flaw that will destroy a man. For your own sake, never forget that.

From here on, I will write, but not frequently.

But it is signed "Father."

Alyiakal feels the burning in his eyes. He slips the letter under his oiled waterproof and walks out into the rain, not that he feels it.

*   *   *

On a cool Spring morning the entire group of candidates, who had entered training the previous fall, stands mustered outside the barracks for inspection, as is the case every sevenday. The inspecting officer, one of the captains, is always accompanied by a squad leader with a stack of cards on which to note discrepancies . . . and there are always discrepancies, although Alyiakal has accumulated fewer than most, but not so few as Baertal.

As the inspecting officer walks toward the front of the formation, Alyiakal stiffens. Even without looking, which he cannot do, not and remain at attention, with his eyes forward, he can sense that someone else is with the officer, someone infused with the white of chaos.

A magus! The only reason a magus might wish to inspect the candidates is to determine if any of the candidates have discernible abilities with chaos.

While Alyiakal has continued working to improve his abilities, particularly concealments and shields, he's been careful to do so in the dark, although he carries a light shield all the time, except when involved in arms practice. Still . . .

As he stands there, he contracts his shield closer to his body and does the best he can to match the pattern of order and chaos that other candidates manifest, if with a touch more order. Then he waits . . . and hopes.

"Candidate Alyiakal," declares the captain, "uniform and boots satisfactory." Then he looks to the white-clad magus.

"Slightly higher levels of order," states the magus. "Additional training in field healing might be warranted, depending on practical abilities."

Alyiakal maintains the slightly artificial levels of order and chaos in his shield until the magus is too far away to detect anything and the inspecting officer orders, "Dismissed for instruction."

As Alyiakal walks toward the instructional building, Hyrsaal and Liathyr join him.

"What was that all about, do you think?" asks Liathyr. "Why was a magus inspecting us with the captain?"

"Looking for someone with chaos-using ability who might be a candidate for the Mirror Engineers," suggests Hyrsaal. "Anyone with really strong abilities with order and chaos is likely already being trained as a magus."

"They said something more to you, didn't they?" Liathyr asks Alyiakal.

"The magus said I had slightly higher order levels and that I should be considered for additional training in field healing . . . if I turned out to be smart enough to learn it," says Alyiakal wryly. "He didn't say it that way, though."

"Is that bad?" asks Hyrsaal.

"My father said that it never hurt for an officer to know more about field healing."

"Makes sense," says Liathyr.

Alyiakal still worries about field healing, but all full healers are women, and not Magi'i, but if he is selected for such training, he knows he'll have to be very careful.

At least the magus didn't discover too much.

* * *

Out of habit, after the evening meal, some two eightdays past midsummer, Alyiakal checks his message box. It is, of course, empty. That is not surprising. He never receives letters from anyone, except his father, and then only a few days after seasonturn. Five letters a year. To each, Alyiakal replies, informing his father of his progress.

Officer candidates are limited to four letters per season paid for by the Mirror Lancers . . . and as many as they can pay for beyond that, at a cost of a silver a letter, but most can't afford many, given that their pay is five coppers an eightday. The only other people Alyiakal might consider writing are Magus Triamon and Adayal, but he wouldn't have the faintest idea of where to send a letter for Adayal, except through Triamon. Nor would he wish to entrust what he might write to the eyes of anyone besides her, or, as a last resort, Triamon. *And Adayal does know where you are and could write if she wanted.* As for Triamon, there will be a letter, but only after Alyiakal becomes an undercaptain.

As he turns away from the message box, he stops short, sensing Hyrsaal, and that the other candidate is disturbed.

Hyrsaal looks up. "Oh, it's you. I was afraid it might be Baertal or Ghallyr."

"What about them?"

"They'll make some comment about my unfortunate choice of friends."

"You mean about Khaarl?" All Alyiakal knows is that Khaarl had disappeared between lamps-out and morning muster, but that is always the way it is with a candidate who is found unsatisfactory.

"I knew he was having trouble with reading the material and keeping up," replies Hyrsaal, shaking his head, "but I didn't realize it was that bad."

"He'd likely still have made a better officer than Ghallyr." Alyiakal also knows that there are other reasons, not all of them fair.

"He would, but we don't make those decisions," replies Hyrsaal. Then he offers an amused smile. "I do have something for you."

Something for me? Alyiakal hasn't the faintest idea why Hyrsaal, even as the closest person to a friend he has, would have anything for him. He gestures to the letters Hyrsaal holds. "I see you're fortunate tonight."

"Not exactly."

"I'm sorry. I don't mean to pry . . ."

"You're kind." Hyrsaal pauses. "They're all from family. My older brother . . ."

"The one who's posted to Isahl? Has something happened?"

"It could have been worse," says the redhead heavily. "He'll get a stipend."

Alyiakal waits.

"He lost his right leg at the knee. The letters are from my mother and my sisters."

"I'm so sorry."

"If you're a Mirror Lancer officer, that's always a possibility." Hyrsaal forces a smile. "I said I had something for you." He hands Alyiakal a smaller letter. "It's from my younger sister Saelora. I mentioned you in one of my letters. She said I was boring and sent this, hoping you'd respond." Hyrsaal grins. "I haven't read it. I wouldn't dare."

Alyiakal looks down at the letter. Then he smiles. "Thank you."

"Thank Saelora. It was her idea."

"I will."

Once back in the barracks, Alyiakal sits on the edge of the raised pallet bed, breaks the seal, and begins to read.

Alyiakal—

   I hope you don't mind my writing you. My brother has mentioned you, and that you had no sisters to write you. If you like, pretend I'm your sister and write back. You don't have to. This is just an invitation . . .

Alyiakal shakes his head in amusement. *How can you not write back? Besides, it would be nice to get an occasional letter.*

* * *

In the heat of Harvest, seemingly hotter than even midsummer, Alyiakal is working with weights while the other candidates spar with each other, since neither Squad Leader Ghaud nor Captain Zuhland happens to be available. While working with the weights is boring, it has brought results in greater arm and upper-body strength. It also helps that Alyiakal has grown several digits and broadened, as his father predicted.

Alyiakal senses two candidates behind him, moving toward one of the practice circles. One is Baertal, whom he can recognize by his chaos patterns.

". . . doesn't spar too much . . . thinks he's too good for us . . ." Baertal's voice is quietly scornful.

"You think you're as good as he is?" asks another voice, that of Captain Zuhland.

Alyiakal suspects that Baertal knew Zuhland was nearby and made the comment to have the chance to spar with Alyiakal.

"Candidate Baertal," says Zuhland quietly. "Go to the circle there. Candidate Alyiakal will be there shortly."

"Yes, ser."

Alyiakal can sense the feel of triumph in Baertal, but lowers the weights and turns to see what the captain has to say.

"Give him some bruises. Then disarm him."

"Yes, ser." What Alyiakal knows, and what the captain likely does as well, is that Baertal will not stay within the parameters of sparring, and if caught, will claim that any untoward move was unintentional or merely a reaction to Alyiakal's attack. All that makes Alyiakal's task more difficult, but he merely picks up the sabre wand and walks to the circle. The captain stands, observing.

"You may begin, Candidate Alyiakal, since you were challenged," declares Zuhland.

Alyiakal has watched Baertal enough to know that the moment he lifts his blade, Baertal will attempt an immediate and violent thrust. So he brings his wand up quickly, moves past Baertal's wand, and strikes the back of Baertal's arm below the shoulder hard, then steps back, knowing that will enrage the other.

"Sneaky bastard," murmurs Baertal. "Son of a worthless majer."

Alyiakal ignores the taunt, holding his guard for an instant, until he senses Baertal's next move, which he counters, then slips past, jamming the padded blunt tip of the wand into Baertal's chest before darting back.

"Frigging dancer, never survive a real fight."

Alyiakal anticipates the other's strike at his knee and again strikes Baertal's sword arm, before slamming his wand down on the other's wrist.

Baertal's wand hits the dust.

"Enough!" snaps Zuhland.

Alyiakal steps back quickly, but does not lower his wand.

"Candidate Baertal," declares Zuhland, his voice cold. "If you'd been using cupridium blades, you'd have been dead in moments. Go see a healer about that wrist. Now." Almost without stopping, he goes on, "Candidate Alyiakal, you could use some understanding. From here on, you will spar with your left hand."

Despite the coldness in Zuhland's voice, Alyiakal can sense no anger at all, a feeling more like grim satisfaction.

Even as Baertal picks up the fallen wand with his left hand and moves away, his smoldering fury is likely obvious to everyone.

"Candidate Alyiakal . . . left hand. Candidate Fuhlart, take the circle."

Alyiakal takes the wand in his left hand. It feels awkward, but he knows Fuhlart is only adequate with the wand. He only hopes he won't have too many bruises before he becomes at least adequate left-handed. If not, the nearly two years left in training will feel even longer.

* * *

Alyiakal frowns as he extracts the letter from the message box, wondering who could have written him. Certainly not Saelora, because he had written her more than three eightdays ago, and had heard nothing. So who could it be?

He slips the letter inside his uniform tunic and walks back to the barracks and his bed, where he sits on the edge and breaks the seal, immediately noticing the precise and beautiful penmanship.

> *Alyiakal—*
>
> *I'm so glad you wrote back. I'd hoped you would. I'm late in replying, but that is because Mother withheld your letter from me until Karola persuaded her that Hyrsaal would not have mentioned you if you didn't meet his standards. His standards for friends are high, and he's almost never wrong about character. He told Karola you were quiet, but honest, and very determined.*
>
> *Right now, I'm an apprentice of sorts to the local scrivener here in Vaeyal. It's a little town some ten kays south and west of Geliendra on the Great Canal. I can't be an official apprentice because I'm a girl, but it was a way to help Buurel, and for me to learn more . . .*

Alyiakal smiles as he continues to read.

* * *

As Alyiakal, Hyrsaal, and Liathyr leave the barracks for the mess and breakfast, Alyiakal can see that light snow has fallen across Kynstaar, which is unusual, even in mid-Winter, and which will likely melt as the day passes, despite the raw wind out of the west, which feels as though it has come directly from the Roof of the World.

Not that far behind walk Baertal and Ghallyr.

Baertal's voice is loud, deliberately so, Alyiakal can tell.

"If you're good with the sabre, or even the firelance, all that gets you is immediate duty fighting barbarians." Baertal laughs sardonically. "The better you are, the more the Majer-Commander will keep you fighting barbarians, and the less likely you'll ever see Cyad. The barbarians breed like coneys, and no matter how many you kill, even with blades in both hands, there are always more. Even majers with experience can die if they're posted to the borders enough."

Alyiakal smiles faintly at the backhanded reference to his growing ability to use a sabre effectively with his left hand.

"It takes more skills than weapons and tactics," agrees Ghallyr sagely . . . and loudly.

"How would Ghallyr know?" mutters Liathyr. "He can barely spell 'tactics.'"

"It's also not wise to patronize your peers," continues Baertal. "They might have better contacts and hidden talents."

"So declares the greatest patronizer in the whole training corps," murmurs Hyrsaal.

"He does have some points," says Alyiakal quietly, "even if he doesn't realize they apply to him as well." Although he understands Baertal's intent, Alyiakal still worries about what contacts and talents Baertal may have.

"Do you think they'll have more than overcooked porridge and dried ham strips this morning?" asks Liathyr.

"Dream on," replies Hyrsaal.

* * *

Outside the mess, Alyiakal checks his message box. There is a letter, from his father by the seal, not surprisingly since it is little more than an eightday after Summerturn, but he does not open the letter until he is back in the barracks.

Alyiakal—

My life here in Jakaafra continues much as it has. There are occasional incidents of trees falling across the Forest walls, with incursions by various creatures. The only occurrence of note has been the disappearance of a local magus, Triamon, I believe. No one knows quite what to make of it, but there are rumors that he was revealing Magi'i knowledge that disturbed the First of the Magi'i. If so, that was most unwise on his part, for the Magi'i keep their skills and secrets to themselves and apply strict discipline, if not worse, on any who discover or use those skills outside of their purview.

Alyiakal keeps an impassive expression as he reads those words, clearly as much a warning as "news" of Jakaafra, especially since his father has never been much interested in local events.

My tour at Northpoint is nearing its end. It's likely I'll be posted to command a border outpost in the north. It could be Inividra, Pemedra, or Lhaarat, or it could be something unanticipated. They won't send me back to Isahl. I've heard nothing official to date.

I trust you're paying close attention to your studies, especially to subject areas which do not presently interest you as much as others. Over the course of years, I've discovered that I have come to regret not paying close attention to all the subjects that came before me. I would urge you not to repeat my errors.

Two warnings in the same letter. Alyiakal pauses. He had earlier written that he enjoyed tactics and even logistics more than other subjects. Among the "other subjects" was the manual laying out basic administrative procedures, a manual he'd seen on his father's desk and once glanced through and immediately turned from.

He also realizes that his father's regular but infrequent letters have been written cautiously. Even the warning about Triamon does not reveal that Alyiakal had studied with the magus. *But now there's no way at all to write to Adayal.*

Although Alyiakal has broken the seal, as he considers the caution with which his father has written, he studies the pieces with his order/chaos senses. He thinks there is a touch of chaos in the wax, as if chaos had been used to soften the wax to remove and then replace the seal.

You'll need to study all the seals on letters from now on.

* * *

The air is damp and sticky as Alyiakal reins up his mount, looking out at the obstacle course stretching across twenty hectares, waiting for orders from Undercaptain Faaryn, the only undercaptain Alyiakal has seen in Kynstaar, possibly because Faaryn is a former senior squad leader, and definitely a rarity. Behind Alyiakal is a half squad of ranker trainees, some of whom may even have failed out of candidate training. Formed up in double file, they carry mock firelances, as does Alyiakal.

While the officer candidates have been given real firelances, some rudimentary training, and exercises in firing them, that training has been limited. Alyiakal suspects that he might be able to direct the chaos with his abilities, beyond merely aiming the firelance, but that is not something he is about to try at present, not under close supervision.

The exercise to come looks simple. Alyiakal doubts that it will be. He's never been in command of ten men before, but he has to guide them through the course, an exercise designed to give candidates and rankers-in-training a slight feel for what will be required when they face barbarians.

The undercaptain drops the signal flag.

"Squad! Forward!" orders Alyiakal. "On me!"

He leads the half squad to the first set of banners. "Squad left!"

Once the half squad is through the banners, heading south, Alyiakal senses that the rankers in the rear are lagging. He glances back, then orders, "Rear ranks! Close it up."

For close to a glass, Alyiakal guides the rankers around the training course while Faaryn observes. Once the undercaptain signals the end of the exercise, Alyiakal gives the orders to return to the stables, then begins sensing each of the mounts, something he would have liked to do earlier, but he had to concentrate too much on keeping track of the rankers.

After all the mounts are groomed and Undercaptain Faaryn has dismissed the rankers to their other training, the undercaptain turns to Alyiakal.

"Your orders were clear and timely. Adequate, but not outstanding. You did a solid job of keeping track of your squad. Several times you got too far in front of them. You do that on a real patrol and you risk getting cut off. That never ends well . . ." When Faaryn finishes his debriefing, he asks, "Do you have any questions or anything to add?"

Alyiakal definitely feels that he should add something and says, "Ranker Zaudaal's mount . . . I wonder if there's a soreness or something. Toward the end of the exercise, there was something with the horse's gait . . ." Actually, Alyiakal had sensed a bit of dull red in the muscles of one leg and then noticed the gait.

Faaryn nodded. "Good. You actually remembered his name, and noticed something wrong. If that had happened earlier, I would have pulled him out of the formation, but it happened just before I ordered you back."

From the dull redness, Alyiakal knows that the injury occurred earlier. "Could it be a reinjury? I'm asking because there weren't any tight turns or galloping immediately before I noticed it."

"That's possible. I'll have the trainer look the horse over." Faaryn pauses. "You're out on patrol, and that happens. What would you do?"

"It would depend on where in the patrol it happened. If we were returning, and there was a spare mount—"

"What if you're well away from the post and you don't have any spare mounts? And you usually won't, unless you've captured one."

"I don't have a good answer, ser."

"Why not?"

"Because, if it's a patrol, and I send him back alone, that's one danger. If he stays, the same thing can happen. So much would depend on the circumstances."

"You're right, but . . . in those circumstances, you have to do what's best for the squad or the company."

"Then unless we were close to the post, I'd keep him with the company and watch closely."

"Usually that would be the best course . . . and usually it won't turn out well, whatever you do." Faaryn pauses, then says, "That's all, Candidate Alyiakal. You're dismissed to your scheduled studies or duties."

As he walks from the stables back toward the main part of the post, Alyiakal hopes that he hasn't created expectations he cannot meet. *But if you hadn't mentioned the problem . . .*

Even with less than a year left in training, nothing is certain.

*   *   *

There is a chill Autumn wind blowing out of the west when Alyiakal sees the letter in his message box, almost certainly a letter from Saelora, since the only letters he ever receives are from her and his father, and he has already received and replied to his father's seasonturn letter. Still, he waits until he returns to the barracks to open the missive.

> *Alyiakal—*
>
> *Congratulations! Hyrsaal wrote Karola that you and he and Liathyr are now in real officer training, not just candidate training. He said that meant it was very likely you'd all become officers if you didn't do something stupid. Please don't!*

Alyiakal smiles wryly at the last two words because his father has already written a letter to the same effect, as well as informing Alyiakal that he has received orders to take command of the Mirror Lancer post at Inividra. Alyiakal continues reading.

> *I have some news of my own. Buurel consulted with the Merchanters and discovered that I could be certified as a scrivener because there aren't enough scriveners here in Vaeyal. So I'm now a certified scrivener, and they can't take it away even if more men become scriveners. That won't happen, though. Most of the men work on the Great Canal, and they make more than scriveners do.*
>
> *I'm working part-time for a small trader. He thinks I could even become a junior enumerator if I work hard . . .*

Thinking about how hard it appears Saelora works, Alyiakal smiles again. *Someday, you might even meet her.*

*   *   *

"Candidate Hyrsaal, why do we have to spend so much effort fighting off the barbarians to the north?"

"Because they keep attacking us, ser."

"And why do they keep attacking Cyador?"

"Because they think that we took their land, ser?"

Majer Phannyl turns. "Did the First really do that, Candidate Baertal?"

"No, ser. The first and second Emperors of Light wrested the land from the Accursed Forest. The barbarians believe that because that's what the Merchanters and rulers of the scattered lands to the north tell them."

"Why would they do that?" presses the majer. "And why would the barbarians believe them?"

"It's to the advantage of those rulers and Merchanters," replies Baertal in an assured tone. "That way the barbarians are less likely to attack them. The barbarians can also feel better about not attacking their own people. More important, our people have more goods of value, and our women are in better health. So, when the barbarians do succeed, their plunder is better."

"All that is logical, Candidate Baertal, but why are there barbarians at all? Wouldn't it make more sense for the local rulers to wipe them out?"

"If they could, ser, it might. It takes a significant force of Mirror Lancers to keep the barbarians in check. We have better weapons, better commanders, and better-trained men. I doubt that the scattered local rulers can muster that kind of effort."

Phannyl shakes his head. "You're half right, Candidate Baertal."

Alyiakal considers what Phannyl and Baertal have said, and the only logical conclusion he can come to is that it makes no sense for the local rulers to eliminate the barbarians.

But why? After a moment, he wants to nod. He does not, because he does not want the majer to ask him, although, put in context, it's obvious. *Leaving the barbarians where they are protects the rulers in a way nothing else they could do would.*

"Candidate Vordahl, you look like you might have some inkling of an answer."

"Ser, no one local ruler can remove the barbarians. They'd only move."

"That's true, but there's more to it than that, Candidates. I'll leave you all to think about it."

* * *

As the candidates approach their mess for the evening meal, an undercaptain steps toward the group. "Candidate Alyiakal, this way."

"Ser?" asks Alyiakal politely.

"Subcommander Ciasyrt would like to see you. It's not a disciplinary matter. Beyond that, he did not say."

Not a disciplinary matter? Then why does the subcommander wish to see me? Alyiakal does not question. He just follows the undercaptain to the sunstone headquarters building, not that he has ever been inside, and to a study.

As he enters, Subcommander Ciasyrt stands and says quietly, "Candidate Alyiakal, please take a seat."

As the subcommander sits back down behind the goldenwood desk, Alyiakal takes the straight-backed chair directly facing the subcommander. He still worries what he may have done wrong.

"You didn't do anything wrong or even misguided. In a way, I wish you had. An occurrence like that can be corrected, especially in the case of a candidate who works as diligently as you do."

Alyiakal can sense a touch of chaos, of feeling, not of force or illness, and he fears what the subcommander will say next. He waits.

"You know your father was posted to Inividra?"

"Yes, ser," Alyiakal manages, even though he knows those words from the subcommander signify that something has happened to his father. "How bad is it?"

"He was riding a routine patrol. His heart . . . just stopped. He clutched at his chest . . . and he was gone. There were no barbarians around. There were no healers, either."

While Alyiakal can sense that the subcommander is withholding nothing, for the next several moments, he also does not hear anything the subcommander might have said.

His heart just stopped. No battle. No storm. No lightning. No chaos bolts. His heart just stopped.

"Ser?" Alyiakal doesn't know what else to say. *What is there to say?*

"Your father was an outstanding officer. Because of his death and because you are his only heir, you can request to be released from training and from any further obligation . . . if you choose."

Alyiakal can also sense the truth of that statement. *But what else would you do? The Magi'i won't have you.* He also knows that while he may be able to enter the Great Forest, that is not his future.

"Alyiakal?" prompts the subcommander.

"Thank you for letting me know that, ser, but I belong here."

"I'll leave that option open, in case you change your mind."

"Thank you, ser." But Alyiakal knows that his decision was made even before his father's death.

*   *   *

At the end of the morning formation announcements, right after Harvestturn, Undercaptain Faaryn announces, "Candidates Alyiakal, Jhoald, and Naeyal remain here."

Alyiakal cannot sense any chaos or disturbance, but that means nothing. Removing candidates from consideration can happen at any time. All he can do is wait.

Once the others are dismissed to duties, Faaryn approaches Alyiakal first. "You don't need any more arms or academic training, Candidate Alyiakal. There's a magus recommendation that you be given a short but intensive training in field healing. You're to report to the infirmary immediately. You'll be spending most of your eightdays until commissioning there."

Alyiakal's first reaction is relief, the second puzzlement. "Ser?"

"Why so late when that was recommended over a year ago?" asks the under-captain. "Because there's no point in wasting field-healing training on someone who's not getting his bars." His smile turns wry. "It's not light duty. You'll be working harder there than the other candidates will be. But if you're good, it might save your life, one way or another."

"Yes, ser." Alyiakal nods. He recalls what both his father and Triamon had said. *And they're both dead.*

"I thought you'd understand. On your way, Candidate."

* * *

Alyiakal focuses again on his reflection in the mirror, letting the recollections recede in his memory, not that he will forget any of what he has learned in the past three years. Then he nods, turns from the image that represents only a fraction of who he is and what he has learned, and walks from the barracks toward the formality of the ceremony to come.

XII

Standing at attention in his green-edged formal whites in the late-Harvest heat, his white visor cap firmly in place, Alyiakal concentrates not only on what the graying Mirror Lancer commander is proclaiming to the score and a half of newly coined undercaptains formed up on the sunstone pavement before the nearly empty seats of the arena, but on the surroundings and any possible order or chaos flows that he might sense.

As first of the graduated undercaptains, Baertal stands at the left end of the initial rank. Next is Vordahl, the son of Commander Dahlvor, who is addressing the undercaptains. Third is Alyiakal. Hyrsaal is sixth and stands at the far left in the second rank. All in all, there are twenty-nine junior undercaptains, less than half of those who arrived nearly three years ago remaining, and but a third of those who had attempted only the final year.

But the ones who only trained a year weren't obligated to become rankers for four years. That rankles Alyiakal, even though he understands the political reality associated with the privileged sons of elthage, high altage, or wealthy Merchanter families.

He forces his attention back to the necessary platitudes being earnestly delivered by Commander Dahlvor.

". . . you are here to defend a land that offers more to its people than any ever has . . . to protect the eternal light of Cyador against the darkness and unfocused chaos of the barbarians of the north . . . you are the heirs to a proud tradition of duty and sacrifice, heirs to a greatness that carved a land of peace and prosperity out of forest darkness and bestial cruelty. May you all carry on that proud tradition . . ."

When the commander finishes his speech, he pauses, then declares, "Step forward when your name is called."

"Undercaptain Baertal'alt," announces Subcommander Ciasyrt. Once Baertal comes to attention before the commander and subcommander, the subcommander presents the silver bars and says a few words quietly.

Then the same happens with Vordahl, although the commander is the one to present the bars to his son.

"Undercaptain Alyiakal'alt."

Alyiakal steps forward.

Subcommander Ciasyrt presents the bars, then says, "Your father would have been proud of you. You also have a recommendation from the head healer. That's never happened while I've been here. Congratulations." He lowers his voice and adds, "I'll need to see you before you pick up your orders, say, in a glass or so."

"Yes, ser. Thank you, ser."

"You earned those bars, Undercaptain." The subcommander's voice is more than perfunctory.

Alyiakal returns to his place in formation, wondering about why he's been ordered to see Subcommander Ciasyrt before picking up his orders. *It has to be something about the orders, but what?*

He still smiles when Hyrsaal and Liathyr receive their bars . . . and wonders slightly how Ghallyr ever managed to make it through, even next to last. *Because Baertal helped him more than a little?*

Once the final undercaptain has received his bars and the formation is dismissed, Alyiakal turns to Hyrsaal. "We made it, and so did Liathyr."

As the two walk toward Liathyr, Alyiakal cannot help but notice that Baertal is talking with Vordahl and his father the commander, definitely an officer of influence, given that there are fewer than a half score of commanders in the entire corps of the Mirror Lancers.

"Baertal didn't waste any time getting to the commander," says Hyrsaal quietly.

"That surprises you?" replies Alyiakal. "He's been close to Vordahl since he arrived last year."

"They'll still have to deal with barbarians or the Accursed Forest," interjects Liathyr as he joins them. "So where will they send us?"

"The ones who aren't quite hopeless, like Ghallyr," says Hyrsaal, "will get assigned to port detachments and end up as dead-end overcaptains . . . sub-majers at best."

"Doesn't seem quite fair," replies Liathyr. "We're not that well-connected, and most of us will be fortunate to make sub-majer."

Those the barbarians don't get. Alyiakal doesn't voice the thought he knows the other two share.

"Taking a lot more risks," agrees Hyrsaal. "But we'll at least have some hope of doing better. Those like Ghallyr likely won't."

Liathyr looks to Alyiakal, and then to Hyrsaal. "You two won't have to wait long tomorrow to pick up your orders from Majer Phannyl. You're near the head of the list."

"You're nowhere near the bottom," counters Hyrsaal. "There won't be more than two glasses between when we find out and when you do."

As the other two continue their repartee, Alyiakal wonders why the sub-commander wants to see him before he receives his orders. The only reason he can think of is that there's something unusual or different from what he should be able to expect from being one of the top three out of all the graduating un-dercaptains.

After a time, he excuses himself and heads back to the barracks, where he goes over his kit, with all the new uniforms. He thinks about writing Saelora but decides against it until he knows where he'll be posted. Finally, he walks to the headquarters building and to the subcommander's study.

The ranker at the desk looks up.

"Undercaptain Alyiakal'alt, reporting as requested."

"One moment, ser." The ranker rises and knocks on the door to the inner study. "Undercaptain Alyiakal."

"Have him come in."

Just as Alyiakal has felt the ranker's initial doubt, he also senses the surprise at the subcommander's order.

"You're to go in, ser."

When Alyiakal enters, Subcommander Ciasyrt gestures for him to close the door and then to the chairs in front of the goldenwood desk. He waits until Alyiakal seats himself, if on the front section of the chair, before saying, "You're quite prompt, Undercaptain, but that's not surprising. You're doubtless wonder-ing why I requested you come to see me."

"Yes, ser."

"As all of you who were commissioned today know, it's usual for the top five undercaptains to receive orders to a post such as Syadtar, Assyadt, or Geliendra, where they have the opportunity to show their worth directly to more senior Mirror Lancer officers. In your instance, I felt such a posting was unwise." Ciasyrt pauses. "Would you care to speculate why I feel that way?"

Alyiakal has his suspicions, but he is certainly not going to give the subcommander additional reasons, in case his suspicions are incorrect. "No, ser."

Ciasyrt laughs softly, but not unkindly, then says, "Very wise of you. I knew your father briefly. He should have been a subcommander, possibly more. But he was honest and effective without looking heroic and without high-positioned officers looking after him in his early years. Those are difficult obstacles to overcome . . . and then when he consorted a woman not of the altage . . ." Ciasyrt shakes his head.

That was something his father had never mentioned to Alyiakal.

"You have an outstanding record," continues the subcommander, "but you're not politically sociable enough, especially to those you don't care for or see through to their underlying character. If I recommended that you be sent to one of the more prestigious posts for junior officers you'd likely receive a marginal assessment report, even if your accomplishments were solid or even excellent.

"Despite what we've tried to do, Undercaptain Baertal has convinced the more politically connected staff officers and many of the undercaptains who were commissioned this morning that you are merely a training undercaptain . . . that you really can't stand up to the rigors of a border post or any other difficult assignment. I'm convinced otherwise, but what I, Captain Zuhland, or Undercaptain Faaryn know won't change a perception that's too widespread among your influential peers. The only things that will change that are, first, that you perform well in a difficult situation, and, second, that you build a solid reputation wherever you're posted.

"You're being sent to Pemedra. It's not prestigious, but it has one advantage. It was originally built when the previous emperor planned to expand the borders of Cyador. It was planned as the main post for another line of posts to the northeast, but those plans were never fulfilled, for reasons we all know."

Alyiakal allows himself a nod. *The early and untimely death of the Emperor Kieffal, a death many suspected was not the accident it appeared to be.*

"As a result, the majer in command still reports directly to the Majer-Commander of the Mirror Lancers. Sooner or later, I imagine, the post commander at Pemedra will report to the commander at Syadtar, but that hasn't happened yet. So . . . for very practical reasons, that majer in command at Pemedra is almost always in his last assignment and is more interested in holding the barbarians at bay than in attempting to obtain a prestigious staff position in Cyad. That could work to your benefit. It will certainly not harm you. You may even find other officers there more interested in strengthening the Empire of Light than in bolstering their immediate or future reputation in Cyad."

Alyiakal can sense not a shred of chaos or deception in the words that the subcommander has spoken. "Thank you, ser. I appreciate the explanation." Left unsaid is the fact that repeating what the subcommander has conveyed will undermine any benefit such a posting could have for Alyiakal.

The question Alyiakal would like to ask is why Ciasyrt has told him. *Because he doesn't want you to be bitter and turn against the Mirror Lancers? Because it is all he can do, given Baertal's and Vordahl's ties to high officers? Because he couldn't do more for your father? Or for some other reason?*

"Do you have any other questions, Undercaptain?"

"Not at this time, ser." Alyiakal manages a wry smile. "I'll likely think of such questions only after I can't ask them." He pauses. "I do appreciate the explanation and what you've done."

"You may not once you first arrive in Pemedra. Don't be quick to judge." The subcommander stands.

Alyiakal immediately does as well and inclines his head.

He can sense a mixture of order and chaos swirling around Ciasyrt as he leaves the study.

When he reaches the area outside the mess, Hyrsaal breaks away from Liathyr and Fuhlart and immediately says, "Ghallyr was telling Baertal that you must already be in trouble because he saw you headed into headquarters."

Alyiakal shakes his head. "It was personal. He wanted to tell me how much he respected my father, and he hoped that I could be as good an officer." The last sentence had been implied, rather than spoken, but Alyiakal doubts that the subcommander would have disagreed. "He said that wherever I was posted I'd be judged by my behavior and my accomplishments."

"Won't we all?" replies Hyrsaal.

"Some might be judged more by their political behavior," says Alyiakal dryly. "The rest of us need to rely on the performance of our duties."

Hyrsaal laughs sardonically.

XIII

The heavy-laden firewagon continues toward Syadtar, and Alyiakal feels that they must be drawing close, only because it is late afternoon and the sun hangs low over the Grass Hills west of the road, not that there aren't similar hills to the east. Scattered farmhouses lie closer to the road. The off-white shades of the walls of houses and outbuildings differ from stead to stead, but they all share the green tile roofs and their external green ceramic privacy screens and green shutters.

He looks around the forward compartment, first at the sleeping figure of Fuhlart, who is being posted to Isahl, and then at Naeyal, also sleeping, who is posted to Syadtar, and at a silver-haired woman in a Mirror Lancer uniform of healer green without rank insignia, who had joined them at the last stop. The silver hair is not of age, but a natural shade some few children are born with. The healer sits on the same side of the compartment as Alyiakal and has to be at least a good decade older than any of the undercaptains.

There is something about the aura of the healer that reminds him of Adayal, but that's not surprising, given that Adayal has magely talents and could most likely have been a healer. Despite her parting words, he still feels that there should have been some way they could have stayed together.

Except she isn't truly alive away from the Great Forest, and the Forest isn't really for you, not without her, anyway.

Besides Alyiakal, the healer is the only one awake. He has already sensed that she has shields that reveal nothing, and such shields suggest as great an ability as many of the Magi'i. Although he is familiar with Mirror Lancer healers from his field-healing instruction, none of those healers had showed shields. That this healer does puzzles him, as does the fact that he'd never heard anything about healers in any of the border posts, but he isn't about to say anything, not when other lancers are around.

"You're being posted to Pemedra, aren't you?" says the healer quietly.

"I am," he replies softly. "How did you know?"

"You have too much order and chaos behind that shield."

"Is it that obvious?"

She shakes her head. "Only to the most able of the Magi'i. But you'll need to strengthen your shields—and you should develop two—if you ever want to get to Cyad . . . and survive there. The Magi'i don't tolerate competition, and the Mirror Lancers don't allow those with order/chaos abilities to become or remain senior officers."

"But how can you—"

"Because I'm a woman?"

Alyiakal inclines his head. "I apologize. I did not mean to cast aspersions on your abilities, only upon those who will not recognize them."

The healer laughs softly.

"Where can I find you in Syadtar?"

"In the infirmary. Just ask for the healer."

Fuhlart yawns, opens his eyes, then stretches and straightens himself on the barely padded seat. "Are we getting close to Syadtar?"

"Perhaps another five kays," says the healer.

Fuhlart closes his eyes again.

Before that long—perhaps two quints—the firewagon approaches the white-stone city walls and passes through the open white-oak gates.

"You've made it easier for me," says the healer, as the firewagon reaches what seems to be the central square and turns north.

"How so?" asks Naeyal.

"If most of the passengers in the front compartment are officers, and if most of those in the rear are rankers, the drivers have to go all the way to the post gates."

"Easier for us, too." Fuhlart looks to Alyiakal and adds, "Baertal's got another day before he gets to Assyadt."

"That's what he wanted, I imagine." Alyiakal keeps his voice pleasantly noncommittal, looking out the window as the firewagon passes the green and white awning of a coffee shop, and then a square containing a statue, most likely either the first or the second Emperor of Light, since Alyiakal has never heard of statues of any emperors besides those two. Then the firewagon turns north and comes to a small circle, where it slows to a halt before the open gates.

Moments later, the driver opens the door. "Syadtar Post, Lady Healer, sers."

The healer pulls a small satchel from under the seat and steps out of the firewagon, nodding to Alyiakal, and then turning and walking through the gates past the pair of guards, who incline their heads to her.

"You talk much to the healer?" Fuhlart asks Alyiakal.

"Not much. She got on at the last stop and immediately took a nap. Then I did."

"What's a healer doing here?" asks Naeyal.

"I have no idea," replies Alyiakal, "but the gate guards know her."

Unlike the healer, each of the three undercaptains has to show his seal ring to the guards before entering the post.

"If you're posted to Syadtar, you go to the headquarters building," explains one of the guards. "If you're posted anywhere else, you go to the smaller building to the north of headquarters."

Lugging his duffel, Naeyal hurries ahead to the headquarters building, vanishing inside before Fuhlart and Alyiakal pass the entrance on their way to the second building.

Immediately inside the second building, Alyiakal and Fuhlart find an anteroom with several benches and a single desk, without anyone around.

"I have the feeling we weren't expected," says Fuhlart.

"Or not at the moment," adds Alyiakal.

Even as he speaks, he hears boots coming from one of the side corridors that branch out from the anteroom.

Then a senior squad leader appears, accompanied by a ranker.

"Undercaptain Alyiakal, reporting."

"Undercaptain Fuhlart."

"You're a bit early, sers. Firewagon bring you all the way to the gates?"

"Everyone in the front compartment was coming here," adds Alyiakal.

"That explains it." The grizzled senior squad leader looks to Fuhlart. "They've been waiting for you and several of the rankers. Ghausyn, here, will take care of you, Undercaptain Fuhlart. You'll only be here one night, and you'll ride out with the replacements, firelances, and supplies for Isahl first thing tomorrow morning."

"This way, if you would, ser?" the ranker says to Fuhlart.

Once Fuhlart and the ranker have departed, the senior squad leader turns to Alyiakal. "Ser, it's going to be almost an eightday before the supplies and replacement rankers will be ready to leave for Pemedra . . ."

Alyiakal nods. "That might be for the best."

"Ser?"

"I got some training in field healing at Kynstaar, but it would be good if I could work with the healers here."

"I don't know about that, ser. Overcaptain Usaahl's in charge of transfer undercaptains."

"Then it has to be his decision. I'll ask him. If he agrees, that's what I'll do. If I'm supposed to do something else, I'll do that."

"Just a moment, ser."

The senior squad leader turns and heads down the corridor to the right, returning almost immediately with a narrow-faced and balding overcaptain.

"The senior squad leader said you wanted to do temporary duty with the healers until the replacements and supplies head out for Pemedra?"

"If that's possible, ser. If not, I understand."

"You do any healing work at all?"

"Not quite a season at Kynstaar, ser, half a day every day. But I didn't have much experience with wounds."

The overcaptain looks to the senior squad leader.

"It's in his transfer orders."

Usaahl takes the folder and looks through it, then closes it and hands it back to the senior squad leader. "Even a recommendation. It's still up to the senior healer." From Usaahl's tone of voice, Alyiakal can tell the undercaptain doesn't think much of the idea.

"If I can learn even a little more here," says Alyiakal, "it might make a difference to wounded lancers."

"Your job is to kill barbarians and survive, Undercaptain."

"Yes, ser. But after the fighting, there are still wounded men."

Usaahl does not quite sigh, but says grudgingly, "True enough." After a moment, he adds, "There's not much else you could do here that'd make much difference in an eightday. But it's up to the healer."

"Yes, ser."

Usaahl looks to the senior squad leader. "I'll be back shortly." He turns to Alyiakal. "Leave your kit here. Even if she agrees, you'll need to take care of things here. No sense lugging your gear over there and then back."

Alyiakal appreciates that, especially once they reach the infirmary, because it is almost half a kay from the transfer building.

A ranker sits at the table in the entrance hall of the infirmary, a modest one-story sunstone structure.

Alyiakal can faintly sense something, almost like ancient wound chaos. *Can that seep into the stone?*

"I need a few moments with Healer Vayidra," declares the overcaptain politely.

"Yes, ser. She just got back. I think she's still in her study."

In moments, the ranker returns with the healer.

As Alyiakal suspects, the senior healer is the woman who had been in the firewagon with him and the others, but her eyes remain on Usaahl. "Yes, Overcaptain?"

"Healer Vayidra, Undercaptain Alyiakal is posted to Pemedra. While he is waiting, he believes he can learn something while helping you . . ." Usaahl explains briefly.

Alyiakal is pleasantly surprised that the overcaptain mentions not only his brief training but the recommendation.

"We'd be happy to have him help around here, Overcaptain. Anything he can learn will be of benefit in the field, and we are shorthanded at the moment. He can certainly help with the basics." She turns to Alyiakal. "You'll need to eat at the early duty mess and come here immediately. We'll find some old greens for you, and you can change here."

"Yes, Healer Vayidra." Alyiakal doesn't know what else to call her.

A faint smile crosses Usaahl's face, then vanishes. "I need to get his paperwork taken care of."

"Always the paperwork, Overcaptain." Her eyes go back to Alyiakal. "I'll see you in the morning, Undercaptain."

Alyiakal inclines his head to her respectfully, then walks back to the transfer building with Overcaptain Usaahl. There he receives his quarters assignment, and then carries his kit to his quarters—a narrow room with a single bed, a wall desk, and a chair, the most space he has had to himself in three years.

He barely has time to use the cold-water shower at the end of the hall and change into a clean uniform before heading out of the officers' quarters. He meets Fuhlart outside the mess.

"Overcaptain Usaahl thinks you're chaos-touched," says Fuhlart.

"Maybe I am," replies Alyiakal, "but several officers told me that looking out for your men pays off. Most officers know more about that than I do." He glances to one side where he sees Naeyal nearing the building with another undercaptain. Naeyal appears engaged with the other undercaptain. At least, he doesn't acknowledge either Fuhlart or Alyiakal, who lag back slightly, then follow the two into the mess, where slightly fewer than twoscore officers are gathered.

At first, Alyiakal is surprised at how comparatively few officers appear, given the size of the post, but as he takes in the ranks of those standing and waiting for the senior officer to appear, he is reminded that there are actually more patrols operating out of the smaller border posts than at Syadtar, which is more of an administrative and logistics center.

"Informal seating!" announces someone.

Alyiakal interprets that, from what he sees, as meaning taking seats roughly, but not scrupulously, by rank. He and Fuhlart sit almost at the foot of the table for junior officers.

"Which of you two is headed to Isahl and which to Pemedra?" asks the undercaptain seated beside Fuhlart. "Not that it makes much difference. One's as bad as the other."

Since it doesn't seem to make any difference to the undercaptain, Alyiakal doesn't answer the question and asks his own. "Do the patrols operating from here run across many barbarians?"

"Enough," replies the undercaptain. "There are more barbarian towns, if you can call them that, to the north and northeast, as well as some beyond the eastern hills. They try to raid the smaller towns and hamlets east and southeast of here."

"Are there more raids than usual?" asks Alyiakal.

"I've only been here a year, and I don't see much change. Subcommander Munnyr has to know, but if there's much difference over time I haven't heard."

"What about raids around Isahl and Lhaarat?" asks Fuhlart.

"Except in Winter and early Spring, the barbarians'll keep you busy. Angelfire, they keep all of us busy."

"Why?" says Alyiakal quietly.

"What do you mean 'why'? Because they're barbarians."

"They have more than enough land," replies Alyiakal.

"They don't have enough women, and the ones they have would leave in a moment if they could. A cupridium sabre's worth five of those iron bars they call swords, maybe more, and so are lots of things we take for granted that they don't have."

Alyiakal is about to ask what else might be so valuable to the barbarians when one of the ranker servers delivers his platter, and another fills the heavy wineglass.

"Why don't they trade for them?" asks Fuhlart.

The other undercaptain snorts. "What do they have to offer in return?"

"I can see that," replies Fuhlart.

There must be something that they could trade. While Alyiakal has that thought, he is too tired to think what that might be. Then, perhaps the other undercaptain might be right.

He concentrates on eating, and on not drinking too much wine.

Then, after eating, he makes his way back to his temporary quarters. When he steps into the small room and sees the wall desk, he thinks about writing Saelora, but he can hardly keep his eyes open.

Tomorrow . . . I'll write her tomorrow.

XIV

Tired as he is, Alyiakal wakes early enough to make it to the early duty mess with time to spare, where he finds Fuhlart and sits next to him.

"Why are you up this early?" asks Fuhlart.

"I could say I'm here to see you off," replies Alyiakal with a smile, "but getting a little more healing experience means I have to wake early, possibly every morning until I leave for Pemedra." The healer hadn't made that clear, but Alyiakal has the feeling that was what she had meant.

Fuhlart laughs. "I hope it's worth it."

"So do I. It might be seasons before I learn that." *If not longer.* Alyiakal shrugs. "But I might never get another chance to work with healers, and I'd be doing some work here anyway."

Breakfast consists of ham strips embedded in some sort of egg and cheese casserole with fresh-baked bread and a choice of ale or redberry juice. Alyiakal takes the redberry, but doubts he'll have that choice once he gets to Pemedra.

They both begin to eat quickly.

As they finish, Fuhlart says quietly, "If you don't want to answer, I'll understand, but why did Naeyal get assigned here, and you're being posted to Pemedra? You ranked higher than he did."

"Apparently, the Mirror Lancers feel I'll do better in Pemedra than here."

Fuhlart frowns. "Did Baertal have anything to do with it?"

"Not directly," lies Alyiakal, "but I suspect that it has to do with the fact that I've always tried to let accomplishments speak for themselves. Others have a different approach."

For a moment, Fuhlart looks puzzled; then he offers a wry smile. "Like when you made Baertal look like an idiot sparring and the captain made you spar left-handed with me? I could barely keep from getting hit even then, and you were better than anyone using either hand by the time you got your bars. But you never said anything."

"My father was insistent that acts spoke for an officer better than words."

"Not always," replies Fuhlart. "Especially in Cyad, or so I've heard."

"We'll have to see. I won't worry about that unless I get to Cyad." *And that won't be soon for any of us.*

"Until you get to Cyad."

Alyiakal grins. "That, too."

Fuhlart shakes his head. "We'd better get moving."

The two leave the mess, and once outside, Alyiakal says, "Best of fortune . . . and take care."

"You, too."

Alyiakal watches Fuhlart for a moment, then heads for the infirmary. As he walks quickly, he finds he is surprised that the early-morning air is not noticeably cooler than at Kynstaar, even though Syadtar lies hundreds of kays farther north.

When he steps into the infirmary, the ranker at the front desk immediately stands and says, "Undercaptain Alyiakal, ser, this way," then escorts him to a small room with open wooden cabinets, some holding ranker uniforms. Beside an empty one hangs a set of greens. "You'll need to change here, ser. All the men wearing greens use this room."

Meaning that there aren't any other officers involved in healing duties. "Thank you."

"Once you're changed, Healer Vayidra wants to see you in her study. I'll take you there."

Alyiakal nods to the ranker, then changes. He does keep his wallet and seal ring with him and makes his way back to the entry. In moments, he is stepping into Healer Vayidra's study.

"Ryndaar, if you'd close the door."

"Yes, Healer."

Vayidra motions for Alyiakal to sit down.

Alyiakal looks intently, if momentarily, at the silver-haired healer, who definitely reminds him of Adayal, although Healer Vayidra appears considerably older than Adayal. *The sense of power and of order more than chaos?*

"You're here on time. That's a start," says the healer dryly. "Did you have any healing training before your basic field-healing training?"

"Some very basic training before I was sent to officer candidate training."

"What sort of training?" The healer seems almost relaxed, as if the question is one she has to ask.

Alyiakal begins, "How to distinguish the various kinds of wound chaos . . ." From there he summarizes what Triamon had taught him and what he has learned from sensing various animals.

"A magus taught you all that?" Her tone is not quite believing.

"I don't think he was supposed to. He vanished over a year ago."

"That's not surprising, but why didn't anyone test you?"

"I'd been gone for almost two years. A mage at Kynstaar screened all of the candidates. He said I had somewhat higher order levels."

Vayidra shakes her head, then says, "Knowing that, are you willing to take the risks of having someone learn that you're more than you seem? There won't be any risk here. I can take care of that, but later you'll be on your own."

"You'd know better than I would, but I would think that the more I can learn, in time, the risks will be lower."

"In time. But you'll need to survive."

"I'll take that risk."

Vayidra nods. "Then we'll begin. There are some basic rules you need to follow. All the time. First, you wash your hands after working with any patient, if you even barely touch them, and before working with the next one."

Alyiakal raises his eyebrows.

"For some reason, it reduces the amount of wound chaos," replies the healer. "You may not be able to do that in the field, but dusting your hands with traces of order helps. Second, you will not use any order or chaos manipulation on a patient except under my supervision or at my express direction."

"I can certainly see that."

"Third, in return for what I can teach you, you will undertake whatever tasks I ask of you. That's another reason for the greens. Some . . . individuals might find it . . . beneath the image of an officer to have him doing distasteful tasks on patients he outranks."

That also doesn't surprise Alyiakal.

She stands. "Now, we'll take a tour of a few of the current patients. You're to observe each both visually and with your order and chaos senses. You are not to comment until we are alone and away from any patient—or anyone else. Is that clear?"

"Yes, Healer."

The first patient is a fresh-faced young man with his left leg bound in a splint.

"How are you feeling today, Waaltyn?" asks the healer.

"About the same, Healer. Maybe a little better."

Vayidra looks to Alyiakal and says, "He lost an argument with a wagon when a wheel collapsed. He was lucky it happened here. He could have lost his leg."

"Or more," says the ranker almost cheerfully.

Alyiakal lets his senses range over the leg and the rest of the man's body. There is a massive amount of red-gray chaos in the leg, even around where the ends of the broken bones seem to be set, but he does not sense the whitish red of severe wound chaos.

Once they leave the room and are alone in the hallway, Vayidra looks at him.

Alyiakal tells her what he has sensed.

She simply nods.

The next chamber holds two men. One is unconscious or sleeping, the other moaning and loosely restrained.

Alyiakal studies the unconscious man first, noticing that a dull red mist seems to surround him, something he has never sensed before. He concentrates more intently, before he finds dull reddish wound chaos at the end of the man's right arm—and that the hand is missing, most likely recently amputated. The second man moans again, and Alyiakal turns to him, discovering tiny bits of orange-reddish-white chaos seemingly everywhere in his body. He wonders how much longer the man will survive.

"Do you need any more time?" asks Vayidra.

"No," replies Alyiakal quietly.

Once back in the hall, he relates what he has sensed.

After that, the healer takes him through several more rooms, with less seriously ill or injured patients, after which she says, "Back to my study." Her tone is clipped.

Alyiakal wonders what he did wrong. Once they enter her study, he closes the door, knowing that whatever she has to say is between the two of them.

She does not sit down, but stands beside the desk. "You shouldn't even be a lancer. You're more suited to be a magus." She pauses, then says, "Show me what you did when that magus screened you."

Alyiakal does.

She smiles sardonically. "*That* is the shield you should carry all the time, with a stronger one hidden behind it. That's if you want to survive as a Mirror Lancer officer."

"I've never tried to carry two shields at once."

"You should have time to figure that out here and at Pemedra. After that, it will likely be too late."

The cold certainty in her voice chills Alyiakal, but he says quietly, "In the meantime, what can I do here?"

"First, hold the shield you just showed. All the time. Second, if you ever use chaos, always surround it with order, and keep all free chaos away from your body. Otherwise, you'll die young . . ."

The matter-of-fact way in which she offers the warning confirms what Triamon had once said, but in a colder way.

". . . Third, you're going to learn something about being a healer. Right now. You'll accompany me to the morning sick call. I'll explain that you're a beginning healer, and we'll go from there." She pauses. "Have you ever used free order to lessen wound chaos?"

"Not with people," Alyiakal confesses. "Only dogs and cats."

"Did it work?"

"It changed the whitish-red chaos to dull red, and they got better. They might have without what I did."

Vayidra nods. "That's possible, but unlikely, if the wound chaos was whitish-red and much more than a small point. At least you didn't use too much order, either. That can kill the tissue, and it will putrefy from inside the body."

That was something that Triamon had not mentioned. "Couldn't free chaos destroy the putrefying tissue?"

"It could, but the heat released would likely kill the patient. That's why healers have to be cautious, especially young healers. We need to get to sick bay." She heads for the study door. "At sick call, all you're to do is to watch. Carefully. Don't say anything, and save any questions for later."

Sick bay consists of an anteroom where lancers wait to be seen and a pair of small treatment rooms off the corridor behind the anteroom.

The ranker at the anteroom desk looks up, quizzically.

"He's a field healer who will be helping for a few days," replies Vayidra to the unasked question. "Is there anyone who needs immediate treatment?"

"Not this morning, Healer."

Alyiakal follows Vayidra to one of the treatment rooms, which contains little but a raised pallet bed, a chair, a doorless cabinet containing dressings and supplies, and a high table with several cupridium trays on which are various instruments, also all of cupridium.

Alyiakal quickly studies the room and everything in it, then turns his attention to the older lancer ranker who enters, his left arm in a splint.

"Let's take a look at that arm." Vayidra touches, barely, the dressing above the point where the bones are splinted together, as she draws together a tiny black point of order and eases it into bright red chaos surrounding the point where the bones are splinted together. The bright red fades, but not to the dull grayish red. She glances at Alyiakal, who nods.

Then she eases an even smaller amount of order to the same point, and the last of the brighter red vanishes. She says to the older ranker, "That should feel a little better now. Come back tomorrow."

"Thank you, Healer." He nods to Vayidra, ignoring Alyiakal.

That's fine with Alyiakal. He'd rather not be noticed.

The next lancer has a heavy dressing over his left hand, which Vayidra deftly cuts away with a pair of cupridium scissors. She checks the stitches across the man's palm, then cleans the area, dusts it lightly with order, and re-dresses it. After the ranker leaves, Vayidra murmurs to Alyiakal, "Some of them are careless with the dressings, and it's easier to spend a little time each day until the skin heals enough to seal the wound."

Alyiakal wonders how the man could even get cut that way, but does not ask.

For the next glass or so, he watches closely everything that the healer does, saying nothing.

Then, two lancer rankers bring in a lancer limp on a stretcher with the shoulder area of his uniform covered in blood.

The squad leader behind the three immediately says, "He was unloading crates from a supply wagon. He tripped over something. He must have hit the side of the wagon, because he gashed his head, and fell on a produce crate. The crate must have had a weak board, 'cause it jammed into his shoulder . . ."

For all of the improbability of that explanation, Alyiakal can sense no chaos surrounding the junior squad leader. *Sometimes, the improbable does happen.*

For the next half glass, Alyiakal observes and stays out of the way, while Vayidra stops the bleeding, cleans the jagged but not terribly deep shoulder wound, and then infuses order to keep the chaos beneath the skull from expanding.

After that, she turns to him. "If you'd help Saakkyn clean up the room. Then come find me."

"Yes, Healer."

With the blood and everything else tracked in, it's almost a glass later before he and the other aide finish. He then finds Vayidra in her study, but he waits outside in the hall until a captain he has never met departs. Then he knocks.

"You can come in."

Alyiakal enters and closes the door.

"We'll make another set of rounds, now. I'll watch you try to deal with wound chaos in one or two patients."

"The one who's dying?"

Vayidra nods. "If you're good, you can reduce the level of pain. He'll be more comfortable for a little while."

The two return to the second room they had visited.

The bed of the man who had lost a hand is empty, but the other man is still occasionally moaning.

"Go ahead. See if you can reduce some of that chaos."

Alyiakal senses a larger concentration of chaos in the dying man's shoulder. Following Vayidra's example, he gathers tiny concentrations of order and targets specific points. Because the healer's shields are so good, he cannot tell what she feels.

"That's enough," she says gently. "Any more won't make any difference."

"You wanted to see what I could do, didn't you?"

"Of course. Now, we'll finish the rounds."

Over the next glass, Alyiakal accompanies her. In two cases, she quietly asks him to reduce wound chaos, and he does.

When they are back in her study, she looks at him. "You could be a healer, but there aren't any men healers."

"Just like there aren't any women Magi'i?"

She nods, then says, "Now, you're going to help with changing beds and laundry."

Alyiakal can't say he expected otherwise.

XV

For the next five days, even on eightday, Alyiakal's schedule at the infirmary is essentially the same as it was on fourday. He manages to write Saelora in between those duties and studying the healers' manual that Vayidra has lent him. He also wishes, far from the first time, that he had a safe way, or any real way, to write Adayal.

He has barely finished changing into his uniform late on oneday afternoon when Ryndaar enters the changing room.

"Ser, Healer Vayidra would like to see you before you leave."

"I'll be right there, Ryndaar. Thank you."

When Alyiakal enters Vayidra's study, she motions for him to take a seat, then says, "Overcaptain Usaahl stopped by earlier this afternoon. He wanted me to convey to you that you're to report to him immediately after you finish here today. He also wanted my written evaluation of your performance as a healer aide. I provided it. I wrote that you were as well-trained and capable as possible without combat experience, and that you'd worked long and hard here." She pauses and offers an amused smile. "What I didn't say was that, in handling order and chaos, you're better than most beginning healers and many who have years of experience. From what I've seen, your bonesetting experience is adequate." She pauses once more. "I'd recommend that you limit your surgery to wound cleaning and closure. Unless the patient would absolutely die."

Alyiakal has no intention of getting involved in any major surgery. *And you hope you're never faced with that possibility.*

Vayidra points to a small satchel on the corner of the desk. "That's for you. Officially, on our records, it's a replacement of medical instruments for Pemedra. But since no documentation will be sent to the post, it's essentially yours to use as you can." She stands. "It's been a pleasure to have you here, even if we did work you hard. Now . . . you'd best not keep the overcaptain waiting."

Alyiakal immediately stands as well. "Thank you, Healer Vayidra. I've learned a great deal over the past days. I'll never be able to adequately repay you."

"Everyone you heal is part of that repayment. I don't envy you. You are a healer and a self-trained magus required to be an effective lancer. Being successful at all three will be difficult."

Alyiakal understands what she is really saying—*that if you don't succeed at all three, you likely won't survive.*

"You've seen much more than I have. Have you encountered . . . others . . . like me?"

"Not that I'm aware . . . and you do need to go, Undercaptain."

He inclines his head respectfully. "Again . . . my thanks and appreciation."

"You're welcome." She pauses, then adds, in an amused tone, "You need more work on those shields."

He smiles, picks up the instrument satchel, then turns and leaves the study.

Once outside in the afternoon sun, he walks quickly to the transfer building, where he says to the duty ranker, "Undercaptain Alyiakal, reporting as requested by Overcaptain Usaahl."

"This way, ser."

The balding Usaahl barely looks at Alyiakal before motioning for him to take a seat and returning his attention to a sheet of paper on his desk.

Alyiakal sits down and waits.

After a time, the overcaptain looks up. "You came here straight from the infirmary?"

"Yes, ser."

"This late every day?"

"Yes, ser. A little later today. Healer Vayidra debriefed me on my strengths and weaknesses as a field healer. Or in real terms, an after-the-fight healer."

"She said that?"

"No, ser. You emphasized that."

Usaahl shows a trace of a smile that instantly vanishes. "Keep that in mind, although I doubt circumstances will leave you any real choice. Tomorrow morning, be at the stables with your gear immediately after the early mess. The replenishment force for Pemedra will leave from there. Captain Draakyr will be in charge. He'll be taking over a company at Pemedra, as will you, at least technically. There will be three squads' worth of replacements and four horse-drawn wagons of supplies. I'd suggest you go to the stables now and pick out your mount. It will make things easier for you tomorrow."

"Yes, ser."

Usaahl extends a large envelope to Alyiakal. "I'm returning your orders with the endorsements of your time and training duty here."

"Thank you, ser." Alyiakal pauses, then asks, "Do you know where Captain Draakyr might be at the moment?"

"He said he was going to the stables. If you hurry you might catch him there."

"By your leave, ser?"

"Of course."

Alyiakal hurries toward the stables, satchel and orders in hand.

Once inside the stables, he sees a short and wiry captain talking to one of the ostlers, and he moves closer, but does not approach, not until the other officer turns and gestures.

As Alyiakal catches sight of the captain, he realizes that the captain is much older than almost all the junior officers he has met, except Undercaptain Faaryn.

"What is it, Undercaptain?"

"Might you be Captain Draakyr, ser?"

"I am." The indifferent expression turns to one of mild interest. "Undercaptain Alyiakal?"

"Yes, ser."

"We arrived over a glass ago. What took you so long?"

"I didn't finish my training duty until a quint ago, and I had to pick up my orders from Overcaptain Usaahl."

"Training duty?"

"Field healing, ser. Since I had to wait almost an eightday, I was working as a healer aide in the infirmary."

"I think Majer Klaavyl will be more interested in your blade skills, Undercaptain."

"Yes, ser," replies Alyiakal, feeling that any other response would be inappropriate.

"Top of your graduating group? Or bottom?"

"Number three, ser."

"What makes you a problem, then?"

"I'm not especially political, ser, and I don't scheme."

"You mean you don't scheme well?"

"No, ser. I don't scheme. I do my best, and let what I do speak for me."

For the first time, Draakyr looks amused. "Would the subcommander at Kynstaar agree with that assessment?"

"Yes, ser."

Draakyr shakes his head. "Why are you here, now?"

Alyiakal suspects that the captain is not totally pleased, but somehow not personally upset with him. "To meet you and to pick a mount, if that's possible."

Draakyr nods. "Good idea. I need a mount as well. The ostler said that we can choose from the horses on the south side of the stable."

Alyiakal slips the envelope with his orders into the satchel as they walk toward the nearest stall.

"What do you think of this one?" asks Draakyr casually.

As he nears the chestnut gelding, Alyiakal studies the mount. The gelding edges back. "He looks healthy, but we're not threatening him, and he's backing off."

Draakyr says nothing, but keeps walking.

The next horse is a smallish mare who studies Alyiakal intently, but Alyiakal senses something about her back, and shakes his head. The third horse is a dunskin gelding who lifts his head from the manger.

"This one looks promising," says Draakyr.

Alyiakal can sense nothing obviously amiss, but doesn't feel particularly attracted.

The two officers walk the length of the stable. Alyiakal is most interested in a slightly smaller bay gelding, whose order and chaos balance suggests that the gelding is stronger than he looks, but he goes through all the possible mounts before he goes back. "This one, I think."

"Those runt bays sometimes have attitudes," offers Draakyr.

"I suppose I should find out now," says Alyiakal, setting down the satchel before opening the stall door and stepping inside. He is careful not to move quickly and creates the same warm order mist that has worked with other horses.

Then he stands quietly by the gelding's shoulder for a time before patting it firmly. "I think we'll do just fine."

Several moments pass, and the gelding nuzzles his arm.

After a short time, Alyiakal leaves the stall and retrieves the satchel.

"Have you worked a lot with horses?" asks the captain.

"Not much more than in training, ser. I tried to pick up what the better riders did."

Draakyr frowns momentarily, then heads back to the dunskin gelding, finally deciding on him. Then they find the ostler and convey their choices.

The ranker looks at Alyiakal. "Did you enter the stall?"

"I did. We talked for a bit. He seemed fine."

The ostler and the captain exchange glances, and the ostler says, "We'll have them ready in the morning."

"Thank you," returns the captain, who then gestures toward the stable doors.

They haven't quite reached the open doors when a squad leader walks swiftly through them.

"Here comes Juast," says Draakyr. "He's from Pemedra, and he'll be riding back with us and the replacements."

"Good afternoon, sers." A cheerful smile accompanies the words.

"The same to you. Juast, this is Undercaptain Alyiakal. Pemedra will be his first permanent assignment."

"I'm pleased to meet you, Squad Leader."

"Just Juast, ser, unless you're giving orders."

Alyiakal smiles in return. "Most of the orders will be from the captain."

"Never can tell, ser. Not even on resupply runs."

"True enough," says Draakyr, adding, "We've settled on our mounts. I won't have the final supply manifest until first thing in the morning, but I've been told there won't be anything unusual in the wagons." He adds dryly, "Supposedly."

"The replacements are settled for now," reports Juast. "They'll draw mounts in the morning. We'll have a few spares, and we'll work out any problems on the way. We've got four scouts who escorted the officers and rankers being transferred from Pemedra and the wagons with the depleted firelances."

"How many of the replacements have any experience?"

"Half score, roughly."

Draakyr frowns. "Discipline cases?"

"Yes, ser. Mostly from the Forest companies."

"At least they'll know one end of a firelance from the other. What about replacement firelances?"

"Five hundred. Take up pretty much all of one wagon. They might last until Winter, but I wouldn't count on it. Be a help if the Magi'i would build a Mirror Tower somewhere out here."

"It would, but they can't. All the towers were built by the First of the Magi'i. They say it can't be done now."

"I've heard that." Juast's expression conveys more than a little doubt.

"You've seen the effort it takes to transport spent lances and then ship back the recharged ones," says Draakyr. "If they could avoid that, don't you think they would?"

"Still makes a man wonder, ser."

Draakyr's laugh is sardonic and harsh. Then he smiles and says, "We'll see you early tomorrow."

"Yes, ser," replies the squad leader, smiling back.

When the two officers are well away from the stables and the squad leader, Draakyr says, "If you're fortunate, you'll get a senior squad leader like Juast. Even if you don't, listen to your squad leaders. They'll have more experience than you'll have for years. Or ever, if you don't listen."

"Yes, ser."

"And save the 'yes, ser' for when it's absolutely necessary."

"For when you need to know that I actually understand and will follow orders?"

"That's right."

Alyiakal resists the urge to say "Yes, ser" again.

"I'll see you first thing tomorrow. I still have a few matters to take care of. You have any questions, we'll have three long days to get to know each other better."

"Until then, ser."

Draakyr nods, then strides off.

As he walks back to his temporary quarters, Alyiakal thinks about Draakyr. The captain seems competent and effective, and it's obvious that Draakyr has spent time as a ranker, and squad leader.

XVI

On twoday morning, Alyiakal makes certain that he is up and at the officers' mess the moment it opens. He eats quickly, occasionally looking around, but even when he finishes and leaves, he doesn't see Captain Draakyr. He returns to his quarters only to pick up his kit and the healer's satchel, then hurries to the stable, where he finds his mount and straps his gear in place, spending a little time talking to the bay before leading him out to where the supply wagons are formed up.

Alyiakal sees a cart to one side and right before the lead wagon, with two mounted Mirror Lancers posted beside the cart, their presence making immediate sense, given the firelances the cart contains. Another lancer stands beside the cart.

At that moment, Squad Leader Juast rides up, followed by Draakyr. Both ride toward the cart. Alyiakal mounts and follows their example, receiving a firelance from the lancer standing beside the cart after Draakyr does. He slips the firelance into its leather holder.

"Follow me," says the captain. "Juast will form up the replacements."

Alyiakal does as Draakyr orders, and when the captain reins up, so does Alyiakal, if beside the captain, rather than behind.

"We're three days' ride from Pemedra," says Draakyr. "There aren't likely to be any barbarians within a day of Syadtar. So why are we having the replacements pick up firelances now?"

"Squad Leader Juast said that only ten or so of the three score had any experience," says Alyiakal. "You could give them some training in at least basic formations along the way."

Draakyr nods. "We could, but they'll likely be split up and go to different companies once they get to Pemedra."

Alyiakal considers for several moments what Draakyr said earlier, then says, "We have four wagons of supplies. We're into Autumn, after Harvest. The weather isn't that bad yet. You said that there aren't any barbarians within a day of Syadtar, but that leaves two possible days—"

"That's right. What you wouldn't know is that the whole north had heavy late-Spring rains and a dry, hot Summer. The barbarians likely had an early and poor harvest in most places. They know we try to supply the outlying posts in mid-to-late Autumn. That raises the odds that there will be some raiders looking to ambush any resupply group. Even seeing troopers carrying lances at the ready will discourage most, but you never know."

"And not carrying lances at the ready might tempt them even more?"

"We always want to fight on our terms, not theirs. Sometimes, we don't have that choice, but it's stupid not to put the odds in our favor. We will do a little formation training along the way. Enough that the replacements will resemble a company, at least from a distance."

Once the replacement lancers have been issued their firelances, and Juast has them formed up three abreast, Captain Draakyr nods to Alyiakal, and the two officers ride to a point in front of the main column, but behind the scouts. Juast eases his mount up beside the captain's mount.

Then Draakyr nods to the squad leader.

"Company! Forward!"

The de facto replenishment company leaves the post by the north gates in the wall on a sunstone pavement that ends in less than a kay, where it splits into two roads, one heading north-northwest to Isahl, the other going north toward Pemedra. Both roads are of gravel packed into clay, what Alyiakal's father had called metaled roads, a term Alyiakal never quite understood, but which his father had explained by saying, "It's a term that came from the Rational Stars."

None of the scattered men working in the steads flanking the north road near Syadtar gives even a passing glance to the column. For another two kays or so the road remains wide enough for three mounts abreast. Then it narrows, and the roadbed changes to mostly clay.

"Re-form! Two abreast."

Juast drops back behind the officers.

Alyiakal notices that only three scouts remain ahead of the column, and they are widening the distance between themselves and the head of the column. "Ser, is the fourth scout in the rear?"

"He is, along with two experienced rankers."

Alyiakal has the feeling he shouldn't have asked the question, given how obvious it was.

Draakyr says quietly, "Right now, you can ask questions that seem dumb. Some aren't, and you'll learn from the others. But now is about the only time you can."

"Thank you, ser."

After a time, the captain asks, "What's the longest you've been in the saddle, how many days of more than six glasses?"

"Six days, but only once, and that was three years ago."

"How did that happen?"

"I rode with the Great Forest wall patrols from Jakaafra to Geliendra. There wasn't any other way to get to candidate training."

Draakyr offers a short and amused laugh. "You're one of the few undercaptains who has that kind of experience—even once. You're the only one I've run across. Any other surprises?"

"I don't know about surprises. My father and grandfather were both majers. Both died on duty."

"How's your mother feel about that?"

"She died when I was eight." Anticipating the next question, Alyiakal adds, "I don't have any brothers or sisters."

"Your father died recently, then?"

"Not quite a year ago."

After another long pause, Draakyr says, "I usually don't offer undercaptains advice because they usually don't take it. I will offer you one observation. It's an old saying, but true. There are bold officers, and there are old officers. There are no bold old officers . . . for many reasons." He smiles wryly and adds, "By the same token, there are no old cowardly officers. Success for a Mirror Lancer officer is a narrow and dangerous path."

"I've thought that, ser, but no one ever said it that clearly. What else can you tell me that junior undercaptains think they know and don't?"

Draakyr laughs loudly. "That might take more time than the ride to Pemedra."

As Alyiakal waits to see if the captain will say more, he studies the road, and the lands bordering it. The traces of winter graying color the scattered bushes dotting the Grass Hills through which the road to Pemedra passes—a road meant to be temporary. The ill-fated Emperor Kieffal had planned for Pemedra to be a post like Syadtar, with a town growing around it and a sunstone highway branching off the narrow north highway, a highway never built because of the emperor's death.

Finally, Draakyr speaks again. "Success and failure have one thing in common. They're made of smaller details. There are exceptions, but they're rare. That's why discipline, especially self-discipline, is so important. You do everything right all the time, you're not going to make many mistakes. Quick and careless, on the other hand . . ."

Even as Alyiakal studies the road, and the land, he listens . . .

XVII

Slightly after noon on threeday, the wind shifts. Rather than having a gentle, cool, but not unpleasant breeze at his back, Alyiakal finds he's riding into a colder wind with a bite that blows in from the northeast. For some reason, that requires more effort to maintain his inner shield, but he persists, largely because he recalls the absolute ordered feel of Healer Vayidra's observations about the need for two strong sets of shields.

The road follows ridgelines wherever possible, which allows the lancers the high ground, but leaves the column exposed to the wind. Alyiakal notices that the wind picks up the dry dust from the scouts ahead and blows it toward him. The distance is great enough that the dust settles before reaching the main body, but whatever dust his bay kicks up is certainly being blown into the riders behind him.

"If this wind's any sign," observes Draakyr, "it might be a long cold Winter. But by eightday, it might feel like Harvest. You never know. Like the barbarians."

"When do you expect them to show up?" Alyiakal shifts his weight in the saddle, since he's still unaccustomed to riding so many glasses at a time. As he moves, the bay offers a sound that might be a snort or a sigh, but his ears remain alert but relaxed.

"If we see them at all, it will be this afternoon or early tomorrow. I'd also be surprised if they don't have a few scouts, out far enough that we can't easily spot them."

"Looking for an opportunity?"

"Or waiting for reinforcements."

If not both. "Do you know if the barbarians have ever used a magus in battle?"

"Not that I've ever heard, but it wouldn't make sense. A firelance throws chaos stronger than almost any magus, except the highest."

And with sixty Mirror Lancers in a company, that would be a waste of a magus. Alyiakal nods. His legs and thighs feel sore, as he knew they would, but not as sore as he'd been on the ride from Jakaafra to Geliendra. Even so, he'll be glad when they stop for the day. The road from Syadtar to Pemedra lacks way stations, according to Draakyr, because the barbarians would strip them of anything of possible value, but the scouts do know the best sites for stopping.

A quint passes, then another, before one of the scouts rides back toward the column. The other two scouts rein up at the end of a rise, beyond which the road descends into a long swale or valley. Alyiakal cannot see what lies below the end of the rise. His order/chaos senses offer no help because his eyes can see farther than he can sense—a great deal farther. *During the day, anyway.*

"They've spotted something," says Draakyr. "Question is whether it's scouts or a larger force."

The one scout backtracks along the dusty road toward the resupply force, finally easing his mount in beside the captain, who has kept the column moving.

"Barbarians ahead, ser. On a rise west of the road where it runs through the valley. Looks to be about a score of 'em. No signs of any others. Looks like they've been waiting there for a while."

"Are there any other places where they could have other riders hidden?" asks Draakyr.

"No, ser. The valley widens and flattens north of here. Goes on for kays that way. Stays pretty flat until the road gets closer to the post. There's a spring on the north end of the rise where they're drawn up."

"That's one of the places where we could stop?"

"Usually stop there on the way to Syadtar, ser. Ten kays farther is where we usually stop going north."

"If we stop where the scouts are, they'd have to come uphill at us?"

"Yes, ser. It's a long and gradual slope."

"But there's no water close by except where they are or farther ahead?"

"No, ser."

Draakyr looks to Juast. "Then we'll see what they do. First, we'll form up just above where the road begins to slope and give the men and mounts a little rest. I'd like a good look at the road before deciding."

"Yes, ser," replies the squad leader.

When the column comes to a halt at the point where the road slopes down, Alyiakal studies the gradual incline that extends a good two kays. The rise holding the barbarian force looks more like a hillock to Alyiakal, its top only a few yards higher than the road.

After a brief time, Draakyr turns to Juast. "You said the experienced lancers are up front?"

"Yes, ser, except for two with the scout in the rear. You want the others in the front, ser?"

"We'll wait here for a quint, and if they don't ride toward us, we'll start down toward them. I'd guess they won't attack until we're near the end of the incline. If they do, we'll halt and let them come to us."

"Yes, ser."

Draakyr then turns to Alyiakal. "How accurate are you with a firelance?"

"Better than most other undercaptains in training, ser."

"We'll see how that works here. If they start an attack, you and I and Juast will fire first. If we hit enough of them, they might break off the attack. If not, they'll lose a lot of men, and we'll waste a lot of firelance chaos." Draakyr offers a resigned smile.

After what seems far longer than a quint, during which the barbarians do not move at all, Juast reports, "Lancers in position, ser."

"Time to see what they have in mind, Squad Leader."

"Yes, ser. Company! Forward!"

Alyiakal notices that the three scouts have moved back behind the first ranks of lancers and that he, Draakyr, and Juast lead the column.

"When the barbarians attack, we'll move to the right of the column," says Draakyr, "to give the front ranks clear fire. Only if necessary."

"You think they'll attack, then?"

"They'll at least start an attack to see if they have a chance at those supply wagons. With barbarians, you never can tell. You have to be prepared for anything. The one thing you don't want to do is back down. There are times to avoid fighting, and you have to recognize those times and learn how to do that without giving the appearance of backing down."

Alyiakal watches the riders on the hillock below for the more than the two quints it takes for the head of the column to near the point where the road flattens.

Abruptly, the barbarian force rides down from the hillock, turning onto the road, heading south toward the Cyadoran force, initially at a walk, given that almost a kay separates the two forces.

"Company! Halt!" orders Juast. "Eight-man front! Flank formation."

The resupply company immediately halts, and the first three ranks of Mirror Lancers re-form into a line across the road and the shoulders on both sides. Alyiakal stays beside Draakyr as the captain eases his dunskin to the right of the column. For good measure, once they are in position, Alyiakal leans forward and pats the bay on the shoulder, giving the gelding a touch of what he now knows is reassuring order.

Alyiakal can't see all the barbarians closely, but they appear to number about a score. As they near the Cyadoran force, they spread out. For a moment, Alyiakal wonders why, then realizes that if they ride too close together a firelance bolt has a much better chance of hitting someone, even if badly aimed.

"We want to give them every opportunity to break off," says Draakyr. "Our first bolts will be at the edge of effective range. I'll tell you when to fire."

"Yes, ser."

Alyiakal has been told that while firelances can be effective at slightly over two hundred cubits, most Mirror Lancers do better at half that distance. He wonders how close Draakyr will let the barbarians get before giving the order.

At a distance of three hundred yards, the barbarians urge their mounts into a gallop. When they reach a point that looks to be well over two hundred cubits from Alyiakal, Draakyr snaps, "Fire now!" His bolt leaves the firelance even as he finishes the order.

Alyiakal makes certain his first burst is short. He succeeds, but the chaos bolt barely misses the barbarian, who leans away from it.

"Aim for their guts!" snaps Draakyr.

Alyiakal does just that with his short second bolt, his third, and a fourth. One barbarian drops from his mount. The other two slump in the saddle, but Alyiakal can sense three brief cold mists, mists that mean death. He doesn't get off a fifth bolt, because Draakyr orders, "Cease fire! Cease fire!"

Almost absently, Alyiakal realizes that the barbarians have turned and quickly retreated north along the road. He has the definite feeling that they will not stop as they pass the hillock. After a moment, he eases the firelance into its holder.

"Three out of four," says the captain to Alyiakal. "Not bad. Even better that you kept the bolts short."

"I appreciated the advice," replies Alyiakal. *And I won't make that mistake again.*

"They got the message," says Juast dryly, then orders, "Scouts! Recover those mounts! Straak! Duclaas! Take care of the bodies!"

Alyiakal hadn't even thought about recovering mounts, but he immediately realizes that two barbarian mounts are down, one screaming, and four are in various places, seemingly unhurt.

"You'd think that they'd learn," says Draakyr conversationally. "They lost eight men in moments, but they'll keep trying."

"Against firelances?" asks Alyiakal.

"They wanted the supplies. To them it was worth an attempt. Most of the time, they attack hamlets and steads, for livestock and women, or the few coins that the steadholders have. We patrol to keep them from attacking the most vulnerable, and they try to avoid our patrols."

Alyiakal watches as Juast orders a handful of lancers to take the weapons from the dead men, and the tack from the fallen mounts. The squad leader uses a quick firebolt to kill the horse that had been screaming.

Alyiakal looks more closely at the nearest body, that of a youth, years younger than himself, as several lancers drag the bodies out into the tall grass. He turns to Draakyr.

Before he can speak, the captain says, "The grass cats will take care of the bodies in glasses, if not sooner."

Alyiakal asks, "They start fighting that young?"

"Sometimes younger. They have no position, and no girl or woman will look at them until they prove themselves in raids or battle. The older and successful warriors have their pick of the most desirable young women. Those that there are."

Barbarians, indeed.

Draakyr snorts. "They're a plague on the land, but it's not worth the cost in lives and chaos to wipe them out. Besides, another bunch would show up in a few years, and we'd have to do it all over again and waste more men and chaos."

Alyiakal wonders if any Majer-Commander of the Mirror Lancers will ever think differently, but pushes that thought away. There's nothing he can do about a situation that's existed since almost the beginning of the Empire of Light.

But the image of the young barbarian lingers . . . as does the suddenness of death, and the cold black order mists that accompanied those deaths.

Less than two quints pass before the resupply company is again riding north toward Pemedra.

XVIII

. . . the Great Forest kept the riches of the lands that are now Cyador from use by the peoples of the north and the east. Now that Cyador has been able to contain the Forest, those peoples feel that we are usurpers who arrived from the Rational Stars and wrested the lands, not from the Forest, but from them.

They ignore the fact that they had neither the ability nor the will to constrain the Forest and can only see the prosperity of the Empire of Light as a theft from them. When Cyador falls, many centuries from now, I would hope, for in time all cultures and empires fall, the barbarians of the north and northeast will again fail, and the Forest will regain its former primacy, for only the marshaling of mastered chaos and order will contain the Forest, and only a people determined and united can create a large enough concentration of order and chaos.

That principle applies as well to Cyador itself, in that the Magi'i, the

Mirror Lancers, and the Merchanters must remain united and steadfast, with each upholding its role in maintaining the internal dedication and discipline. None of the three can dominate the other two if Cyador is to remain whole and prosperous. In that respect, the role of the Emperor of Light must always be to assure that no one of the three becomes predominant, for the strength of each is vital . . .

Fragment, Mirror Lancer Archives
Zaenth'alt, Captain-Commander
Cyad, 45 A.F.

XIX

About a glass after noon on fourday, the de facto resupply company passes a small hamlet west of the road nestled between two low ridges covered with grass and sparse clumps of bushes with graying leaves. A mud-brick wall, slightly more than three cubits high—enough to stop a group of riders, but not a determined attack—surrounds the houses and low barns. A short line of scrub trees on the south side of the hamlet suggests a stream. Several kays farther east and west of the hamlet, the Grass Hills rise higher than they have been farther south.

Alyiakal wonders if the hamlet has a name, but then, from what he has heard, most don't.

In the distance, rising above the dried tan grass that covers the largely flat terrain directly ahead, is a white spot, behind which are yet more of the Grass Hills, hills more rugged than those Alyiakal has seen so far, covered more by reddish rock and scrub evergreens than grass.

"That white point is Pemedra," says Juast. "We won't get there until sunset, maybe later. This time of year, we won't see many barbarian raiders, if any. There's a fair number of hamlets like that one, and you never know when they'll take a liking to attacking one, even if there's not much to raid. That's why the majer sends patrols south every so often."

The company has traveled for another glass when Alyiakal sees a trace of smoke several kays ahead to the left of the road, which runs straight as a lance toward Pemedra. "That smoke ahead?"

"Another hamlet," replies Juast. "Herders. They supply mutton, beef, pork, and fowl to the post. There must be a score here and there. Never kept track, except for those closer to the post. One has orchards—pearapples, even."

"How do they get other supplies?" asks Alyiakal.

"They take advantage of supply runs. They follow us a couple times a year.

Or they'll ride to Syadtar during Spring planting time when there's not much chance of being raided. There's also a lot of trickle trade."

"Trickle trade?" Alyiakal has never heard that term.

"Trade between hamlets. Stuff from Syadtar works its way north. Less often the other way," replies Juast.

Over the next three glasses, Alyiakal sees four more hamlets, all with mud-brick walls around the buildings, but all at least a third of a kay from the road. As Juast has said, one does boast orchards, possibly because of a stream, its course indicated by a straggly line of trees, a type he does not recognize.

As the company nears Pemedra in the fading light, Alyiakal sees two more hamlets, one a kay or so west of the post, along what Alyiakal suspects is the same stream that bordered the last hamlet they passed, and another more than a kay to the southeast.

Alyiakal now understands why the Emperor Kieffal situated the post where it stands. It dominates the narrowing area immediately south of more rugged and taller hills, many of which show more rock bluffs and scree than grass or other vegetation.

"There aren't many trees on the hills to the north," he says.

"You'll see why when the wind blows," returns Juast. "Especially in the Winter and at Springturn."

Smooth-finished gray stone walls, close to ten cubits high, completely surround the post, and form a hexagon, each section roughly half a kay on a side. A short stone watchtower tops each of the corners of the walls, although Alyiakal has the feeling that those towers are unmanned. The last half kay of the road leading to the white-oak gates is also stone-paved.

"It's not exactly the usual border post," says Juast dryly, as his mount's hoofs click on the first stones of the pavement.

"Keep that in mind," adds Draakyr, looking at Alyiakal.

While Alyiakal understands that from what the other two have said on the ride from Syadtar, he can't help but wonder why both of them have emphasized the point.

Two Mirror Lancers on foot guard the gates, each with a short firelance.

"Resupply company, returning," says Juast to the two guards. "Is there anyone else out on patrol?"

"First Company, Squad Leader."

"Thank you."

Neither lancer looks happy, and Alyiakal tries to sense why from their order/chaos. After they pass the guards, he asks, "Is gate guarding extra duty?"

Both Draakyr and Juast smile.

"Often, but not always," replies the squad leader.

Once inside the gates, Alyiakal manages to keep his jaw in place, because most of the space within the walls is empty. Although the avenue from the gate leads to a circular plaza or square, the pedestal in the center is vacant.

Meant for a statue of the Emperor Kieffal?

Behind the square, a group of stone-walled buildings sits on both sides of the avenue, including obvious barracks and stables. Beyond those, the avenue stretches north to another set of gates through ground empty of anything but the walls and a series of corrals more like wood-fenced pastures. Alyiakal can't help wondering from where the timber for the pasture fences came, given the scarcity of nearby trees.

Pemedra really was meant to be much more. He shakes his head.

"I had the same feeling, ser," says Juast, "when I first came through the gates."

Alyiakal glances toward Draakyr, whose face is impassive. *He's been here before. As a ranker?* That's a question Alyiakal will not, cannot, ask.

The massive, long stables are a good third of a kay from the other buildings, but built of the same gray stone, suggesting that the construction of other buildings had once been planned for the intervening space.

"The Winters here are hard?" Alyiakal asks as they near the stable doors, on the west side of the stone-paved avenue that runs to the north gates.

Draakyr nods. "The pasture corrals are for the good weather. Better for the horses. Winter can get cold enough to freeze a horse."

Even so, when Alyiakal leads the bay into the stables, he almost gapes. The number of stalls could easily accommodate the mounts of eight companies, and from what Juast has said, Pemedra has never had more than five, but only four in recent years.

"I'll handle the supplies, sers," declares Juast. "After you take care of your mounts, get your gear and report. Majer Klaavyl will likely be waiting."

"We appreciate it, Squad Leader," says Draakyr as two ostlers hurry up.

"The stalls for officers' mounts are on the left. Take any one that doesn't have a mount or a name on the stall door."

Alyiakal lets Draakyr pick a stall first. He takes the adjoining stall, putting the bay in the farthest stall from the stable doors. His bay seemed to get along with Draakyr's dunskin, and most horses seemed to like being close to other horses, or those they like or tolerate.

After setting his gear outside the stall and racking the saddle and tack, Alyiakal begins grooming the bay, talking to him quietly as he does. He doesn't take that much longer than Draakyr, then picks up his gear, and joins the captain, who waits by the stable doors.

"We'll drop our gear in the officers' quarters," says Draakyr, "and then go straight to the headquarters building and report to the majer."

"What can you tell me about the majer, ser?"

"I've never met him. He has to be good to be in command here. I understand he can be harsh on what he regards as incompetence or foolishness."

Since most Mirror Lancers are harsh that way, the majer is likely more so. "Thank you."

The headquarters building faces the square on the east side of the avenue. The stone masonry looks even more polished and crisp than the headquarters building in Syadtar, but the bronze main door, for all its gleaming finish, looks worn.

At the back of the entry hall, an older squad leader sits at a small, plain oak table, watching as the two officers approach.

"Captain Draakyr and Undercaptain Alyiakal reporting for duty," declares Draakyr.

"The majer's expecting you, sers. He'll see you first, Captain. The first door on the left, ser." The squad leader then turns and gestures to the chairs to one side of the desk. "Undercaptain, you can take any of the chairs or stand, as you wish."

Alyiakal takes one of the chairs and seats himself.

Draakyr reappears in roughly a quint. "He said for you to go on in. I'll see you in quarters or at the mess."

Alyiakal stands and makes his way down the corridor to the first door, which is open, and steps inside. His eyes center on the majer behind the desk, a broad-shouldered but spare figure with short-cut iron-gray hair and watery gray eyes. On one side of the desk is a map, angled so that the majer can read it while writing.

"You can close the door, Undercaptain." Klaavyl gestures to the chairs before the desk.

Alyiakal lays his orders on the desk, then takes the center chair and waits. Announcing himself would be superfluous. Instead he uses his senses to study the post commander, but finds nothing remarkable about the senior officer in terms of order and chaos.

The majer begins to read through the orders Alyiakal has handed him. He frowns once, finishes reading, and sets the papers aside. He looks intently at Alyiakal, then says, "Your father was an excellent officer. He might have been my successor, but there's no point in mourning over might-have-beens. He trained you in bladework, didn't he?"

"Yes, ser."

Klaavyl nods. "Your records show that you're too good to have learned it all in training. Why did you request additional healing instruction in Syadtar?"

"I thought I could learn more, ser."

"I'd normally say it would have been better to work on other skills, but with your training record and Captain Draakyr's assessment of your skills with a firelance, that healing training may not have been a total waste. Remember that healing has to wait until all immediate combat threats have been destroyed. You've doubtless been told that, but never forget it."

"Yes, ser."

The majer's lips quirk. "What do you think is the greatest danger for a young officer here at Pemedra? Don't give me a general saying, either."

"Thinking I know things that I really don't, ser."

"Who told you that?"

"In those words, no one, ser. But my father told me there was always more to learn, and that, if I weren't careful, I'd think I know more than I actually do."

The majer gives a short, harsh laugh.

Alyiakal waits.

Abruptly, Klaavyl states, "You'll be in command of Fourth Company. You and Fourth Company will be riding patrol with Captain Lyung on sixday. After that, Fourth Company will initially go on two-company patrols. You will follow all commands of the senior officer and listen to your senior squad leader. Fourth Company's senior squad leader is Maaslar."

"Yes, ser." *Maaslar.* Alyiakal fixes the name in his memory.

"That's all I have for you, Undercaptain. I'll see you at the mess shortly."

"Yes, ser." Alyiakal rises, inclines his head politely, then turns and leaves the majer's study. The matter-of-fact way in which the majer had read his orders and accepted his assignment has definitely surprised him.

Then, what else could he do? But Alyiakal had detected no signs of tension or anger.

The greater surprise lay in the words about his father, brief as they were, which suggest some level of acquaintance, although Alyiakal is fairly certain he had never heard the majer's name from his father.

After leaving headquarters, Alyiakal walks back to the officers' quarters, where a ranker gives him the key to his room and directions to the mess. He carries his gear to the room, then brushes his uniform and washes up before hurrying to the mess in the building adjoining the officers' quarters.

The officers' mess is a modest chamber, paneled in aged but well-oiled golden oak, with a polished gray stone floor. The mess table, likely dating from the time of Kieffal, could hold fifteen or more officers, but is set for five, all around one end. Alyiakal sees Draakyr talking to two other officers, another captain and an overcaptain.

The lanky overcaptain immediately turns and walks to meet Alyiakal. The lines on his face and the mixed white and black hair suggest to Alyiakal that the overcaptain is even older than Majer Klaavyl.

"Undercaptain, welcome to Pemedra, the best-appointed border post in all Cyador. I'm Overcaptain Tygael, the titular deputy commander. What that means is that I handle all the paperwork that goes to the Majer-Commander as well as procurement and supply matters."

"Undercaptain Alyiakal, ser." He smiles warmly. "About as inexperienced as any fresh undercaptain."

"You last a year here and you'll have more useful experience than any of this year's undercaptains. That's why Subcommander Ciasyrt sent you here." Tygael's lips curl into a sardonic expression that somehow conveys warmth. "That's true of all the undercaptains who are sent here." He turns toward the door. "Here comes the majer. We should take our seats. No precedence, except that the majer's at the head of the table."

Even so, the overcaptain and the captain to whom Draakyr had been talking sit next to the majer, while Draakyr is beside the overcaptain and Alyiakal beside the other captain, who immediately says, "I'm Lyung."

"Alyiakal, ser."

Lyung laughs. "At mess, the only 'ser's are for the majer and overcaptain, and then only in response to duties or responsibilities."

Once the ranker server has filled all the wineglasses—and Alyiakal is more than glad that it's wine and not ale—the majer lifts his glass. "To our new officers."

After the brief toast, a platter of a fowl slices in a white sauce circulates, followed by one of cheesed lumps that might be potatoes, and a large bowl of buttered beans—an amber speckled variety that Alyiakal has never seen. Out of caution, he takes a small helping.

"They're spring beans," says Draakyr. "They call them that because they'll grow all Summer and well into Harvest if they get enough water in the Spring. They're not bad."

After taking a small bite of the beans, Alyiakal agrees that they aren't bad. They're edible, but not particularly good, unlike the fowl, which is better than decent. By comparison to the beans, and only by comparison, the might-be potatoes taste good.

XX

On fiveday morning, after arranging for all but one of his duty uniforms to be washed, that being the one he wears, Alyiakal is at the mess as soon as it opens, and so are Draakyr and Lyung.

Breakfast consists of ham strips, fried eggs over something like oatcakes, and ale. The ale is different from anything Alyiakal has tasted, but then, supposedly ales vary from place to place, and he hasn't been many places.

For a time Alyiakal listens as Draakyr and Lyung talk, mainly about the weather and how it affects what the barbarians may do, but also about the replacement lancers.

". . . only ten with any experience . . ."

". . . life's getting too easy in Cyador . . ."

". . . used to be that younger sons of steaders flocked to be lancer recruits . . ."

Alyiakal is thinking about how to leave gracefully when Overcaptain Tygael appears and heads toward Alyiakal.

Alyiakal is immediately on his feet, waiting.

"Undercaptain . . . the majer forgot to give this to you." The overcaptain extends a key attached to a belt clip. "It's to the Fourth Company strongbox in the officers' study. That's where your copies of the company rosters and patrol reports are kept."

"Thank you, ser. I was wondering about records."

"You'll find everything there. By midmorning, we'll have a list of the Fourth Company replacements in your box, along with their orders and files for you to go over with your senior squad leader." Tygael smiles pleasantly, then turns and moves to join Majer Klaavyl.

Alyiakal says to the two captains, "I think I'm already behind. If you'll excuse me?"

"Every undercaptain starts out behind," replies Lyung cheerfully.

Draakyr just offers an amused smile.

From the mess, Alyiakal makes his way across the hall to the officers' study. The study is empty, but he notices that there are five desks, and four of the five have locked strongboxes on them, each topped with a brass plate. He finds the desk holding the strongbox bearing the plate inscribed FOURTH COMPANY. The key fits the lock, and he opens the strongbox.

The strongbox is separated into three sections. The largest contains thin folders. Alyiakal picks up the first folder. On the outside is a name—Atkaar. Under the name is written "First squad."

Alyiakal flips through the folders, counting them as he does. There are thirty-eight for the three squads. Given that the standard squad contains twenty lancers, that means Fourth Company is twenty-two rankers short.

The second section contains a short stack of directives from Mirror Lancer headquarters, outlining various policies. At first glance, none seem of immediate concern, and the most recent is dated threeday, third eightday of Summer, 95 A.F., nearly two seasons ago. Alyiakal decides reading those in detail can wait, and turns to the third section of the strongbox, which contains a set of maps and a bound book the size of a standard sheet of paper. He opens it to the first page, entitled "Patrol reports, Fourth Company, Pemedra." The first report is dated oneday, first eightday of Spring, 94 A.F. It is signed by Prekius'alt, Undercaptain.

While Alyiakal knows he needs to read through all the reports in the book, he turns to the last one, which is written in a different hand. The report is short . . . and chilling. His eyes go to the last lines.

> . . . *Undercaptain Prekius was killed by the landslide started by the barbarian force. Half the mounts of first squad were also so badly hurt they could not be saved. Thirteen lancers were killed, three injured or wounded.*

Landslide? How in the name of the Rational Stars did Prekius get caught in that? His eyes go to the signature—"Shaalt, Squad Leader."

After sitting there for several moments, Alyiakal turns back to the previous report and reads it, and then the one before that . . . and a few even before that. Then he shakes his head and stands.

Time to find Senior Squad Leader Maaslar.

Alyiakal doesn't have any difficulty with that, since Maaslar is alone in the large study shared by the four senior squad leaders and seated at a table desk under a placard stating FOURTH COMPANY.

Maaslar—a short and muscular figure with flame-red hair—stands the moment Alyiakal enters the study. "Undercaptain, ser."

"As you were, Squad Leader." Alyiakal picks up a nearby chair, sets it at one end of the narrow desk that faces the wall, and gestures for Maaslar to sit back down. "For the record, I'm Undercaptain Alyiakal. I'm presuming you're Senior Squad Leader Maaslar."

"Yes, ser." Maaslar's tone of voice is pleasant, but not enthusiastic.

"I've taken a brief look through the Fourth Company records, but right now, and for some time to come, you know more than I do. After reading the last patrol report, it's clear that I need to hear what you think I should know immediately, especially things that I probably don't." Alyiakal smiles ruefully.

"Ser, you make it easy, starting that way. Most undercaptains say something like that. Too many of them don't really mean it."

"My father told me that fresh undercaptains don't know sowshit, and that a good senior squad leader could teach me more than I could possibly learn on my own. He also said that listening to that senior squad leader would keep me from losing lancers unnecessarily." Alyiakal grins. "Now, where do you suggest we start?" He tries to sense Maaslar's reaction to his words . . . and thinks the squad leader is warily accepting.

"With the company, ser."

"The other two squad leaders, first?"

Maaslar nods. "Yurak's the most senior. Been a squad leader for four years. Last tour was at Westend. Elbaar got his stripe this past Summer."

Alyiakal waits, looking at Maaslar attentively.

"They're both solid," adds Maaslar.

Alyiakal suspects that Yurak and Elbaar will follow orders exactly as issued, but decides not to question further. "Right now, which squads do they lead?"

"Elbaar has second squad, Yurak third."

"What happened to Shaalt?"

"His legs were so messed up that he was stipended out."

"He was the senior squad leader?"

"Yes, ser."

"Were Yurak and Elbaar both on that last patrol?"

"Yes, ser." Maaslar pauses. "Might have been worse if Yurak hadn't been there."

"No one's said anything to me, but, after reading the patrol report, was Undercaptain Prekius . . . just unfortunate? Or am I missing something?"

"Ser, I wouldn't know. I was transferred from First Company three eightdays ago. I'm not sure anyone who would know survived. I did hear that the three squads were somewhat separated."

Meaning that Prekius was likely as careless or stupid as you think, but that no one wants to say so and there's no point in saying more about it. "Then you're one of the most experienced and likely the best senior squad leader here at Pemedra?"

"Some might say that Nyltaar is, ser."

Alyiakal suspects that Majer Klaavyl would not be among those who think that way.

"Overcaptain Tygael told me we'd get the names of replacements sometime around midmorning. Then we'll need to decide how to balance the squads." Alyiakal offers an amused smile. "That means you're going to balance the squads and explain to me why we should be doing it that way—and I'll learn something in the process."

"We'll both likely learn something in the process, ser."

Alyiakal has no doubt that he'll learn more, but he only asks, "What should I expect from the barbarians?"

"That would take more time than we've got before tomorrow's patrol, ser."

"Then . . . the one or two most important things. The things that are so obvious to you, but that I wouldn't necessarily know or think of."

Maaslar frowns, then says, "They won't accept mercy, and they won't give it. They'll die before being captured. You could torture them to death or promise them freedom and a hundred golds, and they still wouldn't tell you an angelfired thing."

"Are there any conditions when they won't fight?"

"If it's Winter and they're massively outnumbered . . . or if they're dead. They will avoid a stupid battle or confrontation. Unless they don't have any way out."

In short, don't back them into a corner unless it's necessary and you can kill them all with few, if any, casualties.

Alyiakal can feel that Maaslar doesn't want to talk much more, and he stands. "Thank you, Senior Squad Leader. I appreciate it. I'll find you when I get the information about the replacements."

"I'll be here or in the stables, ser."

After leaving Maaslar, Alyiakal heads back to the stables to check on his bay before returning to the officers' study. He has a lot of reading ahead, some maps to study, and more than a little thinking to do. He also needs to meet both Elbaar and Yurak, but that will come after he gets the list of replacements and meets again with Maaslar.

XXI

Early as Alyiakal gets to the mess on sixday, Captain Lyung is there earlier and gestures for Alyiakal to join him.

"We need to go over a few things," says the other captain as Alyiakal sits down across the table from him.

"Yes, ser."

"I saw you studying the maps yesterday. That's good, but you'll find that even the most accurate map doesn't show everything you need to know. Today will be a single-day patrol, but a long day. With the wind, you'll likely be cold. What we'll be doing is as much an exercise and a way to get you and the new lancers familiar with the area around the post and the way we do things. We might run into a barbarian scouting party or a small group of raiders. That's always possible. It's less likely right now because we won't be going as far from the post." Lyung pauses, then asks, "Why do you think we get new undercaptains and replacements in the fall?"

Alyiakal hasn't even considered that.

The captain smiles, then says, "Because that gives them more time to learn. Raiding's cold and dangerous in late Autumn and Winter. Early Spring is when the barbarians plant. The raids get dangerous in late Spring and Summer. That's when they're short on food and more men are free to raid. That doesn't mean there aren't raids now, but they're fewer. The barbarians are unpredictable. You can count on that . . ."

As Alyiakal eats, he listens intently to the captain.

After he leaves the mess, he returns to his quarters, where he retrieves the healing satchel, dons his winter riding jacket, and tucks his gloves into the inside pocket. When he reaches the stable, he sees that Maaslar and Captain Lyung also wear heavy riding jackets. Neither looks in his direction.

Before saddling the bay, Alyiakal spends a little time talking to him, quietly, as he worries about how Fourth Company will perform. While all three squad leaders are experienced, he certainly has no experience, and more than a third of the lancers don't, either.

Once he saddles the bay, he straps the satchel behind the saddle and the daypack that contains an oilskin and a blanket. He fills the water bottles and adds the slightest touch of order to them to counter any possible chaos in the water, a technique mentioned in passing years before by Triamon. Then he leads the bay to the stable entrance, where he picks up his firelance from the junior squad leader, and uses his senses to make sure it is chaos-filled, after which he mounts, riding to where Maaslar and the other two squad leaders are mustering and forming up Fourth Company.

Shortly, Captain Lyung rides over to Alyiakal, and Maaslar immediately joins them.

"Third Company will lead," declares Lyung, looking at Alyiakal. "We'll take the north road until we reach the fork below the barrier hills. From there we'll head west. Along the way, after we clear the north gates, I expect you to shift formations from three abreast to double file and back to four abreast. Keep varying the formations so the replacements get used to shifting quickly."

"Yes, ser," replies Alyiakal.

After Lyung rides back toward the head of the formation, Elbaar and Yurak ride up, and Maaslar reports, "First squad, formed up and ready, ser."

"Second squad, formed up and ready, ser."

"Third squad, formed up and ready, ser."

"Once we clear the north gates, we'll be ordering formation shifts to accustom the replacements to such shifts."

All three squad leaders reply, "Yes, ser."

"Return to your squads."

Once Elbaar and Yurak leave, Alyiakal turns to Maaslar. "How far is the road wide enough for four- or five-man fronts?"

Maaslar offers an amused smile. "About a kay. There are a few places later that will allow shifts to a three- or four-man front."

"In what order would you suggest we shift?"

"Two to three, then back to two, up to five, back to two, up to four, and then back to two. That's if the replacements can manage it."

Alyiakal understands the rationale behind Maaslar's recommendation. Because the company will usually be riding two abreast, most formation shifts would start from that formation.

As Fourth Company rides north past the fenced corral pastures toward the north gates, Alyiakal says to Maaslar, "The maps show a river to the northwest of here."

"That'd be the West Branch of the Jeryna River," replies Maaslar. "Barely a stream. Rocky, and the hills are more stone than grass. No one lives there. Farther east is the South Branch. Good grassland. That's where most of the raiders live."

"And beyond that?"

"Some call it Cerlyn, I'm told. Most don't call it anything."

"They mine copper somewhere in that area," says Alyiakal. "But they send it downriver to Rulyarth and then ship it to Summerdock or Fyrad. I always wondered why, but looking at the Grass Hills, it makes sense."

"I wouldn't know, ser."

"Are there any barbarian hamlets in the hills?"

"Not on our side, ser."

Alyiakal says nothing, but waits to see if Maaslar will say more.

"Three years ago, the overcaptain took Second Company to the north side of the highest hills. Nyltaar—he was with Second then—he said they could see a bunch of hamlets. Some of them new. A lot more than what you'll see north of here before you get to the real hills."

"Thank you. I wondered."

"We don't go that far. Most of the barbarians aren't raiders. Our job is to stop the ones who are. Not turn the rest of them into raiders."

Alyiakal suppresses a frown. While what the majer, the overcaptain, and Maaslar have told him all fits together, he has the feeling something is missing.

Whether it is or isn't, you'll find out in time, and right now you need to concentrate on learning how to be a good undercaptain.

Once past the north gates, following Maaslar's recommendations, Alyiakal orders the various formation shifts, which are accomplished awkwardly, but without mishaps, before the sunstone pavement ends.

"They're going to need more practice," he says quietly.

"Yes, ser," agrees Maaslar.

The two companies continue north, and Alyiakal orders formation shifts from two abreast to three abreast and back again while the dirt road on which the company rides remains wide enough for a three-abreast formation.

They pass several more hamlets, walled and spread apart, and with buildings and walls built largely of mud brick, before he says to Maaslar, "There must be a reason why the hamlets are so small and separated."

"Water, ser. There aren't any rivers here, and the streams are tiny. Pemedra holds the only spring."

Recalling what Draakyr had said about beans, Alyiakal asks, "Then there's little snow, and most of the rain comes in early Spring?"

"There's snow. It's so dry that when it melts it barely wets the dust."

Alyiakal decides against more questions about anything except barbarians or matters directly related to Fourth Company and orders another formation shift. He does notice, however, if from a distance, that none of the dwellings feature the privacy screens before their doors, unlike most dwellings in Cyador.

A glass later, the two companies reach the point where the main road splits into three roads, or rather two trails and one road. One dusty trail heads north-northeast toward a pass or valley between two taller hills, about a kay or so away. The second trail leads north-northwest toward a similar gap in the hills. Third Company takes the third way, more of a road, heading mostly west, roughly a kay from where the ground begins to rise.

All Alyiakal sees to the south is grass and more grass in the process of turning winter-gray, while the red rock hills to the north occasionally sport scrub bushes and scattered low and gnarled evergreens.

What's the point of even having a post here? There's nothing of value to protect. He doesn't voice this.

Some three kays west of where the roads separate, Alyiakal sees a collapsed mud-brick wall and some charred timbers, partly covered by bushes and tan and gray grass, on the south side of the road.

Surprisingly, Maaslar answers the unasked question: "That was the closest successful raid ever on a hamlet south of the hills. Happened before my time. Almost ten years ago."

Another half glass has passed when the bay lifts his head slightly, turning to the right and into the light breeze, then snorts. Alyiakal senses a touch of chaos in the gelding's order/chaos aura. "There's something different to the left."

"Most likely a grass cat," says Maaslar. "They're everywhere, but they don't attack groups. They'll go for single riders, though. That's why couriers ride in pairs. Over a quarter kay or less the cats can outrun a horse."

Alyiakal takes in the information, but has his doubts. "What about a barbarian scout? Do they post scouts along the trails out of Pemedra?"

"In the Spring and Summer. Never run across one in late Autumn or Winter."

The remainder of the patrol is as uneventful as the first few glasses, but, at least by the time Fourth Company returns to the post, the formation shifts that Alyiakal orders aren't as ragged and he feels as though he has a slightly better feel for Maaslar and the area closer to the post.

Just slightly.

XXII

The early-evening wind moans, rather than howls, as Alyiakal leaves the stable after grooming the bay. During the previous two-day patrol just completed, the only thing moving north of Pemedra the entire time had been smoke plumes from the chimneys of herder hamlets and winter-gray grass swaying and flattening in the wind. He had seen older hoofprints in the road, most of them made by lancer mounts, and a few sets of cart tracks.

He knows that he'll need to write up two copies of his patrol report immediately after the evening meal and leave one copy for Majer Klaavyl, but so long as that report is ready before midnight on the day the patrol is completed, neither the majer nor Overcaptain Tygael will say anything.

He stops by the message box on the way to his quarters to wash up before dinner and is pleasantly surprised to find a letter addressed to Undercaptain Alyiakal'alt. He smiles as he recognizes Saelora's elegant but precise script, but carries the unopened missive to his room and leaves it on the night table while he washes up. Only then does he pick up the letter, letting his senses range over the seal, which has been loosened and reheated, he can tell, from the order/chaos patterns in the wax.

He shakes his head. *As if there'd be anything of interest to the Mirror Lancers in the thoughts of a young woman.* Then he breaks the seal and begins to read.

> *It was so good to hear from you and to know that you arrived safely in Pemedra. Sooner or later, that additional training in healing will prove useful. Hyrsaal is envious that you got a patrol assignment. They sent him to Summerdock. He's in charge of a company that patrols the coast to catch smugglers. He wrote that they even caught some when he'd only been there an eightday.*
>
> *I was surprised to hear that you haven't run into many barbarians so far. Everyone talks about how awful they are. Just be careful.*
>
> *I do have some news of my own. I passed the test to become a probationary junior enumerator. Vassyl was as pleased as I am. I don't get paid that much more, but I can wear enumerator blues, and I'm one of the few women . . .*

Alyiakal smiles as he reads about what she has been learning and what is happening in Vaeyal and along the Great Canal. *Right now, her life is more interesting than yours.*

But then, Alyiakal knows that could change at any time, and certainly will in the Spring, if not sooner.

He adds the letter to the small file with her previous correspondence, because he likely won't be able to write her back until the following evening, since the patrol report comes first. Much of tomorrow will be spent going over the patrol with the squad leaders and dealing with supply issues. He wants to work on the map he's slowly drawing, based on the ones in the Fourth Company officer's chest and on his personal observations. The map helps him remember details, and he'd like to have one that's his, although he couldn't say why he feels it's important.

There's no hurry to write Saelora because it will be two days before the dispatch riders make their next trip to Syadtar.

When he reaches the mess, Draakyr and Lyung are already there. Thallyr, Tygael, and the majer arrive within moments, and all six seat themselves.

After the server fills all the wineglasses, and the majer lifts his glass, Alyiakal and the others follow the majer's example, while the server brings out the serving platters and the large basket of bread. Alyiakal can see that the meat looks to be lamb or mutton in a white gravy, with more spring beans, and false potatoes, which, to Alyiakal, taste like they're half turnip, half potato. With the gravy, they're better than merely edible.

"You got back late this afternoon," says Draakyr to Alyiakal. "Did you see anything up north?"

"Not anything moving. There were some cart tracks heading north."

"Likely those traders that came by here yesterday."

"Traders? Isn't that dangerous for them?"

From beside Draakyr, Lyung laughs. "Everyone leaves them alone. Well, at least inside Cyador. Traders are too scarce to kill. They're also the only source of coins for folks in the hamlets, and sometimes, even the barbarians. If anyone robbed or killed them, they wouldn't last an eightday."

Alyiakal wonders about that, but asks only, "What do the barbarians have to trade?"

"Wool and hides mostly," replies Lyung. "Sometimes, grass-cat pelts. They're scarce and valuable. The cats won't get near anything that people have touched so they're hard to trap."

"Smart, too," adds Tygael.

"It's clouding up to the northeast," says Draakyr. "We might get a bit of snow."

The majer shakes his head. "Enough wind to blow off loose shutters, and maybe a finger's worth of snow so light it'd barely wet the ground."

"Except the ground's not warm enough to melt anything now," returns Lyung.

"Still say it's colder here than in Inividra, even if it's maybe a hundred and fifty kays farther north."

"Doesn't matter," says Tygael. "In Winter they're both colder than an angel's heart."

Not for the first time, as he helps himself to a healthy helping of the mutton, Alyiakal wonders how that phrase came to be.

XXIII

Under a clear and cold green-blue sky, the wind cuts through Alyiakal's winter jacket, gloves, and even the garrison cap with earflaps, as Fourth Company rides up the trail through the Grass Hills following the tracks of raiders who had made a quick strike at one of the few hamlets in the grasslands north of Pemedra.

Why did the majer send an entire company to track little more than a half score of raiders? Especially since they weren't that successful? Because he thinks that they're a lure? Or because we need more experience?

Whatever the reason, Majer Klaavyl hadn't explained and sent Alyiakal and Fourth Company off with the order to find out what they could along with the admonition not to waste lancers.

How can I waste lancers when we haven't so much as seen a barbarian rider in almost a season? But then, over the past season and all the generally uneventful patrols, the majer and every other officer in the post had cautioned Alyiakal that the barbarians were anything but predictable.

He studies the trail and the uneven ground on each side. The ground gradually rises into barren slopes containing only flattened tan and gray grass, rocks, and low bushes and scrub evergreens too sparse to hide a man, let alone a horse. His eyes go back to the trail. For the first time, the tracks in the near-frozen ground look far clearer. "Those tracks look more recent," he says to Maaslar.

"Might only be a few glasses old. Maybe less," replies the senior squad leader. "Thought they might have stopped back in that vale."

Alyiakal nods, although he wouldn't have called the rocky flat behind them where the valley narrowed slightly a vale.

As the company reaches a slight rise, Alyiakal sees tracks heading northwest away from the trail along a path toward the crest of a smaller hill overlooking the main trail two kays farther north. He can't discern how the path reaches the hill as it twists behind a rocky outcrop. "Some of them broke off."

"Looks like half of them left the trail and headed up that slope," says Maaslar.

"Could they get up higher and roll rocks down?"

"They've done that before. They could also be trying to split us up, or get us strung out single file. Doesn't look like that path they're on will allow two abreast for much more than a few hundred cubits. Can't tell beyond that outcrop. Best we send a scout. See if he can determine where they've gone."

"We're on higher ground here. Halt the company," orders Alyiakal.

"Company! Halt!" commands Maaslar. "Rear scout to the company!"

As the scout turns and rides back up the trail separating him from the rest of the company, Alyiakal looks again beyond the prints on the side path. He sees no sign of any trail or path nearing the top of the smaller hill. *But it could curve back around closer to the main trail.*

The scout reins up facing both Maaslar and Alyiakal.

"Baaryn, follow those tracks for a bit," orders the first squad leader. "See if you can tell where they're headed. Don't get too close to that outcrop, and be ready to head back if there's any sign the raiders might be close."

The scout nods. "On my way, Squad Leader."

While the scout rides slowly up the path taken by some of the raiders, Alyiakal looks at the tracks on the main trail, which curves slowly downhill and to the northeast along the north side of the ridge where Fourth Company has halted.

The bay gives a quiet snort as the wind picks up out of the north-northeast, and Alyiakal feels unease in the gelding. He says evenly, "They're closer than we thought." He tries to sense ahead around the downhill curve, but feels only a vague sense of chaos, and cannot determine how far from the company that chaos might be.

Maaslar frowns. "Ser?"

"Hold here," says Alyiakal. "Have first squad set up a five-man front and have the files behind face outward with lances ready. I'm riding back to check something." That's true, but only so far as it goes, because he has a feeling that there's something . . . more than a rider or two . . . to the east of the trail.

Alyiakal has just about reached the end of first squad when he sees and senses riders galloping along the ridge to the east. "Second squad, right file! Outward face! Ready! Lances! Left file! Outward face! Ready! Lances!" He glances back to the front of the company, but can't see or sense riders nearing from the north, not that they couldn't be riding up the trail or back down the side path toward Fourth Company.

The rankers in second squad pivot and raise their lances.

Almost belatedly, Alyiakal raises his, but he waits until the raiders are less than a hundred cubits away. "Second squad! Open! Fire! Short bursts!" Then he aims at the chest and legs of the lead raider's horse.

The horse goes down, as does the mount following closely.

Alyiakal picks off two riders, then turns and urges the bay back toward the front of the company, where Maaslar has re-formed first squad into a five-man front to face what looks to be almost twoscore raiders riding up the gentle incline, along with riders coming back down the side path.

The leading riders coming up the main trail go down, but the raiders continue to charge—until the number of downed men and mounts make progress impossible. Alyiakal targets the last raider moving forward and fires—*willing* the short burst toward the barbarian. The rider ducks, but the chaos burst drops and flares into the rider.

How did I do that? Alyiakal has no idea, but worrying about it can wait. He looks for another target, but, suddenly, there are no more barbarians—mounted, in any case. He glances toward the northwest path, but only two charred forms lie there, as if the raiders realized that they'd failed to catch Fourth Company unaware and had immediately withdrawn.

He eases the bay up beside Maaslar's big white gelding and halts. Farther downhill, beyond the northeastern curve where the road becomes visible heading northward, he sees riders. "They're not staying to deal with their wounded or dead?" Even as he says that, Alyiakal realizes he sounds stupid, and quickly adds, "Or will they come back later?"

"Firelances don't leave many wounded," replies Maaslar. "They don't have much use for wounded or dead warriors, and they figure we'll collect any weapons. The grass cats and the other scavengers will take care of the bodies within days, maybe sooner." Then he turns his mount. "Third and fourth ranks. Search the bodies for anything usable. Make it quick. First and second ranks. Lances ready! Give them cover."

The order for cover turns out to be unnecessary, and in less than a quint, the company has loaded the blades and other usable items on three captured mounts.

"No casualties for first squad, ser," reports Maaslar. "Eight barbarians killed. No mounts recovered."

Elbaar reins up short of Alyiakal and Maaslar. "Second squad. No casualties. Seven barbarians killed. Three mounts and gear recovered. Spoils turned in."

Yurak reports, "Third squad. No casualties. No spoils."

Left unsaid is that third squad hadn't been in a position to be attacked.

But if we'd continued down the trail, it would have been different.

The few coppers and pieces of personal jewelry recovered from dead raiders have been turned over to Maaslar.

Except for small items likely hidden by the collecting rankers.

Once Elbaar and Yurak return to their squads, Maaslar turns in the saddle. "Now what, ser?"

"Unless you suggest otherwise, I'd say we've done what the majer had in mind, and it's time to head back to Pemedra."

"Ser?"

"The majer was clear: Find out what they're up to and don't waste lancers. The whole point of that ineffectual hamlet raid was to get a company out here for an ambush. Fortunately, my horse has a sensitive nose and I realized it." Alyiakal smiles pleasantly. "I'm new to this, Senior Squad Leader. You aren't. Are we likely to find out any more by following these raiders all the way through the hills? Except perhaps getting caught in another ambush?"

Maaslar offers a wry grin. "Not that I can see, ser."

XXIV

Because Fourth Company does not reach Pemedra until after dark, Alyiakal does not finish his log entry for the patrol until close to midnight. He is less than surprised to find himself summoned to meet with Majer Klaavyl little more than a glass after the morning mess, while he is updating and adding to his personal maps.

He stops at the doorway to the sparely furnished office and raps on the half-open door. "Majer, ser?"

Klaavyl gestures for Alyiakal to enter and says, "Close the door."

Alyiakal does, then takes the chair to which the majer has gestured.

"What were my orders, Undercaptain?"

"You ordered me to take Fourth Company to follow the barbarian raiders. We were to follow them and discover their purpose, and to destroy them if possible, but not to waste lancers in doing so."

"How many barbarians did Fourth Company face?"

"Roughly two score. There might have been another half score concealed by the terrain that we did not see."

"Why didn't you check, Undercaptain?"

"Because trying to find out would have risked losing lancers unnecessarily. The attack on Fourth Company made it clear that the small group of raiders that attacked the hamlet were a lure and that they intended to attack us on terrain unfavorable to us. By pursuing downhill into an area offering conceal-ment—"

"That's enough, Undercaptain. I read your patrol report. I also took the liberty of talking with Senior Squad Leader Maaslar. He was blunter than you were, but you both agree on what happened. He also said that you handled the matter effectively."

Meaning that you did it differently from the way he would have, but that you didn't screw it up. Not too much, anyway.

". . . He also said that you realized they were near before he did. How did you know that?"

"I didn't. My mount did. He's sensitive to any strange smells or sounds before the other mounts are, I noticed that after the first few times I rode him. I can't always tell what it is, but if he notices something, it's there."

Klaavyl half shakes his head. "I'd discount that, except Undercaptain Faaryn put a note in your file that you're better than most undercaptains with mounts. From him, it means something." The majer hesitates, then asks, "You've suggested that the raid and the attack were planned. Why do you think that?"

"Ser, you'd likely know better than I, but my thought is that the raiders who attacked the resupply company reported the number of replacements to someone. They might have learned in previous years that the Mirror Lancers send new and replacement officers in the fall. Someone might have put the two together and decided that they could inflict significant losses by making an unexpected attack."

Especially on a company with an inexperienced undercaptain and a large number of lancer replacements.

"To what end?"

"Perhaps to reduce the number of lancers available later in the year so that later raids would be more productive?"

"That suggests a great deal more thought and planning than we've seen before," says Klaavyl evenly.

"I wouldn't know, ser. That was the only possibility I could think of."

"You may be right. We'll have to see." Klaavyl gives a short harsh laugh, then says, "That's all for now, Undercaptain."

"Yes, ser." Alyiakal stands, inclines his head, and leaves the study.

As he walks from the headquarters building, Alyiakal can't help but wonder what Maaslar told the majer . . . and what the senior squad leader might be saying in other circumstances.

But how can you find out?

After what Healer Vayidra had told him in Pemedra, Alyiakal has been working to improve his shields, but shields or order/chaos fluctuations won't reveal thoughts. *What about using the kind of concealment you used in the Great Forest?*

He shakes his head, knowing that he will need something different. Then he turns his steps toward the mess kitchen.

Once he's inside the kitchen, one of the mess orderlies appears.

"Do you have a spare carrot or turnip? Raw?"

"Ser . . ."

"I'm sure it won't be that big a problem."

"Ah . . . yes, ser."

Shortly, the orderly reappears with a midsized carrot.

"Excellent. Thank you."

From the mess kitchen, Alyiakal makes his way to the stable.

As he enters the main door, one of the ostlers immediately walks toward him. "Ser? Do you need something?"

Alyiakal shakes his head. "I want to thank my mount. Even if he won't understand why."

The ostler looks puzzled.

"He smelled raiders before we saw them." With a smile, Alyiakal continues toward the bay's stall.

As he enters the stall and closes the door behind himself, the bay turns his head.

"I brought you a bit of a treat."

The bay nuzzles Alyiakal, but clearly smells the carrot, and Alyiakal offers it. The gelding makes short work of it, then gives Alyiakal another insistent nuzzle.

"That's all I've got."

As he stands beside the gelding, Alyiakal works at creating a concealment, something he hasn't done for some time. The bay doesn't seem to notice that much, except he nuzzles Alyiakal, as if to make sure that he is still there. Then Alyiakal eases toward the stall door and extends his senses. He can't sense the ostler anywhere close. So he eases the door open, by feel and by order sense, since he can't see anything; steps out; and closes the stall door, walking slowly in the direction he'd seen the ostler go.

He moves deliberately and slowly because what he senses isn't as clear as what he could see, but after possibly a score of steps he can sense two figures talking by a doorway. Belatedly, Alyiakal realizes it must be the doorway to the tack room and he halts, moving back against the wall.

So far they haven't seen or sensed you.

"Undercaptain Alyiakal came in. Said he had to thank his mount."

"For what?"

"He said the horse smelled the barbarians before he or anyone saw them."

"Why not? Horses smell everything, and the barbarians stink. Wouldn't think an undercaptain would notice, though."

"He talks to that bay."

"Glad he can. That gelding barely tolerates any of us." The second ostler turns. "I need to get that saddle from Captain Lyung's stall."

Alyiakal has to step back as the second ostler turns back. Clearly, neither man has seen him. He eases away quietly, back the way he had come. He doesn't drop the concealment until he stands by the bay's stall door. Even if anyone is looking, they'll think he stepped out of the stall, but from what he can tell, no one is nearby.

Besides, no one is that interested or concerned with raw undercaptains.

From the stables, he walks to the building holding the mess and the studies for officers and squad leaders. As he nears the entrance, he sees Juast going through the door.

Alyiakal decides to follow Juast, since there's a good possibility he's headed to the same place as Alyiakal. Once inside, Alyiakal glances around. No one is in the corridor except Juast, who doesn't look back. Alyiakal raises a concealment again, then carefully makes his way into the study through the half-open door.

By the time he eases into a position against the wall and near enough to overhear, Juast is already talking to Maaslar.

". . . heard you got called in to see the majer. He want to hear about your patrol?"

"What else?"

"How did it go?"

"He asked a few questions. He always does about new undercaptains."

"You still wary about your undercaptain? He hasn't done anything stupid yet, has he?"

Alyiakal has the impression that Maaslar shakes his head, but he can't tell for certain.

"Not yet. He's polite. Careful and asks me."

"So what's the problem?"

"He's the kind that won't make any of the little stupid mistakes. Because he won't, his first mistake will be big. I don't want to be there when it happens."

"Why do you think that?" asks Juast.

"He sees too much, and he's angel-fired good with a lance."

"I saw that on the supply run. Didn't seem to me that he's the cocky type. He listened."

"Now. I've never seen an undercaptain that cool who wasn't full of himself behind that shield they all have."

Alyiakal stiffens at the word "shield," but relaxes somewhat at the words that follow, although he is aware of a headache that gets more painful moment by moment.

"I'll be interested to see how he turns out over the next year."

"Two'll get you five," replies Maaslar, "that he's either killed or loses more than a squad . . . if not both."

"I'll risk a silver on that," counters Juast.

The tone in Juast's voice suggests, at least to Alyiakal, a smile of sorts.

"Your loss," replies Maaslar.

"My gain," answers Juast, with a laugh, "and yours, because, if I win, you're more likely to be alive to pay me."

Alyiakal eases away, moving slowly and carefully, trying not to make a sound as he leaves the squad leaders' study and also struggling to hold on to the concealment. Once he is out in the corridor and clear, sensing no one near, he releases the concealment, sighing quietly. Then he massages his forehead with his left hand, though it doesn't help much.

Absently, he wonders why his head aches, since it hadn't when he'd used a concealment to walk through the Great Forest.

I wasn't carrying two levels of shields . . . and I'm out of practice. He resumes walking toward the officers' study and makes his way to the Fourth Company desk, his until he's given another duty assignment . . . or until Juast has to pay Maaslar.

Thankful he's alone, he takes out his maps and begins to compare what the map shows and what he recalls of the patrol, then looks at what the map indicates farther to the north and northeast. Then he begins to add the details to the company map and to his own maps. He is still working on the maps when a voice calls from the study door.

"The maps aren't everything, remember?"

Alyiakal senses that the speaker is Captain Lyung even before he turns and replies, "I know, but they help me recall."

Lyung walks from the door to stand beside the desk. "I heard Fourth Company was attacked. Mind telling me about it?"

"We'd stopped at the top of a rise in the trail . . ." Alyiakal goes on to give a brief description of what happened.

Lyung frowns, then says, "First time I ever heard an undercaptain give credit to a horse." He smiles warmly.

"He deserved it."

"Doesn't matter. Keep paying attention to him." After a pause, the captain asks, "Did you see anything out of the ordinary?"

"Ser . . . I haven't been here long enough to know that. They didn't yell or make any noise, they just rode toward us with blades out."

"How did you know to face the lancers out?"

"It made sense. There wasn't any place else the raiders could have come from."

"What about spoils?"

"Except for blades and three scrawny horses, only a few coppers."

"It sounds like they were desperate."

"There were around two score of them."

"Didn't they attack the resupply force?"

"Yes, ser."

"The hamlets to the north might see raids even before Spring. We'll have to watch for that." Lyung steps back. "Keep that in mind."

"I will."

"I need to get moving," adds Lyung. "The majer's accompanying us on patrol."

Better you than me. But Alyiakal knows his turn will come as well.

After the captain leaves, Alyiakal closes his eyes for a time, trying to let his headache subside. In time, it does, but he still feels tired, as if holding the concealment takes more effort.

He stands and walks into the mess, passing a tray of hard biscuits and a small keg of ale. He takes two biscuits and pours half a mug of the cool ale. Then he slowly chews one biscuit, with the help of the ale, which still tastes slightly odd to him, followed by the other before walking back to his desk in the officers' study. In less than a quint the headache is gone, and he feels far less tired.

Another frigging thing to keep in mind. And something neither Triamon nor Vayidra had told him.

He shakes his head and goes back to the maps.

Neither Overcaptain Tygael nor Captain Thallyr appears in the mess at the evening meal, and Alyiakal finds himself seated across from Draakyr.

After several bites, Draakyr looks across the table. "You didn't lose any men. Don't think it'll be that easy again."

"I know we were fortunate. If we'd gone any farther, they'd have caught us where it would have been difficult to use firelances."

"That's always their strategy. One way or another."

"I read the patrol report about their rolling boulders down on Fourth Company last year."

"That's why you need to avoid narrow passages unless you already control the higher ground."

"I didn't see any bows or archers," says Alyiakal.

"You likely won't. Not here. There aren't any trees suitable for self bows, and the barbarians can barely afford to buy or forge swords."

Alyiakal frowns. "Self bows?"

"Made out of a single length of wood. There are two kinds of bows. Self bows and horn bows. Horn bows take time and craft. Also, there aren't that many horned animals around here because of the grass cats. The most numerous are the grass antelopes, and their horns aren't that good . . ."

Alyiakal takes a sip of the wine and continues to listen.

XXV

The Grass Hills of the north will not remain as unpopulated as they now are, not when the peoples of Jerans and the petty warlords west of the great peaks of the Westhorns continue to breed like the rodents they are. The Second Emperor of Light foresaw that probability and began the building of Mirror Lancer posts to protect the northern borders of Cyador . . .

Those posts effectively define the extent of Cyador, both at present and for the future, given the limited, if large, number of chaos towers, now that it has been conclusively determined that those towers cannot be duplicated or replicated, either through technical methods or through any known application of magery, even by the strongest and most capable of the Magi'i. In his wisdom, the late emperor decreed that the chaos produced by the towers be limited to those uses already established. Those edicts do not forbid any use or application of chaos gathered or created by individuals of the Magi'i, provided such uses are in accord with the laws and customs of Cyador and do not adversely impact the chaos towers, especially since such a proscription might inhibit future advances in applied magery that could conceivably extend the existence of the towers.

As always, the use of chaos in firelances should be restricted to where absolutely necessary to maintain order or to defend borders against incursion, as determined by the local Mirror Lancer commander . . .

Fragment, Mirror Lancer Archives
Zaenth'alt, Captain-Commander
Cyad, 45 A.F.

XXVI

Although the green-blue sky is clear, the late-winter white sun offers little heat even in midmorning as Alyiakal and Fourth Company follow First Company along a trail leading northwest from Pemedra. While the trail winds around, and occasionally over, the hills, the map Alyiakal has studied indicates it will take them to the valley holding the springs that are the headwaters for the West Branch of the Jeryna River.

Over the course of late Autumn and Winter, Alyiakal and Fourth Company have made almost a score of patrols—long and short through wind and snow—with only the one attack in late Autumn by raiders. On two other patrols Alyiakal caught his only other sight of any barbarians, and in both instances, a handful of riders immediately rode off when they caught sight of Fourth Company. In the second instance, Majer Klaavyl had accompanied Fourth Company, but he had made no suggestions, nor had he even summoned Alyiakal to discuss his patrol report. Not that there was a reason to, Alyiakal supposes, not unless Alyiakal had misstated something.

This patrol is different. According to a dispatch from Syadtar, conveyed by Captain Thallyr, the barbarians have built hamlets and even a town in the valley, and those communities have supported a continuing series of raids on Cyadoran hamlets.

So . . . because the barbarians here are behaving themselves, we've been ordered to look into the situation and take appropriate action, if warranted.

Given what Alyiakal has heard of Captain Thallyr, "appropriate action" will likely require firelances and dead barbarians—assuming that the reports about hamlets and raiders are in fact correct. Perhaps even if they're not.

When Thallyr orders a brief rest stop at noon at the top of a rise, from which anyone approaching would be visible for close to a kay, not that the scouts have seen anyone, Maaslar eases his mount up beside Alyiakal's bay and says, quietly, "Ser . . . there wasn't much of a briefing this morning."

Alyiakal smiles wryly. "I didn't get any more of a briefing, either, except that the orders came from Mirror Lancer headquarters. I'd guess, and it's only a guess, that, Winter or no Winter, there have been more raids around Isahl, and that they've taken heavy casualties. We're the closest other post to Isahl, and we haven't suffered any casualties so far this Winter. What do you think?"

"Pretty much the same, ser."

"What else, Maaslar? You have that worried expression."

The senior squad leader's face has been expressionless, but from working with Maaslar, and sensing his order/chaos patterns, Alyiakal is now able to discern more of what the senior squad leader does not reveal through words or body posture.

"Don't know as Pemedra's ever gotten an order like this, ser, even from Mirror Lancer headquarters."

"Meaning that it's much worse than anyone's telling us?"

"Could be, ser."

Alyiakal also knows what Maaslar is not saying—that it's likely Fourth

Company is accompanying First Company because Majer Klaavyl doesn't want unnecessary casualties to more than one of his more experienced companies.

Although he'd claim that it's to give us experience.

By late afternoon the wind from the east picks up, and it feels to Alyiakal as if it comes straight from the heights of the icy peaks of the Westhorns.

After the two companies make camp, with mounts picketed, and sentries posted, Alyiakal gathers his squad leaders together, but before he can say anything of import, Thallyr approaches. "Undercaptain . . . a word with you."

"Yes, ser." Alyiakal steps away from the squad leaders and joins the square-faced captain.

"I'm sure you know this isn't just a scouting patrol," begins Thallyr.

"I had some doubts, ser. Two companies seem excessive for scouting, but, given my lack of experience, I wasn't about to offer that opinion."

"Wise of you." Thallyr pauses. "The barbarians have done considerable damage to the Cyadoran hamlets near Isahl and inflicted significant casualties on the companies there."

Significant casualties? Against firelances? "Are they doing something different, or are they attacking in greater force?"

"They have some kind of device that flings giant arrows or light spears at a much greater distance than we've encountered before. They concealed the spear-throwers behind the first riders, who used some sort of buckler or shield to deflect firelance bolts. The bucklers aren't completely effective, of course."

In the momentary silence, almost belatedly, Alyiakal recalls that Fuhlart is posted at Isahl. *Was he one of the casualties?*

Before Alyiakal can fully consider that possibility, Thallyr asks, "How would you defend against such an attack?"

"Take out the horses first," replies Alyiakal. "That should expose the spear-throwers."

"That was my thought as well, but I can't believe that experienced captains wouldn't have immediately adopted that tactic. That suggests there's more to the matter." Thallyr fingers his very square chin. "Considerably more."

"Did they have archers as well?"

"There was no mention of archers, but no bow could launch even a small spear. We don't see many archers among the barbarians around Pemedra, but those along the rivers may have more resources for making and using bows. Or they may have some other tactic or weapon. The dispatch to Majer Klaavyl was . . . less than explicit. I wanted you to be aware of the possibilities."

"I appreciate the information, ser."

"We'll be heading out early, Undercaptain."

"Yes, ser. Fourth Company will be ready."

Once Thallyr turns and walks away, Alyiakal returns to the three squad leaders. "Captain Thallyr is concerned that the barbarians along the West Branch may have a greater range of weapons . . ." When he finishes, he asks, "What are your thoughts?"

"More archers," suggests Yurak. "Has to be something that strikes from farther away than a firelance."

"Might be the shields, especially if the lancers didn't know about them, or if they've got a lot of green replacements," adds Elbaar.

Since the senior squad leader has been quiet, Alyiakal looks to him. "Do you have anything to add?"

"No, ser. I think it has to be something else. I don't have any idea what that might be, though."

"All of you might be right. I tend to agree with Maaslar, but I don't have the faintest idea, either."

Except that it's effective and something Subcommander Munnyr doesn't want to put in writing. "Captain Thallyr also said that we'd be moving out early tomorrow," adds Alyiakal. "Not that any of us expected otherwise."

Maaslar nods, as does Yurak. Elbaar offers a sardonic smile.

XXVII

Before sunrise, First and Fourth Companies are back on the trail that serves as a road, and Alyiakal's bay gelding exhales white puffs in the Winter air. Captain Thallyr has not provided additional information, telling Alyiakal only that he will brief him and all the squad leaders at the first rest stop.

Three glasses later, Thallyr calls a halt and, true to his word, gathers together the six squad leaders and Alyiakal.

"We're being sent to teach the barbarians a lesson," begins the captain. "Unlike the patrols from Isahl, we should have some element of surprise. We'll be making our approach to the valley from the east. The forces from Isahl always approached from the south or west roads as there's no feasible way to circle and attack from the north from Isahl, and it would take longer than a day for them to use our route. They've never been attacked from this direction, even before the establishment of Pemedra."

Perhaps because the "road" we're following is barely a trail, even by barbarian standards. Alyiakal sees no point in voicing the obvious.

"We do know," continues Thallyr, "that when the lancers from Isahl attacked the barbarians outside the largest hamlet, they encountered a great number of spears that were effective from a greater distance, and that shield-bearers protected these assets. That suggests this site was carefully prepared, and that it would be to our advantage to avoid such a situation."

In short, the lancers from Isahl likely rode in with firelances leveled, thinking that superior weapons would make short work of the barbarians. Alyiakal avoids the sardonic smile he feels, because, if the barbarians refuse to move from a prepared site, First and Fourth Companies aren't exactly equipped to spend days waiting them out.

"We will not be attacking," concludes the captain, "until we fully understand the situation. Then . . . we will do what is necessary. Now . . . back to your men."

The two companies ride for another glass, along the trail that curves to the west and is now wide enough to be called a road, with blurred hoofprints in places. After two more glasses and another stop, the two companies gradually descend through a valley too narrow for Alyiakal's comfort, even though Thallyr sends out additional scouts, along the road as well as the higher ground to each side.

The scouts discover nothing, but continue to flank the companies, riding through flattened grass, bushes, and the occasional isolated squat evergreen.

Alyiakal's bay occasionally raises his head, if briefly, but does not seem disturbed. Alyiakal himself cannot see anything out of the ordinary ahead, and he has no sense of anyone following.

Less than a glass later, at the top of a slight ridge, Thallyr halts the column and sends a ranker to summon Alyiakal to join him. Even before Alyiakal reaches the captain, he sees that the road ahead flattens out, and the valley the companies have followed opens onto a broader expanse. A meandering line of trees perhaps some five kays to the northwest marks the course of the West Branch of the Jeryna River. To the west, some bare fields look to have been tilled, with small huts adjoining them.

Farther west, Alyiakal sees what might be a large hamlet or small town, backed by rising hills beyond. Thin trails of smoke rise from the nearer huts, trails that dissipate quickly. As he reins up, he sees that the captain is studying the wide valley—and frowning.

"Ser?"

After shaking his head, Thallyr turns to Alyiakal. "Good example of why you can't always trust maps. We're almost ten kays from the town where the raiders are based, and it's late afternoon. We'll have to use that stead off the road ahead as a place to stop. On the way down, keep a sharp eye out. Don't let anyone get around you, even if it means killing them. I may have additional duties for Fourth Company once we're settled in."

"How long do we plan to be here, ser?"

"As long as it takes, and that depends on the barbarians." Thallyr pauses, then adds, "That's all for now, Undercaptain."

"Yes, ser."

Alyiakal turns the bay and rides back to Fourth Company, where he relays Thallyr's orders for first squad to Maaslar.

"Yes, ser," replies the senior squad leader. "Did the captain say how long we'll be here?"

"As long as it takes. Those were his exact words."

"Thank you, ser."

Alyiakal can definitely sense that Maaslar isn't happy with Thallyr's words. Neither is Alyiakal, but the raiders started the problem by attacking Cyadoran hamlets and refusing to stop raiding. They didn't have to raid. In fact, over time some of the barbarians have slipped into Cyador and become growers and herders, and the Imperial policy states that, so long as they pay their tariffs and taxes, they are welcome.

For those who continue to raid, what else can we do? They can always attack when and where we're not patrolling.

"Company! Forward!" Alyiakal orders.

On the ride down the last slope, he studies the larger valley, noting other steads to the west, but the closest appears to be at least two kays away. As the road flattens, Alyiakal sees another less prominent road angling back to the northeast from a point several hundred yards east of the stead that Thallyr has selected as temporary quarters for the night, hopefully not longer.

Even before Fourth Company reaches the flatter land of the large valley, the squad from First Company has moved well west to control the eastern road, and Alyiakal finds himself again summoned to meet with Thallyr. He has barely ridden up beside the captain when Thallyr speaks.

"There's another stead half a kay east of this one, Undercaptain. As soon as we reach the side road leading to that stead, Fourth Company is to move out and occupy it. Send one squad farther northeast on that road to make sure there's no other road leading to the town. Also look for any steads farther out who could inform the town of our presence without using the roads we control. Holding two steads won't leave us as cramped. Make certain no one leaves that stead and no one passes on that road."

"Yes, ser."

Alyiakal immediately returns to Fourth Company and passes on the captain's latest orders.

"This valley's bigger than I thought," offers Elbaar after Alyiakal finishes.

"I suspect it's bigger than the captain thought," replies Maaslar dryly, "with more barbarians."

Yurak's only comment is an almost inaudible grunt.

Before long, Fourth Company rides northeast on the side road.

"Maaslar, first squad might be the best for scouting and securing the road beyond the stead ahead. Or would you suggest third squad?"

"First squad, ser. Might be a good idea to hold back third squad on the road short of the stead. That way, Yurak can cut off anyone who's away from the stead house and might try to sneak off."

"Then that's the way we'll do it."

When Fourth Company is still several hundred yards from the stead house, Alyiakal turns in the saddle. "First squad! Secure the northeast road!" He waits until first squad is well away before his next order. "Third squad, hold the road. Don't let anyone pass!"

Alyiakal and second squad ride toward the oblong stead house, a strange mixture of shoulder-high turf walls topped with peeled logs covered by grass thatch. The entire dwelling measures seven or eight yards long and five wide. Unlike even the meanest dwellings in Cyador, there is no privacy wall in front of the door. Several other small and low turf enclosures, possibly for animals of some sort, nestle around a larger turf building, likely a stable.

At less than a hundred cubits from the house, he orders, "Lances ready!"

Nearing the front of the turf and log dwelling, he senses someone leaving from the far side, hidden by the dwelling itself.

"Right file on me! Left file! Control the front of the house!" He urges the bay around the dwelling, where a man with a bow turns toward him, nocking and then drawing an arrow.

Instantly, Alyiakal fires a short burst of the firelance.

Bow and man drop in a charred heap, and Alyiakal senses a cold death mist. For a moment, he's stunned by the suddenness of it all.

"You killed him!" screams a woman, running from the rear door toward Alyiakal, a long knife in her hand.

Raaymon, the file leader, turns his mount and catches her in two long strides, slamming the back of her head with the flat of his sabre.

The woman sprawls on the frozen ground, the knife flying from her fingers. She does not move, but Alyiakal can sense that she is still alive . . . for the moment. "Tie her up!" he snaps, gesturing to the nearest ranker.

From what Alyiakal can sense, there might be one or two people in the dwelling, but no one emerges.

"Elbaar, have someone check the place. Carefully."

"Yes, ser."

Alyiakal takes another, longer look at the charred remnants that had been a man moments before. *But what choice did you have?* His eyes continue to survey the area around the crude dwelling.

Before long, the squad leader returns. "Two children, ser. Boy and girl. Girl maybe eight, boy . . . five or six, I'd guess."

"Any signs of older children?" asks Alyiakal. "Did anyone else try to get away?"

"No, ser. I asked the girl if she had any other brothers and sisters. She said that they went away a long time ago."

"They likely died of some flux, and their parents told them that," says Alyiakal. "Put the woman inside, but have someone watch her so that she doesn't have the children untie her when she wakes up."

"Yes, ser."

"Look around for any grain for the horses or any other useful supplies."

"Doesn't look like much so far, ser."

"Most likely not, but it won't hurt to look."

Two quints pass before Alyiakal spies a single lancer riding toward the stead, doubtless a ranker bearing a message from the senior squad leader. In time, the ranker rides up to Alyiakal.

"Ser, Senior Squad Leader Maaslar reports that there's only one stead in the next few kays along this road, and it's been abandoned for some time."

That doesn't surprise Alyiakal, given that the side road points toward rugged hills and that grass is encroaching on the road. "Convey my orders that first squad should return here."

"Yes, ser."

Alyiakal sees no point in having all of third squad guard the road leading to the large hamlet to the west. He orders Yurak to post two guards and return with the rest of third squad. Then he waits for Maaslar.

In the meantime, Elbaar reports, "This is a poor stead. One horse, might have been two once, five pigs, a boar and a sow and three decent-sized piglets, and a bunch of grass rats in one of those enclosures. Not any real grain, but a barrel of grass seeds in the stable. Maybe half a barrel of spring beans, and a third of a barrel of dried maize. Likely cooking and heating the turf house with braided dry grass bundles."

Alyiakal can only imagine the difficulty of surviving on such a stead.

Almost two more quints pass before Maaslar and first squad return.

"There's not much out there except grass, grass cats, rodents, and snakes, and maybe some wild dogs," reports the senior squad leader. "Not enough bushes and trees for antelope or red deer."

"What was the other stead like?" asks Alyiakal.

"Didn't look like it was even finished." Maaslar shakes his head, then says, "I saw a body in back here."

Alyiakal explains.

"Not much else that you could do."

"We'll need to send a report to Captain Thallyr, even if there's not much to say."

"Sometimes, that's best, ser. Might be good to send Elbaar with a pair of rankers."

After briefing the second squad leader and sending him off with two rankers, Alyiakal knows he has to deal with another unpleasant detail. He has to stoop to enter the sod and log dwelling. The odor inside is sour, close, musty, and damp. The woman, hands and feet bound, sits propped against the earthen wall. Maaslar follows him inside.

"Where do you want your man buried?" Alyiakal uses the word "man," because he has no idea of the relation of the man he killed to the woman. He also suspects that with the lack of wood in the area, burials are usual, rather than the pyres used in Cyador.

"Anywhere you want. Won't bring him back."

Alyiakal steps away and says to Maaslar, "Some of their children died. If one of the rankers can find if and where they're buried . . ."

"I'll have someone take care of it."

As Maaslar quickly leaves the dwelling, Alyiakal moves back to the woman, not certain what to say, if anything.

"Demon soldiers," mutters the woman.

"We wouldn't be here if your men hadn't attacked our hamlets," replies Alyiakal.

"What else are we supposed to do? There's little enough wood here, and the traders want coin for anything, especially salt."

For an instant, Alyiakal wonders about why salt is so important, then almost shakes his head. How else can they preserve the meat from the pigs and rodents?

Although they'll have a bit less after we leave . . . quite a bit less.

XXVIII

At dawn, First and Fourth Companies are already riding west toward the small town set in the southwest corner of the valley holding the headwaters of the West Branch. That town sits about a kay north of where the narrow road emerges from the hills that separate the town from Isahl and the hamlets and borders that Isahl was built to protect.

Captain Thallyr's battle plan is simple. Between first light and sunrise, the two companies should be able to cover half that distance. Then at sunrise, with the rising sun at their back, early detection will be more difficult, at least until they near the town. Neither Thallyr nor Alyiakal doubts that the barbarians have scouts posted on the road to Isahl. As the sun rises over the Grass Hills to the east, the Mirror Lancer scouts can discern no traces of scouts or anyone on the narrow road.

No sooner has Alyiakal made that observation, for perhaps the fifteenth time, than a rider emerges from a side path or lane and gallops toward the town whose first dwellings look to be some three kays away.

Thallyr does not order pursuit, but he does send out scouts, as well as dispatch a ranker to Alyiakal. The message is simple. "Have your senior squad leader proceed as planned. Join me."

After Alyiakal turns Fourth Company over to Maaslar, he rides forward to meet with Thallyr.

The captain immediately says, "There are three possibilities. They'll scatter to the winds, making pursuit infeasible. Or they'll form up and fight as a body. Or they'll fight in groups. What we do depends on what they do. If they scatter, we'll have to destroy the town. That will stop their raiding for a while, possibly for several years. If they choose to fight, we'll have to find a way to destroy them. Right now, ride with me until we know more."

Alyiakal isn't in the slightest surprised by the idea of destroying the town, especially since direct attacks against what sounded like the equivalent of fixed emplacements had turned out badly. He does wonder what the captain will do if the local barbarians manage to form up in a defensible position.

Maaslar calls a halt roughly a half kay from where the first houses of the town seem to begin. Less than a quint later two scouts ride back from the town.

Thallyr waits until the two rein up, then asks, "What did you find out?"

The older scout replies, "They've got half a mounted squad on the road just west of the first houses at the edge of the town, with shields and spear-throwers behind. We circled and got a look farther into the town. The main force is forming up in the open space in the center of the town. Big shields and lots of long lances. Men and some women in the center with strange spears. As many as five score there. Might be archers hidden nearby."

"Spear-throwers protected by lances and shields," says Thallyr. "Those spears likely have the range of a firelance." He turns in the saddle toward Alyiakal. "Undercaptain, it's going to be Fourth Company's task to get them to move. Your task is to avoid that road force and set every house, hut, or hovel in this misbegotten town on fire, until the barbarians break out of that formation in the center of town. Don't split your company into groups smaller than a squad. First Company will take a position close enough to the barbarians on the road to attack if the opportunity arises. Don't attack any individual unless they threaten you or your men, and don't break up your squads to pursue anyone."

"Yes, ser." Alyiakal pauses, then says, "The wind's coming out of the north-east. It might be best if we start on each side of the road—away from the shielded riders—and then move out to see if the wind carries the fires toward the center of town. If it doesn't, we can move in toward the center."

Thallyr nods, then says, "Do that."

"Yes, ser."

Alyiakal rides back to Fourth Company and has Maaslar call in Elbaar and Yurak. Once they ride up, Alyiakal shares his briefing with his squad leaders, explaining the situation and Captain Thallyr's orders, adding, "Use as little chaos as possible because the barbarians could move against us at any time."

"What if the barbarians attack?" asks Elbaar.

"We're to destroy them, but not to pursue or break formation."

"Pursuing plays into their hands," adds Maaslar.

"More of the town seems to be on the north side of the road," says Alyiakal. "Maaslar, first squad will handle the south side. If there's any overwhelming force, pull back. The captain also pointed out that those spear-throwers reach as far as a firelance, if not farther."

For the first time, a momentary expression of surprise appears on Maaslar's face. "No one raised that before."

Alyiakal decides not to mention that he'd raised the possibility earlier and says, "The captain was quite clear."

Alyiakal barely hears Yurak's muttered, "Frig," but does not react, instead adding, "I got the impression that it's best to catch them by surprise where there aren't any obvious spear-throwers. Our job is to set as much of the town on fire as possible. If you can take out fighters without pursuing or incurring casualties, so much the better. But destroying the houses and other buildings is the first task."

"Does the captain think that will get the raiders to come after us?" asks Elbaar.

"If they do, their shields and spears won't be as effective," replies Alyiakal. "If they don't, they'll be in no shape to raid Cyador for some time. Any other questions?"

"No, ser," replies Maaslar firmly.

"Then, we'd better start," says Alyiakal. "When we've done what we can, re-form here."

Maaslar immediately orders first squad to follow him.

"Second squad! Third squad! Forward!" Alyiakal leads the two squads along the shoulder of the road past First Company and then follows Maaslar toward the town ahead.

"Pass the word back for Squad Leader Yurak to join me," orders Alyiakal.

Before the squads have covered another fifty yards, Yurak eases his mount up beside Alyiakal's bay. "Ser?"

"Second and third squads need to target different sections of the town. After we circle to the right, when I turn second squad toward the houses, you keep heading west to get separation before you ride toward the dwellings and start firing the buildings. If you run into a large body of raiders, don't engage them in the town. Pull back to open ground where they can't shelter archers or spear-throwers. If they follow and you're confident you have the advantage, you can then engage."

"Yes, ser."

"Then I'll see you later, Squad Leader."

Alyiakal keeps a wry smile to himself as Yurak returns to his squad. Yurak knows what he's doing better than Alyiakal does.

About two hundred yards from the first houses, Maaslar angles left across a bare and turned field. Alyiakal angles right, and checks to see that third squad has followed. Behind him the light increases as the white sun eases above the Grass Hills. He looks to where the road passes between two hut-like dwellings. For a moment he sees a flash of light, but it doesn't recur.

Sunlight on a polished shield? But how could barbarian raiders afford such shields?

He pushes the question away. The real question is how to deal with such a shield. His eyes go to the structures ahead on his left. Unlike the half-turf dwelling at the stead where Fourth Company spent the night, these houses, although some appear little more than huts, are constructed of rough-hewn timber, but they do have grass-thatch roofs. Smoke trails rise from the rough-mortared stone chimneys. Most of them aren't close together, which suggests to Alyiakal that the fire from one dwelling can't be counted on to travel to another, especially in the light wind.

Still, he has his orders. He picks a slightly larger dwelling some hundred yards away and turns toward it. "Second squad! Lances ready!"

Although he watches the dwelling closely, no one leaves it, but that isn't surprising, given that it's just after sunrise on a late-Winter morning, and the heavy board shutters over the single window facing Fourth Company are fastened shut.

Alyiakal reins up some thirty cubits from the slant-roofed dwelling, then aims his lance at the planked wall, giving it the quickest touch of chaos. The firebolt strikes the rough wood, immediately creating a charred and ashen circle slightly more than a cubit across with small flames at the edges that begin to spread.

That might be a little too short a burst.

He turns the firelance toward the corner of the building with a slightly longer burst, then nods as he notes the rapidity with which the flames spread.

After turning to Elbaar, Alyiakal says, "It looks like the houses take a burst a shade longer than what you need against barbarians."

The squad leader nods.

Alyiakal is about to turn the bay when he senses someone on the other side of the dwelling hurrying toward the corner. A slender figure steps around the corner, with bow in hand and arrow nocked.

Whhsssst! The firelance bolt flares into the figure, consuming the archer, bow, and arrow before the shaft could be released.

"Quick there, ser," says Elbaar.

"I thought I heard something," Alyiakal lies. He studies the house, where the flames are growing fast enough that whatever water may be nearby will not be enough to quench them, then says, "We need to move faster now. Rotate the use of the lances among the men. There are close to a hundred houses and huts here." With those words he urges the bay toward the next house to the west, then says to Elbaar, "Take the left file, and fire the houses to the left of this one. The right file and I will take the ones on the edge of town."

"Yes, ser."

While Alyiakal is disobeying Thallyr's orders, he doesn't see how they can flame enough houses to force the locals out of the center of town without splitting the squad.

The second dwelling he approaches seems empty. At least, there's no smoke from the chimney. Alyiakal has Rumbaar, the right-file leader, use his firelance, then moves on.

When the half squad reaches the fifth house, he sees a woman and two children running, and he's relieved that they're running away from town, rather than into it. He glances once more to his left and realizes that Elbaar and the other half of the squad have fired two more houses than his file has. He looks over his shoulder and sees that the houses behind them are now burning strongly, if not yet fiercely.

We need to move faster.

He barely slows the squad for the fifth house, and the sixth, but he sees two older men with bows emerge from the seventh house. He urges the bay forward, leaning low against the gelding's mane, trying to get closer before using his lance. He's still a hundred fifty cubits from the two when he fires off one burst, then a second, *willing* each to strike.

Both figures topple. At the same time, a sharp pain flares through Alyiakal's skull, and his eyes water at its intensity, momentary as it is. "Rumbaar, fire the house!"

"Yes, ser."

Alyiakal blinks, trying to clear his blurred vision. As Rumbaar uses his lance on the house, Alyiakal looks ahead, then realizes that the next house ahead of them is already burning, and Elbaar's half squad is riding toward him.

"Second squad! To the right!"

In less than half a quint, the re-formed second squad is riding back eastward. To the south, it appears as though more than half the town is aflame.

In another half quint, Yurak and third squad join second squad, and Yurak reports to Alyiakal, "Burning accomplished, ser. We had to take out two locals, a young fellow and a woman."

"Thank you, Squad Leader. We're heading back to First Company to await further orders."

Once Yurak rejoins his squad, Alyiakal surveys the town, where most of the dwellings are in flames.

When Alyiakal and the two squads near the east end of the town, he sees that Thallyr has withdrawn First Company almost half a kay and that Maaslar has Fourth Company's first squad drawn up behind First Company.

"Elbaar, you and Yurak continue toward Senior Squad Leader Maaslar and Fourth Company. I'm reporting to Captain Thallyr and will rejoin the company shortly."

"Yes, ser."

Alyiakal rides to Thallyr and reins up. "Ser, most of the town is in flames. To avoid fragmenting forces and following your orders not to seek out raiders, we didn't attempt to fire the houses bordering the center of town, but it appears that some of them have caught fire from those already aflame."

"Carefully done and stated, Undercaptain," replies Thallyr. "Now we wait. If they decide to attack, First Company will slowly withdraw as they move toward us. Fourth Company will withdraw as well along that lane to the east. If it appears we can attack successfully we will. Fourth Company will then attack their rear. If they merely break into groups, First Company will enter what's left of the town and deal with those groups. In that event, Fourth Company will move forward to the edge of town to protect our rear and deal with any groups or individuals attempting to circle behind us or to attack you. You're not to enter the town without direct orders from First Company. Is that clear?"

"Yes, ser."

"Dismissed to your command, Undercaptain."

"Yes, ser."

As he rides past the rankers of First Company, Alyiakal has the feeling that Thallyr had wanted him to go beyond the captain's orders, and that Thallyr was slightly displeased with Fourth Company's ability to accomplish what was necessary without apparently disobeying orders.

When Alyiakal reins up beside Maaslar, he asks quietly, "How did it go? Did you encounter any resistance?"

"We burned enough hovels and huts," replies Maaslar. "Had to flame four barbarians. Two older men and two women. What about you?"

"Two older men, one youth, and two women that I know of." Alyiakal then sends for Elbaar and Yurak and conveys Captain Thallyr's plans.

When Alyiakal finishes, Maaslar nods and says, "They can't hold that formation for long."

Almost two glasses pass. The flames are dying down, and Thallyr sends out three scouts, who return in less than a quint, after which First Company begins to ride toward the town.

"Fourth Company! Forward!" orders Alyiakal.

Less than a quint later, some fifty yards from the first houses, Alyiakal halts the company, then turns to Maaslar. "Dispatch scouts about a third of a kay to the north and south of the road."

"Yes, ser."

Even once the scouts are in position, Alyiakal remains uneasy, hoping that Thallyr is successful and considering what he should do if First Company fails to return.

Another quint passes.

Then the scout to the south of the road signals and rides back to Alyiakal and Maaslar.

"Ser, there are raiders with shields coming from the south, along the edge of the houses. Half a squad, it looks like."

"I'll take second squad," says Alyiakal. "First squad needs to watch the main road here."

Maaslar frowns, but says, "Yes, ser."

In moments, Elbaar and second squad follow Alyiakal, who has a definite feeling that something isn't quite right, yet wonders if it's only his imagination.

Even before Alyiakal reaches the point where the scout had been posted, he sees a group of barbarians toward the southeast, well away from the still-smoldering houses ahead to Alyiakal's left. He counts five, each with an oblong, polished, bronze shield about a cubit and a half wide and more than two cubits tall. Behind them stand a half score others, some with long lances, others with what look to be feathered spears.

Upon seeing second squad, the shield-bearers immediately close and three men with lances move up, so that second squad faces shields and grounded lances.

"Split files! To each side! Right file on me! Left file on Squad Leader Elbaar. Flank the shields." Alyiakal's orders are unconventional, but he wants second squad moving and splitting the barbarians' attention because acting quickly will keep them off-balance, and avoiding engaging them isn't what Captain Thallyr—or Majer Klaavyl—would want, no matter what Thallyr might claim.

As soon as Alyiakal is within two hundred cubits, he fires a quick chaos blast into the barbarians behind the shield-bearers. "Open fire! Ignore the shields! Fire behind them."

He glances farther to the south but sees no other barbarians and no lancers from First Company, then continues to use short bursts on those behind the shield-bearers.

He can sense several spears being thrown, but none are that close to him and the bay.

Once well past the barbarian group, he turns the bay. "Second squad. Re-form on me!"

Most of the spear-throwers appear to be down. One runs straight south, but a firelance blast from Elbaar cuts him down.

The shield-bearers swiftly turn, as do the three men with lances, as if daring second squad to charge again.

"Second squad! Forward. At a trot!" orders Alyiakal.

At some fifty cubits from the shields, Alyiakal orders, "Second squad! Halt! Elbaar, take five men south and flank the shields. Then fire at will."

"Yes, ser."

In less than half a quint, the shield-bearers and lancemen are dead.

Elbaar and the five lancers return to the squad.

"Hamrach took a spear in the shoulder. Looks bad, ser. Those points have nasty barbs. Nomaar's mount also took a spear. Mount won't survive, bloody froth from his mouth."

"We need to return to the rest of the company. Then I'll see what I can do for Hamrach. Have Nomaar ride that far with someone else. Also, have someone pick up those bronze or brass shields."

"Spoils, ser?"

"Pick two men. Have them be quick and rejoin us, and have them count the bodies."

"Yes, ser."

Alyiakal doesn't want the company split any longer than necessary, and he well knows that his tactic would have been far more costly if they'd faced a full company with more shields and spear-throwers.

The squad is halfway back to the other two squads when Elbaar rides up beside Alyiakal and reports, "No real spoils. Some twenty coppers, a few rings. More bodies than I thought, twenty-three in all."

"Thank you, Squad Leader."

As soon as Alyiakal and second squad rejoin the company, he asks Maaslar, "Any trouble here?"

"No, ser. No sign of any locals, either."

Alyiakal quickly summarizes the quick clash with the barbarians, then says, "Send out scouts as before. I need to see to Hamrach's shoulder. Have someone let me know if First Company is returning."

After riding back to Hamrach, Alyiakal gestures to the two nearest riders.

"Help him out of the saddle." Then he dismounts, hands the reins of the bay to another lancer, and unstraps the healer's satchel from behind his saddle.

Hamrach's tunic is bloody, but not soaked, and the lancer is definitely pale. Alyiakal senses the chaos around the wound, the opening of which someone has packed with cloth. Since the cloth is working, Alyiakal concentrates on using his senses to remove the angry whitish-red point of chaos deep in the wound, then on cleaning the area around it, before removing the top layers of blood-soaked cloth, dusting the remaining cloth with order, and putting a more secure dressing over the wound.

"Doesn't hurt so much," says the lancer.

"It's going to hurt for a while," replies Alyiakal as he finishes. "I'll need to see you twice a day. That's the best I can do."

"You a healer, too, ser?"

"I had some extra training," replies Alyiakal as he replaces the satchel behind his saddle and then remounts. He gestures again to the two other unmounted lancers. "You three don't need to remount right now. When the time comes, help him mount. If he uses that arm, it could cause more bleeding."

"Yes, ser."

Alyiakal rides back to the front of the column, where he reins up beside Maaslar. "Any word from First Company?"

"Not yet, ser."

"Have the men stand down, then. They need a break."

"Company! Stand down. Stay close to your mounts!"

Almost a glass passes before Alyiakal catches sight of a single rider who makes his way toward them.

"Ser, First Company will join Fourth Company shortly. Both companies will begin the return trip to post once First Company arrives. First Company will lead."

"Thank you," returns Alyiakal. "Can you tell us what happened?"

"We broke up the barbarian formation, ser. Captain Thallyr would have to brief you on the details."

"I understand," replies Alyiakal dryly. "Convey to Captain Thallyr that Fourth Company is ready to ride and awaits First Company's arrival."

"Yes, ser."

Once the messenger has turned his mount and headed east along the road to the center of what remains of the town, Alyiakal turns to Maaslar. "How would you interpret what the messenger said?"

"I'd only be guessing, ser."

"Guess, then," says Alyiakal quietly, but firmly.

"First Company had more difficulty than anticipated, but succeeded. Any of the locals who couldn't flee likely died."

"Then it looks like Captain Thallyr won't be that displeased with second squad's handling of those who escaped his attack." *Provided you downplay it.*

Maaslar only offers a cynical smile.

Alyiakal doesn't press, but sends word to Elbaar and Yurak that, when the order to remount is given, the squads are to re-form to ride east with first squad leading.

Less than a quint later, when Alyiakal sees First Company approaching, he orders, "Fourth Company! Mount up!" Then he and Maaslar lead first squad past the other two as they re-form before halting, and wait for First Company to take the lead.

As Captain Thallyr nears, he gestures brusquely for Alyiakal to join him.

"You have the company, Senior Squad Leader."

"Yes, ser."

Alyiakal rides to join Thallyr, who halts both companies once First Company is positioned in the lead.

"Two of your men are riding double. What happened?"

Alyiakal gives a brief summary, with as few details as he dares, adding, "Hamrach took one of those feathered spears in the shoulder, and so did Nomaar's mount. Because those bronze shields seemed out of place, I had the men pack them up as well."

"So did I. Last thing we need is for other raiders to use them." After a hesitation, Thallyr asks, "Can Hamrach ride? All the way back?"

"So long as he has help mounting. Using that arm could rip open the wound, although I made the dressing as secure as possible."

"*You* did, Undercaptain?"

"I trained in field healing, ser." Alyiakal adds, "It was emphasized that I could only do that after the fighting was over." After the slightest pause, he asks, "Did the townsmen have more of those shields?"

"Too many of them, and some were even women. We lost four men, and three others are wounded, but this town isn't going to do any more raids. Not for years, if ever." Thallyr hesitates once more, then asks, "How many did you take care of?"

"Twenty-three bodies, ser. No one escaped."

"That's something."

"Would have been much different if they'd had more shields and lances, more like what you encountered."

Thallyr nods, then turns in the saddle. "Traan, detail that spare mount to Lancer Nomaar."

"Yes, ser."

Thallyr says nothing for several moments, then says, "You were rather . . . light on details of how you managed with so few casualties."

"They didn't have many shields and lances. I split the squad and ignored the shields. We concentrated on everyone behind the shields first. After that, we picked off the shield-bearers and lancemen. That wouldn't have worked if they'd had more shields and lances."

"No, it wouldn't," replies Thallyr, "but at least you understand that."

Since Thallyr doesn't say anything more, and Alyiakal isn't about to make conversation, he considers events. What if he angled a firelance upward and loosed a quick chaos bolt? Would that give the chaos bolt greater range while lobbing the chaos over a shield wall?

He's still mulling over the idea when Thallyr's senior squad leader returns and reports, "Mount detailed, ser."

"Good. Companies! Forward!" He adds quietly, "The sooner we're out of this cursed valley, the better. You can return to your company, Undercaptain."

Later, as Alyiakal rides slowly back along the road eastward where it becomes a narrow trail, he wonders if the young archer he killed was male or female. Given the youth of some of the dead raiders who had attacked the resupply company, he has the feeling that the first archer was a young woman.

Does it make any difference? She could have killed you just as easily. According to Thallyr's report, many of the barbarians holding shields and using the spear-throwers were women.

But it still bothers him.

XXIX

As the two companies pass the stead where First Company had spent the previous night and continue toward the side road holding the stead where Fourth Company overnighted, a lancer rides back along the road, easing his mount in alongside Alyiakal's bay.

"A message for you, ser," announces the lancer. "At the next stop, ser, before we enter the hills, Captain Thallyr would appreciate it if you would look at the three wounded men in First Company."

Through the lancer's matter-of-fact words, Alyiakal senses more behind them. What that might be, he cannot tell, and he replies, "I can do that."

"Senior Squad Leader Traan will send a lancer to guide you to the wounded." Then the lancer turns his mount and rides along the shoulder of the road toward the front of First Company.

Alyiakal turns in the saddle toward Maaslar. "How did that strike you?"

After a moment, Maaslar says, "There aren't many officers who do field healing, ser."

Alyiakal keeps looking at the senior squad leader.

"Only a guess on my part, ser, but Senior Squad Leader Traan might have suggested it couldn't hurt."

Meaning that Thallyr's dubious about your abilities or doesn't want to order you to do any healing . . . or feels he can't make that an order. Which of those surmises might be correct, Alyiakal has no idea, but he says pleasantly, "Your surmise is likely far more accurate than any I would have."

Less than a quint later, Thallyr calls a halt. Almost immediately a lancer rides up to escort Alyiakal forward past some captured horses and the four mounts of the lancers killed in the attack on the unnamed town. All of the horses carry baggage, including the brass shields and provisions.

When Alyiakal reaches a position just forward of the horses used for baggage and provisions, Senior Squad Leader Traan stands waiting.

Alyiakal dismounts and removes the healer's satchel, as well as his water bottle, which contains order-treated water, then follows the senior squad leader to a spot beside the road.

Traan gestures to the lancer lying on the makeshift stretcher that must have been fastened between two horses.

"Kaentyl, here, took one of those barbed feathered spears to the gut. Not real deep, but . . ."

Alyiakal sets down his satchel and kneels beside the lancer. Even without sensing deeply, he knows there is little he can do for the gray-faced lancer. The dressing over the wound isn't that bloody, but he senses white-red chaos throughout the man's abdomen. He touches the skin above the dressing and infuses a little order before stepping back.

"That . . . helps . . . ser."

Traan frowns momentarily, but says nothing.

Alyiakal rises and steps away, motioning to Traan, then says softly, "No healer could save him. There might have been something on the spearhead, poison or a corrupt substance."

"Thought it might be something like that," replies the senior squad leader. "Good man." The resigned words hold a slight bitterness. He turns and leads Alyiakal to a second lancer sitting on the side of the road, who starts to stand.

"Stay seated," says Alyiakal. "It's easier for both of us that way."

Alyiakal examines the dressing over a wound similar to the one incurred by Hamrach. There's more chaos and blood in the dressing than he would like. Cutting away nearly all of the cloth, he uses some order-treated water to clean the area, not that it will suffice, but at least it gives cover for what will, as he uses order to remove the growing point of whitish-red chaos deeper in the wound. After that, he re-dresses the wound and stands.

"Feels better, ser."

"Good." Alyiakal turns to Traan. "I'll need to see him tonight and again in the morning."

"Ser . . ." begins Traan.

"Not a word, please. If I can see him, he has a good chance of healing. Now, let's see the other one."

When Alyiakal examines the third lancer, it's clear that the slash to the thigh comes from one of the barbed spearheads, and there's a chaotic fragment in the wound. Alyiakal doesn't like reopening a wound, but whatever the fragment is contains chaos. Keeping the incision as narrow as possible, he removes the thin sliver of what might be wood and cleans the wound with water and order before re-dressing it.

"How did you know . . . that was there?" asks Traan.

"From the shape of the wound," lies Alyiakal evenly. "There had to be something more there."

"You'll need to see him as well?"

"I will."

"Thank you, ser."

Alyiakal doesn't quite know what to say, but manages, "I'm only a field healer, but the men deserve the best I can provide." *After the fighting is over.* "I'll see the men again tonight."

"Yes, ser."

Alyiakal replaces the satchel and water bottle, then remounts and rides back to Fourth Company.

"How bad are they, ser?" asks Maaslar from where he stands beside his horse, water bottle in hand.

"One won't make it. The other two should."

"So First Company will lose five men, with two wounded, and Fourth Company has one wounded and lost a good mount."

Alyiakal can almost see Maaslar's skepticism, and he certainly senses it. "As a junior undercaptain, I have to assume that the losses to hamlets around Isahl were significant or senior officers wouldn't have ordered us here." He pauses, then adds, "Or that there are other reasons that no one has yet shared with me."

Maaslar offers a sardonic smile. "Something like that, I'd guess, ser."

"I'm going to check on Hamrach before we get the order to resume riding. I want to make sure he hasn't opened that wound." That isn't the real reason, of course, but it will do.

He turns the bay back toward second squad, thinking about the patrol and recalling what the now-widowed woman at the stead had said. *"What else are we supposed to do?"*

Then he thinks of the dead lancers from Isahl, one of whom might be Fuhlart, and shakes his head.

XXX

After another two long days of riding back to Pemedra, and a short night's sleep after writing up his patrol report, Alyiakal walks into the officers' mess, glad to have had even a cold shower and definitely grateful to be in a clean uniform. He also looks forward to a hot meal in a moderately warm chamber.

Draakyr is the only officer in the mess. Alyiakal sits down across from him.

"I heard the barbarians you and Thallyr faced gave you some trouble," says Draakyr quietly.

"First Company got the worst of it," replies Alyiakal. "The barbarians had a lot of odd weapons—polished brass shields, long lances, and spear-throwers. The spears had barbed iron heads smeared with poison or something corrupt."

"Word is that Fourth Company didn't do much."

"Thallyr ordered us to cover the west end of the town and not let any raiders escape. We weren't to enter the town unless I received orders to do so. We never received orders. We did intercept more than a score of raiders retreating from First Company. They also had shields, lances, and spear-throwers . . . but not enough to stop flank attacks. We killed them all, as ordered."

Draakyr nods, as if he already knew. "How many did you lose?"

"One wounded—he'll recover—and one lost mount."

"Did you do any field healing?"

"Four of the wounded. Later. One died of a poisoned gut wound on the ride back. So far the other three look good. Two shoulder wounds and a deep spear slash to the thigh."

Draakyr glances toward the doorway, where Thallyr enters. "Interesting. When you talk to the majer, stick to the facts. Only the facts."

"Thank you." Alyiakal smiles wryly. "Isn't that always best for junior officers?"

"For all officers," replies Draakyr, "except some tend to forget after a while."

Thallyr takes a seat beside Draakyr. "It'll be good to have a hot meal."

"Absolutely," agrees Alyiakal, understanding that the senior captain has no desire to talk about the patrol.

The only other officer to enter the mess is Overcaptain Tygael, who takes the seat at the head of the table, signifying that he is the presiding officer, and Lyung's absence means he is out on patrol.

While Alyiakal knows he'll end up being questioned by the majer, he doesn't let that spoil his appreciation for the fried ham strips and egg toast with berry syrup, a combination that isn't frequent at breakfast. He indulges himself with seconds, knowing that the day could turn out to be very long.

After breakfast, he and Maaslar conduct a gear inspection. Alyiakal returns to the officers' study just long enough to be summoned to meet with Majer Klaavyl.

He immediately makes his way to the administration building and the majer's study, where Klaavyl motions for him to take a seat.

"I've read your patrol report, Undercaptain. I appreciate, as always, your diligence in quickly reporting. I do have a few questions."

"Yes, ser."

The majer leans forward a trace and looks intently at Alyiakal. "Captain Thallyr ordered you not to enter the town?"

"Yes, ser. Except if I had direct orders from him."

"Did you enter the town in dealing with the armed barbarians you encountered and dispatched?"

"No, ser."

Klaavyl frowns. "How did you know that you weren't in the town?"

"Towns or hamlets are where the dwellings and other buildings are. We encountered the raiders to the south of any buildings."

"What if Captain Thallyr and First Company had not returned?"

"I would have sent scouts to determine the situation and acted on what they discovered. But by the time Fourth Company had dispatched the raiders trying to escape we received word that First Company was returning and orders to prepare for immediate departure from the town."

"Captain Thallyr said that you treated all of the wounded men. Is that correct?"

"I treated Hamrach, one of the Fourth Company lancers, only after we killed all the barbarians we encountered and returned to position. Later that day, at Captain Thallyr's request, I also treated his three wounded men. One was too badly wounded to survive. He took one of those feathered spears in the gut. From his reaction and quick death, I suspected that the barbed spearhead was also likely smeared with poison or some corrupt substance. That is a judgment, not a certainty."

"Captain Thallyr agrees with that judgment. Why didn't the other three wounded succumb to poison? They were also wounded by spears."

"I can't say for certain, ser, except that gut wounds usually are fatal, in time. I did remove a sliver of something ugly from the thigh of one of the wounded men, and I cleaned all the wounds as well as I could. We'll have to see if what I did works."

"Did Captain Thallyr personally request you treat his men?"

"A messenger from First Company informed me that the captain would appreciate my looking at them. When I rode to where the wounded were, the senior squad leader was there and informed me of their injuries. I did not see the captain then, or when I checked the wounded on three other occasions."

"Did you ask for him?"

"No, ser."

"Why not?"

Because he clearly didn't want to see me. "He had to be aware of what I was doing, ser, and he must have had his reasons. I wasn't about to intrude on his handling of First Company. I wanted to do what I could as quickly and quietly as possible."

"Which you obviously did."

Alyiakal waits, knowing the majer wants him to say more, but since he doesn't know what the majer wants, he isn't about to guess.

"You realize, Undercaptain, that your apparent skill in healing could create a certain conflict or divided loyalty?"

"Ser, I have no intent in that way whatsoever. I did not impose myself or my limited abilities on the captain or First Company. I did want to do my best because the men deserve my best, both as an officer and as a field healer, and those abilities could result in having more experienced lancers over time."

Klaavyl nods slowly. "That is as it should be, and I'm happy that you appear to understand the situation. Captain Thallyr thought you did, but I wanted to confirm his impression." The majer straightens slightly. "There is one other thing. Those brass-plated shields count as spoils, and once we receive the silvers from their sale—after Mirror Lancer headquarters studies them to determine their origin—all those in First and Fourth Companies will receive a share."

"Perhaps I'm missing something, ser, but it strikes me as rather strange that a town of barbarians that can hardly scrape a few silvers together could afford all those polished brass shields."

"You mentioned that in your report. So did Captain Thallyr. I agree with both of you. That's why I'll be sending the shields to the Majer-Commander in Cyad. It's definitely a problem."

All the way to Cyad? Then Alyiakal remembers that the majer reports directly to Mirror Lancer headquarters.

After a pause, Klaavyl says, "That's all, Undercaptain. You and Fourth Company will have a few days before your next patrol."

"Yes, ser. Thank you for the clarifications."

Klaavyl offers a wryly amused smile. "That's one of the reasons for a post commander. Get some rest. You look like you need it."

"Yes, ser." Alyiakal rises from the chair and inclines his head before leaving the study.

In addition to getting some rest and some efforts to update the company map and his personal maps, he'll have some time to write a letter to Saelora, and even to Hyrsaal, although it might be an eightday or longer before any letter will reach either, possibly even later for Hyrsaal. He wishes he could write Adayal as well, but he has no way of contacting her except in person . . . and that won't be possible for years, if not longer.

Yet she and Healer Vayidra are the only ones you can trust to talk about magery.

XXXI

The wind outside Alyiakal's quarters is little more than murmuring, but despite the snug shutters there's still a chill radiating from the window. He glances at the table by his bunk and realizes that he's left Saelora's letter out. He picks it up and smiles as his eyes take in the words.

> *. . . now officially a junior enumerator. I still do some scrivening for Buurel, but I'm thinking of trading on my own. Well . . . through Vassyl, of course. Before he went to Kynstaar, Hyrsaal used to make greenberry wine. It was awful, but he always wondered what would happen if he mixed it with ripe-pearapple juice and distilled the mixture . . .*

Alyiakal winces at the thought of ripe-pearapple juice, which is excessively sweet to him . . . and to most people.

> *. . . around here we have plenty of both. Some of the mothers and widows have a little time on their hands, but there are more than a few, and I organized them. You wouldn't believe how good the raw brandy tastes, and I think it will be even better if we age it. Good brandy fetches a fair price. Vassyl is interested in selling it and even shipping it up and down the Great Canal . . .*

Much as Alyiakal would like to reread the entire letter, that will have to wait, or he'll be late to the morning mess and rushing to get ready for the patrol. He slips the letter into the single table drawer and hurries out.

When he reaches the mess, all the captains are there, as is Overcaptain Tygael. Because it's still Winter, if late Winter, fewer and shorter patrols go out, and Fourth Company is the one scheduled for the day.

Majer Klaavyl enters the mess moments after Alyiakal. All the officers take their seats, but the majer remains standing.

"Among yesterday's dispatches was one from the Majer-Commander. He congratulated Pemedra Post and First and Fourth Companies for removing the threat of armed attacks from the West Branch valley and for providing physical proof that Jeranyi traders had provided shields and other arms to the barbarians previously living there."

The majer pauses and clears his throat. "Imperial fireships have turned most of the city of Jera into a charred waste. The Majer-Commander believes that it is unlikely that other lands will pursue such a strategy." Klaavyl smiles wryly. "I thought you all ought to know . . . before you eat." Then he seats himself at the head of the table.

Almost absently, Alyiakal wonders when the spoils coins from the shields will be distributed to Fourth Company, not that he particularly needs them. Much of his pay remains in his lockbox, since there's little to spend it on, except his share of the mess bill, but he knows that the rankers will appreciate whatever they get.

"That should teach the slimy Jeranyi," says Thallyr, lifting a mug of ale and then taking a healthy swallow.

"For a few years, anyway," replies Draakyr. "They still want to take over Cerlyn so that they can get their hands on the copper mines, rather than paying the Cerlynese."

"Cerlynese'd be better as part of Cyador," says the majer. "Not that the current Emperor of Light will try anything like that after what happened to his predecessor."

"Ser . . ." ventures Alyiakal, "why wouldn't it be better for Cyador to have control of the copper mines?"

"Better for whom?" returns Tygael. "The Merchanters in Cyad make far more by shipping copper they buy from Suthyan traders. If Cyador controlled the mines, the markups would be much less, even if the copper had to be shipped along the same routes."

"Don't say that too loudly in Cyad," counters the majer.

Do the Merchanters have that much power? How could a more cumbersome trading system be more profitable? Alyiakal isn't about to ask those questions, not after seeing Tygael and Draakyr nod.

"You're heading out right after breakfast?" asks Lyung, a question that's clearly rhetorical.

Alyiakal nods.

"Be careful," Lyung continues. "Sometimes, when we get this eerie quiet cold, it's right before we get thundersnow. Not often. Most times, it just warms up a bit."

Alyiakal has read about thundersnow, and from what he's read, he really doesn't want to get caught in such a storm.

"A bit early for thundersnow," says Thallyr. "Usually hits closer to Spring or after Winterturn. Then, you never know."

Alyiakal manages not to comment on the fact that there are far too many aspects of a Mirror Lancer's life where an officer never knows. *Not with any certainty.*

Still, because of what Lyung has said, after eating, when Alyiakal returns to his quarters, he slips some travel biscuits into his winter jacket, along with a spare pair of gloves. The patrol isn't that long, north to the base of the higher hills. The only likely directions for raiders after their attack on the West Branch town would come from slightly east of the hills. They could return by a side trail on the east side of the valley.

When Alyiakal reaches the stable, he immediately checks on the bay, spending a few moments talking to him before saddling him and leading him out of the stall. Only then does he offer a biscuit. The bay nudges Alyiakal as if to suggest that a carrot, or even a turnip, would be preferable, but he takes the biscuit.

Once outside the stable, Alyiakal mounts and rides to join Maaslar.

"Not all that cold," says the senior squad leader. "Not as windy or chill as the last patrol."

"So far," replies Alyiakal dryly, looking to the north and northeast. The sky there is hazy, as it often has been during the late fall and Winter, but he doesn't see any clouds, which is a good sign. He turns back to Maaslar and relays what the majer had said at the mess.

"Does that mean the men might get their spoils coins soon?"

"They'll get them, but since no one's told me, it likely won't be until we get another dispatch or supply run, or the one after that."

"Figures."

Alyiakal nods. Words of congratulation are cheap. The men appreciate the coins far more.

Less than half a quint later Alyiakal rides toward the north gates of the post at the head of Fourth Company. The corrals are empty of horses, as they often are in Winter, except on warmer sunny days, and that's often so that the ostlers and lancers on disciplinary duty can clean the stalls and stables more easily.

Two scouts ride half a kay ahead, the distance they'll maintain in flatter terrain.

Before long the company passes the first of the nearby steads, where a thin line of white smoke rises into the hazy green-blue sky. Outside of the smoke, nothing moves, but then, if he weren't patrolling Alyiakal wouldn't be out in the cold, either, or not for long.

Little over a glass later, Fourth Company reaches the point where the road splits. They take the northeast trail, though not all the way to the gap in the hills. Alyiakal can feel that the wind has stiffened and gotten colder, and there's a hint of darkness over the hills to the northeast.

"The wind's picking up, and it's getting colder," he says to Maaslar.

"Always is colder when the wind blows harder," replies the senior squad leader.

Alyiakal glances to the northeast. The hazy sky is definitely darker, but he still doesn't see any sign of clouds.

Roughly three kays later, after a brief rest stop, he directs the company onto a narrower trail that runs to the stead immediately north of the post. By now the wind is even stronger and colder, and when Alyiakal glances over his shoulder he sees that a greenish-black line of clouds has appeared over the hills to the northeast, and those clouds are moving quickly.

"Does that look like thundersnow coming to you?" Alyiakal asks Maaslar, gesturing back at the clouds.

"Might be, ser. Never seen one up close. If a storm is coming," replies the senior squad leader, "it'll be quicker going this way than trying to go back the way we came."

Shorter, but not necessarily quicker.

Punctuating Maaslar's words, a low rumble of thunder echoes out of the northeast.

Alyiakal looks southwest, in the direction of Pemedra, then back at the clouds, where a greenish-black curtain reaches down behind the leading edge of the black clouds to the hills. Beyond that curtain, Alyiakal can see nothing. He shakes his head. There's no way that Fourth Company can make it to the post or any stead that he knows of.

"We need to find a low hill or a rise where we can shelter on the south side," Alyiakal says to Maaslar as he glances to the hills on his left, the closest of which are more than a kay away over ground that tends to get uneven close to the lower sandy slopes.

"As I recall, there's a bit of a rise about a kay ahead on the hill side of the track."

"Company! Fast walk!" Alyiakal glances back. The greenish-black curtain of what has to be thick snow already shrouds most of the hills beyond the northeast corner of the wide valley. Then a flash of lightning flares, muted by the snow.

Alyiakal concentrates on the trail, but finds it hard to believe that the sky to the southwest, certainly over Pemedra, remains clear and bright in the early-afternoon sun. Even as he looks, the light seems to dim somewhat.

Another long rumble of thunder rolls over Fourth Company.

Close to a quint later, the icy wind at his back, Alyiakal spies the low rise to the left of the trail ahead. "Keep everyone mounted and close together," he orders Maaslar as he turns toward the rise, which isn't as high as he'd hoped, only slightly less than two yards. "Facing southwest . . . toward Pemedra, backs to the wind."

"Yes, ser."

As Alyiakal reins up, and the rest of the company takes position, a blast of wind slams into Alyiakal's back, strong enough to push him almost into the bay's mane and driving icy needles into his neck above the collar of his winter jacket. In moments, he feels as though snow is packed between his jacket collar and his winter cap, and he has no doubt that without the ties from the cap's earflaps his cap would have been torn off and carried for kays.

Within half a quint, the three squads pack into a tight formation, lashed by wind and snow that's so thick Alyiakal can barely see the lancer closest to him. He turns to see those behind him and is immediately blinded by the snow. Closing his eyes, he concentrates on sensing the lancers. So far as he can discern, there are no outliers.

Above him he can sense flows of order and chaos, power far stronger than he's felt in firelances and far stronger than any mage. The amount of chaos is massive, yet it is confined by order.

Alyiakal frowns. It's more like chaos channeled by tubes of order, but that isn't quite right, either.

CCCRAACK!!!

Even though the lightning bolt strikes to the west of the rise, Alyiakal shudders, as much from being somehow drawn to the combination of order and chaos as from the proximity of so much power.

Could you do something like that?

All that order and chaos would likely char him worse than a firelance would—except he suspects that his shields might be strong enough to block a short firelance burst.

You really need to work on strengthening your shields. Then a second thought intrudes. *Couldn't you do that in a smaller way, one that your shields can handle?*

Since there's nothing else he can do but wait out the thundersnow, he concentrates on sensing the order/chaos patterns above him, and then attempts to replicate them, if on a far smaller scale, in the open space well in front of him, knowing that the snow is thick enough that, if he succeeds, no one will be able to link it to him.

After a time, how long he has no idea, he is able to create a tiny little flash of light or lightning.

"That was close!" declares a lancer behind Alyiakal.

Afraid that he cannot repeat the process, Alyiakal does it again, if farther away. The second attempt creates a momentary headache.

Because of the greater distance?

He is still working with order/chaos patterns when, abruptly, the vicious pelting of the snow lessens, and in a quint stops, and the northern half of the sky clears to chill green holding a trace of blue. A large portion of the southern sky retains a greenish blackness extending all the way to the snow-covered grass. The air is much colder than before the storm, and a stiff wind blows out of the northeast.

Alyiakal looks around. For all the intensity of the storm, the snow looks to be little more than calf-high, although he can see drifts more than knee-high. "Slow ride back."

"Good thing we've got more than a few glasses," says Maaslar. "It'll be harder to pick out the track with all the snow."

All that will make for a long day for both lancers and their mounts, Alyiakal knows, but at least they'll be following the storm.

Maaslar looks at Alyiakal, curiously.

Alyiakal suddenly realizes that, unlike Maaslar and most of the other lancers, there's almost no snow on him or the roan. *Shields or all the effort with order and chaos?* "I must have been more exposed to the wind."

"Must be," replies Maaslar.

Alyiakal looks a score of yards to the north where he thinks he can make out a long, slight indentation in the snow and grins wryly. "Do you have a scout who can follow the track back to that stead?"

"Rumbaar might be best at that, ser."

"Then we might as well get started."

Rumbaar is as good as Maaslar suggested, but a ride of three to four glasses takes almost five by the time Alyiakal leads the bay into his stall and grooms him. After finishing with the gelding, Alyiakal is fairly certain that the bay is in better shape than Alyiakal himself.

Alyiakal walks slowly from the stables to the mess, and although the evening mess is over, the duty mess steward has a plate and hot wine waiting.

Draakyr appears as Alyiakal seats himself. "Mind if I join you?"

"Not at all."

"You got caught in that thundersnow. Lose anyone?"

Alyiakal takes a bite of the warmed-up mutton and brown sauce, then shakes his head. "We formed up tight behind a rise and waited it out, then plodded back after it passed."

"You ever been in thundersnow before?"

"No, but I read all the previous company reports and the Winter procedures. They all suggested that trying to go anywhere in thundersnow was a good way to lose men. I just followed procedures, especially when I saw that the snow was so thick you couldn't see much of anything."

"You were still riding, then?"

"No, I was watching the clouds as they approached. We were almost to where we took cover before the snow hit us."

"That will please the majer."

"Oh?"

"He suspects you didn't follow procedures against the barbarians."

"I didn't disobey a single order."

Draakyr smiles. "I'm sure he knows that, but you couldn't have killed that many barbarians that quickly without splitting your squad. That's effectively double-splitting your forces. Since you didn't mention that in your report . . ."

At Alyiakal's raised eyebrows, Draakyr grins. "Years ago, I was a senior squad leader for a certain majer, when he was a senior captain. He had me read your report."

"And?"

"Junior officers need to learn when to follow procedures and when to . . . bend them. Post commanders need to know if junior officers have learned that."

Alyiakal takes another bite of his meal, followed by a sip of the warm red wine.

"So far, you're doing fine," adds Draakyr, "but don't let it go to your head. It only gets harder as you get more senior."

Alyiakal has no doubts about that. He also knows what else to put in the patrol report he has yet to write. At least he doesn't need to update the maps.

XXXII

Early Spring has passed into what seems like continual days of drizzle when Alyiakal enters the stable just after morning mess. He isn't looking forward to the day. The patrol will consist of riding to the hills at the northern end of the valley, then heading west before turning south along the foot of the Grass Hills on the west side of the valley. They are to look for raiders or indications that the barbarians have started scouting for future raids. The Spring sun feels almost as hot as Summer in Kynstaar, so Alyiakal carries three water bottles filled with the odd ale.

The moment he enters the stall, the bay turns his head and nickers softly.

"Yes, we're headed out again," says Alyiakal with a smile as the bay nudges him. "No carrot until we go through our new exercise."

Once he has the bay saddled, with the water bottles, healing satchel, and day-pack in place, he steps up to the bay and puts his hand on the gelding's shoulder. "Just be calm, now," he says quietly in a reassuring tone, after which he puts a concealment around them both, standing there for a time, patting the bay.

He's about to drop the concealment when he hears Maaslar's voice and senses the senior squad leader's approach. He decides to leave the concealment in place.

Maaslar stops outside the stall and calls to an ostler. "Have you seen the undercaptain?"

"He was in the stall a bit ago."

"He's not there now."

"He must have gone out already, then."

Once Alyiakal senses that Maaslar is well away from the stall and leaving the stable he drops the concealment, gives the bay a solid pat—and the baby carrot. "I know. It's small. It's Spring."

The bay nudges him.

"You only get one," replies Alyiakal with a smile. Then he opens the stall door and leads the bay out but walks to the farther door to leave the stable. After mounting, he rides back to where Maaslar is forming up the company.

"Oh . . . there you are, ser. Falltyr has some sort of stomach flux. Can't keep anything down. So third squad will be a man short."

"Is he in sick bay?"

"Yes, ser."

"I'll ride over there. I shouldn't be long."

Alyiakal turns his mount and rides to sick bay, a few rooms on the north end of the barracks, where he ties the bay before walking inside.

The ranker aide looks up from the table where he sits. "Ser?"

"Ranker Falltyr?"

The aide looks puzzled. "Ah . . . he's in the first room, ser."

"I'll likely only be a moment." Alyiakal steps around the table and walks into the tiny space, barely large enough for the single pallet bed.

The lanky lancer is curled on his side, clearly uncomfortable, with sweat on his face.

Alyiakal steps closer, hoping he will not sense a mass of whitish-red chaos in or around the lancer's stomach. He can discern only the faintest traces of reddish gray. "What did you eat that caused this?"

Falltyr groans. "Some pickled stuff . . . Hragaah . . . Third Company . . . think he's sick, too."

Alyiakal touches the lancer's side and extends a tiny touch of order. "Next time, be a little more careful."

"Yes . . . ser."

Alyiakal leaves sick bay, relieved that Falltyr doesn't have a chaos-swollen appendix. He also hopes he never encounters one. While he had watched Healer Vayidra remove one, he certainly doesn't want to have to try, with his marginal surgical skills, but not trying would mean certain death.

Maaslar waits at the head of Fourth Company, where Alyiakal rides to join him.

"How's Falltyr?" asks Maaslar.

"Food poisoning. He should recover. He says he ate pickled stuff Hragaah picked up somewhere."

"You know more than field healing, don't you, ser?" says Maaslar.

"A bit," admits Alyiakal.

"A little more than that, I think, ser. About half the lancers who get wounds like Hamrach don't make it. All three of the ones you treated did."

"Kaentyl didn't," replies Alyiakal, faintly surprised that he remembers the lancer's name.

"That was a gut wound," counters Maaslar, "and it was poisoned."

Alyiakal isn't about to dispute that, for many reasons. "I did the best I could. We need to head out." He pauses, then orders, "Company! Forward!"

While the sun barely crests the hills to the east as Fourth Company rides along the wide sunstone avenue leading to the northern gates, Alyiakal has no doubt that the day will be unseasonably warm.

After a time, the senior squad leader says evenly, "We got off fortunate this Spring, you know, ser."

"Because there weren't that many raids, you mean?"

"Because there weren't any raids when it was raining."

Alyiakal nods, understanding what Maaslar means. Firelances often don't work, or don't work well, in the rain. "It's good that most of the barbarians are busy planting at the time during the rainy season."

"It hasn't always been that way, ser."

And you're telling me that it won't continue that way. "You think we might get more rain later this year?"

"Doesn't look that way, but you can never tell."

"It looks to me like the rest of Spring and Summer will get hot and hotter," replies Alyiakal.

Maaslar chuckles.

By the time they reach the point where the road splits in three directions, the weather confirms Alyiakal's feelings. He calls a halt, has the company dismount, except for the scouts he sends up the three roads to look for hoofprints and/or cart tracks.

A quint later the scouts return.

"No tracks to the northeast, ser."

"No tracks to the north, ser."

"No tracks to the northwest, ser."

Alyiakal nods. "Take a break."

A quint later, the company remounts and takes the northwest trail, which, after a time, turns south at the edge of the low rises below the higher hills. Before long they ride past the trail leading to the West Branch valley, a route Alyiakal never wants to take again, and likely won't. *At least on this tour of duty.*

As they ride, Alyiakal practices carrying even heavier shields, strong enough to stop a firelance bolt—he hopes—while also trying to stretch his range for sensing order/chaos patterns.

After a time, he discovers scores of small order/chaos concentrations that he hadn't noticed earlier and wonders what they might be, until a big-eared coney hop-sprints across the trail behind a scout. For a moment, he wonders why he hadn't sensed them earlier, then realizes that he hadn't been trying to sense patterns in the fall, and that in the Winter, they likely all burrowed underground.

Ahead, Alyiakal senses a larger pattern, possibly a grass cat. The bay's lifted head and curled upper lip reinforce the feeling, but the grass cat clearly senses the large number of men and mounts and retreats behind a low rise. Belatedly, Alyiakal realizes the cat was more than half a kay away.

You're getting better at distance sensing.

Yet another glass passes, and Alyiakal calls another halt.

Maaslar points ahead. "See that low space between those two ridges?"

"Where the south edge has a tree?"

"That's where raiders sometimes hole up for a few days. Nyltaar mentioned it to me a while back. No recent tracks, but wouldn't hurt to send scouts up the path, just in case."

When the break ends, Alyiakal orders the company to remount and continue south. He studies the area Maaslar has pointed out, and asks, "How would they get there without coming along this trail? Is there a back trail between the two lines of hills?"

"Nyltaar thought so, but the dry, rocky ground there doesn't show much."

"And since it's been years . . . no one has looked into it?"

"That'd be my thought, ser."

"It can't hurt to look for tracks," says Alyiakal.

Reaching the path that Nyltaar mentioned takes another glass. Once there, Alyiakal halts the company and dispatches scouts. They return in less than half a quint.

"Ser . . . someone's swept the trail clear of tracks for maybe a hundred yards. Not recently, but there are tracks beyond that. I'd guess maybe three mounts. Might have been an eightday ago . . . or longer."

"I'll take a look," says Alyiakal.

"Maybe take first squad, ser?" suggests Maaslar.

"Good idea. Even if no one's there, we'll at least find out more about the path and where it goes." *And if someone is there, you won't be surprised.*

Alyiakal turns the bay and leads the way through the low Spring grass, grass that could be up to his knees—mounted—by Summer.

Once he reaches the point where the grass dwindles to sparse sprouts, he sees that the narrow path, barely wide enough for a single mount, winds through scrawny bushes and scattered reddish rocks set in sandy red soil too poor for almost anything except occasional scrub evergreens. He rides a few yards farther, then reins up and studies the ground. While he can make out a hoofprint here and there, the continual winds have erased or filled most of the shallow prints. He can't sense any order/chaos patterns except for a few small creatures he cannot see or identify.

He carefully turns the bay and rides back to where Maaslar and first squad wait. "They haven't been here in a while, and we wouldn't want to follow or fight any closer to the hills than right here. Farther along, up into that defile, they could pick us off one by one." With a sardonic smile, he adds, "It's good to know, and we can report that there's a possibility of a raid from this point sometime later this year—and the dangers of following that path into the hills."

Once Fourth Company returns to the southward trail, Alyiakal turns to Maaslar. "Do you think anyone has reported on that path in years? It's not mentioned in the recent Fourth Company patrol reports."

"I wouldn't know, ser."

Maaslar's response tells Alyiakal that he'll need to be very careful in the way he mentions the path and the hoofprints in his report. He will need to add it to the maps. Absently, he blots the sweat oozing from under his visor cap, thinking about how hot the coming Summer will be.

XXXIII

The late-Spring sun beats down on Alyiakal as he leads Fourth Company south on the only real road in the valley—the road that eventually leads to Syadtar. Because there have been sightings of raiders both to the north and to the south of Pemedra, First and Third Companies are heading north, while Fourth Company is the one chosen to go south.

Because you're the most junior and least experienced company officer, no doubt.

But Alyiakal knows he might not be the most junior come Autumnturn because Thallyr's tour at Pemedra will be over, and he'll be rotated elsewhere, possibly promoted to overcaptain, but Alyiakal will be the last to know that. Then, too, Thallyr's replacement might be a junior captain or even another senior captain, possibly one close to being stipended out.

"We're approaching the side road to the midvalley hamlet, ser," says Maaslar quietly, but firmly.

Alyiakal knows that Maaslar's statement really is a suggestion that the company head east to stop by the hamlet in a vale short of the hills where a small stream little better than a brook flows—and sometimes barely dribbles—out of the hills, which explains the stone-walled pond or reservoir above the hamlet. He also understands why the lower walls of the houses are stone, given how close the hamlet is to the rocky lower slope of the eastern hills, but he wonders at the effort required to get the timber for the upper walls.

In response to Maaslar, Alyiakal smiles and says, "You're thinking that if there are any raiders around that's the most likely place. In this part of the valley, anyway."

"I did have that thought, ser."

"It's a good thought, and that's where we'll be heading."

Almost half a glass passes before Fourth Company turns east on the narrower side road, covering almost four kays before Alyiakal sees one of the scouts turning and heading back.

"Looks like Aasnar's seen something," says Maaslar.

"It's too early for traders, especially from the north," adds Alyiakal.

When the scout draws up, joining Alyiakal and Maaslar, he immediately says, "There's dust coming south on the trail along the hills, ser. North of the hamlet."

And dust means raiders, because the steaders aren't going to push their horses like that.

"We'll pick up the pace to a trot," declares Alyiakal, knowing that they're too far from the hamlet to canter or gallop—not and have the horses in shape to deal with possible barbarian raiders, especially if they have to pursue them. "Company! Forward!"

When Fourth Company nears the midvalley hamlet, Alyiakal sees that the raiders have battered their way through the wooden gate in the mud-brick wall that surrounds the hamlet, a wall that's more for confining and protecting domestic animals than for deterring raiders, although the gate has doubtless slowed the attackers.

"See only a score of them," declares Maaslar.

"Send word to Elbaar to have second squad cover the road and move east, in case they try to escape on the trail along the hills," orders Alyiakal. "That way he can cover our rear and deal with raiders who flee. We'll ride straight in through the gate. First squad will take the south side, third squad the north side. Scouts keep watch outside the hamlet in case there are more raiders somewhere."

"Yes, ser."

Maaslar dispatches two rankers with the orders, and Fourth Company continues toward the hamlet walls, now less than three hundred yards away. When Alyiakal and first squad ride across an area of bare ground and then through the sagging open gate, none of the raiders are even looking in that direction, with several beating at the door of the nearest dwelling and others scattered throughout the hamlet.

Suddenly, someone yells out, but Alyiakal can't understand the words, although two raiders beside the nearest dwelling leap onto their mounts. Almost without thinking, Alyiakal triggers two quick bolts from his firelance—both lethal. Then he senses an order/chaos disruption behind the second dwelling on the right and urges the bay that way, with first squad behind him. As he rides around the side of the dwelling he sees a raider on foot holding a girl struggling to get away. Another raider is using an ax on a door, while two others remain mounted, each holding the reins of another horse.

Alyiakal reins up but keeps the firelance leveled in the general direction of the full-bearded raider holding the girl in one hand and a long knife in the other.

The raider has the knife at the girl's neck, but then raises it for a moment. In that instant, Alyiakal triggers the firelance, *willing* the bolt to narrow and to penetrate the forehead of the raider. Alyiakal ignores the flash of pain through his skull and next fires at the raider with the ax. Although his vision blurs for an instant with the intensity of the pain, his shot takes the ax wielder in the chest, and the raider doesn't even have time to look surprised as the ax drops from his lifeless hand.

The two mounted raiders charge toward Alyiakal.

Even before Alyiakal can move his lance, chaos bolts from the rest of first squad char the two attackers into ash, as well as their mounts, but not the two riderless horses. The girl shudders and, with an effort, pushes herself clear of the full-bearded and very dead raider, whose body topples into the dust.

"Next dwelling!" Alyiakal urges the bay past the small timbered dwelling and toward a larger house some fifty yards to the southeast, where he sees several more raiders scrambling to mount up.

"Fire at will!" he orders, following his words with two quick blasts from the firelances. The first slams into the chest of a raider, while the second misses because the man has ducked.

That raider doesn't escape a second firelance blast from behind Alyiakal.

Alyiakal keeps riding and leads first squad past the fallen raiders toward the last dwelling to the south, perhaps twenty yards from the mud-brick wall, only to find that raiders are riding out through another gate in the wall.

Maaslar fires his lance before Alyiakal can trigger his, and the trailing raider falls from his mount, just before the gate, with the other three lost to sight because of the wall and the small orchard beyond the gate.

Alyiakal reins up, knowing that while second squad might catch the fleeing barbarians, he and first squad aren't in position to do so. He glances around, but doesn't see any other raiders. Nor does he sense any order/chaos patterns that suggest violence or someone hiding. Only then does he turn in the saddle and say to Maaslar, "Excellent shot!"

"Not nearly as good as the one you made to take out that bearded raider," says Maaslar quietly.

"I couldn't afford to miss," replies Alyiakal. *For several reasons.*

"No, you couldn't," replies the senior squad leader.

Alyiakal knows exactly what Maaslar means.

"Laaskyn," calls out the senior squad leader, "strip that raider, and close the gate. No sense in having any more of the fowl or livestock escape."

Laaskyn immediately rides toward the gate.

Alyiakal looks at one of the almost scrawny captured mounts, where he can't help but notice that there is an ax strapped behind the saddle—barely more than a leather-bound and padded frame. "That's the second ax I've seen," he says to Maaslar.

"Bride-stealing," replies the senior squad leader. "Most of them were young."

Alyiakal manages not to shake his head.

"Looks like we got most of them," says Maaslar, "except for the three that got through the southeast gate. We'll finish here, ser. Best you go talk to Zakaar. He's the hamlet headman. Burly fellow. Square-cut beard."

When Alyiakal turns the bay he sees the girl who'd been held by the dead raider step inside the house, where, for a moment before the door closes, he can see an internal privacy wall. He slowly rides back toward the center of the hamlet, where a burly bearded man who can only be Zakaar stands looking up and talking to Yurak, still mounted.

"Here comes the undercaptain," says Yurak loudly.

Alyiakal reins up short of the two.

"Good thing you got here when you did, Captain," says Zakaar. "Could have been even nastier."

"How bad was it?" asks Alyiakal warily, fearing what he might hear.

"The bastards killed Kerres's younger son because he ran back toward the hamlet and yelled out a warning. He was out east with his flock. They broke old Kallya's arm and beat her some because she held them off long enough that her daughter could bar the door to the house. There might be others . . . How many did you get?"

"I don't know yet. First squad killed six or seven that I saw. Three others got away. For now, anyway, but the squad I left on the lane might have gotten them. I don't have a report yet." Alyiakal looks to Yurak. "What about third squad?"

"Eight dead so far," replies Yurak.

"Did anyone here see anyone riding farther south?" Alyiakal asks Zakaar.

"No, ser. They came from the north."

Alyiakal can discern no hint of deception. He sees a lancer riding in through the gate, headed toward him, one of Elbaar's men. He waits until the lancer reins up.

"Ser, Squad Leader Elbaar stands by for further orders. Second squad killed three raiders. Another one escaped by riding straight into the hills."

"Thank you. Tell Squad Leader Elbaar to have second squad join us." Alyiakal looks to Zakaar. "I trust you won't mind if we water our mounts before we resume patrolling?"

"We can certainly spare the water, Captain."

"I'm an undercaptain," replies Alyiakal, "but we appreciate the water." He nods to the second squad lancer, who turns his mount and heads out to convey the orders.

"It is your right to take spoils . . ." ventures Zakaar.

"But?" asks Alyiakal, keeping his voice even.

"There were some axes . . . they aren't the best, and they're not weapons . . ."

"We'll need one," replies Alyiakal, "as proof of the raiders' intent. Any others we will leave." At Zakaar's crestfallen look, he adds, "I know there's at least one you can have."

"Two, at least," adds Yurak, a touch of humor in his voice.

Zakaar's expression clears. "Thank you."

In less than half a quint, Maaslar returns with first squad and reports, "No casualties, ser. Eight raiders killed. First squad captured four horses. I suggest leaving two. They'll require more fodder and recuperation time than they would be worth."

Alyiakal looks to Zakaar. "Is that acceptable?"

"Most acceptable, Captain."

In the end, Fourth Company ends up with four decent, barely acceptable mounts, and the hamlet gets three, as well as the ability to butcher and scavenge the fallen horses . . . and possibly two others that are running free.

More than a quint later, as Fourth Company prepares to ride out, Maaslar turns to Alyiakal. "Orders, ser?"

"Unless you have reservations, Senior Squad Leader, I think we should head back to Pemedra along the trail the raiders took."

"I would have suggested that, ser, if you hadn't."

Alyiakal smiles. "I thought you would."

Maaslar doesn't bother to conceal a faintly amused expression.

Once the company is in formation and riding north, Alyiakal says quietly to Maaslar, "I didn't notice any good weapons carried by the raiders. None of those brass shields, either."

"One way or another, they also have to obtain or earn their weapons."

"Was it a mistake to let the hamlet have the three axes?"

"Ser, it would have been a mistake not to let them."

Alyiakal has thought that, but he appreciates Maaslar's confirmation.

After a time, Maaslar clears his throat. "Ser?"

"What am I missing this time, Maaslar?" asks Alyiakal in a tone that is both cheerful and wry.

"Ser . . . we were very fortunate today. Very fortunate."

"We could have come across a more heavily armed force and suffered significant casualties? I did think about that."

"Not exactly, ser. We don't often run up against raiders as well armed as the ones we saw in the West Branch valley." Maaslar pauses, then says, "More than once, we've gotten there after the raiders have left . . . and we couldn't do anything because they've been gone so long we couldn't even pursue."

While Alyiakal has considered that possibility, the certainty underlying the senior squad leader's words is chilling.

After a moment, he replies, "Thank you for reminding me, Maaslar."

"Just thought I should, ser."

"I appreciate it."

Alyiakal wonders how long it will be before he sees what Maaslar has described.

XXXIV

Alyiakal wakes early, drenched in sweat, despite the open window, not that the slight breeze helps much. What little of the early-Harvest air enters his quarters seems more like heat radiating from a stove or a forge, except it's everywhere. Washing up before donning his uniform helps a bit, but by the time he steps outside and starts to walk toward the mess, he's sweating profusely.

The hot, western wind cuts across the Summer-dried tall grass, and Alyiakal glances toward the hills on either side of the valley, then to the north, for any hint of clouds. In every direction, the early-morning sky is already a hazy green-blue that will wash out as the white sun climbs and the day gets hotter and hotter—as it has for more than an eightday.

Alyiakal definitely hadn't realized the extremes of heat and cold that occurred at the post, not until he'd experienced them. He can't help but think the weather might have influenced decisions not to build further border posts, at least not in locations like Pemedra.

Both Lyung and Draakyr are already seated in the officers' mess, and Alyiakal seats himself beside Lyung and across the table from the older captain.

"It's stifling out there, even this early," says Draakyr. "Might be the hottest day yet."

"Seems strange that Harvest is hotter than Summer," ventures Alyiakal.

"Not really," declares Lyung. "There's some rain in Summer, and the grass doesn't dry out until Harvest. That's why the locals plant early."

"It's also why they build, or make those mud bricks, in Harvest," adds Draakyr.

Alyiakal takes a swallow of ale, which is cool, if only in comparison to the way he feels. "At least the ale is cool."

"That's because the brewery is belowground," replies Lyung. "Couldn't drink it if it were warm."

"Is it just me," asks Alyiakal, "or is the taste . . . off?"

Both captains laugh.

"You didn't know?" asks Draakyr. "They use the seeds of the local grass instead of barley. Barley doesn't grow here. Didn't you see that wagon last eight-day, filled with grass seed? The locals harvest it for us, both for the ale and as grain for the horses."

"That must have been during our patrol," admits Alyiakal, saved from saying more about his ignorance by the arrival of Majer Klaavyl.

The majer does not seat himself immediately, instead announcing, "Given the extreme heat, and the apparent lack of raider activity, all patrols for today will be canceled—unless nearby hamlets or steads report any barbarians." Then he seats himself at the head of the table, with Thallyr on one side and Tygael on the other.

"About time," murmurs Lyung.

"It's not about us," returns Draakyr in an even lower tone. "He wants to spare the horses."

"You're absolutely right, Captain," responds Klaavyl cheerfully. "Good mounts shouldn't be wasted. Captains and undercaptains occasionally, but never good horses."

Alyiakal smothers a grin.

Draakyr laughs and replies, "Glad to hear it, ser."

Lyung winces.

After finishing a breakfast with fried oatcakes, which Alyiakal suspects are likely grass-seed cakes, he makes his way to the marginally cooler officers' study and sits at his desk. He thinks about writing Saelora, but he'd sent her a long letter less than an eightday earlier, as well as one to Hyrsaal. He would have sent one to Liathyr, except he doesn't have an address, because, somehow, he never heard where they posted Liathyr, but he did ask Hyrsaal in his latest letter about Liathyr.

Far from the first time, he wishes he had a way to write to Adayal, but there's no safe way for a Mirror Lancer to correspond with a female mage living in the Great "Accursed" Forest with no known address.

Instead, he takes a deep breath, makes a brief entry in the Fourth Company log about the cancellation of daily patrols, and reviews the upcoming schedule.

Finally, after making sure all his reports are up to date, he gets up and makes his way from the study, heading toward the stable to check on the bay, to ensure the gelding has enough water. Once outside, he glances west, noticing a line of clouds drifting toward Pemedra. The clouds aren't high and thin, like the few he's seen in the past eightdays have been, but neither are they low and dark at the base, which might mean rain.

He shakes his head and makes his way into the stable, which is somewhat cooler than the mess building and definitely cooler than outside.

The bay is glad to see him, offering a soft nicker and a nudge.

"No treats today. Just me." Alyiakal checks the feed and water, then pats the gelding. "No patrols today. Too hot for both of us."

After spending some time with the bay, Alyiakal lets himself out of the stall and starts back toward the building holding the mess and the officers' study, realizing that it's already midafternoon. As he leaves the stable, he hears the low and distant roll of thunder. He quickly looks west and sees the darker bases of the oncoming clouds along with a flash of lightning, followed by more thunder. He doesn't see any darker haze beneath the clouds, suggesting little or no rain, and precious little cooling, if any, but the clouds are clearly darkening, and the hot wind from the south has picked up.

More dry thunderstorms. Wind, lightning, and thunder—everything but rain.

He shakes his head and continues on to the officers' study. When he enters, only Lyung is present, clearly writing something. Alyiakal seats himself at his table desk and takes out the map of the area north of the valley. He hasn't had that many patrols there.

Roughly a quint later, the alert bell in the short tower at the top of the administration building begins to ring. Lyung immediately stands and says, "That has to be a fire alert. Not surprising with the dry Summer and Harvest and all that lightning."

Fire alert? Everything here is built of solid stone. Even as he thinks that, Alyiakal stands.

His confusion or lack of comprehension must show on his face, because Lyung adds as he hurries toward the front of the building, "Grass fire. We need to get all the horses into the stables. Good thing only about half are in the corrals."

When Alyiakal steps outside into the hot wind, he finds the entire post shadowed by the thunderclouds almost overhead. The wind carries the acrid scent of burning grass, and he sees smoke rising to the south, although from where or how close the fire is he can't determine because of the stone wall surrounding the post.

Already, lancers and ostlers lead horses into the stables, while others have ridden to the fenced corrals serving as pastures on the northern reach of the post and are moving horses back toward the stables. Lancers also close the heavy northern and southern gates. Yet other lancers shutter the windows.

"Might as well watch," says Lyung. "The overcaptain has it well in hand."

"There's nothing here that will burn, is there?" asks Alyiakal. "I mean here in the post?"

"The dry grass in the northern corrals will go up in smoke, and some of the shutters might get a little warm or blistered. Once the fire gets near the walls, you don't want to be outside. Gets hotter than an oven."

"None of the buildings are within a hundred yards of the walls," says Alyiakal. "Won't that be enough?"

"The winds can carry embers farther than that," replies Lyung. "That's why everything gets buttoned up. Not much to catch fire inside the walls. Walls are stone, and roofs are tile or slate, and the grass embers don't last long. The flames and heat pass, but we're not stone or tile." His last words are wry.

Alyiakal hears a faint roaring, and the fire-driven winds strengthen as the last of the mounts are shepherded into the stables and the doors closed. In less than a quint, all the building shutters are fastened tight.

Now, Alyiakal can see flames above the post walls, thick black and gray smoke swirling up, and hears the increasing roar of burning grass that had stood almost two yards tall. Even though the flames have to be hundreds of yards away, he can feel the growing heat. He also senses the swirl of order and chaos around and intertwined with the flames, a swirling that has no real pattern, at least none he can discern, unlike the almost formal pattern of the thundersnow.

He also senses that the order and chaos of the fire are more diffuse than had been the case with the thundersnow. *There's more order and chaos in a stove or a fireplace than in the same amount of space out here.*

"Time to get inside," says Lyung, pointing to the figure of Overcaptain Tygael running toward them.

Alyiakal pushes the thoughts of how concentrated order and chaos are in different chaotic settings and follows the captain. Both Alyiakal and Lyung enter before the overcaptain, who immediately orders, "Bar the doors."

After doing so, they follow him to the mess.

"Might as well have a mug of ale," declares Tygael. "We aren't going anywhere for a bit. This one's bad."

Alyiakal waits until the other two fill mugs before filling his own and joining them at the mess table.

Even inside the stone walls of the post and of the building, Alyiakal can hear the increasing roaring.

"It sounds worse than it is," says the overcaptain after several swallows of ale. "Not that it's not bad. When it's over, everything outside the walls will be either black and gray or bare earth. By next Summer, the grasses will be back, but not as tall."

"What about the people in the hamlets?"

"It depends. Fires usually don't hit all of them, but those around here will suffer. It's late enough that most of the harvesting is done, but they'll still be short on food by Spring. Grass cats will move where the grass wasn't burned, and they'll kill more of the antelope, or stray sheep or calves they can find."

As Alyiakal listens to Tygael, his thoughts go back to the amount of free chaos and order released by different kinds of fires, realizing how it all fits together. The harder and heavier woods burn hotter and generate more free chaos. Because grass is far lighter, especially dry grass, when it burns there's less chaos for the amount of fuel burned.

But when a good chunk of an entire valley burns, that's a lot of heat and chaos.

After thinking about what all that might mean for his own use of order and chaos, he senses that the roaring outside is beginning to die down, but another half glass passes before the overcaptain stands and says, "Time to see how bad the damage is."

Lyung and Alyiakal follow him to the main doors. There Tygael places his hand on the back of the door before removing the heavy bar, then opening the door and stepping out into the sweltering heat and the acrid air.

Once outside, Alyiakal looks to the north, where a wall of flame with black and gray smoke continues to swirl. Closer to where he stands, the grass in the pasture corrals has been turned to black ash, and some of the fence posts are also blackened. Ash covers everything, even the sunstone roads of the post, but the nearby shutters don't seem charred or blistered.

"Nothing we can't clean up." Tygael laughs and adds, "Old Emperor Kieffal might have been wrong about building Pemedra, but I'm angel-fired happy he insisted on the way it *was* built."

So is Alyiakal, especially after what he has just heard and seen.

XXXV

Between the heat, the lingering grit in the air, and the omnipresent odor of smoke and burned grass, Alyiakal doesn't sleep well and wakes early. Small particles of ash and grit cover the room, but he manages to remove most of it with a damp rag before washing up and donning his uniform. Then he makes his way toward the mess. Pemedra Post doesn't look any better in the morning light than it had the evening before, and the air is at least as hot as it had been before the storm and the grass fire.

For once he arrives first and takes a seat near the foot of the table. Draakyr arrives next and sits down across from Alyiakal.

"Your first grass fire?" asks the older officer.

"First large fire of any sort. I grew up mostly near the Great Forest. It doesn't burn."

Draakyr looks surprised. "It doesn't?"

"According to my father, there's no record of any fires."

Draakyr fingers his chin, then says, "When you think about it, that's not surprising. The Forest has to have certain powers or the First wouldn't have gone to such lengths to confine it. Supposedly, it was far larger, but the First burned it back and then confined it. Something like that, anyway."

"They must have used chaos-fire," says Alyiakal.

"What else could they have used?" says Lyung as he sits down beside Draakyr.

"Order," replies Alyiakal. "Pure order in large amounts would be just as bad as chaos to anything living."

"Even in small amounts, some of the Magi'i aren't fond of it," Lyung points out.

"Why do you think we have cupridium blades?" replies Draakyr wryly.

"I thought that was because they can be cast, rather than forged," says Alyiakal.

"That's half of it," says Draakyr. "The other half is that forged iron blades retain order, and there's enough there to kill a mage who uses a lot of chaos."

"Only if he doesn't flame you first," counters Lyung.

"True," admits Draakyr with a rueful smile.

Within a few moments, Thallyr, Tygael, and Majer Klaavyl enter the mess.

The majer remains standing at the head of the table, indicating that he has an announcement. The other officers wait.

"Today, several of you will be involved in damage assessment and resupply efforts. First Company will follow the north road and survey and report on any damage north of Pemedra and on both sides of the valley. Fourth Company will ride down the main road, as far south as the fire extended, and check on the midvalley hamlet in addition to surveying and reporting all damage from east to west. Captain Lyung will take a squad from Third Company and two wagons to Syadtar to pick up additional supplies. None of the hamlets around here will have enough to provide what they usually do. Second Company will do a thorough inspection of all fences and gates within the walls to determine what, if any, repairs are necessary."

Without further explanation, the majer sits down.

"Aren't you the fortunate one," Lyung says dryly to Draakyr.

"I suspect it's because I actually know what a fence post is," replies Draakyr with a sardonic grin.

"And can even talk to them," adds Thallyr with an amused smile.

"And understand what they say back," counters Draakyr.

Alyiakal can't help but smile.

Lyung turns to Alyiakal. "You're smiling. Could you hear the fence posts?"

"No, ser. I can only hear the trees." *And certain Forest creatures.*

All three captains laugh. Even Tygael and the majer smile.

Alyiakal isn't quite sure how he managed the quip, but it might be because he actually spoke the truth, in a way. He takes a swallow of the grass-seed ale, still amazed, not that it has a taste that's different, but that it's drinkable. Then he cuts one of the ham strips.

Little more than a quint later, the majer stands and departs, a signal that the other officers need to finish up, if they haven't already.

"Undercaptain," says Tygael as Alyiakal rises from the table, "I'd like a word with you."

"Yes, ser." Alyiakal immediately steps toward the overcaptain, then halts about a yard away.

"Do you know why you're being sent south?"

"Not specifically, ser. My guess is because I was one of the last officers to see the hamlet closely."

"Precisely. I hope your memory is good. But that isn't why I wanted a word. No matter how bad the situation is there, and I hope it's not, you cannot promise them anything. Your job is to view and assess the damage and to report back to the majer. The majer will make any and all decisions. The only thing you can promise is that you will report fully and accurately to the majer. Is that clear?"

"Yes, ser."

"Do you know why that is important?"

"My thought would be that we're at the end of a very long supply line, and we're not likely to get any more than we absolutely need, if that."

Tygael nods. "The majer and I will read your report carefully. Provide as much detail as you can."

As if the majer doesn't read everything I write closely and carefully. "Yes, ser."

Immediately after leaving the mess, Alyiakal heads for the squad leaders' study to see if Maaslar is there, or already on the way to the stables, but Maaslar turns and stands as he sees Alyiakal.

"The day's orders were just posted, ser."

"Overcaptain Tygael assigned us to cover the southern part of the fire because Fourth Company was the last one to see the midvalley hamlet."

"Thought it might be something like that, ser."

"Extra water bottles?"

"Might be a good idea, ser."

"Anything else you'd suggest?"

"Extra kerchief. If the wind picks up, the men can wet it and tie it across their nose and mouth. Won't breathe as much ash and grit that way."

"Anything more?"

"No, ser. Strong stomach. Some of what we see won't be pleasant."

"Then I'll see you at muster."

"Yes, ser."

Alyiakal quickly returns to his quarters for a spare kerchief and another water bottle. Before heading to the stable, he fills both bottles with ale at the mess, and manages to snare a slightly wilted small carrot for the bay, which the gelding doesn't get until he is saddled and ready to go.

Even so, Alyiakal is at the muster area almost as soon as Maaslar.

Already, Lyung and his squad have the two wagons out, although Alyiakal isn't familiar enough with Third Company to know which squad will make the supply run. Thallyr and Traan begin to muster First Company as well.

When Fourth Company rides out through the south gates, Alyiakal realizes that, in the near year he has spent at Pemedra, he's ridden through those gates only twice. He also realizes that everything he can see on either side of the road is black or gray, if not both, or bare earth, except the hills to the east and west. Even there, while he cannot see the lower reaches of the hills, patches of black show amid the reddish rocks on the higher parts of the hills.

Perhaps a kay ahead, and several hundred yards off the road, he sees vulcrows circling. As he rides closer, he sees four of the scavengers picking at a carcass.

"Likely a yearling antelope," comments Maaslar. "The older ones know to make for the hills. So do the grass cats. The antelopes have to watch out for them even more because there's no cover."

"What about coneys?"

"Most stay in their burrows, deep enough that the fire doesn't burn them. They can eat the grass roots. The vulcrows will get some of those that venture out without grass cover."

Farther to the southwest, Alyiakal sees more vulcrows circling, but not to the southeast. He hopes that means that the steaders of the midvalley hamlet haven't had significant losses of livestock.

With all the grass burned, Alyiakal notes that the valley is indeed flat on both sides of the road, at least as far as he can see, suggesting that the only rises are those near the Grass Hills that enclose the valley. Except around Pemedra, the Grass Hills might as well be called the stone hills. Absently, he wonders if once they were grassier, or if they were called that by those of the First who never traveled as far as Pemedra.

With each kay Fourth Company rides, the air seems hotter. A slight breeze is just strong enough to carry tiny particles of ash and grit that stick to the sweat on Alyiakal's face. In little more than a glass, his spare kerchief is streaked with black and gray that he's wiped away.

Fourth Company is almost upon the side road that leads east to the midvalley hamlet before the scouts point it out.

"I thought the grass looked all the same, but so does this," says Alyiakal quietly. "At the same time, its absence changes everything."

Maaslar only nods.

Alyiakal looks to the south. In the distance, perhaps three or four kays, possibly longer, the blackness ends, and the tan shade of Harvest wildgrass resumes. *At least the whole valley didn't burn. This time.*

Along the narrow road to the hamlet, Alyiakal sees a few more charred carcasses, some the size of coneys, and one that of a sizable grass snake.

Once Fourth Company reaches the point where Alyiakal can see the hamlet, he realizes the hamlet itself doesn't look all that different from what he recalls. There are even smoke trails from the chimneys. What he does notice is the bare ground outside the mud walls.

Was that there before? Then he recalls that part of the gate the raiders had battered down had been lying on the dirt outside the wall.

When the company nears the now repaired and closed gate, Alyiakal can see the hamlet headman—Zakaar—walking down the lane to the gate.

"Company! Halt!" orders Alyiakal, who waits for Zakaar to reach the gate.

As Zakaar approaches, Alyiakal studies the hamlet, noting the mud-brick tiles on the dwelling roofs, and that many of the low structures holding animals have turf roofs. He does see a few singed shutters, but no significant damage.

Zakaar peers at Alyiakal, then nods abruptly. "You are here again, Captain."

While both Alyiakal and Yurak had earlier made it clear that Alyiakal is not a captain, but an undercaptain, it's equally clear that Zakaar would continue to call him "Captain." Alyiakal sees no gain in correcting the man again. "We are."

"You'll not be seeing any more raiders, seeing as the grass fire swept north from here."

"The majer dispatched officers in various directions to survey the damage to different hamlets. Fourth Company was sent because we were here most recently. You look to have survived the grass fire without too much damage."

"We lost a few lambs and the two gardens outside the walls, but we can replant them. The ash will make them more fertile. The Winter will still be long."

Alyiakal nods and waits.

Zakaar says nothing.

"Was anyone badly hurt?" Alyiakal asks.

"No, Captain. We suffered more from the raiders. What have you come to ask of us?"

"I'm not here to ask for anything except to know how you fared. Some water for our horses would be welcome, if you can spare it."

"If we need food this Winter . . . ?"

"Send someone to the post, and tell the majer. He is the one who decides such matters."

"But you are a captain. You have power."

Alyiakal smiles wryly. "You are kind, but my only power lies in the arms my lancers carry and their ability to use them as ordered by the majer. I will tell the majer that you may be short of food this Winter if matters go badly."

"You will tell him?"

"I will."

Zakaar slowly opens the gate. "There is a water trough on the lane below the pond. You and your horses are welcome. I will send someone to open the sluice as necessary."

"Thank you."

"You saved many. No thanks are necessary. I will close the gate after your men ride through. We do not wish to lose any more animals. We will have to butcher and salt earlier than we would, even if we can obtain wildgrass from the south of the valley."

Of course . . . with the grass gone, they're short of fodder. That raises the same question for all the horses at Pemedra. Except Draakyr mentioned that the post had received wagonloads of grass grain, and the post does have wagons and horses. Still . . .

Alyiakal nods to Zakaar as he rides past, following the lane to the water trough.

ALYIAKAL'ALT,

Captain, Mirror Lancers

Pemedra

XXXVI

The cool mid-Spring rain drizzles out of the greenish-gray sky, dripping off Alyiakal's visor cap, in front of his eyes and down his neck, as well as off his seldom-used oilskin waterproof. While this is Alyiakal's third Spring in the wide valley of scattered hamlets and unpredictable onslaughts by barbarian raiders, each Spring has seemed to last forever, because the only significant rainfalls are in early and mid-Spring, and when the rainfall stops, the barbarian raids begin.

As the bay continues the necessary trot, Alyiakal looks at the trail in front of Fourth Company, the tracks in the damp earth heading south, and then at Yurak, now his senior squad leader, ever since Maaslar had been posted to Dellash, about the time Alyiakal had made captain. "We're catching up, but there are more tracks than I'd like to see this early in the year."

"Almost a score, ser, the way I see it."

"Looks like they're headed for the midvalley hamlet."

"They likely figure that no one would see them if they took the trail next to the hill and that we wouldn't be out in the rain."

"We wouldn't be," replies Alyiakal, "if the overcaptain hadn't figured the raiders might take advantage of the late rain and posted scouts." *But then, he's where he is because he's survived his experiences.* Alyiakal can only hope that he'll be as skillful and fortunate over the years to come.

"Have to say, ser, it worries me that we might have to deal with them *and* the rain."

"No one's pleased, Yurak, especially the holders." *Or they won't be if we don't get there fairly soon.* A trot will get them there as fast as practically possible, and without exhausting the mounts.

Another glass passes before Fourth Company reaches the trail leading west past the hamlet to the only true road in the valley—the one that runs south from Pemedra all the way to Syadtar.

No sooner does Fourth Company turn onto the trail than Alyiakal feels that the drizzle has turned into a steadier rain that further reduces how far he can see. The rain also limits how long and how well the firelances will work. He can't sense the intense order and chaos in the clouds above that indicate a thunderstorm, and that restricts what he could possibly do with order and chaos, not that he's had that much practice with storms except for one thundersnow.

"Friggin' rain would get worse now," mutters Yurak.

"We've got less than half a kay before we reach the lane to the hamlet." Alyiakal thinks he should hear something from the scouts when he sees one of them riding at a gallop toward him.

The scout reins up short to match pace with Alyiakal and the bay. "The raiders just went through the gate into the hamlet, ser."

"We'll keep going. You and the other scouts keep watch, in case there are more raiders." Alyiakal definitely doesn't want to be surprised in the rain.

"Yes, ser."

Alyiakal turns to Yurak. "Have third squad cover the area inside the gate, but short of the buildings. Second squad takes the south side of the hamlet, and first squad the north. I'll be with first squad. Have the men keep firelance bursts close and short. The rain might give us cover, so keep quiet until we attack."

"Yes, ser." Yurak immediately turns his mount to pass the word.

Alyiakal continues riding, looking out for the lane leading south into the hamlet. By the time he reaches it, leading the company, Yurak has returned from conveying his orders to the other two squads.

With all the mist and rain, Alyiakal can't even make out more than the outlines of the hamlet until he is within twenty yards of the gate, which is open, not battered apart as it had been two years earlier.

"They got in without breaking it," says Yurak.

"No one could see them, and there likely hasn't been an attack in the rain in years." *But this rain was light and later, and the overcaptain had a feeling about it.*

The bay's footing is sure on the wet but packed earth of the lane leading to the hamlet's center as Alyiakal takes first squad to the north side of the hamlet, dominated by the house of the head holder, Zakaar. There, the raiders are on foot, one using an ax on the door, and another trying to pry open a set of shutters.

Alyiakal gets off three short blasts from the firelance before it gives out. That takes care of the axman and two others, but a fourth lunges with a spear—a thrust that Alyiakal barely parries with the nonworking firelance. As he jams the useless weapon into its holder, he draws his sabre to block a second thrust, urging the bay forward and inside the tip of the spear.

"Those firelances aren't working!" shouts another raider. "Give 'em cold iron." He immediately starts to swing a broadsword, but Yurak cuts him down from his blind side.

Alyiakal slices into the neck of the spearman and pushes forward, hardly able to see clearly for more than a few yards.

When Alyiakal rides clear of the area before the larger house because all the raiders there are down, either dead or wounded, or have fled, he immediately charges a raider trying to mount, cutting him down as he has one foot in the stirrup.

Then he sees two raiders, one with a woman, or girl, over his shoulder, the other with a weapon, running for a pair of horses. Alyiakal turns the bay to intercept them. One immediately turns and brandishes a broadsword. Alyiakal urges the bay to the side, pulling out the firelance with his free hand, triggering it, and *willing* it to fire. A short blast slams into the chest of the sword wielder. In two more strides of the bay, he pulls even with the raider carrying the woman, but realizes that any sabre thrust risks injury to the woman.

Again, he tries *willing* the firelance.

Darkness flares over him, for an instant, followed by searing pain through his eyes and skull. Several moments later—he *thinks* it is several moments later—he discovers the bay has pulled up. He looks back, his vision blurred from pain and heavy rain, and sees the woman struggling out from beneath the dead raider. She looks to him, seemingly undecided, when Yurak rides up.

"It's all over, ser."

"How bad?" manages Alyiakal, who still cannot see clearly, because, this time, the burning in his head has definitely not subsided.

"The raiders got Ruuvyt, and three other men have slashes. Waark from second squad looks to have a broken arm. They got his mount, and it crushed him against the side of a barn."

"Did anyone get away?"

"I'm not sure there's any way to tell in this rain," replies the senior squad leader wryly.

"Good point," replies Alyiakal, tiredly.

"You all right, ser?"

"I got a jolt from the firelance . . . must be the rain," says Alyiakal. "Not something I expected."

"And you're still alive?"

"Must have been a little jolt. Happened when I dealt with those last two raiders." Alyiakal manages a deep breath. "I'll need to talk to the headman." He turns the bay toward Yurak, and the two ride back toward Zakaar's dwelling.

Zakaar stands in the doorway when Alyiakal reins up.

"Once again, it is you, Captain," says Zakaar. "I do not know whether to fear you or be grateful." The burly headman offers a ragged laugh. "You come only when there is trouble, but you keep the trouble from being worse."

"You should thank the overcaptain. He posted scouts on the trails from the north because he thought raiders might attack when there was a rain this late. We came as quickly as we could." Alyiakal takes another deep breath, trying not to wince at the increased pain in his head, then asks the question he must. "How many were hurt . . . or worse?"

"They killed Tokull, and Murgana is bruised everywhere. She was the one you saved. She is grateful she was not carried off."

"So am I," replies Alyiakal. "Anyone else?"

Zakaar shakes his head. "Because of the rain, everyone was inside, except Tokull. He warned us. We got most of the doors barred. Then you arrived." He pauses. "I would offer shelter . . . but there is no place to shelter so many men and horses."

"Before we leave," says Alyiakal, "I'll need space out of the rain to dress the wounds of my men."

Zakaar frowns. "You?"

"For better or worse, I'm also a field healer."

"Then bring your wounded here."

"Thank you." Alyiakal looks to Yurak. "If you would . . ."

"Yes, ser."

In less than half a quint, Alyiakal stands in Zakaar's kitchen, splinting Waark's broken arm, thankful that it's not a compound fracture. Then he dresses wounds on the forearms and thighs of four other men, quietly infusing a touch of order, for a touch is all he dares give, the way he feels. Hopefully, that will be enough to keep wound chaos at bay, and he'll be able to do more in the days ahead.

Once the wounded have been helped out and to their mounts, Alyiakal turns to Zakaar. "Thank you. I'm sorry for intruding."

Zakaar shakes his head. "Go in light, Captain."

Alyiakal inclines his head, then leaves the dwelling. He mounts the bay, glad that the rain has diminished to a slight drizzle, and leads Fourth Company down the lane. Rankers in third squad lead four of the best raiders' mounts, and a fifth carries Ruuvyt's body strapped over the saddle. The remainder of the raider mounts Alyiakal leaves for the hamlet's use, since standing orders only require keeping the best mounts, and only when feasible.

Once Alyiakal and first squad are on the side trail leading back to the main road, Yurak clears his throat.

"Yes?" asks Alyiakal.

"If you don't mind my asking, Captain, how did you get your firelance to work? At the end, there, in the downpour?"

Alyiakal has to struggle to offer an uneven laugh. "I don't know. I knew that I couldn't stop those two using a sabre, and I was angel-cursed if I would let them get away. I don't remember a couple of moments after, and I'm still a little shaky."

Yurak nods. "Thought it might be something like that. Glad the rain's letting up. Going to be a slow ride back, even so."

Of that, Alyiakal is certain.

XXXVII

Alyiakal wakes at dawn the next morning, washes, shaves, and dresses quickly, and then hurries to sick bay, noting that the sky is cloudless, but a hazy green-blue, suggesting that warmer weather is definitely on the way. While most of the pain in his head has subsided, he still has a headache, but not the burning, cutting sensation that had persisted until he fell asleep.

When he walks into sick bay, the duty aide looks up. "I thought we might see you early, ser."

"How are they?"

"Seem to be fine, ser."

"Let's hope so." With that, Alyiakal heads for the ward holding the four wounded lancers. Three of the four are sitting up, unsurprisingly, since Caarthyn and Laarth have slashes with deep bruises to their upper arms and Waark has a broken arm, while Faerll has a deeper cut in his left thigh.

Alyiakal examines Faerll first, because he worries about the depth of the wound. As he suspected, there is more reddish-white wound chaos than he'd like to see, chaos that he treats. After re-dressing the wound, he administers more order, an amount limited to less than he'd like because more would create enough heat to kill the healthy tissue bordering the wound.

"How is it, ser?" asks Faerll.

"You're going to be here a few days," replies Alyiakal. "It should heal fine so long as we keep the wound clean."

"Doesn't feel that bad, ser."

"A grass fire isn't hot, either," says Alyiakal dryly.

There's less chaos in the arm wounds of Caarthyn and Laarth, but Alyiakal still worries about the bruises around the slashes, and those bruises limit the order he can apply after re-dressing both wounds. "I'll see you three late this afternoon."

Then he turns to Waark, checking the splint. "You can leave sick bay, but that arm is going to take eightdays to heal. That's if you don't bang it into anything. If you do, it might not heal properly."

"How come he can leave, and Caarthyn and me can't, ser?" asks Laarth. "We can walk, too."

"Because he doesn't have a wound opened by a chaos-tinged barbarian blade," replies Alyiakal.

Laarth opens his mouth, and Caarthyn says, quietly, "Not a word."

Laarth shuts his mouth.

Alyiakal turns to Waark. "I'll tell the aide that you're on the no-duty list for the next eightday, and then we'll see whether you're no-duty or light duty."

"Yes, ser."

Alyiakal escorts Waark out to the duty aide, explaining the situation. While the two fill out the reports, Alyiakal steps back into the hallway and, seeing no one around, raises a concealment and quietly makes his way back to the ward, listening as he nears and steps inside.

". . . don't complain and don't say a word," says Caarthyn, "or you'll pay for it. More than you want to pay."

"Don't see why you told me to shut up," mutters Laarth.

"Because the captain's more than a field healer. Ever notice that Fourth Company wounded don't die later? He might even be a real healer, and if anyone finds out, they'll either cashier him or stick him in an infirmary somewhere, and some of us will die. Don't mess with a good thing, Laarth."

"They'd do that?"

"Real healers are like Magi'i, and senior officers don't like Magi'i."

"The captain's not like that."

"That's right. He leads, and he takes the same risks as we do. More sometimes. You want him pulled out and we get a green undercaptain like Kettaur?"

The silence that follows suggests to Alyiakal that Laarth is shaking his head.

"Thought not," declares Caarthyn.

Alyiakal holds the concealment until the moment he opens the door and steps out of sick bay. That way, anyone who might be looking will assume they missed seeing him step out. From there he makes his way to the officers' study, where he immediately sets to work finishing the patrol report he'd begun the previous night.

He finishes before morning mess and hurries to the headquarters building, where he places it in the post commander's inbox on the duty desk before making his way back to the mess. He is the last to arrive except for the overcaptain, the acting post commander until the arrival of Majer Klaavyl's replacement.

Once in the mess, Alyiakal sits beside Draakyr, now the senior captain. Across from Draakyr is Wherryl, a captain only a year senior to Alyiakal who had arrived from a posting at Westend the previous fall, along with Undercaptain Kettaur, seated beside Wherryl, as he often is.

"I still don't see why headquarters recalled the majer to Cyad," declares Wherryl. "He was due for reposting this Autumn. It would have made more sense to wait until his replacement arrived."

"It might be," says Draakyr dryly, "that they wanted to hear what he has learned here in Pemedra. It has been a number of years since any of the senior commanders in the Mirror Lancers have had any recent experience along the borders." After the briefest hesitation, he continues, "Especially majers with extensive experience in dealing with the barbarians."

Kettaur frowns.

"You disagree, Kettaur?" asks Alyiakal.

"What about officers like Subcommander Grevyll at Syadtar?"

"He's been there a year," returns Draakyr, "and he hasn't taken a border patrol since he was a captain. Majer Klaavyl took a couple of patrols every season."

Alyiakal finds himself nodding.

"As Alyiakal well remembers, and as you should," adds Draakyr.

Kettaur's blocky face stiffens, but Tygael's arrival in the mess saves him from any response.

"No announcements this morning," says the overcaptain as he seats himself, "except to note that Fourth Company successfully kept the damage from a raider attack on the midvalley hamlet to a minimum. One lancer was lost, but the heavy rain greatly limited the use of firelances." Tygael takes a swallow of ale. "That's all."

"How many wounded?" Kettaur immediately asks Alyiakal.

"Four," replies Alyiakal tersely. "With a little fortune they'll all recover fully."

"Five casualties," says Kettaur. "Minimum damage?"

"Only one death in the hamlet and sixteen dead raiders," replies Alyiakal.

"There's a reason why we'd rather not patrol in the rain," says Draakyr. "When we can't effectively use firelances, we lose more lancers. Sometimes, it's unavoidable. Without what Fourth Company did, the raiders might have killed most of the men there and made off with the women. Protecting them does happen to be our duty . . . even in a downpour when firelances don't work."

"Well put, Captain," says Tygael evenly.

Kettaur's face stiffens again, and Alyiakal gets the feeling, not for the first time, that Kettaur isn't used to reprimands, even indirect ones, and that the undercaptain definitely doesn't like them. He also has the feeling that Tygael has been waiting, possibly for eightdays, for such an opportunity.

Why? Because Kettaur or his family has some influence in Cyad or because Kettaur is more influenced by his peers than by his commanding officer? Or something else?

"You think we'll get more rain?" asks Wherryl quickly.

"Not much," says Tygael. "We might not see any until Autumn, if then. That's the usual pattern."

The remainder of breakfast conversation centers on the weather and when and where the next barbarian raid might originate and what area the raiders might target.

When the overcaptain rises from the table, he looks to Alyiakal and says, "In half a glass, Captain?"

"I'll be there, ser."

That makes the rest of Alyiakal's day simpler, although he does want to conduct a gear and tack inspection, and he hopes he'll have time to answer Saelora's latest letter, although he has several days before the next dispatches are scheduled.

Almost exactly a half glass later, Alyiakal enters the overcaptain's small study. Tygael gestures for him to take a seat, then says, "I noticed that you handed in your report this morning. Usually you turn it in the night before."

"I had four wounded men, as I reported, ser. I checked them again after dinner, and it was late. I started writing up the report last night, but . . . I was falling asleep. So I got up early this morning and finished it."

Tygael smiles. "Sometimes, for routine matters like reports, it doesn't hurt to wait, especially if you're dealing with more important things, like the health of your men." The smile vanishes. "Why do you think I chose Fourth Company for the patrol yesterday?"

Alyiakal has thoughts about that, but he's not about to voice them, unless pressed.

"Come now, Alyiakal," says Tygael. "You must have thought about it."

"I can see why you wouldn't send either Wherryl or Kettaur, and I'd guess you chose me over Draakyr because Fourth Company is closer to full strength than Second Company."

"That's one reason. Care to come up with a second?"

"No, ser," replies Alyiakal with what he hopes is an amused smile.

"I can see why you wouldn't want to speculate. I'll save you the trouble. I knew there would be casualties. More of your casualties survive. That may be because you're a field healer, and early treatment makes it more likely that casualties survive. There may be other reasons, but that's not my province to investigate. You fight first and fight well." Tygael barely pauses before going on. "You suggested that the aim of the raid was to obtain women, based on the comparative youth of the dead raiders. Were there any other reasons that came to mind?"

"It's possible that older leaders among the barbarians wanted to get rid of young hotheads, but that's an unsupported guess, ser."

"That's certainly a possibility. That's all I have for you. As always, your report is thorough, but concise. Do you have any questions for me?"

"Is there any possibility that you will be promoted to command here, ser?"

Tygael offers an amused laugh. "Hardly. First, command here is a majer's billet. Even if I were to be promoted, I'd still only be a sub-majer, and I doubt that Mirror Lancer headquarters would look favorably on either a double promotion or giving the position to a sub-majer. Also, there's a . . . reluctance, you might say, to promote officers who come up from squad leader to ranks beyond overcaptain or sub-majer."

"I'd see that as a waste of experience, ser."

Tygael smiles. "If you make it to being a commander in Cyad, you might be able to change that, but I'll be a bit too old to benefit from it." He pauses again. "You'll be up for reposting this Autumn. Where would you like to go?"

"You know I have no family," replies Alyiakal. "What assignment would you suggest to develop the additional skills to benefit the Mirror Lancers and my future?"

"The way you phrased that is interesting."

"If what I do doesn't benefit the Mirror Lancers, ser, I may have no future advancement."

"Most junior officers don't see it that way. They should . . . if they want to be successful as a lancer officer." Tygael fingers his chin. "Let me think about that. You already have a set of . . . interesting skills."

"I'd appreciate that, ser." Alyiakal pauses, then asks, "When do you think we'll hear about the new commander?"

"Most likely about the time you get orders for reposting."

"That long?"

"Pemedra is not the greatest concern of Mirror Lancer headquarters. We have the barbarians under control. There are . . . other matters. Headquarters has not seen fit to clarify those, except to say that they do not involve those of us along the northeast borders of Cyador." Tygael's voice turns dry. "Such words are less reassuring than they might be." He shrugs, then stands. "I will give some thought to your question."

Seeing that the overcaptain has effectively ended the meeting, Alyiakal stands as well. "Thank you, ser."

He senses Tygael's gaze on him as he leaves, but only discerns interest of a sort. *It could be worse, much worse.*

As he leaves the administration building, heading for the squad leaders' study, Alyiakal puzzles over what Tygael has said . . . and not said—and over his clear wish to think over what next duty might benefit both the Mirror Lancers and Alyiakal.

He shakes his head. At least he should have a little time to himself later in the day and possibly a chance to write to Saelora. He also wishes there happened to be a way to write and deliver another letter.

XXXVIII

On twoday afternoon after mid-Summer, Alyiakal finds himself in the over-captain's small study, with no real idea of why Tygael has summoned him.

The overcaptain's first words are, "I have no problems to discuss with you."

Alyiakal has his doubts, but merely nods and waits.

"But . . . Pemedra Post has a problem. It's been well over five years since we sent a company far enough to determine the barbarian activity beyond the Grass Hills to the north. You and Fourth Company are the best suited for such a patrol." Overcaptain Tygael does not smile.

"Is that because I'm due for a change of duty, ser?" asks Alyiakal.

"Not directly. Besides Captain Draakyr, you have the most experience in this part of the border. A successful patrol that gathers new information would be most useful to the new commander of Pemedra, as well as to Mirror Lancer headquarters. It would also be useful to you personally. If it is successful, of course."

Alyiakal understands not only what Tygael is saying, but what he is not—that while Alyiakal has a more than successful record as a company commander, what he has accomplished will still not overcome his background and lack of political contacts. "I can see that, ser." He debates asking exactly what kind of information the new commander and Mirror Lancer headquarters might find most useful and decides against it, given that failure to provide the smallest detail about what Tygael might ask for could be used against him.

"Since such a patrol could last at least four or five days, if not longer," says Tygael, "I thought sevenday would afford you a few days to prepare."

"Thank you, ser."

"I do wish you well, Captain, for many reasons. Do not underprepare for this patrol. That's all I have for you."

Meaning that it's not going to be easy. "Yes, ser." Alyiakal stands and then leaves the small office, his steps heading toward the armory, where Yurak has the Fourth Company rankers going over their blades and personal equipment, everything except their firelances.

Alyiakal hasn't taken more than three steps into the armory before the senior squad leader joins him.

"What did the overcaptain want, ser?"

"We've got a special patrol on sevenday," says Alyiakal.

"*How* special, ser?" asks Yurak warily.

"So special that it might take even longer than a certain patrol to the West Branch . . ." Alyiakal explains the overcaptain's orders, without the personal references. Then he waits for his senior squad leader's reaction.

"Sounds like someone's afraid the northern barbarians might be building up a force like the one in the West Branch valley," says Yurak.

"*Or* that they want reassurance that it *isn't* happening, as well as an unsaid suggestion that we make sure that it can't," replies Alyiakal.

"That's the nasty part," points out Yurak. "Doing something like that could cause more raids before long." The senior squad leader offers a sardonic grin. "You sure you didn't piss off the overcaptain, ser?"

"I'm fairly sure I didn't. I'm not so sure I trust those higher in the chain of command."

Yurak snorts. "You're sounding polite, ser."

"Well . . . if you were the overcaptain, would you send First or Third Company?"

The senior squad leader shakes his head, then says, "So it has to be Second Company or Fourth. Why us?"

"Apparently, it's our turn, and we need the experience," replies Alyiakal dryly.

"Thought we got enough experience in that Spring rain. We just got Waark back."

"We can never have enough experience, don't you know?" Alyiakal's laugh is sardonic.

Yurak shakes his head.

XXXIX

Early on sevenday morning, Alyiakal makes his way to the morning mess. He had thought about writing to Hyrsaal and Saelora, but since he'd written both two eightdays earlier, he hasn't that much new to relate, and he's heard nothing from Liathyr for some time. As the first officer there, he takes the opportunity to fill his three water bottles with grass ale. Given the taste of the ale, he's never been tempted to overindulge on any patrol.

He's about to sit down when Kettaur appears.

"Three bottles of ale?" asks the undercaptain.

"It's going to be a long and hot patrol."

"Aren't they all?" replies Kettaur. "I can see why, though, after almost three years, one might overindulge."

"I think you're speaking for yourself," replies Alyiakal cheerfully, "but then, you usually do." He sets the bottles on the table in front of his place and seats himself.

Kettaur stiffens, then turns and walks toward the door of the mess. He stops as Draakyr enters.

Draakyr heads for the table, where he sits beside Alyiakal. "Tygael told me you're headed beyond the hills to the north to see what the barbarians have been doing."

"Every so often, someone does," replies Alyiakal. "This time, it's Fourth Company. We're not to be casual about it, either."

"He said that?"

Alyiakal offers a wry smile. "Not in so many words, but when a senior officer says the patrol and survey might take four to five days, if not longer . . ."

Draakyr nods. "I'd guess someone doesn't want a repeat of what happened at Isahl."

"What was that?" asks Wherryl as he sits down across from Draakyr.

Kettaur immediately sits down beside Wherryl, but says nothing.

Alyiakal manages not to frown, although he is certain that Wherryl has been informed about the barbarians in the West Branch valley and the casualties they inflicted.

Draakyr summarizes the events and the role of the Jeranyi traders in helping the barbarians acquire brass shields, special spears, and throwers.

For reasons he cannot explain, Alyiakal remains skeptical of the purported role of the Jeranyi traders. Not that he has a particularly high regard for traders and Merchanters, but he doesn't see any reason or profit in essentially giving arms to the barbarians, not when the Jeranyi traders compete with traders from Cyador. At the same time, after what little he has heard about the unexplained death of Emperor Kieffal, he sees no point in airing his suspicions.

"Serves the dirty Jeranyi right," says Kettaur.

Wherryl looks to Alyiakal. "What do you think you'll find?"

"Barbarians, dwellings they call houses, fields of a sort, horses . . . beyond that I'm not about to speculate. We've tried to prepare for a range of possibilities."

"It doesn't matter," declares Kettaur. "One way or another, they'll fight. The only question is how many you have to kill and how many of your men they kill."

Although Kettaur may well be correct, Alyiakal smiles, then replies, "Who knows? Maybe they'll have built an actual town or two."

"After last Spring? Hardly. They aren't capable of anything that civilized."

Before anyone can respond to Kettaur, Overcaptain Tygael enters the mess and seats himself. "Good morning."

"Good morning, ser," reply the officers.

"Another hot day. Fourth Company ready, Captain?"

"Yes, ser."

"Good." Tygael takes a swallow of his ale. "No reports of any raider tracks recently. They're not usually quite as active in mid-Summer, but you never know."

Alyiakal smiles politely, reflecting that the unofficial motto of Pemedra might well be "You Never Know."

Little more than two quints later, Tygael stands and leaves the mess.

Alyiakal has long since finished his breakfast of ham and egg casserole and bread, but before he can even stand Kettaur leaves, followed by Wherryl.

"What did you say to Kettaur?" asks Draakyr.

Alyiakal quickly relates the interaction.

Draakyr shakes his head. "Don't know that I'd have been even that civil. Don't worry about it."

From Draakyr's tone of voice, Alyiakal decides that he definitely won't worry about Kettaur, at least not until he gets back from the coming patrol. "I appreciate it."

"It'll be my pleasure." Draakyr grins, but only for a moment, then adds, "Be careful."

"We'll try."

As Alyiakal stands and is about to leave the table, water bottles in hand, the mess aide appears.

"Captain, ser?"

Alyiakal stops.

"Heard you were going on a long patrol, ser." The ranker aide hands Alyiakal a carrot. "Otherwise, it might be a while before your horse gets a carrot."

Alyiakal smiles warmly. "He'll appreciate that, and so do I. Thank you."

"Have a good patrol, ser."

Alyiakal is still smiling as he heads for his quarters to get the rest of his gear. He isn't smiling by the time he carries all his gear and the healing satchel to the stable, where he saddles the bay, fastens his gear and water bottles in place, and gives the gelding the carrot.

"There's only one, and it's the last one for quite a while," Alyiakal tells the bay, knowing that, as soon as the horse finishes the carrot, he'll still nudge Alyiakal for more—which he does.

Alyiakal pats him on the shoulder. "I said that was all." Then he leads the bay out of the stable and mounts, riding to where Yurak is mustering Fourth Company. Given what they might face, Alyiakal has added three spare mounts to the company, both in case of injury to other mounts and to carry additional supplies, as well as a sack of grass-seed grain as emergency fodder.

"Morning, ser. Any word?"

"It'll be hot, and there haven't been any recent raider tracks. That was all the overcaptain had to say."

"Could have been worse."

"There wasn't much else he could have said. Any problems with mounts or men?"

"Had to change out Rumbaar's mount. Cracked hoof. Doesn't look that bad, but there's no reason to risk problems."

"Not on a patrol as long as this one," agrees Alyiakal. "Anything else?"

Yurak grins. "I managed to get more trail biscuits. Cooks are right fond of you, ser. I hope we won't need them, but it can't hurt to have them, and they don't weigh much."

Alyiakal looks back at the formation, then sees Elbaar, now third squad leader, and Renkaar, the second squad leader, riding forward.

They rein up, and all three squad leaders report.

"First squad, ready to ride, ser."

"Second squad . . ."

"Third squad . . ."

In mere moments, Fourth Company rides through the post on the sunstone road toward the north gates. The three scouts have ridden well ahead, although it's unlikely they'll spot any potential problems before Fourth Company enters the hills.

"Any new thoughts on what to expect, ser?" asks Yurak.

"As I told you before, I don't know what to expect, and I don't think the overcaptain does, either. I suspect someone in Mirror Lancer headquarters is worried about better-armed and better-trained barbarians." Alyiakal isn't about to mention his concerns that the Mirror Lancers are being used as counters in some political or power game of which he is unaware, but he's scarcely surprised at the possibility.

XL

On twoday morning, Alyiakal calls a halt on a ridge overlooking a rolling plain covered with greenish-gold grass that stretches for kays, if not farther. From where he sits on the bay, the Grass Hills seem to angle to the northeast while the wide expanse of grass seems to widen to the north and northwest. He can vaguely see trees in the distance to the north, probably bordering a stream or small river. Beyond the watercourse, he can barely make out the squares and rectangles of fields, and brown lines of roads.

He does clearly see a series of hamlets dotting the nearer plain. They're separated by roughly ten kays and joined by roads somewhere in between straight and winding. Those hamlets closest to the Grass Hills are markedly smaller than those farther away, with small plots of cultivated ground around the dwellings.

"What do you think?" Alyiakal asks Yurak.

"Doesn't look much different from hamlets around Pemedra, except they're not walled," replies the senior squad leader.

"We're not raiding them all the time," replies Alyiakal.

"Not worth the bother," says Yurak. "Their raiding us isn't, either, but they're too dumb to realize it."

"Or there's something going on that we don't know. That's why we need to see what we can. Pass the word that no one is to use a firelance unless ordered." Alyiakal shouldn't have to give such an order, but he doesn't want anyone killed who's not a threat.

"Yes, ser."

Alyiakal continues to study the plain below as Yurak passes the word to all the squads. He doesn't see dust on the roads or in the fields, not that he'd expect any tilling in late midsummer.

When Yurak returns, Alyiakal orders, "Company! Forward!"

The trail leading down to the plain shows no recent hoofprints and certainly no footprints, but then there haven't been recent tracks anywhere on the trails for the past ten kays.

Too early to raid for harvest coins . . . and no reason to risk men needed for harvest?

No scouts out, that he observes, but that's not surprising, since Mirror Lancers haven't traveled this far across the Grass Hills in years. When Fourth Company leaves the lower hills, the road forks, one trail running northeast parallel to the base of the Grass Hills, while the other turns westward toward the nearest hamlet. There are a few hoofprints on both rudimentary roads, but not enough to indicate large groups of riders. Alyiakal decides to follow the road westward toward the nearest hamlet.

More than two quints later, Alyiakal and Fourth Company finally approach the hamlet, barely visible over the tall grass. Before too much longer, the plains grass gives way, in places, to small fields and plots, with crude dwellings built of mud brick beyond. They have higher front walls and shorter walls to the back and woven grass-thatch roofs slanting between the two. Most of the small dwellings have a mud-brick chimney roughly in the middle of the back wall.

"Those look even worse up close," says Yurak.

A woman hoeing a patch of ground that appears to be a garden looks up, then grabs the child beside her in one hand, and with the crude hoe in the other, hurries inside the small dwelling, closing the narrow door behind her.

"Didn't even look to see who we were," offers Yurak.

"She acted like all riders are dangerous." That bothers Alyiakal, because no lancers he knows of have been this far north in years.

At the sight of the lancers, the various people outside scramble to get inside and close doors and shutters . . . until Fourth Company reaches the far side of the hamlet, where a gray-haired and bent man leaning on a stick stands, apparently waiting, not far from a tiny mud-brick hut.

Alyiakal reins up and says, "Good day."

The older man replies.

Alyiakal has trouble understanding some of the older man's words, but one phrase is definitely clear. "Why are you here?"

Alyiakal speaks slowly and deliberately as he replies. "We came to find out why your young men keep trying to raid our lands."

"Those are the men who do not want to plant or harvest, and they have nothing better to do. They do not live here. We avoid them, as we can."

"Where do they live?"

"That way." The man gestures almost in the direction from which Fourth Company has come.

Alyiakal suspects that Fourth Company might well have run into the raiders had the company taken the other fork in the trail when it came out of the hills, and says, "They have horses. Horses are hard to come by."

"They cross the river and steal them. Some of them are killed by those of Cerlyn."

"I see few horses here," says Alyiakal.

"Most have donkeys. They cost less, and no one wants to steal them."

"How far is Cerlyn from here?"

"Beyond the river."

"How far is that?" asks Alyiakal.

The man shrugs.

Alyiakal waits, then says, "How long on a good horse?"

"Four glasses, they say."

"Which road goes there?"

"Any road that goes north. I have not been there in years. It is not safe."

"Why not?"

"It is not safe. You go there and you will see." The older man turns and limps back toward his hut.

"Ser?" asks Yurak.

"We'll head for the river. We can always deal with raiders. I have the feeling the overcaptain will be more interested in what might be happening with Cerlyn than another fight with raiders. Besides, if we have to, we can always deal with them on the way back. That's *if* they cause trouble."

"They likely will," predicts Yurak.

"I won't wager against you, Senior Squad Leader, but there's something odd going on here. The overcaptain won't be happy if we don't find out more."

"An unhappy overcaptain usually leads to unhappy lancers."

"It has been known to happen. Company! Forward!"

For the next three glasses Fourth Company follows the road leading mostly north, going through two other, larger hamlets, where the reaction to the presence of the Mirror Lancers is similar to that in the first hamlet.

As he rides, Alyiakal reflects on the differences and similarities between the steads near Pemedra and those through which Fourth Company has just passed.

They're really not that different, except those near Pemedra are better off.

Then again, holders farther from the borders are even better off, and most people are much the same anywhere. Some few are not. Certainly, Adayal was, and surely still is, far different from those who wrest a living from the ground.

Because she is part of the Great Forest and lives and works with it?

Alyiakal shakes his head. While he can see, even respect, her choice, he would feel trapped by the Forest, as he would if he were one of the men laboring to make a living from the land. Adayal, on the other hand, feels freer in the Forest, just as he feels freer as a Mirror Lancer. *Being consorted to you would have destroyed her . . . and made you miserable. And she saw that when you didn't.*

Almost absently, he wonders why the seemingly endless grass and the poor hamlets have reminded him of Adayal, not that he hasn't thought of her now and again. *Or is freedom the combination of having the ability to do what you want that is meaningful to you?*

Alyiakal continues to ponder those questions until, finally, he can see the tops of the trees that usually signify running water. The plain grasses actually are shorter nearer to the water. What surprises Alyiakal the most is that the road comes to an end thirty yards short of the stream. The second surprise is the number of tree stumps on the south side of the stream. The stream itself isn't that wide, perhaps three cubits, but the banks drop steeply almost a yard to the water, suggesting that at times the stream might resemble a small river. On the far side, there are trees and almost no stumps.

Alyiakal halts Fourth Company well short of the water and surveys the opposite bank, and its almost ankle-high grass. Farther west along the bank he sees a small herd of goats, with a youthful herder who could be male or female. Perhaps sixty yards north of the stream is a field, but Alyiakal cannot tell what grows there. A narrow road ends short of the low grass and trees on the north side of the stream.

A bell being rung vigorously breaks the comparative silence of the mid-afternoon.

"First squad!" orders Alyiakal. "Five-man front. Staggered formation! Ready firelances!" That formation will allow ten lancers to fire simultaneously, not that Alyiakal intends such—unless the Cerlynese immediately attack.

The bell continues to ring for almost half a quint.

Almost another half quint passes before Alyiakal hears the sound of hooves and then sees mounted riders coming. The six men who ride up to the end of the road have polished brass shields and sheathed sabres. All six carry strung bows.

All six look surprised as they take in Fourth Company and the firelances leveled at them.

Finally, one man rides slightly forward, closer to the grass, and calls out, "What are Cyadoran lancers doing at the border of Cerlyn?"

"We're here looking for the raiders who keep attacking our holders," replies Alyiakal, raising his voice. "We heard that they sometimes raid Cerlyn for horses."

"You're looking in the wrong place. We allow none of those in the wild plains to cross the river . . . on pain of death."

"Then where do they get their mounts?" asks Alyiakal, sensing that the other is not entirely truthful.

"I have no idea. You'd have to ask them."

While the man's first statement is a lie, Alyiakal doesn't want to start a fight with another land over a lie, especially without knowing more. "Are all the grasslands south of the river what you call the wild plains?"

"That is so."

"And everything north of the river is Cerlyn?"

"It is."

"Then we will look for the raiders in the wild plains," declares Alyiakal. "We will withdraw, peacefully, provided you do not attempt any attack."

"That might be best," says the other, condescendingly.

"I would not speak quite so arrogantly," replies Alyiakal, triggering his fire-lance with the shortest of bursts, sufficient to turn a small bush to the right of the speaker into flame and instant ashes. "Cyador is to be respected."

The Cerlynese leader immediately says, "I meant no disrespect."

"Then you withdraw, and so will we."

The leader turns his mount and gestures; the other five follow him.

"Have the company withdraw," Alyiakal says quietly. "Leave two lancers with me. We'll rejoin you once everyone's out of range of those bows."

While Alyiakal does not trust the Cerlynese in the slightest, none of the six Cerlynese riders return, although they have withdrawn only a few hundred yards up the narrow road. He keeps watching over his shoulder as he and the two lancers ride back to rejoin Fourth Company.

Once he is at the head of the company, heading south, he turns to Yurak. "Your thoughts about what happened?"

"He was telling the truth about the border. I think he was lying about the horses and the raiders."

"Those are my thoughts as well, but it's definitely not a good idea for a relatively junior captain to start an attack on another land. Especially when he's been ordered to find out about raiders."

"Still would have liked to flame that sow's ass," mutters Yurak.

"That makes two of us." Alyiakal laughs, then adds, "It'll be a long ride back to where I think the raiders' hamlet is. Where do you think a good campsite might be?"

"There was a stream and a bit of a ridge near the second hamlet . . ."

Alyiakal nods and looks out at the unending grass, as much a confinement in its own way as the walls that enclose the Great Forest. He leans forward and pats the bay on the shoulder.

XLI

Threeday morning, Alyiakal wakes up early and stiff, deciding that he much prefers a hard lancer officer's pallet bed to uneven matted plains grass. Less than three quints later, Fourth Company rides south toward the second hamlet through which the company had passed on twoday.

A glass later, as the company approaches the hamlet, Alyiakal's bay lifts his head slightly. Wondering what the gelding has scented, Alyiakal reaches out with order/chaos senses to the east, since the light wind comes from the northeast. He senses something several hundred yards to the left, but the deep golden-green grass conceals whatever it is, although Alyiakal suspects it's a grass cat, and the amount of patterned order and chaos is too great to be an antelope. The pattern does not move as the company rides past.

When the company appears at the edge of the hamlet, those few individuals who are out early immediately retreat to the small dwellings. Alyiakal feels a certain scrutiny as he rides through, but it has to be through the cracks in the narrow shutters. Almost absently, as he sees the narrow doors and shutters, he recalls the tree stumps on the south bank of the stream to the north and shakes his head.

Almost two glasses pass before Fourth Company again passes through the hamlet closest to the Grass Hills, with the same retreat by the inhabitants.

When the company nears the way back to Pemedra, Alyiakal studies where the roads join, then looks to Yurak. "I don't see any tracks besides ours. Do you?"

"No, ser. Just ours from yesterday."

Alyiakal nods, feeling most grateful, since raider tracks heading to Pemedra would have made his task much, much harder. Instead he can focus on the trail and anything he can sense ahead or in the high grass on either side of the narrow road, a road that contains a few hoofprints heading to the northeast.

"If the raiders have a hamlet in this direction," Alyiakal says, "there's not much sign of anything."

"There weren't any tracks or any signs of them going the other way, ser," Yurak points out.

Alyiakal still wonders, but less than a quint later, at the top of a low rise in the road, only a few yards above the surrounding grasslands, he sees dwellings nearly a kay ahead, far more than in the last hamlet they'd passed through. The mud-brick buildings are slightly larger than the grasslands dwellings he's seen in the other hamlets, with thatched roofs that look pitched rather than single-sloped. The outbuildings might well be stables. The road leads to a central open area among the houses.

"That looks a bit more prosperous," Alyiakal says to Yurak. "Think it might be our raiders?"

"I'd say so. Folks with horses and weapons are bound to be better off."

"Ready firelances!" orders Alyiakal, hoping that he doesn't have to use them, but suspecting that he will. He urges the bay forward.

Fourth Company, still slightly less than half a kay from the nearest dwelling, continues on the road when a bell begins to ring, a sound somehow familiar to Alyiakal. He realizes the bell sounds much like the one he heard at the border to Cerlyn. Pushing that thought aside, he turns to Yurak. "First squad will take the west side of the hamlet, second squad the east, and third squad will hold the road as our rear guard. Pass the orders! Don't fire unless fired upon . . . or I order it."

"Yes, ser."

When Yurak returns from passing the orders, Alyiakal commands, "Company! Forward!" Then he urges the bay into a trot, since he doesn't want the raiders to get that organized, and the use of the bell suggests that they've planned in some fashion for intruders or attack.

As Alyiakal nears the cleared area surrounding the houses and outbuildings, he sees men sprinting toward the scattered stables, and two men on mounts already flee northeast, both seemingly armed.

Alyiakal sees what could happen. "First squad on me! Second squad! Hold the square!" Urging the bay into a canter, he heads straight through the hamlet toward the northeast to block the road before too many of the raiders escape. The high, thick plains grass will certainly hamper or slow other avenues of escape.

Another rider makes the road on the far side of the hamlet where the high grass begins before first squad reaches it. "First squad! Re-form! Five-man staggered front. Take down any mount if the rider won't stop."

Alyiakal senses Yurak's confusion and snaps, "Dead men don't talk!" *And without horses they'll have trouble raiding—until they get more from Cerlyn.*

An older bearded man, seeing first squad blocking the road, turns his mount toward the grass.

Alyiakal immediately fires a short burst at the mount's chest. The horse goes down, and throws the rider forward. He doesn't move, but Alyiakal also doesn't sense a black death mist. *Not yet, anyway.*

Yurak brings down another mount, but riders keep trying to escape. Two men on foot charge Alyiakal with broadswords, and Alyiakal uses two bolts to kill them both.

In little more than a quint, ten mounts are down, and Alyiakal counts eight dead and close to a score of wounded or captured men. From what the squad leaders report, somewhere between five and ten men have gotten away, mainly on foot, and are somewhere in the high grass. Alyiakal doesn't sense any close by.

Second and third squads patrol and keep watch so that none of the escapees will surprise the lancers, and so that no one leaves the score or so dwellings. First squad has tied up eleven captives, who sit in the dirt of what passes for a central square.

Alyiakal dismounts and hands the bay gelding's reins to a mounted lancer. He walks toward the first of the captives, a man who looks to be possibly fifteen years older than Alyiakal himself.

"Who leads the hamlet?" asks Alyiakal.

"Domraak. You killed him."

"Why do you raid Cyador?"

"What else can we do?"

"The other hamlets don't raid Cyador."

"They live like peasants. They have no worth. They have no honor. They grub in the dirt." The man spits to the side.

"Where do you get your horses?"

"Where we can."

"Where is that?"

"It is where we can."

Alyiakal is tempted to flame the man, but asks, "Why does Cerlyn give you horses?"

"Because it works better that way."

Alyiakal steps forward, extending unseen order and chaos. "That's not an answer." His words are cold.

"What will you do? Kill me?"

"No. You might lose your right hand and left foot."

"I'll die then, anyway."

"No. You won't. I'm a healer." Alyiakal smiles as cruelly as he can, while projecting absolute certainty.

The raider looks to Yurak. The senior squad leader nods. "He is."

The man swallows, then says, "We get so many from Cerlyn every year."

"Blades as well?"

The man nods.

"And women?"

"Sometimes . . . the ones who won't do as they like."

"And sometimes their young men who cause trouble?"

"If they're strong. If not, we leave them with the peasants."

"Food?"

"They give nothing."

"Do you get anything from traders?"

The man spits to the side again. "Cerlyn kills any traders they find who cross the river."

"You must have a way around that," says Alyiakal. "Someplace where those of Cerlyn do not go or know."

"They have mages who talk to all the traders. They can tell if they lie. If they lie, they die."

The conviction in the older man's voice, and in his order/chaos balance, chills Alyiakal.

"Why did you become a raider?"

"It is better than being a peasant and tilling the dirt for almost nothing."

"How long has this been going on?"

The man shrugs tiredly. "Many years. Since before I became a man."

"Did anyone ever try to tell anyone in Cyador?"

"Many years ago, it was said. Mirror Lancers killed them."

The man believes that to be true, and, unfortunately, Alyiakal can see that as a definite possibility. "Are there any other hamlets like yours? With horses and good blades?"

"We are the only one. The peasants have no will and no honor."

"What if someone wants to leave?"

"Where would they go? If they go south, you kill them. If they go north, those of Cerlyn kill them. If they go east, they die in the hills. If they go west, the Jeranyi enslave or kill them."

Alyiakal turns to the next man. "You heard what he said. Is it true?"

"Yes, ser. Except sometimes, the bastards in Cerlyn torture people."

"Have you seen that?"

"Once, when we went for horses. Before they delivered the horses, they chopped off a trader's fingers. Then they took his manhood. They said worse would happen if we ever crossed the river."

For the next glass, Alyiakal questions the rest of the captives. While he learns a few more gory details, all of the raiders tell the truth as they see it. While he could break into some of the dwellings and question the women, he sees little point in it, except to terrify and/or anger them further. He's learned more than enough to give a solid report to the overcaptain. Visits to more hamlets won't add much, except time in the grasslands.

After the questioning, he orders, "Gather up all the blades and spears, and find enough healthy mounts to carry them."

Then he mounts the bay gelding and watches as the lancers go to work. Once the loading is finished, he turns in the saddle and says to Yurak, "We've learned enough. We'll head back."

"What about us?" asks the older man, still bound and on the ground.

"I'm sure that the women or those who escaped into the grass will be back before long," replies Alyiakal, who then orders, "Fourth Company! Form up! Keep an eye out for armed raiders!" He hopes the men in the high grass have enough sense to remain hidden until Fourth Company is well away from the raiders' hamlet.

Once the company has ridden a good kay west of the hamlet, Yurak says slowly, "Almost feel sorry for the poor bastards."

"I feel sorrier for the women," replies Alyiakal. "And children."

"What do you think the overcaptain will say, ser?"

"He won't be happy." *For more than a few reasons.*

XLII

During the three days it takes Fourth Company to return to Pemedra, Alyiakal thinks over how he should write his patrol report. He also makes notes for the maps and works diligently on carrying a better concealment shield and a much heavier inner protective shield, one where the elements of chaos are firmly linked in order. He suspects, but does not know, and certainly doesn't want to test the suspicion, that the inner shield might deflect not only order and chaos, but also weapons such as spears and arrows. While he hopes his next posting will not be around Magi'i, he certainly cannot count on such, and that is why he redoubles his shielding efforts.

Although Fourth Company arrives after evening mess on fiveday, Alyiakal stays up late writing up his report, thankful that he has composed most of it mentally while riding, and makes sure it is in the overcaptain's inbox before he goes to bed. Even so, he rises early on sixday, cleans up, shaves, and dresses, glad to be in a clean uniform, then makes his way to the mess.

Draakyr and Wherryl arrive shortly after Alyiakal does, but Alyiakal knows he won't see Kettaur, because the undercaptain is patrolling to the northwest, looking for possible raiders from the West Branch valley.

The two more senior captains seat themselves across from Alyiakal.

"That was a long patrol," says Wherryl. "What happened?"

"A fair amount of the unusual," replies Alyiakal. "I'd rather not say much until the overcaptain has a chance to read my report."

"The duty ostler said you brought back seven or eight mounts loaded with weapons. That so?" presses Wherryl.

"It was an unusual patrol," replies Alyiakal cheerfully.

"I think that's all we're going to get for now," says Draakyr, with a chuckle. "Probably all we should for now."

"That's right, Captain Draakyr," says Tygael as he slips into the chair at the head of the table. "I do prefer to be the first one to get the entire report."

"What's been happening here?" asks Alyiakal.

"Not that much," replies Tygael. "We did get a report from Subcommander Grevyll advising us that the barbarians to the west have been rebuilding the town at the end of the West Branch valley. First Company is looking for signs that the barbarians have been scouting or riding in our direction." Tygael offers an amused smile. "We received an interesting dispatch on fourday." He takes a swallow of ale, then helps himself to the strips of meat, which Alyiakal recognizes as antelope, rather more gamy than ham, and then the cheese-egg scramble.

Alyiakal waits for Tygael's next words, although he has the feeling that the other three all know what was in the dispatch.

"Captain Draakyr's duty here has been extended two years, and in late Autumn, when I depart, he'll be promoted to overcaptain."

"Congratulations!" Then Alyiakal says, "At least, I hope it's congratulations."

Draakyr smiles. "It is . . . and I'll get two eightdays' home leave, plus travel time, before I take the position." His smile widens as he adds, "After I'm promoted."

From the feelings he senses, Alyiakal has the impression that there have been times in Draakyr's past when supposedly good news or dispatches were not so good as others thought. Following Draakyr and Wherryl, he fills his platter and takes a chunk of warm bread from the basket.

"Home leave where?" asks Wherryl.

"Summerdock." Draakyr begins to eat.

"You'll be gone almost four eightdays, then," says Wherryl musingly.

"Pemedra will be getting another senior captain before Captain Draakyr goes on leave," says Tygael, "and shortly after that, a new undercaptain or captain to replace Captain Alyiakal. We don't know Captain Alyiakal's next post, and likely will not until mid-Harvest, possibly a little later."

"Quite a change coming here," says Wherryl. "Any word on the replacement for Majer Klaavyl?"

"Not yet," replies the overcaptain.

The rest of the breakfast conversation is scattered, but pleasant, possibly because Kettaur isn't present. At least, that's Alyiakal's feeling.

As Tygael rises from the table, he looks to Alyiakal and says, "In half a glass."

"Yes, ser."

Alyiakal isn't totally looking forward to the overcaptain's questions, but given what he saw and experienced in the grasslands, he'd have been even more worried if Tygael hadn't summoned him.

Once he's seated in the small study, Alyiakal doesn't have to wait long for Tygael to speak.

"I read your report. It appears quite thorough . . . and timely. As usual. I do have a few questions."

More than a few, I suspect. "Yes, ser." Alyiakal waits.

"Do you believe you covered enough of the grasslands for your report to be generally accurate?"

"As I reported, we did not visit every single hamlet we could observe from the vantage point on the northern edge of that part of the Grass Hills, but so far as we could see, we only missed visiting three others. We could see six such hamlets and the one that held the raiders. None of the three we visited differed that much from each other. The area south of the river is smaller than the area here north of Pemedra."

"You're suggesting that the grasslands south of the river cannot support that many more hamlets, then?"

"Not without trade, better tools, and coins . . . I don't think so. It does appear that the area has more streams and seems to get more rain. The grasses are still partly green."

"Did the raiders you questioned give any other answers for raiding Cyadoran hamlets besides the fact that they had to?"

"No, ser. The Cerlynese have set it up so that there's not much choice. I'd guess that they're clever enough not to encourage the raids directly."

"Did anyone mention the Jeranyi?"

"Only the older raider. All he said was that the Jeranyi would kill anyone heading west."

For the next quint, Tygael asks what seem to Alyiakal to be variations on the questions the overcaptain has already asked and that Alyiakal had put in his patrol report.

Then Tygael pauses for several moments, before saying, "Did you think about . . . just destroying the hamlet and the surviving raiders?"

"I didn't see much point in doing more, ser. We killed eight of them and two died of wounds before we left. We destroyed eleven horses. We took all the blades and spears, and eight of their best mounts. There were close to a half score who fled and hid in the high grass. It would have taken days to track them down." The last part is a partial lie, because Alyiakal could have found some of the fugitives, but even with order/chaos sensing, he couldn't have found them all in that sea of grass. "The houses are built of mud brick. You can't fire them, and it's too early in the season there to start a grass fire. Besides, that could have killed many of the people in the other hamlets who aren't raiders."

Tygael fingers his chin and then nods, slowly. "I can see that. You wrote that the Cerlynese border guards were initially dismissive and required a slight demonstration of power. I'd like to hear about that."

Alyiakal describes in detail the situation over the stream and the condescension of the Cerlynese speaker.

"You didn't think that was a deliberate provocation?"

"It might have been, but it was clearly out of ignorance, and I didn't think a comparatively junior captain should be taking an action that could have killed Cerlynese border patrollers in their own territory."

Tygael chuckles. "Much as they deserved it, I appreciate your restraint. So should headquarters." The amused expression vanishes. "What is your feeling about the Cerlynese?"

"I trust them far less than the raiders. They've encouraged if not effectively forced some of the grassland people to raid this part of Cyador. They apparently torture and kill traders who try to sell to or trade with the grassland people. I don't see why that's necessary. The people can't afford to buy much, and there's little to sell. The Cerlynese also exile 'difficult' women and young men to the raiders. The fact that they also have those polished brass shields and archers with what looked to be identical bows I think should be a concern for Mirror Lancer headquarters."

"So do I, I have to admit." Tygael takes a slow, deep breath. "This all bears some thought before I forward your report and my observations and recommendations to Mirror Lancer headquarters." After a long moment, he adds,

"Very good report, Captain. You seem to have handled the patrol as well as possible in a difficult situation. Fourth Company will have at least six days off before your next patrol."

"The men will appreciate it, ser."

"They deserve it. So do you." He pauses. "That's all for now."

"Yes, ser." Alyiakal stands, inclines his head, and leaves the small study.

Once he is out in the corridor, the duty squad leader says, "Captain, ser?"

"Yes?"

"You have two letters that came in while you were on patrol. We kept them here rather than put them in your box in the officers' study." The squad leader hands both to Alyiakal.

"Thank you." Alyiakal takes them and looks at the names, Saelora'mer and Captain Hyrsaal'alt—not that he's surprised, but he is pleased. He wishes he could read them immediately, but he needs to meet with Yurak and convey the news, as well as plan the company schedule for the next eightday, because, even without patrols, there are necessary tasks and duties. Then he pauses and thinks. *Saelora'mer?* Has she consorted a Merchanter? Or become one?

As it turns out, much as he wants to discover what Saelora has been up to, he doesn't get a chance to open the letters until well past midafternoon. He starts with the letter from Hyrsaal.

> *Alyiakal—*
>
> *I'm glad to hear that you're continuing to guard the northwest and surviving barbarians, raiders, and grass fires . . .*
>
> *Here in Summerdock, it's the same all year round. Patrol the coast roads north of the port. Patrol the coast roads south of the port. Catch the stupid smugglers. See traces of the smart ones but rarely get there in time. Then do it in reverse.*
>
> *It looks like my next posting will be a border post like yours. I have no idea which one it might be. When I find out, I'll let you know. Then I hope you can pass on some helpful advice. The raiders you've encountered seem deadlier than smugglers . . .*
>
> *After my next posting, Catriana and I plan to be consorted. She has a small inheritance and has been working at a healers' center in Fyrad. She's been able to save some because she's living with her older sister. Her older sister's consort is a smallholder . . .*

Alyiakal smiles. *Hyrsaal deserves someone who loves him.*

After he finishes reading Hyrsaal's letter, he opens the second letter and begins to read.

Alyiakal—

I always enjoy reading your letters. I'm so glad you keep writing.

We're selling more of the greenberry brandy now that I have the new distillery complete. I also bought a five-hectare plot that was already mostly covered in greenberries. The nasty-tasting wilder ones make better brandy. The plot also has a little house that I'm having fixed up so I can have my own place. Since Gaaran came back and has recovered, I don't think Mother needs me so much, and the house won't be so crowded.

I still have trouble realizing that I'm officially a Merchanter now— Saelora'mer.

Alyiakal smiles. *She's certainly worked hard for it.*

I'm the only woman Merchanter in Vaeyal, but Vassyl sponsored me, and he pointed out that since I was already an enumerator and owned a growing business, how could I not be a Merchanter. No one objected. I guess that's good. Vassyl helped me negotiate an agreement with a trader out of Lydiar. The first sales look promising. We're also going to meet with another trader out of Valmurl next fourday.

I don't know if Hyrsaal wrote you, but he and Catriana are planning to get consorted. I don't think it will be soon, but when he says he's going to do something, he does, just like Karola. She said she'd consort Faadyr, and she did . . .

Karola? Then he remembers—Saelora and Hyrsaal's older sister. Neither has mentioned her often . . . or recently. Alyiakal has no idea who Faadyr is or what he does, possibly because no one's ever mentioned him before.

He continues reading, occasionally smiling.

XLIII

Predictably, after Fourth Company's patrol into the northern grasslands, patrols for all companies posted at Pemedra remain uneventful for the rest of Summer and the first five eightdays of Harvest. There are no raids from the north and only signs of possible scouting from the west, but those tracks never actually enter the valley, and none of the Pemedra companies encounter raiders.

As a result, Alyiakal spends most of his time on patrol strengthening his shields, extending his ability to sense, and improving his ability to hold concealments and move quietly while under one. He also works on making fair copies of his personal maps.

Late on twoday afternoon of the sixth eightday of Harvest, Alyiakal sits at his table desk in the officers' study poring over maps of Cyador when a ranker messenger approaches.

"Ser, Overcaptain Tygael would like to see you at your earliest convenience."

Meaning immediately. Alyiakal stands and says, "Thank you. I'm on my way."

He walks swiftly, but not hurriedly, from the study to the headquarters building and to the small study beside the still-vacant study of the commanding officer of the post.

"Close the door, Captain," says Tygael as Alyiakal enters, motioning to the two chairs before the desk.

Alyiakal seats himself and waits, assuming that Tygael might have his posting orders. *Either that, or another long scouting patrol.*

Tygael smiles enigmatically, then says, "I've received your orders."

"Ser?"

"Your handling of the northern grasslands patrol was apparently influential in assuring a . . . useful . . . posting. You won't think so when I tell you what it is, but I can assure you that it will allow you to develop your capabilities in ways that would not be possible anywhere else."

Alyiakal nods slowly. "But?"

"If you fail . . . well, you won't have to worry about the future."

Alyiakal manages not to wince. "I haven't the faintest idea what or where such a posting might be."

"Neither do most field-grade Mirror Lancers. You're being posted to Guarstyad."

"That's a port town almost two hundred kays northeast of Fyrad. Is there even a Mirror Lancer post there?"

"There wasn't, not until earlier this year. By mid-Autumn there will be six companies there. You'll be in command of one of them."

"Is the town being threatened? By the Kyphrans? Kyphrien is more than five hundred kays northeast, and Ruzor is almost that far to the east." Alyiakal frowns. "If I recall correctly, Guarstyad is in a river valley partly surrounded by the Westhorns."

"It is. It's a very fertile valley, if prone to flooding every Spring, but it has a very good and sheltered harbor, one that the Kyphrans would very much like to obtain. There's also a silver mine several kays north not far from the river. The Kyphrans have been landing troopers on the coast southeast of Guarstyad at the edge of their territory and at the eastern edge of the Westhorns. They've established a fort there. It's built well enough and far enough from the ocean that fireships wouldn't be effective against it."

Alyiakal begins to see where Tygael is leading. So he asks, "Does that mean that I'll need to be in Guarstyad rather quickly?"

"As a captain, you're due four eightdays' home leave, and travel time. You likely won't be able to take all the leave you have, possibly only two eightdays, depending on where you intend to take leave. Have you thought about where?"

"I have," replies Alyiakal, "but the only places I really remember are Jakaafra and Pyraan—that's a little town near Westend. My great-aunt lived there, but she died some years ago."

"As a Mirror Lancer officer, you can take the leave anywhere that's accessible by firewagon, or no more than a day's ride from such a point—unless you want to use leave time to travel farther. Also, if it's where there's a post you can use the visiting officers' quarters. That wouldn't be a problem if you took leave in Geliendra."

Alyiakal refrains from pointing out that he knows what the overcaptain has just said, partly because that would be rude and unnecessary, and partly because he has the feeling the overcaptain has something else in mind. "I understand that I don't have to take all the home leave I'm due."

"That's true. You can carry over two eightdays' worth to the next time you're reposted or due leave."

"So if I took two eightdays in Geliendra, and after a full tour of duty at Guarstyad," says Alyiakal carefully, "I'd have six eightdays of leave on the books."

"I won't mislead you, Alyiakal. After a full tour at Guarstyad, you might need six eightdays of leave." Tygael pauses, then goes on. "If you're as capable as I believe, you might even leave Guarstyad as an overcaptain, or be promoted shortly after you leave. That's certainly not a promise, but it is a possibility."

"You suggested that it would be a good assignment for me, didn't you? Might I ask why?"

"Because you know how to combine unconventional initiative and Mirror Lancer imperatives. I also suggested it because you're suited for such duty. Unless someone has worked closely with you, from reports and mere observation, they would only see a quiet and very competent officer."

In short, you won't get noticed and promoted that far without excelling in unconventional duties.

"You, of course, have an option that can only be used once in your entire career as an officer, and that is to reject these orders. You already know that, but I am required to formally inform you, and you will sign a letter that says you have been so informed and that you either accept or reject the orders."

"If I accept them, and I will, when do I leave Pemedra?"

"No later than the last eightday of Harvest. Travel to Guarstyad will take almost two eightdays, possibly more, since the last part of your travel will be aboard a fireship from Fyrad to Guarstyad, and it's best to accomplish that before the year-end storms make sea travel uncertain. That only allows you to take two eightdays' leave in Geliendra."

Alyiakal nods. "That's the way it will be, and I do appreciate your guidance and work in making it all possible."

"I think it will be good for you and for the Mirror Lancers. That doesn't always happen."

"I appreciate it. I do have a question . . . about personal logistics. I'd like to visit the family of one of the officers I went through Kynstaar with. They live in a small town close to Geliendra. Is it possible to use a lancer mount . . . ?"

"That is a privilege for officers on leave. Use of a mount for the day, when mounts are available, is customary. For longer periods, you have to get permission from the officer handling logistics at that post."

"Thank you. I wondered about that."

"Where is that officer serving, if I might ask?"

"He has a company in Summerdock patrolling the coast to deal with smugglers. He doesn't yet know his next posting . . . or he didn't the last time he wrote."

"Guarstyad won't be that tedious," declares Tygael. "Now . . . since you've decided to accept your orders, you have a few papers to sign."

A half glass later, Alyiakal leaves the overcaptain's office, half wondering if he has done the right thing, yet knowing that rejecting the orders would have meant he'd likely never rise above overcaptain and would be rotated between combat-related duties and assignments that Tygael would definitely have termed as tedious.

He'd hoped to be able to get to Jakaafra to see if he could track down Adayal, but getting to and from Jakaafra from Geliendra would take almost an eightday, if not longer, and trying to get there from anywhere else that had a firewagon stop would take even more time traveling.

She could have written you earlier. She knew you'd be in Kynstaar for several years. She even said you'd do great things in the Mirror Lancers.

With that thought, Alyiakal smiles sardonically. *Great things? Protecting impoverished holders from even poorer raiders that you've had to kill to stop more raiders . . . or killing other raiders being used as game pieces by outlanders?*

He shakes his head as he continues to walk toward the officers' study. At least he can write Saelora and Hyrsaal and tell them he plans to visit Vaeyal on his home leave. He doubts that his home leave will overlap much with Hyrsaal's, but it's possible.

XLIV

The next three eightdays pass slowly and methodically, and Alyiakal takes Fourth Company on four more patrols, during which they discover no signs of barbarian raiders or horses other than those of local holders and of Mirror Lancers.

As Alyiakal leads the company back through the northern gates of Pemedra on sixday of the eighth eightday of Harvest, Yurak clears his throat.

Alyiakal does not smile, but maintains a pleasant expression, as he says, "Another uneventful patrol."

"That's because of you, ser." Yurak clears his throat again. "This is your last patrol with Fourth Company?"

"It is. I'm leaving with the dispatch riders on eightday."

"Hardly an easy ride, going that way." Yurak pauses again. "Don't know how to say this, ser. But there's not a man wouldn't serve under you again. Can't say that about many, especially junior captains."

"I'd serve with any of them again," replies Alyiakal, "especially you, Elbaar, and Renkaar."

"I heard it said you're going to Guarstyad to fight Kyphrans."

"I'm being posted there. The Kyphrans have built a fort close to the border. What that will mean isn't certain yet."

Yurak shakes his head. "The Kyphrans anywhere are nasty bastards. Worse than the Cerlynese. You can't trust them except to be bastards."

Alyiakal senses and knows what the senior squad leader is trying to say beyond a mere warning. "I won't ever turn my back on them. I appreciate the warning." He smiles.

"You know who'll replace you?"

"I haven't heard. I'm leaving earlier than usual because of the situation at Guarstyad and worries about Autumn weather. The overcaptain may take Fourth Company on a patrol or two until my replacement arrives. I suspect you'll get a captain, possibly even a senior captain, rather than an undercaptain." *Because Wherryl isn't that senior, and Kettaur's still green, and Draakyr's moving up to overcaptain.* "But I don't know, and I don't think the overcaptain does either. Not yet." After a pause, Alyiakal adds, "Whoever it turns out to be, he'll be getting a good company."

"Might be because someone spent time working with it."

"More likely that someone was fortunate to be able to work with good squad leaders," replies Alyiakal cheerfully.

Once Fourth Company reaches the stables, Alyiakal dismisses the company to duties for the last time and then leads his mount into the stables. After he unsaddles and carefully grooms the bay, he stands in the stall, talking quietly to the gelding. "I'm going to miss you. You saved me when I was too green to know better. I hope that your next rider appreciates you as much as I have."

His eyes burn when he finally leaves the stall, and he walks quietly to his quarters. After a time, he washes up and then makes his way to the officers' study, where he begins his patrol report. Given that little occurred and less has changed since previous patrols, all he can note is limited, and he finishes writing it up before evening mess.

He steps into the mess behind Wherryl and Kettaur, but Draakyr is already there, and Alyiakal sits down beside him.

"Last patrol, right?" says Draakyr.

"I don't think the overcaptain's going to send me out tomorrow, and I leave on eightday. It was very quiet."

"Likely will be until next Spring when the Cerlynese give more weapons and horses to the barbarians," replies Draakyr.

"That's a waste of silvers," says Kettaur, with a snort.

"Not from their point of view," replies Draakyr.

"How do you figure that?" asks Wherryl. "The barbarians don't harm that many of our men."

Tygael slides into the place at the end of the table and says, "They tie up lancers. The Cerlynese also get rid of their own troublemakers there. Cerlyn uses the barbarians as a buffer between them and Cyador. That makes it harder for us to deal with Cerlyn. Why do you think Emperor Kieffal wanted to build more posts to the north?" He smiles sourly. "And don't bother to ask why it didn't happen, especially in Cyad."

Kettaur immediately replies, "I can't believe that Merchanters—"

"The only value Merchanters hold dear," interrupts Tygael, "is that of golds. Assassins also value golds greatly. We won't say more." His eyes fix solidly on Kettaur for several moments.

Kettaur closes his mouth, but his eyes hold anger that Alyiakal can feel even without sensing the chaos swirling around the undercaptain.

While Tygael can see the anger as well, Alyiakal suspects, the overcaptain smiles and says, "Our job is to protect the people within the borders of Cyador, no matter who they happen to be. All of you have been most effective in doing that, and I'm confident that all of you will continue to do so no matter where you're posted after you leave Pemedra. Now . . . if you'd pass that platter of lamb cutlets . . ."

While the platter really doesn't need to be passed, Draakyr eases it fractionally closer to Tygael.

"You're going to spend your leave in Geliendra?" the overcaptain asks Alyiakal.

"It's as close to home as anyplace, and I can't take that much leave because of the travel constraints." Although Tygael knows that, Alyiakal understands that the overcaptain wants to change the subject and suspects he also wants to point out that sometimes officers don't get all the leave that they've accrued.

"Travel constraints?" asks Kettaur, predictably.

"The captain has to travel by fireship from Fyrad to Guarstyad," explains Tygael, "and after mid-Autumn, the seas can get quite rough, sometimes for eightdays. Since Fyrad is surrounded by the lower Westhorns, the passes get snowed in early, sometimes even by mid-Autumn."

Given what Tygael had said earlier and what he just revealed, Alyiakal wonders why he hasn't been detached and sent to Fyrad earlier. It's not as though the Kyphrans would be any threat until late the next Spring, if then.

Tygael chuckles, then says, "All of you captains have similar thoughts behind those pleasant smiles. The reasons for the situation are simple. First, headquarters didn't find out what the Kyphrans were up to until late Spring. Second, it's not as though the Mirror Lancers have six companies to spare. Neither the Magi'i nor the Merchanters have ever supported excessive numbers of Mirror Lancers, especially anywhere close to Cyad. Headquarters has barely a company's worth of rankers, largely clerical and administrative. There are less than twoscore officers in all of headquarters. It's taken three seasons to recruit more rankers and find the right mix of squad leaders, rankers, and officers to create those six companies and to transport them to Guarstyad . . ."

Alyiakal can certainly see that. While he doesn't know the exact numbers, he doubts that the Mirror Lancers have more than eighty companies, possibly less. While district guards train and can be called up, they certainly wouldn't be suited to handling border duties eightday after eightday, or for the extended and more isolated duty required at Guarstyad.

". . . Third, which I wouldn't mention outside this mess, headquarters is rather resistant to sudden change."

"What about the Magi'i?" asks Kettaur.

"The number of Magi'i is considerably less than the number of lancer officers," replies Tygael dryly. "The amount of chaos most could summon in a battle is possibly the same as a single firelance. Perhaps a handful might have chaos powers equivalent to a single company armed with firelances. Their powers are best used in creating our weapons and tools . . ."

As Tygael speaks, Alyiakal wonders, not for the first time, why Kettaur doesn't already know all that, or is the undercaptain a dunderhead from a high altage family who was tutored and trained intensively enough privately to scrape through officer training?

While Vordahl definitely had those advantages, he was also intelligent and worked hard, not that Alyiakal has thought that much about either Baertal or Vordahl since they all left Kynstaar. A second thought strikes him as well. Since he can gather chaos, why couldn't he recharge a firelance in a pinch? He wishes he'd thought of that earlier, but there had never been the necessity.

"So, as a company commander," says Draakyr, "you have more chaos at your command than do most Magi'i. That's a sobering thought."

Another indirect and polite way of telling Kettaur he needs to think about what he blurts out.

"Indeed," adds Tygael. "I think I'll have a bit more of that lamb."

Almost immediately, Draakyr turns to Alyiakal. "You going to visit anyone on your leave?"

"Another officer I went through Kynstaar with and his family. They live near Geliendra." What Alyiakal doesn't mention is that, based on Hyrsaal's last letter, Hyrsaal's leave is later than Alyiakal's, and they'll likely only have a few days when they're both there. *If that.* At least Saelora sounded pleased that he was coming in her letter. *Reservedly pleased, which could mean anything.*

"Sometimes, it's good to keep in touch, and sometimes," says Draakyr, "you find that you no longer have quite the same outlook."

"I appreciate the caution," replies Alyiakal. "What about you?"

"I'm going to Summerdock. I'll have to stop by the post there, but I'll stay with my brother and his consort. He's the foreman at a trading warehouse. My mother lives with my sister, who has three children. That would be crowded, but they're not that far from each other."

"That's good, I take it?" Alyiakal does not ask about whether there's someone else Draakyr might be hoping to see. His own father had told him that some officers who come up from being squad leaders are very sensitive about consorts . . . or even about whether they have one.

"It is. I get to see everyone, and I'm there long enough to be reminded why that kind of life isn't for me."

"Most Mirror Lancer officers wouldn't be happy doing anything else," says Tygael. "From what I've seen anyway."

Wherryl nods.

Kettaur just looks bored.

"Well, if you do stop by the post, you might say a word to a friend of mine," says Alyiakal. "Hyrsaal. He's a junior captain."

"We'll see."

After Tygael leaves the mess, Alyiakal stands, then makes his way back to the officers' study, where he writes the second copy of the report and places it in the Fourth Company file. Then he takes the overcaptain's copy and walks to the headquarters building, where he leaves the report for Tygael.

Tomorrow, he'll go through his gear and pack, including his notes and maps. He'll need to attend to arranging for new uniforms in Geliendra, but he's certain there will be a tailor on the post or nearby . . . and that he'll have plenty of time.

ALYIAKAL'ALT,
Captain, Mirror Lancers
Geliendra & Vaeyal

XLV

By threeday morning, after a hard two-day ride to Syadtar, ending after sunset on twoday, Alyiakal is in a firewagon headed for Ilypsya. While he has hoped to see Healer Vayidra while he is in Syadtar, it turns out that she has been sent to Cyad, although no one at the infirmary can tell him more than that. He also wondered if he'd run across Naeyal, but he doesn't see him at morning mess before he catches the firewagon.

Late on threeday evening, he arrives at Ilypsya Post, where he spends the night before catching another firewagon. In the end, he arrives at the Mirror Lancer post at Geliendra late on eightday afternoon. When he walks through the gates, carrying his gear, the walls and gates don't seem as imposing as they had the first time he'd come to Geliendra. It takes him more than a glass to report his leave and transit status, to arrange for firewagon passage to Fyrad after his leave, and to obtain a room in the visiting officers' quarters, a chamber not that different from the one he occupied in Pemedra, just, unsurprisingly, far warmer. He quickly washes up, shaves, and makes his way to the officers' mess, where he stops and informs the mess orderly.

"Yes, ser," replies the orderly. "Captain Riegar informed us you'd be here. Two eightdays, ser?"

"Yes. I'll be leaving two eightdays from tomorrow morning. I might miss a few meals, since I'm visiting friends."

"That's not a problem, ser."

Alyiakal makes his way to the junior officers' table, since Geliendra has enough officers for two tables, although the senior officers' table is only set with five places. As he nears the table, he doesn't recognize any of the officers standing around the table, but he does see three very young men waiting at the end of the table—clearly officer candidates on their way to Kynstaar.

Or, as someone told you more than six years ago, merely candidates to be officer candidates.

There's a separation between the ten captains and the five undercaptains, three of whom look to have been former squad leaders, and Alyiakal moves to join the captains, introducing himself: "Alyiakal, on leave and in transit to Guarstyad."

The captain beside Alyiakal volunteers, "Talaan, Forest patrol."

The captain across from Alyiakal, considerably older, says, "Ghrennan, Geliendra." He frowns. "Have we met?"

"I don't think so. I went straight from Kynstaar to Pemedra. You might have known my father, though—Majer Kyal."

"I did, in fact. You do look a bit like him. That must be why I thought we might have met. I was sorry to hear that he died on patrol several years ago. He was a good man and an excellent officer."

"Thank you. His death came as a shock, even though I knew it was always possible. He died right before I was commissioned."

"Then he knew you'd be commissioned. At least he knew that." Ghrennan pauses. "Guarstyad? They're sending a lot of people there, I've heard. All of the officers have combat experience."

"So I understand."

"Has to be the frigging Kyphrans."

At that moment, a tall and impressive-looking majer enters the mess, joining two overcaptains, and immediately declares, "As you were." Then he seats himself at the senior officers' table, and all the other officers seat themselves.

Captain Talaan asks quietly, "I heard that the Jeranyi armed a bunch of barbarians with shields and other weapons, and inflicted some severe casualties."

"They did," replies Alyiakal, taking a sip of the wine, far better than anything served at Pemedra.

"Were you . . . involved?"

Alyiakal smiles. "In a way. I commanded one of the two companies who destroyed them and fired the town. I was the junior captain. Captain Thallyr was in overall command. He might be an overcaptain by now. Solid officer."

Ghrennan nods. "That might explain why you're headed to Guarstyad. Do you have family around here?"

"I don't have any living family left. I spent time growing up around here, and I thought I'd visit the family of a friend nearby. Our leaves will cross for a few days, if we're fortunate."

"Better reason than for some leaves," offers Ghrennan in a bemused tone. "Never saw why some officers take leave in Cyad. Everything costs twice as much, and no one cares about junior officers. Have to be a subcommander to get much respect."

"Or an acclaimed majer," adds Talaan sardonically.

"Even they don't count much in Cyad," says a captain farther up the table.

Alyiakal serves himself firm-fleshed fish in a white sauce and a healthy helping of cheesed potatoes. The fish is clearly river trout, which Alyiakal hasn't tasted in years. He much prefers shellfish, but any kind of fish makes a good change, especially since the food at Pemedra had been bland and monotonously repetitive, if filling.

After a time, he asks Talaan, "Forest duty, patrolling the wall?"

"The southeast wall between here and Eastpoint."

"Does the northeast wall still have the greatest number of treefalls and Forest cats getting out?"

Talaan looks surprised. "You've had duty here?"

Alyiakal shakes his head. "Years ago, my father commanded Northpoint. He told me that then. I wondered if it had changed."

"We all get breakouts of a sort. There are more in the north, but not by much." Talaan pauses. "There's talk about not having a majer in command in Jakaafra, just having the captains in the north report directly to the commander here in Geliendra."

"That's still only talk," says Ghrennan. "Might happen, might not."

"When there's talk," replies Alyiakal, "there's either something behind it, or someone stirring up trouble. Sometimes both."

Ghrennan chuckles. "Something to that."

Alyiakal senses the older captain's amusement, and a certain discomfiture from Talaan.

Before anyone else can say anything, Ghrennan clears his throat and says to Alyiakal, "How cold does it get in Pemedra? I've served in Assyadt and Inividra. They didn't get much snow, and I hear Guarstyad does, even if it's a port town."

"Pemedra doesn't get that much snow, but it does get what they call thunder-snow. It comes over the hills in a quint or so and can drop knee-deep snow in less than a glass. Then it's gone. I had my doubts until my company got caught in one."

"How do you handle that?" asks Talaan.

"You gather the company tight and wait it out. The snow comes down so thick you can't see much more than a yard."

"Can't say I'm sorry to have missed that," replies Ghrennan.

After that, Alyiakal concentrates on finishing his meal.

When the majer signifies the end of the evening meal, Talaan immediately stands and then leaves with the captain with whom he'd been sitting.

Alyiakal turns to the older captain. "A pleasure meeting you."

"You be here for a bit?"

"Two eightdays, on and off."

"Then we'll likely be talking again." Ghrennan smiles warmly.

Alyiakal leaves the mess, then sees Talaan and his seatmate standing inside the outer door, talking in the dim light. After looking and noting that, for the moment, no one is watching, Alyiakal raises a concealment and moves closer to the two captains.

"What do you think of Alyiakal?" Talaan asks the other captain.

"He's had combat experience with two different kinds of barbarians. As the son of a majer, he likely knows more than most captains his age. He also had to be recommended for Guarstyad by someone who's evaluated combat officers."

"You're saying there's more there than I saw."

"Likely more than either of us saw. You heard his comment about talk. Most junior captains don't think that way. That kind of officer is dangerous." The other captain laughs softly. "That's another reason why he came recommended. Headquarters doesn't like dangerous officers. Don't worry about him. If he survives Guarstyad, he'll still be fortunate to make sub-majer."

Alyiakal flattens himself against the wall and waits until the two leave the building and for another pair of captains to pass and depart before he drops the concealment.

Dangerous officer? For doing things as well as you can?

He shakes his head and walks toward the visiting officers' quarters. More than anything else, at the moment he needs a good night of uninterrupted sleep.

XLVI

At the morning mess on oneday, Alyiakal carefully keeps his conversation innocuous, pleasant, and short. He ends up sitting beside Ghrennan and another captain and lets them do almost all the talking. He does ask about a tailor for new uniforms.

"They're all about the same," replies Ghrennan. "The post tailor costs a little more, and the fit's a little better. He also makes slightly more durable uniforms."

"What about boots?"

"Stay with the post cobbler."

After an entire morning occupied with various necessities, like having his dirty uniforms washed, Alyiakal takes both recommendations, first visiting the post tailor and commissioning four sets of uniforms, two of them winter uniforms, then going to the cobbler, where he orders a pair of heavier winter boots, because, between snow and flooding, having a spare pair of dry boots might be extremely useful in the seasons he will likely spend at Guarstyad.

He then makes his way to the stables, where he meets with the head ostler and arranges for a mount on twoday, given that Vaeyal is likely a two-glass ride, one way.

Since Geliendra Post itself doesn't look to have changed much since he last explored it some six years ago, Alyiakal decides to explore the town. The front gates are slightly more imposing than those at either Pemedra or Syadtar, and the guards incline their heads as he walks past them, if only in recognition. More than a few captains are posted at Geliendra, and captain is the most common officers' rank, since more than a few officers spend almost all their time in the Mirror Lancers as captains.

Which is fine if you start as a ranker, but not if you begin as an undercaptain.

He turns right outside the gates, in the direction of Vaeyal. The majority of the commercial establishments in the first block consist of those designed to relieve lancers, especially rankers, of their pay in some fashion. He counts three alehouses, two brothels—and has no doubt that two of the three boardinghouses also partly serve the same function—two coin lenders, and an actual bakery. By the time he walks three blocks, he sees the green and white awning of a coffee shop, which looks well-furnished and clean.

He decides to stop there. An older woman in green and white escorts him to a table for two. "Are you expecting someone, ser?"

"Just me. Coffee and the best pastry you have that doesn't depend on the filling."

"You sound like you appreciate quality in the basics."

Alyiakal smiles and says, "I hope so."

"You recently posted here?"

"I'm on leave. My great-aunt lived nearby. Well . . . not close. A town near Westend. I'm between postings and thought I'd visit friends."

"I hope they're expecting you. I've known officers to be . . . disappointed."

"They are. The family is that of a fellow officer."

"Better that than thinking some young woman will wait for you." She pauses. "But you're good-looking enough that one might. I'll be right back with your coffee and pastry." The server turns and walks toward the back of the shop.

Alyiakal surveys the shop, and the only other patrons. Two white-haired men at another table for two, playing Fyrr, and barely sipping their coffee, and two well-dressed women, possibly older than his server, who sit chatting over empty platters that suggest a long-finished meal of some sort.

The server returns with the coffee in the customary tall and narrow mug and a small platter holding a single pastry—composed of a thin strip of phyllo wound in a spiral from the center and then obviously baked until flaky-crisp and lightly sprinkled with small crystals of glazed pearapple syrup.

"Thank you. What do I owe you?"

"Four coppers."

Alyiakal gives her five.

"Enjoy the spiral."

"I'm sure I will." After the server leaves, Alyiakal takes a sip of the dark, strong, but not bitter coffee, followed by a bite of the crispy spiral. The light, flaky, and buttery pastry almost melts in his mouth, and the pearapple-syrup crystals are sparse enough that there's just enough sweetness.

Even before he finishes the spiral, he has the feeling he'll likely be visiting the coffeehouse again before he leaves Geliendra.

Then again, you haven't had much to eat except Mirror Lancer fare for the last six years. With that thought, he finishes his coffee and stands.

He might as well see what else Geliendra has to offer.

XLVII

On twoday, Alyiakal wakes early, thinking about the day ahead. While he knows a fair amount about Saelora's successes as a scrivener, an enumerator, and a junior trader, all he really knows about her is that her hair is reddish, but darker than that of Hyrsaal, and that she's somewhat above medium height, and has brown eyes. She's never mentioned any men besides her brother and those she has worked for, let alone a consort, but Alyiakal has never asked, either.

And you've never mentioned any women except working for Healer Vayidra.

Then he rises, washes, shaves, and dresses. He carefully checks his sabre, doubting that he'll need it, but since he'll be traveling a road between towns, there's always a possibility of trouble. Even if it's highly unlikely, he'd rather be prepared.

At breakfast, he sits with several captains he hasn't met, one of whom is on his way to take command of a company at Westend. Alyiakal is pleasant, but reveals as little as possible. After breakfast, he makes his way to the stable, where he meets and then saddles his mount, an older mare, under the watchful eye of the ostler. As usual, Alyiakal spends a little time, effort, and reassuring order on the mare.

When he leads her out of the stall, the ostler nods, then says, "Looks like you know a little about horses."

Alyiakal smiles. "I try to listen. They've saved my life more than once."

"You take care of them, and they'll take care of you."

"They already have."

Once mounted, Alyiakal rides out through the south gates and turns west on the main sunstone avenue, passing the green and white awning of the coffee shop. Less than a kay later, he reaches the last of the close-set houses and enters an area of small steads and smaller houses, where he sees men and women performing various harvest-related chores. The high trees bordering the steads are numerous enough that he can't see the white walls enclosing the Great Forest, but he can certainly sense, if faintly, the patterns of order and chaos.

At that realization, he stiffens in the saddle, recalling that he hadn't been able to do that when he was within yards of the walls. *But that was when you were younger and hadn't worked much with order and chaos.* Still, he wonders if he's grown more perceptive or if the Great Forest has grown in power.

He rides another kay, and the road forks. The left fork is sunstone, the right fork is a narrower worn gray stone road. At the fork, there is a kaystone. Below the arrow pointing to the southeast are the words SHAARN/FYRAD. Below the arrow pointing northwest is the word VAEYAL. Alyiakal turns the mare toward Vaeyal.

More than a glass later, the trees alongside the road thin out and the small steads give way to small fenced areas. Ahead he sees low houses and beyond them taller buildings.

Saelora's directions are simple. "Take the road from Geliendra until you reach the street closest to the Great Canal. Turn right and keep going until you reach the building with Vassyl's name on it."

When Alyiakal reaches Canal Street, he can finally see the Great Canal, almost adjoining the whitestone tow-roads that top the levees on each side of the canal reserved for the compact firetows to pull the barges up and down the canal. Between the east tow-road and Canal Street is a waist-high stone wall, unbroken except at designated loading/unloading areas. Except for the loading docks, the west side of Canal Street is bare of structures, and all those on the east side are constructed of either stone or brick, or both.

For several moments, Alyiakal admires the Great Canal, which he has not seen since he was a boy living with his great-aunt. Then he turns the mare to the right, away from the loading station and the wagons lined up there. While there are scattered wagons and carts along Canal Street, he doesn't see another rider. Three blocks later he sees a three-story building with a modestly large façade signboard—VASSYL, FACTOR & TRADER. Below the larger signboard is a smaller one that states: GREENBERRY SPIRITS.

Alyiakal smiles, then reins up the mare and dismounts, tying her to the sole hitching post he can find.

"Alyiakal! Or should I say 'Captain Alyiakal'?" says a woman who can only be Saelora. She stands in the doorway to the factorage.

Saelora isn't exactly as Alyiakal has imagined, since she's broad-shouldered, and only a few digits shorter than Alyiakal, who is slightly taller than most Mirror Lancer officers. She might even be taller than her brother. Her mahogany-red hair frames her strong, handsome, rather than pretty, face. Deep brown eyes focus on him, and he can't help but look straight back at her and smile.

After a moment, he realizes that she wears tailored blue trousers, with a matching blue vest—the colors and inside working garb of a Merchanter enumerator—over a cream shirt. Her smile holds the same infectious warmth as her brother's, however, and Alyiakal can see and sense that she's clearly pleased to see him.

"No sister would ever call a brother 'captain,'" he replies happily, grinning as he adds, "You were the one who said I should treat you as a sister."

She grins back. "I said '*write* me as you would a sister.' Don't stand on the street. Come in. Vassyl insisted that he has to meet you." She steps back from the doorway and gestures.

"Will the mare be safe here for a bit?" he asks.

"Certainly during the day."

"Is this also the primary place of business for Greenberry Spirits?" he asks as he approaches the door.

"For now. I've moved the distillery to the land with the greenberries. We needed more space. We can talk about that later."

Alyiakal follows her inside the factorage, carefully closing the door. The small and spare front of the factorage contains a waist-high oak counter with a polished, if battered, top extending across the entire front of the factorage, except at one end. Roughly four cubits behind the counter is a brick wall with a single iron-bound door—open for the moment.

Obviously, Vassyl handles valuable goods . . . or Vaeyal is more dangerous than it looks.

"Vassyl! I told you he'd be here today." Saelora walks around the counter, motioning for Alyiakal to follow.

"You don't have to shout," comes a raspy voice from beyond the open door.

"You wouldn't hear me if I didn't," returns Saelora, stepping through the door behind the counter.

Alyiakal follows . . . and is almost stopped in his boots. He has expected an expansive and dusty storeroom with rows and rows of shelves and more than a little clutter. Instead, the front section of the warehouse, for, given the size, it cannot be called anything else, contains two tasteful walnut desks, one on each side, with a Merchanter-blue carpet between them. A small walnut conference table stands in the middle of the carpet, with four matching chairs around it. Behind the tastefully furnished area that functions as a study there are rows and rows of shelves, but they are constructed of time-polished oak and look spotless.

The goods on them are neatly arranged as well. Alyiakal spots two sturdy, long ladders, well back along the shelves that stretch at least thirty yards back. A polished wooden staircase leads to the space over the entry area.

The man rising from the desk on the right is almost as tall as Alyiakal, but wiry and a good twenty-five years older. His Merchanter blues are of good quality, but are not of the shimmersilk purportedly worn by Merchanters in Cyad and those elsewhere of great wealth. He offers a pleasant and friendly smile, although Alyiakal senses a certain reserve. "Always glad to meet a man who keeps his word, especially to this Lady Merchanter. Oh . . . and I'm Vassyl."

"I've heard a great deal good about you," replies Alyiakal. "Saelora has written me about all you've done for her."

"No more than she's done in helping me return all this to what it should be. It took years."

"It only needed a tidy," says Saelora.

Vassyl shakes his head. "More than that. She's earned those blues. The bigger Merchanters are much friendlier these days. That's because they want access to the brandy . . . and now she's working on a special liqueur to go with it."

"No," says Saelora. "It's because you have unique goods people want."

"Which I couldn't find until you came along."

Saelora offers an amused headshake.

Alyiakal turns to her. "You didn't mention the liqueur."

"It's not ready, and we're not sure how well it will sell," she admits.

After a long moment of silence, Vassyl speaks. "Why don't you two go have something to eat at the coffee shop?" He looks to Alyiakal. "You can stable your horse in back in one of the empty stalls."

"You can do that," adds Saelora, "while I change." She drops her eyes for a moment. "I thought you'd be later. I'll meet you at the stalls." She hurries toward the back of the warehouse.

"Ride to the lane two doors up and turn right," suggests Vassyl. "Then take the first alley back down. I'll unbar the doors."

"Thank you. I would feel better about the mare." Alyiakal inclines his head, then walks back through the door to the front room of the factorage and then out to the mare.

A white-haired man in well-tailored Merchanter blues turns from where he had been looking at the mare and says, "I thought that was a Mirror Lancer mount. You posted at Geliendra, Captain?"

Alyiakal shakes his head. "I'm on leave, but the mare is theirs. I'm visiting friends."

"All sorts of folks be visiting Vassyl and the lady Merchanter these days. It's good to see. A pleasant day to you, Captain."

"The same to you."

Alyiakal unties the mare and mounts, following Vassyl's directions to the rear of the warehouse, where, true to his word, the Merchanter has the doors open. Alyiakal dismounts and leads the mare to the open end stall, reassuring her with kind words and a touch of order, before closing the stall.

Vassyl has left, and Saelora has closed and is barring the stable doors.

Alyiakal looks again at the four stalls, three of which now hold horses, the fourth of which holds hay and likely grain. Then he looks back to Saelora, now clad entirely in Merchanter blues, the tunic not that of an enumerator, but of a full trader. "You look most impressive." He gestures toward the horses. "I take it one of these is yours?"

"The roan gelding. I needed a way to get to all my growers. He's also strong enough that he can carry me and two kegs of the raw greenberry juice. Sometimes, I have to hire a wagon, but it's cheaper than owning one and another horse."

She turns and leads Alyiakal back through the spotless shelves of the warehouse and out into the counter area, where Vassyl speaks with the white-haired man Alyiakal met out front.

Alyiakal says nothing until they are on the side of the street walking north. "Do you know the white-haired man?"

"That's Rhobett. He and Vassyl grew up as neighbors. He owns one of the canal warehouses, but his two sons do all the work now. He stops by every so often. Sometimes, he even buys something."

"The greenberry brandy, I'd wager."

Saelora laughs. "Of course. He doesn't need much of anything else. He's always pleasant, though. Mostly, he talks to Vassyl."

Alyiakal sees the green and white awning ahead, several storefronts past the lane he'd taken to stable the mare. "I see we don't have far to go."

"We don't, and the fare is good."

Alyiakal has the feeling she isn't saying everything, but he nods and says, "After years of mess food, almost anything is welcome."

"You sound like Hyrsaal."

"I suspect he feels the same way."

When they enter the shop, only two of the half score of tables are occupied; an older woman server appears and looks questioningly at Alyiakal, and then Saelora.

"Celuisa, this is Captain Alyiakal. He's visiting on his leave. He's a friend of Hyrsaal's."

"I'm pleased to meet you," offers Alyiakal.

"At least you're good-looking," says Celuisa. "This way." Once she seats the two, she turns to Saelora. "You know the fare. I'll be back."

Alyiakal smiles, then says, "I take it you know her. She's not impressed with Mirror Lancers, it seems."

"She and Mother used to be . . . acquaintances. In a town this small, people get to know each other. Her consort was a lancer ranker, but he was killed. So her son was accepted for possible officer training. He wasn't as successful as you and Hyrsaal. He's serving in Biehl."

"It could be worse."

"Don't tell her that," replies Saelora softly and dryly.

"How are the pastries?" asks Alyiakal, thinking of his visit to the coffee shop in Geliendra.

"The spirals are good if you like crispy and flaky. My favorite is the almond-custard roll."

"That sounds decadent." He grins. "I'll try one."

When Celuisa returns, Alyiakal nods to Saelora.

"Coffee and the almond-custard roll."

"I'll have the same," says Alyiakal.

Celuisa nods and leaves the table.

"You look much like I thought you would," muses Saelora, before smiling and adding, "but I pestered Hyrsaal to describe you in detail."

"How am I different from what you pictured?"

"You're a little taller, and your hair is true black, not just dark. Hyrsaal said your eyes were green, but not the intense green they are. Most people with green eyes have watery green eyes. Your shoulders are broader, too."

So are yours. "Anything else?"

"My turn," she replies. "How am I different from what you thought?"

"You're taller. You said you were slightly above medium height."

Saelora blushes, if but slightly. "Most men don't like tall women."

"Your hair is . . . more alive. You said it was a darker red than Hyrsaal's. I'd say the same thing about your eyes. They're not muddy brown, but a strong piercing brown." Before she can press, he goes on, "I really wasn't trying to picture you. What you wrote"—*and that you kept writing*—"was far more important to me."

The return of Celuisa with the coffees and rolls saves Alyiakal from further questions about her appearance.

"That'll be six," says Celuisa evenly.

Alyiakal immediately comes up with seven coppers. "Thank you."

Celuisa nods and leaves the table.

"She'll have it all over Vaeyal that you had a young captain visiting you," speculates Alyiakal.

"Most likely, but since everyone knows Hyrsaal's a Mirror Lancer officer, it won't be much of a surprise. Besides, we're talking in midday at the coffee shop."

"Is Vassyl a widower?" asks Alyiakal. "From the way he talked . . ."

"He is. Farsella and his son got the red flux around eight years ago when they visited her mother in Jaarn. Elinjya, his second child, has never been interested in the factorage or trade, and she consorted a widower with a fair amount of land and a large house outside of Shaarn."

"How did you come to work for him?"

"I never planned it. Buurel asked me if I'd help Vassyl three years after Farsella died. She'd been the one who handled the coins and the shipping. We got on. I'm sort of the daughter Elinjya couldn't be."

Alyiakal notes the slight emphasis Saelora places on the word "daughter," but only says, "It sounds like he was really distraught."

"He was. But it's worked out for the best. Elinjya visits him now more than she ever did and brings her two little ones. She even thanked me. She told me that I'd done what she couldn't, and that she didn't have to feel quite so guilty about not wanting to work at the factorage."

"Can I ask about his son?"

Saelora shakes her head. "They were always at odds. Buurel told me that Evaant was too sloppy and never wanted to work hard. Vassyl seldom says much about him. Once in a while, he'll say something to the effect that he was likely too hard on both of them. I don't think so. I listen, and say something like we all have to do the best we know how, and no one is perfect."

"That's certainly true enough."

"How did you come to be a Mirror Lancer? All Hyrsaal said was that your father was a majer and that he thought you lost your mother young." She pauses, then says quietly, "I tried to let you know what I felt when Hyrsaal wrote that your father died."

"Your letter helped . . . it helped more than I could let you know then. You know about how it is."

"Not as much as you. I was so young when Father died. I just felt the emptiness in Mother."

"You felt enough, I'm certain. I was eight . . . when my mother died . . . that emptiness still comes back at times." Alyiakal pauses, then goes on. "You asked how I came to be a Mirror Lancer. I suppose the simple answer is I couldn't conceive of being anything else. My father hoped I could be of the Magi'i, but my talents there aren't suited to being more than a field healer."

"You're more than that." Saelora looks directly at him. "I don't know how much more or what, but Hyrsaal said that there was something about you. He's usually right about people . . . and I feel the same way."

Alyiakal offers an embarrassed smile, then says, "It's dangerous for me to say much or reveal much, but I can do a bit of real healing. That scares senior Mirror Lancer officers." Alyiakal knows there's a certain risk in revealing even that, but most of that is in his records, and he doesn't want to lie to Saelora.

But what you don't reveal is deceptive as well. For now, he can only avoid outright untruths, but perhaps . . . in time. If not, then what he has said isn't fatally damaging, although he is fairly certain that Saelora keeps confidences.

Her smile is amused. "You're being careful. I understand. I also appreciate your being as truthful as you can. Hyrsaal has mentioned how certain other officers tried to make your future more difficult."

Alyiakal is, again, thankful for Hyrsaal. After a moment, he goes on. "From what I've seen so far, I don't think I'd be better suited for anything else. What about you?"

"As I wrote you, I owe so much to Buurel and Vassyl. They're like favorite uncles. I don't know anything else that I'd like doing better." She pauses. "I can't say that to Mother, but I never wanted to stay home and raise children."

"Don't you think she knows that by now?"

"She does, but I still couldn't say it. It would belittle everything she's done, and it wouldn't come out right."

"I can see that." Alyiakal takes a sip of the not-quite-steaming coffee, then a bite of the almond-custard roll. "This is good. It's definitely decadent and fit for Cyad. That's a guess, because I've never been there, but all the officers hint that it's expensive and decadent."

"Someday, you'll be posted there."

"Most officers never make it," he points out.

"You will."

"You're kind . . . and don't tell me you're not."

She smiles ruefully. "How did you know I was going to say that?"

"It was a calculated guess, based on almost six years of letters."

"What did you do? Study them?"

"I had a great deal of time in the evening."

"Hyrsaal wrote something like that."

And he was posted in an actual city. "Junior officers have to get used to that. Most of us, anyway." He smiles. "Please tell me more about how you actually built a distillery from nothing."

"It started with little things. There are so many greenberries around here, but they're so bitter that even traitor birds and vulcrows won't eat them. I wrote you about Hyrsaal's idea, but even mixing the juice with pearapple juice didn't work . . ."

For the next glass, Alyiakal mostly listens, prompting her with occasional questions.

Then, abruptly, she stops talking and says, "I've enjoyed this so much, but I have to check the distillery. There's also a trader who sells spirits to an Austran Merchanter, and he'll be coming by sometime after fourth glass."

"I'd say I didn't mean to spend so much time with you, but I'd rather not lie." He stands. "What if I came back on fourday?" He'd rather come back on threeday, but that might be pushing it.

Saelora stands, more athletically than with studied grace. "Fourday . . . after second glass of the afternoon. We could have an early dinner. That way, you wouldn't have to ride back in the dark." She pauses, then adds, "You wouldn't want to stay at any of the inns here, and I wouldn't want you to."

And you can't really invite a strange man to stay with you and your mother . . . and your stipended and disabled brother.

Alyiakal leaves another copper on the table because of all the time they have spent and then walks out with Saelora. He can't say that he escorts her, but rather that they accompany each other.

When they enter the front door of the factorage, Vassyl stands behind the counter, listening to a burly bearded man. He nods to Saelora, but continues to listen to the other man.

". . . wouldn't know a graving iron from a bower if you showed him both . . . doesn't see the difference between a maul and an ax . . ."

". . . some folks are like that," replies Vassyl.

Saelora is the first into the study area and quietly closes the door, so that Alyiakal can no longer hear the conversation. Then she leads the way through the warehouse shelves to the stable.

Alyiakal stops short of the stall holding the mare and says, "Second glass on fourday."

She nods. "I'm so glad you came."

"So am I."

She unbars the stable doors and then opens them.

Alyiakal can sense her watching him as he leads the mare from the stable and out into the alley, where he mounts. Then he looks down at her and says, "On fourday," largely because he doesn't know what else to say.

"I'll be here."

He rides back along the way from the stable and to Canal Street, then past the factorage. Saelora is not out front watching.

Why should she be? Besides, she had to close up the stable.

As he turns onto the street that will become the gray stone road back to Geliendra, he discovers, realizes, really, that while he instinctively likes Saelora, and definitely wants to see her again, he is wary of saying too much.

Is it because you've never been that close to an attractive woman since Adayal?

Adayal had been very clear. *We have different paths.* And he had sensed the absolute firmness of that statement.

Alyiakal shakes his head as he rides eastward out of Vaeyal.

XLVIII

On threeday, Alyiakal takes out the mare again, but only to ride around Ge-liendra outside the post walls in order to get a better feel of the town. Unlike Jakaafra, the only buildings within half a kay of the Forest wall are those within the post walls, but Geliendra is unquestionably a much more prosperous town than Jakaafra, if the number of large houses is any indication.

He locates the market square, but does not enter because he would have to leave his mount, and while he can sense how trustworthy most people are, he worries about others he does not meet or know about. Besides, the square isn't that far away from the post gates.

You can come back on foot later.

Then he rides slightly west and takes a lane to get closer to the white sun-stone wall that stretches northwest from Geliendra. He reins up a good hun-dred yards from the wall, in the shade of a tree beside the lane, and, for a time, just looks at the wall and the Great Forest towering over the white barrier. Then he uses his order/chaos senses to discover what he can discern, and is surprised to find that he can indeed sense both the power of the Great Forest and the blackness of the flows of order and the tumbling whiteness of chaos behind the walls, as well as the curtain-like mixture of order and chaos created by the wards—an almost ugly combination.

Is that why the wards work? Or for some other reason.

For a time, he attempts to locate specific patterns within the walls, those that might be stun lizards or panther-cats, or giant snakes. Some patterns are clearer than others, but with some effort he can generally pick out most of the creatures.

When he hears a cart approaching, he halts his efforts and turns the mare.

The older man leading the horse and cart looks up to Alyiakal and says pleasantly, "I'd think you'd seen enough of the walls."

In return, Alyiakal smiles. "I grew up near the walls. I haven't been posted here. Not yet, anyway. I'm on leave, passing through."

The carter shakes his head.

Alyiakal rides back to the post and to the stables, where he dismounts and leads the mare back to her stall. He unsaddles and grooms her, quietly talking as he does. When he finishes and closes the stall door, he sees the head ostler walking toward him.

"How was she?" asks the ostler. "You have any trouble?"

Alyiakal shakes his head. "She's a good mount. Very responsive. She's in good condition. That has to be your doing."

"Thank you, ser. We all work with all the mounts. You have a good ride?"

"I did. I rode around the town to get familiar . . . in case I'm ever posted here." Alyiakal pauses. "Tomorrow, I'll need a mount for the afternoon and early evening, but I should be back before sunset. Will that be a problem?"

"No, ser. You could take her overnight if you have a safe place to stable her."

"I won't need that now. I might in a few days. My friend might get back on his reposting leave, but we'll have to see."

"You said you're headed to Guarstyad?"

"That's what my orders say."

The ostler shivers. "Too cold for me, from what I hear."

"I'm sure I'll find out," replies Alyiakal pleasantly. "Thank you. Until tomorrow afternoon."

"Yes, ser."

The ostler turns and walks back toward the tack room.

Alyiakal moves close to the stall and glances around. When he's sure that no one is looking, he raises a concealment and uses his senses and follows the ostler because his senses tell him that the ostler hasn't come to talk just by happenstance.

He stops outside the open tack room door, but he can hear clearly enough.

". . . went and talked to him like you asked, ser."

To Alyiakal, that suggests that the ostler is talking to an officer, but he can only discern that the other figure is a man.

"What did he have to say?"

"He said that he'd ridden around Geliendra to get familiar with the town in case he was ever posted here."

"Nothing else?"

"He's waiting to meet a friend—another officer who'll be on leave soon. That's what he said. He said the mare was a good mount. Not much more than that."

"You've seen officers come and go. What was your feeling about him?"

"He's good with horses. They like him. That says a lot."

"I don't care what the horses think. What do you think?"

"I go with the horses, ser. They're more often right than I am."

Alyiakal can't quite make out the officer's quiet return, but he definitely senses the man's unhappiness with the ostler's views. He eases his way back to the mare's stall, and when he's alone, he drops the concealment and says a few more words to the mare before leaving and making his way back to the visiting officers' quarters.

Once back in his temporary room, he ponders who at Geliendra is interested in him and why. The unnamed captain he'd met the first night? Alyiakal is certain that he had never met the man before, and the brief conversation the two captains had suggested that neither knew him prior to their meeting.

You don't know enough. But then, junior captains never do.

He returns to thinking about Saelora. From her letters, he had the impression of intelligence and ambition, but, as with some people, she doesn't write as well as she speaks. It's clear that she has a talent for organizing people and things without being overbearing and offensive.

That's a rare skill.

Later, after more thought, and not just about Saelora, Alyiakal arrives at evening mess looking for Ghrennan, but doesn't see the older captain and finds himself sitting across from another captain roughly his age, although Alyiakal is certain that they've never met.

"I'm Alyiakal, on leave, before reporting to Guarstyad."

"Jaenstyd. I'm on my way to Northpoint."

"It's not a bad post. Jakaafra is a decent town."

"You've been posted there?"

Alyiakal shakes his head. "No. My last post was Pemedra, but my father was the commanding majer at Northpoint years ago. Where were you posted before?"

"Dellash."

Alyiakal frowns. "I'm not familiar with Dellash, except that it's on Esalia." Esalia is the large island off the coast west of Summerdock.

Jaenstyd laughs. "Not many people are. It's the only port on Esalia, and the only town of any size."

"The post handles port security and smugglers?"

"Exactly. Not terribly exciting."

"A friend of mine has a similar post at Summerdock. From what he's written, his company's had to deal with quite a few smugglers."

"We had to deal with some smugglers, but we also had to support the Imperial enumerators. Some of the outland traders weren't too interested in paying tariffs . . ."

Alyiakal mostly listens.

Then the captain beside Jaenstyd says, "Pemedra. Did you ever run across a Captain Prekius?"

"There was an Undercaptain Prekius. He was killed in an ambush by barbarian raiders before I arrived."

"Oh . . . I never heard about that."

"I'm sorry," says Alyiakal. "I wouldn't have known except I was his replacement. If you don't mind, what was he like?"

"I really didn't know him. We were at Kynstaar together. By the way, I'm Nyell. Temporary duty here."

Alyiakal nods. Temporary duty is usually in an administrative position while an officer recovers from a wound or injury. He gingerly extends his senses, but doesn't find any chaos or anything unusual.

"It's not from an injury." Nyell smiles wryly. "I was due to go to Luuval, you know, where two companies watch almost a hundred kays of coast for smugglers. Most of the town slid into the ocean after a storm in the middle of Harvest. It sort of . . . slumped, I heard. Most everyone in the post survived. The town wasn't so fortunate, and headquarters hasn't figured out what to do with the post."

"I hadn't heard about that," says Alyiakal.

"How would you," replies Nyell amiably, "you were on the other side of Cyador at one of the most isolated posts." He pauses. "You obviously survived the barbarian raiders. Are they that bad?"

"Some are so hopeless you almost feel sorry for them, and some are both good and angry enough to inflict considerable casualties. When you're patrolling there, you run across both. At least, I did."

"It sounds like Prekius wasn't so fortunate."

"From reading the patrol report, I got the impression he hadn't expected an ambush."

"I heard there were more than a few things he didn't expect," says Nyell. "He came from a wealthy Merchanter family in Cyad."

Jaenstyd winces.

Nyell nods. "He should have gotten smuggling duty, but . . ." He shrugs.

The family golds made sure he got what he wanted, at least partly.

Then Nyell says, "I overheard you're on leave before you go to Guarstyad. Back here to see old friends?"

"Actually, to see a newer friend and his family. He and I went through Kynstaar together. Quarters at his family are cramped, though. So I've been riding there. I've been impressed by the mounts and stables here."

"I imagine they have to be good, handling all the Forest patrols."

"I haven't met the officer in charge, only the ostlers."

"Oh . . . that's Captain Warbaan. He's an older captain. He seems solid. Doesn't say much."

"Sometimes, results tell you more than words," replies Alyiakal, fixing Warbaan's name in his mind.

"Results always tell you more," agrees Nyell.

For the short time remaining before the senior officer stands to signify the meal is over, the three captains trade agreed-upon generalities.

When Alyiakal walks back to the visiting officers' quarters, he can't help thinking about the meal, and who was and wasn't in the mess and at Geliendra. So far he has not seen any officer he met or can remember from six years earlier, but Nyell's question about Prekius suggests the officer corps is small enough that in any gathering there's a good chance some of those present know others or of them. That understanding doesn't tell him why Warbaan, most likely, but not definitely, is interested in him.

XLIX

The greatest Magi'i of the First and the late Emperor of Light all cautioned that the Great Forest must remain inviolate, not for its sake, but for the sake of Cyador. The amount of order and chaos held within those walls, if unleashed, could remove most of Cyador from existence in less than a glass, if not in moments. The walls and wards represent no more than a truce between the Great Forest and the Magi'i of the First. Should any organized force of Cyador attack or encroach upon the Great Forest, that truce is voided, and the Forest will no longer be bound. In a similar fashion, if Cyador can no longer maintain the walls and wards, the truce is also voided.

The use of magery against any aspect of the Great Forest within the walls is absolutely forbidden, and the penalty for such efforts is death because such efforts hazard all that is and will be Cyador . . .

For these reasons, the Mirror Lancer patrols of the walls are as much to keep those of Cyador from despoiling the Forest as to keep any creatures who escape from the Forest from harming the people of Cyador . . .

Some individuals live within the warded walls, but they are creatures of the Forest. Should they emerge, they should be first encouraged to return from whence they came and only if they refuse should they be destroyed, as with other creatures of the Great Forest . . .

Fragment, Mirror Lancer Archives
Zaenth'alt, Captain-Commander
Cyad, 45 A.F.

L

On fourday afternoon, Alyiakal leaves the post stables at Geliendra roughly a quint after first glass. While he talks briefly with the head ostler before saddling the mare and leading her out of the stable, he doesn't see any officers in or around the stables, which is understandable in early afternoon. Mounted patrols depart early and usually return late, and officers inspect early in the day and check again late in the afternoon.

Usually, anyway.

He wears his lighter riding jacket because, by the time he'd returned from Vaeyal on twoday evening, he'd definitely felt chilled by the damp early-Autumn breeze, and he suspects he'll be at least a little later. He does wonder what Saelora has in mind for the early dinner.

Not only what, but where, since she mentioned it being crowded at her mother's house.

As he nears the south gates of the post, he sees a firewagon coming through, and a firewagon inside a post is something he's never encountered before, although it suggests to him that the firewagon carries someone of import, possibly at least a commander from Mirror Lancer headquarters. He eases the mare to the side of the sunstone pavement and waits for the firewagon to pass.

As it does, he senses a significant amount of chaos surrounding someone in the forward passenger compartment. That puzzles Alyiakal, because from what Vayidra had told him, any mage who carries that much chaos around his body without shielding himself is likely to have a very short life—and Alyiakal can detect only a comparatively minimal amount of order amid all the chaos.

The firewagon does not stop or even slow, and Alyiakal can only assume his shields have kept the mage from sensing that Alyiakal has some abilities of the Magi'i. Or that the mage's order/chaos senses are so blinded by all that free chaos that he can't sense at any great distance. Or possibly, he simply isn't paying attention.

While Alyiakal would like to know which might be the reason, he's happy to go unnoticed. After the firewagon passes him and heads toward the headquarters building, he eases the mare forward and toward the gates.

He slows the mare as he approaches the closest guard and asks, "Do you know who that was?"

The guard glances up. "No, ser. We were told a commander and one of the high Magi'i were coming this eightday. No one gave names."

"Thank you. I wondered. I've never seen a firewagon enter a post before."

"Me, neither, ser."

Alyiakal continues to wonder if, by high Magi'i, the one in the firewagon might be the Third Magus, simply because he can't imagine the First or Second Magus coming all the way from Cyad to visit a Mirror Lancer post, even one as important as Geliendra.

Except the First of the Magi'i designed the chaos towers and wards.

He shakes his head and turns the mare onto the street that leads to the road west out of Geliendra.

As he rides, his thoughts go back to the firewagon and the near encounter with a powerful magus. After being posted to Pemedra, he's now on his way to Guarstyad. Syadtar or Pemedra didn't have mages, and, given the situation at Guarstyad, he doubts that there will be any there, either.

Did Majer Klaavyl try to make sure that you weren't stationed near mages? Or Tygael? Or is all that coincidental because they tried to give you another posting where you have a chance to establish a solid record of accomplishment?

While it could be coincidental, Alyiakal isn't a great believer in coincidences. He also wonders, not for the first time, why Majer Klaavyl was ordered to Cyad so abruptly, with no replacement selected.

Over the next glass, he encounters several wagons, one of which is high-sided and covered, and requires a four-horse team. The side of the wagon proclaims, in plain letters, FYRAD TRANSPORT. While there is an armed guard seated beside the teamster, there aren't any mounted guards escorting the wagon. He eases the mare to one side of the sunstone-paved road twice for Mirror Lancer dispatch riders, one pair headed to Geliendra and one pair headed away and most likely to Fyrad. Once on the road to Vaeyal, he encounters only two carts until the town is almost in sight, when he passes several women pushing empty handcarts and heading away from the town, suggesting that they'd brought produce to sell at the market square and have been successful.

When he reaches Canal Street, he sees several barges moored at the unloading area, and a handful of wagons being either loaded or offloaded, perhaps both. He turns the mare toward Vassyl's factorage. When he reaches it, as he starts to dismount, Saelora appears in the doorway wearing full Merchanter blues.

"Just ride around to the stable. I'll meet you there." She smiles, then steps back inside the factorage and closes the door.

When Alyiakal reaches the rear of the factorage, he finds Saelora waiting for him, mounted upon the roan gelding. The stable doors are closed.

"We have to ride somewhere for dinner?" he asks with a smile.

"If you don't mind," she replies. "It's not that far."

"Which way?"

"North on Canal Street."

"You lead the way."

Once on Canal Street, where they ride almost abreast, with Saelora slightly in the lead, Alyiakal has the definite feeling that more than a few eyes turn to them, but almost immediately lose interest. For a moment, he wonders why, but then laughs.

"Something amusing?"

"As a matter of fact, yes. A number of people have been looking at us, and then they lost interest."

"Of course. You're in uniform, wearing your visor cap. I'm the only woman who can wear Merchanter blues, but when they see your uniform, they think I'm riding with my brother."

"You haven't told me where we're going."

"I thought you'd like to see the distillery before we eat."

Alyiakal can sense that she's not telling him everything, but there's no feeling of chaos, which suggests she wants to surprise him. So, as they ride past the coffee shop, he says, "I'd like that."

"We'll turn left in two blocks."

The street on which they turn is also stone-paved, but older than Canal Street and the main road to Geliendra.

"This is the old road, but it ends about three kays out."

"Old road? But it ends?"

"About thirty years ago a whole section of it collapsed into a sinkhole," explains Saelora. "The Mirror Engineers investigated. They said there was no point in trying to rebuild it because it would happen again. They were right in a way. It's become a swampy lake that's slowly getting bigger on the east end. The west end is rocky and solid. You'll see."

Alyiakal studies the buildings and houses along the old road, which look older than those along the Vaeyal road. After riding about half a kay, Alyiakal sees only small houses on modest plots flanking the road, and grass grows between the stones near the edges of the paving. The ground and the road begin a gradual rise.

Ahead on the left are two brick buildings. The nearer one is long and narrow and looks to be two stories high. The long side parallels the road and is only three or four yards from the road. The second is a dwelling with an attached stable.

"The long building is the distillery?"

"It is. We're going to ride almost to the end of the road first, though."

Almost? The road seems to level off at the top of the rise several hundred yards ahead. Alyiakal says nothing, and the two keep riding, first past the distillery, then past the house, where he notices smoke coming from the chimney, although the day isn't all that cool.

As the mare carries Alyiakal to the top of the rise, he realizes that, first, there are no more trees ahead, and second, a pile of stones blocks the road. The mare lifts her head, and he can sense her unease. Then he sees that, beyond the stones, the ground slopes unevenly down to what Saelora accurately described as a swampy lake. He reins up and looks to his right. The ground to the east of the small house slopes more gradually, but unevenly, and almost everything is covered in greenberry bushes, which extend to just short of the swampy water and at least two hundred yards to the north.

"So these are your personal greenberry fields?"

"They are."

"You obtained the land at a much lower price because it's not much good for anything else?"

Saelora nods. "I can use bruised pearapples for the syrup as well. If we're careful."

Alyiakal shakes his head. "I can see why Vassyl backed your selection as a Merchanter."

"Now, we need to go and have dinner at the house. It's not finished, not the way I want, but I'm sure you'll understand."

"You're cooking as well?"

Saelora offers a sheepish grin. "No. I'm . . ." She pauses. "I'm an awful cook. No one in the family will eat anything I fix. I wanted you to have a good home-prepared meal, and I wanted us to have some quiet time together. Laetilla minds the distillery, and *she's* an excellent cook. It's a benefit for both of us." She turns the roan gelding and starts back.

Alyiakal rides beside her. "How did you get the distillery building built so quickly?"

"I already had some older masons working on it when I first wrote you. The distillery walls are built of old brick they knew where to get. The roof is of whatever slate I could get cheaply."

"How did you get masons—"

"Vaeyal is an old town. There are more masons than work."

Some of them doubtless wanted to help an attractive and ambitious young woman—or their consorts wanted them to.

"Has your mother seen all this?" Alyiakal gestures toward the distillery and then the small house. "Or Karola?"

"Hardly. Mother is appalled that I'd even consider living close to the angel-cursed swamp. She knows I have the distillery here. A distillery close to a swamp makes sense to her. Karola wouldn't be impressed with a building that looks like it was built of leftovers and a small run-down house."

As they near the house, Alyiakal sees that the shutters and iron-bound front door look sturdy, and paving stones cover the area in front of the stable with a walk from the stable to the front door and to the road. Then he glances back at the distillery building and sees that the space between the loading doors and the road is also paved. "I see you found a use for the paving stones that I assume came from the end of the road."

"It seemed like a good idea." Saelora reins up in front of the stable and dismounts.

Alyiakal does as well. Before he leads the mare into the space that is half stable and half barn and attached to the house, Alyiakal notices that the heavy timbers of the stable doors look recently replaced, although the wood is certainly not recently milled. The heavy bars and slot timbers would make breaking in close to impossible.

"Take the second stall," calls Saelora from inside the stable.

"Thank you." Alyiakal leads the mare to the indicated stall in the very neat and well-swept barn. "I can tell this is definitely your stable."

"There's more to do, but that will have to wait."

By the time Alyiakal has the mare in the stall and the door closed, Saelora stands beside a narrow door into the house.

"We'll go in this way. I hope you don't mind coming through the kitchen."

Alyiakal thinks about saying that such an entry is usual for family—and decides against it. He follows her into the kitchen, which, although scrubbed and clean, definitely looks old and worn. A small graying woman standing beside an old iron box stove turns.

"Laetilla, this is Captain Alyiakal."

"I'm pleased to meet you," Alyiakal replies warmly. "I understand you've been a great help to Saelora."

Laetilla inclines her head. "She's been a great boon to me, ser."

Alyiakal can sense the total honesty behind those words and wonders how bad life had been for the older woman.

"Laetilla's too modest," says Saelora. "She's made everything so much easier. Without her, some things wouldn't have been possible."

"It's good, but rare," replies Alyiakal, "when matters work out that way."

"I'll let you know when dinner is ready," says Laetilla to Saelora.

"Thank you." Saelora leads the way into the front room, sparsely furnished with two wooden armchairs, softened by matching blue cushions. A low table sits between them, and there is no other furniture. Again, the room is worn, but clean. She takes the chair closest to the door into the kitchen.

Alyiakal settles into the other chair.

"As you can see," says Saelora, "the house needs a great deal more work, but the roof and walls are sound. I haven't really changed much. This front parlor is the same, and so is the kitchen. I turned the bedroom behind the kitchen into a dining room by adding a table and chairs and an old sideboard. That way the kitchen has space. The main bedroom is the same, and the other bedroom is part study . . . or will be. Right now, it's empty. About all that's in my bedroom are a bedstead, two small tables, an old chest, and a stool."

Alyiakal nods. "Are the heavy doors and shutters for her or you or both?"

"Both. They seemed wise. Laetilla has quarters at one end of the distillery. She prefers it that way. Those doors and shutters are even stronger. She's from Fyrad. Her consort leaves something to be desired, especially if he spends too much time at the alehouse. Once their son joined the Naval Marines, she left him and came here."

"Why here?"

"Because she knew no one here. Neither does her consort. She was working at the Vaeyal Inn, making almost nothing. I could pay her more, and I really needed someone most of the time to work at the distillery."

"So she gets paid more and has a clean and safe place to live, and you have someone dependable to handle the distillery . . . and occasionally cook." After a moment, Alyiakal adds, "You amaze me with all you've done in the last six years."

"Not quite six," she protests.

"All I've done is to learn about horses and how to ride them and listen to them, how to kill raiders effectively while not getting killed, and a bit about how to heal people who aren't too badly injured."

"How about leading lancers so that they don't get killed either?" she asks gently.

"The ones who died under my command might disagree with you on that."

"Hyrsaal wagered that your company more than held its own and had fewer casualties. He told me to ask you if that was so."

Alyiakal isn't quite certain how much to say. "I don't know"—*not for certain*—"about how effectively I dealt with raiders as company officer. I was told that I had the fewest casualties."

Saelora offers an amused smile. "Did anyone complain about your not being effective enough? Ever?"

"No," admits Alyiakal sheepishly.

"So, you were at least as effective as other captains, and possibly more. And you had fewer casualties. That says you're very effective. Or am I missing something?"

"I don't think you miss much," replies Alyiakal wryly.

"She does not," says Laetilla from the kitchen doorway. "Dinner is ready."

"Then we should eat." Saelora stands.

So does Alyiakal, following Saelora into the narrow hallway and then into the dining room, which contains only what Saelora has mentioned. Except that a Merchanter-blue tablecloth covers the table, lit by a three-taper candelabrum in the middle. The two places are set across from each other in the middle of the table, with silver cutlery and utensils and two blue-tinted crystal wineglasses. A single white porcelain platter edged in blue is at each place setting.

Saelora takes her seat even before Alyiakal has a chance to seat her.

"It's a simple dinner—roasted game hens with a wine and herb glaze, rice and raisins with a thicker version of the glaze, and green beans with crushed nuts in butter."

Alyiakal manages not to burst into laughter as he sits down. "You may call it simple, but it's the most elegant meal I've had in more than six years." *More elegant than I've ever had.*

Saelora lifts her wineglass. "To a good dinner and better conversation."

Alyiakal lifts his glass in return. "To the most excellent Merchanter Lady I've ever known and likely ever will."

Saelora blushes. "You don't know that."

"The first half is absolutely true. I'd still wager on the second."

"Don't say more until you taste the wine . . . and the dinner."

He takes a sip of the pale, almost colorless, gold wine. "This is excellent." He would have said that it was the best he's ever had, but that means little because he knows, from what other officers have said, that he's never tasted a really outstanding vintage.

"It's a good wine. The dinner should be better."

Alyiakal still waits until she begins before he samples his game hen. "This is not only elegant. It's the best fowl I've ever tasted." The rice is equally good, and after tasting the green beans, Alyiakal wonders if he'll ever again be able to swallow the spring beans such as those grown around Pemedra.

He eats slowly, enjoying each mouthful. After more than a few mouthfuls, he stops and says, "If anyone let Laetilla go, they weren't very smart."

"Those at the inn never asked if she could cook."

Alyiakal almost shakes his head, then says, "Her skill would be wasted there."

"That's what she thought."

"I can't tell you how much this dinner . . . everything means to me."

"Alyiakal . . . your letters have meant more than you know. You deserve a few good things in life."

"I suspect you do as well."

"People have helped me. You wrote me and encouraged me. Buurel helped me, and so did Vassyl. Laetilla has helped me, too."

"You helped them as well."

Saelora laughs softly. "Just enjoy the rest of your meal."

Alyiakal does, even if he does offer more than a few additional compliments, which Saelora deserves.

When he finishes the last morsel of rice, he says, "Thank you . . . again. It was all wonderful."

"You're not done. We do have a modest dessert. A special tart."

Catching a touch of amusement in Saelora's voice, Alyiakal asks warily, "What kind of tart?"

"We'll let you decide for yourself."

Laetilla appears and removes the platters, then refills the wineglasses. She leaves the dining room and returns with two smaller plates. In the middle of each is clearly a tart, with pearapple slices embedded in a greenish glaze. She smiles and leaves.

Alyiakal looks at the tart and grins. "I have a strong suspicion . . ."

"Just try it."

"I will if you will."

She smiles in return and cuts a section of the tart, then slips it into her mouth.

Alyiakal does the same. The taste isn't the cloying sweetness of ripe pearapple syrup, nor is it bitter, but there's a sharpness that somehow makes the pearapple intense without it being sweet. The second bite is even better, and before he knows it, there are only a few crumbs and smears of glaze on the plate.

He looks across the table. Saelora's plate is equally bare. "That . . . it's dessert magery. How? Baking the greenberry brandy into the glaze?"

"It's more than that, but mostly." Her smile fades a bit. "It's too good and different for Vaeyal, Laetilla says."

"She might be right." Alyiakal straightens in his chair. "This has been the most wonderful meal."

"You said that before." Her tone is warm, and so are her eyes.

"I meant it both times." Despite what Saelora has said about his letters, Alyiakal can't help but wonder why she has gone to such lengths. Finally, he says, "I don't know how to say this. You've been wonderful . . ." He can immediately feel apprehension. "No. I'm not going to disappoint you. I wouldn't want to hurt you in any way. I'm overwhelmed. You've been so open, and this dinner . . . everything. I feel like I don't deserve it."

"You do. For six years, you've written. Every season, you've been in danger in some way. You've written. You've been encouraging—"

"So have you. When there was no one there, your letters were there—"

"Exactly." Saelora smiles warmly again. "So were yours, and you've never asked for anything."

"Neither did you."

"I'm not asking now, either. This evening . . . the coming days . . . are what they will be. I don't know what comes next, and neither do you. I do know some things. I can't cook, and I don't want to learn. I do know I want to be a successful Merchanter with her own Merchanting house. I don't even know if I want to be consorted. I don't know if I want children. I certainly don't want them anytime soon. I do know that I want to be close to you in some way . . . always."

Alyiakal swallows, and finds his eyes are burning. "I know less than you, in most ways."

"I know that, too. The very strictness and dangers you face mean that there's much you haven't thought about or felt. You couldn't. You need to now. When you're not in danger. It wouldn't be right or fair if you don't. I can't do that to you, and I won't let either of us do it to me."

"So . . . day by day?"

She smiles softly.

"Tomorrow or sixday?"

"What do you think?"

"Tomorrow. Then we'll see."

"Third glass of the afternoon, then." She stands. "You need to leave. I don't want you on the road late."

Alyiakal stands as well. "I don't want to be on the road late." *But then, I don't want to be on the road at all right now.* He steps around the table and takes her hand, then lifts and kisses it. "This . . . all this . . . was special. No one . . . has ever . . ."

"You deserve special."

"So do you."

She smiles broadly, but with a hint of the impish. "Who said it wasn't special for me, too?"

LI

Alyiakal sleeps well on fourday evening, but wakes early on fiveday, thoughts circling through his head. In some ways Saelora is exactly like her letters, but in others, she turned out to be much more than he realized.

Far more ambitious, and definitely far more able . . . and with an understated but very good sense of humor.

Saelora is also incredibly different from Adayal, the only other woman he has known closely. Alyiakal also realizes, after a moment, that while he has much to learn about Saelora, after almost six years of corresponding, he knows far more about her than he does about Adayal.

So why do you still think about Adayal? He smiles wryly. *As if you don't know.*

Since he's awake, and unlikely to go back to sleep, Alyiakal gets up and makes ready to go to the officers' mess for breakfast.

When he enters the mess, he sees Ghrennan, and the older captain is already seated with officers Alyiakal has seen before, but never met. Alyiakal ends up sitting across from Nyell and beside another captain, who gives his name as Dhenaal.

"We didn't see you last night," offers Nyell.

"I was visiting friends in Vaeyal. I didn't get back until after dinner."

"If you got fed, you likely did better than here," says Dhenaal.

"I have to say it was a very good dinner." Alyiakal doesn't want to talk dinner or Saelora, or mislead the other officers, so he immediately goes on, "As I was leaving the post yesterday, I saw a firewagon coming in. I've never seen a firewagon enter any Mirror Lancer post."

"It doesn't happen often," replies Dhenaal. "Subcommander Zaentyl appeared briefly at evening mess to announce that the Third Magus and a senior commander from headquarters are visiting Geliendra as part of an inspection of the chaos towers and the wards confining the Great Forest. I'm more than happy they're doing it."

"I can't imagine why," says Nyell dryly.

"Have you had any major treefalls or large numbers of Forest creatures?" asks Alyiakal.

"Hardly a patrol goes by when we don't see something, but in the last year we've only had one large trunk come down. There were at least three cats, and one stun lizard. We were fortunate to lose only one man. Another had his thoughts so scrambled he couldn't think straight for almost an eightday."

Alyiakal offers an appropriate wince.

"I'm happy you're handling that," says Nyell. "I'd rather deal with smugglers and barbarians and weapons I can see."

After that, the conversation covers handling smugglers and barbarian raiders, which is fine with Alyiakal.

As Alyiakal gets up from the table, an overcaptain approaches and gestures, "Captain Nyell, Captain Alyiakal, Subcommander Zaentyl would appreciate seeing you both in his study. It will only take a moment, but he likes to be familiar with all the officers at the post, even those here only for short periods." The overcaptain turns, clearly expecting the two captains to follow him from the mess to the post headquarters building.

From the chaos flows around the overcaptain, Alyiakal knows that the senior officer has not conveyed everything. The fact that the summons included Nyell suggests that Alyiakal isn't being singled out. But he still worries. Knowing that there is a powerful magus on the post, he also checks and strengthens his outer camouflage shield.

After they enter the post headquarters, the overcaptain stops in what has to be the anteroom to the subcommander's study and turns. "He'll see each of you individually. Captain Nyell, you go in first."

Even before the overcaptain speaks, Alyiakal can sense the strong flows of chaos behind the closed door. He's known for years that, sooner or later, he'd have to face the Magi'i, and he's not exactly looking forward to it, but he can only hope that his shields will suffice to conceal the full extent of his abilities, especially since he doubts they're a match for the Third Magus.

Nyell enters the study, and the overcaptain closes the door before turning to Alyiakal and saying, "These meetings are usually short."

Alyiakal senses nothing being withheld or evaded and nods.

"You're headed for Guarstyad?"

"I'll be leaving for Fyrad on the oneday after the next."

"You couldn't take all your home leave?"

Alyiakal shakes his head. "Not if I wanted to accept the posting."

"Sometimes it happens that way. More than sometimes, if you want to advance."

"I've seen that, ser."

Neither says more until Nyell opens the door and steps out into the anteroom.

"Captain Alyiakal." The overcaptain gestures.

Alyiakal steps into the study, closing the door after he enters. He finds himself facing three men standing beside the polished goldenwood desk that is Subcommander Zaentyl's. Beside the subcommander stands a commander, and beside him a lean man in the white tunic and trousers of the Magi'i with a cloud of unseen chaos surrounding him and with the crossed lightning bolts on his collar—the sign of a high magus.

Alyiakal thinks the commander is familiar, but he is far more concerned about the high magus.

"Captain Alyiakal," says Zaentyl, "I'd like you to meet Commander Dahlvor and Third Magus Verinaar. They're here to inspect the operation of the chaos towers, and since I wanted to meet you, I thought it might be useful for you to meet them."

"I'm honored, ser." Alyiakal inclines his head respectfully.

"You're on home leave before assuming a post at Guarstyad?"

"Yes, ser."

"You must have considerable combat experience then."

"Three years at Pemedra, ser."

"Were you involved in the successful expedition against the Jeranyi barbarians in the West Branch valley?" asks Dahlvor.

"Yes, ser, but there were two companies. Captain Thallyr—he might be an overcaptain now—was in overall command."

"I imagine," continues Dahlvor, "your company was also deeply involved?"

"Yes, ser, but not quite so much as First Company."

"There was also an expedition dealing with Cerlyn?"

"Yes, ser. That was my company."

"Just your company?"

"Yes, ser."

"That explains your posting." Dahlvor inclines his head to the Third Magus.

"Captain Alyiakal," says Verinaar, "you hold more order than most officers."

"I've been told that, Highest. That was why I was given additional training in field healing."

"Has that training proved useful?" asks Dahlvor.

"I believe so, ser, although my use of that training has been limited to times after fighting."

"As it should be." The commander frowns. "You look familiar but I don't believe we've met."

"There are two possibilities, ser. My father was Majer Kyal, who commanded at Inividra and Assyadt. I'm said to resemble him somewhat. I was also commissioned at Kynstaar standing next to your son Vordahl, when you spoke to all the new undercaptains."

Dahlvor smiles wryly. "Both possibilities are correct. I did meet your father briefly." He turns to Verinaar. "My apologies, Highest."

The Third Magus smiles pleasantly, although Alyiakal can sense the expression is practiced and does not reveal a certain irritation with the Mirror Lancer commander. Then Verinaar addresses Alyiakal again. "When we arrived at Geliendra after midday yesterday, we passed a mounted officer. Were you that officer?"

"I left to visit the family of a fellow officer somewhat after first glass yesterday afternoon when I saw a firewagon coming and moved aside. If you were in that firewagon, then I was that officer."

"Excellent," declares Verinaar, in a tone of satisfaction as he looks to Subcommander Zaentyl. "Captain Alyiakal is close to having the capabilities of a healer. He's probably done some healing without knowing it. It's rare in men, but not unheard of. You're fortunate to have him."

Zaentyl nods, and Alyiakal can sense that, in some fashion, the subcommander is pleased.

Because that explains to him why you're being posted to Guarstyad? Or for some other reason?

Alyiakal waits, not knowing what to expect, hoping that his shields are sufficient to hide the full scope of his abilities.

Commander Dahlvor smiles. "A pleasure to meet you, Captain. I wish you well in Guarstyad."

"Thank you, ser." Alyiakal again inclines his head.

"We won't take any more of your time," adds Zaentyl.

"By your leave, sers, Highest?"

"Enjoy your time here," says Dahlvor.

Alyiakal turns and leaves the study. He is careful to close the door behind himself as he steps into the anteroom.

"That's all, Captain," says the overcaptain.

"Thank you, ser."

Alyiakal doesn't take a deep breath until he is out of the headquarters building. While he *thinks* his shields may have hidden his abilities, there's also the possibility that the Third Magus is so much more powerful that he finds Alyiakal's abilities almost beneath notice.

That is the most likely possibility.

Since there's nothing he can do about it, he keeps walking toward the post gates because he wants to go through the market square to see if he can find something appropriate and special for Saelora. After walking five long blocks, under the warm Autumn sun, he's glad he didn't wear the light riding jacket, although he will need it for the return ride from Vaeyal. When he passes the green and white awning of a coffee shop, he smiles. Two blocks later, he reaches the market square, where he immediately notices two patrollers in green strolling along the edges of the square.

Alyiakal stands back for several moments, trying to determine if different sections of the square hold different goods or whether everything is mixed up, the way it had been in Jakaafra. He thinks he sees mostly produce to his right, and because he isn't interested in that he heads toward the tables and carts set up on the left.

Not knowing where to begin, he starts down a row of tables presided over by older women. As he looks closely, he sees they all are selling lacework of some sort or another, all of which seem intricate, many of which catch his eye, but he doubts that Saelora would be enthralled by lace. Some tables hold only rings, and others have pendants and necklaces of silver and gold, and still others bracelets and pins. By the time Alyiakal has looked at everything, he's overwhelmed and ready to leave.

He doesn't, but instead moves to where several vendors sell scarves in a variety of colors. The vendor at one small cart even has an array of shimmersilk scarves, in shades of green, red, yellow, and blue, but not Merchanter blue.

"I imagine these are not inexpensive," he says.

The gray-haired woman seller smiles. "Shimmersilk is costly because it takes tens of glasses to harvest the fibres and spin the thread. Its cost means that it's a gift of love or care. You shouldn't purchase shimmersilk on price, but because of a desire to please someone."

Thinking of the single blue shimmersilk scarf that had been his mother's, Alyiakal can see that. For a moment, his eyes burn, but he says, "You make a good point, but I've heard that the wealthiest of Merchanters in Cyad often wear shimmersilk."

"They do so to please themselves," the seller replies dryly. "That only shows their contempt of others."

"How much do these run?" He manages a smile and adds, "So I'll know how much to save for when there's someone who deserves it."

"The smallest are several silvers. The large shawls can cost as much as a gold. Those I don't sell in the square."

Alyiakal inclines his head. "Thank you."

As he leaves the shimmersilk vendor, he marvels, not necessarily favorably, at those who would clothe themselves in shimmersilk.

From the square, he walks down an adjoining street as far as an alley that appears empty, then takes several steps into the shaded side of the alley before looking around. He sees no one near, although he can sense people in the building he stands beside. Then he lifts a concealment around himself and slowly makes his way back to the market square. The inadvertent meeting with the Third Magus has made it more than clear that he needs to stretch his abilities considerably.

As he nears the square, he sees a figure strolling along the edge of the square and realizes that it's likely one of the patrollers he has seen earlier. He decides to follow the other, if several steps back. After a score of steps, the patroller stops. So does Alyiakal.

The patroller half turns and mutters something.

Alyiakal waits silently, but keeps sensing the area around him, knowing that someone could walk right into him.

Then the patroller continues his rounds.

Alyiakal lets the distance between the two of them increase by another yard or so, but the patroller does not stop again until he nears another figure, one Alyiakal suspects is the other patroller.

"See anything strange?" asks the patroller Alyiakal has followed.

"Can't say I have. Unless you count the Mirror Lancer officer who was looking at jewelry and silks. Why?"

"I had the feeling someone was following me. But there wasn't anyone close."

"You had too much ale last night. Sometimes that'll leave strange feelings."

"Maybe for you. I can't afford to drink like that. Let me know if you feel anything strange."

"Why not?" says the other with a laugh.

Then the two resume their patrolling.

Alyiakal steps away from the square, deciding that trying to navigate through the square under a concealment might not be the best idea. He does hold the concealment until he returns to the post and slips into a corner of the stables where no one is around. From there he makes his way to his temporary quarters, where he sits in the wooden straight-backed chair and considers other exercises he should try.

The most obvious is to gather order and chaos within a shield so that the power cannot be easily discerned.

But that will require holding three shields at once. He smiles wryly. *If that's what it requires, that's what you have to do. You might as well start trying now.*

He begins by gathering a small amount of order and chaos, the chaos within a thin coating of order, and then creates a shield around both. After perhaps a third of a quint, he drops the shield and gathers additional order and chaos. Creating the larger and tighter shield is more of an effort, and in little more than half a quint, sharp needles of pain jab at his skull. He releases the third shield, and then gradually lets the chaos bleed away. His head still aches.

Since he has time before he needs to leave for Vaeyal, he makes his way to the officers' mess.

The mess orderly immediately approaches. "Can I get a few biscuits and a little ale?"

"Yes, ser. On the small table in the corner."

The ale and biscuits definitely help, and Alyiakal makes a mental note that, on future patrols, he needs an additional supply of both.

He's about to leave the mess when Ghrennan appears, heading for the table with obviously the same thought.

"Oh, I thought you were out visiting friends."

"I'm about to leave. It's a bit of a ride, and I thought a few biscuits and a bit of ale might be a good idea."

"Any lancer who's ridden patrols learns that lesson early." Ghrennan chuckles, then says, "Quite something to have the Third Magus here."

"I saw the firewagon coming into the post and didn't know what it meant at the time."

"You weren't the only one. Must be more than routine to get a high magus here."

"I'd guess so, but they're not about to tell junior captains."

"Or old senior captains," replies Ghrennan. "Young Talaan said the other day that you must have done something special to be assigned to Guarstyad."

"I haven't done any more than's expected of any captain dealing with barbarian raiders. The thing that might be different is that I'm a qualified field healer."

Ghrennan frowns, but nods. "Might be. I was thinking more about arms and tactics. How do you do with that?"

Alyiakal wonders how much to say. Too little is as bad as too much. "For what it's worth, I was the best at Kynstaar with both blades and firelances."

"You one of those who only sparred with the best of the officers?"

Alyiakal nods. "I got a lot of bruises that way."

Ghrennan laughs. "All that makes more sense." Then he shakes his head. "Talaan'll be fortunate to survive to even be considered for overcaptain."

That might also be said of any captain going to Guarstyad right now. "I wouldn't know. I do know that judging others when you know nothing about them is unwise . . . and often dangerous, one way or another."

"That it is." Ghrennan smiles. "Won't keep you from your friends."

"I'm sure I'll see you before I leave. I appreciate your thoughts and kindness."

After Alyiakal leaves the mess, he is more than certain that Ghrennan didn't happen to be headed to the mess. At the same time, Alyiakal hadn't sensed anything other than curiosity and openness. He hopes he has answered the older captain's questions in the best way possible, and he also appreciates the other's assessment of Talaan.

After returning to his room for his light riding jacket, Alyiakal heads for the stable. Once there, he confirms his use of the mare for the afternoon, saddles her, and leads her out of the stable, where he mounts. He doesn't see any officers on the way to the front gates of the post, not that he expects to in early afternoon.

The ride to Vaeyal is uneventful, although he sees a few more riders, wagons, and carts than he has on his last two trips. Once he turns onto Canal Street he checks the unloading area. While a barge is moored there, it appears fully loaded, and since there are no wagons at the loading docks, Alyiakal surmises that the barge is waiting for a firetow.

He knows he is arriving early and intends to hitch the mare in front of the factorage and walk inside to announce his arrival, but he only gets as far as dismounting before Saelora appears at the factorage door, wearing Merchanter full blues.

"I'll meet you in back."

Alyiakal smiles. "I'll be there."

By the time he reaches the stable doors, Saelora is mounted and waiting and the doors are closed, and he asks, "Where are we going?"

Saelora smiles sweetly, but Alyiakal senses something behind her smile, which is confirmed by her next words. "Into combat . . . and an early dinner."

He considers her words, then asks, "Your mother's house or Karola's?"

She laughs, if with a touch of harshness. "Mother's. It takes almost half a glass to get to Karola and Faadyr's house. Well . . . maybe not that long, but it feels that way."

Alyiakal decides against asking for an explanation. "Has your mother been asking about me, or is this a preemptive attack?"

Saelora turns the roan gelding north and replies, "She's been asking about you for years. I've told her that I wrote you because Hyrsaal suggested it and because I liked getting your letters. She would have heard you were here before long. So, I suggested it might be good to have an officer who was Hyrsaal's friend for dinner."

Once again, as he eases the mare alongside her, Alyiakal senses the truth of her words, but also something more. "And you didn't want to create the impression that you're hiding something."

"I don't like deliberately hiding anything."

He grins. "What about just not revealing? What haven't you told me?"

"Quite a lot. Where should I start?"

The absolute truth of that reply silences Alyiakal for a moment. He finally says, "Wherever you like."

"Mother was fine with writing you at first. Then she asked if we intended to be consorted. I told her what I've told you. Then she said I was leading you on."

"You weren't," replies Alyiakal. "I worried that I was leading you on."

"You didn't." She turns the roan north on Canal Street, and Alyiakal and the mare stay with her. "We're heading north on Canal Street, past the old road to the distillery. Quite a way past." When Alyiakal doesn't say anything, she adds, "You made it clear that you weren't thinking about consorting."

"I didn't write anything like that."

"You didn't. You didn't mention or hint about consorting in any way. The only time you mentioned consorting was when you said you were glad about Hyrsaal and Catriana."

"I was, and I still am." Alyiakal pauses. "How did he meet her? She lives in Fyrad, and that's not exactly the next town."

"She grew up here. She hated it. Her older sister met a young man from Fyrad who accompanied a shipment of goods. One thing led to another, and they consorted. A year later, the sister had problems after childbirth, and Catriana said she'd help. She went and helped her sister through two children. We all knew she had no intention of returning, especially after she got that inheritance from her great-aunt Ilsyen." Saelora smiles. "Catriana was the only girl who got anything. That might have been because Ilsyen always wanted to leave Vaeyal and couldn't. That's a guess on my part."

"What about you?"

"For me, it's not where I live. It's what I do."

"I can see that. Right now, being here has given you the chance to do what you value doing."

"I like the way you said that," Saelora replies. "You didn't say 'enjoy.' You said 'value.'"

"You've made it very clear that what you do and how you do it are important." *Possibly more important than being consorted or where you live.*

"Isn't that true for you . . . and most men? Why shouldn't it be true for me?"

"It should be. That's one of the things I admire about you."

They ride for another block before Alyiakal asks, "What should I know about your mother?"

"You never asked before." She offers an amused smile.

"I wasn't going to meet her before, and I didn't know I would need recon before going into combat."

"It really won't be that bad. I was teasing you a bit."

But not entirely.

"I think, deep in her heart, she wishes she could do what I'm doing."

"She's very organized, then?"

"Oh, yes. In that, we're alike."

"That suggests that you're not in other ways."

"We're not. I'd rather not say more. It might be better for you to meet her before hearing who I think she is."

"Will your older brother be there?"

"He should be, although he might not be, or he and Charissa might be."

"Charissa?" Alyiakal had never heard that name before.

"She's the youngest daughter of Traybett. He's Rhobett's younger brother. Charissa likes Gaaran, and he dotes on her. She won't get anything much from her family, because her father's the younger brother, and a match with a stipended Mirror Lancer captain is better than any other possible consort in Vaeyal."

"And consorting with Gaaran maintains her . . . position?"

"Exactly. In time Gaaran will inherit the house. He's mentioned building a smaller house for Mother on the land behind the house. She might like that. I'm not sure Charissa would."

Alyiakal nods, although he has a much better idea why Saelora is fixing the small house next to the distillery, something he's reminded of as they ride past the road leading to the distillery and house.

As they continue north, Alyiakal notices that the buildings containing tradesmen and shops have given way to small neat dwellings. "We're getting to the better part of town."

"We are . . . if you mean the part where people have a few more golds."

"You phrased that more accurately than I did," Alyiakal concedes.

"I'll take that as a compliment."

"As it was meant."

"Mother's house is on the next corner."

Alyiakal straightens as he looks ahead. The house isn't a mansion, not that he'd seen many, but it is a good-sized, two-story brick structure, with a pale gray slate roof and sturdy shutters painted gray. As they ride closer, Alyiakal also sees a barn capable of holding at least four horses and a carriage.

"Does your mother have a carriage?"

Saelora shakes her head. "Only a one-horse chaise."

While Saelora let slip the fact that her father had been a Mirror Lancer major, she has never written anything about his death. Given the size of the house, Alyiakal wonders if he'd consorted Saelora's mother near the end of his service and retired with a healthy stipend. "Was your father . . . a bit older than your mother?"

"More than a bit. Almost twenty years. He died right after Gaaran received his commission. He was . . . cautious . . . with his golds."

"Like a daughter I know."

She smiles. "It runs in both sides of the family." She turns the roan down the stone way to the barn.

Alyiakal lets her lead the way.

They haven't quite reached the stable doors when a flame-haired lean man limps quickly toward the barn. While the man has boots at the end of his trousers, Alyiakal can see that he has a wooden leg of some sort.

That has to be Gaaran. Alyiakal catches sight of a full-figured but muscular blond woman standing at the top of the low steps leading down from the roofed wraparound porch. *And Charissa.*

After opening the stable doors, Gaaran looks up to Saelora. "You said he'd be on time." Then he turns to Alyiakal. "I'm Gaaran, as if you haven't guessed."

"Alyiakal . . . as I'm sure you already know." Alyiakal dismounts and leads the mare into the barn, every bit as swept and clean as the stables at the rear of Vassyl's factorage.

"The end stall is for your mount," says Gaaran.

"Thank you. You don't mind if I unsaddle her?"

"I'd hope you would."

Dealing with the mare doesn't take that long, and Gaaran waits for Saelora and Alyiakal.

As the three walk toward the house, Gaaran says, "Hyrsaal wrote that you're quietly impressive. I can see what he meant."

"Hyrsaal's impressive in his own right," replies Alyiakal.

Gaaran chuckles. "Hyrsaal's not quietly anything."

"Have you heard anything lately? His last letter to me said that he didn't know his next posting."

"He has orders to Lhaarat. At least it's not Isahl."

Or Inividra.

Gaaran pauses, then says, "Saelora told me you were at Pemedra. I understand two companies from there . . . were sent . . ."

Abruptly, Alyiakal recalls that Gaaran had been wounded while serving at Isahl, and he finishes Gaaran's sentence. "To deal with the Jeranyi-supplied barbarians? That's right. I was in command of the fourth company. We didn't leave much."

"Good!"

Saelora looks to Alyiakal. "You didn't mention that."

"I thought I did. I wrote you about the West Branch valley barbarians who had shields and other Jeranyi weapons." Alyiakal pauses. "I might not have mentioned that we were sent because of the casualties suffered at Isahl." He turns to Gaaran. "That was more than two years after you were there."

"They were trouble then. The subcommander at Syadtar didn't believe what we reported."

"Was that Subcommander Munnyr?"

"It was. He was a manipulative idiot. I understand why some idiots get promoted when better officers don't, but I still don't like it."

"That makes sense," replies Alyiakal. "Somehow Munnyr got Mirror Lancer headquarters to order companies from Pemedra to attack the West Branch valley. We were told that we could attack from the east and that would provide greater surprise."

"That sounds like Munnyr," says Gaaran. "Get someone else to take the casualties." He pauses. "How bad was it for you?"

"Out of the two companies, we lost five men and had three wounded."

"What about your company?" Gaaran presses.

"We lost one mount and had one man wounded, but we fought a smaller band of raiders. Just over a score."

"You're too honest, Alyiakal," declares Gaaran as they reach the porch steps. He gestures to the blond woman standing in the shade at the top of the steps. "Charissa, this is Alyiakal. You've heard a little about him."

Charissa steps back as the three come up the steps to the porch. Her smile is pleasant and honest. "Only a little." She glances to Saelora. "I can see why you might not want to share him."

"I suspect she was being cautious," says Alyiakal quickly. "We hadn't ever met until twoday."

"But you've been writing each other for years," replies Gaaran.

"She might have wanted to see if the man presented by my letters was the same man in person," suggests Alyiakal.

"You're all guessing why I did what I did," declares Saelora with a wry sharpness. "You might ask me."

"Why did you hide everything about Alyiakal?" asks Gaaran, trying to keep from grinning.

"Because, just because," replies Saelora. "Or maybe, because I wanted to keep you all guessing."

"Guessing about what?" asks the woman stepping out of the house, who has to be Saelora and Gaaran's mother.

Alyiakal studies her. She is shorter and more slender than Saelora, more like Hyrsaal and Gaaran, but with graying flame-red hair, and has a critical but amused expression on her face as she looks back at Alyiakal, who says, "I'm Alyiakal, as you obviously know, and I'm pleased to meet you."

"After all these years, it's good to put a face to the name. I'm Marenda, and the mother of the rowdy one and the recluse." Then she turns to Saelora. "You were right. Handsome is as handsome does, and he couldn't be other than handsome."

Alyiakal is far from sure, even sensing Marenda, that her words are exactly a compliment.

"We might as well all go into the parlor and have some refreshments," continues Marenda. "That way I might even get in a few words." With that, she turns and steps into the house, leaving the door ajar.

Gaaran and Saelora exchange sardonically amused glances, as he gestures, and Saelora moves toward the door. In turn, Alyiakal motions for Charissa to follow Saelora, before following the two women. Gaaran acts as rear guard and closes the door.

The parlor is spacious, but not overlarge, with two matching settees upholstered in a green too dark to be termed Imperial, and four matching armchairs upholstered in the same shade of green.

Marenda has already claimed one of the armchairs.

Alyiakal takes a seat on one of the settees beside Saelora. He can smell the odor of something being roasted. Fowl of some sort, he thinks.

After everyone seats themselves, Marenda looks to Gaaran. "If you wouldn't mind dealing with the refreshments." Her words are not a question.

"We have ale, a white Alafraan wine, and redberry," says Gaaran. "The greenberry brandy is better after a meal."

"You know my preference," declares Marenda.

"The white Alafraan, please," says Charissa.

"The same," says Saelora.

"I'll also try the Alafraan," adds Alyiakal.

As Gaaran leaves the parlor, Marenda says conversationally, "We did have a good red wine—Fhynyco—I believe, but it's not always easy to come by."

"Any good wines are hard to come by at the Mirror Lancer border posts," replies Alyiakal, "but I imagine Gaaran has made that point."

"Often," replies Marenda tersely.

"I don't know much about wines," says Alyiakal. "What others have a good reputation?"

For a moment, no one speaks. Finally, Charissa says, "My father and uncle both speak highly of Cillaryn. It's a red wine. I've seldom tasted it. It comes from the hills north of Ruzor."

"A Kyphran wine, then?" asks Saelora.

Charissa nods.

At that moment, Gaaran returns with a tray on which are a beaker of ale and four glasses of Alafraan. He presents the beaker to his mother first, then serves Charissa, Saelora, and Alyiakal, setting the tray on a side table and taking the last glass for himself, after which he sits in the armchair beside the settee across from his mother where Charissa has settled. He lifts his glass. "A toast to our guest, who has survived the barbarian raiders of the northeast."

After everyone sips their drinks, Alyiakal says, "Thank you all. I'm very glad to be here, but it wouldn't have happened if Hyrsaal hadn't gone out of his way to befriend me years ago. I hope he returns home before I leave for Guarstyad."

"Any of us will be fortunate to see him," replies Marenda. "He'll likely spend most of his time in Fyrad."

"As he should," replies Gaaran cheerfully. "Catriana is his consort-to-be."

"Ah, yes," replies Marenda, "I forgot." She turns to Alyiakal. "No one's ever mentioned your mother."

"She died when I was eight," replies Alyiakal evenly. "When I couldn't accompany my father, I stayed with my great-aunt. She died before I went to Kynstaar."

"What was she like?" asks Saelora.

"She was very kind." Alyiakal smiles wryly. "She also insisted that I read a lot and practice my calculations."

"Good for her . . . and you," declares Marenda.

"It was good for me," Alyiakal agrees.

"She sounds like my aunt Rhenna," volunteers Charissa. "She's always asking if I'm still reading."

Alyiakal looks to Saelora.

"We don't have any aunts," she replies, "not by birth. Our uncles both live in Wendingway."

Alyiakal has heard of the town and knows it's on the west side of the Great Canal not all that far from Westend, but not exactly where.

The conversation for the next quint or so centers on the various familial relations, but when that topic comes to a silent end, and an older-looking serving woman appears in the archway to the front hall, Marenda says, "Our early dinner is ready. We don't want Captain Alyiakal riding back to his post in the dark."

"You have to ride back this evening?" asks Charissa.

"I arranged to bring the mare back tonight," replies Alyiakal. "I can't afford to do otherwise."

"No . . . you can't," agrees Gaaran.

Charissa offers a puzzled frown.

"Officers who don't keep their word don't get promoted, especially junior captains," explains Gaaran.

"For a little thing like that?" Charissa asks.

"For quite a few little things like that," answers Alyiakal.

"You'll find, Charissa," says Marenda coolly, "that so-called little things often count for more than those that most people think are important." Then she stands and walks from the parlor across the center hallway to the dining room, where she stands beside the chair at the head of the table until everyone follows her.

Marenda gestures to the place at her right, and says to Alyiakal, "If you would," then to the place at her left, adding, "Gaaran."

Saelora takes the seat beside Alyiakal, and Charissa the one beside Gaaran.

Alyiakal notices that the serving woman has already filled the wineglasses at the table, with what looks to be the Alafraan white, and in moments she serves Marenda, then Alyiakal and Gaaran, ending up with Saelora. As Alyiakal has suspected from what he had smelled entering the house, the meat is sliced fowl with a white sauce, cheesed lace potatoes, with sliced baked quilla. There is also a large basket of dark bread.

Alyiakal waits until Marenda begins before he samples the fowl and the white sauce, which has a nutty but agreeably buttery taste. The potatoes are excellent, and the lime-basted quilla is acceptable, although he'd never choose the bitter cactus strips.

"What will you be doing at Guarstyad, Captain Alyiakal?" asks Marenda.

"Whatever duties I'm assigned. There's a possibility of having to deal with Kyphran raiders."

"By deal with," replies Marenda, "I assume you mean killing?"

"Since Cyador, at present, is not invading other lands, any dealings we have with the Kyphrans will be if they're invading Cyador. In that case, some of them will likely be killed."

"Are you good at that?" asks Marenda.

"As good as I have to be. I'd prefer that the Kyphrans remain in Kyphros."

"Have you actually killed people?" presses Marenda.

"Yes."

"How many?"

"I don't keep track of things like that."

"Surely, you must have some idea."

"Fourth Company likely killed over threescore raiders under my command. I personally accounted for a number of deaths. Other company officers would likely have similar raider casualties."

"You look so polite and well-mannered," observes Marenda.

"I try to be so, unless I'm facing armed attacks with lethal weapons," replies Alyiakal with a cheerful smile. He can sense a certain malice or spitefulness, but he has no idea of the reasons behind Marenda's feelings. For Saelora's sake, especially, he intends to remain calm and controlled.

"My late consort would approve." Marenda's tone is that of sardonic amusement. "I've always found it, shall I say, amazing that he—and you—can do what you have done and remain so . . . civilized in other settings."

"That's what's required of a Mirror Lancer officer. It may be why so few make it through training and get promoted to higher ranks."

"Exactly!" interjects Gaaran. "Now that you've established that all the men in the family, and Alyiakal, are polite trained killers, I believe it's time to move on to another subject, Mother."

"Of course, dear." Marenda turns to Saelora. "How are the renovations coming on your swamp-side abode-to-be?"

"The roof and window repairs are done. The doors and shutters have been replaced, and there's now a stove in the kitchen. Laetilla's quarters in the distillery are finished. Everything's clean. The more elegant refurbishing will be done bit by bit."

"Do you really want to live there?" asks Charissa.

"I like having my own house and being a successful Merchanter," replies Saelora. "That property allows me to do both."

"It is rather close to the angel-cursed swamp," says Marenda, "but that has the advantage of discouraging unwanted visitors. Only those who wish to see you will take the old road."

"It strikes me," Alyiakal offers, "that the solid pavement of the old road will prove to be a great advantage, given how much it can rain here."

"Most people judge on image, rather than practicality," replies Marenda.

"You're right," says Alyiakal, "but they only judge what they see. They'll never see the distillery. They'll see the long-standing and reputable factorage of Vassyl and Greenberry Spirits."

Gaaran smothers a smile that Marenda does not—or chooses not—to see.

"I do believe it is time for dessert," declares Marenda.

The serving woman clears the plates away, and then serves each person a small square of paper-thin baked pastry sheets soaked in honey with crushed thin layers of nuts seasoned with a mixture of spices Alyiakal cannot identify. He finds it good, if a touch too sweet for his taste, but neither he nor anyone else leaves even pastry flakes.

"Everything was excellent," Alyiakal says as he looks directly at Marenda. "I do appreciate both the invitation and the fare."

"Thank you. I did so want to meet you." Marenda eases back her chair and stands.

Alyiakal does the same. "And I you." *If not for the usual reasons.* "But I really should be going."

"It's not a short ride," says Gaaran.

"I do hope you're staying, dear," declares Marenda, looking at Saelora, standing beside Alyiakal.

"I need to check the distillery. Alyiakal can escort me there. It's on his way," declares Saelora. "With him, I'm quite sure I'll be safe. Besides, it's still light out."

"I'll see you both off," says Gaaran.

Charissa eases closer to Marenda. "You never did finish telling me that story. The one about how you decided on this house."

"I suppose I should," says Marenda casually, before saying to Alyiakal, "It was refreshing to meet you." Her eyes go to Saelora. "Do be careful." Those words are almost emotionless.

"Of course," replies Saelora.

Once Gaaran, Saelora, and Alyiakal are out of the house and walking to the stable, Gaaran smiles and says to Saelora, "I know you didn't intend it that way, but thank you both."

"Give my best to Charissa," replies Saelora. "As I've said before, she's much nicer than Mother deserves. Have you decided on a date yet?"

"The eightday after yearturn."

"That will give me time to finish more of the house and move the rest of my things. Not that I've ever had that many."

"You don't have to—"

"Charissa doesn't need another woman in the house," says Saelora firmly. "What made Charissa finally agree?"

"Your success as a Merchanter."

Saelora nods thoughtfully.

Alyiakal can see that, since Saelora's success means that Gaaran will have no obligation or need to offer any assistance to his still-unconsorted younger sister. Not only that, but a successful woman Merchanter in the extended family in a town as small as Vaeyal is bound to be perceived in a largely favorable way.

Besides polite but honest farewells, neither Alyiakal nor Saelora say anything until they are mounted and well away from the house, heading south on Canal Street.

"I like Gaaran," says Alyiakal quietly. "Otherwise, it's been an interesting afternoon and dinner."

"That's *one* way of putting it," replies Saelora ironically. "I thought you handled Mother quite well."

"I had a great deal of practice growing up." After a moment, he asks, "How do you think the dinner went?" He smiles wryly. "Preemptively, that is?"

"About as well as could be expected. You're handsome, intelligent, and capable. If, from her point of view, worse comes to worst, no one will look down on her if we consorted. If we don't, then she can simply say that you are a friend of Hyrsaal's who visited on your way to your next posting."

"And from your point of view?"

"Things haven't changed, and that's good. We need to know more about each other." She smiles warmly. "Whatever happens, I'm glad you came."

"So am I." Alyiakal pauses, then asks, "Tomorrow or sevenday?"

"Tomorrow isn't good for me. There are several traders and factors coming by, and I don't know when, only that they promised they'd be here. What about third glass on sevenday?"

"Third glass on sevenday it is."

LII

At the morning mess on sixday, Alyiakal ends up sitting in pleasant conversation with Ghrennan, Nyell, and Dhenaal. About the only thing interesting he learns is that Commander Dahlvor and the Third Magus have not yet left Geliendra, which means that Alyiakal needs to be careful.

After breakfast, Alyiakal returns to his room, where he dons his light riding jacket because there's a cool wind out of the northeast. Then he makes his way to the south gates out of the post and walks a good half kay west before he reaches the west wall of the post. He continues for several long blocks before turning north toward the Great Forest. While he has to walk several kays farther than if he'd used the north gates, he doesn't want any Mirror Lancers, especially officers, observing him walking straight from the post to the wall, and with the Third Magus still around, using a concealment while inside the post walls wouldn't be a good idea.

The farther north he walks, the smaller and less well-kept the various dwellings he passes are, but that makes a certain sense, given that some Forest creatures do occasionally cross the wall. After almost a kay and a half, he leaves the scattered ragtag dwellings behind and enters an area of small plots and fields, divided by a mixture of fences and hedgerows. He continues north until he nears the wall, where he stops under a tree and studies what lies before him.

Farther to the northwest, woodlots and larger fields parallel the Forest and the white sunstone wall that stretches for ninety-nine kays. The ground between the sunstone road and the wall that it parallels is bare earth, blackened in places by firelances used on shoots or plants or aimed at Forest creatures. At the moment, he sees no lancers on the road, and certainly no wagons or carts, given that few growers would risk themselves or their horses or donkeys to the possibility of an attack.

Alyiakal extends his senses to the wall only about a hundred yards away. Since he can neither see nor sense anyone, he raises a concealment and begins to walk through the calf-high grass that stretches to the edge of the road.

He has almost reached the road when he hears hoofs on the sunstone and senses a pair of dispatch riders coming from the northwest, possibly from Westend. Alyiakal halts and waits. The riders pass within ten yards, but don't slow. Once they are well past, Alyiakal crosses the road at a deliberate pace. He's not about to run. While he may be concealed, any puffs of dust or tracks he may leave are not.

He continues until he stands a yard or so away from the base of the wall, realizing that it has been more than six years since he has been this close to the Great Forest. He feels the looming power of order and chaos beyond the wall, and the comparatively thin curtain of separate flows of order and chaos that run from ward to ward, flows created by the chaos towers located at thirty-three-kay intervals. For whatever reason, the power of the Great Forest has a greater depth, one that overshadows the power flowing from the chaos towers.

He cannot sense any person or large animals near him outside the wall, and while he can sense patterns on the other side of the wall, the wards distort his perceptions. Finally, he decides to climb the wall. He finds it easier than he recalls.

You're older and stronger in more ways than one.

Once he sits on the top of the wall, his perceptions of the forces within the wall are clear and precise, but interpreting those patterns without sight is difficult. Still, he cannot afford to drop the concealment. The last thing he needs is a report of a Mirror Lancer sitting on the top of the wall—especially with the Third Magus still at Geliendra.

For perhaps half a quint, he attempts to make sense out of the patterns below and around him inside the wall. He perceives an open space below and to his left, and he eases himself down. As soon as his head is below the top of the wall he drops the concealment and finds that he is above packed earth, suggesting that a large creature might have created it for resting or ambushing other creatures.

As his boots hit the ground, he glances around in the dim light filtering through the leaves and branches, but sees no sign of such a creature. The taller trees stretch well over a hundred yards above him and the comparatively smaller trees of the understory.

A flow of unheard noise carried by a blast of chaos strikes his shields and melts away. While the power shivers him, it only momentarily affects him, and he turns in the direction of the blast. A stun lizard, perhaps as long as a horse, and a third as tall, waits beside the trunk of a massive tree.

Just a young one.

A massive overwhelming power, neither chaos nor order, but partaking of both and something else beyond, encircles Alyiakal, and he has an impression of a question, possibly an inquiry as to why he has entered the Forest.

He attempts to create the feeling of wonder and curiosity.

Out of nowhere, an enormous serpent appears, its open mouth big enough to engulf Alyiakal. He decides instantly that responding with chaos would not only anger the serpent and/or the power behind it, but also be futile. Instead, he strengthens his shields and anchors them to the order he feels somewhere beneath his boots.

The serpent vanishes, replaced by an equally large stun lizard, which confirms Alyiakal's impression that the creatures are a creation of the Forest, a form of illusion, but illusions with great power.

Power great enough to destroy you if you didn't have shields.

Abruptly, he switches his outer shield to the one he'd used years before, when he'd sought out Adayal . . . or to one as close as he can recall.

Even so, another flow of unheard noise carried by an even larger blast of chaos washes over Alyiakal. Both shields hold, against a blast from a stun lizard much larger than the first one and against the second blast that follows.

Alyiakal forces himself not to strike back.

An image appears, before Alyiakal or in his mind, he cannot tell which. The feel of reality is strong enough that, for all practical purposes, the image is real. Tall, dark-leaved trees stretch as far as the eye can see, yet beneath those trees, Alyiakal senses an understory of more trees, and beneath this are all sorts of creatures—giant black panther-cats, stun lizards, bears with long curved claws living in the trees, medium-sized cougars, great serpents, water lizards with enormous teeth. The trees stretch for kays and kays, with no signs of roads or dwellings or structures.

Then, flashes of brilliant light fill the blue-green sky, and giant white metal spears plunge toward the Forest, their tips pointed skyward, the ends burning with white chaos-fire, fire that burns away trees, leaving vast patches of dark ash.

A shimmering figure in white appears at the edge of a burned patch. The figure stands next to something resembling a firewagon. Chaos flows in ordered streams from the sun to the shimmering figure, building around him. Great flying lizards dive at the shimmering figure, but chaos-fires from his fingers burn them from the sky. Stun lizards throw chaos noise at the figure, but his fires sear them out of existence, and the blackened area grows and grows.

Another image appears—a healthy forest surrounded by white walls—and that image settles between the burned edge of the Forest and the towering figure in shimmering white. The fires disappear from the fingers of the figure in white, and white walls appear around a smaller forest.

Alyiakal swallows. This has to be the Great Forest's vision or memory of opposing the powers of the First.

Another image appears, this one of a time when the white walls sag and the trees begin to grow beyond the walls and to cover them.

Then, that image vanishes, and there is a sense of quiet anticipation.

Alyiakal struggles to create a simple illusion of himself sadly climbing the wall and leaving the Great Forest.

He waits.

Another image forms, showing him standing in the Forest beside a pool. Two tawny cougars approach. The Alyiakal image turns toward the wall, and the cougars follow close behind him as he walks to the wall, climbs it, and then descends. As the image of Alyiakal walks away from the wall, it lifts its arms, and fires flow from its hands. Then the image fades.

Alyiakal smiles, nervously. "Thank you." He tries to project that feeling, then slowly turns to the wall. Climbing it the second time is much harder, but as he reaches the top, he looks back. Two tawny cougars stand beneath the wall, as if they had escorted him to it.

Alyiakal inclines his head in respect, then raises a concealment before he climbs onto the top of the wall and then down.

He has to walk slowly, carrying a concealment, as he crosses the sunstone road, because his legs feel unsteady. When he reaches a hedgerow shielding him from any direct view, he releases the concealment, and his jaw drops as he realizes it is midafternoon.

That long?

He shakes his head, slowly. No wonder he feels exhausted. He looks down at his jacket and uniform. Both are mussed, not stained, but his uniform feels sweaty, as if he's run a good kay—or farther.

More than a few thoughts circle through his head, which aches with a dull throbbing pain he hadn't even realized he had.

The images projected by the Great Forest had been so real, including the amount of power demonstrated by the magus of the First. The representation of ordered chaos flowing from the sun to the magus intrigued him, as if it augmented his power.

Enough power to force the Great Forest into submission . . . or an agreement?

But the last images had bothered Alyiakal. They suggest that, when Cyador can no longer maintain the wall, the Great Forest will return and reclaim its place.

And the two tawny cougars? Two had been present years ago when Adayal had sent him away. Did the Great Forest know that, too? And the fires from his hands, or from the fingers of the image of himself.

Does that mean you can throw order and chaos? Or that you should use it any-where but in the Great Forest? Or that you're somehow linked to that great magus of the First?

Those questions circle through his thoughts as he walks, putting one foot in front of the other, heading back to his temporary quarters. As he nears the post gates, he swallows, then remembers he needs to change his outer shield back to create the impression of a Mirror Lancer officer with slightly higher order abil-ities than most. If the Third Magus remains at the post, the Forest-mirroring shield would scream who Alyiakal really is and where he has been.

Despite his tiredness, Alyiakal finds the shift surprisingly easy, and that puzzles him, too.

LIII

When Alyiakal returns to his room, he stretches out on the narrow bed to rest, but immediately falls asleep and doesn't wake for almost two glasses. He has to hurry to wash up and get to the evening mess on time, where Dhenaal and Nyell both gesture for Alyiakal to join them.

No one says much until they've served themselves—river trout fried in a nut batter along with fried quilla, of which Alyiakal takes only a small portion, and buttered brown rice.

"You out visiting friends today?" asks Nyell.

Alyiakal shakes his head. "I spent most of the day walking around." He smiles wryly. "I came back in midafternoon and fell asleep."

"You get back late last night?" asks Nyell.

"Not that late, but it takes almost two glasses each way. That's one reason why I'm not visiting every day."

"Is she pretty?" asks Dhenaal. "You wouldn't be traveling that often if a woman weren't involved."

"She's a handsome woman," replies Alyiakal. "I never met her until now, but she started writing me when I was at Kynstaar. She's impressive. She's a Merchanter." He takes another mouthful of the trout, which is better than passable, followed by the quilla, which is not, then some of the brown rice.

"From a Merchanter family?" asks Nyell.

"No. She earned it on her own."

"That is impressive, even if it's easier around here than in Cyad," says Nyell. "You serious about her?"

"I'm serious about getting to know her better."

"How much better?" asks Dhenaal with a grin.

"Not that way," replies Alyiakal, adding, "Both her brothers are also Mirror Lancer officers. They're very protective."

"Ah . . . I can see why you're being careful," says Nyell.

"Did the Third Magus ever leave?" asks Alyiakal.

"He and the commander left around midmorning. Subcommander Zaentyl looked a bit relieved after that." Nyell offers an amused smile. "I can see why. If I were in command, I'd be worried, too, if a headquarters commander and the Third Magus showed up at my post."

"I wonder if there's been trouble with the wall wards," says Alyiakal.

"Not that I know of," replies Dhenaal.

"One of the dispatch riders said he saw tracks coming from the wall this afternoon, but no one saw anyone," says Nyell.

"Boot tracks or animal tracks?" asks Dhenaal.

"Boot tracks. The tracks went straight to the road, but there weren't traces beyond the road."

"Someone or something coming out of the Accursed Forest? Can't say I like that at all," declares Dhenaal.

"I wonder how the First ever managed to wall up the Forest," offers Alyiakal. "You see all those creatures . . ." He shakes his head.

"They could do things that none of the Magi'i today could come close to doing," says Nyell. "Of course, the Magi'i won't admit it, and it's not wise to even hint at."

"They must have been incredibly powerful," replies Alyiakal, thinking about the clarity of the Great Forest's images.

"We could use some of that power now," Dhenaal declares. "Sometimes, it takes three firelances to take down one of the big cats."

As Dhenaal speaks, Alyiakal realizes, almost absently, that behind the older captain's words are a healthy respect and tempered fear . . . and that his own awareness of what others feel is somehow sharper than it has been. *Because of what happened in the Forest.* After a moment of silence, Alyiakal says, "I've heard that there are giant serpents as well."

"How would anyone know?" asks Dhenaal. "I don't see how a serpent could climb the wall."

"It could if one of those giant trees fell across the wall," Alyiakal points out.

Dhenaal frowns, then nods. "I could see that—the same way most of the big cats get out. I think I'd still worry more about them. They're fast."

"In your position," says Nyell, "I'd worry about everything connected to the Accursed Forest. Nothing good comes out of there."

While Alyiakal could dispute that, saying that there are good aspects to the Great Forest isn't something he can do, not as a Mirror Lancer.

"You lived near the Forest for a time, didn't you?" Dhenaal asks Alyiakal. "What's your feeling about it?"

Alyiakal smiles wryly. "Let's say I wouldn't get in an all-out battle with the Forest and any of its creatures. The best you can do is survive, and sometimes that's what Mirror Lancers have to do."

Dhenaal nods. "You're right about that. There are always more creatures. Even the First couldn't destroy the Forest. The best they could do was to confine it."

Nyell frowns, then nods. "I wouldn't have thought of it that way."

Alyiakal finishes the brown rice and the trout, but not all the quilla.

A little later, as he leaves the mess building and starts to walk toward the temporary officers' quarters, he immediately senses the presence of the Great Forest—and even the flows of order and chaos—a feeling he has only felt in the past when he was far closer to the walls.

Because you entered the Forest?

He shakes his head. It has to be because he did not attempt to fight the Great Forest, but merely held his ground and accepted the Forest for what it is.

He smiles, an expression somehow both wry and sad.

LIV

Alyiakal's dreams are vivid, yet when he wakes early on sevenday morning, he cannot remember most of the details. The one absolutely clear image is walking away from the Great Forest with order-and-chaos bolts somehow radiating from him.

First the Forest plants that image and now it's in your dreams. Should you try to see if you can do more than merely gather order and chaos?

He sits up slowly, thinking, wondering if the Forest had been suggesting . . . or foreseeing.

Then he shakes his head. *It might be a good idea to see if you can even do something like that, or you'll always wonder.*

Then he realizes that he definitely feels rested, and he stands, begins to ready himself for the day.

Breakfast is much like other breakfasts at the mess, where both the fare and the conversations are bland.

He spends more than a glass at the tailor's shop, trying on his new uniforms and then paying for them. Most, but not all, of the cost comes from the uniform allowance granted to all officers when they are posted to a new duty station after at least two years in their previous post. After that, he makes his way to the cobbler's shop, where he tries on his new boots, after which he carries the uniforms and boots back to his quarters.

He thinks about going back to the market square, but decides against it. He still has no idea what sort of gift would be most appropriate for Saelora, and he does have an eightday in which to decide.

He debates whether he should try throwing or projecting order and chaos, but immediately decides against attempting anything within the post.

At a quint before the first glass of the afternoon, he rides the mare out through the south gates of the post. This time, he decides to see if he can use his order/chaos senses to discern where the old road from Vaeyal joins the current stone road.

More than a glass later, some four kays past where the roads to Fyrad and Vaeyal diverge, Alyiakal concentrates on the left side of the gray stone road, looking for traces of the older road. He rides another two kays, laughing quietly when he reaches what he'd thought was a lane leading off to several steads. The lane is unpaved. That doesn't surprise Alyiakal because the road builders would likely have used the paving stones on the newer road. This hadn't occurred in Vaeyal because it would have taken too much effort to cart the stones all the way to the new road, especially since it also would have meant removing a paved street in the town.

Or perhaps the locals here may have used the stones for other purposes.

Alyiakal still senses an underlying order beneath the packed earth, an order he doubts he could have perceived days earlier, and he wonders what else has changed in his order/chaos abilities . . . and why.

Just because you stood up to the Great Forest . . . or because doing so opened up your perceptions and abilities more?

He is still mulling over those possibilities when he reaches Vaeyal and nears the Great Canal, where the sunstone blocks, reinforced with order and chaos, comprising the walls and tow-ways seem strangely out of place, a balance of order and chaos that is, paradoxically, somehow out of balance.

The feeling is strong enough that, for a moment, Alyiakal himself feels unbalanced, but with a deep breath and a little concentration, he regains his equilibrium and guides the mare north on Canal Street.

As on fiveday, Saelora appears at the front door of the factorage as he nears it.

"In back again?" he asks.

"For now," she replies before reentering the factorage and closing the door. Alyiakal continues riding up Canal Street to the next lane, where he turns. When he reaches the factorage, Saelora stands beside the open stable doors in her Merchanter blues. As he reins up, he asks, "We're not going anywhere?"

"Not immediately, but I thought we'd eat at my house."

"Excellent," he says cheerfully as he dismounts.

"You don't want to go to Mother's?" Her smile holds a hint of mischief.

"The fare at your house is better, and we don't have to spar for it." He leads the mare into the open stall. After he settles the mare, steps out of the stall, and closes the door, Saelora says, "Gaaran stopped by this morning. He likes you. So does Charissa."

"And your mother?"

Saelora lifts her eyebrows, clearly asking why he worries about Marenda.

"I don't want to be the cause of any disruption."

Saelora laughs softly. "You worded that so politely and carefully. What have you been doing since I last saw you?"

"Among other things, eating with other officers, and trying on and paying for new uniforms. My old ones are a bit worn. What I'm wearing is one of the few remaining in decent condition. Next time, I'll wear one of the new ones."

"Other things?"

"I'll tell you over dinner."

"Is that to make certain I feed you?"

"I hadn't thought of it that way, but if that's what it takes . . ."

Saelora shakes her head, then moves toward the stable doors.

Alyiakal takes the door she doesn't, and then slides the bar into place. "Where are we going now?"

"To see Vassyl. He asked if he could talk to you."

"We can do that." *Especially since he's been so good to you.* Alyiakal follows Saelora through the organized and clean shelves of the warehouse section to the part that looks more like a study.

Vassyl immediately stands and gestures to the small circular table. "We can all sit here. It's easier that way."

As he seats himself, Alyiakal says, "Saelora says you'd like to talk."

"No," replies Vassyl with an amused smile. "I'd like you to talk. I'm only a factor and a trader. I haven't been all that far from Vaeyal. Fyrad's the farthest I've been, so I like to talk to people who've been places I haven't. Would you mind telling me about Pemedra? And about who lives around there and what their lives are like?"

"I'm afraid that it won't be that interesting, but I'll be happy to tell you what I know and what I saw."

For almost a glass, prompted by Vassyl's questions, Alyiakal conveys his observations about the post, what the Mirror Lancers ate and did, the local steads, the barbarians, the weather, and the way the Cerlynese deal with traders who don't follow their dictates.

When Alyiakal finishes, he says, "I don't know what else there is to tell. Except for the barbarians, the raiders, and the weather, there's not that much else of great interest."

"You're very observant," replies the factor, "especially about copper and how it's traded."

"I'm not a trader, but I don't like the idea of Cyadoran traders buying copper, then going to Jeranyi smiths who forge polished copper or brass shields that they then supply to barbarian raiders." Alyiakal offers a sardonic smile. "I also don't like the idea that any officer who mentions that in Cyad is endangering his future or possibly his life."

"You're telling me," replies Vassyl.

"You're not a trader in Cyad, and you're honest. And trustworthy."

"How do you know that? Except for today, we've only talked briefly a few times."

"I just know," declares Alyiakal.

"Hyrsaal told me years ago that Alyiakal was never wrong about his judgment of people," adds Saelora.

"I've been wrong about what people might do," replies Alyiakal.

"But not about what kind of people they are. You understood Mother in moments."

Alyiakal almost replies that seeing Marenda's character wasn't that hard, but decides against it.

Before he can say something else, Saelora adds, "And don't say that you're fortunate or something like that."

"Well, you're right," says Alyiakal.

"She usually is," adds Vassyl.

"Is there anything else you'd like to know?" Alyiakal turns to Vassyl. "Besides Pemedra?"

"I have a small favor to ask. You're being posted to Guarstyad. I've heard rumors about a spice, some kind of underground mushroom, that they harvest there from the roots of certain trees. They only trade with certain important Merchanters from Fyrad . . . but not Cyad. If you hear anything about it, if you'd convey that to Saelora, I'd appreciate it."

"I can do that. I'll have to mention you knew about traders going to Guarstyad, or something like that. Is there anything else?"

"You lived close to the Accursed Forest before you were a Mirror Lancer, Saelora told me. What are your impressions about the Forest? Have they changed?"

"Impressions change as we learn. I always thought that the Great Forest held a great deal of power. The only change in my feelings is that it's more powerful than I realized."

"Why do you think that?"

"I can't say." *Not without revealing more than I should.* "It's a feeling."

"Sometimes, feelings are more accurate than reasoned thought," observes Vassyl.

"But it helps to know when that's so," replies Alyiakal sardonically, "and when people won't accept feelings as a reason."

"I imagine that's often the case for lancer officers."

"Usually is more like it." Then Alyiakal smiles and adds, "Except when we're out on patrol." Before either Saelora or Vassyl can say more, he asks, "Why are you interested in my feelings about the Great Forest?"

"It was here before we were. Everyone accepts that it will remain behind the walls and nothing will change. I look for things that people think won't change, but could."

"I have the feeling that the Forest isn't about to change anytime soon."

"Why do you say that so confidently?" asks Vassyl.

"Because the Third Magus was at Geliendra yesterday and the day before, presumably to check the wall wards. After that he left quietly. That suggests to me that he found nothing amiss. There would have been an undercurrent of feelings and unrest if he had been worried."

Vassyl frowns, then fingers his chin. After a moment, he says, "I can see that." Then he smiles broadly and stands. "I've kept you long enough. You two need to enjoy the rest of the day."

Saelora is on her feet as quickly as Vassyl, but Alyiakal isn't far behind, and she leads the way through the warehouse to the stable. When they get there, he notices immediately that her roan is already saddled.

"Are we headed to your house and the distillery, or do you need to go somewhere else first?"

"We don't, but thank you for asking."

"Do you need me to lead the roan out front so you can bar the stable?"

"No. We can close the doors. Vassyl will be along shortly to bar them."

Before long the two are riding north on Canal Street, which doesn't seem as busy as it had on fiveday, but then, it is sevenday, and more than a few people try not to work late or even in the afternoon on sevenday.

"You're a bit like a magus, aren't you?" asks Saelora quietly.

"Why do you say that?"

"They picked you for field healing. Reading between the lines of your letters, I'd say fewer of the wounded in your company died from wounds. Don't tell me that you were fortunate, either."

"The training helped. What I learned from Healer Vayidra in Syadtar did as well. I wrote you about her."

"You did. I have to say I'm glad she's much, much older."

"I never thought of her that way. I had too much to learn."

"And you did. You're more than a field healer, Alyiakal."

"At least a bit more," he concedes. "Why do you think so?"

"You're very practical and capable. Yet you talk about feelings as if they're so real that you can touch them. That means, to you, they are."

Alyiakal manages a soft laugh. "You are a very dangerous woman, Saelora, but I imagine all good Merchanters are."

"So are all good Mirror Lancer officers. I have no doubt that you're good in a quietly effective fashion."

"Several senior officers have mentioned that. They've also hinted that it's a disadvantage."

"Of course it is. When you're really good at something, it seems effortless to others. They don't realize how much skill and effort is involved."

"Like building a spirits-trading business and a distillery?"

Apparently to avoid comment on that, Saelora says, "We turn east on the old road ahead."

"You don't like to talk about your success, do you?" Alyiakal makes it a question.

"I try to let the brandy speak for itself. Anything resembling boasting by a woman doesn't set well with many men . . . or most women."

"Vassyl praises what you do."

"He and Buurel are about the only ones besides you." Saelora turns the roan onto the old east road, and Alyiakal does the same with the mare.

He suspects there are others who think highly of Saelora, but since she's obviously worried about saying much about what she's done, he says, "Vassyl mentioned a special liqueur. How is that coming?"

"Laetilla and I are still working on it. It needs to be a bit sweeter, I think. We have a couple of different versions at the house."

"And some of the greenberry brandy?"

"Of course." She pauses, then asks, "Is my company so wearing that you need brandy to bear it?"

Alyiakal can hear the teasing tone, but says mournfully, "I think you're being hard on me."

She doesn't laugh, but there's a hint of a smile.

"I'd like at least a sip of the greenberry brandy. I'd like to be able to recommend it, but I'd be deceptive if I've never tasted it."

"There's some. It's only been aged a year or so. It's drinkable, but we're trying to age most of it longer. We're behind on that because it took longer to find a cooper who would make enough barrels."

When they reach the barn, they settle both horses quickly and enter the house through the door from the attached barn to the kitchen.

Laetilla immediately turns and smiles. "It won't be that long."

"We're not going anywhere else." Saelora leads the way to the front parlor, where she takes one of the armchairs.

Alyiakal takes the other. Since Saelora doesn't say anything, he asks, "Is there anything about me that you haven't already deduced and would like to know?"

"I have a thought or two, but I'm curious. Were there any boys or girls your age in Jakaafra?"

Alyiakal debates how much he should reveal at the moment, then says, "I lived at the post in the commander's quarters. I was the only young person there." He pauses. "As you've guessed, I do have a little ability with magery. I don't talk about it or show it because lancer officers aren't supposed to have or use those abilities, unless they become Mirror Engineers. I had some instruction from a mage in Jakaafra. My father hoped I could become a magus, but the mage felt my abilities were based too much in order, and unsuited to being a Mirror Engineer. I got the field-healing training because the mage testing the officer candidates at Kynstaar noticed that I had higher level of order than usual. They're a bit higher than he thought because I learned to shield them. Healer Vayidra later helped me with that as well." Alyiakal holds up a hand. "I'm getting to the girls, or girl."

Saelora grins. "I knew there had to be someone. Go on."

Alyiakal decides not to ask how she knows that and says, "I was walking the road beside the Forest wall one evening—"

"You *walked* there all alone?"

"I did carry a sabre."

Saelora shakes her head.

"Anyway, I saw a black panther that somehow wasn't quite that . . ." Alyiakal recounts meeting Adayal, how he found out she was also Triamon's student, and his efforts to find her name. "I thought Adayal must be near my age, but she was actually at least several years older, and she taught me about the Great Forest. This all happened the Summer before I went to Kynstaar. The last time I saw her, she told me she was at least half a part of the Great Forest, and that I was meant for a different life, and destined for great things she couldn't and wouldn't share." He shrugs. "Until you, she was the only girl or woman in my life. But she would have been miserable consorted to a Mirror Lancer. As powerful as the Forest is, that's not who *I* am. So we both would have suffered."

"You're both fortunate to have realized that."

Alyiakal offers a wry smile. "Give her the credit. I didn't realize it until I was posted to Pemedra. Actually, until I'd been in Pemedra quite a while, and started to really think about the way people live—or have to live."

"You never tried to write her?"

"I couldn't, not directly anyway. She lived in the Great Forest, and the magus who taught us both disappeared when I was at Kynstaar. My father wrote me a letter, carefully impersonal, not mentioning that Triamon had taught me, about the disappearance of a local mage."

"A warning, you think?"

Alyiakal nods. "No doubt of that. Triamon taught me skills I wasn't supposed to know."

This time, she is the one to shake her head. "The more you wrote, the more I *knew* you were different."

"I didn't want to deceive you, but most letters to lancer officers are secretly opened and read. At least, many of mine have been. So, until I could talk to you in person . . . and I didn't want to say much until I knew you a little better."

"You're taking a risk in telling me, aren't you?"

"It's a risk only if you tell anyone else. I trust you. Even if we're only friends. Even if we weren't friends, you wouldn't break that trust." He pauses. "Am I wrong?"

In the muted light of the small parlor, he can see the hint of tears. "I hope I haven't upset you."

She shakes her head, then swallows. "No one . . . no one has given me what you have."

"No one's ever done what you have," he replies quietly. "I can't tell you how I've looked forward to your letters."

She manages a shaky smile. "I look for yours."

"Then we need to keep writing, although I understand there may be delays to and from Guarstyad during the Winter. The only way to get there is by ship once the passes are snowed in, and sometimes the seas are too rough." He stops speaking as he senses Laetilla coming into the parlor.

"Dinner is ready."

"Thank you, Laetilla," says Saelora as she stands.

Alyiakal admires the athletic grace in her movements, then stands as well and follows her into the small dining room, where the three lit candles in the candelabrum supplement the late-afternoon sun.

They both sit, and Alyiakal looks at his wineglass and his plate.

"The wine is Alafraan, the same as last time. The dinner is baked chopped lamb combined with various spices and other savories, rice and raisins, and roasted turnips."

"And the glaze or sauce?" he asks.

"It's special. We hope you like it."

Alyiakal offers an amused smile, suspecting he knows at least one element of the sauce, but he waits for Saelora to begin. Once she takes a bite, so does he. A small bite, so that, if he detests what he is tasting, he can suppress any physical reaction. Except he doesn't have to. The chopped lamb morsels are tender, with a hint of mint. The glaze adds a touch of a sweet yet sharp, but muted, "greenness" that he cannot describe in any other way and gives the rice and raisins a piquancy that makes Alyiakal want another bite. It also helps with the turnips.

"This is magnificent." *Except for the turnips, but they were even edible.* "You could sell that glaze or sauce as well."

Saelora beams. "Laetilla and I came up with the sauce. We'd thought about selling it, but some of the spices are expensive."

"Put it in smaller bottles. Give one bottle to each of the larger traders, and then sell additional bottles for a hefty price." Alyiakal frowns. "Maybe you should make a few bottles and see how they age before you put any of it up for sale. Wine and distilled spirits age mostly predictably. Something like the sauce . . . that might be different, and it might not age well at all."

"We'd thought about that."

Alyiakal nods and happily returns to enjoying a tasty and very special dinner. He leaves not a morsel or the smallest trace of the glaze sauce on his plate.

"I can see that you didn't like the dinner at all." Saelora smiles broadly.

He looks at her equally empty plate. "Neither did you."

"I may be a terrible cook, but I do like food, especially good food. I'm fortunate that Laetilla enjoys cooking more than eating."

"Cooking for you . . . and for the captain," adds Laetilla from the doorway. "May I take the plates?"

"Please," says Saelora.

As Laetilla leaves the small dining room with the plates, Saelora stands. Alyiakal pushes back his chair and starts to get up.

"Please sit down. I'll be back in a moment."

Alyiakal eases his chair forward. He senses faint amusement from Saelora, but no strong adverse emotions.

Shortly, if more than a few moments later, Saelora returns with Laetilla. Saelora carries two bottles, and Laetilla two wineglasses and two smaller glasses, which she sets at Saelora's place before leaving the dining room.

"The smaller glasses?" asks Alyiakal.

"Cordial or liqueur glasses. We didn't plan a dessert. You said you wanted to taste the greenberry brandy, and Vassyl mentioned the liqueur . . ." Saelora reseats herself and fills the wineglasses only about a third full, before handing one to Alyiakal. "This is the brandy. See what you think."

Alyiakal lifts the wineglass and sips the clear, greenish-tinted liquid. There's both a smoothness and a sharp edge to the brandy, and that small sip goes down his throat easily and warmly. The taste resembles the glaze, but is more direct. He tastes the familiar underlying hint of pearapple, and something completely different, which has to be the greenberry.

"What you're drinking is the oldest brandy we have. It's barely two years old, and we don't have much of it. We're trying to balance what we sell with what we'd like to age longer, because the taste gets smoother over time."

"This tastes smooth to me. Much smoother—and a lot stronger—than most of the wine lancer officers get."

"We'll never be able to make large volumes of the brandy. That's why Vassyl thinks we ought to age most of it longer, so that it's of higher quality and we can sell it for more."

"I'm no Merchanter, but that makes sense to me."

Alyiakal takes another sip of the brandy, deciding that it is too strong for him, especially after the wine he had with dinner, and sets the glass aside. He watches as Saelora fills the cordial glasses half full and extends one to him.

They both sip, and she looks to him inquisitively.

"The liqueur has the same basic taste as the brandy, but I taste other subtle flavors beyond the greenberry and the hint of pearapple. I couldn't tell you what those flavors are, only that they're present."

"You're tasting more than the few others who've had it."

"I'd wager they wanted more."

"They did, but not necessarily for the subtle flavors," she replies wryly. "Outland traders are known for liking strong spirits."

"So are some lancer officers."

"You're not one of them."

"No, I'm not." For one thing, Alyiakal has never been fond of spirits stronger than wine or ale, and he's never wanted to lose control of his thoughts or tongue. "How did you come to that conclusion?"

"Hyrsaal said you never overindulged, but I also got that impression from the way you write your letters."

"Have you heard from him lately?"

"No, but he's supposed to be here next sixday or sevenday."

"Did Gaaran say any more about your mother?"

"You mean, did she say anything more about you?"

"Or about you, for setting up the dinner at her house."

"She never says much about me. I'm not feminine enough."

"You're very feminine, and not simpering or manipulative, and I like that."

"You're kind."

"No, I like you the way you are. I think you've always been like that."

Saelora frowns.

"You don't think so?"

"I think I was less determined and more self-centered before Father died. I never realized how much warmth and light he brought into the house. Not until he was gone. He wasn't boisterous or loud—just quietly warm and cheerful."

"And he loved and warmed your mother?"

Saelora nods. "No one else can."

"I'd guess she won't warm to anyone else, not because you and Gaaran aren't warm people." *I can see why Gaaran wants her close, but in separate quarters.*

Alyiakal glances to the single window and takes in the late-afternoon light.

Saelora follows his gaze. "You need to go soon."

"Unhappily . . . yes. What are you doing tomorrow?"

Saelora smiles. "Tomorrow is eightday, remember?"

"I could come earlier."

"You could." She pauses. "I'd thought about inviting Karola and Faadyr for a midday dinner."

"At your house, I take it?"

"Faadyr and Mother are cordial at best."

"Because Karola consorted him without your mother's approval?"

"She thought a smallholder was beneath Karola."

Alyiakal isn't about to comment directly on that, instead saying, "Karola obviously disagreed or didn't care."

"Both. Besides that, Faadyr holds more lands than most holders. They're productive lands, too."

"So he's fairly well off?"

"More than fairly, I'd judge. But he's quiet about it."

"I'd be happy to meet them, if it won't be too much work for you."

"It won't be for me, and I'm paying Laetilla extra for the dinner."

Alyiakal refrains from pointing out that Saelora seems exceedingly sure that everyone would agree to the dinner and says, "When should I arrive?"

"Noon would be good. That way we could eat at first glass."

"I can manage that."

"You can manage anything you put your mind and skills to."

"Not everything." *And definitely not dealing with a magus of the highest level.*

"Most things, I'd wager."

"There are some I'd rather not try."

"Those are the ones we usually have to face, sooner or later." She offers a resigned smile and stands. "We need to get you on your way."

LV

There are only a handful of officers at the mess on eightday morning, one of whom is Ghrennan. He and Alyiakal talk cheerfully about matters of no immediate consequence. After finishing breakfast, Alyiakal dons his light riding jacket, because the air is definitely cooler than usual for early in Autumn, and he strolls around the post to familiarize himself with where everything is. Then he goes to the stable, talks to the duty ostler, and leaves riding the same mare as before.

Once he is on the old stone road to Vaeyal, he glances around. He can't see anyone nearby, and the occasional trees bordering the road will shield him from anyone seeing what he is about to attempt.

First, he gathers a small amount of free chaos, keeping it within a web of order, and then he throws the chaos as far as he can ahead of him—and, especially, the mare—slightly to the left.

The chaos strikes the paving stones some twenty yards in front of the mare and flares into a pillar less than a yard high, before dissipating, leaving a circular patch of polished stone. The mare doesn't even break stride. Then again, Alyiakal wouldn't have expected anything less since lancer mounts are accustomed to firelances.

On the second try, Alyiakal uses less free chaos, and a bit more order to increase the range, but the chaos burst lands only a little farther away than the first.

For the next quint, as he rides, he continues to experiment, but by the time his head begins to ache, he has still extended the range of his small chaos bolts to only forty yards, less than the range of a firelance.

You definitely need more work and more practice.

His headache slowly subsides and is almost gone when he reaches Canal Street at nearly two quints before noon. He continues on and reins up before Saelora's stable more than a quint before noon. Since the stable doors are unbarred, he opens them and leads the mare inside, settling her in the same stall he's used before. He closes the stable doors and is about to knock on the kitchen door when Saelora opens it.

"I thought you might be early. I'm glad you are." She steps back so that he can enter, and adds, "Try not to peek at what Laetilla's doing. It's always better if dinner's a bit of a surprise."

Alyiakal avoids looking either at Laetilla or at what's on the stove and the worktable, as he follows Saelora into the parlor.

Saelora does not sit in one of the armchairs, but turns to him. "I'd hoped to have a settee by now, but it's taking longer than I'd hoped. We'll have to go to the dining room and have a drink there, while Laetilla finishes up with dinner."

"Can I help?"

She shakes her head.

"No matter how well you plan, when you depend on others . . . well . . . sometimes they're not as disciplined as you are, or something happens that they can't control."

Saelora merely nods.

She has kept glancing to the parlor window, Alyiakal notes, and abruptly she says, "Here come Karola and Faadyr." She turns, walks to the front door, and opens it.

Alyiakal follows, and they both watch as Faadyr guides the single-horse chaise up to the front of the stable, where he and Karola alight, and then tie the horse to the sturdy hitching post. The chaise appears solid and well-made, but displays no ornamentation at all, a statement of prosperity without presumption of position as full holder or a Merchanter.

Alyiakal takes in both Karola and Faadyr as they walk toward the front door.

Except for her cheerful and open smile as she sees her sister, Karola looks the way her mother, Marenda, might have in her youth, with the flame-red hair and slender build, but her midsection is broader—and Alyiakal realizes from the separate pattern of order and chaos that she is with child.

At first glance, Faadyr doesn't look like a smallholder, not with his lanky, wiry build, but his brown jacket and trousers are of fine polished cotton, as is his cream shirt. He looks to be a few years older than Alyiakal. He also smiles as he sees Saelora. "We're here and on time."

"As if Karola would let you be late," replies Saelora, from where she stands in the doorway, with Alyiakal beside her.

"As if I'd ever want to be late when we're coming to see you."

Alyiakal can hear Faadyr's slight emphasis on the word "you," but he keeps the smile he feels to himself.

Karola's eyes turn to Alyiakal. "It's good to see you. I've heard so much." She smiles again and says to Saelora, "You were right."

"Dare I ask what you were right about?" Alyiakal asks Saelora.

"Wise man," says Faadyr as he follows his consort to the front door. "You'll notice he didn't ask what, not directly."

The two sisters exchange glances.

After a moment, Saelora says, "That you're five cubits tall and made of stone."

"I'm not that hard," replies Alyiakal in mock protest, understanding that, if Saelora wants to tell him what she really said, it will be later. *Possibly much later.*

"Do come in to my all-too-humble abode," says Saelora, stepping back inside.

Alyiakal steps to the side to allow the couple to enter.

Faadyr looks around the sparsely furnished parlor and nods, approvingly, then says to Saelora, "You've done the important things first. Windows, doors, shutters . . . and the distillery building looks solid. Karola told me, but it's good to see."

"And the kitchen," adds Karola.

"Because I did those first," says Saelora, "we have to go into the dining room to sit down."

This time the table is set for four. As before, each place setting holds a single white porcelain platter edged in blue, set off by the Merchanter-blue tablecloth, the silver cutlery and utensils, and four blue-tinted crystal wineglasses. Given that it is midday, the tapers in the candelabrum remain unlit.

Alyiakal senses Faadyr and Karola's slight surprise, and that Saelora speaks quickly.

"I'll sit at this end, and Alyiakal will be at the other end, with you two across from each other. The porcelainware and wineglasses came from Vassyl as a housewarming gift. He had a score of place settings and dinner cutlery from his old house on the north end of town, and he said he'd never use it, and Elinjya can't."

Faadyr frowns for a moment, then nods. "You're effectively his Merchanter heir."

"That's almost exactly what he said. He did add that he wanted me to use them to my advantage." Saelora comes up with an impish smile. "He didn't specify what advantage." She gestures to the chairs and immediately seats herself.

Alyiakal understands. Saelora is a Merchanter, not a woman subservient to any man.

Laetilla appears and fills each wineglass exactly half full, then leaves the dining room.

Alyiakal immediately lifts his wineglass. "To the Lady Merchanter who made this dinner possible."

Saelora flushes slightly, but nods as everyone drinks, and then lifts her glass. "And to the Mirror Lancer captain who encouraged me from the first."

After that, there is a moment of silence before Karola looks to Alyiakal and asks, "You'll be here for another eightday?"

"I have to leave for Fyrad an eightday from tomorrow morning." Alyiakal briefly explains his itinerary and duty station.

Karola shivers. "It has to be cold at the foot of the Westhorns."

"I'm told it can be quite chill. But Hyrsaal's going to Lhaarat, and that's also at the foot of the Westhorns, and it's farther north."

"He didn't mention that," says Karola. "Is it dangerous?"

"It's not supposed to be as dangerous as the northern and northeastern border posts," replies Alyiakal, "and there aren't any good passes between Cyador and Kyphros. But there are always brigands in the hills beyond the borders." He turns to Faadyr. "I've heard your name more than a few times, but not enough for me to know much." He grins. "Except that Karola was most interested in you."

"I was always most interested in her as well." The smallholder blushes. "I've been fortunate in inheriting some land and more fortunate in obtaining additional parcels."

"Fortunate," snorts Karola. "He's taken worn-out and overused lands, and made them bloom again."

"Over time," adds Faadyr.

For the next two quints or so, the conversation is mostly about lands and planting, for which Alyiakal is grateful, and then Laetilla serves the midday dinner and says, "This is a dish popular in Hamor. I've always liked it, and I trust you will, also."

"Thank you so much," says Saelora. "I'm sure we will."

Alyiakal looks at his plate. Thin strips of braised fowl breast laid on a bed of sticky rice. After waiting for Saelora, he cuts a morsel and tastes it. The meat is tender, moist, and piquant—with a touch of smokiness and a hint of pearapple sweetness. The rice carries the same flavors, with a hint of crunchiness.

"This is really special." Karola looks to Alyiakal. "We wouldn't be here having this if you weren't here. We're so glad we could meet you."

"I wouldn't be here if Saelora hadn't written a lonely officer candidate almost six years ago," Alyiakal says quietly but warmly.

"And if you hadn't replied with such wonderful letters," answers Saelora.

Alyiakal wants to protest that his letters weren't that wonderful. "We both did what we could."

From her end of the table, Saelora offers a mischievous smile.

He smiles back.

"Do you think you'll be able to come back here anytime soon?" asks Karola.

"I won't get home leave for at least another two years, maybe three."

"That's awful."

That's one reason why your father didn't get consorted until he finished his obligation and was stipended out. "We all know that's the way it is."

"Letters are such a poor substitute," presses Karola cheerfully.

"Alyiakal can't change the way the Mirror Lancers function, dear," says Faadyr patiently. "Just like I can't change the rhythm of the seasons."

"But . . ."

"He can't, and I can't." Faadyr's tone is gentle, but firm.

The rest of the dinner conversation deals with comparisons of various foods, a few questions about Mirror Lancer duties and postings, and assorted recollections of past events.

Two cheerful glasses later, Faadyr and Karola leave.

Saelora takes a deep breath and sinks into one of the parlor armchairs.

"A bit of a strain?" asks Alyiakal dryly, sensing the tension leaving Saelora.

"She's sweet, and I love her, but . . ."

"She believes she can arrange the world the way she thinks it should be?"

"It's more that she's arranged her life to suit her, and why can't I do the same."

"Faadyr seems kind and caring. Is he?" Alyiakal thinks that the smallholder is from what he's perceived, but he knows that differing circumstances can bring out less desirable characteristics and behavior in people.

"He's not only prosperous, but he's a dear man, better than Mother could have hoped, and all Mother can think of is that he's a smallholder."

"Even though Karola will have a better and happier life with him than with men of supposedly higher position?"

"She will. In time, Faadyr will be even better off than most of them. I wouldn't be surprised if he's recognized as a holder." Saelora smiles sardonically. "Even if it might be after Mother's gone."

For several long moments, neither speaks.

"You're the quiet one, aren't you?" asks Alyiakal. "That's why your mother referred to you as the recluse."

"Mother's always wanted to make a personal impression on people. I'm happier doing things that are meaningful."

Alyiakal nods. "Even in your choice of whom to write. You do things because they feel right. For you, what's meaningful in a constructive way is what feels right."

She frowns. "Can something destructive be really meaningful?"

"Unhappily . . . yes. If I'm reading history correctly, Emperor Kieffal, the previous Emperor of Light, wanted to expand Cyador's rule beyond the Grass Hills. That's why he built Pemedra. Before he could take further steps, he had an untimely accident. Many suspect it wasn't an accident. Whether it was or not, the accident was destructive and meaningful because it affected trade and borders, not to mention who profited and how from the trade of copper mined in Cerlyn."

"You never wrote about that."

"A senior officer suggested quite strongly that junior officers should not speak of it. Putting it in a letter that might be read by someone other than you wouldn't have been wise."

"I can see that. It doesn't speak well of—"

"Any number of people in power in the Triad."

"Triad?"

"The higher levels of the Mirror Lancers, the Magi'i, and the Merchanters."

"I don't think I'd want to be a Merchanter in Cyad."

Alyiakal laughs softly. "You might not like it, but you'd do well because you focus on what's meaningful." He pauses, then asks, "Do you know if your father was ever posted anywhere close to Guarstyad?"

"I don't think so. Why?"

"I thought it might be useful to study maps of the area."

She shakes her head with a rueful expression. "Do you always think about duty?"

"Not always. I've been here an eightday, and it's the first time I thought about maps when I've been with you."

"The first time you thought about them or the first time you asked?"

"Both."

"I'm glad to hear it." Saelora sits up straighter in the armchair. "You should be on your way." She stands. "I need to get something. Wait here. I'll be right back."

Alyiakal still stands, but does not attempt to follow her toward the rear of the small house, much as he would like to.

She returns almost immediately and hands him a heavy cloth bag with an amused smile. "You did ask for this."

"Greenberry brandy?" he asks.

"Three bottles, each wrapped in cloth."

"I'll save them for where and when they'll do some good." He pauses, then asks, "Tomorrow?"

Saelora shakes her head. "There's too much to do on oneday and twoday."

"Third afternoon glass on threeday?" he suggests.

"I'd like that." Then she guides him toward the kitchen and the stable. "Third glass on threeday."

"I'll be here."

LVI

Once he finishes breakfast on oneday morning and the officers stand to leave, Alyiakal decides to follow Ghrennan and Nyell under a concealment. He has to duck into an unused side hall to raise the concealment, and by the time he catches up, the other two captains are outside, walking toward headquarters.

". . . definitely has to be a woman he's visiting in the area. Likely not in Geliendra, either."

"He can't be sleeping with her, or not at night," replies Nyell. "He gets back too early in the evening, usually around sundown. What do you really think of him?"

"He's young for his rank. Means he went through the whole three years at Kynstaar. Overheard the subcommander say Alyiakal was one of the top undercaptains. It also means," says Ghrennan, "that Alyiakal isn't the boasting type. There's more to him. I can't figure out what."

"He wouldn't be posted to Guarstyad if there weren't," replies Nyell with a sound that could be either laugh or snort. "He sounds perfect for dealing with the Kyphrans. A good company officer who's excellent with weapons, mounts, and men and too junior to be able to use his accomplishments for his own benefit."

"Most of the company officers being sent to Guarstyad are like that," says Ghrennan cynically. "Only the best, and sometimes the most fortunate, survive such duty unscathed."

As the two reach the low steps to the headquarters building, Alyiakal halts and waits until both enter before turning and making his way toward the southern gates, where, in a niche where the walls meet the massive gatepost, he removes the concealment before heading out into the small city of Geliendra.

He walks quickly past the establishments catering to rankers and then turns south at the next cross street, which contains a variety of shops. Since he hasn't seen anything in the market square that strikes him as a suitable gift for Saelora, he hopes the shops will offer more variety—except he discovers that most of them are not open yet. He smiles wryly and keeps walking, taking his time and window-shopping for an idea of what each sells. Two blocks farther south, he sees a silversmith's shop, and the next block a goldsmith's, with iron gratings across the windows, as well as a shop that sells all types of cloth, and possibly scarves. When he reaches the point where the shops give way to modest houses, he retraces his steps and then makes his way to the coffee shop he had visited the previous oneday.

The shop holds a handful of older men, two of whom look at Alyiakal and immediately lose interest.

The blond woman who greets him is young, certainly several years younger than Alyiakal, and offers him a wide, warm smile that includes her eyes. "Just you, Captain?"

"Just me."

She guides him to a table beside one of the numerous small windows. "Do you know what you want?"

"Coffee and one of those flaky spirals."

"That's a good choice."

He smiles pleasantly and asks, "Is there anything better?"

"For this early in the day, I'd say not. You wouldn't be on leave, would you?"

"How did you guess?" Alyiakal's tone of voice is wry.

"You're a captain, and not one of the old captains. Younger captains on duty aren't usually free to go to coffeehouses this time of day."

"You obviously know about the Mirror Lancers. Anyone in your family serve?"

She shakes her head. "We're all involved with the coffeehouse. Everyone who works here is family. We're very good at listening." She follows those words with an amused expression that's not quite a smile. "Let me get your coffee and spiral."

In moments, she returns with a tall narrow mug and a small plate holding the flaky pastry. "Here you are. That will be three."

Alyiakal hands her four coppers. "A quick question before you go. I was thinking to do some shopping . . . a thank-you gift for the family I'm visiting. Besides the shops east and south of here, are there other good shops nearby?"

"Those are good. So are the ones two blocks west and south of the market square."

"Thank you."

"My pleasure."

Alyiakal takes his time with the coffee and the pastry, then makes his way to the shops beginning to open near the market square. The only places that interest him are a bookstore, because he has never seen many, and the coppersmith's shop, where he sees nothing that he feels might be appropriate for Saelora. So he returns to the street he visited earlier.

He decides to enter the cloth shop, but most of what is offered consists of bolts of various fabrics, except shimmersilk. There is a small display of shimmersilk scarves, but the colors are limited to a deep red, pink, forest green, and lavender. The older male shopkeeper watches Alyiakal with a skepticism that's definitely not concealed, and Alyiakal leaves without speaking.

His next stop is at the silversmith's shop. Alyiakal is immediately taken by a small silver bird perched on a silver limb, then smiles as he realizes it is a miniature of a traitor bird, and even the bird's posture captures its mischief and calculation. He turns to the older woman behind the counter. "A display piece?"

"Good for you, Captain. Most men your age don't see that."

"The artistry is excellent, but you know that."

"I'll pass that on to Geillant."

"Has anyone tried to buy it?"

She smiles sardonically. "The only use it would have would be as an elegant insult, and it could be traced far too easily."

Unless someone bought it now and saved it for years.

"Would you sell it?"

"We'll sell almost anything at the right price."

"Hypothetically . . . how much?"

"Four silvers."

Almost half a gold . . . but . . . "I'll have to think about it." Alyiakal immediately senses the polite skepticism behind the woman's pleasant expression. "Thank you very much."

"You're welcome, ser."

Alyiakal knows he'll be back, assuming that what he purchases for Saelora doesn't exhaust his funds, but she comes before his whim. *But is it a whim . . . or a calculated purpose for a time yet to come?*

His next stop is the shop of the goldsmith. The iron gratings have been folded back, but as he sees when he walks inside, far more is on display than he has expected. A muscular middle-aged man stands behind the small display case.

"Good morning, Captain."

"Good morning." Alyiakal's eyes go to the display case.

"You looking for jewelry with green stones? Some pieces here with malachite, green garnet, or tourmaline."

"I was actually looking for something with blue stones."

"Over here, ser. That ring is sapphire. Most expensive, ser. The bracelet here is lapis."

Alyiakal nods, but the lapis doesn't speak to him.

"And there's this . . ."

"I take it that the gold of the setting is worth more than the stone?" asks Alyiakal.

"That's the problem with blue stones, Captain. You've got sapphire, and anything with a good stone, even a very small stone, will be over a gold. The other blue stones, well, they can be pretty, but pretty's not enough for those with golds to spare."

Alyiakal listens, but a bracelet in the corner of the case catches his eye, a circlet of silvery gold with brighter blue stones, not quite as intense as the sapphires, but with a definite crystalline depth. "What about that bracelet?"

"It's too big for most women's wrists. It was a special piece. His consort didn't like it. Sent it back from Fyrad. The stones are blue zargun, and the bracelet proper is electrum."

"How much would it be?"

"Ser . . . blue zargun is . . ."

"Usually worn only by Merchanters or their consorts?"

"Ah . . . yes, ser. You understand that there is no prohibition, but a woman not of the Merchanters might be . . . uncomfortable."

Alyiakal nods. "I understand. How much is the bracelet?"

"Almost a gold."

"How about four silvers?"

The goldsmith shakes his head. "Not for that."

Alyiakal feels that he won't have to pay a gold, but he can't tell how far the other will go down. "Five then."

"Not less than seven."

"How about six and five."

"For you, ser, I'll take that."

"For your peace of mind, it is for someone whom no one could fault for wearing it."

Alyiakal senses a certain relief from the goldsmith, possibly because he won't have to rework the bracelet or because he can claim it went to a Merchanter. *Or maybe both.*

For a few additional coppers, Alyiakal purchases a small black wooden box to hold the bracelet, and the goldsmith throws in a soft woolen cloth to wrap around it.

Then Alyiakal walks back to the silversmith's.

The older woman looks up in surprise as she sees him enter the shop.

"What about three silvers for the bird?"

She turns and looks toward the rear of the shop.

An amused voice calls out, "Three and two. Final."

Alyiakal counts out the coins, then accepts the miniature traitor bird, which fits neatly in the wooden box with the bracelet, for which he's grateful.

He smiles as he walks back toward the post with his two successful purchases, one of which he hopes will brighten Saelora's days, and the other of which he has no idea of when or where it may be useful, only that, somehow, it will be.

LVII

Alyiakal wakes to find himself in an enclosed space, reminding him of a fire-wagon, except that he can sense that the contained chaos that powers the conveyance is far more compressed, and far deadlier. His limbs move, and he opens the vehicle's odd door and steps out.

Less than fifty yards away, a handful of men, and some women, in odd greenish uniforms, are building a whitestone wall.

Alyiakal turns to see a lanky man, flushed and angry, walking toward him.

"It's a waste of power and people! A total waste. Just because you say there's an agreement. An agreement with a stupid forest. If you won't call it off, I will . . . one way or another."

"You won't," Alyiakal finds himself saying. "Without the agreement, in days, we'll have nothing."

"Since you won't listen to reason—" The other man lifts a wand of some sort, and bluish chaos flares toward Alyiakal.

It never strikes. Alyiakal wields a tight, compressed white knife of chaos that cuts through the blue fire and the man who tried to kill him. In an instant, the attacker is less than ashes. The power so casually wielded staggers Alyiakal, even as he struggles to understand and capture the structure and essence of that tightly coiled chaos.

Coiled chaos?

With that single question, the Forest, the wall, and the conveyance all vanish, and Alyiakal discovers he is standing beside his bed in but his smallclothes.

That had to be the same magus who bound the Forest.

Alyiakal shudders at the recollection of the power the man wielded.

But why are you remembering his acts? Because he was linked to the Great Forest? Am I?

Before he forgets, Alyiakal concentrates on pressing chaos into a tight coil, bound in order, tighter and tighter . . . focusing a line of it on the stone floor.

Hssst!

Heat flares from the cubit-long slit in the stone, and Alyiakal steps back, swallowing.

But you did it!

He forces himself to do it again. And yet again, fearful that he will not remember in the morning.

When he finally lies down again, exhausted, he can only hope that he will recall what the dream—or vision—has taught him.

When he finally wakes on twoday morning, yawning and wondering if he had dreamed the part about using chaos, he immediately looks at the floor.

The clean-cut slits in the stone are still there.

Then he tries to gather and coil chaos . . . and does, but at the cost of a dull throbbing in his skull, and he lets the chaos dissipate—mostly, binding a bit to his inner shield to strengthen it, before realizing, belatedly, that he'd never done that before, nor known how.

He shivers and looks at the slits once more.

No one will enter his quarters until he leaves, and whatever ranker who's later assigned to clean the quarters will be mystified.

The throbbing in his skull doesn't go away until he's eaten a large breakfast, another reminder that working with order and chaos has a price.

After leaving the mess, Alyiakal sees no point in exploring Geliendra further and thinks any immediate exercises with order and chaos are likely not the best idea. Instead, he decides to find maps of the area around Guarstyad.

His first thought is to ask the senior squad leader serving as Subcommander Zaentyl's clerk, but when he reaches the headquarters building and asks, the response is disappointing.

"Maps of Guarstyad? No, ser. We have maps of all of this part of Cyador, but they only go so far as the foot of the Westhorns."

"Do you know of anyone who might?"

"I couldn't say, ser."

"Thank you."

Alyiakal smiles pleasantly and then makes his way out of the headquarters building, thinking. While the Mirror Engineers might have some maps of the harbor area around Guarstyad, such maps would be available only in Fyrad. Then he recalls the small bookshop near the market square.

It can't hurt to ask. Besides, the bookseller might know where else to find maps. *If not, you might have time to see if you can get maps in Fyrad.*

Glancing up at the gathering clouds, Alyiakal realizes that he is actually sensing the flows of order and chaos, flows strong enough that there will be a thundershower before long, but not as powerful as a thundersnow. He lengthens his stride as he walks out of the southern gates and turns west.

The name of the shop turns out to be Books and Rarities, and when Alyiakal stops outside the narrow door, it is smaller than he remembered, little more than four yards across the front, although he suspects it is likely far deeper. He also notes the large glass windows across the front, placed too high for anyone to peer in or to look out and fixed so as not to be opened, and he wonders at their purpose.

He opens the heavy door, and a bell chimes. It chimes again as he steps into the shop and closes the door.

"Be right there!" calls out a raspy voice cheerfully.

Alyiakal glances around. Books line the walls on both sides of the shop, and the shelves extend from about a third of a yard above the stone floor to roughly three yards high, but the shelves extend only some four yards back from the door to an interior wall, in the middle of which is a heavy door. In the area between the shelves are a bench against the front wall and two wooden chairs on each side of a small oblong table.

Abruptly, Alyiakal recognizes the purpose of the high windows: to provide enough light so that potential purchasers can read the books—or as much as the seller will allow.

The door to the back part of the shop opens after a moment and a broad-shouldered and muscular gray-haired man a good cubit shorter than Alyiakal steps through the doorway, closing the door behind him.

"A Mirror Lancer captain. I can't say I've seen many lancers looking for books. Fewer even for rarities. How might I help you, ser?"

"I hope what I'm looking for isn't a rarity," says Alyiakal. "I'd like maps of Cyador east of Fyrad, including Guarstyad and the coastal area of Kyphros east of Guarstyad, if you have any."

"Maps . . . almost a rarity in their own way. I don't see many of them. They're rare, but they're not expensive."

"Rare, but inexpensive?" asks Alyiakal, since in his experience most things that are rare are not inexpensive.

"The best maps are almost never sold. They're too valuable. Those that are old, maybe outdated, aren't as useful, and almost no one wants them."

"Do you have any of either?"

The proprietor frowns. "I used to have an old atlas of Candar. I don't remember selling it. From what I recall, there's not that much detail about Cyador except for the larger ports and harbors. Maybe more on the area around Lydiar. Let me see if I can find it, and anything else like it." He looks to Alyiakal. "It might take a bit."

"That's fine. I have the time."

"On leave?"

Alyiakal nods.

"You can look at the shelves and see if there's anything else that catches your eye."

The proprietor retreats back through the door in the middle of the wall, and Alyiakal heads for the bookshelves. The first section he approaches deals with various aspects of raising crops, livestock, managing orchards, methods of irrigation. Then he sees several books on anatomy, one of which he leafs through, but puts it aside when he realizes that he can sense more than what the book tells him. The next section contains material on ships and sailing, but nothing on fireships, although Alyiakal would have been surprised to find that knowledge anywhere except in a library held close by the Mirror Engineers.

The roll of thunder and the patter, then the splatter, of rain on the high windows cause him to look up, and, at that moment, the door to the back section of the shop opens, and the proprietor emerges with a single volume in his hand. "Didn't take as long as I thought. I didn't see anything else about Guarstyad, but I didn't have to go through everything to find this."

Alyiakal judges the volume to be roughly a half cubit high and a cubit wide, considerably larger than most books. The dark leather binding is worn and scratched, even gouged in places on the spine. As large as the atlas appears to be, he fears the maps will be too small to be of much use.

Anticipating Alyiakal's fears, the proprietor sets the atlas on the table and opens it, then carefully unfolds what appears to be a single page into almost double its size. "Each map is close to the width of four pages." He pauses. "Let's see if we can find Fyrad."

"What part of Cyador does that show?" asks Alyiakal as he steps up beside the proprietor.

"Rulyarth and the coast for about fifty kays on each side. It's remarkably detailed for the coast, but very few inland details. On this map, anyway."

Alyiakal senses that the bookseller is moderately intrigued, but also almost detached, as if the atlas is an interesting curio.

The bookseller turns to the back of the volume and opens another fold-out page. "Worrak, but with the old spelling. Means this was drafted more than fifty years ago. Likely out of date in other ways." He carefully refolds the page and then goes to the front of the volume. "Ah . . . here we are. Closer, anyway. This map is centered on Luuval. Definitely dated there. Not much left of the town, I hear."

"Luuval's about a hundred kays west of Guarstyad, isn't it?"

"A bit more, I think." The bookseller turns to an adjoining page. "Here we are—Guarstyad. Map's pretty much like I recall. Harbor's detailed, even some good rendering of the lower Westhorns and the coasts on each side. Inland—except for the mountains—not so much." He steps back to allow Alyiakal a better look.

Alyiakal steps forward and studies the map. The details are mostly as the bookseller has described, but the maps do show a road from Guarstyad winding through what has to be a mountain pass to Luuval, or what's left of the town, and eventually to Fyrad, and another pass through the eastern part of the Westhorns to the high plains of Kyphros. "I see what you mean." He steps back and turns to the bookseller. "Is the atlas for sale?"

"Everything's for sale at the right price." The bookseller smiles, but his expression and the feelings behind it are more of amusement than greed.

"The problem with that," replies Alyiakal, "is that I don't know what the right price might be . . . or if I could afford to pay what it's worth."

The proprietor laughs. "Some say that a book is only worth what people will pay. This atlas is worth a great deal more than anyone is likely to pay. It's also worthless if it's not being used. I have the feeling you have a use for it. Is that so?"

"I do. I'm being posted there."

"Then you can have it for a silver and five."

"I'd like to have the atlas, and I can afford that," says Alyiakal, although he's beginning to worry about coins, having laid out more than a gold in the past two days, and that wasn't counting what he paid for new uniforms and boots.

"Then it's a deal."

Alyiakal extracts the coins and hands them over. "Thank you."

The bookseller takes them, carefully folds the open map back into the volume, and hands the atlas to Alyiakal. "I have the feeling you'll get more worth from it than most, Captain."

"I hope so." Alyiakal smiles. "I do appreciate it." He pauses then asks, "How did you become a bookseller?"

"By accident and opportunity. How did you come to be a lancer officer?"

"Family tradition, and a feeling that I should be."

"Do you still feel that way?"

"More than ever." Alyiakal offers a wry smile. "Even if I can't tell you why."

The bookseller nods thoughtfully. "That is why I sell books. I wish you well in Guarstyad."

"Thank you." Alyiakal gestures toward the windows and the rain that is still coming down. "Would you mind if I sat at the table and read until the rain lets up? I'd rather not risk the chance of getting the atlas wet."

"Be my guest. I'll be in back. If you happen to see anything else that catches your eye, pound on the door."

"I'll do that."

For the next glass or so, Alyiakal studies the atlas, looking at each map, then returning to the map of the Guarstyad area. As the bookseller has said, only the major geographic features of the interior of Candar are shown, with several exceptions, such as the area around Lydiar and the interior of Suthya.

When the rain stops, Alyiakal knocks on the inside door and says, "I'm leaving now. Thank you."

"You're welcome, Captain. Best of fortune in Guarstyad."

As Alyiakal heads back to the post, he silently thanks the bookseller.

LVIII

On twoday afternoon and after breakfast on threeday morning, Alyiakal studies the maps in the Candar atlas, comparing them to his own maps, but the atlas maps of the area south and east of Jera, including the northern borders of Cyador, have little more inland detail than the rivers and the general outlines of the Grass Hills.

Well before first glass on threeday he is riding out of Geliendra, wearing his sabre, not that he expects trouble, but he prefers to be prepared, although he knows he can also rely on order/chaos bolts to some greater extent than before. He also carries a water bottle filled with ale and a handful of trail biscuits, as well as the black wooden box, which holds only the bracelet.

When he can, after he turns off the main road onto the way to Vaeyal, he resumes working on the control and power of his order/chaos bolts, and he soon discovers that what he learned in the dream—or vision—allows him to project chaos in a straight line as far as a firelance.

He also discovers that he needs the ale and the biscuits, all of both, but his head does not ache, despite the greater power he uses, either because of the extra nourishment or his slowly improving control, or possibly both.

He also can't help thinking about the vision. Was it something the Great Forest observed and somehow passed on to him? While he has no doubts about the Forest's powers, it's definitely unclear why it has chosen to help him develop his abilities.

For its own interests, most likely, but are those interests for the best of Cyador?

Yet, for his own survival, Alyiakal would be foolish to turn his back on what he has learned. Still . . .

He shakes his head.

As before, after Alyiakal enters Vaeyal and nears the Great Canal, he sees barges moored at the unloading areas and wagons at the docks, although he can't discern what is being unloaded. What he can discern, even more clearly, is the feeling of contrasting senses of balance. While the order-and-chaos-reinforced sunstone blocks that comprise the walls and tow-ways of the Great Canal seem solidly balanced, as a whole the Great Canal feels out of balance with what lies beneath and around it, although those depths seem balanced as well.

Contrasting powers out of balance? That's something to keep in mind, although he has no idea what he can or should try to do about it. His immediate thought is to leave the matter well enough alone. *At the very least until you have far better understanding and control of your abilities.*

Alyiakal turns the mare north on Canal Street, but because Saelora isn't waiting when he reaches the factorage, he hitches the mare in front and walks into the empty front area.

"Saelora? Vassyl?"

In moments, Saelora appears. "I didn't realize it was so late. I have a few unexpected details to deal with. There are problems with invoices from one of the traders. I hope you don't mind."

"You need to do what you need to do. Can I stable the mare in back and wait, or take a walk so I don't distract you?"

"I'll unbar the doors." She offers a wry smile. "I might get finished faster if you aren't around."

"Then I'll put the mare in a stall and walk up the street."

"Thank you for understanding."

Alyiakal leaves the factorage, unties the mare, mounts, and rides around to the back of the factorage. After taking care of the mare, and securing the doors, he walks through the warehouse area into the section with the conference table, at which Saelora is seated with stacks of paper on both sides. The box is already tucked inside his riding jacket.

"A glass or so?" he asks.

"A quint less than that."

"I'll see you then."

When Alyiakal leaves the factorage, instead of walking up or down Canal Street, he crosses it and makes his way to the tow-road at the edge of the Great Canal. There he stops and watches, using his order/chaos senses, as a firetow slowly pulls a barge north, taking in the wooden crates stacked high in the well deck, as well as several score amphorae, most likely from Hamor and containing oils of various kinds. Four guards with bored expressions scan the sides of the canal.

When Alyiakal senses nothing out of the ordinary on the barge, he concentrates on the firetow. At first, he can discern only a mass of concentrated chaos, more chaos than he's ever sensed in such a small area, but further study reveals that order confines the central mass of chaos, but an order more concentrated than any he's ever sensed before. It feels a shade darker and somehow *deeper*.

He puzzles over what he has sensed well after the firetow and barge have continued northward past Vaeyal. *Are firewagons the same?* He suspects they are, but since he hasn't studied one since his encounter with the Great Forest, that has to remain a surmise until he does.

After a bit more thought, he returns to Canal Street and walks north. He's a few yards past the cross street he took to reach the rear of the factorage when, behind him, he senses a figure stepping out of a building.

Then the figure calls out, "Captain, a moment, if you would."

Alyiakal turns to see the white-haired Rhobett approaching, accompanied by another man who has left the same building. The second man's face looks similar to Rhobett's, and Alyiakal surmises that he is Rhobett's younger brother. "What can I do for you, sers?"

Rhobett grins and says to the other, "I told you he was polite." Then he addresses Alyiakal. "Captain, I'd like you to meet my brother Traybett."

Alyiakal inclines his head. "I'm pleased to meet you."

"And I, you," replies Traybett. "I understand you're familiar with the brothers of Saelora'mer."

"I'm more familiar with Hyrsaal. He and I went through Kynstaar together. I have met Gaaran."

"Might I ask your opinion of the older brother?"

"I've only spent a few glasses with him, and with your daughter Charissa, just once, but my impression is favorable. It's also clear to me that he is extraordinarily fond of your daughter."

"You've also met his mother?" asks Traybett.

"She was kind enough to invite me to dinner. She has a strong personality, but she seems to look on your daughter favorably." *Possibly more favorably than her own daughters.*

"There are always considerations when a widowed mother has daughters," says Traybett cautiously.

"From what little I've seen," replies Alyiakal, "both daughters like Charissa. Karola doesn't live that close, and Saelora'mer has spoken most favorably of Charissa. As I'm sure that you both know, Saelora is not given to deception."

Both men offer smiles, but Alyiakal can sense a hint of embarrassment from both.

"You understand," says Rhobett, "that we value your observations because you're likely to have fewer . . . established feelings about people."

"I thought that might be why you asked."

Rhobett inclines his head. "We appreciate your forthrightness, Captain, and your taking the time to talk with us. We hope the remainder of your leave is pleasant, and we wish you well in your next posting."

"Thank you," replies Alyiakal. "I can see why Saelora has spoken favorably of both of you." *Even if your approach was rather rude.*

After the two brothers reenter the building, Alyiakal continues north on Canal Street, past the coffee shop, keeping his eyes open to see if there might be a bookshop along the way, although he hadn't noticed one before, but then, his attention had been largely on Saelora.

He takes his time and makes his way slightly past the road to Saelora's house and distillery and then back. While he passes a tinsmith's, a coppersmith's, a dry goods store, several fabric shops, a tiny cobbler's shop, a large and busy cooperage, and a pottery shop, as well as three inns, two of which are likely partly brothels, he sees no goldsmith's and no bookshops, not that he would have expected either in Vaeyal.

When he reenters the factorage, Vassyl stands at the front counter, talking to a young bearded man in well-worn brown garb.

Vassyl motions Alyiakal to the door to the back. "She's expecting you."

"Thank you."

Alyiakal hears only ". . . don't see many lancer officers here . . ." before he closes the door.

The conference table is empty of papers, and Saelora stands and turns from her desk. "It didn't take as long as I feared," she says.

"I'm glad."

"Did you see anything interesting?"

"A barge and a firetow, several inns whose appearance confirmed your statements about them, and I had a brief conversation with Rhobett and Traybett, who hailed me."

"About Gaaran?"

"They wanted my opinion, about him *and* your mother. I expressed favor and support for Gaaran, and said that your mother seemed most receptive to Charissa, as did Gaaran's sisters. Those are my honest feelings, and I hope I'm not mistaken."

"Your comments certainly can't hurt, even if accosting you was uncalled for." After a brief hesitation, Saelora adds, "You asked about maps. Gaaran came by the factorage on oneday. I asked him if he'd look into whether there were any maps of Guarstyad at the house. He looked through the study and came by this morning. There weren't any maps that showed Guarstyad, but there were some of the area between Biehl and Jera."

"Do you think I could borrow them and possibly use the conference table to copy them? Tomorrow or on fiveday?"

"I don't see any problem with that . . . but you're going to Guarstyad. Is there a reason why you also want maps of Biehl?"

"I've discovered that good maps are hard to come by. Even the ones we had at Pemedra left something to be desired. I ended up making my own personal maps. Someday, I might be posted to Biehl or near there, and the maps might not be available then."

Saelora smiles. "Making your own maps. That doesn't surprise me."

"They help me remember places. I can usually remember about people I've met or places I've been, but maps let you relate places you haven't been to places that you have, and that can be very useful."

"You're very practical."

"Impractical officers don't live long, *but*," Alyiakal draws out the word, "speaking of the immediate practical, do you have anything planned for the rest of the afternoon?"

"Do you?" she counters with a mischievous smile.

"Only that I'd planned to spend it with you. I don't know enough about Vaeyal to be very creative about what we might do."

"You've already discovered the extent of Vaeyal's attractions and diversions."

"But I have yet to know all of yours." Alyiakal grimaces and blushes. "I think what I just said could be taken in ways I didn't intend."

Saelora laughs. "That's the first time I've seen you flustered. As for diversions, there aren't any. We're going to go to my small house and have dinner and talk. Then you'll ride back to Geliendra. We'll do this a few more times before you depart for Guarstyad, and then, I hope, we'll continue to write each other."

"And see what happens?"

"Did you have something else in mind?"

He grins. "Not yet."

She blushes.

"I was hoping for dinner and more time with you."

"Then we should leave and ride to the house. Dinner and conversation are what I planned." Saelora stands.

"Then we're in agreement."

By the time the two ready their horses, ride to Saelora's house, stall the mare and the gelding, and get settled in the front parlor, almost two quints have passed.

Alyiakal leans forward in his chair and says, "You've written me for years. Now that I'm here, you've arranged your schedule to see me. You've fed me better fare than I've ever had, and I've enjoyed being with you incredibly." He holds up a hand to forestall any objections. "I'm not going to press you on anything, but I do want to express my thanks in more than words."

"You don't have to—"

"I want to." He eases out the black wooden box and hands it to her. "This is just a token of my appreciation."

"I can't—"

"I'm asking nothing, except that we keep talking and writing. You've expended coins and effort to make me welcome. The past eightday has been the most enjoyable of my life. Compared to that, what's in the box is a mere token. So please open it."

Alyiakal watches and senses her feelings as she lifts the top of the box, then eases the bracelet from the cloth in which it is wrapped.

"It's gorgeous!" Saelora's eyes widen, before she turns to him and says, "A mere token?"

Alyiakal smiles ruefully. "How about a heartfelt token? It's not sapphire and gold. It's electrum and blue zargun."

She smiles, with a warmth Alyiakal can easily see, but her words contain wry amusement. "Just electrum and blue zargun? Some Merchanter consorts never get something like this."

"You're not a Merchanter consort. You're a Merchanter. Wear it as a statement of who you are." *Not as a statement of to whom you belong.*

Saelora's eyes are bright, but she says only, "I will. Thank you." She swallows. "And thank you for giving it to me before dinner."

Alyiakal raises his eyebrows. "Do I have to worry about dinner?"

Saelora's laugh is half amusement, half relief. "No. Laetilla's still cooking. You only have to worry if I'm cooking."

"Why don't you try it on?"

She looks down at the bracelet. "Most bracelets . . ."

"Try it."

Carefully, she eases it onto her left wrist. "It's perfect." Her voice is a mixture of pleasure and relief.

"I'm glad. I'd thought it would fit, but I still worried." He adds, "It goes well with your blues, but then that was the idea. I wanted you to have something that conveyed the right sense."

"That I'm successful, but not pretentious?"

"That was my thought."

"I like your thoughts." She turns as Laetilla appears in the doorway from the kitchen.

"Dinner is ready."

Saelora stands, extending her arm slightly toward Laetilla to display the bracelet, then says, with a hint of amusement in her voice, "The bracelet is a token of appreciation from Captain Alyiakal."

"Good. He should appreciate you. It's also beautiful, but it should be."

Alyiakal is already on his feet and replies, "You're right."

"Since we're all agreed on that," Saelora says, "we should have dinner."

"And pleasant and intriguing conversation," replies Alyiakal.

"How could it not be?" Saelora gestures toward the small dining room.

Alyiakal smiles and joins her as she walks from the parlor.

LIX

The early dinner and conversation on threeday are both to Alyiakal's satisfaction, and to Saelora's, so far as Alyiakal can determine. Fourday he spends in Geliendra, but he leaves for Vaeyal on fiveday a good glass before noon, because Saelora has agreed that he can arrive earlier, so long as he spends the time copying the maps of the Biehl area. On the ride, as he can, he practices with order/chaos, working on narrow and short blasts, so that he can be more effective with less use of order or chaos.

Copying the various maps takes longer and is more tedious than he expected, but that turns out for the best. The various meetings that Saelora and Vassyl have last much longer than the two Merchanters have expected, and while they meet, Alyiakal ends up doing much of the copying on the front counter of the factorage. In the end, Saelora and Alyiakal eat at the coffee shop very late in the afternoon before he rides back to Geliendra.

Since Hyrsaal arrives on sixday, Alyiakal and Saelora decide it would be best if Alyiakal did not return to Vaeyal until the second afternoon glass on sevenday.

When he reaches the factorage on sevenday, Saelora does not come to the door. Alyiakal ties the mare outside and enters.

Vassyl immediately comes to the front counter. "Saelora asked me to tell you that everyone will be meeting at her mother's house, and you're expected to join them. Her brother—the one you served with—arrived yesterday afternoon, and he's looking forward to seeing you."

"Thank you for letting me know, and for all you've done for her."

The factor shakes his head. "She's done more for me than I'll ever be able to reciprocate."

"I know that feeling," replies Alyiakal, adding, "at least for now."

"She's not ready for more right now."

"I know. Neither am I. Even if I were, it wouldn't be right, or fair, to her." *For more than a few reasons.*

"You'd better not keep her waiting." Vassyl smiles. "Besides, I don't want her thinking I delayed you."

"She'd never think that, but I appreciate the thought." Alyiakal inclines his head, then turns and leaves the factorage.

In little more than half a quint, he is riding up to the stable, where both Saelora and Hyrsaal come out to greet him. Saelora wears her full Merchanter blues, rather than just the vest and trousers.

"I could tell it was you from a block away," calls out Hyrsaal. "Not many ride as well as you."

"I'm fortunate with the mounts I'm given."

Hyrsaal laughs boisterously. "That's what you say about everything."

"You work every bit as hard." Alyiakal reins up outside the stable and dismounts.

"Enough!" declares Saelora emphatically, but humorously. "You're both fortunate and hardworking, and I'm happy that you're both here."

"How is Catriana?" asks Alyiakal as he follows Saelora into the stable and leads the mare to the open stall.

"According to the letter waiting here for me, she's fine. I'm just sorry you won't be able to meet her."

"I might have a chance," replies Alyiakal. "I'm leaving for Fyrad on oneday. How long I'll be there depends on when a fireship or another ship leaves for Guarstyad." He finishes with the mare and closes the stall door.

"I promised Mother I'd stay here through twoday. I won't get to Fyrad until late on threeday at the earliest. We'll have to see."

Alyiakal doubts that he'll see Hyrsaal or Catriana in Fyrad, but he nods.

The three start back toward the house, with Saelora between the two captains.

Alyiakal notices that Saelora is wearing the electrum and blue zargun bracelet and smiles briefly.

"Mother has afternoon refreshments set up," Saelora says quietly to Alyiakal, "since she insisted on a late dinner to accommodate the family."

"That's very thoughtful," replies Alyiakal.

"Not really," says Hyrsaal wryly. "We had to insist."

"You didn't have to. Seeing you both is refreshing enough."

"You're kind," retorts Saelora, "but Mother can be difficult, as we all know."

"By the way," says Hyrsaal, "before I left Summerdock, an overcaptain came by. Draakyr, I think."

"I told him to look you up. He was the senior captain at Pemedra, and he was promoted to overcaptain about the time I left. Good solid officer. He taught me a lot."

"He said you were the best junior captain he'd seen in years."

"*Don't* say he was just being complimentary," declares Saelora before Alyiakal can respond.

Hyrsaal laughs. "She has you figured out."

"How are things going with Gaaran and Charissa?" asks Alyiakal.

"Apparently, her father and her uncle liked what you said," replies Saelora. "Everyone has agreed to the consorting. Mother even likes the idea of having her own cottage."

"She didn't put it quite that way," says Hyrsaal. "Her words were more, 'Saelora shouldn't be the only woman in the family to have a cottage where she can do as she pleases.'"

Alyiakal represses a wince as he follows Saelora up onto the side porch. "Your mother does have a way with words."

"That's one way of putting it." Hyrsaal opens the door to the parlor, where Marenda, Gaaran, and Charissa sit waiting.

"Karola and Faadyr won't be here until around fourth glass," says Saelora before Alyiakal can ask, although he didn't have that thought in mind until Saelora spoke.

"As you can see," announces Hyrsaal cheerfully, "Alyiakal is here."

"Yes, dear," says Marenda—too sweetly, Alyiakal can tell—"we can all see that."

Gaaran immediately stands, using the straight-backed chair as an aid, and says to Alyiakal, "It's good to see you again. I understand you went through a bit of an interrogation the other day."

"More like a pleasant inquiry."

"With Uncle Rhobett, I doubt it," says Charissa dryly.

"They're just looking out for you," replies Alyiakal as he takes one of the straight-backed chairs. "That was my impression, anyway. That is one of the advantages of having family." He hesitates slightly, then adds, "And sometimes, I understand, one of the disadvantages."

"You understand?" asks Marenda before saying, "That's right. You're the only one left in your family."

Alyiakal senses that Marenda isn't surprised, even though her tone suggests it. "That can happen when your father and mother are only children and your mother dies young and your father is a lancer officer who dies on duty."

"Oh. I didn't know. I'm sorry," says Charissa, with a sympathy she actually feels.

"You couldn't have known, but that's one of the reasons why Hyrsaal and Saelora are as close to family as I have. They were both very supportive when my father died, and I can't say how much I appreciated it."

"Since I'm on my feet," says Gaaran, "can I offer you something to drink?"

"If you have any of that Alafraan?"

"We do, indeed. I'll be right back."

"It must have slipped my mind," says Marenda, looking at Alyiakal, "but when are you leaving for Guarstyad?"

"Early on oneday morning, I'll be taking a firewagon to Fyrad. From there I'll take the next available ship to Guarstyad."

"That's sometimes a rough voyage," says Gaaran, returning with a wineglass that he hands to Alyiakal before reseating himself on the settee beside Charissa.

"So I've been told." Alyiakal raises the wineglass, looks directly at Marenda and then Gaaran. "I'd like to thank you both for letting me borrow those maps so that I could copy them. I appreciate it very much. As I told Saelora, sometimes, even in the Mirror Lancers, the maps aren't the best, and, if I'm ever posted to Biehl, the copies of those maps will be most useful. In fact, whether I am posted there or not, they'll be helpful."

"You're welcome," replies Marenda. "I'm glad someone else can make use of them."

"That's Alyiakal for you," says Hyrsaal cheerfully, "always thinking ahead."

"And acting," adds Saelora. "Thinking ahead isn't that useful unless you do something about it."

"So says the woman who took her brother's suggestion and worked hard to create a profitable enterprise and to become, if I understand correctly," says Alyiakal, "the only Lady Merchanter in Vaeyal in her own right."

"It is a definite distinction," agrees Marenda.

Suggesting you'd rather have her consorted unhappily to a wealthy holder than happily establishing and building her own Merchanting house. Alyiakal only smiles pleasantly and nods, then turns to Hyrsaal. "How much home leave are you taking?"

"Two eightdays. That way, I'll have six eightdays after the coming posting, and Catriana and I won't have to rush anything involved with consorting." Hyrsaal grins and adds, "I know. That doesn't sound much like me, but the Mirror Lancers have made me more patient, and by then Catriana and I will have more saved."

"Your father felt the same way."

Alyiakal has the feeling that Marenda isn't necessarily approving, but it might be that she likes the idea, but not the person for whom Hyrsaal is saving. He looks to Charissa. "What about you two?"

"Father accepted Gaaran's proposal, but we haven't agreed on a date. It will likely have to be after yearturn with all the details."

Alyiakal nods, recalling that Gaaran had mentioned a specific date earlier.

"The angels designed details," says Gaaran sardonically.

"Or at least, the First would like to have us think so," replies Hyrsaal. "Sometimes, I think Mirror Lancer headquarters could have taught the angels a bit about unnecessary details."

"Especially in dealing with smugglers?" asks Alyiakal.

"And a few other matters, but . . . let's not talk about that now." Hyrsaal turns to Saelora. "How are you coming with the distillery and the greenberry brandy?"

"We're doing well. We're holding back on selling all of it so that we can age more."

Saelora expands on what Alyiakal knows, and adds more about the various traders and houses expressing interest, and about the future possibility of other products that might come from the distillery.

When she finishes, Hyrsaal says, "You've done more with that than I ever could have, and done it better."

"You could have done it as well," says Marenda, "if you'd shown any real interest in being anything besides a Mirror Lancer officer."

"It's rather difficult to do something well," offers Alyiakal, "if you don't like it or you don't think it's important."

Gaaran immediately says, "That's why so many sons of senior officers don't do well at Kynstaar. A handful do really well. Most fail or barely get their commissions."

Hyrsaal looks to Alyiakal, then says, "If you'll excuse us, I need some time with Alyiakal to get his thoughts on dealing with barbarians. We don't have much time. We'll be out on the porch."

As Hyrsaal finishes, Alyiakal stands and follows his friend onto the porch, toward the front of the house, well away from the side door.

When Hyrsaal stops, Alyiakal smiles. "Do you want to start with Saelora or the barbarians?"

"Saelora. She's the most important. She says that, right now, there's nothing physical between you two."

"I've kissed her hand. I wouldn't say that there's nothing physical. We simply haven't expressed anything physical."

"That bracelet you gave her?"

"For all she's meant to me. It's not a consorting gift."

"She said the same, but I wanted to know—"

"If we both saw it that way?" asks Alyiakal. "She said she's not sure what she wants, or if she even wants to consort anyone, let alone think about children. I'm not about to coerce her or press the issue. It will be some time, possibly years, before I can see her again, and that would be cruel and unfair to both of us. I have enjoyed being with her—incredibly—and I'm going to miss her more than I realized."

Hyrsaal shakes his head. "She's fortunate it's you."

"I'm fortunate she's who she is." He pauses, then asks, "Has your mother said anything about the bracelet?"

"Saelora's worn it at least ever since I got home. Mother hasn't said a word, not to me, anyway. I never mentioned it to Gaaran, and I doubt he's even noticed. I saw Charissa eyeing it when she came in this afternoon, but I doubt she'll say anything to Gaaran until later. She wants everything to go smoothly, and so does he."

Alyiakal nods.

"What about the barbarians?" asks Hyrsaal.

"The biggest problem is that the Cerlynese and the Jeranyi manipulate them into attacking us. I suspect there's much more behind it." Alyiakal details his own experiences, and relates what he's observed about tactics and weapons. Then he adds, "I don't think the Cerlynese will be involved with the mountain raiders you'll be facing, but since the Kyphrans are moving to attack Guarstyad, it's possible that they might use the mountain people in the same ways against Lhaarat, equip them with better weapons, shields, that sort of thing."

When Alyiakal finishes, Hyrsaal nods. "You've thought this out, as usual, and I appreciate it."

"I'm sure you know this, but talk to the squad leaders, as many as you can, and listen at mess."

"You always listen, and I've tried to follow that example." Hyrsaal shakes his head. "Listening is harder for me."

"It's harder for everyone, except maybe Saelora. Your mother calls her the recluse. Has it always been that way?"

"She's the youngest, so that might be part of it. It just might be her." Hyrsaal gestures toward the house. "We should rejoin the others." He laughs softly. "You're a brave man, Alyiakal, to come here a second time."

"How else would I get to see you?" Alyiakal won't mention the fact that he's not about to avoid Marenda, not when avoidance might reflect badly on Saelora.

"I appreciate that." Hyrsaal turns toward the door.

Alyiakal follows.

As soon as the two captains return and seat themselves, Marenda asks, "Are you quite sure you're finished?"

"Alyiakal has valuable information, which I trust," replies Hyrsaal.

"Trustworthy and honest information is hard to come by," adds Gaaran.

"What did we miss?" asks Hyrsaal.

"Nothing involving Mirror Lancers," replies Marenda pleasantly.

"We were wondering when Faadyr and Karola might arrive," says Saelora, "and whether Karola would bring any late-harvest vegetables, as she did the last time."

Hyrsaal turns to Alyiakal. "Speaking of food and vegetables, how was the fare at Pemedra?"

"We did well with meat. Everything else was less satisfactory. They brewed the ale using wildgrass seed. Spring beans were the vegetable at most meals."

Gaaran nods, and Hyrsaal winces.

For the next glass the conversation centers mainly on food.

Abruptly, Marenda smiles and says to Alyiakal, "I'm so glad that you came to see Hyrsaal before you have to leave for Guarstyad. I do hope we'll see you on your next leave, but we'll have to begin to get ready for dinner."

Alyiakal senses the surprise from almost everyone in the parlor, but he manages a smile as he stands. "I appreciate your hospitality. As for when I might return, I won't speculate. We all know how unpredictable the life of a lancer officer can be."

"I'll walk out with you." Saelora stands. "I'm sure I won't be missed in preparing dinner."

Alyiakal turns to Hyrsaal, who looks uncomfortable, and who, Alyiakal senses, definitely is also upset. "We'll see if our schedules match in Fyrad."

"I'll check at the post, once I get there. If not, take care."

"I will."

Alyiakal addresses Gaaran and Charissa. "It was good to meet you both. I wish you well, especially over the next season." Then he walks from the parlor, accompanied by Saelora.

Neither speaks until they are off the porch.

"I didn't expect that from Mother." Saelora's voice is low and hard, and Alyiakal can also sense her fury. "Not so quickly and blatantly, anyway. I did tell Hyrsaal she might try something like that. I also told him not to say anything if she did. He's having enough trouble with Mother."

"Over Catriana?"

"More over the fact that Catriana lives in Fyrad and that Mother can't influence her."

Alyiakal can certainly see that. "She doesn't much care for me."

"She doesn't care much for anyone who shows me favor, or more favor than she receives. She avoids speaking to Vassyl and Buurel as much as she can."

When they reach the stable, Alyiakal stops and asks, "When can I see you tomorrow—alone, at least for a bit?"

"If you don't mind coming early, I'll be at my house until noon. As I told you earlier, Mother's planning a big family dinner."

"That's why I asked," says Alyiakal gently. "What about three glasses before noon?"

"But you'll have to get up early—"

"Getting up early isn't exactly unknown to lancer officers," he says warmly, but dryly.

"Then I'll see you then." She smiles. "I'll also tell Hyrsaal you'll be there, but that I'll need time with you. He'll understand."

"I'm sure he will." Alyiakal enters the stall and leads the mare outside.

"Alyiakal," Saelora says gently. "Thank you. You handled yourself so well."

"I didn't want to put you or Hyrsaal in an uncomfortable position. It would have made matters worse."

"I saw that. Most men wouldn't." She takes his free hand in hers and squeezes it. "I'll see you tomorrow?"

"You will." Rather than kissing her cheek, which he'd prefer, he squeezes her hand in return before letting go, and then mounting the mare. "Tomorrow morning."

He can sense her eyes on him as he rides away and turns south on Canal Street. He can't help thinking about families and how complicated matters can get. *Mother was never like Marenda and never would have been.* He shakes his head.

LX

On eightday morning, Alyiakal rises early. After washing, shaving, and dressing, he stops by the mess, where he grabs several biscuits and fills a water bottle with ale before heading to the stable. It's early enough that there are few carts or horses on the streets of Geliendra or on the road to Fyrad, although he sees the early firewagon heading toward the post, most likely one on the same schedule as he'll be taking the next morning.

Even the Great Canal seems quiet as he rides into Vaeyal, but then, it is eightday.

Alyiakal doesn't quite make it to the stable doors before Saelora steps out of the house with a broad smile.

"I thought you might be early."

"I didn't want to be late," Alyiakal admits. "Not for you, especially not for you." He dismounts.

"I'm glad you added the last few words," she replies impishly. "You don't like being late for anyone, including Mother."

"That's my lancer upbringing."

"Hyrsaal's already here. He walked over."

"He doesn't have a horse?"

"He arranged for the firewagon to stop on the other side of the canal. They'll do that for officers. They'll pick him up when he goes to Fyrad. It saves the Mirror Lancers silvers and it saves him time."

"Trust your brother to find that out. I'll have to keep it in mind."

"The stall is open."

Alyiakal gets the hint and leads the mare into the stable, where he puts her into the stall and then follows Saelora into and through the kitchen to the front parlor, where Hyrsaal stands next to one of the dining room chairs, clearly moved in anticipation of Alyiakal's arrival.

"I'm sorry about yesterday, and Mother. Saelora said you understood."

Alyiakal hears Hyrsaal's unease and immediately answers, "I hoped you'd understand that I wasn't being curt with you. I didn't see any point in arguing or disrupting what your mother planned. It was clear, even before you got to Vaeyal, that she wasn't happy about your spending so little time here. Saelora said she'd tell you—"

"She did. Both of you have been far more understanding than Mother."

Your mother doesn't want to be understanding. She wants you to put her above Catriana. "She hasn't seen you in years." Alyiakal's words are gentle.

"That's why I came to Vaeyal first. Arranging it took some doing because it's extra travel."

"I even told Mother that," explains Saelora, "so Hyrsaal wouldn't have to."

"It didn't mollify her?" asks Alyiakal.

"Not much," says Hyrsaal. "Enough about Mother." He gestures to the chairs. "You told me all about the barbarians and the Cerlynese behavior and tactics. What about you?" Before Alyiakal can respond, Hyrsaal looks to Saelora and says, "I won't take all his time, not even most of it."

"I told you a bit about Draakyr. I did my best to follow his guidance." Alyiakal continues for a little more than a quint, mentioning his suspicion that he'd been assigned the patrol beyond the Grass Hills so that Tygael could recommend him for a posting like Guarstyad.

"That makes sense," replies Hyrsaal. "They're trying to establish how good you are so that the political commanders in Cyad have to pay attention to you."

"What about you?"

"I avoided making any major mistakes, although I almost protested the majer canceling a patrol, except I realized it was because the smugglers were associated with a well-known Merchanter clan in Cyad. At least, I think they were."

"The majer is about to be stipended?" asks Alyiakal.

"His last day was the day before I left. He received quite a number of farewell gifts, and many, I suspect, that few know about."

"How can they get away with that?" asks Saelora.

"Because some of the Merchanters have ties to the Magi'i. Mirror Lancer port commanders who have been too . . . *enthusiastic* in pursuing certain smugglers have been known to suffer unfortunate accidents."

"So the tacit operating plan is to watch outland ships, from Hamor, Austra, Nordla, or from other parts of Candar, rather than Cyadoran ships."

"It wasn't that blatant," says Hyrsaal, "but something like that."

"So those with power and influence could smuggle, but not outlanders or smaller Cyadoran traders?" asks Saelora.

Hyrsaal nods.

"What about the other officers?" Saelora's voice is even.

"There's no way to prove anything," says Hyrsaal. "The priority is to begin with foreign shipping. We seldom dealt with Cyadoran shipping. If you aren't patrolling where the smugglers are, you won't find them. If you disobey orders and don't find smugglers, you'll be discharged at the end of your current posting. If you disobey orders and find smugglers, you'll be flagged as insubordinate and either suffer an accident, be posted to dead-end duty, or, if you're good in combat, you'll spend the rest of your career on the borders and possibly make overcaptain or sub-majer, if you survive."

Saelora winces.

"Of course," says Hyrsaal humorously, "if Alyiakal can make it to being a senior commander or even Majer-Commander of the Mirror Lancers, he might be able to change things."

Alyiakal shakes his head. "Dream on."

Hyrsaal stands. "I've taken enough of your time." He looks to Alyiakal. "Be careful in Guarstyad." Then he says to Saelora, "I'll see you later."

Both Alyiakal and Saelora stand.

After a parting smile, Hyrsaal leaves the small house. Both Alyiakal and Saelora watch from the open doorway until he is well beyond the distillery.

Then she closes the door and turns to him. "He was furious with Mother, but he didn't say anything. I'd be surprised if he ever comes back to Vaeyal to see her again."

"I don't want him mad at her because of me."

"That's only a part of it. She's been quietly cutting about Catriana as well. Even Charissa was uncomfortable."

"She's pushing everyone away from her. Doesn't she see that?"

Saelora shakes her head. "She thinks that we're all turning away from her when we just want to lead our own lives. One of the reasons I wanted her to meet you is because you're part of my life. You will be, as far as I'm concerned, no matter what happens. You saw how she reacted."

"It doesn't seem likely that any of you can change that." Seeking to change the subject, he says, "The bracelet looks good with Merchanter blues. I'd hoped it would, but I never really had a chance to see for certain."

"It does. Vassyl says that you have excellent taste. One of the things I love about it isn't the bracelet itself. It's that you chose something that suits me, as I am." She pauses. "You didn't give me a delicate bauble that I could only wear to a dinner party of the kind I'll likely never attend."

"It would look good there as well, but I'm selfish," Alyiakal admits. "I wanted something you could wear anywhere." *And hopefully think of me occasionally.*

"And I can. That means so much. Too many men pick gifts to show who they are. You didn't."

Thank the Rational Stars! "I tried."

"You more than tried." She gestures toward the dining room. "Laetilla picked up some pastries from the coffee shop this morning—for us and for you. As early as you had to get up, I doubt you had time to eat much. There's also some decent ale."

"You're right. Pastries would be wonderful."

The two walk to the dining room. Alyiakal smiles as he sees a platter filled with both spirals and almond-custard rolls, at least four of each.

"I'm hungry, too," she says. "I . . . I wasn't earlier."

"You weren't?"

"I worried. Mother . . . everything . . ."

"I said I'd be here."

"You did, and you are. And I am hungry." Saelora seats herself at one of the set places, with an empty plate and mug.

Alyiakal sits across from her, deciding that she looks striking. Not pretty, but striking. He half stands to pour ale into her mug and then his before re-seating himself.

Saelora takes a healthy bite out of her almond-custard roll, while Alyiakal begins with a crunchy spiral. Neither speaks for a time.

Finally, he says, "You *were* hungry."

"After you got here."

"Thank you. This is so thoughtful, and I was very hungry." He picks up a second spiral. "I still am." After several more mouthfuls and some ale, he asks, "Where should I write you?"

"After what you've seen on your visit?" Her momentary smile is sardonic. Then she hands him a card across the table. "I wrote out both the factorage address and this one. I'd prefer that your letters come here, but they'll take a day or two longer. So . . ."

"I write you at the factorage if it's something urgent."

She nods. "Tomorrow morning, Hyrsaal will help me move the rest of my things here. I'd planned to do it before long, but not so soon. After yesterday though . . ." She shakes her head again.

Alyiakal looks at the card, studies the address, and finally puts it in his belt wallet. He takes another swallow of ale. "Did this come from the distillery, too?"

"Light, no! It came from Faadyr and Karola. One of his tenants brews the best ale in Vaeyal. They keep me supplied."

For the next glass or so, they simply talk, exchanging stories of their child-hood.

In time, they make their way to the stable, where Alyiakal leads the mare out and ties her to the post by the stable door. Then, he leans toward Saelora and brushes her cheek with his lips—only to find her arms fiercely around him.

He reciprocates, murmuring, "I didn't know . . ."

For a time, they hold each other. Then Saelora eases back, although her hands take his. "I don't know where we're going, or where I am, but I couldn't let you leave with just a brotherly kiss. You mean too much for that."

"I had to leave that to you," he says quietly.

"She taught you well."

"How—"

Saelora puts a finger to his lips. "I've seen and heard enough to know how most young men act. I also felt how you wanted me, but never insisted or pressed. Since she was the only one for you, she had to be the one."

"You don't mind? I've worried about that, and whether I should have told you."

She smiles. "You've written for almost six years. When you first saw me, you looked into my eyes—not elsewhere. If I'd been attracted to someone else when I was younger, I would have told you. I don't like secrets between people who care for each other." She grins momentarily. "Besides, you would have known. You sense what people feel. That's probably because you're a mage and a healer."

"Is it that obvious?"

"Not to most people, I'd think. After years of reading and rereading your letters, I've watched you closely with others this past eightday." Her voice lowers. "I have to say that worries me a little."

Alyiakal tries to keep his voice reassuring yet cheerful as he says, "I can't tell what you're thinking."

"That's probably for the best at the moment." Her hands tighten around his. "I wish we had more time, but you need to go now."

"In a moment." Alyiakal wraps his arms around her tightly, then kisses her gently, but not too long, and then just holds her.

He can feel the tears, and not all of them are hers.

In time, they separate, and he mounts the mare. "I'll write as soon as I can after I get to Guarstyad. I don't know how long it will take for letters to get to you."

"I'll be here."

"Stick close to Hyrsaal this afternoon."

"I won't be anywhere else." Her smile is wry.

As he turns the mare away from Saelora, Alyiakal knows that the ride back to Geliendra will be long, but not nearly so long as the afternoon facing Saelora.

LXI

Once Alyiakal returns to Geliendra, he spends the remainder of eightday organizing and packing his uniforms and gear, except for the time he spends at the evening mess, which is lightly attended. After the morning mess on oneday, he lugs his gear to the front gates of the post, where he waits for the firewagon to Fyrad.

As Alyiakal stands waiting, another captain approaches, a Mirror Engineer from his collar insignia, and Alyiakal says, "Good morning."

The older captain replies, "The same to you. I'm Taeland. From your gear, you're heading for a new post. Fyrad?"

"Alyiakal. I'm headed to Fyrad to catch a ship to my new post in Guarstyad."

"Aren't you the fortunate one."

"What about you?"

"Posted at Fyrad. General maintenance. I had a temporary assignment here for the last eightday."

"Was that the result of the visit of the Third Magus here?"

Taeland frowns.

"I happened to be here when he came, and I was introduced to him. When a senior commander and the Third Magus show up at Geliendra, and then there's a Mirror Engineer on temporary duty . . . I thought there might be a connection."

"Might I ask how . . . ?"

"Subcommander Zaentyl had all the officers at the post introduced. I was staying here on leave so I could visit friends. For some reason, the Third Magus wanted to meet everyone."

"That seems odd."

"To me as well, but comparatively junior captains don't ask why."

Taeland chuckles. "Wise of you."

"Your temporary duty?" prompts Alyiakal.

"Oh, nothing to do with whatever the Third Magus was here for. The sixday before last, all the wards in a one-kay stretch of the wall failed. It might have been somewhat earlier, but late on that sixday a number of tawny cougars were seen outside the walls. The local Mirror Engineers discovered the failure, but couldn't find any physical reason for it. There weren't any breaks in the conduits or the wall itself. The wards just burned out."

The sixday before last? "I'm only a company officer, but that seems strange to me."

"Subcommander Zaentyl thought so as well."

"Are wards your specialty?" asks Alyiakal.

"Chaos-flow systems, really, but the wards rely on maintaining flows."

"What was the problem, then?"

Taeland shakes his head ruefully. "It wasn't with our systems. There was an order/chaos overload of some sort, most likely inside the Accursed Forest close to the walls. They've happened before, but it's been years." Abruptly, he looks past Alyiakal. "Here comes the firewagon."

Unlike on Alyiakal's previous firewagon journeys, he and Taeland are the only officers, and have the front section to themselves.

Once inside, with their gear stowed, Taeland says, "If you'll excuse me, it's been a long eightday." He stretches out on the forward, rear-facing, seats, leaving the rear, forward-facing, seats to Alyiakal, who isn't particularly sleepy.

The firewagon follows the whitestone road that Alyiakal had been using to get partway to Vaeyal, but then takes the left fork until it reaches and crosses the Great Canal, where it turns south along the road that is actually part of the west side of the canal and that runs south to Fyrad. The northern part of the road parallels the canal to its end north of Westend, where it turns northwest to Ilypsya, which was doubtless the way Hyrsaal had gotten to Vaeyal.

Alyiakal senses a certain amount of excess order and chaos surrounding Taeland, but the Mirror Engineer seems almost unaware of it and certainly doesn't seem to have any shields or separation of order and chaos. Out of caution, Alyiakal waits until Taeland has dropped off into a doze before he lets his senses study the firewagon.

As he has previously surmised, the firewagon operates in the same fashion as the firetows of the Great Canal, with the order/chaos flows turning a device linked to the rear wheels. He'd expected the device to be bigger than those in the firetows, but realizes that the loads pulled by the firetows are far greater than those conveyed by the firewagons. But then, the firewagons travel much faster.

A trade-off between speed and load.

His next thoughts turn to the Great Forest. He'd certainly felt the power of the Forest when it had been directed at him, but he'd had no idea that the confrontation, if that was what it had been, had been strong enough to burn out all the wards in a kay of the wall.

But what else could it have been?

As he sits in the firewagon heading toward Fyrad, he again feels that there is too much about magery that he does not know but that he needs to work on however he can.

LXII

After turning off the whitestone road, essentially part of the Great Canal, and traveling perhaps a hundred yards west on another whitestone avenue, the firewagon comes to a stop just before noon on twoday outside the gates of the Mirror Engineer post at Fyrad. At least, Alyiakal presumes that is where he is, especially with the engineer's words.

"Here we are. It's good to be back. The Great Forest . . . it's unsettling."

"I've never been here before. Where do I go from here?" Alyiakal asks Taeland as a Mirror Lancer guard opens the firewagon door.

"I'll show you." The Mirror Engineer steps out of the firewagon, waits for Alyiakal to disembark, and then points to a low tower several hundred yards beyond the gates. "The port headquarters and operations center. They can tell you—"

"Ser . . . are you Captain Alyiakal?" asks someone.

Alyiakal turns to see a squad leader standing beside a small horse-drawn cart. "I am."

"We're here to take you to the *Kief*."

"The *Kief*?"

"The *Kief*. The captain's waiting on you. We'll handle your orders when we get to the ship."

Alyiakal turns back to the Mirror Engineer. "A pleasure meeting you, Taeland. I'm sorry I have to rush off."

"I certainly won't keep you. Best of fortune."

By the time Taeland has said those few words, the squad leader has carried Alyiakal's two duffels and placed them in the cart, resumed his place in the second row of seats, behind the teamster, and gestured to the space next to him.

Alyiakal immediately climbs up beside him. "I'm sorry to be a little slow. I just spent a day and a half in a firewagon."

"I was told that, ser. The captain's worried about the weather and wants to cast off as soon as possible."

The gate guards nod to Alyiakal as the cart passes, but don't appear terribly interested.

"What can you tell me about the fireship?" Alyiakal asks the squad leader.

"It's one of the older fireships. That doesn't mean much, though. They're rebuilt every thirty years, except for the chaos-flow mechanism. That's sealed."

"They're never opened?" asks Alyiakal.

"No, ser. I heard a magus and an engineer talk about that. Magus said that if they ever opened one of them, it would never work again. Said the First discovered that."

Alyiakal finds that hard to believe, but decides not to question it, since the squad leader clearly believes what he has said. "How long will the voyage to Guarstyad take?"

"Two days, usually. Sometimes three or four, depending on the weather."

Once inside the Mirror Lancer post, Alyiakal tries to take in everything. The stone tower containing headquarters and operations looks out on the harbor, which contains a half score or so of piers, all extending westward from the peninsula that juts out into the waters of the Great Western Ocean. A paved causeway runs from east of the tower along the west edge of the peninsula and connects the piers.

From what Alyiakal can see, there are only three or four ships moored at the piers.

"The *Kief* is at the end of the next-to-last pier, ser," offers the squad leader.

"Thank you."

As the cart nears, Alyiakal studies the white ship, somewhat less than a hundred yards in length with the main deck a little over three yards above the waterline. There are two turrets, one forward, one aft, each containing a single large firecannon, with two lighter firecannon on each side. Belatedly, Alyiakal realizes that the ship is built of iron.

Of course. Only iron could resist the chaos that powers the screws and the firecannon.

When the cart stops at the foot of the gangway leading up to the main deck, the squad leader takes one of the duffels and Alyiakal the other, and the two climb the gangway.

An older Mirror Engineer, an undercaptain by his insignia, is waiting. "Captain Alyiakal?"

"The same." Alyiakal presents the envelope containing his orders and his seal ring.

"Thank you, ser. If you and the squad leader would wait here. I'll be as quick as I can."

While Alyiakal waits, he can see that, around him, the ship's crew has become more active.

From somewhere, he hears the order, "Single up! Stand by to cast off!"

Then the undercaptain returns. "Captain, if you'd sign here, and in the same place on the second copy as well. This acknowledges that you've boarded the *Kief.* It will go to the port commander. We'll add the endorsement to your orders shortly."

Alyiakal quickly reads the sheet, the formal language of which boils down to what the undercaptain has said, and signs both copies.

Then the undercaptain hands one sheet to the squad leader, who takes it, then nods, and says, "Permission to leave the ship."

"Granted, and thank you."

"Our pleasure, ser." The squad leader turns to Alyiakal. "Best of fortune, ser."

"Thank you."

The squad leader turns and heads down the gangway.

The moment he is on the pier, three sailors pull the gangway aboard and swing it into a long narrow locker.

"Cast off all lines!"

Alyiakal feels the iron deck vibrate beneath his boots as the *Kief* begins to move away from the whitestone pier.

"If you'd come with me, I'll show you your quarters and give you a quick tour. I had one of the crew take your gear to your stateroom. I'm Sublieutenant Naartyn, by the way. The officer in command of every fireship is the captain. You'll be called Lieutenant Alyiakal while on board. It's the naval equivalent of your rank."

While Alyiakal recalled that, once reminded, it was still a surprise.

"The *Kief* can carry sixty naval marines on the lower decks, or if we're transporting Mirror Lancers, sixty lancers. Those compartments are separate from the crew spaces. Ship's officers' staterooms are forward on the deck below the main deck, and there are two staterooms for marine or lancer officers. You'll have one to yourself, because you're the only Mirror Lancer officer, and we don't have any naval marines aboard. We're carrying thirty Mirror Lancers. You and they are the last of the post complement at Guarstyad." Naartyn turns and walks aft until he comes to a hatchway. "This is the easiest way below. I'll take you to the wardroom first."

Wardroom? Then Alyiakal recalls that is the naval equivalent of the officers' mess.

A quint later, Alyiakal has at least a basic understanding of the fireship's layout, and he returns to the main deck.

The ship has begun to pitch slightly as it makes its way through the low waves, and Alyiakal looks aft. The *Kief* is well clear of the harbor, heading south-southeast, perhaps three kays offshore, so that the port tower looks almost minuscule, and the cold wind off gray-green waters chills his hands and exposed face, despite the cloudless but hazy green-blue sky.

He walks toward the stern, trying to see if he can sense any order/chaos flows, but he has to strain even to locate them. For a moment, he wonders why, then abruptly shakes his head, thinking about all the layers of iron between him and the order/chaos device that powers the ship, not to mention that the power chambers are well below the waterline and that the water would absorb any free chaos escaping the ship, although the chances of that are slim, given all the iron in the ship.

He stops and looks at the aft turret, an iron box, three yards on a side. He faintly senses the chaos contained in the turret, but that chaos, he knows, has to be replenished by the power source below after each blast from the firecannon.

After a time, he makes his way to his stateroom, a chamber anything but stately, that is two and a half yards long, and two yards wide, with two bunks, one over the other on one side, and two small fold-down desks, one on each side of the short wall. There is only one chair, but that may be because he is the only officer using the stateroom.

He extracts the atlas of Candar from his gear, folds down one of the desktops, sets the atlas on it, and opens the atlas to the page featuring the area around Guarstyad. He can't seem to concentrate, however, and he puts the atlas away and stretches out on the narrow bed, with his feet almost touching one bulkhead and his head close to the other.

He wakes to a rap on the door.

"Evening mess," says a voice.

Alyiakal struggles up and makes his way to the wardroom, an oblong space three yards wide and roughly five long, with a narrow table in the middle covered by a green cloth and seven chairs to each side and one at the head.

"Permission to join?" Alyiakal asks the senior officer at the head of the table, with the collar insignia equivalent to a majer, suggesting he is the executive officer, because Naartyn had mentioned that all fireship captains were the equivalent of Mirror Lancer subcommanders. Although Alyiakal has already talked to the wardroom section leader, he'd been instructed to make that request the first time he entered for a meal.

"Granted, Lieutenant."

Alyiakal takes a place in the middle of the table that will be his until he leaves the *Kief*.

The executive officer says, "For those of you who don't know, Lieutenant Alyiakal is headed to Guarstyad to take command of one of the Mirror Lancer companies there. He spent three years fighting barbarians on the northern borders at his previous post. Welcome, Lieutenant."

"Thank you, ser."

Two other officers slip into the wardroom and seat themselves, and the executive officer lifts his wineglass. Then a single steward serves each officer a plate containing lamb chops, boiled sliced potatoes, and carrots, all glazed with a kind of wine reduction.

"Have you ever been on a fireship before?" asks the lieutenant to Alyiakal's right.

"I've never been on any ship before."

"You might like it, unless you're the type to get seasick."

"I'll have to see."

"What was your last post?" asks an officer across the table.

"Pemedra. It's north of Syadtar. It's the post closest to Cerlyn."

For the remainder of the meal, finished with a dessert of oversweet pearapple tarts that remind Alyiakal of Saelora, the conversation is largely about posts and ports.

Alyiakal is more than glad to retreat to his stateroom, hoping he can get a good night's sleep.

ALYIAKAL'ALT,

Captain, Mirror Lancers

Guarstyad

LXIII

Around noon on sixday, the lookout calls out, "Guarstyad, ho!"

Alyiakal has been able to see the white-tipped mountains just above the horizon for some time, but they don't seem to get any closer, though the *Kief* continues to cut through the choppy gray-green waters at a respectable speed. He wears his winter jacket and gloves to keep warm in the cold wind that blows from the north.

More than three glasses pass before the fireship enters the harbor, roughly three to four kays wide and stretching another five kays north between rocky hills on both sides. The hills end in cliffs that drop to the water, except for a few narrow beaches. The valley in which Guarstyad is located widens north of the port, located on the east side of the River Guar. The general shape of the harbor and valley seem to correspond to the map in Alyiakal's atlas, but the map didn't convey the height of the northern peaks, tops concealed by clouds dark enough that they hold rain or snow.

As the *Kief* nears the port, Alyiakal notes the town has two levels. The lower level holds only the piers and a few wooden sheds. A good ten yards higher and somewhat set back, the upper level contains several hundred structures, mostly dwellings. There are two modest piers. Several small sailing vessels are docked at the inner pier, likely fishing craft. The river mouth doesn't look wide, possibly only thirty or forty yards across. He also sees no sign of what might be a Mirror Lancer post.

But then, why would it be that near the town?

On the west side of the river is a single long pier with a small stone building at the shore end, but Alyiakal can see no other structures nearby. Behind the foot of the pier is a low wall, but inshore of the wall, bog or marshland covers the west side of the river.

The fireship slows as it nears the outer pier on the east side of the river, where two Mirror Lancer officers wait with three wagons lined up at the end of the pier.

Judging that it won't be much longer than a quint before the *Kief* docks,

Alyiakal heads below to get his gear. When he returns, the *Kief* has pulled alongside the pier, and the lines are being doubled up.

At that moment, Sublieutenant Naartyn appears and hands Alyiakal an envelope. "Your travel confirmation on the *Kief.* Sometimes posts want them. Sometimes they don't."

"Thank you," replies Alyiakal.

Naartyn glances northward. "Already snowing up there. You can have it, Captain."

"We each make choices," says Alyiakal. "I'm more inclined to have solid ground underfoot."

"I'm inclined to have a decent bunk every night. Take care." With that, Naartyn turns away and heads aft to where the Mirror Lancer rankers form up.

By the time the gangway is in place, Naartyn has returned and nods to Alyiakal, who then walks down the gangway, carrying his gear, and very glad that he is wearing his winter jacket because the wind becomes brisker the farther he gets from the fireship.

He's met by an overcaptain. "You're carrying a lot, Captain."

"Winter uniforms and spare boots, ser." Alyiakal doesn't mention the healer's satchel in the second duffel.

The overcaptain laughs. "At least you have some understanding of where you are. I'm Overcaptain Shenklyn, in charge of logistics for Guarstyad Post."

"Alyiakal, reporting. Previous posting at Pemedra."

"I understand Overcaptain Tygael is the deputy post commander there."

"He was, but he was due to be reposted right after I left. He didn't know where at that time."

"Do you know who replaced him?"

"Yes, ser. Overcaptain Draakyr. He was recently promoted."

"If I might ask, how did you find Overcaptain Tygael?"

"Very thorough, very knowledgeable, and quietly direct. He was acting post commander for almost a season before I was reposted."

Shenklyn nods.

Alyiakal senses that the overcaptain is not displeased and might even be slightly satisfied.

"The advance on your posting indicates you're also an effective field healer. How accurate is that?"

"I'd say it's accurate, ser, but that's a personal judgment."

"How many men did you lose to wounds?"

"None, ser . . . if they survived the first few glasses after the fight."

"Are there Magi'i or healers in your family?"

"No, ser. Not that I know. My parents were both single children, and my mother died when I was eight."

"What about your father?"

"He was Majer Kyal. He died on duty at Inividra a little over three years ago."

Shenklyn nods again. "I didn't know him, but I heard good things about him." He gestures toward the end of the pier. "We brought you a mount."

As is his habit, Alyiakal does not immediately mount or load the horse provided for him, instead sensing the healthy, but slightly agitated, chestnut gelding, and projecting ordered calm as he approaches. He spends a little time talking to the gelding, patting his shoulder, before loading him with the two duffels, mounting, and easing the gelding up beside the overcaptain, also mounted.

"I see you calmed him down," says Shenklyn.

"I talked to him. It helps."

"I wondered. The advance said you were good with mounts. Majer Jaavor doesn't trust much of what's written about incoming officers. It was his idea to send the chestnut."

While Alyiakal doesn't know the command structure at Guarstyad, Jaavor is likely the deputy post commander, and Jaavor's skepticism, in time, might work to Alyiakal's advantage. *Provided you don't make stupid mistakes.* "He's a good mount. Can I keep him?"

Shenklyn chuckles. "No one else is likely to object."

Once they load the thirty rankers and their gear onto the wagons, the other Mirror Lancer officer, a captain likely several years older than Alyiakal, rides up and addresses Shenklyn. "Rankers accounted for and ready, ser."

"Good." Shenklyn gestures to Alyiakal. "Captain Fraadn, Captain Alyiakal. Alyiakal is the Sixth Company officer. He had an eventful posting at Pemedra." Shenklyn then looks to Alyiakal. "Fraadn is the senior captain and came off a tour at Inividra. His previous tour was at Lhaarat."

"I'm pleased to meet you, ser," says Alyiakal.

Fraadn offers a boyish smile at odds with a stern countenance. "No 'ser's among captains, Alyiakal."

"Wagons! Forward!" orders Overcaptain Shenklyn as he leads the way from the pier toward a long stone ramp with a stone wall on the east side, a ramp that leads up to the town proper.

After the two captains ease their mounts in behind Shenklyn and head up the wide, gradual slope of the gray, stone-paved ramp, Alyiakal studies the area, immediately realizing the reason the town sits higher than the piers has to be due to the frequent floods that Tygael had mentioned. The flat and marshy lands on the west side of the River Guar must experience substantial flooding, Alyiakal reflects.

"How far is the post?"

"Roughly five kays north and a little east. It's about the same distance to the town as to the foot of the road leading to the east pass."

"What about the west pass?"

Fraadn shakes his head. "Way too far. You have to ride a good ten kays north where the ferry crosses the river. That's if the ferry's operating, and it can only take four mounts at a time. Half the time landslides or high waters on one side or the other close off the west pass. Subcommander Laartol said as much when he briefed me. I have taken First Company as far as the ferry when we scouted for other feasible approaches through the mountains to the east."

"I take it that there's more scouting to be done."

"That's how you'll get your company working together. Except for what we've scouted and covered, there's not a decent map or description of anything except the harbor, the road to the mine, and the area around Guarstyad itself."

"What about Kyphran scouts?"

"We saw traces and tracks in late Summer and Harvest, but the snows closed the top of the east pass by mid-Autumn. Since then, the coastal watches see more, small, unflagged sloops along the coast east of here and in the waters off the entrance to the harbor. Most likely Kyphrans looking for places they could land troopers. I doubt they've had much success. You saw the cliffs on the east side when you came in, didn't you?"

"I did. I didn't see any place that could accommodate troopers."

"Neither has anyone else, not even the naval types or the Mirror Engineers." Fraadn pauses, then adds, "We all think they're up to something, but so far we've seen nothing."

When they reach the top of the ramp, the overcaptain turns his mount east on what appears to be the stone-paved main street of Guarstyad, past a sizable factorage on the north side and a modest inn on the south side. Two blocks later, the shops end at a cross street, beyond which are modest and weathered-looking dwellings with steep-pitched wood-shingled roofs. While some dwellings have stone or brick walls, many are built entirely of wood. The overcaptain turns left, again heading north on the cross street. The stone paving ends four blocks later, replaced by dirt covered with small stones and gravel, and the dwellings thin out and largely disappear three or four blocks later, except for houses for smallholders or tenants.

While the ground on each side of the road seems roughly level, when Alyiakal looks eastward to his right, he can see that, farther east, the land is slightly higher and the fields and plots give way to green-and-gray woodlands, signifying a mixture of seasonal trees and evergreens, unlike the Great Forest, which holds no evergreens at all.

"Have you had any snow yet?" asks Alyiakal.

"Only a dusting on oneday, but it's close to freezing most nights."

After a little more than half a glass, Alyiakal sees Guarstyad Post, situated on a low rise overlooking the road, although there are higher hills not that much farther to the east. From a distance the post does not look especially imposing, especially compared to Pemedra or Syadtar. Although its gray stone walls convey authority, those walls appear to be only a quarter kay in length, if slightly higher than those at Pemedra.

But then, the post here isn't meant to be the command center for other posts farther north and east.

The causeway linking the post to the north road is roughly a half kay long and stone-paved, and as the chestnut's hoofs strike the stone, he shies slightly. Alyiakal leans forward and pats him firmly on the shoulder, adding a touch of warm and reassuring order, while also trying to sense if there's anything wrong with the gelding's hoofs or legs. He senses no chaos or lingering wound chaos as he rides through the post gates behind the overcaptain.

Less than twenty yards behind the gates is a square two-story building.

Fraadn gestures toward it. "That's headquarters. The building directly behind on the right has the officers' quarters and study, as well as the mess. The mustering area is to the left with the stables behind it."

Alyiakal listens to the senior captain's description, looking around and trying to fix the buildings in his mind.

Moments later, the overcaptain reins up outside the officers' stable, then turns to Alyiakal. "Once you take care of your mount and drop your gear in your quarters, you need to report to the deputy post commander. That's Majer Jaavor. He'll brief you before you meet Subcommander Laartol."

"Yes, ser."

Shenklyn then dismounts, as do Fraadn and Alyiakal.

The chestnut tenses slightly as Alyiakal leads him into the stable.

An ostler sees the chestnut and immediately says to Alyiakal, "Ser . . . he usually goes in the end stall."

"Is there another stall available?" asks Alyiakal, suspecting that the gelding associates something bad with the stall, although that suspicion is based only on feelings and riding the gelding for less than a glass.

"There's one at the other end. It's farther from the stable doors . . ."

"That will be fine." Alyiakal continues to the last stall, which is clean but without water or fodder. He opens the door and says to the gelding in a reassuring tone, "This should be better."

He takes his time unloading and unsaddling the chestnut, as well as grooming him. During that time, one of the stable boys arrives with water, and Alyiakal watches to see if the chestnut drinks too much.

When Alyiakal finishes with the gelding, and leaves the stall, one of the ostlers approaches.

"Ser . . . you don't have to—"

"I understand there may have been problems with this horse. Is that correct?"

"He's . . . often . . . temperamental, ser."

"I understand," Alyiakal says quietly, "but I don't want force used on him. If there's difficulty, let me know."

"Yes, ser."

"Thank you. I know you have your hands full, and I do appreciate it."

Then Alyiakal picks up his two duffels and lugs them to the officers' quarters, where the duty squad leader shows him to his quarters—a single room farthest from the jakes and bathroom, containing a bed, a side table, a straight-backed wooden chair, a narrow three-drawer chest, and an open armoire for his uniforms.

He deposits his gear, then walks to the headquarters building, carrying only his orders and personal records.

A single anteroom serves the studies of both the subcommander and Majer Jaavor. An older squad leader sits at a desk equidistant from the doors to the studies.

"Ser?"

"Captain Alyiakal, reporting as ordered." Alyiakal hands over his orders and records.

"Yes, ser. I'll tell the majer you're here."

The squad leader has barely moved to the half-open study door when a firm but mellow voice says, "Let me have the orders and records, and have the captain come in."

The squad leader enters the study, then returns to the door empty-handed and gestures. Alyiakal follows the prompt into the study, and the squad leader closes the door behind him.

The blond but partly bald majer stands from behind the desk. "Have a seat, Captain."

"Thank you, ser."

"How was your journey here?"

"Long, ser, but I took two eightdays of leave in Geliendra. So I've only been traveling five days straight."

"How long did it take you to get to Geliendra?"

"Almost an eightday from Pemedra, but I was fortunate. I didn't have to wait long at any of the stations."

Jaavor pauses. "You must have suspected that you're the junior captain here. Why do you think you were even considered?"

"My previous superiors must have found favor with what I did, how I did it, and were able to explain it."

"What about your qualifications?"

Alyiakal can sense that the majer's questions are more than merely curiosity, but he doesn't sense malice, only a certain amount of puzzlement. Still, he decides to be cautious. "I would think that what my previous superiors reported would bear more weight than my impressions."

Jaavor offers a wry smile. "They reported that you're exceptionally qualified—for a junior captain. They also reported that you're cautious about extolling your own accomplishments. Can you tell me why?"

"My father was a Mirror Lancer majer. He disliked junior officers who praised themselves, especially those who did so excessively."

"It's as dangerous to underestimate one's abilities as to exaggerate them. I'd like an honest self-appraisal of your abilities."

Alyiakal wants to take a deep breath. He doesn't. "Since that is a direct order, ser, I'll be as accurate as I can. I am able to direct my men in a way that they understand and obey. I'm excellent with a firelance and good with horses. I'm a better than decent field healer, better than most, but I'm certainly not a fully trained healer. I can see the possibilities of an opposing formation or group of raiders and can usually anticipate their possible actions, but I have almost no experience in combat above the company level."

Jaavor nods. His expression remains pleasant, but all that Alyiakal can sense is that the majer is not displeased. After a moment, Jaavor says, "What you said is close to what both your previous superiors reported. Did they ever ask you what I did?"

"No, ser."

"What have you been told about Guarstyad?"

"That command established this post in the past year because of the threat created by Kyphran forces and their newly constructed fortification." Alyiakal quickly summarizes what he has been told.

"That's correct, if incomplete. I'll get back to that in a moment. For now, your immediate duties require you to ride patrols investigating and discovering any possible, if more difficult, approaches from Kyphros to Guarstyad. These patrols will also get you used to working with your squad leaders and lancers, and accustoming them to your leadership. Because Guarstyad has been over-looked, there's much that's not known about the lands away from the river and the town, especially in the woodlands." Jaavor pauses, then taps all four fingers of his left hand on the desk. "The coastal border post the Kyphrans are building appears to be smaller than Guarstyad Post, with lower walls. It's also located some twenty-five kays from the eastern end of the east pass, but before the snows closed the pass, some of our scouts discovered that they appear to be working to connect their post to the old trading road from the east pass through the high grasslands."

Jaavor does not say more.

"How are they supplying the post?" asks Alyiakal.

"From a cove west of their post. It can take small vessels or boats in calm

seas. They must have built a road down to the cove even before they started
work on the post, because there's no record of anything before last year." Jaavor
offers a cynical expression that isn't either frown or smile.

"Then it appears this has been planned for some time."

The majer then asks, "What's your immediate reaction, Captain?"

"They think there's far more silver in the mine north of Guarstyad, or something else of equal or greater value. Why else would they build a road to a small
harbor that often can't be used and work on a road to the east pass?" *And all that
is far too elaborate just to draw Mirror Lancer troops from other border passes with
Kyphros.*

Jaavor stands. "I've taken too much of your time after a long journey, and I
know Subcommander Laartol wants to meet you."

Alyiakal gets to his feet quickly, following the majer out the study door and
to the open door of the other study.

"Ser," says Jaavor, "you wanted to see Captain Alyiakal."

"I do." Laartol stands, if briefly, before settling back behind his desk, and
motioning to the chairs. He is of wiry build, with silver-shot black hair, and
hazel eyes, and his voice is a moderate light baritone.

Behind Alyiakal, Jaavor closes the door.

Alyiakal sits erectly in the middle chair and waits.

"Welcome to Guarstyad Post, Captain. I'm sure Majer Jaavor has outlined
your duties and I won't go into that."

Not unless I get into a difficult situation.

"I like to meet each of my officers. In your case, I had another reason. I
served briefly with your father years ago, and I found him an incredibly effective
and dedicated officer. I suspect you already knew that, but I wanted to let you
know that is my feeling as well."

"Thank you, ser."

"One of the reasons you—and the other captains—were selected for this
duty is because the situation could become rather . . . *interesting,* for lack of a
better word. You know about the silver mine, I presume?"

"I've been told that a mine exists. That's about all I know, ser."

"What many people don't know is that the mine isn't the usual silver mine.
Most silver contains veins of lead, sometimes copper, or other metals and ma-
terials. Refining such ore is a cumbersome, time-consuming process and takes
hundreds of people. It's also messy and can leach various substances into the
water. This mine produces what they call dry silver, which is remarkably pure.
It was thought to be a small deposit when they began mining several years ago.
It appears it is much larger."

"Is that why the Kyphrans are—"

"Not totally. Another aspect of the problem is the Prefect of Gallos's displeasure with the Duke of Kyphros. Kyphros is not exactly a wealthy land. The high grasslands to the east of the southern part of the Westhorns could be called a grass desert. You can see, I trust, why the Duke might have an interest in Guarstyad?"

"Yes, ser."

"What is somewhat unsettling is that the Kyphrans have moved a considerable number of troopers into their recently constructed fortification, but do not seem to have done much beyond that. The mountains make ascertaining potential activities somewhat difficult, but with the size of their force . . ."

Alyiakal senses that the subcommander is looking for something more. "I was told it took some time to assemble the six companies for this post. I'm not privy to anything beyond that, but it suggests that with the past difficulties on the northern borders and the unrest with the Jeranyi and the Cerlynese—"

"Exactly," says Laartol. "None of you captains can afford to spend men unnecessarily. You, in particular, have a record of accomplishing what was necessary with extremely low casualties. You're also a good field healer. I've told the other company officers to call on your services as necessary, because every ranker may be needed. Your interactions with the rankers of other companies will be strictly limited to wounds and other injuries. Do you understand?"

"Yes, ser, but there is one aspect to this that other officers should know. Certain kinds of wounds can fester unseen. If I say that a man is not ready to return to duty, and his officer overrules me, I do not want to be held accountable for what happens to him."

"You think you can judge that better than a lancer's own superiors?"

"If I can't, ser, I'd be a poor healer," Alyiakal replies evenly.

Abruptly, the subcommander laughs. "Fair enough, Captain."

Alyiakal can sense that his reply actually pleased Laartol, and that worries him, but if he hadn't spoken, he'd likely have faced greater problems in the future.

"That's all I have for you, right now. You need to get settled. You and those of your rankers who arrived with you won't have patrol tomorrow, but after that you'll be scheduled as necessary."

"Yes, ser. By your leave?"

Laartol smiles and gestures toward the study door.

Alyiakal stands, inclines his head politely, then turns and leaves the study.

From there, he walks back to his new quarters, where he unpacks his gear, puts away his clean uniforms, and separates out those that need laundering. Then he looks for the officers' study, where he locates the table desk for Sixth Company. He finds two unused logbooks and a stack of envelopes that contain a significant amount of paper. He'll have to address that later this evening and on sevenday. He decides against opening any of them until after the evening meal.

He walks around the rest of the building to discover what is where, then makes his way back to the mess, where he introduces himself to the duty mess orderly.

He's barely finished when Fraadn appears with another captain, narrow-faced, brown-haired, and gray-eyed.

"Alyiakal, this is Rynst. He's got Third Company."

"I'm pleased to meet you," replies Alyiakal.

Rynst grins. "I heard you're very good with horses. Some of us didn't fare as well. I could make that chestnut behave, but it was a struggle."

"Did the overcaptain try that on all the captains?" asks Alyiakal.

"Only the two of you," says Fraadn, adding in an even lower voice, "That's not something he would have done on his own."

"The overcaptain said it was the majer's idea."

"No harm done," says Rynst amiably.

Before long, all the officers have seated themselves, except for the place at the head of the table. Alyiakal finds himself across the table from Rynst, with Kortyl, the Second Company officer, on his left, and Craavyl, the Fourth Company officer, on his right. Baentyl, the Fifth Company officer, sits across from Craavyl.

Subcommander Laartol enters the mess and stands at the head of the table. "For those of you who haven't met him, the new face at the table is Alyiakal. He comes from an eventful tour at Pemedra. He's also a skilled field healer, which could prove quite useful in our rather isolated situation." Then he seats himself, and the two mess orderlies begin to pour the wine, then to serve the evening meal, which is a poached whitefish served in a wine reduction, accompanied by sliced boiled potatoes in a cheese sauce and roasted quilla.

"You'll see potatoes in every form here," says Rynst.

"We weren't that fortunate in Pemedra," replies Alyiakal dryly.

Craavyl laughs.

"Your supply squad leader must have left something to be desired," suggests Kortyl mildly.

"Potatoes don't grow there," replies Alyiakal. "Neither do pole beans. The local produce was largely limited to carrots, turnips, spring beans, and false potatoes. Oh, and the local ale was made from the seeds of plains grass."

"That must taste awful," says Rynst.

"Not awful, but somehow off. I never got used to the taste."

"What about the barbarians there?" asks Kortyl.

"It all depended on which barbarians and what season." Alyiakal gives as brief a description as he can without elaboration, but he does mention the Jeranyi-forged weapons.

"Jeranyi have always been a problem," says Baentyl. "My uncle had problems with them years ago."

For the remainder of the meal, Alyiakal tries to say as little as possible, without being rude, by asking questions.

After the dessert, a pearapple-custard tart of sorts, and the departure of the senior officers, Alyiakal stands and stretches, and finds that he and Rynst are the last to leave.

"You never said where you served before this," says Alyiakal, stopping in the hallway.

"My first tour was at Isahl, and then I had two years at Westend—the Accursed Forest."

"I know about the Forest. I lived in Jakaafra before I went to Kynstaar. Did you have much trouble?"

"Not that much. Not if you kept yourself ready for anything."

"Did you run across many of the large black panthers?"

"A few. They seemed to respect lancers and firelances. They were more likely to attack traders who risked using the road. The cougars were more dangerous for us—quicker, and they'd hide in the foliage of fallen limbs, especially those that bridged the top of the wall to the ground." Rynst looks to Alyiakal. "Did you ever see any?"

"I saw one panther and two cougars—all on the top of the wall. That was before I went to Kynstaar."

"They didn't come after you?"

"Why would they? I wasn't close to the wall, and I wasn't a danger to them. They seem to focus on horses as much as on people." Alyiakal offers a wry smile. "Of course, that's only if there isn't a fallen tree limb."

Rynst frowns, then nods. "I never thought of it that way. They've gone after mounted messengers, but there weren't any reports about people walking being attacked." After a pause, he asks, "Where are you headed now?"

"To the officers' study. A stack of envelopes awaits me, and I hope somewhere amid them is a company roster."

"There will be. Overcaptain Shenklyn and Majer Jaavor are both good on keeping us informed. The majer likes reports on time, for your information."

"I appreciate the tip."

"I'll see you later," says Rynst, turning in the direction of the officers' quarters.

Alyiakal turns toward the officers' study.

LXIV

On sixday evening, Alyiakal opens, reads through, and sorts the information in the waiting envelopes. In going over the Sixth Company roster, all he learns are the names of the men assigned and of his three squad leaders.

On sevenday morning he rises early. He checks his box in the officers' study. Then he heads out in the chill dawn air for the study in the rankers' quarters reserved for the senior squad leaders, looking for Torkaal, who turns out to be a not-quite-grizzled, but definitely weathered, figure half a head shorter than Alyiakal.

"Good morning, Captain. I figured you'd be here early." Torkaal offers an amused smile. "Didn't think I'd be wrong, either."

Alyiakal smiles in return. "You've had a number of border postings, I imagine."

"Five, ser. Last one was at Lhaarat. Others were at Inividra, Assyadt, Isahl, and Pemedra."

"I've only been at Pemedra."

"Heard that you had one of the companies that flattened the West Branch barbarians. That so?"

"It is."

"Figured it had to be."

"Tell me what you know so far about Sixth Company, if you would."

"Both Maelt and Vaekyn are solid. About a third of the rankers don't have much experience. The others have more. How good . . ." He shrugged. ". . . there's no way of telling yet." After several moments, Torkaal says, "That's about it for now."

"There's one other thing you need to know."

The senior squad leader stiffens. "Ser?"

"I'm also a field healer. *But* I'm under standing orders not to do any healing until the fighting's over."

Alyiakal can sense a certain amount of relief.

"Makes sense, ser. You can't do much for fatal wounds, anyway. Is there anything else, ser?"

"Not right now. I've gone through all the notices and paperwork. So far there's nothing urgent. Muster after breakfast? I'd like to do a walk-through. Not an inspection, but I'd like to see every face and have every man see me."

"Yes, ser. The company will be ready."

Alyiakal is fairly certain that meets with Torkaal's approval. Certainly, the senior squad leader isn't actively disapproving.

"Good." Alyiakal then heads back to the mess, arriving at the same time as Fraadn and Baentyl.

"Good morning, Alyiakal," says Fraadn cheerfully.

"The same to both of you."

"I saw you working late last night," says Fraadn.

"More like getting organized and making sure something wasn't urgent."

"That won't start until tomorrow morning," suggests Baentyl, with a trace of a smirk.

"Or possibly until oneday," adds Fraadn.

Once the three seat themselves below Kortyl and Craavyl, Alyiakal says, "From what both the subcommander and majer told me, it didn't appear that the Kyphrans have made any attacks. Or did I misunderstand something?"

Fraadn shakes his head. "During the last part of Summer, we thought they might. They brought two whole companies partway into the east pass, then withdrew when they saw Second Company. They might have held maneuvers below the pass on their territory, but our scouts didn't see any sign of that. With the pass snowed in, it's unlikely they'll try anything until late Spring. We still have scouts checking the pass on our side. They certainly can't move quickly through snow that's almost waist-high already."

Alyiakal can understand that. He can also see why the Kyphran forces worry the subcommander.

At that moment, the subcommander arrives and says, "Second Company will be patrolling the edge of the woodlands north of the east pass today. No other announcements." He seats himself and pours some ale into his mug, then serves himself some of the fried eggs over the potato cakes.

Once the platters are passed around and everyone has served himself, Alyiakal says, "Once I found out I was being posted here, I started to see if I could find any maps."

The hint of a smile crosses Fraadn's face, but he says nothing.

"Are there any decent maps of the area?" Alyiakal asks, not addressing the question to anyone in particular.

"There weren't any maps at all," replies Overcaptain Shenklyn. "Of anything anywhere in this valley or around it."

"There's a large map on the wall next to the door to the officers' study," adds Fraadn. "We're adding to it almost every day."

For a moment, Alyiakal wonders why he didn't see the map, then realizes that it would have been behind him as he entered the study, and in the dim light he might not even have noticed when he left late the night before. When he'd checked his box earlier in the morning, he'd definitely been preoccupied.

"We might even know our way around Guarstyad before the Kyphrans attack," murmurs Baentyl in a voice even Alyiakal can barely discern.

"It's not that bad," says Fraadn cheerfully.

"What isn't?" asks Shenklyn.

"My potato cake," replies Fraadn guilelessly.

"Your last posting must have spoiled you, Fraadn. This is good food." But Shenklyn grins.

"My apologies, ser."

Alyiakal grins as well and addresses Fraadn. "You would have loved the turnip dumplings at Pemedra."

Kortyl gives the slightest of headshakes, although he doesn't look toward the foot of the table, or at anyone, for that matter, but Alyiakal discerns a sense of dissatisfaction on the part of the more senior captain.

"Are there any duties out of the ordinary?" asks Alyiakal.

"Only wood duty," answers Fraadn.

"Wood duty?"

"Lancers who receive disciplinary punishment have to saw and split wood," explains Fraadn. "It gets cold here in Winter, and the snow can be deep at times."

The amount of silver in that mine must be considerable. But Alyiakal just nods.

After finishing breakfast, Alyiakal retrieves his winter jacket and walks to where Torkaal is forming up Sixth Company.

The walk-through goes as expected, with Alyiakal first meeting briefly with the three squad leaders, then walking through the ranks, asking each man his name and his previous posting, or in the case of recent recruits, their home.

As he finishes, Alyiakal notices that Captain Kortyl and Second Company head out of the post, but he has no way of knowing what their patrol entails. That reinforces his worry about being out of touch with what is occurring. While he knows it can't be any other way less than a day after arriving, he still worries.

After that, Alyiakal walks to the stables, where he spends time with the chestnut gelding. When he leaves the stall, one of the ostlers appears.

"Is everything all right, ser?"

"He seems to be fine, thank you."

Then Alyiakal returns to his quarters to pick up the atlas of Candar before making his way to his desk in the officers' study. Both Fraadn and Rynst sit at their desks. Alyiakal does not disturb either, and settles in for what he knows will be a long day getting his records and files set up.

After that, he plans to spend some time studying the map of Guarstyad in the atlas to see how well it corresponds, or does not, to what he has so far observed—and to the larger map on the study wall.

LXV

Over the remainder of sevenday and all of eightday, Alyiakal discovers the map in his atlas appears to be more accurate than the wall map, at least so far as the coastline and harbor are concerned. Reluctantly, he lends the atlas to Overcaptain Shenklyn to allow the two maps to be compared.

As Alyiakal hands over the atlas, Shenklyn says, "We all appreciate this. It's good to have another source. I don't imagine it was inexpensive."

"No, ser. Though, given how hard it was to find anything at all, I thought the cost would be worth it."

As the overcaptain carries the map book away, Rynst says, "How did you come up with that?"

"I found a bookstore in Geliendra that happened to have it. It wasn't cheap, and I think I got it for less than most would have because the bookshop owner knew I was a Mirror Lancer officer being posted here. He didn't say why, but that he was glad I had a use for it."

"Do you always think that far ahead?"

Alyiakal shakes his head. "I try, but I can't say that I always succeed."

Rynst looks amused, but doesn't say more.

Late on eightday afternoon, Majer Jaavor summons Alyiakal and assigns Sixth Company a familiarization patrol for oneday.

Alyiakal takes the order to the officers' study, where he reads the route and looks at the map. The directions simply state that Sixth Company is to follow the mine road along the east side of the River Guar until it reaches the junction with the trail/road to the east pass. They are then to take the trail road no more than a kay past the lookout post before riding back to the mine road and proceeding to the ferry crossing, then north to the gatehouse to the mine. The return can be in any fashion but should not retrace the outward route except where necessary.

After studying the map and taking notes, Alyiakal looks for Torkaal, whom he finds in the stables, and passes on the patrol order.

On oneday morning, Sixth Company sets out on a clear, chill, and blustery day.

Alyiakal observes that more than a few of the new rankers don't look comfortable in the saddle, and the same was true when he accompanied new rankers from Syadtar to Pemedra. *But then, three days in the saddle made a considerable difference.* He smiles wryly, knowing that he and the squad leaders need to use the familiarization and scouting patrols to get the company working well together.

After leaving the post causeway, Sixth Company turns north on the road from Guarstyad, which is, in fact, the mine road, roughly following the river, if on higher ground several hundred yards east of the river proper. On both sides of the river, Alyiakal notices the profusion of low plants and higher grasses, as well as marshy areas, although the river itself is fairly straight and doesn't appear that shallow. A few bent and gnarled trees edge the lower ground immediately bordering the river.

On the east side of the road are occasional small dwellings, more than huts but less than houses; all have chimneys.

And enormous woodpiles.

Less than three kays north from the post, the mine road shrinks to a track barely wide enough for a wagon and a single horse, side by side.

Alyiakal frowns, wondering about the road, then realizes, if the silver is as pure as the subcommander says, a wider road is scarcely needed, since most of the people in the valley live within five or ten kays of the harbor.

Almost a glass passes before Sixth Company reaches the even smaller track heading eastward. A stone with moss around the edges has one word and an arrow chiseled into it. The single word is PASS.

"They don't like to use many words," says Torkaal.

"Or build roads that are very wide," returns Alyiakal.

Sixth Company heads east on the narrower way.

After riding about a kay eastward, Alyiakal notices that the mostly open ground slowly gives way to the mixed forest, and that the ground gradually rises toward the hills in the east. Beyond the hills, he can see rocky peaks above evergreen forests.

For another kay or so, the road to the east pass remains fairly straight with a modest shoulder, but then, as it curves around a hill, the shoulders shrink, and the undergrowth on each side is nearly head-high and continues for some distance into the trees.

While Alyiakal cannot sense anyone except lancers within half a kay, he doesn't like being hemmed in. The Summer grass in Pemedra had been bad, but the hilly undergrowth would definitely be worse, if it weren't for the fact that he's now able to sense much farther than he could in Pemedra.

Thanks to the Great Forest.

He turns to Torkaal. "Send out another set of scouts, as necessary, so that we have a half kay between the forward scouts and the company, with the ability to report directly."

"Yes, ser."

Alyiakal senses a slight feeling of relief from the senior squad leader before he issues the necessary orders.

Once the company continues, Alyiakal says, "The Kyphrans could be less than half a kay away, and we'd have no way to tell, not if they were quiet. Do you have any other ideas?"

"Might be best if we position ourselves first. Not sure we'll always be able to do that, though."

For the next several kays, neither the scouts nor Alyiakal find any sign of anyone near the road, although Alyiakal has sensed several red deer, and possibly a mountain cat farther into the woods to the north.

Ahead, the road flattens slightly, and Alyiakal sees a recently cleared area. At the west end of the area stands a log watchtower, although he cannot see anyone posted there.

"That must be the lookout post," says Alyiakal. "You and I will take first squad a ways up the road. We need to see what it's like, but I don't see that there's much sense in taking the whole company."

"Not right now, ser."

Alyiakal smiles. "You mean since the snows have closed the pass?"

"Something like that, ser."

"Second and third squads can stand down. Pass the orders."

"Yes, ser."

Before long, the scouts, Alyiakal, Torkaal, and first squad ride past the log tower. The platform on the top sits five yards above the road, which runs straight past the tower for fifty yards before curving northeast along a narrow stream to the right of the road.

After the first curve, the road then curves southeast, and Alyiakal calls a halt, then turns to Torkaal. "The road's going to do this for at least another ten kays before it even gets to the snow line. We've seen enough for today. We'll rejoin the other squads and give first squad a bit of a break."

"Yes, ser."

Alyiakal has no trouble sensing Torkaal's approval.

As first squad heads back down toward the lookout tower, Alyiakal can't help but silently ask himself why Mirror Lancer headquarters has put six full companies in Guarstyad, more than in any other border post, especially since the eastern border seems to consist largely of hills and mountains that are difficult to get through in the best weather and impassable the rest of the time.

He keeps pondering that question after first squad rejoins the other squads and the company heads west toward the mine road and north from there toward the ferry and the rest of the familiarization patrol.

LXVI

Over the next three eightdays, Alyiakal and Sixth Company ride patrols over most of the passable roads on the east side of the River Guar. According to the maps—and Overcaptain Shenklyn—the only usable road west of the river is the one leading to the west pass, which is closed until Spring. It's effectively impossible for the Kyphrans to attack from that direction.

Between patrols and drills, and other duties, Alyiakal spends time with the chestnut getting him used to a concealment and riding under it. He also writes a long and thoughtful letter to Saelora, but he isn't able to dispatch it until the next fireship arrives with supplies on sixday of the sixth eightday of fall—two days after Guarstyad has received a light snow, light being less than four digits.

Less than a glass after Alyiakal has given the letter to the duty desk for dispatch and returned to the officers' study, a ranker appears, breathing heavily.

"Captain Alyiakal, ser! There's been an accident, ser. Squad Leader Torkaal said to get you. Hamstaadt . . . he's hurt bad."

"Where?" Alyiakal is on his feet immediately, although he doesn't know who Hamstaadt is, only that he's not in Sixth Company.

"The loading docks at the supply building, ser."

"Get him to sick bay. I'll be there as soon as I can."

Alyiakal hurries to his quarters, grabs the satchel, and moves quickly to sick bay, arriving before two men lead a third into the treatment room. "We had to help him, ser. Says his head hurts, and he can't keep his balance."

Both those symptoms worry Alyiakal far more than the superficial cuts and gashes on the lancer's forehead and the blood on his face. The injured lancer, presumably Hamstaadt, cradles his right forearm with his left, and staggers as the two lancers set him in the chair beside the examining table.

Ignoring the blood for the moment, since the bleeding no longer seems profuse, Alyiakal senses the arm, then runs his fingertips along the skin. The larger arm bone is broken, if cleanly, roughly midway between the wrist and elbow, but his sleeve is in tatters, and the skin beneath is gashed and cut in more than a few places.

Why wasn't he wearing a winter jacket?

That question will have to wait, Alyiakal knows, as he begins to sense wound chaos, not all of it from the arm. His eyes travel to the lancer's forehead, where a right-angle gash suggests a box or crate struck with considerable force. The points of white-tinged red chaos within the lancer's skull beneath that gash confirm the severity of the impact.

Alyiakal immediately gathers two small points of order and lightly touches Hamstaadt's forehead. The order reduces, but does not eliminate, the white-tinged chaos. Then he says to the duty ranker, "I'll need some clean water and spirits and clean cloths—also a splint and the canvas strips to go with it."

"Yes, ser."

Using his cupridium belt knife, after dusting it with order, Alyiakal cuts away what's left of the right sleeve, being careful not to disturb the injured arm. As he does, he asks, "Hamstaadt, how do you feel?"

"Arm hurts like sowshit. Head . . . like . . . anvil . . . someone hammering . . ."

Alyiakal would like to use more order on Hamstaadt's brain chaos, but he recalls Healer Vayidra's warning about too much too often. As soon as the duty ranker returns, he gently cleans the cuts and gouges on Hamstaadt's arm, then, using his senses and a little order pressure, realigns the arm and splints it.

After that, he dusts the abraded skin's surface with order, and he and the duty ranker move Hamstaadt to one of the vacant beds, not that any are occupied at the moment. Alyiakal folds several blankets and eases them under Hamstaadt's shoulders, neck, and head, something he recalls from what Vayidra taught him about head injuries.

Only then does he return to the squad leader.

"How is he, ser?" The squad leader looks to Alyiakal.

"The arm looks worse than it is, but he won't have much use of it for almost a season, maybe longer. He'll also be spending the next few days here because of swelling, and I can only put a splint on it until the swelling goes down. Then it will need a cast. There's also that head injury. I'm fairly certain he's not himself, and he'll need to be very quiet for several days, possibly longer."

"How bad is the head injury?"

"It's not something to take lightly. If he were hit again at that point, he might not live."

"How can you tell?"

"His pupils are larger, but they're not the same size. He was dizzy and unbalanced, and his head hurts badly. There's a slight indentation on the outside of his skull."

"Can't you do more?"

"Anything else I can do would likely kill him. Right now, quiet and rest are best." *Aided by judicious application of order.*

"Could . . . ?" The squad leader breaks off.

"Could a real healer do more?" asks Alyiakal. "In this case, I don't think so. If we were talking about other injuries, yes."

"Begging your pardon, ser, but did you ever work with healers?"

"I did. Before I went to Pemedra I had extra training at Kynstaar and again at the infirmary in Syadtar. At Syadtar, I worked under one of the best healers in Cyad."

"Thank you, ser."

Once the two lancers depart, Alyiakal returns to Hamstaadt, where he senses the chaos in the other's brain. He adds the tiniest touch of order, then straightens.

Hamstaadt moans, but his eyes are closed.

Alyiakal leaves the ward and goes to the duty ranker, who is seated behind a table desk.

"Ser?"

"Hamstaadt is resting now. I'll be back to check on him periodically. If he has a seizure or convulsions, send for me immediately."

"Yes, ser."

Alyiakal recovers his satchel and walks back to his quarters, then returns to the officers' study, where Craavyl hurriedly meets him.

"How is Hamstaadt?"

Alyiakal takes a deep breath. "He has a broken arm. That should heal, but it will likely take a season, possibly a little less. He took a severe blow to the head. The next few days will tell. I've done what I could. He needs rest and quiet, and he needs to sleep with his head elevated slightly." Alyiakal pauses, then asks, "Do you know what happened? I was more concerned about treating him."

"I don't know all the details. He was unloading supplies from the fireship. Somehow a crate skidded off the wagon and hit him."

"Somehow?"

"I have the squad leaders looking into it," says Craavyl dryly. "There's more to it, I'm sure. Hamstaadt's been . . . a little difficult."

"I wish you well with that," replies Alyiakal. "I'll be seeing Hamstaadt on and off. If he lets anything slip, I'll let you know."

"I'd appreciate that. Thank you."

After Craavyl leaves, Alyiakal makes his way to his desk and sits down, thinking.

He'd managed to use order, somewhat like a shield, to help nudge the broken bones into position. It would have been helpful if he also could have used order to immobilize Hamstaadt's arm when he was splinting it.

You'll likely have some time this Winter to work on that and on strengthening your shields.

Although no one has asked or suggested it, Alyiakal decides to write up a report on his efforts to heal Hamstaadt, both for the record and so there are no "misunderstandings" about what he did and why.

He needs to go back to updating his maps, both the one in the atlas that Overcaptain Shenklyn finally has returned and the one he is drawing for his own use in the field. Later, of course, he'll need to check on Hamstaadt.

LXVII

Over the next eightday, Alyiakal keeps a close watch over Hamstaadt, often checking on him using a concealment so that the apparent number of times he visits the lancer appears low, even to Hamstaadt, because Alyiakal can use order to keep the whitish-red chaos under control without Hamstaadt noticing that he's present or what he's doing. By oneday of the seventh eightday in fall, only a small amount of dull reddish gray remains, and Alyiakal allows Hamstaadt to return to the barracks, albeit with a solid plaster cast on his forearm.

Hamstaadt never lets anything slip about his "accident," and Craavyl never asks Alyiakal.

The sky remains a hazy green-blue, and most of the traces of the previous snow vanish by twoday afternoon, when Majer Jaavor calls in Alyiakal.

"Ser?" asks Alyiakal as soon as he's seated in the majer's study.

"Now that we've mapped and explored all the trails and roads known to cross the Westhorns from here, we need to make sure we're not missing anything," the majer explains. "There are more than a few gaps in what we know. One area is the higher land south of Guarstyad that stretches east to the lower Westhorns. The locals say the road heading south at the top of the bluffs beyond the town ends after a while. No one can say exactly where. It would be useful to know, along with anything else. Tomorrow, Sixth Company will take that road and discover what it can. Plan for several days. That may not be necessary, but no one seems to know how far that road extends, and the few people living there are supposedly . . . odd. They grow some kind of tree-root mushrooms, and they don't like strangers. Individuals who travel there tend to disappear. If they're too hostile, do what's necessary. We don't need trouble here and from the Kyphrans."

"Yes, ser." Alyiakal sees no point in saying more, but he wonders about tree-root mushrooms. He also has the feeling that he's heard something like that before, but he can't recall where.

Once he leaves the study, he finds Torkaal and briefs him, then asks, "Have you heard anything about that area?"

"No, ser. Only that it's rugged, bordering on impassable, especially where it's close to the Westhorns."

"Then the men should be in full winter gear."

"Yes, ser."

On a clear, not-quite-freezing threeday morning, Sixth Company rides through Guarstyad, and Alyiakal easily picks up feelings of puzzlement, as well as resentment, from the handful of people on the narrow streets. Both feelings are understandable, especially the second, given that no town is likely to welcome six companies of Mirror Lancers unasked for, especially a town boasting only three small taverns, at least that he has seen or heard mentioned.

When the company reaches the south side of town, a single dirt road leads up a gradual slope. While the land immediately around the port sits only just above the water, south of the town bluffs border the Western Ocean, and the land rises farther south and east so that the southern coastline east of Guarstyad becomes sheer rocky cliffs eventually merging into the southern end of the Westhorns at an unnamed rocky point.

That is, if the maps happen to be accurate. Alyiakal has no doubt that the rocky point exists, that the Westhorns end there, and that the maps of the coastline are largely accurate, but none of the maps show any detail of the area between Guarstyad and the coastline.

Which is why Sixth Company is here.

The edge of the bluffs is roughly fifteen to twenty-five yards from the west edge of the road. Alyiakal cannot see the eastern side of the harbor, but can easily make out where the waters on the west side lap at the narrow rocky beaches below the bluffs. On the east side of the road, the ground holds a mixture of rocky hummocks, low evergreen bushes, and a coarse, knee-high grass.

While the slope is gradual, it seems unending, and Alyiakal not only watches and senses, but concentrates on creating and holding an even stronger inner shield.

Two glasses pass before the bluffs give way to the sheer, rocky cliffs that angle slightly to the east. The dirt road remains the same, with traces of hoofs and wagon or cart wheels. Belatedly, he realizes that the road has remained well-kept since Sixth Company left Guarstyad.

So who is maintaining it . . . and why?

Ahead, perhaps a kay or so, Alyiakal sees scattered conifers in places farther inland.

"Someone has to live out here, or do some logging—something," says Torkaal.

"It doesn't look like anyone's grazing the grass here," adds Alyiakal. "Not recently, anyway."

"There's grass, but it's sparse. Might not be enough for a large flock," replies Torkaal.

Alyiakal extends his senses to see if there are large cats that may have enlarged their range from the Westhorns, or other large animals, but, so far, he doesn't sense any.

Sixth Company rides another kay, and Alyiakal orders a break, riding the chestnut closer to the edge of the cliff. The stone cliffs drop straight into the water at the base of the cliffs on the west side of the inlet. While he cannot see the base of the cliff below him, he senses that the stone there also goes straight into the water. He eases the chestnut back to the dirt road.

Half a quint later, he gives the order to continue.

Almost another glass of gentle climbing passes before Sixth Company reaches the rounded point joining the north-south cliffs with those running east-southeast. A few yards back from the rounded point separating the inlet from the Western Ocean, someone has piled stones at least three yards high on a stretch of bare stone. The stones don't appear to be shaped for use as masonry, but there are no other stones for at least several hundred yards in any direction, only scattered copses of weathered and bent evergreens and grasses that might conceal them.

The remains of a marker to show the entrance to the harbor, or something else?

Since the dirt road continues along the cliff line, Alyiakal and Sixth Company keep following the road, bordered by sandy and often bare ground on the ocean side, and thicker groves of the scraggly evergreens and occasional clumps of grass on the north side. He's neither seen nor sensed anything but a few small rodents, most likely coneys, which concerns him. The lack of larger game—and sheep—might be a result of the severe weather suggested by the condition of the trees, or it might reflect those who use the road, or both.

Then Alyiakal notices a thin wisp of smoke rising from the evergreen forest bordering the north side of the road several kays farther east. Since Sixth Company has covered at least fifteen kays, he has to believe that there must be more than one stead so far from the town, but all he says to Torkaal is, "That smoke means someone's living out here."

"Doesn't make sense to me," replies the squad leader. "No sign of anything big enough to hunt or trap, and the only grazing land is five kays behind us. The trees don't look to be that good for timber, either."

After Alyiakal and Sixth Company ride another two kays, almost abreast of the location of the smoke, the road becomes a thin layer of dirt and sand over the underlying rock. Ahead, the road turns north at a narrow space between the trees, while a path continues to parallel the cliffs to the east-southeast. Alyiakal can now see the rocky point depicted in his atlas and the map being developed by Overcaptain Shenklyn, but judges that the nearest part of that point has to be more than five kays away, possibly ten.

"Company! Halt!" Alyiakal commands. "Scouts in!" While his orders are to investigate the road, he has the feeling that he also needs to find the path's extent, because, according to Shenklyn's map, the Kyphran base sits on the far side of the rocky point.

The road first.

Alyiakal turns his eyes to the road—and the trees on each side, tiny trees compared to those in the Great Forest, but still with tops roughly ten yards tall. Less than a hundred yards after the turn in the road, the space on each side is cleared. A wall, comprised of a stone base a yard high and a timber wall two yards high above that, runs along the northern end of the clearing. Heavy timbered gateposts flank the road.

Alyiakal makes out structures beyond the open gate and senses patterns of order and chaos beyond indicating people and animals.

"Ready firelances," he says quietly. "Forward."

He understands that a community so isolated needs defenses, but he's also been warned that the people have been dangerous.

When he is less than fifty yards from the gate, he calls out, "We're on a scouting mission. We intend no harm."

As Sixth Company continues to ride forward, the heavy timber gate swings closed.

"I wouldn't do that, if I were you!" Alyiakal calls out. "We're here under the orders of the Emperor of Light."

"He's not here," returns a voice from behind the gate.

"No, but his chaos is," replies Alyiakal. "If you don't open the gate, you'll have to replace it, and people could be hurt."

"You could be hurt, too," replies the voice.

"That would be very bad for you," says Alyiakal, projecting the words with a certain force of order. "You don't want that." He can sense only two people behind the gate.

"Please wait a moment," comes the reply. "I'm summoning someone."

A bell begins to ring, insistently.

A handful of moments pass before the ringing stops, and Alyiakal senses several other figures approaching the gate. Then the gate opens, slightly.

A man of indeterminate age stands in the narrow opening. His expression is one of annoyance, followed by apprehension that Alyiakal senses clearly as the man takes in the company of Mirror Lancers before asking, "Might I ask your intention?"

"Sixth Company has been tasked with following certain roads and trails," replies Alyiakal. "Since this is a road that appears on no maps and might lead eventually to the eastern border, we're following it." As he speaks, Alyiakal eases the chestnut forward slightly and extends his senses. He can ascertain perhaps a half score of men moving toward the gate.

"The road ends here," declares the man standing in the gate.

"Then, once we have verified that, we will depart," returns Alyiakal politely, but firmly.

"The road ends here. That is all you need to know."

"No," replies Alyiakal. "We will see if that is so. Because you fear us, ten men will accompany me to assure that. If anything happens to any of us, you will not have anything left standing."

"That is not acceptable."

Alyiakal can sense chaos building around the speaker and raises his fire-lance, willing its chaos to block the chaos bolt aimed at him. Chaos flares just short of the man, who has to be a mage of sorts, and some cascades back around his shields, but those shields collapse under the force of two chaos blasts.

The second chaos bolt from Alyiakal's firelance turns the semi-mage to ashes and a few pieces of metal.

The gate starts to close, and Alyiakal blasts more chaos at the base of the leading edge of the gate, which sags, grinding to a halt. He can sense no more chaos, but while he can tell that the men behind the gate may hold weapons, he has no idea of what those weapons might be.

"Open the gate and stand aside! Or we'll burn it and everyone around it to ashes!" Alyiakal adds a certain amount of order to his words. He hopes he doesn't have to waste chaos on burning the gate down, but he isn't about to lose men unnecessarily either.

He waits, ready to use the firelance instantly.

Then the gate grinds fully open, revealing a stone-paved way leading between one-story dwellings with separate small barns. Between his sight and senses, Alyiakal discerns at least thirty dwellings, likely more, enclosed by the stone-and-timber palisade. Beyond the rear wall, with a second open gate, the trees look unfamiliar, at least to Alyiakal.

A gray-haired woman appears, wearing a leather jacket and gray trousers. Alyiakal isn't surprised that she carries an unseen amount of order.

"Spare us, ser," she says evenly, without a hint of begging.

"I would have done that to begin with," Alyiakal replies, "if the magus hadn't been so obstinate. We're seeking roads, not to take whatever you have."

"No one has ever bested him. He did not believe it possible."

"What I said stands. I will bring ten men. You will guide us. You will answer questions. If all is as the magus said, we will depart." He pauses. "But you will open the gate to Mirror Lancers, should we come again."

She inclines her head, in agreement, but not in blind obeisance.

Alyiakal turns slightly in the saddle. "Torkaal, the left file of first squad will accompany me. If anything untoward occurs, burn every structure. Spare any who don't resist."

Despite the rudimentary shields the woman has, Alyiakal can feel her shock at his words.

"Yes, ser."

Alyiakal looks to the gray-haired woman. "Lead on."

"You meant that," she says in a low voice.

"I did. I made a reasonable and legal request. Mirror Lancers have the right to every road in Cyador. Your mage not only refused, but tried to kill me. At that point, I had the right to destroy your town." *But exercising that right would have been stupid and counterproductive, although Majer Jaavor likely wouldn't have said a thing.*

The woman turns. "This way." She begins to walk into the town from the open gate, then says to the men standing beyond the gate, "Go back to your houses until the lancers leave. You'll only get us killed. He has more power than Herrak did, and his lancers have more than that."

The nine men back away slowly, their eyes still on Alyiakal and the lancers who follow him.

"I'm sorry I had to do that," adds Alyiakal. "Was he your consort?"

"Does it change anything?"

"No," he admits.

"At least you're honest. He was my brother."

"I am sorry. An officer may have to do his duty, but can still regret the necessity."

She says nothing more.

Alyiakal takes in the very ordered community. The log-walled dwellings are neat, with slate roofs and rock chimneys. He sees no huts or hovels. Nor does he see any markedly larger dwellings. He notes no one else on the main street, but can sense their presence elsewhere. The center street has six dwellings on one side, seven on the other, and the dwellings extend back about a hundred yards on each side. From what Alyiakal can quickly calculate, the walled area of the community is roughly two hundred and fifty yards on a side.

At the north end of the walled area is another gate—open—and the street or road out of the north gate leads across a timber bridge over a small stream to the edge of the trees, where it splits into dirt lanes. As he reins up short of the trees, Alyiakal can see that they are definitely different, with shiny green leaves with pointed tips and edges. He also sees what look to be horned cattle covered with long hair that almost touches the ground grazing behind a split-rail fence to the north of the strange trees.

Stranger and stranger. "What sort of cattle are those?"

"They're not cattle. They're mountain musk oxen," says the older woman dismissively. Then she looks up to Alyiakal and gestures. "You see? This is where the road ends."

"There's no road or path beyond the trees—those kind of trees?" adds Alyiakal.

"No. The land gets rockier and drier as one goes lower."

Alyiakal can sense the truth of what she says. He glances around. The lead lancer isn't that close. "Is magery required to grow the tree-root mushrooms, or only to preserve them?"

The surprise on her face confirms part of his suspicions. She gives the smallest of nods. "Both."

Alyiakal doesn't intend to press. "Don't worry. I have no interest in them. I just wondered." He silently tries to project the truth of his words. "What kind of trees are they?"

"They're holly oaks. They grow only in a few places, and it takes much work to keep them healthy."

"Thank you. What do you get from the musk oxen? Meat? Milk?"

"Some meat. For us. No milk. The undercoat wool is the softest and finest in all Candar, or the world."

Alyiakal nods, then turns and calls out, "We've seen enough. We'll head back now." He looks to the woman. "You'll come with us back to the south gate. Do you know where the cliff path leads and how far it goes?"

"It follows the cliffs for as far as I've ever walked, more than five kays, less than ten. The farther I went, the narrower it got. There are mountain cats farther east, and they make hunting the red deer dangerous."

"Don't the cats hunt the musk oxen?"

"The cats aren't that stupid."

As he turns the chestnut back south, Alyiakal understands why individual travelers may not always return from traveling the cliffs.

The woman says nothing on the walk back through the town, but waits beside the gate a yard away from Alyiakal as the lancers return to first squad.

Then she looks up at Alyiakal with a smile both bitter and amused and says quietly, "They saw it all and still do not understand. My condolences, Captain."

"And mine to you." Alyiakal inclines his head. "I wish you well."

While he slowly turns the chestnut, his senses remain focused on her and the area near the gate until Sixth Company re-forms, facing southeast toward the narrow way that follows the cliffs.

Then he addresses Torkaal. "According to her, the path continues for five, possibly ten kays. There are mountain cats in the area as well. We'll have to follow it as far as we can."

"I thought as much, ser."

Left unsaid is the fact that the majer, and possibly the subcommander, will not be pleased until they know no road exists across the rocky point to where the Kyphrans have built and may expand their post.

LXVIII

For the next five kays, Sixth Company rides east-southeast along the cliff path, mostly sand over bare rock, bordered on the ocean side by cracked and fissured stone and on the south by scattered and gnarled evergreens, ranging from little more than bushes to small trees. The rock on which the path lies gradually rises the closer it gets to the rocky point marking the southern end of the Westhorns. Alyiakal can see that the trees farther to the south of the path have become scrubby and twisted evergreens growing farther apart, irregularly spaced in the rocky terrain only passable on foot. At one point, he feels the slightest trace of an order/chaos pattern that might be a red deer or a mountain cat before the creature turns away. At the same time, thinking about the words of the gray-haired woman, who is more mage than healer, he has concentrated on maintaining a stronger inner shield.

When the path narrows even more, to the point where riding two abreast is barely possible, Alyiakal calls a halt to give men and mounts a short break, and to talk things over with Torkaal.

"What do you think about continuing?" Alyiakal asks.

"Did the majer offer any thoughts on that, ser?"

"Only that he wanted to know more about where it ended." Alyiakal smiles wryly. "I don't think he'll be happy with a report that says that the road ends in a small walled town that keeps to itself and raises mountain musk oxen for very costly wool."

"Strange bunch, ser. How did you know the one who tried to attack you was a mage?"

"He had to be. No one else would have even dared to defy a company of Mirror Lancers."

"Might I ask how you—"

"Managed not to get turned into ashes? I remembered what an overcaptain once told me. He said that most mages—and he was talking about trained Magi'i—couldn't muster much more chaos than is contained in a single firelance. So I figured that, if the moment he started to raise chaos to throw, I used my firelance, all that chaos would be caught around him. It didn't work quite that way, but he was so surprised that he couldn't block the second blast."

"Chancy, ser."

"It was, but striking first against someone like that is usually better." Alyiakal smiles. "It looks like we need to follow this frigging path for a ways, at least to see if it ends or looks impassable. It might be faster if I took one squad, and you stayed here with the rest. Second or third squad?"

"Third squad, ser. More experience."

"Have someone summon Vaekyn, then."

"Yes, ser."

Vaekyn appears quickly, with a worried expression. "Yes, ser?"

"We need to explore that path ahead," explains Alyiakal, "but I'm only going to take one squad, and that's third. It looks like we can go two abreast for a bit, but we'll have to see how long that's possible. Two scouts forward, and you'll ride with me."

"Yes, ser."

Much to Alyiakal's surprise, the path does not narrow, at least not for the next kay or two, but it does level out. Nor are there any tracks of any sort.

He turns to Vaekyn. "Do you see any way we could be easily attacked from the north through those rocks and low trees?"

"No, ser. Not unless there's another path hidden there."

While Alyiakal cannot sense anything resembling a path paralleling theirs, anything could be hidden among the tangle of rocks and evergreens, but getting from another path to his through that tangle would be anything but easy.

An ambush is impractical here, if not impossible.

After another half kay, Alyiakal notes that the path seems to end at the edge of the cliff, but when he rides closer, he realizes that the path doesn't end, but that the line of cliffs turns north. He reins up.

A few yards from where he's halted, the cliffs drop to a small inlet that seems to have no beaches and no way to reach the water, other than jumping and falling over two hundred yards. On the other side of the inlet, about a kay away, is the rocky point comprising the south end of the Westhorns. The rugged top directly across from Alyiakal rises several hundred yards higher than the cliff edge where he is, and extends a good two or three kays into the sea from the northernmost point of the inlet.

"I didn't realize we were that close, ser," says Vaekyn.

"Neither did I," replies Alyiakal, turning his gaze northward, studying the edge of the cliff on his side of the inlet, and the path, which continues northward for almost a kay before it appears to end at a rocky mass a hundred yards higher than the path.

Alyiakal's eyes widen as he discerns what seems to be a white line running east along the rocky mass to a spot above the northernmost point of the small inlet. "By the frigging Rational Stars!"

"Ser?"

"We're on a frigging road. See! It goes to that rocky mass and turns east. It's cut into the stone about to the middle of the inlet. There must have been a landslide, because there's a chunk gouged out of the stone. The gap must be a good fifty yards across, but the road continues past the inlet and there's a depression on the other side. I'd wager that road somehow crosses the point."

"The Kyphrans did that?"

Alyiakal shakes his head. "They couldn't have done that, especially not in the last year or so. The only people who could have done that are the First."

But why? And how?

Except Alyiakal thinks of the Great Canal, which is far longer than the narrow cliff road. Had the First decided against finishing the road when the section of the cliff had given way? Or had that happened later?

"I need to ride to the end of the path on this side, just to get a good idea of where the road on the other side leads. And so do you and two or three lancers."

"Yes, ser."

"If it's lasted since the First, it's not going to collapse under our weight." *And the majer may want to hear this from others besides his most junior captain.* "I'll lead the way."

"Yes, ser."

The closer Alyiakal rides to where the path or road curves into the rocky mass angling westward into the cliff highlands, the more he can see why no one could have seen the old road. It certainly isn't visible from the water, or except by taking the path all the way from Guarstyad. Why would anyone have ridden or walked that far when there isn't a town or anything of value in that part of Cyador or Kyphros beyond the rocky point?

He also wonders whether there's an old stone road under the dirt road that they've followed all the way from Guarstyad.

Although the road cut into the cliff is more than wide enough for a wagon and a horse abreast, Alyiakal only rides the chestnut a few hundred yards along the rock-cut section, out of caution and because he needs to ride that far to get a good look at where that road appears on the other side of the inlet.

Even so, he can't tell how far it extends, only that it appears to pass through the lowest part of the rocky point, and he can see no obvious sign of travelers or of past travel.

He has to admit that he's relieved once he, Vaekyn, and the two lancers return to their earlier observation point. Turning to Vaekyn, he says wryly, "I think we can tell the majer where the road ends." *For the moment, anyway.*

"Yes, ser." Vaekyn's tone is subdued.

Alyiakal knows it's already late afternoon, and that Sixth Company will have to return to where the path narrowed and bivouac there before returning to the post on fourday to report their findings to the majer.

He doubts that the majer will be pleased, to say the least, although Alyiakal can't see how the Kyphrans could possibly cross the gap in the road anytime soon. It's far too wide to bridge, and cutting a road out of the stone surrounding the gap could take years.

But that's something that the majer and subcommander have to worry about. Not you.

At least, Alyiakal hopes so.

LXIX

Sixth Company rides back to Guarstyad Post on fourday under clouds and snow that begins to fall as they go through the town. Before dismissing the company to duties and quarters, Alyiakal tells the squad leaders to caution their men to say nothing about the road for the next day or so. He doubts that what they found will remain unspoken even that long, but he'd like to have a chance to write a thorough report for Majer Jaavor. Alyiakal leaves the chestnut and the stable slightly before the fourth glass of the afternoon, dropping his gear in his quarters, and heading for the officers' study to write up his report. He doesn't even get to the study door before a squad leader intercepts him.

"Ser, Majer Jaavor would like to see you immediately."

Alyiakal turns and heads for the headquarters building, where he's ushered into the majer's study.

"You were gone for almost two days," says Jaavor, even before Alyiakal is fully seated. "Did you need all that time?"

"We needed every quint, ser. How detailed a report do you want now?"

"Whatever's so important that it took two days, Captain."

Alyiakal manages to remain calm, although he would like to point out that the majer was the one who told him to prepare for several days, but such a point would be ill-received. He says pleasantly, "We discovered a fortified community in the woods near the road's supposed end, and an undiscovered mage attacked the company. After that, we went on to discover that the road didn't end, or it was built not to end." Alyiakal then describes in detail what happened at the walled community and what Sixth Company discovered about the road. He confines himself to the facts, and does not include his speculations about the relationship of magery and tree-root mushrooms, but mentions that he had other lancers come with him partway along the road with the missing section.

Jaavor frowns as Alyiakal finishes.

Alyiakal can tell that the majer is disconcerted, and more than a little unhappy at what Alyiakal has discovered. *Because someone should have found that out earlier . . . or because the most junior officer did . . . or because it means there are other implications? Or simply because the importance of the discovery means that Jaavor will have to go see it to verify the finding for Mirror Lancer headquarters?*

Jaavor does not speak for several moments, then clears his throat. "That sounds almost unbelievable, but you're not the type to spin tales, and the fact that you had a squad leader and rankers come with you to confirm it shows that you understood you might not be believed." The majer pauses, then asks, "Have you thought about who built it and why?"

"I don't know that anyone but the First could have built it. The damage to the middle of one section had to come later because whoever built it could have simply cut deeper into the rock where it collapsed had it happened while they built it. When complete, the road would have been much shorter than the way through the east pass and would have been usable most of the year."

"Still . . ." muses the majer, "people build roads to travel or transport goods. There's nothing beyond the point in Kyphros besides what the Kyphrans are presently building."

Not now. "Ser . . . does headquarters know if the Kyphrans built that fortification . . . or if they uncovered it and are rebuilding it?"

Jaavor's eyes narrow, but he says only, "I wouldn't have thought that even possible, but what you're reporting means that's something to be considered." He pauses. "I look forward to your full report, Captain. I'll also be talking to your squad leaders and the lancers who accompanied you. That's all for now."

"Yes, ser. By your leave, ser?"

Jaavor nods.

Alyiakal turns and leaves the study. The majer is more than a little unhappy. That's clear. But, as Alyiakal already knows, sometimes the worse outcome of a patrol is to accomplish the mission successfully.

He takes a deep breath as he walks swiftly from the post headquarters back to the officers' study to write out his patrol report. He spends the time before evening mess, except for a little time to wash up, working on the detailed patrol report. Immediately after eating, he returns to the officers' study to continue writing.

A glass later, Fraadn appears beside Alyiakal's desk. "Obviously, Sixth Company's patrol wasn't as uneventful as most of us suspected."

Alyiakal looks up. "For the moment, let me say that it appears you're better off not having made the patrol." That's absolutely true, Alyiakal thinks, if not in the way in which Fraadn will take it, because none of the other captains would likely have fared as well against even an untrained mage.

"You don't sound like you want to say more."

"It's best I don't. Not until the majer reads this."

"He doesn't know?"

"He knows, but he wants the background and all the details."

Fraadn winces.

"After he's read it, I'll be happy to tell you. But we suffered no injuries and no casualties."

"You make it sound mysterious."

"It is, possibly unfortunately. We'll have to see."

Fraadn nods. "I'll let you get on with it. Best of fortune."

I'll need that and more. "Thank you." Alyiakal turns his attention to the paper before him.

LXX

Alyiakal finishes the second, and final, draft of his patrol report late on fourday evening, then seals it in an envelope and then walks through the still-falling snow to deliver it to the duty squad leader at post headquarters so that Majer Jaavor receives it first thing in the morning.

Alyiakal is tired enough that he sleeps deeply, but he still wakes early on fiveday. That allows him to unpack the remainder of his gear, get his quarters back in order, and get thoroughly cleaned up before breakfast. The snow seems to have stopped falling sometime earlier, but Alyiakal can hear that the wind has picked up.

When he enters the mess and seats himself, Fraadn looks across the table.

Since neither Majer Jaavor nor Subcommander Laartol has arrived, Alyiakal simply says, "I turned in the patrol report late last night. I don't know if the majer's read it."

"You were checking on how far the cliff road goes, weren't you?" asks Craavyl.

"That was the assigned patrol," replies Alyiakal. "There were certain unforeseen developments."

"Unforeseen developments," repeats Rynst ironically. "How can anything possibly be unforeseen at a Mirror Lancer post?"

"When someone doesn't follow orders," says Kortyl.

"Or when they do," counters Rynst, "and what happens doesn't please whoever gave the orders."

"That's a bit harsh, Captain," says Overcaptain Shenklyn evenly, adding in an amused tone, "even if it's too often true."

Alyiakal catches Kortyl's quick frown before it vanishes, as well as Baentyl's momentary unguarded expression of calculation.

The banter stops as both Majer Jaavor and Subcommander Laartol enter the mess. Jaavor seats himself, while Laartol stands behind his chair, then clears his throat, waiting a moment before speaking.

"Yesterday, Sixth Company returned from what was expected to be a routine patrol to determine where the southeast cliff road ends. Instead Captain Alyiakal discovered that it turns into a road cut through solid rock that appears to have once crossed the rocky point separating Cyador and Kyphros. A landslide or the equivalent ripped away a fifty-yard section of that road on the Cyadoran side of the point. Because of that missing section, Captain Alyiakal was unable to determine whether the remaining section of the road continues across the point and into Kyphran territory. The course of the existing road appears largely impassable to large numbers of troopers, whether mounted or on foot, except by the road cut through the stone."

Laartol pauses. "This information should not be shared except with other officers. At the moment, especially at this time of year, it is unlikely to change the military situation. A road was discovered, and presently no signs that anyone has used that road beyond where it is believed to end for years. That is essentially all that we know right now." Without another word, the subcommander seats himself.

Fraadn looks across the table at Alyiakal. "How come no one else found it before?"

"Others probably did years ago," replies Alyiakal, "but you can't get to the last part of the road before the rockslide, except by the road, and you can't get off the road except by jumping into the ocean, and the road leads nowhere except to where you can't cross and can't climb. So people forgot about it, I'm guessing."

"So who built it?" asks Rynst.

"My *guess*," Alyiakal emphasizes, "is that the First did, for a reason we don't know and may never know. The section cut into the rock was originally almost a kay long, wide enough for almost two wagons. I can't think of any other way it could have been done." He pours himself some ale and helps himself to a pair of fried eggs, each plastered to a crispy brown potato cake. Then he tries to eat as the other captains speculate on the reasons for building an impossible road in an improbable location.

". . . has to be the First . . ."

". . . could be early Magi'i . . . earth mages . . ."

". . . lots of Kyphran war captives with chisels . . . they're a savage bunch . . ."

After a time, when Alyiakal has finished eating, Fraadn looks across the table and gives a slightly rueful headshake. Alyiakal senses a combination of amusement and sympathy and returns the gesture with a sardonic smile.

Once the subcommander leaves, Alyiakal stands, stepping away from the mess table. Rynst approaches, but before he can speak Overcaptain Shenklyn moves in.

"Alyiakal, I'd appreciate your accompanying me to the study and outlining on the map, to the best of your recollection, the location of this road."

Rynst steps back and mouths, "Later."

Alyiakal follows the overcaptain to the wall map in the officers' study, where he points and describes the path that likely conceals a wider road beneath and the sheltered cliff-cut section of the road.

"How far do you think it goes on the other end?"

"I couldn't tell, ser. Not for certain. The sun was low enough that there were shadows. At least half a kay up into the rocky point, but I'd guess it goes farther. That's only a guess."

"Did you see any chisel marks on the stone section you rode out on?"

"No, ser. The stone was smooth. Smooth, but not polished."

All in all, Alyiakal spends more than a glass with Shenklyn and the map before he can leave the officers' study to find Torkaal, whom he locates in the Sixth Company barracks spaces concluding a gear, locker, and bunk inspection. He eases away, raises a concealment unobserved, and returns to hear what the senior squad leader might have to say to first squad.

". . . not too bad . . . except some sloppy oiling of your boots . . . want them to shed water once we get more snow . . ."

Alyiakal continues to listen.

". . . one other thing: Any captain, except Captain Alyiakal, asks questions, you got two answers. Either 'I don't know' or 'The squad leader or Captain Alyiakal would know better.' You say anything else, it won't be pleasant. Keep anything you say to the senior officers to what you saw or what you know. Nothing else."

Alyiakal slips away, back inside the barracks door, where he removes the concealment and waits for Torkaal. When the squad leader appears, Alyiakal asks, "How did the inspection go?"

"Better every time, ser."

"Good. I take it that Majer Jaavor asked you and Vaekyn about the road and the difficulty with the one man at the walled town?"

"Yes, ser. He wasn't much interested in the town. Said that you handled that right. Asked a whole lot of questions about the road, especially to Vaekyn."

"I thought he might."

"Ser, who do you think built it?"

"My guess is the First."

"But why would they go off and leave it?"

Alyiakal shakes his head. "I have no idea. After all the effort it must have taken, leaving it doesn't seem to make sense. That might be why the majer and the subcommander have concerns."

"You think the Kyphran bastards discovered something at the other end of the road?"

"I don't know, but it's likely." Another thought occurs to Alyiakal. "But we couldn't see any traces of anyone on the road beyond where the cliff collapsed. I wonder if there's another place where the road is blocked or broken on their side."

"That'd make sense."

In one way, but that would mean that the breaks were deliberate. "We'll have to see. Then, we might never know."

"That happens, ser. We all know that." Torkaal pauses, then asks, "Do you know when we'll be heading out again, ser?"

"There's nothing posted on the schedule, and what we discovered may change anything the majer has planned. I'll let you know as soon as I find out. Are there any troubles with any of the mounts?"

"Might have to find a few replacements. Got the ostlers working on it. If there's a problem, I'll let you know . . ."

For the next quint, Alyiakal and Torkaal go over various administrative and logistical details before he returns to the officers' study, wondering if the majer or the subcommander have more questions, or if he and Sixth Company will even be involved with the mysterious road from this point on.

LXXI

On sixday afternoon, Fraadn appears beside Alyiakal's desk in the officers' study.

Alyiakal looks up, then smiles wryly. "I take it that Majer Jaavor is accompanying you on a follow-up reconnaissance of the cliff road and its extensions."

"I didn't say a word." Fraadn pauses and adds, "But I would have."

"Leaving early tomorrow morning?"

The older captain nods. "I got the impression that the subcommander wants confirmation by a more senior officer."

"That's not surprising. To claim there's a First-built road where no one thought there was one on the word of a junior captain and two squad leaders?

That would likely prompt Mirror Lancer headquarters to order another patrol with a senior officer for confirmation. Along with subtle language suggesting that should have happened before any report to the high command."

"Anything you'd like to pass along?"

"The folk in that walled community are touchy. I have a suspicion that they've got ties to powerful Merchanters out of Fyrad. They sell very expensive wool and possibly other items. Any damage to the town or their herds might not be worth the trouble. I was fortunate to keep the casualties to one poorly trained local mage."

"I don't think that's been mentioned," says Fraadn dryly.

"I did tell the majer that. He didn't say I couldn't mention it."

"How do you know about the Merchanters?"

"A Merchanter I know mentioned a rumor about them. When I asked the town healer about why they kept mountain musk oxen, she told me about the wool and how fine it was. Put the two together . . ." Alyiakal makes a vague gesture.

Fraadn shakes his head ruefully. "We need to talk after I get back."

Alyiakal grins. "I don't think either of us is going anywhere very far for the next season or so."

Fraadn chuckles. "You're definitely right about that. I need to take care of a few things, but I wanted to talk to you first."

"Best of fortune."

After Fraadn leaves, Alyiakal considers the situation, not that he can do anything about it. Yet he has to admit that the largely hidden road seems almost inexplicable. Why would anyone, even the First, want to build such a road, and one so close to the ocean?

Except from what he's seen of the terrain and what the various maps show, the road, when it was functional, covered the shortest possible distance from the Kyphran post to Guarstyad, and likely the one that required removing the least amount of stone.

The Great Canal certainly shows that they could remove stone.

The larger problem with the idea of the First building the road is the fact that there's no indication of any attempt to link Guarstyad to the rest of Cyador by a more convenient route.

Or was that something planned for later that was abandoned?

Alyiakal shakes his head. He doubts that he, or anyone else living, will ever find out everything behind the mysterious road.

A sudden thought strikes him. The Great Forest conveyed to him its version of why the Forest wall was built. Would it recall anything about Guarstyad? He decides that's unlikely, given that all the history and stories suggest that the

Great Forest never extended farther than the base of the lowest hills bordering the Westhorns.

He takes a deep breath and goes back to adding details to his personal map of Guarstyad.

LXXII

Late on oneday afternoon, Alyiakal watches as First Company rides back into Guarstyad Post as scattered snowflakes drift from a cloudy sky. Two scouts lead, followed by Majer Jaavor and Captain Fraadn. Alyiakal, carefully looking over the company, sees no indication of missing or wounded lancers, and he breathes more easily as he walks back to the officers' study.

More than a glass later Fraadn walks into the study, takes a chair from his desk, and sits down beside Alyiakal's desk. He looks at Alyiakal and says quietly, "You really are a persistent bastard."

"When you're the most junior captain among five others who are senior and more experienced, persistence is useful."

"It's almost fifteen kays from where the path looks almost impassable to where the road ends at that gap in the cliff. I had to keep pointing out to the majer the tracks Sixth Company left. He said more than once that the patrol had better turn out to be worth it. Then he thought, right before we reached that corner before you head north beside the inlet, that it all ended there."

"What was his reaction when he did see it?"

"First, he didn't see the part of the road cut into the cliff . . . and when he did . . ." Fraadn chuckles. "It was almost worth it. He just muttered 'Angel-fired sowshit.' We spent some time making more accurate distance measurements."

"That makes sense. It won't hurt to send those off with his report."

"He also told me I had to write a report as detailed as yours." Fraadn shakes his head. "I can do it, but I still hate writing reports."

"Don't we all?" asks Alyiakal.

"Sometimes, it's almost as bad as doing something. Maybe that's because you get the feeling that no one except the post commander really cares, and he doesn't usually even need the report."

Alyiakal nods, then asks, "Did the majer say much about the road itself?"

"He agrees with your feeling that it had to be built by the First, but he doesn't understand how something that big got forgotten, and with no record of it."

"That we know of, but there's not much of a record of how the First built a lot of what they did," Alyiakal points out, "and even less about how they got here from the Rational Stars. But that isn't our problem. I worry more about what the Kyphrans might have found at the other end of the road. Even if the road were intact, they couldn't use it effectively."

For a moment, Fraadn frowns. Then he nods. "I see what you mean. You could put a few lancers with firelances in a score of places and destroy any force with very few casualties on our part—except—if they took the east pass *and* Guarstyad, *and* fixed the road, then they'd be almost impossible to dislodge."

"That's three 'if's," Alyiakal points out, "and they're big 'if's."

"Right now," agrees Fraadn. "We still don't know much about what the Kyphrans are doing. Once Mirror Lancer headquarters finds out about the road, they might be more concerned." Fraadn stands. "Anyway, I need to get to work on that report. The majer wants to have everything ready to send off on the next fireship."

"Thank you for letting me know."

"You're welcome. I also appreciated the cautions about the walled village. The majer took a quick look, more to let the locals know that they need to behave, and then we proceeded."

"They're touchy, and there's not much point in upsetting people in Cyador when you don't have to."

"Most officers would agree with that." Fraadn nods, then picks up his chair and carries it back to his desk. Once there, he seats himself and takes out several sheets of paper.

Alyiakal returns his attention to the end-of-eightday report from Torkaal.

Between that report, other paperwork, and studying the maps, Alyiakal ends up staying in the officers' study until time for the evening mess. So does Fraadn, and the two captains walk from the study to the mess together.

Rynst and Baentyl are already there, but in moments all the officers are present except for Subcommander Laartol and Majer Jaavor, who soon arrive. Both remain standing behind their chairs once they reach the table.

Then the subcommander says, "Majer Jaavor has a few words." Then he seats himself at the head of the mess table.

Jaavor clears his throat. "I'm sure everyone knows where First Company and I have been. And yes, there is a road, an incredible road, even if it's now unusable, but I'd like to offer a toast, and an apology, to Captain Alyiakal. Personally, I couldn't believe that this tiny path cubits from cliffs hundreds of yards above the ocean could possibly lead anywhere, except to a very long fall. But he and Sixth Company persisted for some fifteen kays to discover an amazing feat of engineering, and he wrote it up absolutely accurately." Jaavor reaches down and picks up his wineglass. "To Alyiakal."

After that, Jaavor adds, "Also to Captain Fraadn, who pointed out the faint traces left by Sixth Company and kept assuring me that we'd find something."

Alyiakal raises his glass to Fraadn, along with the others.

Then Jaavor seats himself.

Rynst immediately says, "I'm glad you two had to do it. Mountains are no problem, but drop-offs into the ocean?" He shakes his head.

Kortyl looks down at his plate.

Craavyl asks almost immediately, "How did anything that big get forgotten?"

"That's a question for Mirror Lancer headquarters," interjects Overcaptain Shenklyn. "*We* have to deal with the strange road and whatever the Kyphrans may be trying to use it for."

"Still seems strange," says Craavyl. "If the First built it, that was barely a hundred years ago."

"Not even that," declares Kortyl. "It's like someone wanted it forgotten. That wouldn't be the first time, either."

"Don't most people have things they don't want remembered?" asks Rynst. "Why would the First be any different? Also, Guarstyad's out of the way. Not that many people come here."

"Not all that willingly," murmurs someone, but whom Alyiakal can't discern.

Shenklyn laughs and adds, "And once Winter sets in, even fewer will be coming here, willingly or otherwise."

Alyiakal can't help but smile at the overcaptain's cheerfully sardonic words. He takes another sip from his wineglass and waits for his plate.

LXXIII

Over the next few days, Majer Jaavor doesn't summon Alyiakal for more patrol details, for which Alyiakal is just as happy. On fiveday, when the weather clears and the seas are calm, a fireship ports with supplies.

When he hears that, Alyiakal finishes the letter he's been writing to Saelora, then rereads it, his eyes going to the sections he'd drafted with particular care.

> *. . . this fall, all of our company exercises and duties have been designed to*
> *accomplish several objectives, those being to conduct patrols and drills to assure*
> *that our companies work well together, to familiarize all our lancers with*
> *the roads and trails in the area, and identify and scout all possible ways any*
> *Kyphran forces might attempt to enter this part of Cyador . . .*

. . . Guarstyad is well-laid-out, but does not seem to have grown much in recent years. There are scattered steads north of the town which supply meat, produce, and fodder, but there only seems to be one other hamlet or village besides Guarstyad itself . . . and, of course, the mine at the north end of the valley . . .

. . . are a number of fishing boats, and we have had more dinners featuring fish since I have been here than I've had in the entire rest of my life. While I've not seen any trading vessels, I've heard that Merchanters from Fyrad occasionally travel to Guarstyad and deal in various items, including those that your acquaintance mentioned, and also with a rare fine wool that comes from mountain musk oxen, which I've only seen from a distance, and which appear to be quite capable of dealing with the large mountain cats that can stray from the Westhorns . . .

. . . Although I've mentioned before how much I enjoyed my time with you, your family, and your Merchanter associates, I most relished the dinners where we had a chance to talk, and I look forward to the time when I can again enjoy your company and conversation . . .

When he finishes rereading the letter, he seals it and carries it to the headquarters building and turns it over to the dispatch clerk, along with the silver it costs to send.

Then he heads back to the officers' study to go over Torkaal's latest report.

The fireship is scheduled to leave early on sixday morning, doubtless carrying a full report about the mysterious road that will make its way to the Majer-Commander of the Mirror Lancers. Alyiakal doubts that even the swiftest fireship could reach Cyad in less than ten days in the best of conditions. In turn, there's no way any directives could reach Guarstyad until the second eightday of Winter or that any Mirror Lancer companies could move against the Kyphrans until Spring, possibly mid-Spring if there are late snows in the southern part of the Westhorns.

Alyiakal has no doubt that, come Spring, there will be some sort of action to deal with the Kyphrans and to determine more about the road. Until then, all he can do is prepare as best he can.

LXXIV

Alyiakal tries to push aside the cold mist that enshrouds him, finally using order-bound chaos to force a rift in the mists. Once through, he finds himself standing on a narrow stone ledge above greenish-gray waters far below and looking at the uneven mass of rock before him, then down at a cupridium tube, with an odd-shaped nozzle, extending from a four-wheeled cart that holds coiled and compressed chaos bound by order.

Without any volition on his part, Alyiakal finds his hands adjusting a disk on the top of the tube where it emerges from the body of the device.

"Fire!"

He presses the disk, and coiled chaos shaped into a knife edge flares from the nozzle. Almost two yards of rock vanish while someone holds an order shield to block the boiling cloud of molten rock, forcing it to cascade into the ocean below, sending up gouts of steam as they strike the surface.

Alyiakal shudders and wakes sweating, but the chill air of his room turns the sweat icy in moments.

Another dream? Or am I really recalling what someone else once experienced in building that road?

He sits up, swinging his legs over the side of the bed. He tries to focus his eyes, filled with tears, as if he'd actually seen that brilliant whiteness.

Your eyes tell you that you did see it.

He shakes his head.

He can understand, after his encounter with the Great Forest, how he might have other dreams about that powerful First magus, but to perceive it as so real that his eyes act as if they'd been light-seared? And what possible connection could the cliff road have with the magus who made the agreement with the Great Forest? A magus who could draw ordered chaos from the sun. *If the images of the Great Forest can be trusted.*

He shakes his head, still thinking.

Your dream is your mind trying to work out how they built the road, nothing more.

Alyiakal can still call up the feel of the compressed white chaos, not that he's about to try to gather and direct that power in his quarters in the middle of the night.

After he dries off and climbs back into his bunk, he finally drifts off to sleep. When he wakes, he can still recall how real his dream felt, yet until his encounter with the Great Forest he never had dreams that vivid. In fact, he can't remember ever recalling his dreams before that.

So how—and where—can you try to replicate those feelings and see what you can do without anyone else noticing?

He opens the inner window shutters slightly, enough to see that it's stopped snowing, then closes them, wondering at the fact that Winter has seemingly come so swiftly, yet knowing that it has already been five eightdays since he discovered the hidden road.

Still thinking about that, he washes up, shaves, and dresses in one of his heavier winter uniforms. Then he makes his way to the mess. He's early enough that Rynst is the only one there.

"I see someone else couldn't sleep," declares the other captain. "Or do you have an early patrol?"

"I don't," says Alyiakal as he joins the other captain standing beside the table. "Not that we could get anywhere beyond the main roads. The snow's not that deep here, but it's likely waist-deep on the upper part of the east pass. It'd take all day to get as far as the walled village."

"When do you think the subcommander will get an answer about the road?" asks Rynst.

"It's been four eightdays since he dispatched his report. Since then we've only had one fireship port, and that was two eightdays ago. It's too soon for a reply. Besides, the Majer-Commander has to know we can't do anything dealing with the Kyphrans until Spring."

"Likely late Spring."

"Even if the Majer-Commander knows what he wants, I don't think we'll see another fireship porting for another eightday, and that's if we get clear weather."

"I looked out earlier. You can't see the outer harbor." Rynst glances toward the door as Kortyl enters the mess.

"The locals say that there've been years when they couldn't see the outer harbor all Winter," says Kortyl.

"So why did they need us all here by Autumn?" asks Baentyl, who has followed Kortyl into the mess.

"Because it took a season and a half to assemble you all," says Overcaptain Shenklyn from behind Baentyl. "If headquarters started to move in lancers this coming Spring, by the time we could assemble a force, the Kyphrans would likely already hold Guarstyad."

Alyiakal has already figured that out, and knows all the other captains have as well, but Baentyl hasn't, or is playing a different game.

With Fraadn's arrival, the captains take seats at the table, followed by Craavyl, and then the majer and the subcommander, neither of whom offer any announcements. That's fine with Alyiakal, who is still considering how and where he might experiment with what he thinks he has dreamed.

After everyone has served themselves, Rynst smiles, then asks, "Does anyone have any idea when we'll be ordered to advance on the Kyphrans?"

Jaavor stiffens and says, "Isn't that a bit—"

Laartol says quietly but firmly, touching the majer's shoulder as a signal to stop, "Captain Rynst is most perceptive. I have no orders from Cyad, but there's little point in leaving six companies in Guarstyad indefinitely, while barbarians and others actively probe Cyador's borders elsewhere. Obviously, Captain Alyiakal's rediscovery of the road that apparently linked Cyador to part of Kyphros will affect any decisions and any orders I receive. Until then, it's probably best to keep speculations quietly among ourselves."

Alyiakal keeps his smile to himself, but, as a result of the words spoken in the last quint, he has greater confirmation of which two officers were likely posted to Guarstyad at least partly because of political or personal connections. He also has a very good idea why Laartol was selected as post commander.

"Glad that's out in the open," says Rynst.

"As if we all didn't already know," murmurs Craavyl.

The remainder of conversation at breakfast is prosaic, but pleasant.

After Alyiakal leaves the mess, he checks his box in the officers' study, but finds nothing in it, not that he has expected to, then returns to his quarters. There, he dons his winter riding jacket and cap and pulls on his gloves before venturing into the chill, overcast morning.

The calf-deep snow lies somewhere between dry and powdery, and heavy and wet, and the faintest breeze blows from the northwest. The walks between the buildings have already been shoveled clear by the day's duty company—Third Company, which was likely why Rynst was already in the mess. The main roads to the gate, as well as some fifty yards beyond, and to the stables and the supply warehouse, are also clear.

Alyiakal walks to the officers' stable, where he visits his chestnut, who immediately nuzzles him.

"No riding today, fellow." The weather in Guarstyad has been cold, but not intensely so, and Sixth Company has taken moderate patrols on known roads two or three times an eightday, to keep both horses and lancers in shape. "No treats, either. I didn't realize I was coming here. I know it's already been a long Winter for you, and it's barely halfway through."

After a time, he leaves the chestnut and walks eastward, toward the rear stone wall, along the main thoroughfare dividing the post. He walks past the paddocks behind the buildings and continues on the uncleared road toward the area designated for formation training. So far as Alyiakal has been able to tell, the area is largely unused except for disciplinary exercises. When he reaches the rear wall, he turns north and walks halfway to the corner. This section of the wall remains concealed from the buildings with rear-facing windows because of the placement of the supply warehouse.

Turning to the wall, he strengthens his shields and attempts to concentrate chaos in the coiled fashion he observed and felt in his dreams.

His initial problem is understanding how to coil chaos without the "coiled" sections collapsing into an inchoate mass. He can immediately sense that will lead to a massive chaos blast. Next, he starts to press the chaos into a thin string surrounded by order, but the chaos dribbles out when he removes the order blocking one end of the coil. On the next attempt, he makes the chaos string thicker. The chaos flares away from him and into the gray stone of the wall, but does little besides heat the stone.

Maybe if you made a longer string and compressed it more tightly with order?

He's halfway through compressing the longer string into a much tighter coil when he begins to feel the increase in the pressure of the chaos trying to escape. He nods to himself and keeps compressing the coil, realizing, as he does, that all the order/chaos machinations are giving him a definite headache, but he feels he needs to complete the effort, and he does.

He worries, in part, about releasing too much chaos at once. Concentrating on opening one end of the coil through a space he visualizes as not much bigger than a pinhole, he releases a tiny amount of the compressed chaos.

Hssst!

Alyiakal staggers back as the thin line of chaos cuts into the stone wall and the dissipated chaos and stone fragments slam into his shields. After a moment, he straightens and looks at the wall.

The stone sheds puffs of hot white vapor from a hole, barely as big as Alyiakal's finger, cut into the stone. As the vapor dissipates in the cold morning air, he moves forward and examines the hole, which looks to be at least half a cubit deep, so far as he can tell without sticking something into it.

He smiles sardonically. The results of his effort tend to confirm how the road was cut out of the stone. *And you have another way to use chaos.*

At the same time, his headache blossoms, and he's definitely light-headed. He doesn't retrace his steps, because his tracks, should anyone even notice, would call attention to where he stopped. So he continues his walk along the rear wall, knowing that a dark hole in the dark gray stone won't be noticed, or associated with someone taking a walk. At the next corner, he turns north, making his way back toward the various post buildings. Each step seems more difficult, and his dizziness increases.

He enters the building holding the mess and officers' study and heads for the mess.

"Are you all right, ser?" asks the mess orderly as Alyiakal ignores the question and forces himself to the side table, where he pours a mug of ale and takes a small swallow, and then another. In a bit, the light-headedness gradually vanishes, and he takes several bites of a hard biscuit. Before he knows it, he has finished the entire mug and eaten three biscuits.

"Ser?" asks the orderly.

"I'm fine now. I guess I didn't have enough to eat this morning."

The orderly looks at Alyiakal. "You're sure, ser."

"I'm sure." Alyiakal feels more strength in his voice, but he also knows, at the moment, he'd have a hard time riding a patrol or even running a short distance.

As the orderly turns away, Alyiakal half fills his mug with ale and takes another biscuit.

He can definitely see why the First compacted chaos into their devices instead of relying on personal use of magery. He still wonders how in the world the First magus could receive or gather ordered chaos from the sun.

LXXV

Much as Alyiakal suspected, the Guarstyad Winter is even more dreary than Pemedra's, with continually overcast skies, the snow piling up, and little sunlight to relieve the gloom. The depth of the snow anywhere but on the main road and in the town itself restricts company maneuvers to rides north to the ferry and around the town, giving both horses and troopers some relief and exercise.

Only one fireship docks during the last half of Winter, on sixday of the eighth eightday. It carries no dispatches from Mirror Lancer headquarters, or at least nothing that Subcommander Laartol relays to any of the captains. It does bring another letter from Saelora, informing Alyiakal, again, of how glad she is to have her own house to herself, and that she hopes to have it so improved by the time that he next visits that he won't recognize it.

He rushes through reading her letter, adding a few hasty paragraphs to the reply he has already composed, noting that they are hurried because the fireships never remain in Guarstyad more than a day, and often stay only a few glasses. Almost as soon as the *Rylaan* departs, the clouds lower, and snow once more begins to fall.

Alyiakal is grateful that he bought heavy winter boots, because he only feels secure improving his control of chaos when he's out in the snow where no one can see him. At times, he walks, and at times, he takes the chestnut, under the excuse that the gelding gets irritable without exercise. Perhaps because that fits with the ostlers' prior assessments, no one says anything. Or perhaps no one cares. So far as Alyiakal can tell, Rynst is the only other captain who walks in the snow, if not as frequently as Alyiakal, but none of the other officers mention it.

When oneday of the first eightday of Spring arrives, it snows, and the snow seems little different from what has fallen throughout Winter. Then, on fiveday, a wet snow begins to fall. By late afternoon the snow has turned into a cold rain that continues through the night. On sevenday the sun reappears for two whole days and the temperature hovers above freezing, after which comes another day of rain, warmer rain. Four days later, the ice on the Guar River begins to break up, and the water level begins to rise.

By the end of the second eightday of Spring, the river has swelled its banks and continues to rise. As a result, no maneuvers or exercises outside the walls are scheduled, given that parts of the main road and large sections of land bordering the river are either underwater or a muddy morass.

With the river flowing well over its normal volume, the port is effectively closed, and Alyiakal can see dealing with the Kyphrans will be impossible until at least mid-Spring, possibly later.

Except that the rains stop, and the clouds vanish. By the middle of the third eightday of Spring, the floodwaters of the river begin to subside. Spring flowers rise out of the mud, seemingly everywhere.

Late on eightday afternoon, the ranker aide to the duty squad leader walks into the officers' study and distributes letters to individual officers.

"What ship?" Alyiakal asks after being handed three letters, presumably two from Saelora and one from Hyrsaal, given the handwriting.

"The *Rylaan,* ser. She ported a little over a glass ago."

"Thank you." *That means we'll find out what plans the Majer-Commander has for us and the Kyphrans.*

Within moments, Rynst walks over to Alyiakal's desk. "By tomorrow, we might have some idea of what's going on with Kyphros."

"Or we might find out that the Duke of Kyphros has withdrawn his forces," replies Alyiakal.

"You don't really believe that, do you?"

"It's unlikely," agrees Alyiakal, "but sometimes the unlikely does happen."

"Usually only to our disadvantage," says Rynst cynically. He looks at the three letters Alyiakal holds. "Three letters. Now that's the good kind of unlikely."

Alyiakal grins, but doesn't ask if Rynst received any.

"I only got one," says Rynst, "but if I had to choose, it'd be this one."

"Good!"

After Rynst returns to his desk, Alyiakal opens the earliest posted of Saelora's letters, using his belt knife to avoid breaking Saelora's blue wax seal. He doesn't need to open Hyrsaal's letter immediately. The fact that there is a letter means something in itself. Saelora's first letter is dated fiveday of the sixth eightday of Winter, some two eightdays before the previous fireship ported, suggesting a delay somewhere. He uses his senses to study the seal, senses the chaos, then nods. He checks the seal on the second letter and finds the same chaos.

He begins to read.

Alyiakal—

　I keep telling you how much I enjoy your letters. I hope my repetition of that doesn't upset you, but it's true. I do wish they didn't take quite so long to get here from the time you wrote them, but it's not as though firewagons can get to Guarstyad . . .

Alyiakal smiles at her indirect acknowledgment that someone is reading their correspondence. The remainder of the first part of the letter is about her successes and setbacks as a Merchanter, the successes outnumbering the setbacks, while the last part has some more personal touches.

　. . . Karola had a daughter, and she has her mother's red hair. Faadyr is quite doting, but shows how he feels through his actions rather than his words, like someone else I know. People talk about actions speaking louder than words. No matter what they say, most people pay more attention to words. You speak well, and I love your written words, but what I love most are your actions . . .

Alyiakal smiles, turns to the second letter, and continues to read.

　The weather here is cool and damp. I imagine it is colder in Guarstyad, and snow is still everywhere. As you know, we seldom get snow here, and none fell this Winter at all . . .

　. . . I still can't help thinking about your encountering mountain musk oxen. Vassyl had heard of them, but never saw one. I sent a letter to Catriana, asking her if she'd ever seen any garments or blankets made from their wool. She wrote that she'd heard of it, but never saw anything made from the wool. Only the wealthiest women in Fyrad can afford them . . .

　Hyrsaal wrote me recently. Lhaarat is even colder than Guarstyad, but he still has to lead patrols because the mountain people continue to raid the Cyadoran hamlets in the Winter. Catriana worries about him all the time, as I worry about both of you . . .

　Vassyl had a flux a little more than an eightday ago. He was very ill, but

*he's better now. He's still weak, and I'm handling more of the work and trades
at the factorage. That's not a problem, because we really can't do much with
the distillery, except watch and turn the barrels, until the greenberries begin
to ripen in late Spring. The good thing is that, properly tended, they keep
fruiting until early fall . . .*

Alyiakal frowns. *Vassyl's still weak. That doesn't sound good.*

*. . . I have the feeling you're busier than you say, but you made it clear that
certain Mirror Lancer duties were best not mentioned in letters. Those duties
can be dangerous, I know. I want you to know that I do pray to the Rational
Stars for your safety and health. Those Stars may not answer or heed my
prayers, but that's the least I can do for all you have given me . . .*

All I've given you? *You were the one to reach out to me.*
He reads Hyrsaal's letter before he leaves the study, glad to know that Hyrsaal is well, if enduring a colder and drearier Winter than Alyiakal has experienced in Guarstyad. He stops at his room before going to the evening mess,
leaving the letters in his personal file.

All of the captains are early to the evening meal.

Not surprisingly, given the arrival of the Rylaan. But Alyiakal waits quietly to
hear what the subcommander has to say.

Once Laartol arrives, punctually, as usual, he stands at the head of the table
and offers a bemused smile before beginning to speak. "I've received a great
deal of information from the Majer-Commander. While I know you want to
know what's in store for us, it's going to take several glasses to go over it, if not
longer. I'd like to read and understand it thoroughly before saying anything.
So, while you may wish to speculate, there will be no discussion concerning the
information or its possible ramifications at dinner this evening." Then Laartol
seats himself.

"There must be a lot of information," offers Baentyl.

Kortyl tries not to frown and fails.

Alyiakal hopes he has succeeded at not wincing.

At Baentyl's words, Shenklyn replies, gently sardonic, "I believe that's exactly what the subcommander said."

Alyiakal and Rynst exchange glances, and Alyiakal smothers a smile.

LXXVI

Oneday morning, Alyiakal rises early and makes his way to the mess, then smiles when he sees Rynst and Kortyl already there, standing by the table.

"You think the subcommander is going to say anything of import at morning mess?" asks Alyiakal.

"Since some of the information he has to have received applies to every officer here," replies Rynst, "he might as well provide the overall background."

It also might assure that everyone hears the same information at the same time, without having to cram everyone into his study. Alyiakal just nods.

In moments, Fraadn, Craavyl, and Baentyl join them, followed by Overcaptain Shenklyn, who motions for the captains to seat themselves. They've barely seated themselves before the majer and the subcommander appear. While Jaavor seats himself, the subcommander remains standing.

"You all expect me to have information for you," begins Laartol. "The situation is largely unchanged from what it was last Autumn. The Kyphrans continue to maintain a garrison near, we think, the old road's end, and where they could mount an attack on Guarstyad through the east pass. The *Rylaan* put out shortly to patrol the coast off the natural harbor near a stone pier built to supply the Kyphrans. That harbor is a little less than twenty kays east of their fort. The *Rylaan* has orders to intercept any vessel attempting to offload there. She'll also be taking additional supplies and equipment that can be offloaded by boat when conditions allow. Once you have control of the port."

Alyiakal keeps his attention focused on the subcommander.

"Mirror Lancer headquarters has uncovered certain archival references to 'brief schism of southeastern dissidents' in the early period of the second Emperor of Light. Those scattered records of the first days of the Mirror Lancers suggest that the lands the Kyphran forces currently occupy were once considered part of Cyador. This area may harbor objects of interest, which would be best not left in their hands. It has been suggested that the Kyphrans might be rebuilding a former Cyadoran outpost. Should that prove to be the case, we may have to post a force there until Emperor Taezel and the Majer-Commander determine how to handle the matter. The initial objective is to foreclose any possibility of a Kyphran advance through the east pass. Once that is accomplished, the second objective is to take and occupy the Kyphran fort."

Laartol pauses and clears his throat. "While the Majer-Commander has ordered Guarstyad Post to move expeditiously, given the current conditions in the east pass, the earliest we can feasibly dispatch any companies will be at the end of this eightday. The first companies in will be First and Third. Other companies will follow, based on weather and conditions in the east pass. Various companies will escort supply wagons, since the high grasslands around the fort only offer forage for horses, little local game, and no communities from which to obtain supplies."

After a short pause, Laartol adds, "I will be briefing company officers individually on the specifics for their companies, and I will post a tentative schedule of each company's departure over the next few days. That is all for now." He seats himself at the head of the table and immediately lifts his mug and takes a small swallow of ale.

"Never heard of the southeastern dissidents," says Baentyl.

"I don't think anyone I know has," says the subcommander, surprisingly, since he seldom comments at the table. "It's clearly a part of Cyadoran history that the First didn't want known."

"Or those who came after them didn't," suggests Overcaptain Shenklyn.

"That's also possible," says Laartol amiably.

Alyiakal wonders when Sixth Company will be sent to Kyphros, and how his vision of using a chaos device fits in. Maybe his mind is just trying to make sense of what he's learned from the Great Forest, *if* the Forest is somehow involved.

But how could it be? It never grew here or in Kyphros.

LXXVII

Twoday of the fourth eightday of Spring, just past midmorning, finds Alyiakal sitting in Subcommander Laartol's study, with Majer Jaavor seated in a chair beside the desk and facing Alyiakal.

"Sixth Company's situation has not changed since you were all briefed," Laartol says evenly. "You'll still be leaving tomorrow morning. However, one aspect of the situation has changed. Earlier this morning, a naval cutter arrived with more information. The Duke of Kyphros is assembling a fleet at Ruzor. The Magi'i believe some of the ships hold a modest number of reinforcements for the Kyphran force. The *Rylaan* will leave this afternoon to patrol the coast off the small port established by the Kyphrans and to do what it can until another fireship can be recalled and dispatched."

"Modest reinforcements, ser?" asks Alyiakal as politely as he can.

"They'll need a small fleet against fireships, even to deliver a thousand troopers or so. A thousand or more Kyphrans aren't a match for you. They don't have firelances or discipline."

Alyiakal only nods and focuses his attention on the subcommander, whose order/chaos fields remain calm, suggesting that he is being direct, although Alyiakal cannot understand how he can be that matter-of-fact. While Majer Jaavor is also calm, Alyiakal senses a hint of annoyance, but there's no telling what might be the cause.

"In addition to your command of Sixth Company," continues the subcommander, "you will be responsible for the safe conduct of three supply wagons. As mentioned earlier, while there is adequate forage for your mounts, there is some question about adequate rations until you can take possession of the Kyphran fort. I must reiterate the need to acquire any objects of interest, which should not be left in the hands of other lands."

Thinking about his visions of a small cart with the power to carve solid rock, Alyiakal represses a shiver. "If such objects still exist, ser, I understand the concern."

"I'm sure we all can," says Laartol almost mildly, then adds, "You will carry a dispatch for Captain Fraadn conveying what I have told you, and two more companies will join the three of you over the next eightday or so. Exactly when depends on the weather."

"Yes, ser."

"That's all I have for you, Captain."

Alyiakal stands. "By your leave?"

Laartol nods. Jaavor's visage remains pleasantly impassive.

As Alyiakal turns and leaves the study, he wonders why he's been briefed with Jaavor present. *So that there's no question about emphasizing "objects of interest"? Has headquarters found something of more concern?*

Alyiakal makes his way from the headquarters back to find Torkaal, who is likely finishing up his gear inspection for all the rankers in Sixth Company.

Since Alyiakal can sense the senior squad leader is finishing as he reaches the barracks, he waits outside the main door. In less than half a quint, Torkaal appears.

"Ser? Something new?"

"Three supply wagons and some complications." Alyiakal explains most of what the subcommander has said.

"Sounds like we could be there all Summer. I have to say that I don't like the idea of a fleet bringing reinforcements."

"The subcommander was very matter-of-fact."

"Begging your pardon, ser, but he's not the one who'll be facing them."

"And we'll have to prove him right," replies Alyiakal. *Just to get through it all.*

"How do you think the Kyphrans even knew there was an old post there?" asks Torkaal after a moment.

"Scavengers, I'd guess, and word got back to the Duke. If there *was* an old post there, someone buried it. It's been less than a hundred years, and if they had just abandoned it, someone would have found it almost immediately."

"Maybe they did, and they stripped it," suggests Torkaal.

"Perhaps, but if that's what happened, someone had to find something else recently."

"Think we'll find out, ser?"

"We'll find out something. Whether we'll like it is another question."

"The subcommander's sending five companies. We won't like it."

Alyiakal chuckles sardonically. "You're probably right. I'll let you know if anything else changes, but I doubt it will. Not until we're in the mountains, anyway."

Torkaal shakes his head.

Alyiakal heads back toward the officers' study. He has no more than stepped into the chamber when Baentyl approaches.

"Is there something new about your heading out?"

"We're still leaving tomorrow morning," replies Alyiakal. "Nothing new, but we'll be escorting some supply wagons."

"Sounds like you'll be staying longer."

"That's for the subcommander and the Majer-Commander to decide," replies Alyiakal dryly, deciding not to point out that the subcommander mentioned the wagons an eightday earlier.

"Do you know what other companies might be going?"

"You know as much as I do."

"That's not much."

"Is it ever?" asks Alyiakal sardonically, turning and heading for his desk.

Once there, he takes out his letter to Saelora, quickly reading over the part he rewrote twice.

Sixth Company is going on maneuvers, and it's possible we may be posted
somewhere from which I won't be able to write. So, if you don't receive
anything, it's not that I've been thoughtless or inconsiderate. These unforeseen
events and postings are a necessary, but not always welcome, occurrence for
the family and, perhaps, those more than friends of Mirror Lancers. I'll write
when I have the opportunity and know you understand that you are always
in my thoughts.

He finishes, and immediately posts the letter, returning to the officers' study and settling at his desk. With his map spread out before him, he considers what he faces in the seasons ahead—possibly raids from grassland nomads, the likely need for attacks on Kyphran forces and positions, and the slight, but real, possibility that the Kyphrans have found some weaponry of the First that could be deadly. Not to mention supply problems and inadequate chaos charges in firelances.

How useful will his improving abilities with order and chaos really be? He can match a firelance in terms of a single blast, possibly even two or three, but a heavier use of chaos quickly exhausts him. At least he can target smaller short blasts more accurately without tiring so quickly and sense farther and even behind obstructions. His shields should be some help, but for sustained fighting, the firelance and his sabre are more reliable.

He can't help wondering what the Kyphrans may have found.

Or are they building up a force to try to take Guarstyad?

But they have to know about the road, and how could they not speculate about how and why it was built?

Alyiakal wants to shake his head. There's too much he doesn't know.

But for junior captains, isn't it always that way?

LXXVIII

By early midmorning of threeday of the fourth eightday of Spring, Alyiakal follows his scouts and leads Sixth Company eastward up the road to the east pass across the lower Westhorns. In addition to his own lancers, he carries the responsibility for three supply wagons and the lancer teamsters who drive them, one of which contains enough chaos-charged replacement firelances for three companies, firelances offloaded from the *Rylaan*. First and Third Companies left Guarstyad three days earlier, and Alyiakal suspects that Second and Fourth Companies will be the two companies scheduled to follow Sixth Company over the next eightday.

He calls for a brief stop at the watchtower marking the beginning of the steeper climb to the top of the pass. While the sky is a slightly hazy green-blue and the air is pleasantly cool, with only a hint of a breeze, Alyiakal has no doubts it will become colder and windier the farther they climb.

Torkaal reins up beside Alyiakal. "Those wagons will have trouble."

"Difficulties with wagons are always possible," replies Alyiakal dryly. *That might be why the majer decided to send them with the company commanded by the most junior officer. That way a more senior captain up for promotion won't be responsible if there's a problem. And if you handle it competently, then no one will even remark on the difficulties surmounted.*

That possibility is also why Alyiakal personally inspected each high-sided wagon, with sight and senses, before Sixth Company set out. He didn't discover any weaknesses or problems, but that only means that he likely won't have problems until the wagons struggle over the east pass. He also scanned the unused firelances, comparing the amount of chaos in several of them with the remaining chaos in his own firelance. He discovered that his firelance currently holds less, roughly one part in forty, than the unused firelances.

Alyiakal takes a swallow from one of the three water bottles he'd filled with ale before leaving the post. Once the ale runs out, he'll have to rely on order-dusted water.

After the brief respite, Alyiakal orders Sixth Company forward, past the log tower, riding gradually uphill and following the road northeast along a narrow stream on the right until the road starts to curve southeast above the streambed.

Over the next two glasses Sixth Company travels perhaps five or six kays before Alyiakal again calls a halt, partly because he worries that the horses pulling the wagons need a break.

By late afternoon, according to the maps and the one scout, who traveled the route before being transferred to Sixth Company, the company remains almost fifteen kays from the pass's summit. After climbing for another five kays, Alyiakal calls a halt for the night in a semi-sheltered area, which shows signs of having been used by others for the same purpose.

Fourday morning dawns cold and clear, and the wind blows hard enough to make it feel near freezing. By midday, the company—and the three wagons—finally reaches the summit of the pass, a depression with rocky slopes rising several hundred yards higher on each side.

While Alyiakal can see a vague greenness in the distance, that's to be expected. What does concern him is the steepness of the road winding down through more rocky slopes. He senses the order/chaos patterns of several mountain cats, not close enough for immediate concern, but one is trailing the company, and he turns to Torkaal.

"Send word to the rear guard to watch for mountain cats. If they see a straggler or someone lagging, they'll attack. The Winters are long up here, and any cats are going to be hungry." That's the best Alyiakal can do without revealing more than he can afford to have known.

"Yes, ser."

The descent into Kyphros, assuming the border runs along the highest ground between Kyphros and Cyador, stops after the company has traveled another three kays downhill, when a wagon wheel breaks. Replacing it takes almost a glass, and Alyiakal knows the remainder of the descent will be slower than the climb from his experience in the Grass Hills. He hadn't, however, fully realized how much slower it is turning out to be.

By the time Sixth Company stops for the night, Alyiakal fears it will take close to two more days before they reach the grasslands. On top of that, the map that Alyiakal holds indicates a side trail, south, toward the Kyphran encampment branching off somewhere in the lower hills before the pass road reaches the high grasslands that are at least as dry as the Grass Hills.

Alyiakal can certainly follow the tracks left by First and Third Companies, but he only hopes they know where they're going, because the rocky slopes below look the same from north to south.

When Alyiakal wakes on fiveday morning, the air feels slightly warmer. Even so, the descent continues to be slow, though there are no more incidents with the wagons, possibly because the teamsters have been more careful. Alyiakal is just grateful that the skies remain clear, given that rain would have made progress even more difficult. When the company and wagons stop for the night, Alyiakal suspects another half day before they reach the side trail heading south, to the coast and the Kyphran outpost.

Sixday morning is warmer, no doubt because Sixth Company is farther from the ice and snow still coating the tops of the nearby peaks. By midmorning, the company rides on a slightly wider track through grassy hills that bear scattered bushes, and far fewer rocks. As the company rides farther east and lower, Alyiakal can no longer see the grasslands except by riding up the hillsides, or the Western Ocean to the south, or any signs of roads or trails through the grasslands—which concerns him—even though there have certainly been no side roads or trails they could have taken.

Slightly after midday, the scouts report a trail ahead, splitting from the trail heading east, leading south. The southern trail shows heavy travel, unlike the trail heading due east. While the tracks heading east appear to have been made by Mirror Lancer mounts, they are not as recent.

Alyiakal turns to Torkaal. "I'd say the tracks heading east belong to First Company scouts. What do you think?"

"I don't see how it could be otherwise, ser."

At the point where the trails diverge, Alyiakal again climbs the nearest hill. While the right-hand trail continues south, he can see little more than hills and a bit of grassland. The trail to the east winds around another hill, but where it leads after that, Alyiakal can't see. He shakes his head and returns to the company, where Torkaal sends him a questioning look.

"Since almost all the tracks head south, and since we're supposed to be heading south," Alyiakal says dryly, "we'll take the south trail. It's likely to be the right one, and even if it's not we'll be headed in the right direction."

From what Alyiakal can tell, the trail runs southeast of the rugged rock spine that comprises the south end of the Westhorns and merges into the rocky point that juts into the Western Ocean.

Four glasses later, and more than ten kays farther south, the trail abruptly widens into nearly a road.

Alyiakal turns to Torkaal. "This must be the road that the Kyphrans were working on."

"Shame they didn't get farther," returns Torkaal sarcastically.

"We'll take what we can get."

Less than a quint later, Alyiakal sees one of the scouts riding back with another lancer who, as the two approach, he can tell is definitely not from Sixth Company.

Alyiakal calls a halt and waits as the two join him and Torkaal.

The Sixth Company scout says, "Laarmar here is with First Company."

"Captain Fraadn posted scouts yesterday and today to watch for you," says the older lancer. "He thought you might be here earlier."

"It took us a little longer," replies Alyiakal. "We've got three more supply wagons in the rear."

"Begging your pardon, ser, but that sounds like we'll be here awhile."

"I suspect that's likely. I also have a dispatch for Captain Fraadn from the subcommander." Alyiakal gestures toward the south. "How much farther?"

"Another five kays or so. Captain Fraadn has us set up a little northwest of the Kyphrans. They're holed up in a . . . well, you'd have to see."

While Alyiakal wonders what sort of structure the Kyphrans occupy, he'll find out soon enough without pressing. "Are you our guide?"

"Might be better that way. I'll send Darst ahead to let Captain Fraadn know you're coming."

A little over a glass later, in the deep shadow of twilight, Laarmar says, "Just ahead, past that heap of stones, you go right. We cleared the way, but it's a little rough. The Kyphran road goes straight to . . . their place. It's less than a kay away." He calls out, loudly, "Laarmar here! Sixth Company coming in."

Even before Alyiakal reaches the turnoff, he senses two lancers carrying firelances on a low rise to his left.

Once he's past the sentries, Alyiakal's eyes widen as he nears the Mirror Lancer encampment. Low hillocks, none more than a yard high, ring the east side, while on the west side he sees and senses a stone wall, fifteen yards long, that appears to be about four yards from the base of a sheer bluff. As he rides closer he observes that the top of the wall looks as though the stone had once been melted like candle wax. The northern end of the wall stretches over two yards high, while the southern end is little over a yard tall.

As though a giant focused chaos knife had sliced through the stone at an angle. Alyiakal can't help but remember his dream vision of the comparatively small chaos rock cutter. *But whatever did this was much more powerful.*

"Never seen anything like this," says Laarmar. "We cleaned out the loose rock and spread the tents across. Took some doing. Barely got it done when a bunch of Kyphrans tried to drive us out. We got behind the low walls and used firelances. They didn't like that."

"Did they attack again?" asks Alyiakal.

"No, ser. They've stayed in their fort."

So far.

Laarmar gestures. "Officers' spaces are at the far end, ser."

Even before Alyiakal has reined up, Fraadn strides toward him.

"We were getting worried."

"We brought three more supply wagons," says Alyiakal. "One of them is filled with spare firelances."

"They're welcome, but their inclusion has certain not-so-welcome implications," replies Fraadn sardonically.

"Where do you want the wagons? And where are we corralling or picketing the horses?"

"The wagons go straight ahead, the horses through a makeshift gate fifty yards back. There's a sort of short defile or canyon there."

"I've also got a dispatch for you," says Alyiakal, "and we need to talk."

"Take your gear up to the end there and leave it, along with your firelance. We can talk after you settle your mount."

In the end, it takes more than a quint before Alyiakal can sit on his bedroll in the "officers' spaces" chewing travel biscuits and taking small swallows of order-dusted water while Fraadn reads the orders from Subcommander Laartol by the light of a small travel lantern.

When Fraadn finishes, he looks to Alyiakal. "You suspected what was here from the moment you found the road, didn't you?"

"I thought it was likely. People don't usually build good roads to nowhere. Have you found the other end of the road?"

Rynst's eyes go from Alyiakal to Fraadn and back again, but he says nothing.

"The east end is inside the Kyphran fortification," says Fraadn. "The road continues about a hundred yards south of here, mostly covered in shallow dirt. It's blocked about a hundred yards west, like someone sheared off the stone on each side, dropped it into the road, and melted it into a mass five yards high. I climbed it yesterday. It looks to be clear past the blockage as far as I could see. I'd guess it's that way until it reaches the rockslide area above the inlet." Fraadn pauses. "Do you know what's in these orders?"

"Not precisely. I'd guess that we're supposed to flush out the Kyphrans, discover what they're guarding, and secure the cove below the cliffs so that the *Rylaan* can use its boats to offload various supplies."

"The Kyphrans have also built a solid stone pier in the inlet not quite twenty kays east of here," Fraadn points out. "And there's more."

"About the Duke's small fleet, you mean?"

"I can't say I like the idea of a fleet carrying reinforcements, especially since, according to the Magi'i, many of the troopers are equipped with polished metal shields."

The subcommander glossed over that "small" detail, not bothering to mention it to Alyiakal, or the fact that the Magi'i had discovered it. While Alyiakal hears that some Magi'i can use mirrors to see distant places and events, he hadn't ever known of that knowledge being used by Mirror Lancers. The Magi'i generally remain aloof from Mirror Lancer activities, except for fireships, firelances, firewagons, and restraining the Great Forest.

Another thought strikes him. "Because the pier at that inlet is solid stone, it would be close to impossible for the *Rylaan* or another fireship to burn it down. Did the subcommander say how many troopers the Duke plans to send?"

"A significant number, apparently, with enough ships that the *Rylaan* can't deal with all of them. No other fireship can get here in less than three eight-days. More problems with the Jeranyi and the Suthyans."

Alyiakal thinks even a single fireship could pick them off one at a time, but if the *Rylaan* moves to block the new pier, the Duke's ships, at least the smaller ones, could flank the fireship and use the cove below the fort. *Unless we post lancers there, and that leaves fewer to deal with the Kyphrans here.* "This looks messy." *And that's an understatement.*

"Especially if the Kyphrans find something in the building's ruins they can use as a weapon, or as a defense against firelances. The Magi'i *think* that's possible. At least, something's happening there with order and chaos."

The second mention of the Magi'i being involved concerns Alyiakal, because it suggests worry, and anything that worries the Magi'i suggests significant problems for the Mirror Lancers' force.

"Your scout mentioned one quick sally by the Kyphrans. Have they tried anything else?" asks Alyiakal.

"The scouts haven't seen anyone leaving their fortification. They might have missed an individual or two, but not any large number of troopers. That suggests they've got a spring somewhere in there. There's one up behind here."

Alyiakal nods. That might explain why the First—or the dissidents—located whatever they'd built where they did.

"Since we haven't surrounded them, and they're not leaving the fort, even though we likely outnumber them and have firelances, that suggests they've been ordered to stay put. They expect to be supported and relieved." Fraadn yawns. "Well, we can't do much tonight, and tomorrow will come early."

Alyiakal doesn't find those words reassuring in the slightest.

LXXIX

In the early-morning light of sevenday, Alyiakal steps out from under the canvas-roofed area set aside for officers and looks to the southeast. He looks more intently at the humps he thought were rocks and earth in small hillocks, and on closer inspection he sees that the rocks, earth, and intermittent scattered grasses cover the ruins of a building, or buildings, that had to have been flattened years before.

Almost a century ago.

Rynst joins Alyiakal, and comments, "It's not like this everywhere. There were a few buildings here, then the one bigger building where the Kyphrans are, and a few others around it, but they all got flattened somehow. Then it was buried, like in front of us, until the Kyphrans came and dug it out. There are heaps and heaps of sand and dirt east of the walls. They must have gathered all the unbroken stones to build the wall around whatever they're doing or digging out." Rynst gestures to the top of the short cliff above the improvised quarters. "You have a better view up there. It's a bitch of a climb. They walled an area less than a quarter the size of Guarstyad Post. Maybe smaller. Fraadn's guessing they've got three to five companies there."

"Then they outnumbered you. Why didn't they attack again?" asks Alyiakal.

"They weren't expecting us. They made one sally, but we hit them with firelances. They must have lost forty men before they even got close. Then they withdrew. Didn't take them long to get archers on the walls."

"That doesn't make sense," says Alyiakal. "Everyone in Candar knows Mirror Lancers carry firelances. Didn't the Kyphrans even carry polished metal shields?"

"Fraadn said as much. The only thing that makes sense is that they didn't expect us this early in the Spring. Didn't the dispatch from the subcommander say they were loading those ships with men who had those shields?"

"It still doesn't quite make sense." *Except it does . . . in a way.*

"What are you thinking?" asks Rynst.

"Because of the Westhorns, and the high grasslands here, we've never fought the Kyphrans. They're not on good terms with the Gallosians, either. Cyador hasn't had lancers in Guarstyad ever before. At least not that we know." *Or did know.* "Most likely they didn't see our scouts last Autumn. Those men and ships the Duke of Kyphros is gathering, they're likely being sent to invade Guarstyad, not to fight us. The armsmen here may not have even known who you were. At least, at first."

"That makes a kind of sense," interjects Fraadn as he nears the other two. "So what do you suggest?"

"I think many of those behind that wall might not even be armsmen," ventures Alyiakal. "It might be better if we were the ones behind the wall when the rest of the Kyphran forces arrive."

"We don't have the equipment to scale or break down those walls," says Fraadn. "Even if we did, we'd lose too many men."

We might not have to. Alyiakal then asks, "Would you mind if I took one of my squads and did a little scouting later this morning?"

"So long as it's only scouting," says Fraadn warily. "And you aren't going fifteen kays on a narrow trail."

"I just want to look at the Kyphran walls and gate."

"The gate looks like sturdy wood. Even if we used firelances to burn through it, we'd have to fight at close quarters, and we couldn't use firelances effectively."

"And we'd lose men we can't afford to lose," adds Alyiakal. "We all understand that. I've had to fight in a downpour before where we couldn't use firelances more than once or twice. I don't advise doing it if there's a choice."

"We're not likely to see many heavy rainstorms here, thankfully," says Rynst.

"Like you, I'm in no hurry to lose men," adds Alyiakal. "We have some time. It will take at least four days for the Duke's ships to reach that stone pier, and it's almost a two-day march from there. That doesn't count the time to offload and get organized." What Alyiakal doesn't mention is that a fleet could likely transport more than a "mere" thousand troopers.

After a quick breakfast of sorts—trail rations and order-dusted water—Alyiakal sees that his men are dealing with the mounts, then attends to the chestnut gelding, after which he finds Torkaal, then gives him a general briefing on the situation.

"Can't say any of that's news," says the senior squad leader.

"It's definitely not, but Captain Fraadn has agreed that I can take a squad on a short reconnaissance of the Kyphran fortifications. You're coming, but what about Maelt and second squad?" Alyiakal grins. "Third squad got the last real recon on patrol."

"That makes sense. Second squad's had the lightest load."

"If you'd tell Maelt."

"Yes, ser. Might take a bit longer to get the mounts ready."

"No dawdling, but they also don't need to hurry. It might take me a little more time to get my mount ready."

"That makes two of us, ser."

Almost three quints pass before second squad is mustered, mounted, and ready to ride. The picketing arrangements for the camp, in the small canyon to the north of the ruined buildings, aren't as organized as Alyiakal expected.

As he, Torkaal, and second squad follow two scouts along a dusty track in the direction of the dirt-covered road leading to the Kyphran position, Alyiakal says quietly, "After we get back, I'm going to talk to Captain Fraadn about reorganizing the picket lines so horses can be found, saddled, and mounted in less than a quint, if not sooner."

Torkaal only nods, but Alyiakal has already sensed the senior squad leader's feelings.

Even before the squad reaches the concealed part of the road, Alyiakal senses the residual chaos-locked order of the road's surface beneath the dirt. The road isn't blatantly obvious, but revealed by the lack of any low bushes and the gnarled, twisted evergreens common to the area.

Alyiakal turns in the saddle, looking to the west. Less than fifty yards back, he sees the clean-cut edges of the old stone road through the east side of the rocky point. As Fraadn has said, perhaps a hundred yards farther west, stone, appearing to have been melted off the rock on each side, partly fills the cut. That mass of rock stands four to five yards high, with the tallest point of the melted rock still a good five yards lower than the rock on each side.

Alyiakal turns back toward the Kyphran position and takes in the mottled stone wall toward which the road runs. As Rynst has said, once second squad is away from the building remnants being used by the Mirror Lancers, the ground on either side of the buried road doesn't seem to hold any other ruins, not that Alyiakal can see.

"How do Kyphran archers compare to barbarian archers?" asks Alyiakal as he continues to ride eastward.

"I don't know, ser. There weren't that many barbarian archers where I was posted."

"A good archer—not even a great one—can take down someone at two hundred yards. That's twice the effective range of a firelance." *Unless that firelance is in the hands of someone trained in magery.* Even if Alyiakal can use a firelance to match an archer, he'd still be an easy target for other archers. "I'm thinking about how close we can afford to get to those walls."

"They're likely not that good, ser, but there's no point in trying to find out," says Torkaal dryly.

Alyiakal barks a short laugh.

Out of caution, he orders second squad to a halt roughly three hundred yards from the wall. Only a handful of troopers man the wall, and none of them take out bows, let alone loose shafts, although he can see that all of them seem to be looking in his direction.

The wall, little more than two and a half yards high, is as effective as twice that height against Mirror Lancers without firecannon. Some of the blocks in the patchwork wall are time-aged and stained sunstone, while others appear to be sandstone and limestone. While a modest catapult could break through the wall, entering such a breach would cost men.

What surprises Alyiakal is the lack of a gate in the wall facing second squad. The unseen road runs to and possibly under the almost makeshift wall. *But then, they may not have even climbed over the mass of rock blocking the road. How could they not see that there had to be a road that had been blocked? Perfectly straight canyon walls or defiles don't occur in nature, not in the southern end of the Westhorns.*

Alyiakal extends his senses to see what he can discern while staying out of arrow range. He gains an immediate sense that the Kyphrans have built nothing inside the walls. A fence restricts their horses to the southeast corner, and the gate is in the middle of the east-facing wall, farthest from second squad.

What's missing are the order/chaos patterns he expects. *Where has everyone gone?* With as many horses as he senses, the Kyphrans have to be somewhere. *Underground chambers carved out of the rock by the "dissidents" of the First?*

That's the most likely answer, but without getting closer, Alyiakal can't tell, and logical as his conclusion may be, that doesn't mean it's accurate. *Yet, given the powers of the magus who forced the Great Forest into an agreement, any dissidents would have considered how to defend against those powers.*

"Ser?" asks Torkaal.

"Sorry. I'm just thinking. Some of this doesn't make sense. You and I and Captain Fraadn and Captain Rynst can see where the road goes, but the Kyphrans don't seem to have paid any attention at all to it."

"Maybe they thought it was a dead end, or that the First never finished building it. Maybe someone climbed over the blocked part and walked to where the rockslide is and figured there was no reason to unblock this end."

"They wouldn't have to cut away the block at this end. The walls are high enough above the cut that they could have built ramps on both sides. But you're right. There'd be no point in doing that unless you could find a way to bridge the gap where the rockslide was. Still . . ." Alyiakal shakes his head. "It took us four days to get here, and the way we took isn't usable for a third of the year, and it's anything but easy. I'd wager it only took two days when the road was open, maybe only a day and a half, or less, and it could be used anytime except during a storm. You could also carry more goods or supplies in fewer wagons."

"So why did someone destroy it?" asks Torkaal.

"Supposedly, some of the First didn't want to be part of Cyador, and they may have been the ones that built all this. If that's so, I can't see them destroying the road. I can see the Magi'i, or the Mirror Lancers, destroying it to make it harder, if not close to impossible, for the dissidents to get supplies from Guarstyad."

"But why didn't they take over Guarstyad?"

"Maybe they did, and that was the problem," says Alyiakal musingly. "Maybe they moved out of Cyador and discovered they needed those kinds of supplies." He makes a vague gesture eastward. "Did we see anything out there that would support anything but nomads?"

"From what we saw," says Torkaal carefully, "it doesn't seem likely."

"I don't *know*, but I'd also wager there aren't many other places where there's much water." Alyiakal shakes his head. "Figuring it out can wait. We need to circle around the walls and have a look at the other side."

"Yes, ser."

Keeping a good distance from the walls, Alyiakal leads second squad around the south side of the fortification, noting it is a good half kay from the cliff edge, which fits with what he'd been told about the inability of fireships to use firecannon against it. *Besides, there's little enough to burn.*

As he'd sensed, a timber gate sits in the east wall, and more than a few heaps of dirt on each side of the rough road stretching eastward, presumably to the limited port and pier. The north wall looks much the same as the other three. The sentries looking over the walls watch, but no archers appear.

As second squad rides back toward the Mirror Lancer camp, Torkaal says, "If their archers are any good at all, taking that fort could be a problem. There's no cover, and all those irregular hills make it hard to cover the distance to the wall at any speed."

"We'll have to find a way, or we'll be the ones withdrawing once the main Kyphran force arrives." Alyiakal offers a grim smile. "But then, that might be the best strategy. We could pick them off trooper by trooper on the east pass road."

"If the charges in the firelances last," replies Torkaal.

"Which they won't, especially if we have to use firelances a lot before then," Alyiakal admits.

Neither man says that much more on the return to the lancer encampment.

Fraadn appears before Alyiakal can lead the chestnut into the picketing area for the horses. "Did you discover anything useful?"

"There's something odd about that fort, but I need to get closer. I'm going to need to do a night recon to confirm."

Fraadn frowns.

"It's too quiet. You think that there are more than a hundred troopers there, but there wasn't a sound from the place."

"You think they withdrew most of the troopers and left a handful?"

"I don't know, but I'd like to find out."

"*If* you're careful."

"I'll be very careful." *And then some.* After a moment, Alyiakal says evenly, "I'm also a little worried about the horses. It took more than two quints for one squad to get mounted and ready to go."

Fraadn nods. "You shouldn't have any trouble tomorrow, or now. I took care of that."

"Thank you. I appreciate it."

As Alyiakal leads the chestnut gelding through the makeshift barrier of scrubby evergreen limbs, he keeps thinking about what he sensed—and what he failed to discern within the walls of the Kyphran outpost.

LXXX

While the white sun drops behind the near-impassable rocky heights immediately to the west of the Mirror Lancer encampment in late afternoon, true darkness doesn't descend on the area for another three glasses, and Alyiakal waits for another glass and then some before setting out on his "reconnaissance" with Vaekyn and two older rankers from third squad.

"We'll head south to the road cut's start and then ride toward the Kyphran wall," Alyiakal tells Vaekyn and the two rankers. "We'll stop two hundred yards from the wall. I'll leave you there and go on foot. You're to wait until I return."

"Ser?" questions the squad leader politely.

"I've cleared it with Captain Fraadn. You're here to make sure I've got a mount waiting in case I'm spotted and have to leave in a hurry. I need you to be as quiet as possible." Alyiakal smiles in the darkness and adds, "What I'm looking for is impossible to describe accurately. That's why I'm not sending anyone else."

"Yes, ser."

Though Vaekyn's tone is respectful, Alyiakal can still sense the squad leader's unease at the situation. He can also understand it, because he's never liked it when superiors ordered or said things he's questioned.

Except you know what you're doing. At that thought, Alyiakal stifles a smile, knowing that his superiors likely felt exactly the same way. "Let's see how it goes, Vaekyn."

"Yes, ser."

Alyiakal says only, "Forward."

The ride south to the buried road takes a bit longer in the darkness, as does the ride from there to where Alyiakal quietly says, "Halt."

He eases off the chestnut and hands the gelding's reins to Saavacol, the nearest ranker. "It might take me a glass, even a bit longer." Then he begins to walk down the unseen road. He waits until he is a good ten yards from the three lancers and the mounts before raising a concealment. Even then he senses surprise when he raises the concealment, almost certainly because his cream uniform just vanished.

Knowing there's no help for it, he shakes his head and continues to walk slowly and carefully toward the walls.

Nearing the western wall, Alyiakal concentrates on sensing the order/chaos patterns of the sentries behind the walls. Given what he'd seen during the day, he suspects the presence of a stone walkway behind the wall placed about two cubits lower than its top. It would offer archers some protection—if they duck— and no protection against firelances—provided that the lancers could get closer than a hundred yards without taking heavy casualties. *Which we can't afford.*

As Alyiakal thought likely, and why he walked toward the center of the wall, there is a sentry posted on each corner. Once he stands almost against the wall, he extends his senses. After several moments, he concentrates more intently.

It can't be, can it?

Except it is. The western half of the fort is a building, or what is left of one. The roof, or what might have been the roof, sits three cubits below the top of the wall. Most likely the wall stones have been placed against the remains of the building's west side. The buried part doesn't extend the full length of the wall, leaving a bit more than ten yards between the ends and the wall. From what Alyiakal senses, the building, or its ruins, extends only twenty yards east of the wall. He senses only approximately forty horses in the northeast corner of the fortification. What he can't sense is more than a handful of order/chaos patterns on the walls or elsewhere in the open area.

Should you try to find out more?

He decides to climb the wall. Even if he doesn't enter the makeshift fort, he might be able to discover more.

Slowly, he edges up the wall, not that it's difficult, as rough and uneven as the stones are, until he sits on the top of the wall. An errant thought occurs to him.

You've always found out things beyond walls.

Rather than dwell on that, he concentrates again, sensing more order/chaos patterns—scores of them, if barely discernible, beneath the stone surface some three cubits below him.

So what's left of the building is habitable enough to sleep in, and that's where they are.

Resisting the temptation to push his luck, he eases back down the wall and slowly walks back toward the waiting lancers. So far as he can hear or sense, his early-night visit has not been noticed by the Kyphrans.

When he nears the waiting lancers, he eases to the north so that he won't be where they're looking when he drops the concealment. As he eases closer, he listens to the murmurs.

". . . still can't see him . . ."

". . . disappeared like a big cat . . ."

". . . can't be a cat . . . horses like him . . ."

". . . something different about him . . . don't know . . ."

"There's something different about every officer posted here," declares Vaekyn quietly, but dryly. "They wouldn't be here otherwise."

Almost every officer. When Alyiakal is about three yards to the side of Saavacol, he releases the concealment and says in a low but firm voice, "I'm back."

Both rankers start slightly.

Alyiakal takes the chestnut's reins from Saavacol and mounts. "Keep quiet until we're well away. I'd rather that the Kyphrans didn't know we were close."

Once the four near the road cut and turn north, Vaekyn asks, "Did you find out what you needed to know, ser?"

"Their sentries aren't that alert, and they don't have many mounts. There are a few other things I need to talk over with Captain Fraadn before I say more. I appreciate your support and patience. Waiting in the darkness for your captain when you don't know where he is or what he might be doing can be nerve-racking."

After a moment, Vaekyn says, "Your mount didn't budge when you appeared."

"Why would he? I came back upwind of him, and he could smell me farther than we can see at night."

As with everything in poor light, once the four are back at the encampment, it takes Alyiakal longer than usual to deal with the chestnut, and he is just leaving the picketing area when Fraadn appears.

"What did you find out?"

"Why don't we go back to the officers' area," suggests Alyiakal.

Once there, in the dim light of the travel lantern, with both Fraadn and Rynst watching and listening, Alyiakal describes the layout of the Kyphran outpost, including the half-buried building and the likelihood that most of the Kyphrans slept there, the number of horses, and the ease of climbing the walls.

"Do I want to know how you found this out, Alyiakal?" asks Fraadn.

"I walked up to the walls in the dark, then climbed up the wall in a spot where I couldn't hear any of their sentries talking or making noise. From there I made what observations I could, and returned as quietly as possible."

"How come they couldn't spot you?"

"The walls are mostly sunstone. In the dark, there's very little difference between a cream uniform and a sunstone wall."

"I have the feeling no one else would stake his life on something like that."

"Well, the walls aren't that high, and it's almost impossible to hit someone with an arrow if they're directly under the wall, in the dark, and difficult to hit a running target under faint starlight. Not that either happened, you understand. Since there was no uproar, I'm fairly certain the Kyphrans don't even know I was there."

"On that, I think we can agree."

"From what I saw," Alyiakal goes on, "we could take the place in a night attack with minimal casualties. Get a handful of lancers over the walls and cover the entrances to the building with firelances . . ."

"That sounds possible," says Fraadn cautiously.

"One small problem, however," says Alyiakal. "If we're successful, we'll have almost as many captives as lancers. That's assuming that some of them haven't already left, but I'd think you'd have seen signs of that."

"You're assuming they'll surrender," Rynst says.

"One way or another, it's a problem." Fraadn turns to Alyiakal. "Now that you've posed the problem, do you have any other ideas?"

"How about letting them escape?"

"They don't exactly seem inclined to leave," Fraadn points out.

"We have a little time," replies Alyiakal.

"What exactly do you have in mind?" asks Fraadn.

Alyiakal explains.

LXXXI

Roughly a glass before dawn on eightday, as Alyiakal leads the chestnut out of the picketing area, Fraadn appears and looks at Alyiakal. "I don't know why I agreed to this."

"Because none of us have better ideas. Because doing nothing is likely worse, and because it won't hurt to try," replies Alyiakal.

"Unless you or some of your squad get killed by archers."

"I'm fairly sure they won't be able to react that quickly." *To begin with, but later?* Alyiakal will worry about crossing that bridge when the time comes.

"Let me know as soon as you come back—sooner if it appears they're going to mount and attack in retaliation."

"That might make it easier for us, wouldn't it?"

"Did you have that in mind?"

"You might recall I mentioned the possibility, but after the casualties they took the last time, I doubt they'll try again. That first attack was why I thought my plan might get them to withdraw. They have to know about the new pier, and that we can't afford to follow them that far."

"You're assuming they're logical. How logical are the barbarians?"

"Not very," admits Alyiakal, "but the Cerlynese and the Jeranyi are."

"Let's hope the Kyphrans are more like the Cerlynese."

Alyiakal just nods. He's seen and heard about the cold-blooded side of the Cerlynese. "We'll have to see."

Fraadn steps back, and, in less than a quint, Alyiakal and Torkaal finish mustering first squad, while Maelt and Vaekyn ready their squads to guard the encampment on the off chance that the Kyphrans attempt to attack in retaliation.

Alyiakal doubts the Kyphrans will be foolhardy enough to attempt a counterattack in the darkness before dawn, but he can't discount the possibility. It's highly improbable they can ready a large force quickly, and Alyiakal can send word if that appears likely.

Alyiakal and Torkaal take first squad south for their approach to the Kyphran fortification. Alyiakal leads, because sending scouts ahead increases the chances that the Kyphran sentries will discover the lancers before they're in position.

"Do you think this will work, ser?"

"If it doesn't, it will only cost us a few firelance charges."

"Do you think the sentries are archers?"

"I doubt it, but we'll find out. That's one reason why we're making the first attack before dawn."

In the darkness, Alyiakal sets a moderate pace, and when first squad reaches the buried road and turns toward the Kyphran fortification, he orders, "Silent riding."

Instead of halting when the squad reaches a point roughly two hundred yards from the walls, he gives a second order. "Ready firelances. Do not fire, except on command."

A hundred yards from the walls, Alyiakal slows the chestnut and searches for the sentries, using both sight and order/chaos senses. The one at the southwest corner gives the impression of dozing on his feet, while the sentry at the northwest corner looks in Alyiakal's direction. Alyiakal raises his firelance, aims it, and *wills* the short chaos bolt into the sentry.

The burst of white chaos jolts the southwest sentry alert, but before he can even call out anything, Alyiakal's second burst turns him into ashes.

"To the right. On me," Alyiakal orders quietly but firmly. He's gambling that the other two sentries, if they even saw the quick bursts of chaos and light, will be somewhat confused.

Alyiakal's senses tell him that the sentry on the southeast corner does not move, but the sentry on the northeast corner is moving, possibly looking from side to side. Alyiakal and the chestnut are standing almost opposite the middle of the south wall when the sentry on the northeast corner begins to yell. The sentry on the southeast corner straightens and turns, just in time to be hit by Alyiakal's third bolt.

Since Alyiakal cannot yet discern any movement in the ersatz courtyard inside the fortification, he orders, "Fast walk."

By the time the troopers stir and rush into the courtyard, Alyiakal is opposite the gate, with an even better shot at the remaining sentry, who hurries toward the gate. Alyiakal doesn't even have to use much of his personal order and chaos to guide and extend the chaos bolt to take out the last sentry. Then he angles his firelance up and fires a bolt, guiding it slightly so that it drops into a handful of Kyphran troopers heading for the horses.

Alyiakal, even without his order-augmented senses, can hear the yells and screams.

"To the rear, ride!" he orders, easing the chestnut around the squad and leading the way back to the buried road. Once the squad stops on the road, at the edge of archery range, he calls a halt.

"Now we'll see what they do," Alyiakal says to Torkaal.

"Do you think that last bolt of yours did any good?" asks Torkaal.

"It had to at least injure some troopers. There wouldn't have been screams otherwise."

From what he can sense, the only gate to the fortification remains closed, but he and first squad wait. Then he senses several men moving to replace the previous sentries. The replacements, unlike their predecessors, keep their heads low, quickly peering over the wall, then ducking. While Alyiakal might have been able to direct another chaos bolt, he decides against it.

When light spreads across the eastern horizon, Alyiakal orders first squad to return to the encampment, leaving two scouts to observe and report.

As he rides back, he wonders whether his plan will work, or whether it will be like dealing with the barbarians; a lot of deaths, where nothing really changes, except for the young captains and rankers who do the killing to keep the raiders from killing others.

Fraadn waits as the squad rejoins the other two guarding the eastern side of the encampment. "How did it go?"

"We took out all the sentries on the wall and dropped a chaos bolt into the courtyard. From the screams, there were casualties."

"You realize we're going to have to have a company ready all the time now."

"Yes, ser." *But you knew that.* "Since we're already here, we'll take the first duty. Our scouts are already in position."

"Carry on, Captain."

Alyiakal can sense that Fraadn's concerned, but his only reply is, "Yes, ser."

Once Fraadn leaves, Torkaal eases his mount closer to Alyiakal and says, "Ser, you could have done all that without the squad."

Alyiakal smiles sardonically. "Not if they'd sent a squad against me. And that *will* happen sooner or later. We just don't know when."

"Have you always been that good with a firelance?"

"No. I've gotten better with experience." Which is true, if not the kind of experience Torkaal will think.

"Is that why you came up with this plan?"

"I couldn't think of anything better that would work and keep our casualties to a minimum." *At least for now.* "Apparently, no one else could, either."

"What happens if they attack?"

"A lot of them will get slaughtered, and we'll lose a few men and a lot of chaos charges we can't afford to lose. That's why I hope this will persuade them to leave."

"Won't they run into the Kyphran reinforcements and come back with them?"

"That's very possible, and I don't have an answer for that, but I'd rather have us behind walls firing chaos bolts out than the other way around."

"When you put it that way, ser, it makes sense."

What makes more sense, Alyiakal feels, is to find out what is in the buried building and, if it isn't useful, to withdraw to the east pass. *But even that can't be held against a large enemy force without a constant supply of recharged firelances.*

Those considerations lead to even more disturbing thoughts.

LXXXII

Under the cloudless but hazy blue-green sky of Spring, the sun hasn't even reached midmorning when Saavacol comes hurrying back to the encampment. Alyiakal immediately calls out, "All squads! Stand by to mount!" Then he waits for the scout to reach him.

"Ser! The Kyphrans have formed up outside the gate to the fort."

"How many?"

"Most of them, I'd say. Looks like three foot companies and one mounted. Maybe a third of the foot are archers."

"Any wagons or are any of the horses carrying gear?"

"No, ser."

"Which way are they taking? The one on the north side of their outpost or the way we approached this morning and the other night?"

"On the north side, it looks like, ser."

"All squads mount!" Alyiakal turns to Torkaal. "Get them ready to move out." One way or another, Sixth Company will be riding somewhere. "I need to tell Captain Fraadn. I'll be right back."

"Yes, ser."

Alyiakal doesn't have far to go because Fraadn is already moving toward him.

"Four companies forming up," announces Alyiakal. "No packs or wagons. One mounted. One of archers. Two foot. They're positioned to take the road on the north side of their outpost."

"Congratulations," says Fraadn sardonically.

"You did say you didn't want to have to attack their fort, ser."

"The lesser of two evils is only the lesser of necessary evils," replies Fraadn. "It was a calculated risk. Not that we had or have many decent choices under our orders. With that many foot and archers, we're better off having most of the companies staying behind the walls and picking them off as they come."

Since Fraadn implies which company won't be behind the walls, Alyiakal asks, "What if Sixth Company moves out and then attacks their rear?"

"You'll be exposed to the archers."

"We can stay out of range until the right moment. Also, their mounted might decide to engage us."

"That's a good possibility. Do what you can, Captain."

In other words, try not to lose many men, but do as much damage as you can. "Yes, ser." Alyiakal turns and heads back to where a mounted ranker holds the reins to the chestnut gelding. He mounts immediately, then turns to Torkaal. "We're heading south. We need to flank them or get behind them."

"Best of a bad situation," replies the senior squad leader. "Personally, I'd rather be attacking than defending."

Right now, I'd rather not do either. But Alyiakal says only, "Company! Forward!" Then he eases the chestnut into a trot, heading south.

Sixth Company maintains the same pace and in half a quint nears the Kyphran outpost. Even before Sixth Company is within a fifth of a kay of the Kyphran fortification, Alyiakal senses manned walls, held by archers, and that the main gate is secured.

"To the left, on me!" Alyiakal concentrates on the archers on the west wall, but none of them nock shafts—not surprisingly, given that the company is outside the effective range of the best archers.

He turns his attention to the area north and east of the fort, but detects no Kyphrans there. Nor are there any on the section of the northern road close to the fort, but he can definitely sense horses and riders at the rear of the Kyphran force heading toward the Mirror Lancer encampment. He also doesn't sense order/chaos patterns flanking the northern road behind the Kyphrans.

You'll have to keep sensing behind you, just in case.

Sixth Company rides closer to the Kyphran rear guard, comprised entirely of mounted troopers. Although Alyiakal cannot discern their weapons, they don't carry lances or longbows, impossible to use on horseback. He also doubts that they are slingmen.

From what Alyiakal can tell, the Kyphrans have not sighted Sixth Company, although Sixth Company is less than three hundred yards behind them. *Are they trying to lure us closer?* He says quietly to Torkaal, "They should have noticed us. They've got something in mind, but they're far enough back from the main body that the archers there, even if they turned immediately, couldn't get many shafts back even to the rear guard."

"Then we should pretend we don't realize that they have something in mind," suggests the senior squad leader. "We should get as close as possible and then attack at a fast trot. We can spread from that. The ground on each side isn't that uneven. Not for the first five yards or so."

"Order first squad four abreast."

Torkaal turns and orders, "First squad! Four abreast! Lances ready!" He turns back to Alyiakal. "Looks like the Kyphrans are already four abreast."

"That's going to make it hard for them to turn and face us, if that's what they have in mind."

"They might turn and spread," Torkaal points out.

"Then we need to hit them before they do and be ready to spread as well, depending on their weapons." At that moment, Alyiakal senses chaos bolts ahead, and that means the Kyphran foot is attacking the Mirror Lancer encampment. "Sixth Company! Fast trot!"

In less than a twenty-count, Sixth Company has closed to less than two hundred yards, but by the time Alyiakal is within a hundred yards, the Kyphran rear guard begins to turn and spread, lifting shorter horn bows.

"Archers! Company spread!" snaps Alyiakal, immediately targeting one of the mounted archers, then a second, and a third, urging the chestnut forward and belatedly expanding his shields to protect his mount.

Almost instantly, Alyiakal feels the impact of shafts on his shields, but by drawing their fire, he hopes he spares some of his lancers. He can sense the company spreading, and the black mists of death across the ranks of the horse archers.

By the time he reaches the point of the rear guard's last position, the situation has deteriorated into man-to-man combat. Then, in a fraction of a quint, a scattered handful of the mounted archers have ridden northward, circling back to the Kyphran fort. Alyiakal judges that there might be a score of riderless mounts, although some might be chaos-burned and possibly fatally injured. "Sixth Company. Regroup! Ten abreast! Staggered formation! Forward!" orders Alyiakal.

While he knows there have to be wounded lancers, some possibly seriously, Sixth Company needs to strike the foot archers at the rear before they can react.

In a tenth of a quint, Alyiakal has Sixth Company moving toward the foot archers at the rear of the remaining Kyphran force, although some lancers lag because of the uneven ground on both sides farther away from the northern road.

From where he rides in the middle of the front line, Alyiakal concentrates on the foot archers, who are roughly a hundred and fifty yards from the low walls of the Mirror Lancer encampment and still loosing shafts toward the lancers behind the walls, providing cover to the regular foot charge.

"Lances ready!"

Alyiakal is little over a hundred yards from the rear of the archers when he sees several in the rear rank turn, nock shafts, and release them. He waits for a twenty-count, so that the first line is well within effective range of their fire-lances, before he commands, "Open fire!"

In moments, the Kyphran archers in the rear line flare into ashes, and before long, the company of foot archers has disintegrated into men fleeing northward, not that the short Spring grass will provide any real cover, but the grass is deep enough that it conceals rodent and snake dens that could cripple horses moving at any speed. At the moment, Alyiakal has far higher priorities—in particular, attacking the rear of the Kyphran foot from enough distance that Sixth Company can avoid inadvertent chaos bolts from the two companies behind the walls.

Alyiakal turns to Torkaal. "Have second squad spread on the right flank, and third squad on the left. Fast walk toward the foot. Short bursts."

Sixth Company closes on the Kyphran foot, its chaos bolts striking down those in the rear.

"Sixth Company!" bellows Alyiakal, sensing that he is approaching where chaos bolts from the Mirror Lancers to the west could possibly reach him and his lancers. "Halt! Stand fast! Targeted fire! Short bursts!"

Alyiakal aims as precisely as he can, keeping his chaos bursts almost momentary.

By now, the Kyphran foot are trapped, almost half felled by fire from east or west. A few run straight at the Sixth Company lancers, some with spears, others with blade and buckler. None of those Kyphrans survive. In less than a quint, the few remaining troopers of the Kyphran force caught between fire-lances on both sides flee northward, then to the east. The space between where Alyiakal halted Sixth Company and the Mirror Lancer encampment is littered with bodies and ashes.

As the number of Kyphrans dwindles, Alyiakal feels chaos impact on his shields, almost directly in front of him.

A distance-weakened chaos bolt? A second bolt flares against his shields as well, and he smiles wryly, glad that he has worked so hard on those shields, even if he hadn't expected their first trial would be by misdirected Mirror Lancer fire.

Then he senses that the entrenched Mirror Lancers have stopped firing, with less than a handful of Kyphrans in range, and he belatedly orders, "Sixth Company! Cease fire! Cease fire!"

"What about the survivors?" asks Torkaal.

"Take them prisoner for now and march them toward the encampment. We need to find out more about their force and the fortification. As you can, find out about our casualties, especially the wounded."

"Yes, ser."

As Torkaal moves away, Alyiakal does his best to scan the battle area and beyond, especially toward the Kyphran fortification, but he can see only scattered Kyphran troopers, little more than a score, if that, trying to circle back to their base.

Almost immediately, Torkaal returns. "Two deaths, three wounded, one pretty bad."

"Frig." Alyiakal wants to shake his head, but asks, "All from the archers, I take it?"

"Yes, ser. Could have been a lot worse."

Alyiakal understands that's as close to approval—or acceptance—as he'll get from Torkaal, or any senior squad leader. "Let me take a quick look at the most badly wounded man first, then the other two."

"Captain Fraadn might want you to report."

"There aren't any Kyphrans nearby, and men come before procedures, especially when we likely incurred most of the casualties."

"Yes, ser."

Alyiakal senses surprise, but not necessarily disapproval, as he turns south, following Torkaal perhaps fifty yards to where a lancer lies on the ground on his back, another lancer kneeling beside him.

"Graanish looks to be the worst hurt, ser. He took a shaft in the chest, and the horse archers got his mount. She went down, and he hit his head on something. He's breathing, but he's out."

Alyiakal dismounts and hands the chestnut's reins to the nearest mounted lancer, then studies Graanish. For all the gashes and blood, he doesn't sense more than faint redness in the skull, but the shaft in his chest, close to the right shoulder, is another matter. Blood isn't spurting, but there's more than Alyiakal would like to see. He senses that the arrowhead lies perilously close to the large vein returning to the heart.

Can you put a little shield there to protect it before you remove the shaft? Do you have any choice?

"Get me that satchel strapped behind my saddle," he orders.

Once he has the satchel open and laid out beside the unconscious trooper, Alyiakal inserts the shield, and using both his own strength and order, eases the shaft out, then dusts the area around where the arrowhead had penetrated with order before dressing the wound. He looks to Torkaal. "You can move him now. The gashes on his head aren't that deep, but he'll have to be carried flat."

"We'll manage that."

Then Alyiakal turns to the two other wounded troopers—shoulder wounds. In less than a quint he is back in the saddle riding across the battle area toward the Mirror Lancer encampment.

Fraadn stands waiting in front of a section of the wall that is shoulder-high. He looks up to Alyiakal and asks, "What were you doing out there after you finished wiping out the survivors?"

"Doing some quick treatment of wounds. I'll have to follow up with more later."

"You took time for that?"

"Why not? There are only a handful or two of the Kyphrans left, and we might need every lancer we have if this mess drags out. My lancers are escorting the survivors here so you can question them."

Fraadn opens his mouth, then pauses.

Alyiakal can sense the flash of anger and says, "When it doesn't threaten anyone else, healing can come first."

"What happened before you attacked the Kyphran rearguard archers?" asks Fraadn.

Alyiakal explains briefly about the horse archers.

"How many of them escaped?"

"Possibly a half score."

"How many did you lose?"

"Two dead. Three wounded. There's a chance the three will recover. Did you have any casualties?"

"Not that I'm aware of."

Alyiakal nods. "Good."

Fraadn looks levelly at Alyiakal.

Alyiakal looks back evenly, but says nothing.

After a long moment, Fraadn shakes his head. "The subcommander said that you were effective with minimal casualties for what you accomplished."

"They could have withdrawn or fled. We left them that option."

"We are on their territory," Fraadn points out.

"And we have orders," replies Alyiakal dryly.

"Sowshit situation. Could have been set up by the black angels." Fraadn pauses. "Maybe the black angels built the road and whatever's behind the wall the Kyphrans built."

"We'll find out by tomorrow," suggests Alyiakal.

"You think so?"

"They've suffered massive casualties despite outnumbering us. Now we outnumber them. In addition, by twoday or threeday we'll have two more companies here."

"They won't know that tomorrow, and they still have walls."

"We can repeat what we did this morning." *Was that just this morning?* Alyiakal then realizes that it's only slightly past noon. *You need to eat something. You're barely thinking.* "After my men turn over the captives, permission to return Sixth Company to quarters? Or what passes for quarters?"

"Permission granted, Captain." Fraadn turns and calls out, "Captain Rynst! Ready Third Company for immediate scout and picket duty!"

"Third Company, preparing for duty."

Alyiakal rides toward Torkaal, who leads first squad toward the encampment, with five Kyphrans walking in front of four lancers with firelances. The Kyphrans look fearful and slightly dazed.

As soon as Alyiakal is close enough to the senior squad leader, he says, "Captain Fraadn is waiting for the captives. Also, have third squad remain mounted on watch duty until Third Company finishes relieving us."

"Yes, ser."

Then Alyiakal turns the chestnut and takes over escorting the prisoners to Fraadn, wondering how long he and first squad will have to guard them.

He doesn't have to worry about that for long, because Fraadn has lancers from First Company waiting.

"You and your men can get some rest, Captain," says Fraadn.

"Thank you, ser," replies Alyiakal.

Over the next quint, Alyiakal takes the time to check on Graanish, who is stretched out in the makeshift quarters. He adds a touch of order to reduce the dull redness of the head injury and cleans up the gashes, adding more diffuse order strategically to the shoulder wound, then checks on the other two lancers.

Even so, it's more than a quint before Third Company is mustered and in position and Rynst rides up to Alyiakal.

"Heard you only lost two men and had three wounded. How are they doing?"

"Two look to be all right, but they won't be fighting any time soon. The third? I'm hopeful, but the next few days will tell."

"Fraadn said their horse archers tried to lure you in, but it didn't work."

"It worked. Torkaal suggested we play dumb and get as close as we could so that we only had to cover minimum distance for the firelances to be effective. The squad leaders spread when I gave the order so all the firelances were available. It worked fairly well."

"That's one way of putting it."

"How would you put it?" asks Alyiakal.

"Murderously efficient."

Alyiakal doesn't even have to use his senses to feel the disapproval. "I'd rather not fight at all. But if I have to fight, I don't like losing men, and I don't like having to fight the same enemy twice. We gave them two chances to leave. You repulsed them the first time. Sixth Company showed them early this morning they were vulnerable. How many chances do you give someone? Give them too many and you'll lose men you don't have to."

"You have a point," replies Rynst. "I don't like it, but it's valid. But . . . thinking like that can get you stuffed into poor posts, or continually sent out to kill barbarians."

"You may be right," agrees Alyiakal, "but I won't lose men to further personal ambition."

Rynst winces. "I'd keep that sentiment to yourself."

Alyiakal offers a ragged grin. "I shouldn't wax philosophical when I'm exhausted."

"Go get some rest," returns Rynst cheerfully. "I'm not about to say anything. You likely saved some of my men, maybe even me."

Alyiakal turns the chestnut and rides to the enclosed picketing area. As he dismounts and walks the chestnut to the raised temporary stone pool serving as a makeshift watering trough, he sees two lancers farther down the pool, one of whom looks at him and then quickly looks away. Intrigued, Alyiakal focuses his senses on what they're saying.

". . . swear I saw arrows bounce off that horse . . . and he talks to his mount . . . almost like he hears something in return . . ."

". . . if that's so, I'd talk to him, too."

". . . another thing . . . he never misses with the lance . . . even in the dark . . ."

"I'd be more worried if he missed. Don't worry about that sowshit. He got us where the Kyphran bastards got killed and we didn't."

"Except for Wullyn and Kaastryn. They were good men."

". . . most of us are still here . . . most of them aren't. That takes a good captain."

". . . still say there's something about him . . ."

"That's true of all the good young captains . . . wouldn't be here otherwise . . ."

Alyiakal has to agree with the last words of the older lancer before the two lead their mounts away from the watering area. He pats the chestnut on the shoulder. "You did well today." He wishes he had a carrot or even a pearapple to give to the gelding.

Once Alyiakal returns to the tent-covered area in the walled ruin that comprises officers' spaces, he eats some trail biscuits, washed down with order-dusted water, then lies down on his bedroll, which only softens the hard ground slightly. Even so, he falls asleep.

He wakes up to Rynst's voice.

"Are you going to sleep through what passes for dinner?"

Alyiakal bolts awake. "Is it that late?"

"A glass from real sunset, I'd guess."

"I take it nothing alarming has happened?"

"Not so far, anyway. We've been watching the Kyphran fort all afternoon. Another score of their troopers straggled back. From all he can hear, Fraadn thinks there's something going on behind the walls."

"Preparing for another attack? I'd be surprised. They might be withdrawing to that half port and pier they built."

"You think they'd leave the safety of the walls?"

"It's possible." Alyiakal isn't about to point out that he's already proved that hiding behind the walls isn't all that safe. *Not for the Kyphrans, and possibly not for us, either.* "We can't afford to follow them very far, and they have to know that. So, if they can slip away under the cover of darkness and get to that pier, they may think they have a better chance."

Rynst nods. "That makes sense, since they likely don't know about the fireship."

"Even if they did, the *Rylaan*'s not about to waste firecannon chaos flaming a few troopers on a pier when there's a small Kyphran fleet headed her way."

"So when will we see this Kyphran force, assuming that some of them get past the fireship?"

"It was likely six days ago when the subcommander got word about the Kyphran fleet. From what I know, it will take the Kyphran ships at least six days—and that's with favorable winds—to sail from Ruzor to that pier." Alyiakal shrugs. "But we don't know how long it took them to embark men and supplies or for that information to get to the subcommander."

"I'd guess we have a few days," adds Fraadn, as he joins them. "I've stationed some lookouts on the bluff south of us. They can't see to the pier, but they can watch the cove and see anyone trying to offload from a ship. Or if the *Rylaan* destroys anyone who tries. I don't see that happening. The trail up here from the cove ends half a kay east of the Kyphran fort. It's barely wide enough for a single horse. So, we might as well let anyone who lands there climb the trail and pick them off as they near the top. That tells me that the *Rylaan* will concentrate on the pier area."

"If some of the Kyphran ships have catapults," says Rynst, "they could engage the *Rylaan*. That might allow the others to offload at the pier."

Alyiakal nods. If it comes to that, the *Rylaan* will have to engage any ship that attacks, simply because the fireships are too valuable to take preventable damage. *The Duke of Kyphros has to know that.*

"The Kyphrans here don't know exactly when to expect reinforcements," says Alyiakal. "So whether they stay or withdraw won't tell us much."

"We'll have to watch the fort carefully and see," declares Fraadn.

Nothing happens over the next glass, while the three officers eat trail rations, and the slight headache that Alyiakal almost hadn't noticed vanishes. None of the three speculates on what the Kyphrans might do.

Fraadn assigns Third Company as the duty company for the night, with one squad at a time ready to ride at a moment's notice.

Alyiakal wonders if he'll be able to sleep, but has no difficulty.

Sometime later, Alyiakal wakes in the darkness to voices.

"Ser," says Rynst quietly to Fraadn, "the Kyphrans are pulling out. They're heading east, wagons and all, via the rough road they built. There are still fires and some smoke from the fort."

"They could have set fire to anything they didn't take. Or they might have left fires burning to give the impression that they've left troopers behind. Keep the duty squad ready—and let me know immediately if anything changes." After a pause, Fraadn adds, "We're not attacking in the dark in territory we don't know."

Rynst slips away in the darkness, and Alyiakal follows him with his senses, but he can't discern any order/chaos patterns east of the Mirror Lancer encampment or west of the Kyphran fort.

That should mean that they're really withdrawing.

Even so, for a time Alyiakal lies there, sensing as far as he can, before he finally drops into a restless sleep.

LXXXIII

Oneday morning, Alyiakal awakes before dawn, and immediately senses for order/chaos patterns outside the Mirror Lancer encampment. He finds none except for rodents, possibly a grass snake, and the scouts posted to observe the Kyphran fortification. He gets ready for the day quietly, including checking on Graanish and easing a little order into his wounds and seeing to the other two wounded lancers as well.

Fraadn and Rynst aren't far behind him, and none of the three says much as they eat hard oatcakes for breakfast. Alyiakal finishes first, then asks Fraadn, "Why don't I take a squad and investigate the Kyphran post? My men are the most rested."

"You're really interested in it, aren't you?"

"It's where the old road ends. I have to wonder what's there. There might be nothing left, but if there's nothing, why didn't the Kyphrans fortify this area instead?"

"You can also take over as duty company and relieve Third Company's sentries and scouts."

"Yes, ser."

Over two quints later, Alyiakal leads second squad along the northern approach to the Kyphran base. With the sun still low in the eastern sky, he uses senses as well as sight as they near the silent walls, but he discerns no signs of life. He keeps the squad well away from the walls until they're far enough east to see the gate, barely wide enough for a single wagon. The narrow gate is closed, as he suspected.

All that means is that there's no one on the walls or in the courtyard, and there aren't any horses, either.

"Real quiet, ser," says Maelt. "The gate's closed."

"If they've all left, they'd have closed it, if only to make us cautious and delay any possibility of going after them. We'll move closer, slowly."

When the squad is less than fifty yards from the gate, Alyiakal says, "Send two men to open the gate. There's no one in the courtyard. If there were, there'd be signs, and we'd hear horses."

Maelt looks at Alyiakal.

Alyiakal can sense the doubt, but simply says, "Do it, Squad Leader. Just tell them to be careful. The Kyphrans might have left some sort of trap, or maybe a concealed pit in front of or behind the gate."

As the two rankers ride forward, warily, Alyiakal concentrates on the gate, trying to discern anything out of place. If there is, he's fairly certain it's not something infused or moved by free order or chaos.

The two rankers stop short of the gate, clearly studying the ground, then slowly near the right side.

Then one calls out, "It's not even barred!"

The second adds, "There aren't any pits, either."

Still mounted, the two slowly open the gate, which scrapes across a sand-covered stone surface until it grinds to a halt, suggesting to Alyiakal that the Kyphrans had to lift the gate to open it wide. But then, even getting the timber for a gate would have been difficult.

Which suggests that there's something of interest in there.

"Do you see anyone in the courtyard?" calls Alyiakal.

"No, ser."

Alyiakal turns to Maelt. "We're going in. Detach two men as sentries to warn us if Kyphrans return." Not that Alyiakal expects such, but it is theoretically possible. "And have them keep an eye on where the trail up from the cove ends."

"Yes, ser."

Having positioned the sentries, Alyiakal leads the way, at a deliberate pace so he has time to sense for anything untoward or dangerous.

When he nears the gate, he sees where the ground ends and a smooth stone surface lies just under a thin layer of sand. Alyiakal senses the same stone under the entire courtyard ahead, except for the western half, where stand chest-high, roofless sunstone walls, the tops of which look smooth-melted.

Once inside the walls, Alyiakal glances around, still sensing no one but his own men and mounts. The dung heaped in the northeast corner confirms that section has held horses. His eyes go back to the smooth white walls, whose mortar lines are barely visible. "There was a taller building here, and some-one . . . or something removed its top. Let's see where the stairs to the lower levels are."

"Lower levels, ser?" asks Maelt.

"There's no sign that all those Kyphrans slept or ate or whatever up here in the courtyard. Or am I missing something?" He pauses, then adds, "Unless some slept in the roofless part of the building, but I never heard them when I scouted the walls."

Alyiakal rides to where the walls begin, reining up at an open space in the walls that might once have been an archway or entry. He dismounts and hands the chestnut's reins to the ranker riding behind him. He unstraps the travel lantern from behind the saddle.

"Kaarlyt, you're with me."

After the ranker joins him, Alyiakal walks through the entry and down what once had been the main corridor. He can't tell if a floor had covered the sunstone, and doubts it, before realizing, when the road to Guarstyad had been intact, obtaining woods and goods would have been much easier.

Alyiakal sees square shafts spaced at intervals and walks over to the nearest and peers down. While he can see only a few cubits, he senses that it goes down farther.

In the center of the building, truncated walls surround what used to be a courtyard below, where he sees a makeshift stove and oven of sorts. The center of the courtyard holds a fountain with a basin, from which water somehow drains. Some eight cubits down lie pieces of discarded, or broken, gear on the courtyard's stone floor. Off the main corridor Alyiakal finds not the staircase he suspected, but a long, gradual, and rather wide ramp.

Why a ramp? It takes up more space.

"Let me go first, ser," says Kaarlyt, "just in case."

Although Alyiakal cannot sense anyone beneath them, he steps back and lets the veteran lancer lead the way down the black stone ramp of the sunstone staircase. Following Kaarlyt, he discovers that the ramp is wide enough that his fingers barely touch the walls when he extends his arms. At the bottom is a hallway, too dark to see much, but clearly leading to the courtyard in the other direction. Alyiakal walks to the courtyard, where he finds that the floor of the upper level extends almost two yards from the courtyard walls.

The fountain has significant flow, and no chaos in the water he can sense. He also discovers that it's difficult to sense beyond those walls except through openings. That being the case, he lifts the travel lantern, and removes the striker from its slot. Although he holds the striker, he actually uses a bit of chaos to light the lantern. "We're going to take a quick look at the side chambers."

"Yes, ser."

Only the courtyard chambers on the lower level appear to have been used by the Kyphrans, possibly because of poor to nonexistent ventilation. Several rooms farther from the courtyard, along side halls, look like storage, judging from traces of spilled maize meal and flour. Broken stones and other rubble, in a chest-high pile, fill five of the chambers well back from the courtyard, while another holds discarded equipment, including two broken blades. One other chamber's use is also obvious, from the slight odor emanating from the stone seats. Beneath the open seats, several cubits down, Alyiakal hears running water, and he sees likely drain openings in the floor. *But to where?* The building sits several hundred yards from the cliffs.

From there Alyiakal heads back to the first dark hallway, but it seems to lead nowhere. One opening on the left, however, looks different from the other doorways on the right side of the corridor. As he gets closer he can see why: The doorway's edges are marked—not smooth like the others.

"The Kyphrans did this," says Alyiakal, holding the lantern close to the right edge of the opening, a space roughly as wide as the other existing doorways, "using picks or chisels, sometime recently." Enough of the wall has been removed, and the rubble removed, that he cannot tell if there had been a sealed doorway or the Kyphrans had just cut through the wall.

Holding the lantern high, he walks into the empty chamber.

"They took whatever was in here when they left," says Kaarlyt.

"I think they took it all earlier, as well as anything in the other chambers, most likely last Summer or early Harvest. That may be why they built the pier." Alyiakal steps out of the chamber and begins to examine the wall farther away from the building's center, since the chamber broken into by the Kyphrans is only halfway to the end of the corridor.

The wall section looks smooth, with no masonry joins. *As if the stone had been melted.* He can also sense that order reinforces the surface, but only slightly. *Why? Wouldn't the stone take any more? Or had the order been added quickly and much of it has dissipated over the years?*

Alyiakal moves to the end of the hallway, examining the wall using both sight and senses, and from what he can tell the unbroken sunstone wall is definitely a construction of the First or the Mirror Engineers. Alyiakal has doubts about the engineers' involvement.

He walks back to where he feels there should be a doorway but there isn't. He senses nothing beyond the wall's surface. Finally, he turns and heads back toward the base of the ramp, shaking his head.

"Ser?" asks Kaarlyt.

"Just thinking about what was in that concealed chamber." He shakes his head again. "We'll have to worry about that later. We need to report back to Captain Fraadn."

At the top of the ramp, Alyiakal takes a quick look at the ruined upper level above the dark hallway, but he can't discern another staircase or ramp anywhere. *That will have to wait.*

He returns to the rest of the squad and mounts. Little more than half a quint later, he reins up next to the officers' area and dismounts.

Fraadn is there almost as soon as Alyiakal's boots hit the ground. "They've really left, then?"

"They have, and inside those walls is a ruined building with an old flowing fountain and usable stone jakes."

Fraadn raises his eyebrows.

"You can see for yourself." Alyiakal provides Fraadn with a full description, including the wall the Kyphrans had broken through, and noting in passing that the gate won't stand up for long against any catapult, nor will the walls hold against any sustained assault.

"With what you've said, we may have to split our forces. We'll need to keep a duty company posted here, maybe two, once Second and Fourth Companies arrive. I don't like having all the mounts in that fort. They'll be far too cramped. We'll have to change that when the Kyphrans get close, but there's some forage in that small canyon, and easier access to the plains grass."

Alyiakal nods as Fraadn continues, but half his thoughts remain on the ruined building, as he wonders who built it and for what—and why it had been destroyed.

Except it wasn't thoroughly destroyed—just partly destroyed and rendered effectively isolated and impractical to keep using.

LXXXIV

The three Mirror Lancer companies spend much of oneday and twoday morning relocating some supplies and wagons to the fortification, as well as cleaning up the living and storage spaces, and disposing of all too many bodies by the only practical method—dropping them off the cliff into the waters below. Where possible, the fallen Kyphran mounts have been butchered and cooked, and some of the meat sun-dried.

The dull redness in Graanish's skull has almost vanished, and none of the three wounded lancers in Sixth Company show any signs of reddish-white chaos, but Alyiakal knows he'll have to keep close watch over the three for some time.

Early twoday morning Rynst and his second squad make the arduous trip down the trail to the cove, occasionally used by the Kyphrans, to determine its usefulness and assure that no Kyphrans lurk there. The green-blue sky remains cloudless, as it has since they arrived, but slightly hazy, and the night chill is gone within two glasses after sunrise. Alyiakal suspects the Summer will be brutal, and is not looking forward to it, since he has the feeling at least some of the Mirror Lancers will remain.

Just before noon Alyiakal and third squad ride out east along the rough road that the Kyphrans used to withdraw. As squad leader, Vaekyn rides beside Alyiakal, but neither speaks until the squad is well away from the makeshift fort.

"What do you think we'll find, ser?"

"Very little of use, either in terms of any Kyphran discards or anything in the way of information. Possibly a broken wagon wheel, or a cracked or broken bow. Anything much beyond that would surprise me." Alyiakal smiles wryly and adds, "I'd be happy to be proven wrong."

The road slowly angles toward the cliffs, then roughly parallels them, running over sandy ground south of the wiry plains grass, already knee-high in places. South of the road and extending to the cliffs' edge, some thirty yards or so, the sparse ground cover consists of low-growing plants resembling thin stringy vines, and occasional low evergreen bushes. Alyiakal wonders how they survive. He senses something in the grass ahead and to the north, probably a rodent or a coney. So far, he hasn't seen anything resembling the grass cats he observed at his posting in Pemedra, but that might be because they avoid people when the grass doesn't provide enough cover.

Scarcely two kays from the fort, on the north side of the road, Alyiakal sees a section of a leather strap, judging from its width, part of a harness. He suspects it got tossed into a wagon earlier and either fell out of the wagon or was discarded in the hurry to get away from the fort.

From Alyiakal's observations of the sandy road, the rear guard was small in numbers, given that hoofprints only occasionally mark the wheel traces.

Or does that reflect how few Kyphrans remained, or both?

Over the next ten kays the only other object third squad finds is a wooden bucket with a rope handle, worn through in the middle, that likely fell off a wagon in the darkness.

Alyiakal reins up in early midafternoon at a point where the ground begins a long, gradual slope to the Western Ocean, which he suspects continues to the Kyphran pier. He rides closer to the cliff edge and studies the ocean, but doesn't see the *Rylaan* or any other ships. He rejoins third squad.

Alyiakal can't see any sign of the Kyphrans, and sees no indications that any rider or wagon left the road that third squad has followed. There are also no signs of any hamlets or people anywhere. That scarcely surprises Alyiakal, since the grasslands look even less habitable than the Grass Hills of Pemedra.

"Do you see any signs of anything, Vaekyn?"

"No, ser. The Kyphrans must be more than five kays ahead of us, maybe farther."

"They're likely near or at their pier. We're not going to find anything more unless we go all the way to the pier, and that would take us farther than Captain Fraadn specified. It's time to head back."

"Yes, ser."

On the return ride, Alyiakal continues to scan the surrounding area, but the only order/chaos patterns, besides those of his men and their mounts, are those of small animals.

Once they near the gate to the stone fort, Alyiakal, dismissing Vaekyn and third squad to the picket area to care for their mounts, rides through the open gate and hitches the chestnut at a rail in the northeast corner of the courtyard. He walks to the ruined building, where Fraadn waits under an awning created by a tent stretched across a corner.

The senior captain raises his voice to Alyiakal, still several yards away. "What did you discover?"

"We traveled a bit over ten kays. The road's mostly level to that point. From there, especially to the southeast, there's a gradual slope. The Kyphrans stayed on the road, and the only thing discarded was a wooden bucket with a worn rope handle. The squad brought it back because they thought it might be useful for the pickets. From the tracks, I'd guess less than a company remains."

Fraadn nods. "Not surprising, after your accomplishments with Sixth Company."

"Have you heard anything about Second and Fourth Companies?"

"One of the First Company scouts rode back a while ago. They met up with Second and Fourth Companies, and the other scout is leading them back."

"Well," replies Alyiakal, "they'll be here before the Kyphran force arrives."

"Possibly quite a bit before the Kyphrans, if the *Rylaan* is effective."

"Do you think the *Rylaan* can stop them from landing troopers?"

Fraadn shrugs. "I don't know. I'm not counting on it. Especially if the Kyphrans are willing to lose a few ships. Now that Second and Fourth Companies are here, we might be able to do something about that."

"Send two companies to hold the pier?"

"That, or inflict as many casualties as possible while the Kyphrans are vulnerable. There's no point in letting them get established if we can stop them. We'll send out scouts tomorrow to look for signs of the Kyphran ships, and to see if they can find any streams or water sources. Then at the first indication of a Kyphran approach, we'll dispatch the companies. If there's any significant water, I'll send them sooner."

"In the meantime, what about billeting?"

"Right now, First Company and its mounts will be here. The other four will be where we're already set up."

Alyiakal nods. The fort really can't hold more than the horses of a single company, and separating lancers from their mounts makes no sense. "Is there anything else you need from Sixth Company?"

"For now, stick to the duty roster. That will change tomorrow, but I'll let you all know then."

"Yes, ser." Alyiakal turns and walks back to the chestnut.

In a bit more than a quint, he finishes settling the gelding, washes up at a makeshift water trough made from the diverted spring, and makes his way to the officers' tents.

Rynst immediately asks, "Did you find anything?"

"Only that the Kyphrans stayed on that road for the first ten kays and that not much lives around here in the Spring. What about you?"

"That trail down to the cove is brutal. They can't have gotten that much in the way of supplies. We saw bones below the trail. Horse bones. We didn't see signs of any ships."

"I only looked when we stopped, before we turned back, but I didn't see any, either."

"We'll be waiting, then," suggests Rynst.

"Two days, anyway."

Alyiakal sits on his bedroll, and leans back against the stone wall, his thoughts going back to his suspicion that there may be another hidden chamber in the ruined building. While each of the wagons carries a pick, getting through the wall with just a pick would be a chore.

Still . . .

He'll have to see how matters develop.

Second Company, of the remaining companies, is the first to arrive at the picketing area, followed shortly by Kortyl. He walks to where Alyiakal and Rynst wait under their makeshift awning.

"So these are the officers' tents."

"For now," replies Rynst.

"I have to say I'd rather be here than buried in that strange ruin."

"How was the ride from Guarstyad?" asks Alyiakal.

"Not too bad, except for the wagons."

"Did you bring any spare firelances?" asks Rynst.

"All that there were left, roughly fifty. I heard that you made hash out of the Kyphrans and took over this place." Kortyl glances around. "Not a bad location to fight off an attack."

"Alyiakal inflicted most of the casualties," says Rynst. "He got behind them, wiped out their rear guard and archers. After that, the foot were easy targets. The survivors moved out in the night."

"That so called fort won't stand up to much," observes Kortyl.

"Not without archers or an unlimited supply of firelances," says Alyiakal agreeably.

"Did you find out anything about who built the ruins?" asks Kortyl. "It looks like they used a massive firelance and melted the top off everything."

"It had to be the First or people with the same abilities," replies Alyiakal, "but so far we've found nothing other than the building, the road, and the mess left by the Kyphrans."

"What about the cove?" Kortyl asks Rynst. "Fraadn said you were down there. Could we get supplies there?"

Rynst laughs harshly. "You'd have to offload to a boat, row ashore, then pack them up a trail barely wide enough for a single horse at a time. It would take about as long as to use the Kyphran pier east of here and put the supplies on wagons."

"Which is likely why the Kyphrans built the pier where they did," adds Alyiakal.

Kortyl snorts. "Think I'd rather defend the east pass. Defending here, with no easy way to get supplies or to hunt, seems shortsighted."

"Except the Kyphrans broke into a concealed room and possibly removed something that the Mirror Engineers and the Magi'i would like to see," adds Rynst.

Clearly Fraadn or Rynst looked at that dark hallway and talked it over. "So they think there might be something else hidden somewhere?" asks Alyiakal.

"That's a guess on Fraadn's part," replies Rynst, "but why else would we be here? It'd be easier to protect the silver mine by holding the east pass."

"So we risk men because there *might* be something dating back to the First buried in these ruins?" asks Kortyl.

"Inside the fort, but yes," replies Rynst.

"If it's so frigging important," says Kortyl, "why did it take them a year to get us here?"

"Because there aren't enough Mirror Lancers to do everything that needs to be done," Alyiakal answers. "And because Guarstyad didn't have an existing post."

"*And* because the Magi'i didn't know about the road until Alyiakal found it," adds Rynst. "That probably made them reconsider their findings."

"So why haven't they sent a magus or two?" says Kortyl disgustedly.

"They won't risk a magus until the Kyphrans aren't a problem," suggests Alyiakal. "Then you'll have more Mirror Engineers and Magi'i here than you'd ever want to see."

"I just wish that the Majer-Commander didn't have to bow and scrape to the First Magus." Kortyl shakes his head. "We're always the ones paying for their high-sounding ideas."

"And sometimes for those of the Merchanters in Cyad," adds Alyiakal.

Kortyl snorts. "They all ought to spend a season with us."

"They should," agrees Rynst, "but they won't."

Certainly not any time soon.

All three officers turn at the sound of Fourth Company's approaching mounts.

". . . can't wait to see Craavyl's reaction . . ."

Alyiakal barely hears Kortyl's muttered words, but Rynst hears them as well. They exchange amused glances, but neither says more.

When Craavyl arrives, Kortyl goes out to meet him, and the two walk away, talking, and neither looks exactly happy.

After what passes for dinner, Fraadn gathers the captains together in the officers' area at the original encampment, explaining why only First Company will be quartered inside the fort. Then he continues, "None of our scouts and lookouts have seen any sign of the *Rylaan*. That suggests that the Kyphran fleet has either taken longer to gather and sail or that the fireship has successfully delayed or destroyed Kyphran ships. While there is the possibility that the *Rylaan* might have been damaged, if that has happened, we'd already be seeing Kyphran ships. We'll send scouts tomorrow to see if mounting an attack at the pier is feasible, while the Kyphrans are trying to land."

"You think they can get past the *Rylaan*," asks Craavyl.

"If they have enough ships and are willing to lose some," replies Fraadn. "The problem is that the *Rylaan* is only one ship. If we had two available . . ."

"Why don't we?" asks Kortyl.

"More problems with the Jeranyi and with the Duke of Lydiar restricting access to the Great North Bay. The emperor sent two fireships to Lydiar, and the only way to recall them is to send a courier, which takes time."

As Fraadn speaks, Alyiakal is again struck by how thin the Empire's forces are spread. *Is Cyador so impoverished that we cannot raise more Mirror Lancers?*

Alyiakal understands that the number of fireships is fixed, because their chaos/order power systems cannot be duplicated, but more firelances could be created. Then again, firelances need to have their chaos replenished, and that requires a chaos tower. *But does it? Could you replenish the chaos in your firelance, possibly bit by bit?*

He smiles wryly, thinking that even if that is possible, he cannot replenish the chaos of even a sizable fraction of the firelances of Sixth Company. *Still . . .*

"Because we have no idea where the Kyphran forces are or when they may arrive," Fraadn continues, "we'll see what the scouts report. If there's no water source, we'll have to send two companies at the first signs of a possible landing. If there is, we'll dispatch two companies earlier." When Fraadn finishes the briefing, he asks pleasantly, "Any questions or anything where you'd like more explanation?"

"How long do you think we'll be posted here?" asks Craavyl.

"As long as it takes to resolve the situation."

"Resolve?" presses Craavyl.

"Defeat, drive off, or destroy the Kyphran force, or learn that the *Rylaan* and any war sloops deployed have destroyed the Kyphran fleet. Even so, it's possible that a company will be posted here, on a rotating basis, a season at a time, for years to come."

"No one mentioned that," says Kortyl bluntly.

"No one mentioned it to me, either," replies Fraadn, "but I don't see how we can control access to Guarstyad without maintaining a presence here. That would require building a real post. Not based on the ruin, of course. That is, if it were up to any of us."

"I can agree to that," says Kortyl, almost in a growl, "but will they listen to us?"

"I wouldn't wager on it," declares Craavyl.

"Would any of us?" asks Alyiakal in a cheerfully cynical voice.

Rynst laughs heartily, and even Craavyl and Kortyl show traces of amused smiles as they shake their heads.

"I think we're agreed on that," says Fraadn. "Remember, this is just my opinion, and senior officers seldom listen to strategies offered by even the most senior captains." After a moment he adds, "That's all I have for now. The duty company tomorrow will be First Company, and the scouts will come from the duty company. On fourday, the duty company will be Second Company. After that, depending on what the scouts report, we'll see."

As Fraadn leaves, Alyiakal slips away and joins him.

"You have something in mind, Alyiakal?"

"With your permission, tomorrow I'd like to try something, since Sixth Company is not on the duty roster."

"Oh?"

"When I was investigating the lower levels of the building, I made rough measurements on the dark end of the corridor."

"You think there's another chamber?"

"It's possible. It would be good to find out before we have to deal with the Kyphrans, and since it will be at least a day, if not longer . . ."

"Go ahead. I'd thought about it. As a field healer, you're the closest we have to a magus."

"I'm just—"

Fraadn holds up a hand. "The subcommander told me about the survival rate of men you treated. That doesn't happen if you don't have both good training and at least a touch of ability with order. Let's leave it at that."

"Yes, ser. We will need to borrow two picks from the wagons."

"I'll have them waiting."

"Thank you, ser."

"Thank you. You're the best for that, especially if you find something. I'll see you in the morning."

"Yes, ser." Alyiakal can't help but wonder how much more Fraadn knows or suspects, but it's far better not to confirm or deny anything involving magery, especially given Alyiakal's suspicion. He watches as the senior captain unties his horse, mounts, and rides toward the fort, accompanied by two lancers.

Rynst joins Alyiakal. "Can I ask?"

"I asked for permission to investigate a part of the ruined building. He agreed, so long as it doesn't get in the way of duties."

"You think there's something there?"

"I don't know. Maybe, but I think it's a good idea to find out, one way or another, before the Kyphrans return. I think Fraadn feels the same way, but if it goes wrong, it's my head and not his."

Rynst grins. "Remind me never to roll bones with you."

Alyiakal declares seriously and sonorously, "Officers never roll bones." Then he grins back.

Rynst shakes his head.

Later, once it is full dark, Alyiakal returns to where he has laid out his gear and studies his firelance with his senses, observing how much chaos remains. From what he can discern, it now holds slightly less than half of the original amount of chaos. But was the original amount of chaos what the weapon's reservoir could hold? Or the amount it could *safely* hold, given the conditions under which the firelances are used?

He doesn't have an answer to those questions, but there is another he can see if he can answer. Slowly he begins to gather and coil free chaos within order. When he has enough for his purposes, he needs to figure out how to get it into the firelance reservoir. If he triggers the firelance, that will open the valve to release chaos—definitely *not* what he needs.

Could the order around the coiled chaos be formed into a funnel with a one-way flap from the side of the coiled chaos? Alyiakal smiles grimly, knowing that the coiled chaos *should* have enough power as it hits the flap to force its way into the reservoir. He also knows that "should" and "does" can be *very* different things.

As he forms and moves the order funnel into position, he hopes his speculations are correct, but the coiled chaos performs as he has theorized. Just to be safe, he stops funneling chaos into the firelance before it reaches what he remembers as the full level. He wants as much chaos as possible, and he knows there has to be some margin of safety. Otherwise, there would be casualties among the Mirror Engineers who routinely replenish the firelances.

Then he leaves the firelance with his gear and walks in the direction of the picketing area, gradually releasing the remaining chaos in a tiny stream, so diffuse there's no hint of a chaos bolt or flare.

When he finishes, he, strangely, has only a slight headache. Otherwise, he feels simultaneously stronger and more tired. He eases the headache by eating a few trail biscuits, softened with order-dusted water. He suspects that, before long, he will sleep soundly.

LXXXV

On threeday morning, Alyiakal checks on his wounded lancers and attends them first. He adds a slight amount of order again to reduce the small area of dull red chaos between Graanish's skull and brain, as well as treating the wound chaos of the other injured lancers under the guise of checking their dressings. Then he eats a breakfast of warm oat porridge prepared on a crude stone stove topped by an iron plate, after which he wraps a few fragments of charcoaled evergreen wood from the base of the makeshift stove in a rag to take with him.

After readying and saddling their horses, Alyiakal and three lancers from second squad ride toward the fort.

"We're going to do some digging," he says. "There's a place that should have a doorway and doesn't, and we're going to see if there's a hidden chamber in the lower level of the ruin. The Kyphrans already found one."

"Ser?" asks Fhaquar politely.

"Why Sixth Company? Because when I pointed out what the Kyphrans had done, Captain Fraadn agreed there might be another chamber and suggested that I should take charge of finding out." He smiles ironically. "Junior captains with ideas often are allowed to carry them out."

"That because you found the old road, ser?" asks Naalyn from where he rides behind Alyiakal and beside Escalyn.

"Maybe." Alyiakal laughs softly. "If anything goes wrong, or we've wasted time and effort, there's only one officer to blame."

When the four reach the fort, they ride through the narrow gate to the single hitching rail adjoining the new fence confining First Company's mounts. After dismounting and tying their horses, they walk across the courtyard toward the awning, but Alyiakal doesn't see Fraadn.

The senior captain's voice reaches him from the far side near two of the six wagons. "I'll be there in a moment."

Fraadn appears, carrying two pickaxes and something else. When he reaches the four, he hands the picks to Fhaquar and Naalyn. "There are the picks you asked for. I've also got a wagon lantern for you. It should provide better light." He extends the lantern to Alyiakal.

"Thank you." Alyiakal's response is heartfelt because the three lancers will need that additional light far more than he will, especially since they'll be the ones wielding the pickaxes. He hands the lantern to Escalyn. "We'll see if there's anything to find."

"If there's anything to find, you'll find it," replies Fraadn. "One way or another, we'll need to know."

Alyiakal leads the way to the ramp, struck again by its width, and says to Escalyn, "You might want to light the lantern now. The corridor is dark."

Once Escalyn has the lantern lit, Alyiakal heads down the ramp, followed by Escalyn. When they reach the bottom, he waits for the others, then says, "Toward the dark end. You can lead the way, Escalyn. Stop at the first opening on the left."

"Yes, ser."

As he follows the lancer, Alyiakal concentrates on the patterns of order and chaos in the wall, at least as well as he can, given the slight overlay of order he sensed previously. Abruptly, he realizes not only that the order was most likely placed there to make the wall more resistant to a breach, but that such order, especially after its immediate application, would have made sensing beyond the wall difficult, if not impossible.

But a strong magus, especially one centered in chaos, likely wouldn't have noticed that kind of concealment. Nor would a magus in a hurry.

When Escalyn stops, Alyiakal says, "Hold the lantern close to the edges of the opening. You can see the marks. None of the other doorways have marks."

"There aren't any doors, either, ser," says Naalyn.

"There's no wood left anywhere, not even the chambers where the Kyphrans put rubble and refuse. I'm guessing that over the first years after it was leveled, nomads removed all the wood. There aren't any sizable trees. Then the wind and weather covered most of the ruins until the Kyphrans came along. That's a guess, of course, but it fits." Alyiakal pauses. "Move the lantern along the wall slowly, so I can see if there are any signs of another hidden doorway."

That way, Alyiakal can also sense the wall's surface, and hopefully beyond, without drawing suspicion—*or more suspicion*—to himself. The first six or seven cubits reveal nothing, nor does he expect them to. Then he senses slightly more order beyond the wall, probably the wall between the empty chamber and whatever adjoins it. The next part of the wall feels like the one fronting the empty chamber, but after perhaps another five cubits, Alyiakal senses a difference, a minuscule increase of the underlying order. He still, however, cannot determine what lies beyond the wall.

"Stop," he says quietly to Escalyn. "Bring the lantern closer to the wall. Here." He points. While he can see no difference, he runs his fingertips up and down along what might be the edge of a sealed doorway. Taking out a piece of his makeshift charcoal, he traces along that line. "Now, move the lantern slowly away from that mark."

"Yes, ser."

As Alyiakal has suspected, there is another area where the underlying order feels different, and he marks that and steps back. The distance between the two marks is definitely wider than the other doorways, even wider than the opening created by the Kyphrans.

Alyiakal studies the wall all the way to the wall that abuts it at the end of the corridor. The only places where the order levels vary in the slightest are the places he has marked. He straightens up and takes a deep breath. "Now, we'll see if you can use the picks to remove some of that part of the wall—or doorway. It could be that there's nothing there, but we have to start somewhere." Alyiakal looks to Fhaquar, then Naalyn. "We'll start in between these two marks. Which of you wants to take the first try?"

Fhaquar grins sheepishly. "I'll try."

"Be careful," Alyiakal warns. "That stone is hard. Close to being as hard as iron, I'd guess. The pick might bounce back at you."

Fhaquar frowns, but swings the pick easily, if keeping control. The blunt point of the pick hits the wall and clearly sends a shiver through Fhaquar's arms.

"Whoa! You weren't jesting, ser." Fhaquar lowers the pick.

Alyiakal inspects the wall. The pick has chipped a fragment of stone perhaps the size of his thumbnail, but that allows him to sense that the ordered stone isn't that deep, perhaps only half a digit. *But getting through that half digit is going to be brutal.* He steps back from the wall and says, "Try to hit several blows as close as you can to the first."

"Yes, ser."

Alyiakal spreads a thin layer of chaos around the first point of impact, hoping that the pick will drive some of that chaos against and into the order.

Fhaquar's second blow is several digits from the first but within the circle of chaos. As Alyiakal has hoped, a larger sliver of stone flakes off, perhaps half thumb-sized, but not much thicker than a fingernail.

Less than half a quint later, Alyiakal motions for Fhaquar, sweating heavily, to step back, revealing an irregular oval not quite half a cubit across, with several barely visible nicks in the stone outside the area that Alyiakal has been covering with chaos. Alyiakal surreptitiously blots his own forehead.

Fhaquar looks at the tip of his pick. "Frig! That stone is hard. Part of the end here is gone."

Alyiakal manages not to shake his head. *You idiot! The chaos weakens the pick as well.*

"You can pound at it for a while," says Alyiakal, doing his best to bind order around the tip of Naalyn's pickax.

Naalyn's reaction to his first blow is similar to what Fhaquar's had been. "Stone's frigging hard. Can't believe it's like that."

"I'm fairly certain that a magus strengthened the stone," Alyiakal says.

"Now he tells us," murmurs Escalyn.

Alyiakal simply says, "I did say it might be as hard as iron."

After Naalyn delivers several blows, it's clear to Alyiakal that the order-tipping of the pickax helps—more and larger stone flakes fly off the wall.

After motioning for Naalyn to take a break, Alyiakal inspects the enlarged oval and nods. In a few places, he can sense stone that isn't order-infused. "You're getting closer to the stone that isn't strengthened."

"How can you tell, ser?" asks Fhaquar.

"In the parts of the wall where you've gone deeper, you're getting larger pieces of stone. Stone isn't like that naturally."

"Frigging right," mutters Escalyn.

Alyiakal steps back and motions for Naalyn to continue.

When it appears that Naalyn's efforts are waning, Alyiakal says, "Time for you to take a break, Naalyn. Escalyn, give the lantern to Fhaquar and take Naalyn's pickax."

"Yes, ser." Escalyn exhales with polite resignation.

By early midmorning, the three lancers, with Alyiakal's hidden assistance, create a patch roughly a yard wide, a cubit high, and a little over two digits deep, the bottom of which is all natural stone.

"Why don't you want us to go deeper, ser?" asks Fhaquar.

"Because we need to get rid of more of the strengthened stone. That will make the rest of it much, much easier."

Alyiakal also wants to control the access to whatever might be in the chamber.

By late midmorning, the three lancers have doubled the area of order-strengthened stone they've removed, and Alyiakal steps forward, examines the wall, and motions the three closer.

"You can see the mortar lines now. They must have chaos-melted stone over the entire wall."

"They can do that?" asks Naalyn.

"I don't know if the Magi'i or the Mirror Engineers can do that now," replies Alyiakal, "but that's what someone did here." *This had to have been done before the building was rendered unusable.* He turns to Fhaquar and says, "Now you can deepen the area you've marked out."

"How will we know if there's anything there?" asks Escalyn.

"You might break through this course of stone and run into dirt or rocks," replies Alyiakal. "I don't think that's likely, though, not after a magus went to all the trouble and effort to hide an entry and then seal it off."

"You think there's gold and jewels back there?" asks Escalyn.

"I doubt it. If there's anything here, it will be more valuable than that."

Alyiakal steps back and nods to Fhaquar. "We won't find out if we don't get through that stone."

"Yes, ser."

As Fhaquar chops away at the underlying stone with the order-tipped pickax, which Alyiakal has to replenish periodically, Alyiakal tries to infuse the underlying stone with chaos. That doesn't change the situation much, because the chaos stays on the surface of the unstrengthened stone, as it did with the order-reinforced stone.

Alyiakal wonders how the mages in the time of the First managed to get that additional order into the stone. *Maybe adding order when the stone was briefly molten?*

Still, by slightly after midday, after a break necessitated by the need to replenish the oil in the lantern, the point of Naalyn's pick goes through the stone, leaving a finger-sized hole.

"I'm through!"

"Keep working on widening the hole," orders Alyiakal. "We won't be able to see anything until it's wide enough to get the lantern through." Much as he knows he could likely sense what might be there with a smaller opening, there's no point in even trying, because others will have to see what's there. *Or what's not.*

More than three quints pass before Alyiakal says, "That looks large enough to get an idea of what's there. If you'd hand me the lantern, Escalyn."

"Yes, ser."

Alyiakal eases the lantern up to the hole, which is roughly a cubit on a side, then peers inside. He is stunned by what he sees and senses, but not surprised. Against the wall directly opposite him, there is a waist-high, oblong object with four wheels. A cupridium tube curves out of the device from its smooth cupridium top, and at the end of the tube a nozzle, similar to the one in his dreams, projects roughly half a cubit from the body of the device. He cannot sense or see a disk on or behind the tube. The entire device also seems larger than and slightly different from the one in his dream. *If it was a dream.* He shivers slightly, trying not to show it.

In a wooden rack against the left wall are what look like firelances, although they're shorter than those carried by Sixth Company. Another rack, against the right wall, stands mostly empty, but oval shields fill several spaces. Alyiakal would wager that the shields are mirror shields, designed to reflect and deflect chaos bolts.

"Fhaquar, you look first," says Alyiakal, stepping back, but holding the lantern so that it still shines into the chamber.

"Black frigging angels."

When Naalyn looks, he just whistles and shakes his head.

Escalyn snorts. "Old firelances, shields, and a thing that no one today knows about and can't use."

"Ser, what is that thing in the middle?" asks Fhaquar.

"I don't know," replies Alyiakal truthfully, because he doesn't *know*, only *suspects* what it may be. "It's most likely something the Magi'i and Mirror Engineers would like to get their hands on." He turns to Naalyn. "Go tell Captain Fraadn that I'd appreciate his presence down here. If he asks why, tell him that we have something he should see."

"Yes, ser." Naalyn immediately heads for the ramp.

Alyiakal hands the lantern to Fhaquar and lifts the fully intact pickax from the floor. "Now that you three have done all the hard work, I'll take a few swings." As he swings the pick into the stone on one side of the opening, he adds an order spike to the end of the pick.

The impact on the stone runs from the pickax up his arms almost like a burn. The small chunk of rock that drops might be twice as big as the largest ripped out by Fhaquar, but given the effort, both in sheer muscle and in focusing order, even if he helps with the pick, it's still going to be a slow process to gain access to the chamber.

"Pretty good there, Captain," says Fhaquar.

Before Fraadn appears, carrying another wagon lantern, Alyiakal widens the opening by a few digits, then hands the pick to Fhaquar.

Fraadn looks at the ragged opening in the wall. "A half day's work by three strong lancers?"

"And the captain," adds Fhaquar.

"The stones appear to have been strengthened by a mage," declares Alyiakal blandly, "possibly in a way similar to how the original road was cut. Why don't you take a look in the chamber?"

Fraadn takes his lantern and peers into the chamber for a time. Then he looks at Alyiakal. "How long before you can widen this enough to enter?"

Alyiakal understands that Fraadn isn't about to talk about what he's seen un til the two are alone. "I'd guess the rest of today and most of tomorrow. There's really only room for one lancer at a time and someone to hold the lantern."

"Couldn't someone else start somewhere else?"

"They wouldn't make much progress, ser. The entire wall appears to have been strengthened by a magus. It's a little softer where the entry was. Once we can get it wide enough for someone to squeeze in with a pick, that man can work on the softer stone from the inside, while someone else works on the outside."

"I can't believe . . ."

"Fhaquar, if you'd hand the captain your pick."

"Yes, ser." Fhaquar grins and extends the pickax.

Alyiakal turns to Fraadn. "Just try and scratch the stone away from the entry area."

Fraadn smiles. He doesn't take the pickax. "Let me know when we can get in. Keep up the good work." He pauses and adds, "Sixth Company is relieved of patrol duty. You're to post guards on this hallway until the contents can be safely removed."

"Yes, ser." Alyiakal can tell that Fraadn is amused, and not in the slightest angered, and that concerns him as much as if the senior captain had been angry. "Have we heard from the scouts yet? About the Kyphrans?"

"Not yet, and that likely means they haven't landed yet and aren't in sight of the pier."

"That would be helpful."

"Whether it is remains to be seen." Fraadn offers an enigmatic smile before turning and heading toward the ramp.

"Guards, ser?" asks Escalyn once Fraadn is well away. "For stuff like that?"

"It might turn out to be totally useless," says Alyiakal dryly, "but, if you were Captain Fraadn, and engineering devices from the time of the First went missing or were damaged, would you want to answer to the Majer-Commander or the First Magus?"

"Ah . . . no, ser."

"The next officer they'd be after would be me," adds Alyiakal. "So, we'll post guards. Escalyn, since I need to stay, ride back to the encampment and tell Senior Squad Leader Torkaal that I need him here."

"Yes, ser."

After Escalyn hurries off, Alyiakal takes the pickax from Fhaquar.

"Ser?"

"I don't want it said that the captain only stood and watched." Alyiakal grins and adds, "Even if I don't take as many swings as you do." Besides, his using a pickax will reduce the time it takes, and he wants a good look at a device that is far too similar to what he dreamed for his own comfort.

LXXXVI

Even with Alyiakal's surreptitious use of order and chaos, it is well after sunset on fourday evening before he and Sixth Company hack a narrow entry to the chamber, wide enough and flat enough at the base for lancers to remove the strange device. The firelances either lacked any chaos when stored or have long since lost any chaos they might have had. Alyiakal has noticed that the chaos reservoirs seem larger than those in the current firelances. In addition to Alyiakal's initial assessment, the front left corner holds a small but sturdy four-wheeled cart of cupridium, apparently powered by an order/chaos mechanism and designed to carry something, while the front right corner holds a case containing small firelances designed to be held one-handed. These also have no chaos in their small reservoirs.

Once Fraadn inspects everything in the chamber, and makes certain every officer has been in the once-concealed chamber and seen the contents, he and Alyiakal stand alone. Fraadn turns to the junior captain. "What do you think of the device with the tube?"

"All the workings appear to be cupridium, suggesting it dealt with chaos. If I had to guess, I'd say it's what they used to cut the road out of the cliffs. What do you think?"

"I have to agree. Do you think there was another one in the other chamber?"

"That or something similar," says Alyiakal. "Again, I'm guessing."

"Then, if it's in working condition . . ."

"If the Kyphrans can find a mage who can fill it with chaos, it could be used as a weapon."

"If they have a mage, why use the device at all?"

"Because even a modestly strong mage—one we could destroy with a firelance—could add chaos to the reservoir over time, storing a huge amount. That's *if* he knew, or could discover, how. Stored chaos powers firelances, except I imagine it only takes moments to replenish a firelance from a chaos tower."

"But if they used it like a giant knife—the way these buildings were destroyed."

"I suppose that's possible. I just don't know how they might do it."

Fraadn nods. "That bears some thought on how we should deal with the Kyphrans."

"Have you heard more from the scouts? Besides the existence of a small brook?"

"They've sighted sails to the southeast, and Second and Third Companies left about a glass ago."

"Surprise attacks from spread formations and then a quick withdrawal?"

"Only if they're forced to withdraw. Then we'll have to see." Fraadn clears his throat and adds, "For now Sixth Company's duties are to guard and keep these devices secure."

"Yes, ser." Alyiakal suspects that Fraadn assigned the security to Sixth Company not only because of Alyiakal's background, but also because Sixth Company has had the most open combat and suffered the only losses.

When Alyiakal returns to the officers' tents under the bluff late on fourday, Craavyl is waiting to talk to him.

"How did you know where the entry would be?" asks Craavyl.

"I didn't. I looked for slight imperfections in the melted stone about where I thought a door should be—if there was a doorway—and we started chipping away at the middle."

"You actually used a pick?"

"To give them a break. We're expected to use firelances, I figured it didn't hurt to show I could wield a pickax." Alyiakal manages a momentary grin. "I also thought it would keep them from thinking I didn't understand how hard it was."

"I heard that sometimes the pick wouldn't scratch the wall," offers Craavyl, not quite questioningly.

"Usually it would scratch the stone," replies Alyiakal, "but we never got more than tiny flakes of stone at first. You can see the pile of chips."

"What do you think that thing is?"

"The tube has a nozzle at the end," replies Alyiakal. "My guess is that once charged with chaos, it could cut stone. The nozzle has a slit. That would narrow the chaos, possibly into an edge like a knife." He shrugs. "That's just a guess."

"Are there any Magi'i in your family?" asks Craavyl. "You seem to know a lot about this."

Alyiakal shakes his head. "Not that I know. Just Mirror Lancer officers. I did hear a bit about magery from a Magi'i healer when I trained in healing at Syadtar. She seemed to know a lot."

"You ever meet up with any important Magi'i?" presses Craavyl.

"Once." Alyiakal laughs and tells an edited version of his encounter with the Third Magus, ending with, "After that, I have no interest in meeting with any high Magi'i."

Craavyl smiles faintly, then asks, "You ever find out why?"

"To my knowledge, none of the post officers or those in transit were ever told why he wanted to meet every officer."

"He had to be looking for someone, or something. I wouldn't want to be that officer."

"We might see him or another high magus," says Alyiakal. "After we deal with the Kyphrans, that is. They're going to want to see and take control of what's in that chamber. And if the Kyphrans get their hands on it, none of us will ever make overcaptain." *Most likely because they'd have to kill all of us to get it.* "Why else do you think Fraadn insists on additional lancers guarding it?"

"Why didn't the Kyphrans try to break down the wall the way you did?" asks Craavyl.

"Maybe they only finished breaking into the other chamber a little while ago. Maybe they had orders to wait. Maybe they have a mage that they're sending with the force they're assembling. Maybe they thought there was only one sealed chamber. The marks around the chamber they broke into look like it already had an entry."

Craavyl fingers his chin. "That would make sense. Leave an obviously sealed door and hide the possibility of a second chamber."

Alyiakal nods. That has not occurred to him, but it makes a certain kind of sense, particularly if the original builders thought they might have a chance to return. "I wonder who they were and whether the First attacked them or whether someone else did."

"It had to be the First," declares Craavyl. "If anyone else had that kind of power, we'd know about it."

"The old records did mention," says Alyiakal, "dissidents in the southeast, and that was obviously kept quiet. But you're right. If there happened to be a third group with that kind of power, there wouldn't likely have been any way to keep that secret."

"That still doesn't explain why the First kept it quiet," says Craavyl.

"They didn't want any sign of successful rebels," replies Alyiakal. "The First wanted to create a unified Cyador. If these dissidents—and maybe a few others—vanish before they can use their power against Cyad, then it keeps people from getting ideas."

Alyiakal knows he's missing something important, something flitting around the back of his mind, but he's just too tired to recall what that might be. Two days of quietly and continually using order has taken a toll. "We may never know. Or maybe if the Magi'i send a magus, he can tell us."

Craavyl laughs. "Good fortune with that. You think that the Magi'i, or even the Mirror Engineers, will share anything like that with mere lancer officers?"

"You have a point," says Alyiakal.

Later, as Alyiakal lies on his bedroll, wondering why he can't fall asleep if he's so tired, he almost bolts upright as he realizes what had eluded him earlier.

The number of chaos towers is fixed. There's no way to create more, and any prolonged struggle would have made it harder for the First to forge a united Cyador.

He can't help shivering as he considers what sort of man—or emperor—it took to destroy the dissidents and remove all traces of them. *At least, for almost a century.*

LXXXVII

Alyiakal sleeps soundly enough that he wakes slightly stiff on fiveday morning, most likely because he didn't move all night. He can sense farther, or at least he thinks so, but it's hard to tell. There's nothing distinctive except lancers and their mounts, either close to him or in the Kyphran-built fort.

He's still pondering that when Fraadn arrives to meet with him and Craavyl immediately after they finish breakfast. Fraadn announces, "I haven't heard anything from Kortyl yet, but I wouldn't expect to until later this morning."

"Won't be any fighting today," says Craavyl. "Kyphrans might not even be able to land."

"If there were mirror shields in that other chamber, and they have them," Alyiakal points out, "they might be able to hold off Second and Third Companies."

"I'd be surprised if the Kyphrans attempt to land their forces, outriders, or scouts before late tomorrow, even if they're offshore of the pier now," Fraadn says. "Dark, low clouds are massing in the southwest, and the wind has shifted as well."

"Just our luck," observes Craavyl. "It almost never rains here, but it'll rain on us."

"The fog will be heavier at sea," says Fraadn. "That will make a landing harder."

"If you're wrong, and it really rains," says Craavyl, "firelances won't be worth sowshit. That ruin could flood, too."

"That's unlikely," says Alyiakal. "The lower level has drains, and the fountain basin has emptied into them all along with no backup."

Fraadn looks quizzically at Alyiakal but doesn't say anything.

"Does anyone know how the Kyphrans found out about this place?" asks Craavyl. "There were ruins. Nothing else. No one living here."

"Most likely the fountain," replies Alyiakal. "Water probably pooled in the ruins of the courtyard. Any nomads grazing their flocks here would know that, and maybe they investigated, or mentioned the ruins and the water. If the Duke of Kyphros was already thinking about invading Guarstyad for the silver mine and the harbor, he'd want to know about the routes to the east pass and any water. It could be that in trying to find more, or better, water, some officer or squad leader looked farther. That's just a guess."

"It's as good as any," says Fraadn. "How they found out doesn't much matter now."

What matters now is how we deal with the Kyphrans. Alyiakal sees no point in saying so because they all know that.

After Fraadn returns to the fort, Alyiakal and Craavyl muster their companies and deal with the necessities and routine.

That afternoon, the clouds move in over the area, but with almost no rain, only a foggy mist obscuring everything without dampening the ground.

Craavyl and Alyiakal sit under the tent awning over the officers' area speculating on the Kyphran force and what tactics might be appropriate against such a force when Craavyl says, seemingly from nowhere, "Where'd you come up with the drains? No one thinks about drains."

"I don't know," admits Alyiakal, "except I like to see how things fit together, or why they don't."

"You really think the Duke of Kyphros only wants a silver mine?"

"I think it started that way. When his forces discovered what was hidden here, he got the idea that he could take and hold Guarstyad as well, which would give him another good harbor."

"How could he hold it?"

"That device with the nozzle probably projects chaos in a thin line. If . . . *if* that's what his people found, and if they've figured out how to use it, it's effectively a mobile firecannon. The fact he's assembled a fleet suggests that he believes that he can prevail against Cyador, especially if we aren't expecting it."

"You think he's figured out how to use it?"

"It's easy enough to see how it should work," says Alyiakal. "Making it work is another matter."

"But why else would he attack here or in Guarstyad?"

Alyiakal shakes his head. "Right now, we don't know." *And finding out is going to cost lives, on both sides.*

They look up at Fraadn riding through the mist toward them. After the senior captain dismounts and hands the reins to a ranker, he joins Craavyl and Alyiakal. "I just got a message from Kortyl. This morning, before the fog moved in, their scouts reported seeing flashes of light on the oceans near the horizon. There weren't any clouds to the east. That means that the *Rylaan* engaged the Kyphran fleet. When the fog closed in, the flashes stopped. One way or another, that's going to slow the Kyphrans."

"How long?" asks Craavyl.

"Ask the fog," replies Fraadn.

Craavyl snorts.

"I'll let you know when things change. If anything comes up, you know where to find me."

"Thank you," replies Alyiakal, while Craavyl merely nods.

Craavyl and Alyiakal watch as Fraadn departs.

Craavyl grunts slightly as he stands. "Need to let the squad leaders know." He turns and leaves.

After a moment, Alyiakal heads into the mist to find Torkaal, who is talking with Maelt and Vaekyn.

"Ser?" asks the senior squad leader.

"The fireship engaged the Kyphran ships before the fog moved in." Alyiakal then relays the rest of Fraadn's update.

"So all we can do is wait for the fog to lift and find out what happened?" asks Torkaal.

"For the moment," replies Alyiakal. "Unless anyone comes up with a better idea to present to Captain Fraadn."

"Not right now, ser," replies Torkaal.

"I'll let you know when I know more."

"Yes, ser."

Alyiakal turns and walks back through the thin, impalpable fog to his own tent, such as it is. Then he glances at his firelance, thinking. The smaller and older firelances in the hidden chamber have larger reservoirs. *Was the change to smaller reservoirs because more chaos put too much strain on the cupridium in the firelances? Or so that not as much chaos would be required at a time?*

Another question nags at him. If the buildings near the encampment had been built by dissidents from the First, how had they powered the devices and the firelances in the hidden room?

If there had been a chaos tower in the building or nearby, there should have been some sign or record of it. And why would there have been one so far from Fyrad, Cyad, or the Great Forest?

The only thing Alyiakal can conclude is that some of the dissidents had been Magi'i, and that they had to have laboriously gathered chaos to power the devices.

You were exhausted from half charging a single firelance, and there had to be at least ten times that amount, if not more, in the device that cut the road into the cliffs— and in whatever device destroyed the buildings. There couldn't have been a chaos tower here, not without some evidence or record. So how did they gather all that chaos? And, if the Kyphrans have such a device, how can they fill it with chaos? By exhausting what mages they have for eightday after eightday?

As with some of the other questions facing him, he has no answer, and he has the feeling he'll still be trying to make sense of it all, even after whatever occurs with the Kyphrans is long finished.

Unless matters go badly.

LXXXVIII

When Alyiakal wakes on sixday morning, he recalls something he thought was a dream, but wasn't, not exactly. Rather it was among the images conveyed by the Great Forest—the image of chaos flowing in ordered streams from the sun and building around the shimmering figure of the great First magus.

Could it be possible? Or was that just the way the Great Forest interpreted events? Still, when he stands in the sun, at least not in Winter, he feels the warmth, and since order doesn't generate heat, except when it's used to concentrate chaos, there must be some tiny bit of chaos coming from the sun.

Alyiakal looks around, smiling ruefully. Of course, the foggy mist still hangs over the Mirror Lancer encampment, and trying to determine any relationship between chaos and the sun will have to wait. He stretches, stands up, and gets ready to face the day ahead.

He and Craavyl finish eating, mustering their respective companies, and dealing with other duties and necessities by the time Fraadn arrives.

"What have you heard?" asks Craavyl as soon as Fraadn is within speaking distance.

The senior captain replies, "Let me get close enough so I don't have to shout, Craavyl. With this fog, we don't exactly need to hurry. It's not going anywhere quickly, it appears."

"That could change in a glass," counters Craavyl.

"Right now, according to Kortyl's latest report," declares Fraadn, "the fog is heavier at sea. The lookouts can't even tell whether the *Rylaan* is continuing to engage the Kyphran ships."

"What about troopers landing?" presses Craavyl.

"As of first light this morning, the fog remains heavy near the pier, and there have been no Kyphran ships in sight, and no sounds of approaching vessels. That's hardly surprising. No ship captain is about to approach a largely unknown harbor through a heavy fog. Both companies are at the pier, ready to repulse any attempted landing should the fog lift or disperse quickly."

"Good." Craavyl nods.

"Then what?" asks Fraadn. "What happens when the Kyphrans do attempt a landing?"

"Kortyl and Rynst turn them into ashes."

"What if they empty their firelances before the Kyphrans run out of troopers? Or if it rains or archers prevent the lancers from holding the pier? Or some other defense? What then?" Fraadn turns and asks, "What do you think, Alyiakal?"

"There are two possibilities. The first is that, between the *Rylaan* and Second and Third Companies, the Kyphrans cannot make a successful landing right now. Keeping them from trying again might require posting a company to hold the pier, rotating the company every few days, until it's clear that the Kyphrans have abandoned the idea of attacking. That only works as long as we have chaos in our firelances.

"The second possibility is that they succeed in getting a substantial force ashore. That requires a significant number of archers, possibly mages, and conceivably a device such as the one we discovered. Any form of standard attack against such a force will involve ruinous casualties for us. The best tactics I can see are fast attacks by small numbers of lancers, spread far enough apart that the Kyphran archers would have to waste shafts for an occasional hit. We could pick off their troopers before they can react, and then withdraw momentarily. The more troopers we wound or kill before they reach the fort, the better our chances for defeating them and forcing them back."

"Neither of those suggestions would find favor with Mirror Lancer headquarters, I fear," replies Fraadn.

"We're on Kyphran land," replies Alyiakal. "Our position here is indefensible over time without more lancers and more supplies. Cyador can't presently provide either, without problems on other borders. We don't live in a perfect world with continual replacements and timely resupply."

"Then, in a perfect world," says Fraadn, with heavy sarcasm, "how would you handle the matter?"

"Use the Mirror Engineers to rebuild the original road and make the east pass more impassable. Then put a real fort and gate on Guarstyad's side of the cliffs, before the section of destroyed road. A squad with firelances could hold that position indefinitely. Traders would favor it because it offers another way to trade, and the Imperial tariff enumerators could collect tariffs due. Kyphros might even build a small trading hamlet or post at the stone pier for times when the seas are too rough to enter the Guarstyad harbor." Alyiakal grins. "You did say 'in a perfect world.'"

"You'll never see anything that perfect." Fraadn shakes his head, then adds, "I'll let you know when things change."

When Fraadn is mounted and almost out of sight, Craavyl turns to Alyiakal. "You're right. They'll keep fighting until we leave their land."

"Unless we build a post here and reclaim a small bit of land that would be ruinous for Kyphros to fight over, or fight a war and successfully take over Kyphros." *Which will take more Mirror Lancers than we could ever raise.*

"Who in his right mind would want the place?"

"The Prefect of Gallos apparently does," says Alyiakal.

"That says he's not in his right mind."

"I think it's more that the Prefect wants access to another port, and he's willing to pay a high price."

"Ruzor's not that great a port," Craavyl points out.

"It's better than no port at all."

"Not much. From what I know, Guarstyad has a better harbor."

Alyiakal laughs softly. "You have a point there." Then he frowns. "Two actually. I hadn't thought of it that way. About the dissidents, I mean. If the First had left them alone, they would have taken over Guarstyad. Then they could have expanded east, at least as far as the stone pier, and they would have had two harbors and enough chaos power to become independent of Cyador. At least, they would have had enough to make it very costly for Cyador to conquer them. I'd wager that the First acted before that could happen."

Craavyl shakes his head. "I won't take that wager. From what's in that one storeroom, it looks like they had already built an armory. Do you think they sealed off those chambers thinking they could lay low, then come back later and try again?"

"That might have been their thinking. They obviously didn't understand how brutally efficient the First could be." *Especially the magus who faced the Great Forest.*

"Why show mercy if that allows someone to strike back later?" asks Craavyl. "Something to think about. We can talk more later. You reminded me. I need to check on how much chaos most of the company firelances have."

Alyiakal has already checked the Sixth Company firelances. Most are less than half full; another thing to worry over, especially if dealing with the Kyphrans turns into a drawn-out series of skirmishes or battles. He can't help wondering if lasting times of peace follow brutal conquests because few are left to object, and those who are are fear another wave of efficient brutality.

But what's the alternative?

LXXXIX

Immediately after dawn on sevenday morning, the foggy mist begins to dissipate, and after little more than a glass, it's obvious to Alyiakal the day will be sunny and bright, with some lingering haze in the late morning. Once he's dealt with the chestnut gelding and the other necessities, such as checking on his three improving wounded, and the morning muster of Sixth Company, he walks away from the officers' tents and finds a niche in the rocky slope between the ruins and the blocked road, a niche where he cannot be observed.

Closing his eyes, he concentrates his senses on the white sun, incredibly distant, and unreachable.

But something flows from it, something akin to chaos, or we would not feel warmth.

At first, he senses nothing. Then, after a short time, he feels the tiniest impacts, almost like a chaos mist, on his outer shield, impacts so small he cannot discern them, and barely feels them.

How can you gather them, let alone funnel them into a firelance or the device in the sealed chamber?

He smiles at the thought and begins to create a large but thin funnel of order that ends in a pinhole, with a flap similar to the one he used to replenish his firelance, beyond which is a container of order. In moments, increments of chaos begin to form in the funnel, presumably from tiny chaos bits too small for him to sense joining together, and then to flow down to the flap. In half a quint, he has enough chaos to fill a quarter of a firelance reservoir. But what he finds most interesting is that holding the order funnel takes almost no effort, unlike gathering free chaos.

That could be very, very useful.

He expands the order funnel and immediately senses an increase in the discernible chaos. Then he nods and collapses the funnel. While he can easily hold the chaos he has gathered, holding more would be difficult and possibly painful.

If you funnel the chaos into something else, like the device you found, and if . . .

Alyiakal shakes his head, knowing that's likely a series of improbable "if"s. Then he walks back to the officers' spaces, gathers his gear, and makes his way to the picketing area, where he readies the chestnut.

Less than a quint later, Alyiakal rides to the fort with the third squad rankers who will take over the duty guarding the items in the chamber. After he tethers his horse inside the fort and unstraps his travel lantern, he and the four rankers walk toward the ruined building.

Fraadn meets Alyiakal before he reaches the ramp.

"Has something happened?" asks Alyiakal, gesturing for the rankers to head down the ramp and relieve the lancers guarding the chamber.

"Not yet. Kortyl sent a ranker to let me know that, after dawn, a number of ships gathered offshore, several with catapults, and attempted to engage the *Rylaan*. A glass ago, our lookouts on the rise above the pier reported chaos flashes."

"Then the Kyphrans have already begun to attack."

"That's my feeling." Fraadn pauses, then asks, "Why are you here?"

What the senior captain is really asking, Alyiakal knows, is what Alyiakal has in mind, since there's no need for him to accompany a change in guards. "Craavyl and I were talking last night, and he asked some questions that got me thinking. I wanted to take a look at that device again."

"What sort of questions?"

"Since there's no sign the dissidents had a chaos tower, how did they power that device? Nothing except something like chaos could have cut through the rock and melted the rock."

Fraadn laughs harshly. "I don't think studying the device will tell you much, but it can't hurt for you to try."

"It's a sowshit-poor wager," agrees Alyiakal, "but why not at least look? We have the time now."

"Not for much longer, but go ahead and look."

"I'll let you know if I discover anything." Then Alyiakal turns and waits until the four rankers who have been relieved come up the ramp.

"Ser," says Saavacol, as does Puall.

"Head back and get some sleep," replies Alyiakal. "You'll regret it later if you don't get some rest."

"Yes, ser."

Alyiakal heads down the ramp, worrying about Fraadn's grudging approval. He hopes he'll be able to find a way to make the device work and worries about what to do if he does.

Nearing the chamber, he lights the travel lantern. "I need to inspect the device in the middle."

"What is it?" asks Vuurnyn, one of the junior rankers.

"We don't know, except it used chaos, since the entire device seems to be cupridium." Alyiakal steps into the dry confines of the chamber, and stops short of the device, studying it. He begins with the tube leading to the nozzle, where he finds a cupridium lever where the tube emerges, not a circular disk.

To control the chaos flow?

Then he discovers a small circular opening at the rear of the device. While he cannot see, he can sense that the base of the opening has a cupridium flap of sorts, below which is a cupridium cylinder that has to be the chaos reservoir. The cupridium on one side of the opening is faintly rough. He brings the lantern closer and smiles. Etched into the metal, by chaos, is a circle, with short lines radiating from it. The symbol might be what the First or the dissidents used to represent chaos.

Or it might represent the sun. Either way, that makes matters more interesting—if you can figure out how to get chaos into the device.

He walks to the rack of older firelances, studying the one at the top. It has a replenishment port similar to the one in his own firelance, but there is no symbol beneath the port. He returns to the device, and takes a slow, deep breath before attempting to funnel some of the chaos he has gathered through the flap into the chaos reservoir. The flap doesn't move.

You need more force. But isn't chaos chaos?

He smiles crookedly and begins to coil and compress the chaos.

The second attempt works, at least so far as his ability to store chaos in the reservoir of the device. When he completes the transfer of chaos, he places an order block in the circular depression leading to the flap and steps back, reinforcing his shields.

Nothing happens. Then he removes the order block, but the chaos remains in the reservoir. To his senses, the amount of chaos in the reservoir is only a fraction of what the reservoir can hold, and likely of what it needs to operate.

He attempts to push the device. It moves slightly, and the wheels creak.

In for a copper, in for a gold.

Alyiakal clears his throat, then says, "We're going to wheel this up the ramp into the sun."

"Ser?" asks Yurval, the senior ranker.

"We need to get it up into the sunlight."

The wheels move and the creaking dies away as Vuurnyn and Chaavar push it down the hallway and up the ramp. While Alyiakal sees a set of brackets on the rear, suggesting the device was to be pulled or towed backward, presumably in order not to damage the protruding tube and nozzle, he cannot find any sign of whatever connected to the brackets, and he has no rope handy.

The four rankers, Alyiakal, and the device have barely emerged into the morning sunlight when Fraadn appears.

"What are you doing with that up here?" demands the senior captain.

"Seeing if there's a chance to get it to work," replies Alyiakal.

"And how are you going to manage that?"

"At the moment, I don't know, except it's got an image of the sun etched into the cupridium. It's not going to do us any good down in that chamber. If the Kyphrans have managed to make one work, it's possible we could. If we can't, and they can, there's a good chance they'll get this one as well, whether it's down in the chamber or up here. If they can't, we'll still have this one."

"Majer Jaavor would be giving you a dressing-down by now," says Fraadn.

"That's why he'll never be a subcommander, let alone a commander," replies Alyiakal evenly.

Fraadn raises his eyebrows, then shakes his head. "It's your neck." He turns and walks back under the tent awning.

Alyiakal has the rankers position the device in full sun. Then he creates the largest order funnel he can manage. While it isn't visible, within moments he feels the heat radiating from the flap above the opening as the chaos begins to build.

"Feels like that thing is getting hot, ser," declares Vuurnyn.

"You can step back a bit." Alyiakal inspects the device closely until enough chaos has built up for him to compress and force it into the reservoir. He has hoped that the chaos from the funnel would build and provide enough pressure to open the flap and feed into the reservoir, but it appears that he needs to compress the chaos and force it into the reservoir.

He continues to funnel sun-chaos bits, then coil, compress, and insert them into the device as he carefully studies the lever and the nozzle.

Less than a glass later, Fraadn returns. "Have you discovered anything useful?"

"It seems to gather heat in the sunlight," replies Alyiakal.

"All metals do," says Fraadn dryly.

"More than that." Alyiakal points to the symbol behind the small circular opening. "That has to mean something."

"Probably chaos," suggests Fraadn.

"Most likely," says Alyiakal agreeably, "except I didn't see that symbol on the replenishment ports on the firelances in the chamber. The lever here likely controls the chaos flow, while the nozzle can be twisted to shape how the chaos emerges."

"So what are you going to do? Let it sit in the sun and hope somehow it gathers chaos? How can you tell if it will?"

"By turning the lever and seeing if anything happens."

Fraadn winces. "Just don't point it at anyone or any mount in case you're right." Then he adds, "You stay with it until you take it back down below."

"Yes, ser."

Alyiakal understands all too well. If anything goes wrong, Fraadn wants to make certain that the blame lands squarely on Alyiakal.

After Fraadn heads across the courtyard to the southeast corner of the fort and the lookout posted there, Alyiakal expands his thin order funnel wider, not enough to strain himself, and considers how to use the device. If it works, and it might not, whatever chaos it throws won't last long. His gut reaction is that it ought to be used first to take out any chaos-thrower or chaos-cutter that the Kyphrans have and then to strike at the center of the Kyphran force.

He laughs softly to himself. *You're planning to use a device you can't be certain will work against a force you haven't even seen.*

"Ser?" asks Yurval.

"I was thinking about the situations in which we get involved. We're going to fight a battle against a force that didn't even exist a season ago, with five Mirror Lancer companies that have only been in Guarstyad two seasons or so, over artifacts built a century ago, for reasons we don't know, to stop a threat to a part of Cyador most of us had barely heard of before being posted there. But then, that's a good part of being a Mirror Lancer."

"Do you think you can get this thing to work, ser?"

"It did once. Whether we can figure out how is another question." *So is whether you can replenish the device's chaos reservoir enough to get a blast of chaos strong enough to have any effect.*

The massive firecannon on the fireships have an effective range of only a few hundred yards. The device is far smaller and, even fully charged, wouldn't likely reach that far.

So why are you even bothering?

Alyiakal realizes that he really doesn't know. He only has a feeling that he should, and usually his feelings are at least as accurate as his reasoned decisions.

After Alyiakal spends another glass or so secretly funneling coiled and compressed chaos into the device, Fraadn again approaches. "You still hoping the sun will replenish that device?"

"That. And thinking," replies Alyiakal. "If the Kyphrans have one that works, how could they use it? It probably doesn't have the range of a firecannon, and that's not that much greater than archers can loose a shaft. It would only be effective against a massed charge of lancers, or for burning through the gate. It has to have a limited amount of chaos, and the more chaos it uses, the less time it can be effective."

Fraadn frowns, then nods. "So it's likely, if they have such a device, that they won't use it against Second and Third Companies?"

"Unless lancers attack in close formation. Didn't you suggest that they keep their men spread if the Kyphrans got a large force ashore?"

"I did."

Left unsaid is the fact that Fraadn suggested, but did not order, and Kortyl is definitely an officer of strong opinions.

By early midafternoon, Alyiakal discovers that the device's chaos reservoir is perhaps half full, and he's debating how long he should keep up the replenishment efforts when a lancer rides from the east through the partly open gate and heads straight for Fraadn.

Alyiakal waits until the ranker messenger finishes with Fraadn and leaves to deal with his mount before approaching the senior captain.

Fraadn immediately says, "Kortyl and Rynst engaged the Kyphrans as soon as the first ship neared the pier. The Kyphran marines had large polished brass shields as well as a handful of larger oblong cupridium shields that looked to be identical to the few in that chamber you opened. They poured onto the pier. The Kyphrans lost possibly fifty to a hundred men, but more marines followed and picked up the shields. There were so many that they finally held the pier. Then two more ships came in. One stood off filled with archers who lofted shafts that came down like hail. The other one unloaded foot—all with polished brass bucklers."

"The Kyphrans thought the landing out well," says Alyiakal.

"Too well. Kortyl thinks that Second and Third Companies have killed or wounded over two hundred Kyphrans, possibly more, but there are close to a thousand who've survived. That includes at least a company of archers. More troopers were landing every glass when he dispatched the messenger."

"What about Mirror Lancer casualties?"

"The messenger didn't know, except that there were lancers wounded, and at least three deaths that he saw."

"Is the *Rylaan* still fighting?"

"Kortyl thinks so. There were still chaos flashes out offshore, but he and Rynst are pulling back to re-form. They intend to attack from spread formations as long as their firelances hold out."

"How many spare firelances do they have?" asks Alyiakal.

"Sixty, but those won't last much more than today. Some lancers are already on their second lance."

"The Kyphrans will push as quickly as they can," says Alyiakal. "They won't have that many supplies, not for more than a thousand troopers. There's also not much water available."

"I'd thought that as well. They can't afford a slow and measured approach, not when the nearest supply port is a four-to-five-day sail one way under the best of winds. The problem is," adds Fraadn dryly, "we're in not much better shape, except for water."

"If the *Rylaan* survives the near-suicidal attacks on her," Alyiakal points out, "she'll eventually destroy more of the Kyphran ships, and they won't be able to get supplies."

"That won't help much right now."

"Have Kortyl and Rynst do what they can today, then withdraw. Send out Sixth Company before dawn. We'll do the same thing tomorrow. If they're not close by tomorrow night, send out Fifth Company on oneday."

"What about that device?"

"If it works, and there's no way of knowing that yet, it won't be much good until the Kyphrans mount an attack on the fort—just like the firecannon on the *Rylaan*." Alyiakal pauses, then says, "Whatever you decide on, I would put the order to Kortyl in writing."

Fraadn's smile is both wry and wintry. "I'd already decided on that. Unless the situation changes drastically in the next few glasses, what you suggested makes the most sense. We need to bleed them dry—as much as we can." He steps back and adds, "I'll let you know."

"Yes, ser."

Alyiakal turns and heads toward the device, with the determination to expand his order funnel and see how much chaos he can pack into the reservoir before the sun gets low enough in the sky that the stone walls cut off its rays.

For the remainder of sevenday, Alyiakal crams as much concentrated chaos as he can into the device, while talking to the rankers, and occasionally to Fraadn. His efforts to find out more about the device are futile. As far as he can tell, it is simply a chaos reservoir with a tube and a nozzle, and a lever to control the flow of chaos.

Once shadows fall across the ruined building, he senses how much chaos is in the reservoir. Sensing through cupridium is difficult, even as close as he is, but he thinks that the reservoir is about half full.

Just half full—after almost a full day of funneling chaos.

Then he turns to the four rankers on guard duty and says, "Go down the ramp until I can't see you. Then stop."

Once they're out of sight, Alyiakal adjusts the nozzle at the end of the tube to its smallest aperture and aims the tube at the top of the south wall. Next he strengthens his shields. Finally, he moves the lever.

Hsssst! A thin line of chaos issues from the nozzle, and, as soon as it does, Alyiakal uses the lever to close off the flow of chaos, then tries to determine how much of the chaos that momentary burst took. He can't tell precisely, but it seems as though the quick burst dropped the chaos level somewhat, possibly a tenth of the amount in the reservoir.

Alyiakal is about to inspect the section of the wall he targeted when he hears Fraadn's boots on the sandy stone.

"Was that thin chaos blast from the device?" demands the senior captain.

"It was. Let's go see what it did, if anything. I aimed it at the top of the south wall, away from anyone."

The two officers walk to the wall, where they stop. Both look up at the cut in the topmost stones, almost a cubit deep and half a cubit wide and tall, the stone melted smooth on all sides of the cut.

After a moment, Fraadn says, "It might be better if you stayed here and worked with the device."

"The Kyphrans won't attack here tomorrow. It might not even be until twoday, or later. You need every company to make attacks on them. If Sixth Company goes out tomorrow, I'll have time. Besides, from what we just saw, the device will be helpful, but it doesn't look like it will make a difference. Not by itself." Alyiakal points to the melted cut in the wall. "That may have been a good part of the chaos it absorbed. The device doesn't show how much chaos it has left. That quick blast didn't quite cut through a cubit of stone. The nozzle can be adjusted to be wider, but if it is, it will spread more the farther it goes, and it likely doesn't have an effective range much greater than a firelance. Even if it does, you wouldn't want to use it until the Kyphrans are close enough that you can sweep through larger numbers, because the chaos has to be limited."

Fraadn frowns.

Alyiakal waits.

Finally, Fraadn says, "I don't like it, but you're making sense. Just don't get yourself killed tomorrow." Then he turns and walks slowly back toward the ruined building and the tent awning he has made his space.

After a time, Alyiakal follows, well aware that Fraadn had hoped for something more powerful than what he has seen.

XC

Second and Third Companies return to the Mirror Lancer encampment well after dark on sevenday. Casualties for both companies total four dead and ten wounded, a casualty level that, on the surface, looks surprisingly low, compared to the Kyphran dead and wounded, estimated as a minimum of two hundred by Kortyl and Rynst. But then, as Alyiakal realizes, that's because the Kyphran archers loosed shafts at where they *thought* the lancers were or would be, not at specific targets. Given the spread formations Kortyl and Rynst used, there weren't many lancers in any given area.

Even so, the loss of fourteen lancers is as significant for the Mirror Lancers as two hundred or more casualties are for the Kyphrans, whose landed force looks to have been roughly fifteen hundred, with the possibility of reinforcements, unless the *Rylaan* has been able to close off access to the stone pier.

Once the companies return, Fraadn dispatches Alyiakal to check and treat the wounded.

Six of the ten wounded look likely to recover, particularly since Alyiakal sees them soon enough to deal with their wound chaos before it can spread far. Two are in serious condition, but Alyiakal is hopeful. One dies before Alyiakal can even look at him, and the last one is problematic, but Alyiakal does what he can and hopes it will be enough.

By dawn on eightday morning, Sixth Company is more than ten kays from the lancer encampment and on the downslope leading to the stone pier and the Kyphran force. Neither Alyiakal nor his scouts sees any chaos flashes on the Great Western Ocean, but what that means remains to be seen.

Another glass passes before one of the scouts rides back and reports to Alyiakal. "Ser, the Kyphrans are moving out. They're about eight kays east from here. The lead company is foot with metal shields. There are archers behind the shield company."

"Are there companies following those two?"

"Yes, ser, along with wagons farther back."

"Were there any ships at the pier or offshore?"

"There was a ship at the pier. We didn't see any others."

"Thank you. Return to your scouting. Let me know if anything changes besides the Kyphrans continuing to advance along the road."

Once the scout rides off to resume his duties, Alyiakal summons the third squad leader.

In a fraction of a quint, Vaekyn rides forward and eases his mount up beside Alyiakal's chestnut. "Yes, ser?"

"Vaekyn, take third squad to the northeast. You're to make a flank attack on a foot company, but *only* if you can without taking an attack by archers. Keep your men spread. If they have large numbers of archers, withdraw and rejoin the company. Even if you attack briefly, that will disconcert them. The aim is to make them lose men, without losing lancers. Understood?"

"Yes, ser."

"The rest of the company will work to slow their progress so that their force gets jammed together. There's a slight rise about a kay or so ahead. We'll be somewhere around there. Time is on our side. You can afford to be a bit cautious. Pick off troopers as you can, but try not to risk men."

"Yes, ser." The squad leader nods and returns to his men.

Alyiakal turns to Torkaal, riding on his right. "I'd thought about using that rise that's about a kay ahead for cover, but once the Kyphrans get close enough to loose shafts, they could blanket the road beyond the rise."

"What about using it the other way, ser?" asks the senior squad leader. "Move the rest of the company north, then wait until archers come over the rise and attack the column behind them from the north side. The archers won't be able to see where we are, and the closer we get to any foot company, the less they'll be able to loose shafts without taking out more of their own men."

Alyiakal laughs wryly. "Much better than my original idea." He studies the rise again. "The rise continues for a ways to the north, then angles east. We could follow it a half kay. What if we had a lancer or two ride down the road, stop behind the rise, and then ride slowly off the road some thirty yards? From there, they could pick off any scouts. That might encourage the archers to blanket the area."

"That might waste more than a few shafts," adds Torkaal. "It can't hurt. I doubt they have a full company of archers behind the shieldmen—more likely a squad. They can't have carried enough arrows to supply more than a company or two."

"They had to have lost a few in defending the pier," says Alyiakal, "even if they recovered most of the shafts that didn't hit anyone."

"They'd be fortunate to be able to recover and use more than a third of what they loosed against Second and Third Companies," Torkaal points out.

Alyiakal nods, then says, "Choose the two men who'll do the best at picking off scouts, and then we'll move into the grass to set up the attack."

A quint later, the first two squads of Sixth Company ride slowly east-northeast through the spring grasses that, depending on the ground, range from one to two cubits high. Alyiakal senses, but does not see, a few coneys moving to avoid the oncoming horses.

The two squads cover close to a kay through the grass before Alyiakal spots Vaekyn and third squad headed west on the north side of the road. In turn, Vaekyn sights the other two squads and turns toward them. As third squad nears, Alyiakal counts the riders. Vaekyn started out with seventeen men besides himself, and sixteen men are coming back.

"Company! Halt!"

When Vaekyn reins up next to Alyiakal, he immediately reports. "There's a squad of archers at the rear of the large company of foot. They didn't start to loose shafts until we were within fifty yards. We lost Puall and his mount." Vaekyn pauses. "We made 'em pay for that. Took out most of the archers and half the foot, close to sixty I'd judge. We withdrew before the archers at the back of the next foot company could target us individually. Their captain was moving the archers to the north side of the road when we left. Likely they'll pass the word back."

"Did you see how many more companies they have?"

"Couldn't tell you, ser, but they stretch back almost a kay, including a bunch of wagons back there as well."

"Anyone at the pier? Any ships?"

"Couldn't tell about troopers around the pier, not for sure. There weren't any ships, and we could sight chaos flashes farther out on the ocean."

Suggesting that the Rylaan *is slowly destroying or driving off the Kyphran ships . . . for the moment.*

Once Sixth Company settles behind the grass-topped rise, Alyiakal beckons to Torkaal, and the two ride far enough up the rise for Alyiakal to see the road. While Alyiakal can see the Kyphran force, roughly two kays away, several quints pass before he can clearly distinguish the formations and advance scouts reach the top of the rise—where both fall to firelances, as does a third scout.

While perhaps a score of bowmen march behind the advancing shielded foot, even after the two lancers kill three scouts, none of the archers nock shafts, let alone release them.

Saving their arrows for more targeted use.

The Kyphrans have clearly consolidated what remains of the foot company attacked by Vaekyn with the foot company following, and moved archers to the north side of the road. Alyiakal quickly studies the formation.

He turns to the senior squad leader. "This isn't going to work out according to plan. Withdraw with first and third squads. Make yourselves seen so that the Kyphrans think everyone is withdrawing. Pull back to where the land levels out. I'm taking second squad to pick off a few more archers and troopers, then we'll rejoin you."

"Are you sure, ser?"

Meaning "Are you mad?" "It's necessary, and we have a better chance now than later. You need to get moving, and make some noise."

"Yes, ser." Torkaal heads down the west side of the rise. "Second squad! Hold with the captain. First and third squads! Withdraw on me!"

Alyiakal rides down to join Maelt. "Squad Leader, we'll angle southwest along the back of this rise to get as close as we can to the Kyphrans without alerting the archers. Then we'll charge toward the road and target the archers first. After that, the lead lancers and I will clear a path through the leading foot company and turn up the road. Once we're clear, we'll go five abreast over the rise and take out the archers behind the shieldmen. After that, move to the open ground south of the road and put some distance between the shieldmen and any remaining archers."

"You're trying to take out as many archers as we can, ser?"

"And as many foot as we can after that." *We just need to make it work.*

"Second squad! On me! Forward!" Alyiakal eases the chestnut parallel to the crest of the rise, sensing the positions of the archers and the main body of the foot company. As he turns the chestnut slightly left and comes over the top of the rise, he widens his shields slightly to offer some protection to the two lancers who flank him, then sees that second squad is slightly behind where he'd thought they should be.

There's no help for that. "Target the archers on the edge of the road! Charge!" As he gives the order, Alyiakal uses three short bursts to take out three archers, then keeps targeting them as the chestnut nears the road.

Belatedly, he realizes the Kyphran troopers wear light green uniforms, but that thought vanishes as he feels impacts on his shields. Some of those blows are painful, but not so painful that he cannot use his control of order, turning chaos bursts from his firelance into a thin, cutting beam. Carving a space from the middle of the foot through the front ranks, he turns the chestnut into the space he's created. In moments, he punches through the footmen, and on through the few yards of open road, before reaching the top of the rise. Turning, he begins to pick off the archers behind the shieldmen leading the Kyphran force.

He sees a single mounted individual and targets him with the firelance before returning to taking out archers. Although he feels the cool black mists of death everywhere, he has no idea whether the deaths are lancers or Kyphrans. There's little else he can do but target archers and anyone else while leading second squad to the open ground on the south side of the road and away from the Kyphran force.

Once the squad is well away, he eases the lancers onto the road, but he doesn't slow the chestnut to a walk until he is more than half a kay from the shieldmen leading the Kyphran force. Maelt moves up beside him. "How many did we lose?"

"We didn't, ser. Escalyn took a shaft in the thigh, but it's not deep."

"Not one?" Alyiakal finds that hard to believe.

"Ser, we caught them by surprise. You took out six archers before they could lift their bows. The rest of the squad finished off most of the remaining archers and at least half of the foot, beyond the ones you took out. There might be a fifth of that company remaining. From what I saw, only one of the archers behind the lead shieldmen escaped. We were far enough away from the next archer line that they only got off a few shafts before we were out of range. One of those shafts hit Escalyn."

"How is he?"

"It's not that deep. It can wait until we rejoin the company."

Alyiakal eases the chestnut to the side of the road and glances back. From what he can discern, the Kyphran force has come to a halt. Then he uses his senses to check his firelance. It's almost empty.

That doesn't exactly surprise him.

Since using the order funnel hadn't tired him before, he silently creates another and lets the tiny chaos bits flow down. This time he can sense a little strain, but he turns the gelding west and continues up the slight gradual slope.

Half a glass later, Alyiakal and second squad reach the rest of the company. Once there, Alyiakal checks his firelance, now roughly a third replenished, and then dismounts, checks and cleans Escalyn's wound as well as possible, dusts it with order, and dresses it. The order dusting gives him a slight headache, suggesting that he needs to be careful, so he eats a trail biscuit, partly washed down with water.

Glancing in the general direction of the sun, he is stunned to realize that it's still before midday. He remounts and joins Torkaal.

"Have they resumed marching?"

"The scouts just reported that they have. They've been taking care of bodies and re-forming companies. Maelt said second squad took out almost a company, maybe more. That so?"

"Somewhere around that, I'd guess. Since I was leading and he was farther back, he'd have a better idea."

"He also said he's never seen anyone as accurate with a firelance. Neither have I."

"We all have talents. Your comments kept me from making a bad decision about how to attack. We work well together."

Torkaal offers an amused smile, but only nods, then asks, "What do we do now?"

"We see if the scouts can tell if and how they've changed their marching order. Whatever we do next will depend on how much chaos is left in each squad's firelances."

"That means first squad will have to lead," replies Torkaal. "Some of the lancers in second squad don't have any chaos left. Third squad's a little better."

"It looks to me," says Alyiakal, "like they're willing to sacrifice troopers to run us out of chaos."

"What other choice do they have? We've likely destroyed half their archers, if not more. Without firelances, we'd have to go hand-to-hand. Even after all the Kyphrans we've already taken out, they still outnumber us three to one. That's *if* they don't get reinforcements."

Torkaal pauses. "I still don't see why they want this place."

Alyiakal has pondered that more than a little, until he realized another possibility. "They don't. They want Guarstyad." He goes on. "I think we can count on their having a device like the one we found. We can also count on their having figured out how to use it. What if part of their plan is to rebuild the old road and fortify both ends and to use the device to guard the western pass? They could build another port where the stone pier is."

"And pay for it all with the golds from the silver mine?" asks Torkaal.

"I don't know if that's what the Duke of Kyphros has in mind, but it makes more sense than anything else I've heard. And if they get ahold of two devices instead of one . . ." Alyiakal pauses, then adds, "But something like that may have been what the dissidents had in mind, except they wanted to be independent of Cyador."

Torkaal laughs. "Maybe they wanted to take over part or all of Kyphros."

"You might be right."

After a moment, Alyiakal asks, "How strong are the firelances? Back in training, one officer said that they could be used as regular lances."

"What exactly do you have in mind, ser?"

"Something that the Kyphrans would never expect—a direct charge through their shield front. From what I saw, they're not carrying spears or pikes, just blades of some sort. We break the formation, and they're open to firelances."

"You're asking a lot from whoever leads that attack."

"That's why I'll be the one."

"Ser . . . is that wise?"

"Is it wise to let them use those shields to stop firelance bolts when we're running out of chaos? And when all the shieldmen are concentrated at the head of the column?"

"When you put it that way, ser . . ." Torkaal pauses. "You realize that Majer—"

"Jaavor would deny such a request," Alyiakal finishes, then adds, "If we don't find a way to win, none of us will have much of a future." *Assuming we survive.*

"Which squad?" asks Torkaal.

"The entire company, but I'll lead second squad. We'll attack head-on, and as soon as we break the front shield wall, we'll turn east. The two other squads need to move in close enough to use firelances."

"What if there are more archers?"

"Withdraw immediately."

"That might be hard on second squad."

"It might be, but we don't want to give the archers all three squads as targets." Alyiakal turns the chestnut. "I need to brief Maelt on what second squad needs to do."

When Alyiakal reins up beside the second squad leader, Maelt merely says, "Ser."

"I need two or three lancers who don't have any chaos in their firelances."

"Who *don't* have any chaos in their lances, ser?"

"That's right. I need them to flank me when we charge the Kyphran shield wall."

"Ser . . . ?"

"The shieldmen don't carry spears or pikes, and we need to get rid of those shields. Firelances can be used as regular lances, as a last resort. We *need* to remove those shieldmen." Alyiakal goes on to explain the plan of attack.

Maelt says little, except an occasional "Yes, ser," and Alyiakal can sense his skepticism. He finishes with, "If I didn't think this would work, I wouldn't try it, let alone lead the charge." Alyiakal hopes his personal shields prove strong enough to wedge apart the shieldmen, not that he can afford to let anyone know that.

Another two quints pass before the Kyphran shield company reaches a point on the road some three hundred yards east of second squad.

"Second squad! At a walk, forward!" Alyiakal looks to his left, where Fhaquar rides, and says, "Stay as close to me as you can."

"Yes, ser."

Alyiakal repeats the same words to Sharkal, on his right.

As second squad moves closer, the Kyphrans raise their shields to block any chaos bolts from the oncoming lancers.

He pats the chestnut on the shoulder. "Here we go, fellow." Then he orders,

"Second squad! Charge!" The chestnut sprints forward. Both Fhaquar on his left and Sharkal on his right keep pace.

At fifty yards, Alyiakal fires a chaos bolt over the heads of the first line, which glances off the shields held overhead by the interior shieldmen. With less than twenty yards to contact, he lowers the firelance and directs the chaos bolt under the lower edge of the shieldman in the center of the first line, who topples forward, and a second bolt into the largely unprotected trooper behind him holding a shield overhead.

Within mere yards of the first line of shieldmen, he extends his personal shields into a wedge while linking himself and the gelding together.

The impact of his shields with the oblong cupridium shields of the Kyphrans shivers through Alyiakal and fractionally slows the gelding, as Kyphran troopers either are violently propelled from the horse or fall to targeted firelance bolts. "Second squad, on me! Right!"

More Kyphrans go down, but the gelding slows to a fast trot by the time he and Alyiakal reach the open ground to the south of the road. Alyiakal's whole body aches, and his head throbs as he swings his lance to the left and pulses chaos at the rear ranks of the shield company, as well as at the foot company immediately behind. Then he slows the gelding, ordering, "Second squad, to the rear! Ride!"

As he heads back south, he mercilessly targets shieldmen, and he can see that both Sharkal and Fhaquar are still with him when he brings second squad to a halt a good two hundred yards west of where the front line of the Kyphran shieldmen had been.

Perhaps fifteen shieldmen remain, but they're moving back downhill to provide cover for what remains of the foot company behind them.

Alyiakal sees two downed mounts, but no more as first and third squads break off and ride back up the last few yards of the gentle slope to where second squad waits.

"Who did we lose?" Alyiakal asks Maelt when the squad leader rides up.

"Kaarlyt. Four others have slashes, not too deep, it looks like."

Alyiakal feels light-headed, and his entire body aches. He fumbles out a trail biscuit and manages to chew and wash it down with water. That doesn't help much.

"Are you all right, ser?" asks Torkaal when he rides up.

"Been better," Alyiakal manages, having to force every word. "You . . . need . . . get Sixth . . . Company back to . . . the encampment . . . done what we could . . ."

"Sixth Company! Form up!" orders Torkaal. "Back to the encampment! Fast trot!"

Alyiakal isn't certain how he even manages to stay in the saddle over what has to be more than a glass, but that is about all he can do by the time Torkaal guides the company to the encampment.

Words flow around him as others help him out of the saddle.

"Captain's hurt . . ."

"Black angel . . . he's got bruises on his face . . ."

Bruises on my face . . . but he cannot even finish the thought as hot darkness sweeps over him.

XCI

Chaos bolts flare out of the night, then out of the sun, each one slamming into Alyiakal and the chestnut, going through his shields, no matter how much he strengthens them. Then the hot darkness claims them both, until he feels a cool damp cloth on his forehead and face.

He slowly opens his eyes, to see a tent awning above him. He finds he is lying on his back, likely on his own blanket.

Within moments after Alyiakal opens his eyes, Fraadn looks down at him in the dim light that might be twilight or predawn.

"Thank the Rational Stars you're still here. What in the name of the black angels were you thinking?"

Alyiakal tries to speak, but his throat is so dry that no sound comes out. The ranker kneeling beside him helps him into a sitting position and hands him a water bottle. Alyiakal takes several small sips. Then he slowly asks, "Did it work?"

"Except for almost losing a captain." Fraadn shakes his head. "I never heard of such a sowshit idea. Somehow you made it work. With almost no casualties. Sixth Company destroyed most of the shieldmen and shields, at least their ability to deflect firelance bolts. You also took out most of the foot company following. Close to two hundred Kyphrans."

"What day?"

"It's still eightday, what's left of it."

"What about my chestnut?"

"He's sore in places, too. Torkaal felt he was straining carrying you back here. You both took a beating breaking that shield wall."

Breaking that shield wall? Then the memories sweep over him. "You're sure about the chestnut?"

"He's in better shape than you are."

"What about the Kyphrans?"

"They made camp west of the skirmish. Right where the land levels out. The scouts are keeping close watch. They've got three wagons. We also sent scouts around them to check out the pier." Fraadn shakes his head. "There's nothing much there besides blackened ground. The *Rylaan* must have finished off or driven out the rest of the Kyphran ships, coming in close enough to wipe out whoever and whatever remained at the piers."

"They have a working device," says Alyiakal.

"Torkaal told me you'd said that. How do you know that?"

"I don't." Alyiakal takes a larger swallow of water. "I need something to eat. Trail biscuits, something I can swallow."

"If you don't know—"

"The Duke of Kyphros wants Guarstyad, the silver mine, and the second device. That's the only thing that makes sense. He's got mages who can somehow get chaos into the device they have." Alyiakal blinks as a wave of dizziness assaults him. "Trail biscuits. Need to eat."

This time the ranker hands him one, and Alyiakal slowly eats it, interspersed with water, followed by a second one. The dizziness recedes, but does not vanish.

"That may be," says Fraadn, "but we don't know that."

"Don't attack with lancers close together," says Alyiakal, wincing as he shifts his weight.

"We may not have a choice if they reach us and attack in force. Tomorrow, Fourth Company will work on reducing their numbers. Now that they don't have many shields or archers left, more traditional tactics might be more effective."

Alyiakal is too tired and dizzy to object, especially since Fraadn might be right. He takes another trail biscuit and slowly begins to eat it.

"You need to rest," Fraadn says. "I'll be back later."

Alyiakal just nods, adjusting himself to lean against the ruined half wall, his thoughts returning to the skirmish. He'd anchored his shields around the chestnut so that any impact wouldn't rip him out of the saddle. That part worked, but the shields had transmitted some of that impact to him and the gelding.

Next time, anchor them to something solid. Except that wouldn't work if he or the chestnut was moving. Then, as he is discovering, using order to control chaos has ramifications he hasn't considered.

"You're bruised all over, you know, ser," says the ranker—Naalyn, from second squad, Alyiakal realizes.

"I can feel that," Alyiakal replies.

"How did you do that, ser? Break through those shields, I mean?"

"Rather unwisely, apparently. Some of the shields must have hit me and my mount. I didn't feel the impacts at the time, though."

"Some of those Kyphrans ran away yelling. Until we got 'em with the fire-lances, anyway."

"Next time, I'll have to figure out a better way," says Alyiakal wryly. *If there is a next time.*

XCII

On oneday, Alyiakal wakes sore all over, after a restless night, not that he expected otherwise. The dizziness is gone, and he has a healthy appetite, even for the porridge that passes for breakfast.

"You look better than yesterday," says Rynst.

"Much better," adds Kortyl. "How did your face get bruised? I could see arms, legs, shoulders—but your face?"

"I don't know," answers Alyiakal, because while he suspects, he doesn't really *know.* "I think it happened when we broke the shield wall, but I didn't feel it until later." He quickly says, "I take it that Craavyl and Fourth Company are doing what they can against the Kyphrans?"

"They left before dawn," replies Rynst. "Craavyl said he wasn't about to try anything like your crazy charge, and Fraadn told him he couldn't because you wiped out almost all of the shieldmen. Fourth Company's supposed to probe their flanks and take out as many as possible without losing lancers." He pauses, then says, "I heard you didn't lose many."

"Two dead, four wounded, this time."

Rynst shakes his head.

Before anyone can comment on casualties or the Kyphrans, Kortyl says, "Here comes Fraadn. He has something on his mind."

"Doesn't he always?" asks Rynst.

"You would, too, in his position," replies Kortyl. "Having command under these conditions is a sowshit stew."

Crude as the image is, Alyiakal agrees. The companies are outnumbered, undersupplied, likely facing a device of the First, with no possibility of immediate resupply. Add to that the possibility of losing an irreplaceable device and other artifacts to a duke willing to do anything to regain the ruins that he believes are legally his. The ultimate prize being control of Guarstyad as well, to which he has no legal claim at all.

Not that legality matters that much in war.

The junior captains stand as Fraadn approaches, stepping into the officers' area, though Alyiakal rises more slowly than the others.

"Alyiakal, how are you feeling this morning?"

"Sore and stiff, but much better."

Fraadn nods. "That's good to hear. I'm going to make a change. You and Sixth Company will man the fort. We'll switch over this morning. The way the Kyphrans are moving, I'd guess they'll come up within a few kays today, and then attack tomorrow. They can't afford to wait. Sixth Company will guard the fort, the ruined building, and the devices there, and be the reserve company when the Kyphrans attack. The attack may be gradual and take several days, or it might be an all-out brutal assault. If it takes several days, having Sixth Company hold the fort will be more effective. The longer you and your men recover, the better for all of us," Fraadn concludes.

Rynst nods, as does Kortyl, which surprises Alyiakal.

Alyiakal has his suspicions about that decision, but says only, "Yes, ser."

"Excellent. You might as well start now. I'll have First Company ready to change over as soon as Sixth Company arrives." Fraadn offers a smile, part perfunctory and part enigmatic, then turns and walks back to his mount.

"Aren't you the fortunate one," declares Rynst sardonically.

"It could be worse," replies Alyiakal cheerfully, adding cynically, "It can always get worse."

Kortyl nods to that as well.

Knowing the morning muster of Sixth Company is approaching, Alyiakal makes his way to the open area east of the company area.

Torkaal joins him immediately. "Good morning, ser. How are you feeling?"

"Sore, but much better. Captain Fraadn just briefed us." Alyiakal goes on to explain the situation to the senior squad leader.

Torkaal tries not to frown, but does not totally succeed. "That so-called fort could be a death trap. Be hard to strategize our way out of that."

"It has some advantages and some disadvantages, but orders are orders." *Even from someone of the same rank, if with greater seniority.* "We'll have to see what we can do. When they get closer, we should have all the horses ready to go." Alyiakal adds in an overly polite tone, "After all, what use is a reserve company if the reserve company is not immediately ready to take the field?"

Torkaal smothers an amused smile. "We'll be ready for any necessary action, ser. You just give the word."

"Once we get settled in the fort, you and I need to go over a few things." *More than a few.* "I'll announce the shift in orders at muster."

Torkaal nods.

After muster and his brief announcement, Alyiakal gathers his gear and saddles the chestnut gelding, carefully and taking his time, while using small amounts of order to lessen the faint reddish gray of the gelding's worst bruises. Then he leads Sixth Company to the fort, from which Fraadn and First Company immediately leave. After securing the chestnut, he carries his gear to the ruined building, under the tent awning Fraadn used. He details two of the four rankers who are the duty guards of the lower chamber to wheel the device up into the sunlight close to the tent, where he immediately creates an order funnel to gather chaos from the white sun.

Over the course of the next few glasses, sitting propped against a half wall, he begins to replenish the chaos in his firelance as he builds up the chaos in the reservoir chamber of the device.

Fraadn returns at late midmorning. As he nears the awning and Alyiakal, he sees the device of the First in full sunlight. A brief smile crosses his lips, which immediately vanishes before he reaches Alyiakal, motioning for him to remain seated. "I see you brought the device up into the sun again. Do you think you might be able to use it against the Kyphrans?"

"We can use it," replies Alyiakal. "Whether we can use it effectively is another question."

"I haven't told anyone that you got it to work."

"I managed to get a single small chaos burst out of it. It was stronger than a single firelance, but nothing like a firecannon. It's likely better that no one knows until it's absolutely necessary." *For a number of reasons.*

"I have to agree with you," says Fraadn. "Even if you get some use, it won't decide the outcome." He clears his throat. "The Kyphrans are moving forward, slowly and carefully. They have a handful of archers left, and they're targeting individual lancers. Craavyl's managed to take out around a score of their foot and an archer or two, but he's already lost two men and has three wounded. I sent back word to keep at it, and to try to attack where the archers couldn't see his men until the last moment."

"You're thinking that they'll have a harder time against four companies?" asks Alyiakal.

"With a limited number of archers who have to be running short on shafts, that's more than likely, but we'll still lose men. We need to get closer to hit large numbers of foot. I'm guessing that they'll stop for the day three or four kays from here, then reorganize for an all-out attack tomorrow."

"What about harassing them with a squad tonight, when they can't be seen? A good lancer ought to be able to take out scouts and troopers on the perimeter."

"The flash of a chaos bolt would provide a target for archers."

"Not if the lancer used a short burst and kept moving."

Fraadn shakes his head slowly. "From what I've seen, you're about the only lancer in all five companies who could do that reliably, and I'm not going to risk you for something like that. You're more valuable with that device and as a reserve force."

While Alyiakal doubts he's the only lancer who could make an effective night attack, he knows there's no point in disputing Fraadn, and he needs time to recover and gather chaos for both his firelance and the device.

"I'm sending twenty-five full firelances over for Sixth Company. That's all I can spare."

"Since we're in reserve, I understand." *But I don't have to like it.* "If anything changes, you'll let us know?"

"I doubt it will, or not significantly. If it does, you'll know. Just take it easy. We'll need you tomorrow." Fraadn smiles, then turns and walks back to his mount.

Alyiakal watches Fraadn ride through the gate, open wide enough for a single rider, then returns his attention to collecting more chaos. Based on what he can do so far, he might be able to concentrate enough chaos to almost fill the reservoir of the device by late afternoon and fully replenish his firelance.

But will that be sufficient to make a difference?

That's a question he cannot answer. All he can do is power both weapons and hope he can use them effectively.

He finds Torkaal to tell him about the firelances.

"Twenty-five?" asks the senior squad leader.

"We're not engaging the Kyphrans tomorrow. Or not as soon as the other companies."

"What are your thoughts on distribution, ser?"

"Half to first squad, and half to second. I'll leave it to you." Alyiakal pauses, then adds, "Unless you think there's a better way."

"No, ser. That's about what I'd do. Is there anything else?"

"Not yet. I'll let you know when there is." Alyiakal heads back to the device.

After sunset, Fraadn summons Alyiakal to join the other captains at the encampment. On Alyiakal's arrival, he notices that Craavyl is also there, suggesting that Fraadn has no plans for a night attack.

Fraadn begins his briefing. "The Kyphrans still have almost a thousand foot and roughly a squad of archers stopped a little more than three kays east of the fort. They have a double line of sentries, the first half a kay from their camp, the second at around two hundred yards. They have three wagons, one with armored panels on three sides."

Alyiakal nods. That has to be the wagon carrying the device. He also wonders how many mages may be accompanying the wagon.

"They only have a score or so of mounts, most likely for scouts and officers. It's possible that the *Rylaan* destroyed or drove off any ships carrying more horses."

When Fraadn finishes giving the details reported by the scouts, Kortyl asks, "What's the plan of attack?"

"Attack the encampment at or just before dawn from different directions," says Fraadn. "We need to keep them off-balance, especially if they have a working device such as the one we discovered. The armored wagon suggests that they do."

"So we're supposed to attack, in the open, against something like a firecannon?" asks Craavyl, his tone of voice verging on petulant contempt.

"If they have a device," says Alyiakal smoothly, "they'll be unlikely to have it ready quickly. If they don't, we should be able to remove more of their foot. Keep a squad or two in sight out of bowshot. The other possibility is to place lancers on foot behind solid cover in the line of their foot advance and use their firelances. If they're spread somewhat and withdraw after firing, they'll be far harder for archers to target."

"We're lancers, not foot," declares Kortyl.

"Better to act like foot and destroy them than act like lancers and be wiped out," says Rynst.

"Then what?" Fraadn asks Alyiakal.

"When they get within half a kay of the fort, attack in spread formations from both sides. If they have a device, they'll want to use it on the fort. It won't be effective from that distance. If it's like the one we have, it can't be moved quickly, and the chaos bursts can't be that wide." Alyiakal smiles wryly. "And if they don't have a device, four lancer companies should be able to wipe out that many foot, even if they have a squad of archers left. The archers can't blanket the entire area at the same time."

What Alyiakal isn't saying, and what all the other captains know, is that the archers *can* blanket one area, and whatever lancers in that area will take disproportionate casualties.

"That's probably the best plan for a sowshit situation," says Kortyl.

"First and Third Companies will make the early attack," Fraadn declares. "Then we'll see how matters develop." He pauses. "Any questions?"

"Don't know enough for questions," grumbles Craavyl.

Rynst rolls his eyes, but says nothing.

Fraadn looks to Alyiakal. "Keep the fort gate closed."

"Yes, ser." *Not that it will do much good against a device, if it comes to that.*

As he rides back to the fort in the deepening twilight, Alyiakal can't help but wonder exactly how the Kyphrans intend to use their device and how quickly they can replenish the device's chaos. It's taken him more than a full day to not quite fill the reservoir.

You'll find out sooner than you'd like.

XCIII

Alyiakal sleeps moderately well, until about a glass before dawn when he suddenly wakes. He quickly rises from where he has been sleeping under the awning. The fort remains silent, but extending his senses, he discerns lancers riding eastward, past the fort, and toward the Kyphran encampment.

Since he doubts he'll sleep, he begins to get ready for the day. The first thing he needs to do is move the device into a position from which he can take aim on the Kyphrans, something he should have considered earlier, and hadn't.

He takes a deep breath and goes to find Torkaal. Not surprisingly, the senior squad leader is already checking the wall sentries, and Alyiakal meets him beside the gate.

"Good morning, ser. Are we headed out?"

"Not yet. We need to build a stone platform for the device somewhere on the east wall, south of the gate, but not too close. It should be about two yards high, so the nozzle of the device sits above the wall. Stack stone on the wall so no one can see it or anyone around it. I'd judge we have less than two glasses to get it done. The men can take loose stones from any wall but the eastern one."

"Does that device really work, ser?"

"I managed to get it to work once. Let's hope we can do it again. Now, let's take a look at the wall south of the gate."

In less than a quint, Sixth Company lancers are lugging stones to the location Torkaal and Alyiakal chose some ten yards from the gate.

"What if you can't get it to work again?" asks Torkaal.

"I can get it to work. The question is whether it will work well enough. I'm fairly certain that the Kyphrans have mages to replenish their firecannon. The armored wagon may be to shield them as well as the firecannon."

"A real firecannon?"

Alyiakal shrugs. "I think it's a device to cut stone, but something like that can cut through anything, and it'll be used as a firecannon."

"Why didn't they work to get into the other chamber?"

"I don't know," says Alyiakal, which is true enough. He's fairly sure that it didn't take the Kyphrans seasons to break through the wall, nor did they lack the time to work on the second chamber after they learned what was in the first. Still, it definitely had to have taken them more time than the lancers, given what Alyiakal has sensed. He's not about to volunteer information because the follow-up question would be how the lancers broke into the second chamber so quickly.

"How soon before we'll be called into action, do you think?"

"That depends on how much damage First and Third Companies inflict on the Kyphrans." *And how many casualties the Kyphrans inflict on them.*

"When do you think the Kyphrans will start using their firecannon?"

"Sometime today, when they realize they can't retake the area without using it. All firecannon have limited ranges and need replenishment. I'm guessing, but I think that's why they haven't used it yet."

"That why you haven't tried to use the one here?"

"Partly. We also don't have an easy way to transport and aim it. It wasn't meant for use as a firecannon." *And you're hoping that you can use order to compensate for that.*

"Just our luck," says Torkaal dourly.

Even with forty-some lancers carrying and placing the large stones from ruined walls and other sources, almost two glasses pass before they complete the rough platform. Alyiakal uses the time to saddle and ready the gelding and to funnel more coiled and compressed chaos into the device's reservoir. Once the platform is complete, the lancers carry the device there, and Alyiakal climbs up beside it. Alternating between standing and sitting on the platform next to the device, as well as looking to the east, he cannot see the Kyphrans.

Another quint goes by, and Alyiakal notices a lancer galloping up the fort road. The lancer rides toward the gate, not the encampment, and Alyiakal hurries off the platform, leaving Fhaquar to guard the device.

The lancers at the gate open it enough for a single rider. He walks his horse straight to Alyiakal, but does not dismount.

"Captain, ser. From Captain Fraadn. First and Third Companies are disengaging and withdrawing. Captain Fraadn said to tell you that they have a firecannon in the armored wagon. They open a panel, and a thin chaos bolt comes out, turning anything in its path to ashes. They've also found more archers. Between the firecannon and the archers, neither company can effectively attack any longer. The plan is to pull back and use firelances from locations secure from the firecannon and out of arrow range. You're to use your discretion in defending the fort. That's all, ser."

"How fast are the Kyphrans moving?"

"At a walk, ser. The armored wagon is slow."

"Can't they attack the horses pulling the wagon?" asks Alyiakal.

"No, ser. The horses are hitched behind it and the armor." Before Alyiakal can say or ask more, the ranker says, "Ser, I have orders to convey to Captain Kortyl."

"To get the mounts back and away from the front part of the picketing area and to choose the best positions to use firelances on foot?"

"Yes, ser. If you'll—"

"Go!" returns Alyiakal, gesturing to the lancers working the gate to open it for the lancer.

"Thank you, ser."

Even before the lancer is through the gate, Torkaal is at Alyiakal's side.

"Things aren't going well for First and Third Companies," Alyiakal says before relaying the lancer's report. "When the Kyphrans get nearer, we'll need to make quick decisions. If they lead with their foot, we need lancers with firelances all along the east wall, but not close to either side of the gate. They'll be sparing with the firecannon, but they'll certainly use it to destroy the gate."

"So we just sit tight and wait?"

"One way or another, Sixth Company is going to see plenty of action before this is over," replies Alyiakal.

"Be happier if we were attacking, ser."

"Not against a firecannon. Let them come to us."

"Stone isn't any protection. Look at what they did to the walls in that old building."

Alyiakal shakes his head. "The dissidents had devices like the ones we have and the Kyphrans have. The First had something stronger. Stone should protect us unless they keep aiming at the same spot. The idea is to make them use up all their chaos while not losing many men." *You just hope that's a workable tactic.*

"Never thought about the First that way," says Torkaal, not quite grudgingly.

"They were far more brutal than the stories and records reveal. Now, pass the word to the other squad leaders and the men. We'll likely have a glass before the armored wagon is close enough to attack."

"Yes, ser."

Alyiakal climbs back up to the stone platform and looks at the several courses of stone that the lancers laid on the top of the wall around the device to shield it from view of the road, stones that can still be pushed out of the way when the time comes, another reason why Fhaquar is on the platform with Alyiakal.

More than a quint passes before Alyiakal catches sight of the withdrawing lancers. First Company nears the fort and continues along the road, toward the Mirror Lancer encampment, followed by Third Company, while Fraadn turns his mount toward the gate.

Alyiakal hurries down, gesturing for the lancers at the gate to admit the senior captain. Fraadn reins up inside the gate and Alyiakal reaches his mount in moments.

"They definitively have something like a firecannon. It may have a range of around three hundred yards if they keep the chaos narrow. Maybe two hundred fifty yards when it's wider. At that range, it's a little stronger than a firelance. They're trying not to use it except when they can target multiple lancers. Rynst tried to outmaneuver them with an oblique attack. They wiped out him and an entire squad."

Alyiakal winces.

"I told him to keep his men spread out. They weren't wide enough. I've lost eight men, and three more are wounded. Can you hold them off and make them use all their chaos? If they didn't have it and the extra archers . . ."

"They kept more archers in reserve?"

"It looks that way."

"We'll do all we can to whittle them down and run through their chaos."

"Good. You're on your own." With that, Fraadn turns his mount and rides out through the gate.

After two men close and bar the gate, Alyiakal addresses the lancers. "To the walls with your firelances. Stay at least five yards from the sides of the gate." Then he walks to Torkaal and relays what Fraadn has told him.

The senior squad leader nods. "Hope these walls are stronger than I think."

"They're not," replies Alyiakal, "but they don't have to be. They'll hold up against chaos better than against a catapult, and the Kyphrans don't have a catapult."

"That's some comfort," says Torkaal, "but not much."

"I need to see what I can do from the platform. Have everyone ready to use firelances. If I order 'Down!' get every man off the walls. They'll need to be ready to take the wall again as quickly as possible. I'm wagering that they'll use the firecannon to destroy the gate, then charge."

"Yes, ser."

Alyiakal returns to his perch on the stone platform, looking eastward. He already sees a faint haze of dust from the road. In less than a quint, he can make out a foot vanguard with two riders near the head of the column, followed by the awkward-looking armored wagon that looks as though it is rolling forward without horses.

He studies the wagon, noting the armored wheel guards on the front and sides and the slight gap between the armor's edge and the ground. The wheel is doubtless completely iron-bound, rather than just iron-banded, which would block the chaos from a firelance. All that explains the slow pace.

How can they possibly guide such an unwieldy monster?

After a moment, Alyiakal decides that the wagon has been pulled traditionally until that morning, when much of the armor was fastened in place. The road from the stone pier is far too rough, and the wagon would have hung up on something every hundred yards or so.

Almost four quints pass before the armored wagon reaches a point roughly three hundred yards east of the gate. From there it leaves the road and creeps across the uneven ground toward the fort.

Then at little more than two hundred yards, the monster wagon halts, and the vanguard splits, falling back, half to one side of the wagon, half to the other. Alyiakal can see archers, perhaps two squads' worth, one squad behind each vanguard, along with two foot companies behind the archers, and another, possibly two, farther back.

Two iron-armored panels part, but with little more than a cubit between them, and, as they part, Alyiakal can sense chaos behind them, but not how much.

Hssst! A momentary flickering line of chaos flares from between the armored panels of the wagon and strikes the stone on the north side of the gate, where a hot mist rises from the stone and a few molten droplets of liquid stone drop onto the sandy ground at the base of the outer wall.

Several moments pass before a second quick line of chaos strikes the wall just north of the side of the gate. Alyiakal senses the chaos, but it strikes and vanishes before he can even attempt a shield.

Which wouldn't be the wisest course, anyway.

Knowing what has to come next, Alyiakal says to Fhaquar, "When I yell 'Now!' push away those stones in front of the device. Make sure that they go off the wall away from us, or we both could end up ashes."

"Yes, ser."

The third flicker of chaos strikes the middle of the gate, etching a line of fire that subsides into smoke, Alyiakal knows, only because the chaos blast is so brief. He also knows that the next one will likely obliterate the gate.

The moment Alyiakal senses the concentration of chaos building in the armored wagon, he snaps, "Now!"

In moments, the stacked stones are gone and Alyiakal's fingers are on the lever, as he concentrates on sending his own chaos knife through the narrow opening between the armored panels.

The chaos blast from the armored wagon strikes the gate, and the yard-wide wave turns the wood to ashes, flame, and steam, and a line of blistering heat sears across the courtyard until it strikes the half walls of the ruined building and jets upward.

Alyiakal's return blast knifes through the armored panels, and he senses one death mist—as well as the shield of a strong mage. That mage somehow aims the Kyphran device toward Alyiakal, and chaos flares off Alyiakal's shields.

Grimly intent, Alyiakal sends a second knife-edged blast, and a third. With the third, the other mage's shields collapse, and Alyiakal senses the death mist. Alyiakal also senses that the Kyphran device also still holds chaos. So, the next chaos knife slams into the small section of the right iron-bound wheel.

Nothing obvious happens. Alyiakal tries a second blast, then a third, and a fourth.

The armored wagon explodes, strewing shreds and chunks of armor and wagon in all directions, cutting through the vanguard like hundreds of knives and taking out most of the archers.

Alyiakal tries sending another blast of chaos at the Kyphrans, only to realize that there's no chaos left in the device.

"What happened?" asks Fhaquar.

Alyiakal immediately recognizes that, with all the chaos bursts, Fhaquar has no real understanding of who has done what with the chaos. "The device sent a blast of chaos at the Kyphran armored wagon. Then everything exploded." As he finishes those words, another realization strikes him. *Sixth Company is the reserve!*

He immediately orders, "Sixth Company! Mount up! Now!" Scrambling down from the stone platform, followed by Fhaquar, Alyiakal sprints through the lingering wall of heat from the Kyphran blast and mounts the chestnut.

Despite his best efforts, almost half a quint passes before he and Torkaal lead Sixth Company—or most of it—out through where the gate had been.

By then First Company, with Fraadn in the first rank, is a good hundred yards east of Sixth Company and charging toward the Kyphran foot companies.

"Sixth Company! Forward!" orders Alyiakal, knowing that the Kyphrans' disorganization won't last and that, even with firelances, First Company will be in trouble without rapid reinforcement.

The foot troopers turn to face First Company, whose firelances begin to decimate their ranks.

Abruptly, a majority of the first two ranks of First Company vanish in a wave of flame. Alyiakal blinks, then sees, slightly to the east, ten or so Kyphran troopers on foot, bearing short lances that throw chaos.

Just like the old firelances in the chamber. Before Alyiakal can yell a warning, the ten continue to fire near-continuous blasts at the oncoming lancers.

Alyiakal concentrates, then triggers his lance and forces a thin line of chaos across the Kyphran troopers with the firelances.

Instantly, he feels as though his head splits, but he concentrates on leading Sixth Company through the remnants of the leading foot company, using quick blasts from his firelance to hit anything in pale green that moves, and then on to the next company, ignoring impacts on his shield.

"Ser! Ser!"

Torkaal's penetrating voice forces Alyiakal to turn and look.

"There aren't any more Kyphrans, except the wounded, those who surrendered, and those who ran. Second and Fourth Companies took care of the rear foot."

"Then we need to head back." Alyiakal knows he's not thinking as well as he should be; his head is pounding. He's angry that he didn't consider that a mage who could charge an old stonecutter with chaos and turn it into a firecannon could also charge the old firelances. "How many more did we lose?"

"One, ser. Fraelt, third squad. One of the last archers got him. Saavacol and third squad took out all the others. The other lancer companies . . . they didn't do as well."

After hearing about Rynst and seeing what happened to Fraadn and First Company, Alyiakal isn't surprised, yet what Torkaal says doesn't seem quite real, even as Alyiakal understands that the Mirror Lancer deaths are a very real fact.

When Alyiakal nears the remnants where the armored wagon had been, he looks twice, because all that remains is a blackened circle surrounded by scattered metal.

"What happened to their wagon and device?" Torkaal asks, his voice puzzled. "I heard the explosion, but there should be more left."

"Maybe something went wrong." That's about all that Alyiakal can think of to say. "We might as well go back to the fort." Alyiakal tries not to sway in the saddle.

"Before you go anywhere, you need some water, ser. And something to eat."

Alyiakal starts to object, then fumbles for his water bottle, trying to control the shaking in his hands. He barely manages to hold on to it and take a bite of trail biscuit. His hands aren't shaking when he finishes the second biscuit, but he's still light-headed as he and Torkaal lead Sixth Company back toward the fort.

"Only one casualty? Is that right?" asks Alyiakal.

"From the fighting, ser. We lost Escalyn to the chaos blast that took out the gate. He was looking over one of the half walls opposite."

"That's more than thirty yards."

"Heat and splinters hit him in the face, ser. Hit him hard."

Alyiakal starts to shake his head, then stops as he feels the light-headedness increase.

Torkaal looks to his left and says quietly, "Here comes Captain Kortyl, ser."

Alyiakal keeps riding toward the opening that had once held the gate. "He can come to us."

Alyiakal's head feels different, besides the light-headedness, and he reaches up to straighten his visor cap, then realizes that he's no longer wearing it. His fingers feel damp. He looks at them and sees blood, then drops his hand as Kortyl calls out, "Where are you going?"

"Company! Halt!" Alyiakal orders, then reins up the chestnut and waits for Kortyl to join him. When Kortyl reins up, Alyiakal replies, "Back to the fort."

The senior captain looks from Alyiakal to Torkaal and back to Alyiakal, then asks, "Why are you headed back now?"

"Because the fight's over, and the fort's still the responsibility of Sixth Company. We held the fort, and we were the first company to support First Company's attack on the Kyphrans."

For a moment, Kortyl does not reply. Then he says, his voice edged, "Some of the lancers from First Company said that the Kyphrans used firelances against them. How did that happen?"

"They had firelances like those in the chamber we opened," replies Alyiakal. "You can probably find them among the bodies. We couldn't get close enough, fast enough, to stop them from hitting First Company, but we made sure they didn't hit anyone else."

Kortyl looks at Alyiakal. "There weren't any survivors from the vanguard, the archers, and the first two companies. Was that necessary?"

Alyiakal looks back. "There wouldn't have been any Mirror Lancer survivors if their firecannon hadn't exploded. Even so, it was close. I don't want to fight the Kyphrans again. Ever. Make the survivors from the last Kyphran companies throw the bodies over the cliffs." Alyiakal adds, quietly, "I'd recommend that, ser."

Kortyl looks away for a moment, then returns his eyes to Alyiakal. "Get something to eat. You look like sowshit, Captain. We'll talk later."

"We will," replies Alyiakal evenly, "when I feel less like sowshit."

Kortyl turns his mount and heads northeast, presumably back toward his company.

Alyiakal gestures, then orders, "Sixth Company! Forward!"

XCIV

After returning to the fort and making sure there are no new wounded Sixth Company lancers, Alyiakal takes time to eat, not particularly well, since what he consumes is mutton jerky, trail biscuits, and a fair amount of order-dusted water. Then he washes the blood out of his hair and off his face, realizing that it's only a glass or so past midday.

He's barely finished checking with Maelt and Vaekyn about the condition of lancers in second and third squad, and, belatedly, ordering the device returned to its original chamber, when Kortyl rides into the fort, leading a second horse, saddled but riderless. He dismounts and hands the reins of both horses to the nearest lancer before walking across the courtyard, visor cap in hand, to where

Alyiakal stands waiting. He extends the visor cap. "I believe this might be yours."

"Thank you. You didn't have to make a special trip for that."

"Since Fraadn is no longer the senior captain," says Kortyl politely, "I need to send a report to Majer Jaavor detailing what occurred here."

"I'd suggest sending the report to Subcommander Laartol," replies Alyiakal.

"Jaavor will insist on seeing it first, and it should go up the chain of command."

"That's your decision," says Alyiakal.

"You don't like Jaavor, do you?"

"It's not whether I like him. It's whether *you* trust him. Personally, I'd prefer sending it with a lancer ordered to give it to the subcommander."

"Jaavor would countermand that order."

"I'm sure he would, but Subcommander Laartol might ask why if Jaavor presents him with a report from the surviving senior captain addressed to the subcommander. That is, of course, your decision as the senior captain." Alyiakal hesitates slightly, then asks, "How can I help you with the report?"

"Just tell me what happened here at the fort and in the field with Sixth Company."

Alyiakal begins with hearing First and Third Companies leaving to engage the Kyphrans, reporting the facts up to the point where the Kyphran mage began to range and target the gate.

"How do you know he was a mage?" asks Kortyl.

"I don't *know*, but I don't know anyone else, except maybe a Mirror Engineer, who would be able to replenish chaos in such a device or in firelances."

"Weren't you working on that?" asks Kortyl.

Kortyl's response confirms what Alyiakal has suspected—that Fraadn had indeed kept Alyiakal's small initial success with the device to himself. "I was. I got one blast of chaos out of the device, but that made the Kyphran mage, or whomever, more determined. He sent more chaos our way, and . . . and then the armored wagon exploded. Since Sixth Company was the reserve company and since the device was useless, we immediately mounted up and rode after First Company." From that point, what Alyiakal relates is precisely as he recalls it. When he finishes, he says, "That's about it," and looks to Kortyl.

"How did you manage to get all the Kyphrans with the firelances?"

"We rode toward them, and kept targeting them until there weren't any more."

"The second squad leader in First Company said you wiped them out in moments from more than a hundred yards away."

"I don't know how long it took." *Not precisely.* "I was angel-fired mad at the bastards."

"Apparently," says Kortyl dryly. "From the way you look and likely feel, that's understandable. Still, are you up to doing some field healing?"

"I can do that."

"Good. I brought a spare mount. After everything, I thought it might be best. I can ask a few more questions while we ride back. That way, I can get matters clearer in my head."

"Let me get my satchel, and I'll be right with you." Alyiakal hopes his head is clear enough that he doesn't make any mistakes in treating the wounded from the other companies. He also worries a bit about Kortyl's "few more questions."

The additional questions are an effort to get Alyiakal to provide more details about matters that occurred so quickly that he's already told Kortyl what he knows, but the older officer doesn't appear upset or irritated at Alyiakal's repetitions and restatements.

Once at the encampment, Alyiakal starts with the First Company wounded. The first several lancers he examines will likely survive, but he re-dresses the wounds, adding small bits of order and removing tiny points of whitish red that might have grown larger and more dangerous.

The third lancer, Gaarlynt, has a chest wound from an arrow, which has been dressed, but he has trouble breathing, with a trace of blue in his lips. Alyiakal looks for a moment, trying to recall what to do. He remembers Healer Vayidra talking about it, about the need to seal the chest so that the lung doesn't collapse further. Then he recalls. While he doesn't have any way to remove fluids, not without equipment, he can use order to create a temporary seal that will last for a short while, and if he keeps doing it . . .

He re-dresses the wound in a way to allow what he needs to do next before slowly positioning the bits of order to create the seal, then adds a few more tiny bits of order to deal with the deeper wound chaos.

He turns to Kortyl. "I'll need to see him several times a day."

The lancer whose wound he has just dressed and sealed looks at him and says, barely gasping out the words, "Begging your pardon . . . ser . . . but you look . . . like you . . . use a healer yourself."

Alyiakal manages a smile. "We'll get to that later, Gaarlynt."

"The Second and Third Company wounded are over there," says Kortyl, gesturing.

Once they're well away from the first group, Kortyl says quietly, "The last one won't make it, will he?"

"He has a chance," replies Alyiakal. "I did what I could to seal the wound, but I'll need to check him often."

The next lancer is unconscious, barely breathing, with severe gut wounds and chaos running through his body. Alyiakal turns to Kortyl, shakes his head, and moves on to the next man.

Almost two glasses later, Alyiakal returns to the fort, light-headed, after dealing with another chest wound worse than the first, and a range of other injuries, including a broken arm and a broken leg. His head throbs, and the dizziness has returned. He lies down on his pallet and lets the darkness sweep over him, a darkness that alternates heat and chill, and words he struggles to hear, but cannot comprehend even when he does finally hear them.

Then there is silence, and twilight, before, somewhere in the twilight, Alyiakal hears noises.

Rain? Vulcrows gloating over carrion?

Then the noises resolve into whispers.

". . . you wake him . . . frigging scary . . . never misses with the firelance . . . Captain Kortyl practically shit in the saddle when the captain looked at him . . ."

". . . not that scary . . . takes care of us . . ."

"Here comes the senior squad leader."

Rather than say anything immediately, Alyiakal coughs, then slowly sits up, realizing that it is indeed twilight and that he hadn't dreamed it. *Or you dreamed it, and it's twilight anyway.*

While no longer light-headed, he's definitely sore and stiff in more places than he can count, but he slowly gets to his feet.

On the other side of the half wall, beside Torkaal, stands a ranker Alyiakal doesn't recognize.

"Ser," says Torkaal. "Captain Kortyl requests that you take a look at some of the wounded."

Frig, frig, frig! You slept too long. "I'll be right there."

After taking care of a few necessities, Alyiakal heads for the northeast corner of the fort, but finds Fhaquar and Saavacol mounted and leading the chestnut, already saddled, toward him.

"The senior squad leader thought this would make it quicker, ser," says Fhaquar.

Saavacol nods, but says nothing.

"Thank you. I was a little tired."

"One way of putting it, ser," replies Fhaquar in a genially dry tone of voice. After Alyiakal mounts, Fhaquar hands him a leather pouch. "Some dried fruit, ser. And your water bottle is full."

"I appreciate it." Alyiakal tucks the pouch inside his riding jacket and takes out the water bottle, opens it, and infuses it with a bit of order before taking a swallow. Then he replaces the bottle in its holder and urges the chestnut toward the gateless opening. As he rides out, he smells the odor of charred men and mounts—and ashes. Even so, he forces himself to eat morsels of the dried fruit, chewing and swallowing, thinking about all the death and destruction, much of which he created. *Not that you had much choice.* Not if he wanted to keep the

Mirror Lancer force from being destroyed and, more than incidentally, survive the fight.

While he understands the need for Cyador to keep Kyphros from taking Guarstyad, he doesn't understand why the First destroyed the dissidents and their outpost rather than maintaining the buildings and the old road. *Or were they so short of Mirror Lancers and equipment they felt they couldn't maintain it—and counted on the arid high plains as a barrier to Kyphran incursion?*

Whatever the reason, the First only passed down the cost a few generations, and Alyiakal finds himself angered by their shortsightedness. He says nothing, but continues to chew and swallow the dried fruit, interspersed with swallows of water on the short ride to the encampment.

Once there, he hurries toward Gaarlynt, the first lancer with a chest wound.

As he suspected, the order-based seal is beginning to give way. He partly re-dresses the wound and strengthens the seal, enough, he hopes, to at least last through the night, and infuses it with a bit more order. Then he moves to the other lancer with a chest wound, whose breathing is labored, doing much the same as with Gaarlynt. He steps back and watches. He thinks that the lancer is breathing a little easier.

After that, since he is already at the encampment, he checks the other wounded, and learns that the lancer with the gut wounds has died.

When he finishes, he turns to walk back to where Fhaquar and Saavacol wait with his mount.

At that moment, Kortyl arrives. "Oh, you are here."

"I've seen to the wounded. The two with chest wounds are breathing a little easier. There's nothing more I can do right now."

"Why weren't you here earlier?"

"First, no one told me I was needed. Second, I was exhausted from everything else I did over the last few days, and I collapsed." *Like saving your arrogant ass.*

"We all fought."

"Except First, Third, and Sixth Companies fought more and longer, and that might have a bit to do with the exhaustion."

Kortyl says nothing.

Alyiakal looks hard at the older officer and adds, quietly, but firmly, "You might want to think about that, ser."

Then he turns and walks away, wondering if he should have put a chaos bolt through Kortyl just before the battle ended. *Except you were too tired and confused to think of that. Besides, that would have left Craavyl in command, which might be even worse.*

He shakes his head, thinking about how the entire campaign has caused the death of the two more competent officers and hasn't touched the two least competent.

They are competent. They're just too arrogant to be much more than merely competent.

He's still thinking about the matter when he reaches the fort.

XCV

For the next few days, Alyiakal manages to avoid Kortyl without seeming to do so, although he uses a concealment once, partly because he's still angry and partly because he worries that he'll say worse than he already has.

He continues to monitor and quietly heal the various wounded. But, despite all he has tried, the lancer with the deeper chest wound, whose name he never learned, succumbs to widespread wound chaos, while the other—Gaarlynt—appears to be on the way to recovery, albeit a lengthy recovery, Alyiakal suspects.

By eightday, the smaller bruises on Alyiakal's face have largely healed, but two have only faded to a yellowish purple, and he's discovered that the scalp wound that had bled so profusely actually extended to the side of his forehead, and will likely leave at least a slight scar.

On oneday, Alyiakal has just finished dealing with Gaarlynt when Kortyl appears.

"Ser," offers Alyiakal politely.

"You're a hard man to find," says Kortyl genially, a geniality that Alyiakal can tell is only superficial.

"Subcommander Laartol ordered me to keep my interactions with the lancers in other companies brief and to deal with them in strictly healing terms and to avoid unnecessary contact with either other lancers or officers in such companies. I've found that following his recommendations is a good idea."

"Following the recommendations of knowledgeable senior officers is always prudent," replies Kortyl.

Alyiakal keeps a pleasant expression and waits for Kortyl to say more.

"You know, it's rather amazing," says Kortyl after a moment. "You're supposedly only a field healer, but only three lancers you've treated have died. Are you sure there aren't any healers in your family?"

"I know of none. Both my parents were only children, and the only other relative that I ever knew was my great-aunt, and she wasn't a healer. I did have the good fortune to work for and get instruction from a Magi'i healer at Syadtar while waiting for lancer replacements. She was much older and very experienced, and I learned a great deal in a short time."

"We're all fortunate for that." Kortyl's words are not quite perfunctory. "Especially the wounded."

"I did my best," says Alyiakal, trying not to sound wary, although he definitely feels that way.

"You certainly did." Kortyl pauses only briefly before continuing. "After all that we've been through here, it seems almost a shame for us to return to Guarstyad and then wait for the Kyphrans to make another attack. Any ruler willing to lose so many ships and men isn't going to give up easily."

Alyiakal has an idea of what Kortyl has in mind. "I'd have to agree with you."

"We lost over a hundred lancers, as well as two captains, and had more than fifty wounded. That's the most lancers lost in a single campaign in decades."

"It cost them well over twelve hundred men," Alyiakal replies. "That doesn't include deaths, casualties, and damage from whatever the fireships inflicted."

"Does that suggest something to you?"

Besides the fact that you have something in mind? "It shows that the Duke of Kyphros should be wary of the Mirror Lancers."

"That's if the Mirror Lancers are based where they can act effectively."

"You're suggesting that we should have a base here?" asks Alyiakal, knowing that is exactly what Kortyl wants him to say.

"What else is likely to stop them?"

Alyiakal frowns. "There's the question of supplying such a base."

"There is," agrees Kortyl, "but even if you couldn't get that device to work the way the Kyphrans got theirs to work, I'm certain that the Mirror Engineers could. If they can't, they have similar devices, and they could remove the gaps in the original road. That would resolve the supply problem."

"I imagine it would," says Alyiakal.

"Of course, such a base would need a captain familiar with the Kyphrans and one with a reputation for the efficient use of lancers with minimal losses. One with healing experience would be even better, though."

"You're not suggesting . . . ? What about you? You're more senior."

"Guarstyad will need a new senior captain, and you're far more suited to be in command here. In fact, I recommended that in the report and dispatch to Subcommander Laartol. He'd already mentioned to me the possibility that the Mirror Engineers might wish to repair the old road, and that would require at least a lancer company to remain while those repairs were in progress. Building a small fortified base before the blocked point of the old road wouldn't take that much longer."

Alyiakal manages to look disconcerted, which isn't difficult, because he can't believe that Kortyl is suggesting that Alyiakal remain, even though he understands Kortyl's scheme. "I wouldn't want you to lose—"

"You're definitely the best one to be here. Craavyl, now, he's a good officer, but he's not decisive enough yet."

Meaning that you don't think he's as good at killing Kyphrans and that he won't give you trouble in Guarstyad. Alyiakal frowns again, then asks, "What about Overcaptain Shenklyn? He knows logistics."

"He's on his last tour, and he'll be more effective in handling logistics from Guarstyad." Kortyl shrugs. "I made the recommendation. It's up to the subcommander—and Mirror Lancer headquarters—to decide how to handle the Kyphrans. It seems clear to me, and it will to the subcommander as well, that not having a force in position to deal with the Kyphrans would be a mistake. A very large mistake."

"That seems obvious to us," agrees Alyiakal, "but will it to Mirror Lancer headquarters?"

"I'd say so, but the Majer-Commander will be the one to decide. I did want you to know that I recommended you for command here."

"That was very thoughtful," says Alyiakal. *Thoughtfully designed to consign me to a long and boring tour watching the plains grass grow, given that it will be a while before the Kyphrans recover from this campaign.*

"I do hope so," replies Kortyl, smiling pleasantly. "I won't keep you longer."

"I appreciate your letting me know."

"You'll have time to think about it. I imagine we'll see Mirror Engineers here well before we know what the Majer-Commander decides."

Alyiakal has no doubt that at least one of the Magi'i and a few Mirror Engineers will arrive, if only to inspect the remaining devices and the original road. *Whether they'll do more than that is another question.*

"Until later," says Kortyl with a smile before turning away.

"Until then," replies Alyiakal.

XCVI

Late on threeday afternoon, more than two eightdays after the fighting ended, an afternoon warm enough that Alyiakal has the feeling the Summer on the high plains of west Kyphros will be even hotter than Summers at Pemedra, Kortyl appears at the fort, looking as genial as ever. Alyiakal walks from where he has been brushing the chestnut to meet the senior captain, motioning for the nearest ranker, who happens to be Vuurnyn, to accompany him.

Kortyl dismounts, hands the reins of his mount to Vuurnyn, and extends a sealed envelope to Alyiakal. He says in a pleasant voice, "We need to talk."

Alyiakal senses neither malice nor arrogance, which surprises him. He gestures. "It's a little cooler under the awning."

The two officers cross the courtyard, which now shows almost no traces of the recent battle, except for the continued absence of a gate.

Once in the limited shade, Kortyl says, "The Majer-Commander has decided to accept our recommendation to establish a post. An eightday from now, we, or rather you, will ensure that the stone pier is secure and that all available wagons are there to offload food and other supplies necessary for the Mirror Engineers to begin construction of the post and repairs to the old road to Guarstyad. Once those supplies and Mirror Engineers are safely established, Second and Fourth Companies will withdraw and return to Guarstyad. I imagine that envelope contains your orders as the officer in charge of Oldroad Post, which will take effect immediately upon the departure of Second and Fourth Companies." Kortyl offers an amused smile.

"What about First and Third Companies?" asks Alyiakal.

"As I understand it, from my instructions from the subcommander, the lancers remaining from First and Third Companies will be added to your contingent, in order to form a second company. I suggest you open the envelope. It might clarify matters."

Alyiakal does. Inside are a note and two other documents.

The note reads:

Rarely does the son of an exceptional officer exceed his sire's accomplishments. You have that potential. Do not waste it.

The signature is simply "Laartol."

Alyiakal swallows, then begins to read the next document, which appoints him as officer in charge of establishing and maintaining a Mirror Lancer post, to be known as Oldroad Post, upon or near the east end of the road dating back to the founding of Cyador, with two companies under his command. As officer in charge of Oldroad Post, he will report directly to the subcommander of Guarstyad Post. He is also directed to appoint Senior Squad Leader Torkaal as a provisional undercaptain in command of the Second Company at Oldroad Post.

The third document is the longest, detailing the requirements for receiving and transporting supplies, Mirror Engineers, supporting Magi'i, and engineer rankers.

Alyiakal lowers the documents and looks to Kortyl. "You set this up very well. Congratulations . . . and thank you."

Kortyl looks back evenly. "I don't like you personally. I likely never will. But you give everything you have to do what's necessary. I'd trust my life and any men I command to you. That's more important than what I feel."

Alyiakal smiles wryly. "Isn't that what being a lancer officer is all about?"

Kortyl actually smiles back. "For those who are truly lancer officers."

XCVII

Dealing with the incoming supplies takes longer than planned, but not that much longer, and on fiveday of the tenth eightday of Spring, Alyiakal and all the able-bodied lancers of Sixth Company, soon to become First Company of Oldroad Post, hold the stone pier slightly less than twenty kays from the Kyphran fort. With the company are all seven wagons and four spare mounts.

As the fireship slowly approaches, its side firecannon trained on the pier where Alyiakal stands with the lancers of third squad, Alyiakal catches sight of the nameplate—KIEF—and he smiles.

"Ser?" asks Vaekyn, the new senior squad leader, since recently appointed Undercaptain Torkaal remains at the fort working to combine the surviving lancers from First and Third Companies into the new Second Company.

"It's the same fireship that brought me to Guarstyad. I knew the *Rylaan* and the *Kief* will be alternating supply runs for some time, but I didn't know which one would arrive first."

Before that long, Alyiakal walks to where the crew positions a gangway and waits, holding his strongest shields behind the camouflage shield recommended so many years before by Healer Vayidra. Once the gangway is in place, Alyiakal walks up to the edge of the quarterdeck. He remembers the older undercaptain—or sublieutenant—and asks, "Permission to come aboard, Sublieutenant Naartyn?"

For a moment, Naartyn appears nonplussed. "I'm afraid—"

"Alyiakal. The *Kief* took me to Guarstyad."

"You're the lancer captain in charge of the new post the engineers will be building?"

"For better or worse. We brought every wagon we have. That's seven."

"Oh, permission granted. The Mirror Engineers and the Magi'i are waiting for you in the wardroom."

Alyiakal follows Naartyn from the quarterdeck.

While there are four men waiting in the wardroom—two Mirror Engineers, one a sub-majer and one an undercaptain, and two Magi'i—the two white-clad Magi'i step forward, each roughly ten years older than Alyiakal.

Naartyn immediately says, "This is Magus Thiaphyl, and Magus Ataphi. And this is Captain Alyiakal. When you're ready to begin offloading, please let me know." With that, Naartyn quickly slips from the wardroom.

Alyiakal can sense the probing of his camouflage shield, but says nothing, as if he were totally unaware.

"Amazing," says Ataphi. "Natural shield, elevated levels of order, but not excessive."

"Agreed," adds Thiaphyl. "Certain sense of healing."

"What might be amazing that you both agree upon," asks Alyiakal politely, "besides the fact that I have a slight talent for healing? If I might ask?"

"We wondered, since you were the one who discovered the old road and found a device, if you had . . . other abilities."

"I was screened at Kynstaar and later by the Third Magus when he interviewed all the officers at Geliendra." Alyiakal smiles wryly. "I wanted to be a magus when I was a boy, but I was told that I didn't have the right abilities. Apparently, I still don't."

"The device," says Ataphi quickly, "was it destroyed?"

Alyiakal shakes his head. "The Kyphran device—I think it had to be a device because it instantly turned the solid-wood gate of the fort to ashes—it somehow exploded. I'd hoped to discover how the device we found works or worked, but . . ." He shrugs, keeping his feelings well behind his inner shield.

"You still have it?" asks Ataphi.

"The one we found? Oh, yes, with another device that might be a cart and possibly a half score old firelances. Did you know that the Kyphrans had a half score as well? They killed more than an entire squad before we took them out."

"Do you have those?" asks Thiaphyl.

"They're not all intact, but I believe we have them all. They're all under guard."

"Excellent, excellent. At the very least, it will be interesting to see the differences in design."

The Mirror Engineer sub-majer clears his throat and says quietly, "We have a long ride, honored Magi'i, on which you can certainly interrogate the captain."

"We apologize," declares Thiaphyl, in a tone that has no trace of apology. "We would not wish to delay matters."

Alyiakal turns. "Sub-Majer, we brought seven wagons. That's all we have, along with four spare mounts. We have most of a company for protection as well."

"Most?"

"We lost over a hundred lancers, and there are almost fifty wounded." Alyiakal offers a polite smile. "The Kyphrans landed over fifteen hundred archers and troopers along with what amounted to a working firecannon. I doubt a handful of Kyphran troopers are still alive."

The undercaptain Mirror Engineer stiffens.

"We're ready to help with the offloading and loading the wagons. I have a squad standing by on the pier." Alyiakal pauses, then adds, "I understand that after we have offloaded everything, the *Kief* will transport a squad of engineer rankers to the cove below where the base will be established and will use boats to ferry them ashore. Is that correct?"

"It is."

"It's a long hike up the cliffs, but will be somewhat easier, and take far less time, than walking or riding nearly twenty kays."

The two Magi'i exchange glances.

The Mirror Engineer sub-majer turns back to them. "If you're willing to entrust your equipment . . . ?"

Ataphi immediately shakes his head. "The orders of the Third Magus were most explicit."

Having met the Third Magus, if briefly, Alyiakal can believe that. He also can see that escorting cargoes and Mirror Engineers, and their equipment, is going to be a long and tedious process.

And that's even before the new base is built.

But it is an independent—mostly—command.

XCVIII

On sixday of the fifth eightday of Summer, Alyiakal stands looking westward from the east end of the old road, watching as the Mirror Engineers continue to remove the melted rock barrier, the first step in rebuilding and reopening the more secure and safer route between Guarstyad and Kyphros. Behind him, and to his right, is the stone building partly cut into the rock but largely built of local stone cut by the engineers, a building with barracks for two companies and quarters for three officers, a kitchen, a lancers' mess, and a small officers' mess. An empty square building for supplies adjoins the larger structure.

The furnishings have started to arrive, and the Winter stables for the horses will be built last, after the restoration of the old road. The Majer-Commander has insisted the post buildings be finished first so that the lancers can be supported properly to protect the engineers as they build and the traders who may come. The score of Kyphran prisoners have been used to widen and straighten the trail to the cove, where a pier will be built for fair-weather use.

A small separate building will be constructed at the entrance to the old road on the south side across from the post building, to house a tariff enumerator, once one is deemed necessary.

Alyiakal smiles, partly in amusement and partly in rue, then turns and heads back to the post building, holding a large double-sealed envelope that arrived with the latest wagonloads from the pier, escorted by Undercaptain Torkaal and second squad of Second Company. He makes his way into the small study of the officer in charge, containing three file cases of lancers' records and other documents, a small writing table, and a wooden straight-backed chair. The barracks section and officers' quarters contain pallet mattresses and little else, but after a season of sleeping on the ground and uneven dried grass, the pallets feel like luxury.

Alyiakal sits at the writing table and looks at the official envelope, wondering about its contents, and suspecting another lengthy list of duties and cautions. Rather than open it immediately, he takes out the letter from Saelora he received along with the sealed envelope. He has already skimmed it, but this time he reads more slowly, his eyes lingering on certain passages.

> *. . . so glad to get your letter after not hearing from you for so long . . . told me to expect that . . . still, I worried . . . so happy that you are healthy . . . pleased that you are in charge of the new post east of Guarstyad . . . you've worked hard and you deserve some recognition . . .*
>
> *. . . Hyrsaal wrote me eightdays ago that there was fighting east of Guarstyad. I knew you had to be involved. I felt you would be all right, but it was so hard to hold on to that feeling.*
>
> *When I finally got your letter, I felt that all the stones in the Great Canal had been lifted off me. I know it may be a long time before you can come to Vaeyal . . . or before you're posted somewhere that I can visit. Whatever is meant for us will be, but I cannot imagine us not always being close, even when we are separated by great distances.*
>
> *Since you asked, the distillery is doing well and so is my trading. If matters continue, I might be able to buy out Vassyl in the next year or so. That was his idea, not mine . . . I never would have even brought it up . . .*

Alyiakal shakes his head. *If she's doing that well . . .* He pushes away those thoughts, because there's nothing he can do. *Not at the moment, anyway.* He folds her letter and slips it back into his uniform.

After several moments, he opens the larger envelope, which contains a note card attached to a longer document and a slightly smaller sealed envelope. The note card, signed "Laartol," simply reads:

> *Alyiakal—*
> *Please read this before you open the next envelope.*

Since there's no reason not to follow the subcommander's request, Alyiakal turns his attention to the document, which is clearly a summary of something much larger and likely more formally worded.

TERMS TO WHICH KYPHROS AGREED

1. Cyador will obtain and retain full control of the East Pass and an area five kays east of the base of the pass road extending south to the Great Western Ocean. Effectively, the border between Kyphros and Cyador has been shifted ten kays east.

2. Cyador will maintain full control of the stone pier until the first oneday of Autumn. After that, Cyadoran vessels may freely port there but must pay any usual fees and tariffs, but only if those fees and tariffs are levied on all vessels.

3. Once the old road is restored and passable, it will be the only access to Guarstyad for trade, and the East Pass will be closed to traders. After that, any commercial goods arriving through the pass will be treated as smuggled, with all penalties for such being applied.

4. All traders will enter Cyador through the old road, and will be tariffed under existing laws and tariff schedules at Oldroad Post, such tariffing being applied by either an Imperial tariff enumerator or by the Mirror Lancer officer in charge, who will act as enumerator until one arrives. The necessary tariff schedules and procedures are being sent to the post.

5. Until an official enumerator arrives, the officer in charge will keep accurate ledgers and remit such revenues to the Imperial Treasury on a seasonal basis, once the old road is rebuilt and passable, such revenues to be tendered personally to the head tariff enumerator in Guarstyad no later than one eightday after the commencement of the season.

The additional and less-onerous provisions take up another page.

After reading through all the provisions, Alyiakal finally opens the inner sealed envelope, which contains more than just a document. Inside is a letter on the letterhead of the Majer-Commander of the Mirror Lancers.

Alyiakal swallows, knowing what the letter must mean, but almost not daring to read it. After a moment, he does, his eyes taking in the key words.

> . . . *based on your accomplishments in the Kyphran campaign and commensurate with your selection as officer in charge of Oldroad Post, ratified and confirmed by the Majer-Commander on Threeday, Seventh Eightday of Spring, 99 A.F., in the reacquired lands of eastern Cyador, you, Alyiakal'alt, are hereby promoted to Overcaptain, effective Oneday, First Eightday, Summer, 99 A.F.* . . .

Alyiakal has to smile at the words "commensurate with your selection as officer in charge," because what that means is that his appointment required the promotion. He wonders if Kortyl realized that. Alyiakal has no doubts that Subcommander Laartol knew.

The other items in the envelope are the insignia of an overcaptain, but they are inside another sheet of paper, with several handwritten but unsigned lines.

> *Congratulations on becoming one of the youngest overcaptains. That means more will always be expected of you. You cannot afford to forget that. Ever. Especially since the Kyphrans were informed that the field officer who created most of their casualties would continue as the post commander. You are already known in Kyphros as the Lance of Fire.*

Alyiakal winces. *Talk about more being expected.*

> *Also, you might like to know that Kortyl was promoted to overcaptain as well, with the same effective date of rank.*

Although the lines are unsigned, the handwriting is that of Subcommander Laartol.

ABOUT THE AUTHOR

L. E. MODESITT, JR. is the author of more than seventy books—primarily science fiction and fantasy, including the long-running, bestselling Saga of Recluce and Imager Portfolio, as well as a number of short stories. His newest series is the Grand Illusion (*Isolate, Councilor, Contrarian*).